COMRADES COME RALLY

As Britain decides on its future is someone killing to hide their past?

Phil Brett

All the characters and organisations are fictional. Any resemblance to those living or dead is purely coincidental.

Copyright © 2014 Phil Brett
All rights reserved.

ISBN: 1494788799
ISBN 13: 9781494788797
Library of Congress Control Number: 2013923505
CreateSpace Independent Publishing Platform
North Charleston, South Carolina

Rise like lions after slumber
In unvanquishable number—
Shake your chains to earth like dew
Which in sleep had fallen on you—
Ye are many—they are few

The Masque of Anarchy. Percy Bysshe Shelley

Nostalgia for an age yet to come

Nostalgia. Pete Shelley (The Buzzcocks)

To Jane, for her support, friendship, advice, and most of all, her love.

Contents

1. What Is to Be Done? — 1
2. Problems of Everyday Life — 25
3. Personal and Political Profiles — 55
4. Reform and Revolution — 87
5. The Poverty of Philosophy — 97
6. Their Morals and Ours — 119
7. By Any Means Necessary — 131
8. April Thesis — 161
9. England's New Chains Discovered — 177
10. The Holy Family — 189
11. Infantile Disorder — 211
12. Chaos or Community — 229
13. What Everyone Should Know About State Repression — 243
14. Rebel Girl — 273
15. A Vindication of the Rights of Woman — 291
16. Make Way for the Winged Eros — 309
17. One Step Forward Two Steps Back — 315
18. Up and Down Stream — 341
19. The Mass Strike — 365
20. The Social Contract — 389

21. What Next?	409
22. From the Old Family to the New	425
23. Friends and False Friends of the Working Class	433
24. State and Revolution	449
25. Beware of Spies!	463
26. Through What Stage Are We Passing?	489
27. In Defence of Marxism	501
28. In Search of a Method	517
29. How History Is Written	539
30. The Revolution Betrayed	553

Prologue: Early Works

He looked down and saw the swathes of red obliterating the shirt's abstract design. The shirt was sticking to him, and no matter how often or vigorously he pulled, it would not *un*stick. He needed to dump it as soon as possible, but it did not seem able or willing to come off. Cursing, he tugged, hands slipping off the soaked cotton. He wasn't sure whether it was the sweat or the blood which was lubricating his grip. But then, did it really matter?

"For Christ's sake, come off. Come off. Come off," he muttered through clenched, tense lips, wrestling as much with the ever-growing panic as with the shirt.

He wiped his hands on his forearms. He did so again and again. What fell from him was not liquid but solids, falling onto the sandy, rain-deprived dust. The heat. This bloody heat. It was drying everything out. Not the shirt, though; it still felt damp, sticky, and clinging. Why was that? Now, though, was not the time to ponder the physics of evaporation. He wanted the shirt off, *needed* it off, and then needed to chuck or burn it. He wanted to be rid of it. He was desperate to get rid of it.

Flies were buzzing around the soaked cloth. Flicking away one of the more persistent ones, although they all seemed pretty much in the running—or should that be flying for that particular award—he caught sight of the body, lying at angles with arms crossed in a defensive posture, head facing towards him. Deep, violent cuts had ripped through the face. One was at such a depth that it had all but torn the left eye out. The body was so mangled and torn that it was sexless and anonymous, without life, and as though it had never had life.

It had not always been like that. When the body had had a working metabolism, it had been a she—very much a she and very much full of life.

She had also been the very opposite of unknown. Lying there, she might be unclaimed, unnamed, and innominate, but when she had breathed, she had belonged. She stared at him accusingly with her one-and-a-half eyes. Her dead voice silently accused him. Blamed him. Denounced him.

Word had got around the family Diptera that whilst there was limited fun to have with his blood-splattered hands, the real fun was happening at the orgy going on in the coagulating pool by her head. The flies already partying were being enthusiastically joined by their siblings.

Stepping back, he almost lost his footing and fell. In his head, thoughts were fighting for dominance, like the insects. What had happened; what had he done; what was he *going* to do? The latter question seemed to be gaining in importance. Was the answer to simply remove the shirt or to just run? With or without the shirt. The shirt which used to have the abstract design. Run and escape those imputing eyes.

In the distance, a siren pierced the summer stillness. He listened, turning his head in its direction. It was different from the ones he was used to. Different but somehow the same. He looked back at the woman. Was that all she was now? A woman? Now she was dead, she was just a woman, was she? Her hanging eye glared at him.

He returned to tugging at the cotton. Hysteria was mounting, and he was growing ever more desperate to ditch the offending garment. "Christ, oh Christ. Come off, for God's sake!" Twisting and turning, he stumbled again.

The siren was getting closer. It jolted one more change of mood, and paralysing shock stilled his thumping heart. His pulse dropped, and his breathing subsided. He more fell on his arse than sat down on the ground, the gravel sand clinging to the back of his calves.

He crossed his legs and sat there, like a boy scout waiting for his patrol leader. He felt alone and scared, waiting to be awarded his guilt badge in front of a censorious audience. He sat in the heat, staring at her and replaying in his mind what had just happened. He asked again—what had he done? He gently and with tender care smoothed his shirt, feeling her blood between his fingers.

And the siren got nearer.

CHAPTER ONE
What Is to Be Done?

The dozen, crisply ironed, long-sleeve shirts hung in the wardrobe, all on wooden hangers, three centimetres apart, facing the right, with the iron hook pointing away from me. In front of them were the short-sleeve shirts and behind them, separates of jackets and trousers; following up the rear, my suits, with summer first and then the heavier autumn and winter. All were neatly pressed and hung and facing the correct way.

The clock turned thirteen minutes past eight. During the usual ablutions of shaving, showering, and hoping the power was on (it had been), I had pondered the daily question of *the suit*. Which one? After some thought, I had plumped for the blue, four-button mohair with three pockets. Deciding that blue would be today's colour, I took out the azure, one-finger, button-down shirt, and reached in for a matching silk tie, a smart but not too formal choice. True, not the most politically correct of colours, but then sometimes the diktat of style overrode political allegiances.

This was always the part of the morning I most enjoyed—the feeling of cool cotton on my skin as I buttoned the shirt, always the third button down first, then all buttons above, and finally, those below. Next, the trousers, the navy socks, and finally, the tie. I looked into the mirror, watching myself pull the material up, over, and through as I put on the tie. In all honesty, I didn't need to watch, as I had been tying four-in-hand knots since I was a school kid being forced to do so. Now it was natural, and I will end up doing it in my coffin. No doubt, the knot then would be a half-Windsor. Such an occasion demands more formality.

The shirt and trousers looked like drawn curtains when I took the belt in another notch. It was a four-year-old suit which reflected the waist size I was then, as opposed to the greatly slimmed-down me of the present. Any hope that the jacket would hide this fact was lost, because on buttoning it, it was apparent that there wasn't the chest hug which there should have been; instead, it looked as if I was wearing an older brother's suit, hanging off my shoulders, pretending to be grown-up. The look was less impeccably smooth modernist and more baby bro going to a family wedding.

Not that there was anything particularly youth like about my face. My favourite uncle had been a great believer of *tzedakah*, the Hebrew word he would *endlessly* tell me that meant charity and fairness, and it would take all his fabled *tzedakah* to say that I was looking boyish. I could boast impressive cheek bones, but they were more sallow than callow, and only if you could call pasty and pale interesting, could my reflection be called cool. The barnet hadn't aged too much, though. I had been lucky in not losing any sizeable amount of hair. It still had length at the sides; a high, chipped-in fringe; and a shaped back. Regular use of hair dye had fended off the attack of the greys. The worry was that getting such luxuries was getting more and more difficult.

Vanity addressed (didn't my uncle have a quote about vanity in moderation being a virtue? I am sure he did; he had for most things, but it was so long ago, I couldn't remember), I went into the kitchen, and after sitting out a five-minute power cut, boiled some water. I poured it into the cup, stirred in one sugar, and finally added the milk, not too weak and not too strong, not that I thought this coffee could conceivably ever be strong. The last of the fresh Columbian was long gone, with little hope of getting any more, so it was going to have to be the instant. *Weak* and instant, but at least it would have a semblance of caffeine which might just summon up a little buzz.

Then it was the turn of providing a drink for my dear old friend, Red. He got tap water and dried food. From the way he was purring and looking first at me and then at his bowl, it didn't take a cat shrink to understand that he was hoping for more.

"Sorry, mate, no posh stuff for you, either. You're just going to have to make do with basic rations." If I hadn't known better, I would have sworn that he had given me a surly teenage humph of disapproval.

"But you, my old chum, are no teenager. You're as ancient as I am. The best years are well and truly behind you."

I opened the box and continued the conversation. That it was only one way was no doubt as much to do with its mundaneness as with his inability to speak. "The mouse-catching days for both of us are history. We are just a pair of sedate, old, house cats. Sleeping, eating, and watching the world go by."

On I went with the banalities of our existence. I dished out his food. Boring even myself, I turned the radio on to hear a young man with a Welsh accent excitedly telling us that today was going to be another sunny April day with clear skies and above-average temperatures. I was regaled with the temperatures around Britain and was told that Falmouth was the warmest place in the country today. Well, good for the Cornish folk. One of the presenters joined in with a gusto which suggested that for him, meteorology was the sexiest subject on earth, one that featured heavily in his filthiest of dreams. He excitedly remembered last week's showers in a tone that made them sound as if they had been cyclones, and he wondered out loud how amazing it was that it had changed. I had the answer for that—it's called the weather.

"So very English, hey, Red," I mumbled, as the pussy in question spread the food across the floor rather than eat any of it. We were in the middle of the greatest social upheaval this country had witnessed since Oliver Cromwell separated Charles I from his head, and yet still a key talking point was the weather. Was that true of every country? When the Bolsheviks stormed the Winter Palace in the Russian Revolution, had they paused to look at the morning frost? Or had the students in Paris in 1968, adopting a suitably existentialist pose and stroking their goatees, expounded, "Oh, Jean-Paul, do not throw that petrol bomb; look at those clouds—cumulus, aren't they, monsieur comrade?"

A case of pots and kettles, though. My average day did not involve assembling rifles or programming cyber strikes. It was more gentle walks, poring over novels, and a spot of leisurely media surfing: watching events rather than participating in them.

Still, the weather forecast did mean that my daily hour-and-a-half stroll at a quarter past one would be a pleasant one. Last week's rain had made these walks a rather sodden experience of late. Today, I thought I might swing by, or more accurately amble down, the high street towards the park. There I could get myself another coffee, weak and instant again, but coffee nonetheless. Then on past the old place where Mum used to live. I pondered whether or not I fancied dropping in to see some of the old neighbours. No, maybe not. Not today. I didn't really feel up to small talk and broken, stale biscuits.

I took two thinly buttered pieces of medium-toasted bread. No jam. I was out of that as well. I washed the spoon, dried it, and put it in the drawer. Looking around the kitchen, it all appeared neat and tidy. Perhaps the side window was looking a little grimy; I could see the odd speck of dirt on it. It must have been a couple of weeks since I'd last run a cloth over it. That could be my early evening chore. Yes, there was no doubt that the day was shaping up to be a nice one.

A cacophony of synthesised brass boomed from my lounge as the TV turned itself on to herald the news. That signaled the next part of my early morning ritual. Clutching my plate and cup and with the cat wrapped around my ankles, I went into the room and sat down on my favourite armchair: black leather, all quadrilaterals, sturdy but comfortable.

News had always been my drug of choice, well, alongside the odd Belgian beer and several varieties of fine wine. With the last two on the list becoming rarer and rarer, it was becoming an almost overwhelming and unrivalled addiction. I had always been one to enjoy sitting down and absorbing the revelations of the world, but now without work or *any* other commitments, I had been positively OD'ing on it. In or out: watching and listening to the news. Pete Kalder was indeed an avid, if nowadays passive, observer, and my only interaction with the outside world was virtual. Activity had decreased to zero.

That didn't stop me daily compiling a to-do list. Breakfast could smartly and immediately be ticked off. Not only did I like making them, I felt the need to. It was dumb; rarely was there anything earth-shattering listed. Actually, there was *never* anything earth-shattering. What was even dumber was that often I would include things I had already done. It was sad but true; it gave me a feeling of achievement to see those ticks mount up.

But now was the time to see what was happening in this topsy-turvy world. Predictably, the news began with the bland, well-groomed face of the prime minister emoting all over my floor. I really had yet to grasp what was so wonderful about 3-D TV. Did I really want to feel that I could touch him?

Wasn't it just taunting me with the seeming possibility of giving him a good slap when all that would happen would be my hand disappearing into the electronic image of his moisturised cheeks?

What number PM was he now? Was he the third or fourth in the last twelve months? I started to recount the myriad of coalitions we had been having, but I got rather confused; there'd been so many, of so many variations but all so, *so* alike.

This one was called the National Coalition for Negotiating the Crisis, the NCNC, which made it sound like a public school cricket club. Their names usually had multiple letters, so perhaps it was less cricket-oriented and more phonics? Maybe there was a cabal of early years' teachers in control. Who knows, but whatever the reason, snappy titles weren't their thing. Then again, trying to think of something which differentiated them from the previous coalition was a tough one. What actually *was* their thing? But then, like I said, we had had so many. They had gone from being a rarity in British politics to being as common as a grey suit and politically neutral tie on a minister. You wait for one coalition to come along, and then a whole parade of them trundles past. I tried to steer the metaphor away from the cliché towards the scathing—perhaps the buses being empty, or lost, or belonging to another age, but then I realised I would just have to be satisfied with the cliché.

Fear of using clichés wasn't something that bothered our illustrious *present* prime minister. His pet phrases were coming thick and fast out of his mouth. "We must pull together." It was "a time of crisis." This was "no time for extremism. The middle way is the British way." I took out an imaginary bingo card, or as his nibs, our illustrious premier, would no doubt say with that strange accentless accent of his—the all-new, broad-based NCNC card.

"NCNC? No see, No see, more like!" I growled.

Red ignored me. He was used to me proving my left-wing credentials by hurling abuse at the TV. Instead, he sat on the arm of my chair with an air of injured pride at having to make do with substandard food.

I repeated my attempt at cutting political jokes, but their ineptness only proved that the respite I was presently enjoying was not doing anything for my wit. How could I be aging physically but going the opposite way mentally? But then, didn't everyone ask that of themselves? It was called getting old.

But whatever. I returned to armchair heckling and ticked off the hackneyed phrases. All I needed was, "We, the Conservatives, Liberals, and Labour Party are united in negotiating the severe economic situation" and "trust us," and it would be bingo. And there they were. Bingo! I tell you, at least with this motley collection of cross-party politicians, you were rarely surprised.

I wondered if he spoke like this in his private life. Did his wife put on some smooth soul, slip into something sexy, and demand to be ravished, only to be met by him droning on about she shouldn't touch him there as we must pull together (and no, he would *not do that*), and we must find a middle way! And presumably one with other grey-suited men to form a bloc which would have lots of initials.

The thought of him having sex made me feel rather queasy so I concentrated on the news. Another bank had crashed. More investment was fleeing to Beijing. Prices had gone up again, and more firms were going under. Currencies across the world were dropping like collapsing chimneys. So nothing unusual. Showing the consistency of such a long-serving PM (how long was it now—six, seven months?), he reeled off a list of the day's latest woes with a complete set of policies which would do sweet-sod-all. His to-do list might be more dynamic than mine, but mine would at least get done. The latest economic crisis dwarfed previous ones. Indeed, over the past few decades, they had got steadily worse with the booms becoming ever more fragile; actually, they were less boom and more slightly loud bang.

Red clambered onto my lap. "God, you're easy to please," I said, stroking him. "So I'm no longer in the doghouse, then. Or should that be cathouse?" Yes, indeed, the jokes were becoming truly woeful.

Stretching to get my drink, I took a sip. The movement disturbed Red, who looked at my cup, at me, and then at my lap. Then he settled once more on top of my groin with his gaze averted from the politician and instead towards the large lamp in the far corner. It was off, but he seemed fascinated by it.

I turned my attention back to the PM. He was, I noted, wearing a suit today which was unusual. Usually, they favoured casual-formal with collars unbuttoned and the like, to show us that they were men and women of the people. Yeah, an open-necked shirt really meant that you were one of the proletariat. I preferred the grey suits. The idea of politicians attired in classic-fit, check shirts empathising with me, up close and oh, so understanding, made me feel almost as sick as the thought of the PM bonking. Today's outfit, though, was a sombre black number, which was badly cut and had as much style as you would expect from charity shop undertakers. With it, he wore a maroon-coloured tie; wearing a tie—must be serious.

Crunching the final morsel of toast, I smiled in appreciation as the reporter asked in sarcastic politeness how these policies were going to be pursued when the government was, in reality, not in control of the country. The PM didn't twitch but repeated how the three great parties were negotiating the crisis. The reporter persisted; she might look to these old eyes barely out of school, but she was dogged. What, for example, was he going to do about the fact that, as of yesterday, all power station workers had pledged support to the National Workers' Councils and would follow their lead rather than the government?

Give him his due, he didn't splutter, choke, or even pause, but after the obligatory line on democracy, he firmly said he would be personally talking to the representatives of the power station unions. Did I spy a smirk from the reporter?

If there had been, I was with her—I couldn't see the workers dropping to their knees when the PM came knocking. Even if he was wearing a tie and was dressed in his business best, there wasn't going to be a mass meeting where a member raised the motion of support for the coalition because, "Sisters and brothers, he just looks *so* sharp in that ensemble."

Doesn't this, the reporter noted, follow the same decisions made by the local government, transport, education, and IT workers? Smooth as silk, he replied that, "We do not do extremism" in Britain and would not be controlled by these so-called workers' councils, made up of militant trade unionists. "We prefer Parliament to soviets."

With that, they switched back to the painfully moderne studio with colourful squares seemingly hovering in the background and over my floor. It was like looking at a floating Mondrian painting with thick black lines and irregular polygons all over the place. They blathered on about what it all meant—the news, that is, not the pseudo-arty stage set. The newscaster tossed a question, and the 'expert' batted back an answer. It was worth watching as it cleared up so many things. From the exchange I learnt that our prime minister was not happy that another powerful group of workers was defying Parliament and that now that the British Isles had a Parliament (or more accurately, Parliaments) and a National Workers' Council, it meant that there was a constant power struggle. This was incisive journalism. What next? News that the earth was round and that bears went to the toilet in woody areas?

This time I shouted at the inanity of what passed for contemporary broadcasting: so many outlets, so much happening, and so little understanding. I sipped more of my coffee. God, it really was piss-weak.

It was time for my pill. I leant across, pushing Red off. He looked at me as if this was the final insult. Apologising, I pushed the pill out of the silver-and-cream plastic wrap, swallowing it down with another gulp of the brown water which passed for a hot drink. Mentally, I calculated how many of them I was intending to take today—probably just the two. I reckoned I could cope with that.

Next up on the news was a recorded report from the night before. I missed the beginning as Red had decided to playfully sink his claws into my wrist, and I had to disentangle myself. Otherwise, I would be wearing a cat accessory all day, which might have been fine, but I figured it didn't go with the threads. Although neither did the lumps of ginger hair which Red had kindly left between my legs.

"Marvellous, thanks, mate!"

On the news, they were still discussing the situation with the power workers. Judging from the size of the image of the building hovering in my front room, I guessed it was a much-mentioned power station. Conceivably, it could be a high-tech shopping mall built on the grave of British industry in the wilds of up north somewhere. No, it was a rally at a power station. You could tell from the puns on the placards. Things might change, and technology might advance at ever-dizzying speeds, but puns on cardboard stapled to plywood were still bywords for militancy. They also had to be always cheesy. We Hold the Power! and Turn On with Us! were ones I could see straightaway.

At the front stood a tall, black, well-dressed woman in a blue trouser suit. Blue, it seems, was the must-have colour for us latter-day UK Bolsheviks. Her blouse, though, was cream. Well, I was nearly there. She was standing on top of what looked like the back of an open lorry and speaking with passion and an acute sense of what the audience needed to hear into a hands-free mike.

Despite there being thousands present, everyone there looked as if she was talking to them individually. They didn't feel that they were being spoken at or lectured to, but that they were having a conversation. The people listening were gripped. They usually were. Every so often, there would be thunderous applause or sincere laughter. I smiled. She was a witty woman.

Jackie Payne, elected chairperson of the National Workers' Council and leader of the United Revolutionary Socialist Party, was, in the eyes of a growing number of the population, the *de facto* leader of the country. Some had called her the twenty-first-century Lenin or the British Trotsky. To many, she was the future hope; to others, she was the fear. Whatever one's view, she was carving a huge place in history.

The segment was quite an extended one with no interruption of journalistic commentary or flits back to the studio for expert analysis. Instead, they just let her talk. It was as she was seemingly rising to a crescendo that my doorbell rang. Without a second thought, I switched the set off. There was no need to watch her on TV when she was at my front door. Red scampered off in the direction of the back door, obviously not impressed by the fact that the most talked-about woman in Europe had found time in her busy schedule to pay me a visit.

She was half turning away as I opened the door and looking like she was talking to an invisible associate, but obviously she was talking into her earpiece. She was wearing the same suit as on the telly, but this time it was with a red, round-necked top. Covering her eyes were wraparound brown sunglasses. She mouthed a "sorry," which I took to be intended for me. Then, whilst continuing her phone conversation, which from the snippets I heard concerned energy supplies to the country, she spoke to two burly men in jeans and leather jackets standing close to her. Judging by the sizeable guns—not so discretely hanging off their belts—I guessed these weren't plumbers coming to check up on my boiler. They were bodyguards. It was a dangerous thing to be dangerous. One was looking directly at me whilst the other was scanning my street.

"It's OK," she said to them. "He's a friend. We go way back."

They looked at me, and their faces said, "Sad old git, no danger," and they stepped back. The bigger of the two, bigger as in comparing a super-heavyweight with a heavyweight, nodded and then shouted something to a black vehicle parked in front of my house.

Jackie walked in confidently, attempting a kiss on the cheek but missing, whilst still talking at speed on the phone about technicians. She took a few paces down the hall—with those lengthy legs, she rarely had to take more than that, anyway—turned right into the lounge, and without hesitation, sat down on the armchair. The choice did not surprise me; from there, she could direct the conversation.

She'd been here enough times in the past to know her way around. Her eyes scanned the room, as if trying to register any changes since her last visit. I was pretty certain that she'd been here since the room's reassembly, so aside from Red finding different places to snooze, it all would be pretty much as it had been. I had thought of redecorating, but to be honest, I found the varying shades of green quite calming. I could see one of the bodyguard-cum-boiler repairmen standing directly in front of my window. Not subtle, these ones.

I made a T sign to ask if she wanted a cuppa, but she shook her head. I made a C sign but again, she gave a shake and flick of her wrist to indicate that time was pressing. That was hardly surprising with all that was happening. That was why I had been rather taken aback to get her call last night at just past midnight. I'd been getting ready for bed—twelve thirty was bedtime—and the last thing I had expected was a call from Jackie Payne. She had sounded serious and, I have to say, a little worried. In a tone which had expected no opposition, she had announced that she would be calling around my house between 9:30 a.m. and 10:00 a.m. because she had something important to talk to me about.

My duties as a host duly delivered, I sat on the sofa, feeling like an audience member waiting for the performance to begin. Looking at her, obviously in a conference call about the power-station vote, sitting back, cross-legged, and oozing authority, she looked pretty much the same as when I had first met her.

Maybe the odd line had appeared around the eyes, and the jaw had lost a touch of sharpness, but it was negligible. How long ago had we first met—twenty, thirty years? She had short hair back then. It was longer now. She was studying at uni, philosophy, I think. She was away from home for the first time and spreading her young, militant wings. Back then, I'd been working for a local library, and every Thursday I did a morning sale of the *Revolutionary Worker* outside her university. I was older than her but not by much. She had bought a copy and then another. We had started to talk.

Her longstanding joke was that as I was barely the only decently dressed party member she'd seen, she felt drawn to me. The style faction, she called us. Unaffiliated but politically interested and *very* serious-minded, she had quickly drunk all my knowledge of Socialism. I had tried to answer her questions, but soon they were outstripping my knowledge. After attending a few meetings and instantly hurling herself into the debates, she had joined. To this day, she credited me for recruiting her, but the fact was she had pretty much recruited herself. Still, it was fine by me to take the glory. She had joined, and the rest *is to be* history.

She hung up and smiled at me. Running her hand over her closely tied-back hair and sliding the shades back, she looked her usual cool self, but she was obviously tired.

"Good to see you, Jacks," I said. "Sure you don't need a drink?"

"No, thanks, I can't stay too long. The power workers are wobbling; at any moment, there could be a reversal of their decision. I guess I'll have to pop back there. I've spent half my life there recently." She gave a heavy, exasperated, sigh. "It's not been easy."

"At your wits' end?" I said, setting up an old, private, past-amusing joke.

"Gone miles past that, Pete," came the stock response with a slight smile, which decreased every time it was given a run out. "Anyway, Pete, it's good to see you. It's been a while, I know. How are you?" She didn't wait for a reply and looked around again. "The place looks good. It cleaned up nice, as good as new."

Then she stopped. Her attention wandered from my furnishings to staring out the window. Obviously, she was deep in thought as the view consisted of two uncollected dustbins and the fat back side of one of her bodyguards. They were not going to be making postcards of that anytime soon. Plainly not focused on what she was saying, she absentmindedly tried another small talk standby. "It's a beautiful day; have you had a chance to get out yet?"

There you go—the weather. I tell you, Marx might have wittered on about the industrial working class, but it was the weather forecasters who held the real power. Get them out on strike, and the country would be finished.

"You look good," she said, continuing with the preliminaries. I wondered when she would get to the point and the real reason for her coming here. I didn't for a second think she had put aside building the revolution so she could talk about home furnishings and the weather. Talk about going around the houses; this was like she was trying to find a parking space in this neighbourhood. "Still need to put a bit of weight on, but you look fine." Temptation tugged at me to check again in the mirror to see how I was looking.

She paused. Rarely had I seen her so hesitant. Her eyes scanned the shelves of books and vintage compact discs, and a slight, affectionate smile crossed her lips. "So much music," she muttered.

I returned the smile. "Yeah, but I don't really play them anymore."

"Why keep them then?"

I shrugged. "I like them there. I like their look and feel, the memories they carry. Never did really get into the digital age."

The smile stayed. "You've always been retro," she muttered to herself. For a second, she almost looked as if her thoughts had drifted. She followed the shelves, as if she was memorising the titles. But then the smile dropped, and she looked directly at me. For some reason, I began to feel uncomfortable. She was acting a little odd. OK, I'm sure that running a revolution can make any of us not quite our usual selves, but this wasn't quite the Jackie I knew. And why was she here? I was pretty sure that she hadn't decided to spend some quality time with me and the cat and to admire my collection of classic 1990s Britpop. Maybe I was being melodramatic, but I thought I saw her take a deep breath. It wasn't, though, from a desire to discuss how "(What's the Story) Morning Glory" had stood the test of time.

She uncrossed her legs and moved slightly forwards in the seat. Both her knees and face turned towards me. "Pete, I've got some bad news," she said, finally getting to the point of her visit. "I got a call last night; it's Alan, Alan Wiltshire. He's dead." She had spoken in that hushed library voice people use when speaking of a tragedy, as if the deceased's feelings might be hurt to find out that they had snuffed it. She stopped and seemed to be waiting for me to make a response.

And what one to give? Wiltshire dead? My mind quickly tried to compute his approximate age. He was a leading member of the party when I had joined, and that was thirty years ago. I'd hazard a guess at him being in his mid-seventies—at least. I seemed to remember him talking about being involved in the first Gulf War. When was that? It must have been 1990 or thereabouts, if I remembered my history correctly.

"I didn't know he was ill," I said rather feebly, not knowing what the expected reaction was. I knew Alan Wiltshire from his books and from countless meetings. He had been a leading member for donkey's years. Reflecting on it, I don't think I'd known a central committee without him. I'd even worked on a few pamphlets with him, and I guess you could say I'd known him for decades. Not that we had ever been friends—comrades, not pals. There had been an occasion when he had clumsily tried to show some friendship, but it had only really embarrassed both of us. He was a great man, well, a great comrade, and it was a huge loss, but if I was to be honest, I wasn't going to fall apart. I, of all people, knew all about that, and this wasn't such an occasion.

Jackie sighed and closed her eyes. "He wasn't. It wasn't natural causes. As far as we know, he was fighting fit. Literally so. He committed suicide." Her voice slowed when pronouncing each letter of the word "s-u-i-c-i-d-e."

I dumbly repeated the word "suicide." It wasn't a hard word to say or know what it meant, but I guess it was always one which caused confusion when it was used. Just such a feeling hit me. Suicide? A man who had devoted all his life—and if my memory served me well, since he was a sixteen-year-old in Leicester—to the revolutionary cause decided to end it all now! Now, when this country was nearer to a revolution than at any time since 1688, he decided to top himself? He'd spent decades building the party when membership had consisted of three students and a dog, and yet now, when it ran over a seven-figure number, he ended it all!

"Bollocks!" I said, rather louder than I had intended. Actually, I thought I had said it in my head. Trying to sound at least semi articulate, I quickly added, "We are within reach of everything Alan ever strove for. Why would he commit suicide now?"

She replied that although it was hard to believe, it was sadly the case. Once more, I disagreed. Then for a few minutes we played a game of It Is Not True Vs Oh Yes, It Is." She won on points.

Seeing that she obviously believed he had taken his own life, I grasped at straws for a possible reason. "Are you are sure that he did not have a terminal illness? He might have but kept it from you." The thought had sounded a lot more logical in my head than how it sounded.

Jackie didn't reply and just shook her head. Was there a tear in her eye? I suppose it wouldn't have been a surprise if there was. She *would* call herself a friend of Alan's, and being fellow Central Committee members meant that they would have worked closely, especially in the old days when the CC would have been no more than half a dozen people.

I wasn't buying it and tried another go at the disbelief game. "Are we sure that it's suicide and not murder? The loony Right has been threatening to go further than the odd *Seig Heil* and use of a copper pipe; I wouldn't put assassination past them. There were those two organisers in the Northwest who got killed. And 'course you yourself have received threats!" That sounded a little saner, although it was strange that I found murder more acceptable than suicide.

Leaning forwards, she recovered her poise. "No, we are pretty sure it's suicide. It was an overdose. There was no sign of the pills being forced. No, Pete, I'm afraid to say that Alan committed suicide." She swallowed. "Dave found him and rang me."

Dave was Alan's grandson. Alan had doted on the boy and had treated him as a son and best friend as well as a grandson. He was about the only non political topic you could get Alan to talk about. One of the reasons I was never that close to Alan was that he was a political bore. It seemed to be all he lived for. That is, besides talking about Dave, how the lad was doing at college and then as a trainee solicitor; he could go on for hours. Some cynics might say, and quite possibly I could be included in this, that Alan was overcompensating for his neglect of his actual son, Dave's father.

Jackie rubbed the centre of her forehead. I noted that even in these difficult times, her nails were immaculate—symmetrical and crimson. "He left a suicide message on his computer. I just hope that Dave didn't see it because it's not a pretty piece of viewing."

"These things can be faked," I replied, still not believing a word. Wiltshire, lifelong Socialist, kills himself on the eve of a possible Socialist revolution. It would be like Winnie the Pooh ending it all in front of a bloody honey-bottling plant."

Though, Alan Wiltshire was probably more like Eeyore, but that wasn't the important thing here.

"Couldn't someone have just made it look like suicide? Kill a leading Socialist, but leave no traces."

"No, too sophisticated; it's not their style. I think they—"

"What about the security services?" I snapped, warming to my theme and letting my love of John le Carré at last serve a useful purpose. "We know they've been devoting all their time and energy to us. We all know there must be moles in the party…"

She appeared to wince, but I paid it no mind because I was in full conspiracy flow. "There's been a lot of discussion about them, both in the party and in the workers' councils. There's been talk of sabotage and of sidelining activists—why not begin to start killing them? Decapitate the movement? Make it look like suicide so no one suspects them, and the government can blame unstable extremists! MI5, MI6—whatever combination of letters and numbers they're using now—why can't they have done it?"

I stopped. I thought I had better, before we got to faked moon landings, grassy knolls, and the Loch Ness Monster. "I know it sounds farfetched," I said, as much to me as to her, "but we all know that capitalism is red in tooth and claw. Christ, they've had wars where millions have died to protect it, so a few dead Lefties ain't going to worry their conscience much!"

My breathing had increased, probably from all this exertion; I hadn't spoken so much for years, not to another human being, that is, and one who was actually, *physically*, in the room. I would need a nap at this rate. Because of the exceptional event of my involvement in human social interaction, a blush crossed my cheeks.

Perhaps sensing my unease at spoiling this unusual day of human contact with my crazed theories, Jackie made a half-arsed attempt at sounding conciliatory. "Well, I guess it's a possibility, but we had some people look over the…" She corrected herself. "We had people examine *Alan*, and they called it a suicide. Don't ask me what tests they did, but they were at it for hours, and they seemed pretty convinced that he had taken his own life." She seemed uncomfortable at the thought of what these tests had been, so she moved from the physical to the material. "And they searched his home. Everything was in its place—no upturned chairs or broken plates. No blood traces, nothing at all to suggest a struggle. There was nothing to say that it was anything other than Alan taking his own life."

Her terminology flagged up a few signals. Unlike me, Jackie was no fan of the crime novel, yet that sentence might have lunged straight out of one. As one of those great books might have said, my suspicions were aroused. "What *people* looked?" I asked.

She grimaced. "I know you will not approve, but we got some of the police comrades to have a look. No, don't make that face," she said, rebuking me, as my eyes rolled the speed of a jet doing loop-the-loop. "I am aware of your position on the party's policy, but you know full well that we want to win over as many of the police as we can. A small minority have crossed the divide and joined. We asked three of them to examine the body and do some simple forensic tests; they were pretty basic, as most of the facilities are no-go areas for us because those police officers who are not off sick are, in the main, pro-government."

"Or pro-Fascist."

She held up a hand and gave me a look I knew was telling me that she wanted me to let her finish. "Shut up, Kalder," the smooth palm and those long fingers were saying.

"Well, I can assure you that these police officers are most definitely *pro-party*. They had a detailed look, and they were satisfied that Alan took an overdose of tablets, washed down by a bottle of Scotch."

"Bollocks!" I muttered, again showing my immense vocabulary and my total lack of fear of repeating myself. "I've spent too long in my life being pushed around and worse by our great British police force, and now they decide to fight for a better world. On the picket rather than breaking it—I don't believe a single one of them. What sort of person joins the police? I'll tell you…" Boy, I sounded radical, didn't I?

"Pete," she sighed, the smile sliding. She wasn't overly impressed at the sound of someone so keen to wear his political credentials by spouting off, just to cover the fact that in reality he did bugger all. I was like those dinner-table Lefties who scoff at people's religions because that shows just how radical they are. They then return to worshipping their postcode and their nice cosy life.

"The whole state apparatus is collapsing. Everything we once took for granted is changing. You know that. What about the armed forces? Basically, we have to win them over, otherwise we're doomed."

Yes, yes, I knew the arguments. I had heard them often enough, but my enmity knew no bounds, and maybe it was the excitement of having company who wasn't a ginger tom, but words tumbled out of my mouth. "Scum in blue. Jackie, I am surprised at you. You take the word of a few newly-joins, who at best have seen how the wind is blowing and switched trains or at worst are hoping to derail us." I could feel myself getting angry, and not even mixed metaphors nor were the Payne smile, charm, and raised hand going to stop me. "And they tell you that a comrade you have known for years has killed himself. Crap. How bloody convenient. Perfect for a cover-up, I'd say. Who are these reds in blue? Seen the light, have they? Read some Marx whilst they were fiddling expenses and banging a few heads. Jackie..." The sugar rush of social intercourse was all but overcoming me.

"For God's sake, Pete, be quiet!" she replied in a volume that, if not a shout, contained the power to become one. Irritation was all too obvious in her eyes. "Things have changed whilst you have been..." Her mind instantly edited what she was about to say. "Whilst you have been *resting*. Sorry Pete, but you've been watching the world from the outside. I'm *in* the world; I'm feeling it change. Not reading about it. Not watching it but experiencing it and trying to change it. I really don't want to be rude, but you're out of touch. You sound like you belong to a bygone age. Let's face it; who are you to say whether a comrade is sincere or not?"

Well, that told me. Don't worry about being diplomatic, Jacks—say it how it is! I could see that her anger had still not shown its full force. It was unusual for her to get narked so quickly. Jackie was known for being the queen of cool, and she had known me long enough to take anything I said with a pinch of salt. I was renowned for my rants. I could vent so often that I could be mistaken for air conditioning. But I knew this woman well. She looked pretty calm on the outside, but there was a real anger brewing inside her, and I for one didn't want to see it; I cared too much for her for us to fall out, and, well maybe, just maybe, she had a point. Perhaps that's why it rather stung.

"Theory, Pete, but what about the practice?" she said, poking a finger at my collection of books. I could have pointed out that, in actual fact, the books she was indicating were twentieth-century novels, concerned mainly about the traumas of middle-class life, but now really wasn't the time. She closed her eyes for a few seconds as she collected her thoughts.

When she next spoke, it was in a cooler tone. "Can I?" she asked, nodding to the TV. I consented. She pointed her phone towards it. "Watch this," she murmured.

The screen flashed on, and Alan's face filled it. Thankfully, it was only two-dimensional. His unkempt hair flopped over his heavy, brown spectacles. With his jowls, five-o'clock shadow, and rather naff taste in shirts, I always thought that he looked like a bloke who might be spending his retirement in his potting shed, taking cuttings, and reading *Shrub World*. Not that he talked like one. He looked straight at the cam and spoke in his correct Midlands-meets-London tone.

Jackie, this is my message to you and the Central Committee. It is with a heavy heart that I record it, but I feel that in all honesty, I have no choice.

I have been a Socialist for over fifty years and a Trotskyist for most of that time. I have dedicated my life to building a world which the human race deserves; a world without oppression, without want, without war, and without exploitation. As of now, you and thousands of workers have brought us close to that prize. What has so long been a dream is almost a reality.

We stand within millimetres of washing away millennia of degradation and humiliation and starting a fresh millennium which is clean of the filth of class oppression. So now is not the time for lies and betrayal, and it is for that reason that, with the utmost shame and humiliation, I must tell you, and there is no easy way to say this, that for many years I have passed on information to the British Security Services. I started in 2010, not for personal gain, be it financial or anything else, but, well, the reason matters to me, but it need not to you. It was stupid. I was mistaken, foolish, and wrong. I could say in my defence that anything I ever passed on was of minimal value. Any important information has been kept within the party ranks, and I broke off all communications with them twelve months ago, but that, frankly, is beside the point. I betrayed the party. I betrayed the class. It is unforgivable.

I am so proud of my small part in the growth of this movement. I would hope that this would be remembered and not my disgrace. But to carry on would perpetuate the lie, so I have decided to take my life after this message. I hope that the news of this act does not damage the party. I doubt whether it will, as we are too strong to be harmed by tittle-tattle.

Let me say once again that I have had no contact with British Secret Intelligence Service for well over a year, and I have destroyed anything which might be of sensitive nature.

So, good-bye, Jackie, and good-bye, comrades.

I am proud to have stood shoulder to shoulder with you. I have no doubt that you will be victorious.

Victory to the Socialist Revolution!

Then the screen went blank, pretty much as did my face. Jackie looked at me and patiently waited for a response, but once more I wasn't sure I could give one. After all, there are only so many surprises you can take in a morning. I felt that my stock of vocabulary of amazement had been totally exhausted. Saying bollocks for a third time just did not seem to be enough to articulate my jaw-dropping shock.

I smoothed one of the folds in my trousers. "So you are saying," I said, choosing my words with care, "that Alan Wiltshire was working for the intelligence services?"

She shook her head wearily. "No," she replied almost in a whisper. "Alan is saying this. Or should I say was."

I tried to take it all in. My head was like a US ice hockey game with hulks crashing into other hulks and fights starting across the stadium, the stadium being in this case—my brain. So Alan Wiltshire, author of dozens of influential, politically important—if not particularly brilliantly written—texts of Marxist theory and history, had spent his spare time also being a footnote to internal Special Branch memos! One of the longest-serving Central Committee members was a spy! The man had been at more demos, picket lines, and street battles than pretty much anyone living. If the exploited or oppressed were fighting their rulers—not just here—but anywhere in the world—then you would bet that Alan would be there, in the thick of it—cheering, cajoling, advising, learning, listening, and doing anything to help the struggle. And all the time, he was on their side?

"I can't believe it. Alan a spy? He was devoted to the party. That man gave his life to the struggle. Jacks, you knew him better than me; surely you don't believe this!"

She ignored a bleep of her phone and merely shrugged her shoulders.

"This must be fake—it's not hard to do…"

"We think it's genuine."

A few more ice hockey jocks crashed in my head. "Let me guess—our Bolshies-on-the-beat checked it." This time, Jackie did not reply but just sat regally, looking at me, waiting for me to calm down.

The pills I took daily were to keep me on the level. They were to dampen anxiety and stress, numb anger, tackle depression, and promote a sense of contentment. In other words, these happy pills were designed to suppress every feeling that I was now experiencing. I was instantly regretting cutting down the dosage.

Through teeth which were magnetically being drawn to a gritted position, I hissed, "So to recap: Alan Wiltshire, leading member, has, despite working twelve hours a day building the party, been working for the ruling class. Despite mostly looking like a tramp, he's been James Bond. We accept that and accept that because of this, he chooses now of all times to kill himself. Oh, and whilst we shouldn't have trusted him, we do trust some—"

"Yes, Pete," she interrupted, with quietness but steel-like firmness. "I understand your position."

"Good!" I snapped and moved forwards in my seat. Emotions were swelling in my head and heart, harking back to a bygone time in my life. My long-dormant temper really was now awakening. "'Cos I can't bloody understand yours! How long have you known him? You can't believe he was a traitor. I mean, frankly, why would they bother? We're an open party! We're not terrorists. You've always been able to find out what we're doing by just going along to a public meeting, or if you want to be really cloak-and-dagger, go online and read the blogs!"

Again, she did not say anything. It was obvious that Jackie herself was feeling emotional, and yet she remained silent. It could have been that she found temper tantrums rather undignified and that the sight of a middle-aged man behaving like a spoilt teenager was rather embarrassing. But it was as if she was waiting for something. I assumed it was to wait till I started to act my age. If I had given it a thought and used any of the common sense I possessed, or even if the pills were working, then I would have paused to ponder a little more deeply as to what that might be.

Instead, I spewed out more undirected verbiage. Why I was doing so, I perhaps could, should, also have contemplated. The passion I was experiencing made me feel like a former virgin after the first time—both excited and frightened. For so long I had made myself a zombie, and yet now here I was, fully awake and vomiting out words and gagging on disturbance. Despite being stunned at the news, it was just as surprising that I personally felt so annoyed, insulted even, at the accusation of Alan's betrayal. In the scheme of things, what did it matter? Why did I feel so involved in the allegation? Why did I just not shrug my shoulders, express doubt, and say something pithy and profound about comrades as police, and police as comrades, let her go on her way, and let me return to my day?

But I didn't. "You need to look into this. You can't let this slur go unchecked."

A strange smile appeared across her red lips. "I agree."

I was thrown for a second; it wasn't quite what I had expected. I thought she had written the beginning, middle, and end of this story.

"I agree with a lot, well maybe *some*, of what you say. I think it is strange, as well; it *is* very strange, the whole thing. I have quite a few questions that I want answered; questions I think it is important to have answered, not just to clear Alan's name but for the party, the movement, and his friends and family to know. And that, Pete, is why I'm here." There was something about her voice that made those sportsmen on ice stop bumping into each other and against the sides of my brain.

She looked straight at me. "I want you to look into this."

Dumb struck, I stared at her. "What?"

Her hand lifted, and like a cross between a karate chop and half a prayer, she listed coolly, coldly, her reasons. "I find it as hard as you do to think that Alan killed himself. And if he did, why did he? If it is true that he was a mole, then to slightly echo what you were saying—why end it now? In his message, he says he has broken off all contact with them, so again the question is, why now? Or maybe he was still passing on information…"

I scoffed. It was met simply by her telling me that we must not be sentimental about this. "Not sentimental, Jacks, try loyalty." But that argument had passed, so I did not pursue it. I was more interested in what she had said about getting me involved. "Anyway, that's all fine and correct, but where do I fit in?"

"As I said, Pete, I want you to look into it."

The doctors had said that one of the problems with the pills I had been taking was that emotions, if they did arise, might be confused. That was a possible reason for me somehow having a fairly long list of them right now. Surprise, sadness, confusion, anger, and possibly even pride were fuzzily skipping along at low level, and then occasionally, from nowhere, up one went, hitting the ceiling. This time, zeal jumped up, ricocheting off a desire to avoid involvement. "Why? Why me? Can't you get one of your pet cops to do the investigating?" My opposition had the stridency of stamping my foot.

For the first time since her arrival, she laughed. Well, more like an ironic chuckle, but I guess when you're discussing the betrayal and suicide of one of your friends, you don't expect side splitting guffaws. "Pete, you're not alone in your attitude to police comrades. How would it look if they went around asking questions about someone like Alan? They'd cause outrage and find nothing out whatsoever, whereas, you're known as a longtime comrade. You're trusted."

It was a nice character reference; I'd file it away and use it someday. But however much flattery could usually disarm me, it wasn't so in this case. "There are plenty of other comrades you could ask who aren't wearing pointed hats and carrying truncheons," I muttered.

"But, Pete, they're all busy. We're all working long hours, and we're shattered. I need someone known and someone I trust, and any other candidates are otherwise occupied. You, Pete, you're, well, free right now. You're *available*."

She didn't need to explain that reasoning any further. Which hurt. Still, I could see that our friendship was nagging at her, so she softened me up. Again, presuming that the best way to seduce me was to flatter me, she all but cooed, "Pete, you love a mystery, and you know the history of the party. You are the one who wrote *You're Nicked!* and *Notes of the Vanguard*. Fine books. And as a trained researcher, you have the skills."

If penning books on a Marxist history of the crime novel and a potted history of the party, both years old (and both barely read, I might sadly add), made me an expert on investigations, then we were living in strange days, indeed. She was right; I was indeed a researcher but of art history at a university facility, not of crimes. If we were to look at my CV to find suitable employment in a possible future worker's paradise, then what about the travelling I had done? Was that a good CV item for liaison with international workers' movements? That day trip to Calais surely made me ideal for Anglo-French solidarity! The ability to conduct a computer search and use an index and suddenly I'm bloody Inspector bloody Morse!

"But…" I said, stuttering, not really knowing what I was going to say. "I wouldn't have the foggiest idea where to start!"

For some reason, I have no inkling why, Jackie took that simple, quite sensible question to mean, "Yes, Comrade Payne, I will of course investigate his suspicious death."

Her mood changed; she went from confident, in-control Jackie (with a dash of personal grief) who has a delicate question to ask and who is angered by opposition, to one of confidence, control (still with grief), who has got what she wanted, and now just needs to pass on some instructions.

She sat up and, holding her phone in her hand, said almost as an announcement, "I am transferring everything we know about Alan's death to you now. It's not much, as we only had one night to look into it, but the reports, with photographs from police comrades, are there. I've included some statements which were taken. The forensic reports are there, too. It's basic but a start. Plus there are some useful numbers you can ring and some notes from me. I want you to see what you can find out about this. Alan was a dear friend and an important comrade, and I want someone I can *trust* to look into it." She paused and then with heavier emphasis, "The party wants someone—*needs* someone…"

"But I'm not qualified." I was aware that the whining teenager had lost the argument to tidy up his room. Again, although I had been perfectly clear in what I had said, it appeared to translate into agreement. The adolescent would have to realise that the socks were going to be put away.

To rub it in, I was given a maternal pep talk. "I have faith in you, Pete. Maybe it's time you regained that faith in yourself. I think you will do a good job. Time is against you, as we have managed to keep this quiet for now but for how long, who knows? Only those who need to be, have been informed, but it's only a matter of time before it becomes public knowledge. Once it does, I think we can assume that it will cause a furor, so I think it would be easier if you could do as much as you can before that happens."

Fab. I now had been given my very own You Have Twenty Hours to Solve This, or You're Off the Case speech. It was usually said by some well-meaning but plodding senior officer. Often to be PC—politically correct, not the other one—they would be black, female, overweight, or a combination of all three, which always appeared to be the case on the screen, though not in real life. Well, Jackie was two of the three, but she certainly wasn't plodding or indeed overweight. Unlike those maverick cops to whom it's usually addressed, I was perfectly content not to get the case in the first place, if nothing else, because I had no idea what the case actually was.

All this was irrelevant. She stood up and slipped the phone into her pocket. Obviously her job here was done. All agreed. All arranged and all motions passed. Great. She said a few more things, but I wasn't really listening. The word gob smacked came to mind. Numbness returning, I saw her out before I returned to the sanctuary of my armchair.

Red had also returned, sat on the floor, and looked straight at me. I returned the eyeballing. Yes, mate, you can look, but I saw you scarper pretty quickly when she arrived. The jumping frogs by the pond were more interesting, were they? I ignored him and switched the TV on.

Seconds later, as my head was trying to unravel what had just happened, it went dead—the TV, that is—my head couldn't decide whether or not to. So did the lights and the electric clock. Power cut. Again. I sighed. Was it a strike against the government? Or was it a strike which was pro-government and against the workers' councils? Was it for some demands I wasn't aware of? Or was it a common, garden-variety, and all-too-usual power shortage?

"Shit." Whatever it was, I took it as a sign that my nice, carefully planned day had just changed.

CHAPTER TWO
Problems of Everyday Life

The traffic was minimal between my manor of North London (or in the modern parliamentary jargon—London Sectors) and East London, the latter being Alan Wiltshire's part of town. I say *manor*, because riding the scooter always made me feel as if I was in some cool 1960s gangster flick. 'Course, cool 1960s gangsters wouldn't have been seen shotgun dead on a scooter but rather would be wheel spinning Jags or Rovers. But then, self-delusion doesn't have to be realistic because, well, it's delusional.

The only real snag was a mini-convoy of three armoured carriers loudly and *slowly* trundling down Holloway Road. Dwarfing me and thwarting my many attempts to overtake them had made it more *Lavender Hill Mob* than *Italian Job*. Once they had turned off, taking a corner of pavement with them, it had been pretty clear from then on.

This was at least partly due to the fact that much of the traffic was in lines queuing up and desperately hoping that there was some electricity left in the public storage cells to boost their cars. Files of green cars had drivers with red faces. The Highbury Corner substation was especially busy, with many an anxious driver wondering how long this power stoppage would last. I drove past them with a look of non-fraternal smugness, relishing the benefits of relying on a scooter. This little thing could go a good many kilometres on just a solitary charge. The old petrol heads, who had managed to get hold of some drops of the black gold, drove past feeling superior and wearing welcome-to-our-world looks. The faces of the drivers of the green cars went green.

Swinging into Alan's road, I could see that they still had red flags waving from the front windows from the Worker's Day of last week. Then again, they might be a permanent feature, as we had such days pretty well once a month. Keeping them up saved a lot of ladder work. Although it had been a while since I had been here, remembering which one of the terraced, two-story, Victorian houses was his was not exactly a stretch. His was the one with formidably large iron shutters. Those on the ground floor were closed, somewhat spoiling the bay features and making the house resemble a battleship. I had a similar house, with similar windows, but mine had window boxes—not so macho but a great deal more elegant. More grand design than grand dreadnought.

Further security was being supplied with two people lounging on deck chairs in his small, concrete, front garden. I parked up and turned off the bike. I could see that it was a man and woman, both in their twenties. Both were donned in skin-tight jeans and T-shirts and were in identical, wraparound, black sunglasses. Mine were rather cool, blue, round ones which I noted were becoming popular once more—indeed, dare I say it, even trendy—due to the success of the e-musician AriFat who sported them in every picture. Personally, I thought of myself more of a Lenin or a Lennon. But then we can all dream, blah, blah.

Their look of students on vacation was only slightly spoilt by the incongruous sight of the submachine gun resting on the female's lap. Even in times such as ours, I still didn't think firearms were the gap-year accessory of choice. Both stood up as I dismounted and watched me with suspicion as I approached them.

It was only after I had taken off my helmet and shades that they relaxed. Obviously I had a friendly face. It must have also been a common one, as they appeared to know me. I could see by their lapel badges that they were party members, but in all honesty I couldn't recall ever having met them. Before I had a chance to say anything, the man, a youth of heavily gelled hair and rather acute cheek bones, welcomed me. "Pete Kalder, isn't it? Comrade Jackie Payne said you would be coming and texted a photo over of you; not a particularly flattering one, but we recognise you." They both giggled; obviously, the photograph was not destined for a centrefold of Class-Conscious Hunks of the Month. "We've got the key," he added.

He rummaged deep in his pockets to find it. So Jackie had told them to expect me, had she? Was that before or after she had met me? My guess was that it was before she had even called me. I wasn't sure how I felt about being so predictable. How did she know that I would agree to her frankly boggle-eyed request? I myself didn't know until I was halfway here. And I couldn't really tell you why I had agreed, if indeed I had. It might have been because I felt loyalty to her or to the party. Then again, perhaps her jabs at my inactivity had hurt more than I thought, and guilt had brought me. Maybe it was the very fact that I *had* felt guilt and shock and anger that had done it. Feeling something, *anything*, was still a novelty. Whatever the reason, I was here. And why start here? Well, Jackie had guessed that correctly, as well. Not that it was a great act of clairvoyance on her part, as it was the logical place to do so. Start where he ended it all—the place where he had committed suicide. *If*, of course, it had been suicide.

Finally finding the key, which looked to be somewhere by the back of his leg from the position of his hand, comrade gel handed it over to me. Taking the plastic card, I thanked him and opened the door. I was about to say that I didn't need their help, but noticing that both were already seated and back to enjoying the sun, I realised that I didn't really need to, because none was going to be offered.

I stepped in and entered the front room. Forgetting the power situation, or lack of, I turned on the light switch, but of course, nothing happened. With the shutters closed, there was very little light to illuminate the gloom. It was almost dark. I hadn't thought about that. Hoping that my phone was charged up, and thankful I didn't have an earPC which is "brilliantly compact for all your tech needs," except that is, when you require a torch which right now was exactly what I needed.

The first room lit up to show the dark silhouettes of shelves upon shelves of books. The walls were covered with them in no particular order and not much chance of being even the correct way up. What books weren't on the shelves, whether horizontal or vertical, were in piles on the floor. Tower blocks of them tottered upwards. Whatever Alan may or may not have been, a librarian he wasn't.

Unlike my house, there were no through doors between the front two rooms. Looking next into what nominally was the dining room, I could see the same landscape—books everywhere. To be fair, in a concession to everyday living, there was a dining table, but that had piles of magazines and newspapers covering it. And, of course, books. What was it that an American Trotskyist way back in the 1920s or '30s had once said? Something like, "The only thing Socialists have in common is that they steal your wives and your books."

Ignoring the sexism for the moment and the quandary of where gay male comrades might fit in, it certainly wasn't true of this one; there'd only been one woman in my life. Now Alan, on the other hand…He hadn't actually stolen any, but in his day he had certainly attracted a good few. Women had warmed to his intellect, many finding it compelling, which was probably just as well, as I could not think of anything else which might have done the trick (unless, of course, they had wanted to purloin his books).

I'd have been tempted to a romantic fling if I could have laid my hands on his collection. He had some real rarities here, titles that hadn't been in hard form for half a century. He, like me, was an old-fashioned type who liked to be able to hold the thing you were reading or listening to. Paperless reading had only a limited appeal to him. Taking a step further in, I could see a treasure trove of Penguin classics just sprawling across the floor. Mouth-watering editions from the 1950s: Fitzgerald's *Tender Is the Night*, Wyndham's *Kraken Wakes*, and Jerome's *Three Men in a Boat*. Glorious stuff. Their orange stripes just seemed to be yelling to find a new home. Mine. A naughty thought flashed through my mind, but I quickly banished it. No, helping myself to a few would not be right, even if no one would notice.

Leaving my temptations behind, I went to climb the stairs but paused. A claw dug into my bowels. Involuntarily, I looked towards first the front door and then, as if possessing x-ray eyes, to the pair outside. It didn't help. I could feel a sense of coldness and a little foreboding in venturing further into his house. Being a die-hard materialist, I didn't believe in the supernatural, but was I feeling a wee bit spooked? "Pull yourself together," I muttered to myself and ascended the beige carpeted stairs. Maybe it was the colour making my teeth chatter. I was more a striped-floor kind of dweller, and if it was to be a carpet, then beige it certainly wouldn't be. Who would choose beige? Insipid and uninspired. Then again, I doubted if Alan had even noticed it had existed.

Reaching the top, I breathed a sigh of relief that no ghosts had grabbed me—yet. Yeah, if I kept the smart-arse dialogue going in my head, I might just manage to ignore the concern I was feeling.

The front bedroom, the largest room on the first floor, was the reason for my intrepid expedition because this was where he had set up his office and where he spent most of his time when he was at home. A good place to start, I wisely thought to myself.

With the shutters open, the rooms upstairs were light. This made my visit a little easier, though you had to wonder at Alan's ideas of security—that danger would only come at ground level. Obviously, the baddies never had ladders.

It was a good-sized room, with the obligatory bookcases circling an old IKEA desk which, at a guess, dated from the early years of the century. Some middle-class trendies would pay good money for a vintage classic like that. Although, and I am no expert on such matters, the chipped corners might detract from the value, as would the multitude of telephone numbers, quotes, and statistics, written in blue Biro which covered it. By the bay window were neat piles of past magazines and newspapers as well as yet more books.

I sat myself down on the matching computer chair and stared at his laptop. He'd written scores of articles and a number of books on the old thing. Old being the operative word because this was old-school ICT, as in Tom Brown's school. We did have some things in common, like being pretty well stuck in the technology of several decades ago. Despite its antiquity, he relied heavily on it, and I figured that it would be worth a root about.

If it worked; now, there was a thought. With the power strike, that might be in doubt. Then again, Alan would always leave the mains lead in (yes, it still had such a thing as a mains lead), so maybe the battery was charged up. One thing I wanted to see straightaway was the data Jackie had given me; my eyes preferred the screen size to my phone's, and furthermore, my phone's project facility was screwed after dropping the phone last week on one of my constitutional walks.

After turning it on and feeling relieved that the battery was full, I typed in his password—KARLMARX. An original choice, it wasn't. But it was still his, and it worked; the laptop started up.

The obvious thing to look at first was his video message. I watched it again, trying to take in what he was saying. He said he had started working for MI5 in 2010. Placing it in a timeline by using personal history, I thought back. It was well before I had started working as a librarian. Actually, in 2010, if you had told the youthful me that I would really take a job as a librarian, I would have wet myself laughing. How would that fit into nights and mornings of clubbing, MDMA, and dancing? I had been a history student back then, which had made minimal demands on my time. That was taken up with my social life.

Not that I was a mindless night clubber. I had general feelings of what was right and what was wrong, but I wasn't in the party and would not be so for several years. There had been some courtship, but it had just been flirting, nothing serious. You could say, though, that my political life had been born then, during the anti-cuts campaigns of the first austerity governments. Simultaneously, it could be said that Alan's had died then. It was still an astonishing proposition. It was quite possible that at some uni meeting when I had first heard Alan speak, he had been a police spy! Whilst pontificating about the need for a revolutionary party, he had been an MI5 snitch! That was even more amazing than me becoming a librarian.

Watching him make this confession, I remembered all the times we had met. Was there anything that might have given a clue as to this double life? Lame in its predictability, I tried to think of anything I had found strange about his manner or attitude. Strange, that is, aside from the inadequacies of his personality, some of which could have been explained by his absorption in politics or by his obvious shyness or just that he had been an awkward bugger. In social situations, he would almost shrink into his M&S V-neck rather than talk to people. If it was a political situation, he would battle bravely with a preference of hiding in a corner with a book and force himself to talk—often at length—politics to someone who had shown an interest. He wasn't unfriendly, and he could be kind, but human interaction was always clumsy and graceless. Even his gait, slouched to the point of almost hunchback, gave the impression of being a centimetre off colliding into a vase. Usually unshaven, his wayward hair which resembled a collapsed quiff and nasal hair which needed hedge trimmers to control added to the effect. He oozed slovenliness. You couldn't say that about his work, though. He was unimpeachable at that.

I watched again and again, but nothing jumped out at me. The proverbial wild goose was being pursued. It looked legit; I could not see any hesitation in his speaking, and he kept his eyes at the webcam. It did not look as if anyone was forcing him. But then, how would I know? They were hardly going to be standing there with his arm yanked behind his back, were they?

One thing did strike me: looking at him, I saw total blankness. There seemed to be a total lack of emotion, as if it had been sucked out of him, leaving a deflated balloon. My wife, Caroline, who had worked with him a few times and had known him slightly better than me, had commented on how when he was left alone, he had almost seemed to shrivel. She said that when he was with people, he played the part of a leading member. When that audience went, he became a lonely man. We had often discussed how isolated he appeared to be, and whether for all the convictions to the cause, the cause itself gave him a conviction to live. That appeared to be all but gone in this recording. Perhaps his suicide told us that his act wasn't from solitariness but from betrayal of his convictions.

Certainly seeing him in front of me, blankly looking out, reminded me of somebody I knew well. Me. I knew all about alienation and a feeling of remoteness, of feeling completely detached from the world. Oh, I could write a whole book about the subject. Not that it would be a particularly original one—man loses the two things he most cherishes in life, his partner and his daughter, and so loses interest in that life. Same old story.

But what of Alan? Now there was a twist in the tale. Working for MI5 wasn't the usual thing men did in a personal crisis. Usually they bought a flashy new car, wore far-too-young clothes or got a haircut that looked good on someone a third of their age, that sort of thing. They usually didn't work for the Security Service. Certainly, looking at the total surrender in his eyes, it hadn't worked. He would have been better off with a visit to the hair salon. Only when he said "foolish" did he show any emotion, and that was pure rage. It resembled one of the robots in the old sci-fi movies that the audience had thought was dead, but they realised there was life in the machine when its eyes went from grey to red.

I zoomed in and looked at his face but only saw a broad spread of lines and wrinkles, with greying hair seemingly everywhere. Something I did clock were the books behind him. No surprise, I know, but it did give me an idea. I zoomed in further to see if I could see the titles. They were all in a uniform cream with black bold lettering. Though the picture was slightly distorting as I enlarged, I could easily see some Roman numbering. I knew the books: *The Collected Works of Marx and Engels*. They were behind me. Turning round and looking at them with the sun shining on one end of the set gave me another idea. Looking carefully at them, I could see volumes 5, 7, and 8, and I could see light reflecting off the binding. I played the message again but now enlarged it to its maximum amount, focused on those volumes. I watched closely, but the light remained the same, no jumping or change in angle, direction, or intensity. It didn't look to me as if it had been edited; it looked like one continuous filming.

Feeling that I had exhausted the video (there were only so many times I could watch Alan drone on), I flicked onto what Jackie had saved. Seeing the titles of the folders, the question did pop up: So where to look? Not an easy one to answer, as I still had no idea *what* I was looking for. There were several different types of files, and they had been created at various times through the night. There was one named David Wiltshire. Not that anyone ever called him David; it was always Dave. With the cast-iron logic of not having any idea of what else to do and knowing that Dave had found Alan, I started with that one.

What it consisted of was not what I had hoped for—his thoughts—not video, verbal, or even typed, but a typed, brief report from someone called Vic Cole. The top read that it was from Vic Cole, NW London Police Council, Camden Workers' Council, and Camden United Revolutionary Socialist Party. Well, that was showing his credentials. I was surprised the "Internationale" didn't start up and a couple of red flags thrust out from the screen as I read it. So this was our good friend, Police Comradestable Officer Cole. "I was proceeding in a westerly direction when I observed a rum-looking fellow. I'm not political; I was only doing my job, though now I am political and doing my job."

"Pull yourself together, Pete; we are talking about someone's death here." It was someone I knew, to boot. So I read what Copper Cole had to say.

Dave had arrived at Alan's at approximately six thirty. He hadn't phoned ahead because he thought he would give his grandfather a surprise visit. Impressively, Dave had gotten hold of some fresh croissants. I was jealous. Uprisings were all very well, but you did go without things. Dave said they usually saw each other about once a fortnight, but it had been three weeks since they'd last met, so he had thought that Alan would welcome the visit. He had guessed he'd be at home, as Alan had told him he would be housebound for a few days whilst he did some research for the party.

That was something which surprised me as being a touch unusual—research? *Now?* Surely he wasn't writing a book! I knew he was an academic, but I couldn't really believe him penning a study of Voltaire as the walls of capitalism came crashing down. Then again, would I have ever believed I'd be here in this situation! Dave didn't know anything about what research Alan was doing, and Cole hadn't asked.

Dave hadn't seen anyone except one of the neighbours, Zak at number twenty-three, who was washing his car. I noted that Police Officer Cole had helpfully put a link to statements from the people nearest to Alan's house. Dave had let himself in and, finding no one downstairs but seeing the upstairs light on, had gone up. He looked first in the study; the computer was on, but the room was empty. Then he had gone into the bedroom. It was there that he had found him, lying face up, fully clothed, on the bed.

Why Cole thought it was important that he had clothes on, I wasn't sure, or why he had felt the need to list them. For the record, he was wearing jeans; a red, black, and blue plaid shirt; a pair of grey socks; and black boxer shorts. So, in other words, Alan had not dressed up for the occasion.

Dave had immediately checked Alan's pulse. With a nice line in alliteration, he described Alan as having a "ghoulish, greyish-green colour." He found that he was dead, although in desperation, he did try various resuscitation techniques. These were also listed, noting in passing that whilst trying mouth to mouth, Alan had an unpleasant, metallic taste. That and whatever else he tried were unsuccessful. He thought Alan had been dead for some time, as he felt cold (there was another link to an additional file).

I didn't know whether Jackie had always had me in mind to do this task, but Cole's notes were written as though he had been asked to write in a style aimed at an amateur who required the facts served up in an accessible manner. Nothing was too detailed, and all was easy to read. Think a student guide to a supposed murder/suicide—an idiot's guide to a suspicious death.

At 7:00 p.m., Dave had made his first call. It was to Jackie. That was an interesting choice of person to call after you've found a dead body. Not the police, not the ambulance, but the leader of a political party. Not that Cole questioned the choice—far too arse-licking for that. No doubt he thought, "Who else would you call but Comrade Payne?" He did ask one question, though. "Why the thirty-minute delay?" Dave had said it was from trying to resuscitate Alan, and then he had just sat there in shock. That sounded about right to me. Dave's a sensitive young man, the type to cry after passing a dead fox on the roadside. Finding a dead grandfather would be pretty grim for most of us, but especially for Dave.

Jackie had got there an hour later with two unnamed comrades, followed by a whole militia of people. Phoning them as she travelled (and as I could testify, very few people said no to a command from Ms Payne), Vic Cole had arrived ten minutes later. Then came Asher Joseph, apparently a forensic scientist, then Roijin Kemal, a forensic ICT scientist, whatever that might be, and finally someone I had heard of, Marie Williams. Marie—yet another interesting choice of person to be summoned to the death scene.

Again, Cole had not queried the choice of people. He did state that Dave had spoken to Alan the day before, at approximately eleven in the morning, and he had been in fine spirits. Indeed, so much so, that Cole had quoted Dave. "He sounded like a kid in a sweetshop. Whatever this research was, it was making him happy." There was a helpful note: "David could not think of a reason why Alan Wiltshire would commit suicide." Gee, thanks, Vic. I needed that explained to me.

And that was that. Not much, I had to say. I clicked on one of the links and found brief video statements from various neighbours. None of them had seen anything suspicious that particular day or in any of the proceeding days. Question was: What was classified as suspicious nowadays? Right at this moment, two armed students were sunbathing in the front, and that wasn't even registering a twitch of a curtain. None of the neighbours could recall seeing any visitors in the previous days, which at least two of them, including Zak the car washer, did say was unusual, as often there would be quite a coming and going of people.

Getting up and stretching, I asked myself for the thousandth time, what the bloody hell I was doing here. I mean, what did Jackie want me to find? I needed a break from the *Cole's Guide to Crime Investigation*, so I left the study and opened the door into Alan's bedroom which if not a murder scene, was at least the scene of the death. I had never been in there before, and it surprised me. It was neat and tidy and with no books. This was the only room in the house which did not shout at you with a desire for knowledge, or of a man devoted to politics. Even in the bathroom, there were books, both paper and e-, by the loo; in the kitchen, the two screens had one devoted to e-books, and the other, the news channels.

The walls were painted in a pastel green, and two prints hung opposite his double bed. Taking a closer look, I saw that they were both by the mid-twentieth-century painter Oliver Kilbourn. One was the aptly titled *North Street Corner*, which was a painting of just that in Northern England, and the other was of daffodils in a window, entitled *Spring*. Very seasonal. They were quite sweet and almost naïve and not the artwork I had expected to be on his walls. We party members could usually be relied on for posters of the like of Malevich or Kandinsky or maybe a Diego Rivera. And, of course, Picasso's *Guernica*. Go for the abstract and lacking sentimentality—quite the opposite of these two.

Elsewhere in the room, there was a small wardrobe, a set of drawers, and a bedside cabinet. On the latter were a cheap-looking lamp and a photograph showing a middle-aged Alan smiling, sitting on what looked like a pub-garden bench with a young baby gurgling on his lap. Alan not being one of this world's great paternal types, I guessed that this must be baby Dave. Especially as sitting next to him and holding one of the baby's hands was Stuart, Alan's only son and Dave's father. They looked alike, as did Dave when he grew up. All in the photograph had honest-looking faces, passably good-looking whilst not being drop-dead gorgeous. They had a melancholic air about them, even when quite obviously happy here. The forehead and cheeks seemed to always say, "We have the world on our backs."

I sat on the bed and picked up the photograph. I wondered where Dave's mum, Anisha, was. Maybe she was holding the camera. Perhaps finding it amusing, aiming it at father and son's almost comic shorts which displayed classic English knobbly knees. Alan wore a tatty-looking T-shirt with an enormous clenched fist. I had never met Stuart. Unlike his father and later, Dave, he was not political in any shape or form, and judging from the fact that he was unashamedly wearing a U2 T-shirt, he wasn't really into music, either. Not good music, in any case.

Dave had been brought up on a small farm in Norfolk, and then as soon as he was, at least in the eyes of the law, an adult, Stuart and Anisha had moved up to Scotland and set up another farm. The last I heard was that they were still together and had moved onto an island up there. I could remember Alan once mentioning that he had lost contact with them, although Dave did so, on a regular basis, and would often visit in the summer holidays. Like anyone's kids, you never knew how a comrade's kids were going to grow up, but I have to say, being a son of a leading Trotskyist and becoming Farmer Giles was pretty unusual.

I looked around and saw a disturbingly fresh stain on the bed. I hadn't noticed it when I had first come in—well, you got to be a bit pervy, looking for bed stains, haven't you? It also rather merged into the quilt's garish flower pattern. But whatever the reason for my not noticing it on first entering the room, seeing it now made me stand up pretty smartly.

As I did, I heard children's voices coming from outside. Using it as a convenient excuse not to examine the discoloration on the bed linen, I went over to the window. I could see into next door's back garden. Three children were bouncing as high as they could on a trampoline, whilst two more appeared to be circling it on push cars. All were laughing hysterically. I watched for few minutes, the pure innocent fun bringing a smile to my face.

But I had work to do. Feeling thirsty, I wondered if Dave had left his prized Kenyan coffee downstairs and whether there was any fresh milk before remembering that there was a power cut, so that was a no-no.

I left the room with the stain and returned to Alan's office and his laptop. The screen said I still had two hours of battery time left. Seeing a file marked Photographs, I opened it up and found that it was hardly Robert Capa. It more resembled an unimaginative estate agent's portfolio on a property. There were pictures of the downstairs and upstairs windows, as well as the front and back doors. This, I guessed, was to show no forced entry. Then, there were photographs of the room I was in. What took my attention was the bedroom. That had Alan lying on it, shirt open, and head to one side. You'd never see that in a property portfolio.

Next to it was the 3-D symbol. I paused because I did not really want a better picture of him. I could not really see any point of it. If the professionals were convinced, then who was I to doubt them? Sick-inducing images of what an overdose can do to the human body was not something I really wanted to look at. Still, I pressed it.

A tiny image appeared in front of the screen. Facing me was the macabre sight of Alan's corpse. I slid back so as not to find myself in some virtual nightmare with my ear mingling with his torso. With my hand, I swiped it to go closer. Dave's description of Alan's skin colour was pretty accurate. It certainly wasn't his usual translucent white but was more the colour of potatoes going off. Not pretty.

Neither, although for a different reason, were the photographs of the three-quarter-consumed bottle of whisky and two empty bottles of pills on the bedside cabinet, obscuring the family photo of the male Wiltshires enjoying a pint which were shown as I waived a shift in perspective. I felt something in me. It was a poignant image, and one I didn't want to linger on. I had the whole scene hovering right there to look at, but I had enough of it.

Pushing aside the image and putting it on hold, I went back to the screen. Roijin Kemal's report was concerned with the legitimacy of the video. Neatly listed with asterisks, there were four tests which she—I presumed from the name it was a she—had conducted to verify that the video had been recorded in one session and had not been edited, amended, enhanced, or altered in any way. Basically, fancy advanced ICT tests had confirmed my *Collected Works of Marx* volume 5 test. Roijin reckoned the file was kosher or in her words, "a file of integrity." Considering what it was, I reflected, the description was an unfortunate and ironic way of putting it.

So far, so little. With no clue as what to do next, I minimised the report and waited for inspiration. None came. Idly deciding to nose into what research he had been doing, I decided to take a gander at his computer's directory. Not that I expected anything of worth to be seen or any clues as to why he had chosen to take his own life. It was hardly likely that it had been so dull that he had ended it all. I was just curious.

What was immediately striking was that since a week ago, not a single file of *any description* had been created. Looking at his multitude of different types of electronic mail, I could see that there was an equal silence. According to this, Alan had not touched his laptop for seven whole days. Not to write anything or communicate anything. Indeed, according to this, he had not even looked at the Internet. So whatever research he had been doing, he had not needed to use it. Highly unlikely. Indeed, impossible.

His social network sites were equally silent after what seemed to be pretty regular usage beforehand. Roijin made no mention of that fact. Unless Santa had popped one down the chimney, Alan did not have any other computers. One was all he could, if not master, then muster. He would have used it in that time. Who didn't use their computer daily? Hourly? His history previous to this supposed purdah showed that he used the laptop extensively in all the ways you would expect. I could even see that his favourite tune of choice was Mozart's "Piano Concerto No. 21." That had been played at least twice a day before the week's silence. Odd then, it all goes quiet.

Still, there was one way of checking, even on the old-fashioned hard drives. He had, I noticed, been of sufficient technical suss to have the gHost system, so any electronic activity was copied there. Finding that—predictably (why had MI5 needed spies when we were this unsubtle?)—his password for that was also karlmarx, I got in. It confirmed that for a week, he had seemingly not been in contact with anyone or anything. Puzzling.

The only time and date registered for seven whole days was 11:35, last night. Before that, it was as I had discovered, *seemingly* unused for a grand total of 172 hours. But again I asked myself, if Alan was supposed to have been researching something so important, which took him away from the revolution, wouldn't the computer have shown *some* activity? But there was nothing; not even the video facility registered any use. Which was plainly incorrect; he had taped his confession on it. But by 11:35 last night, he was long dead, and his home was full of a posse of comrades led by Jackie Payne. So where was the entry of the video being made? There wasn't any, which could only mean one thing: that it had been erased.

Stretching my knowledge of such things to the max, I looked in his gHost imprint, which had a facility showing the times of files erased. There it was, a cam video erased at 2:22 a.m. As had been huge swathes of files and done so in such an organised way, that I could not tell what the names of these files were or even what types of files they had been.

That they had been deleted was as far as my ICT skills stretched. If I was honest, I was damned impressed with myself that I could trace the fact they'd been deleted in the first place. But there was no mention of this in the notes from Vic Cole. Surely they would have noticed it straightaway? Wasn't one of them a techie, forensic type of bod? This Roijin Kemal person would have. But of course, there was nothing to notice because the files *were* at that time *there*. Judging by the fact that the computer been turned on at 11:35 and turned off three hours later, they had not been staring at blank space. My bet was that they had been looking at whatever Alan had been doing in those missing 172 hours. In which case, had sister Roijin helped Cole to erase them?

Reverting back to the files Jackie had given me, I scanned them for any mention of this happening but couldn't see any. Was that because she didn't know or that she didn't want me to? I would ask her later.

Leaving aside the erased files, I cast an eye over Asher Joseph's report; it wasn't quite as simply written as Cole's or Kemal's. It was chocker with medical jargon and had every conceivable chart and graph you could think of, enough to bring a satisfied grin to the most die-hard maths teacher. On first reading, I understood one word in twenty. The rest was all but intelligible. I did have a simple way around this. When I had been researching the background to Catholic Church art of Florence in the fifteenth century, I had been lost in the number of saints, so by simply using Explainspeak, I could have instant accounts of the multitudes of Marks, Peters, and Pauls. I did so with this one; instead of martyrs, I was hoping to have the drug explained. Alan's computer was presently visual-only, so I didn't have the joy of the bizarre experience of being spoken to by a computer speaking English with a Brazilian accent.

 Pretty quickly, I began to understand what he had written. Or at least raise it to fourteen words in twenty. Basically, Alan had swallowed one-and-a-half bottles of Xrenanthol Bulinate, which was a drug for recovering cancer sufferers. Seeing that did ring a bell or two; a few years ago, it was being hailed as the wonder drug to cure all cancers. According to the software, it did not quite do so, but it did have a high reputation for helping cure most strands of the disease. Expected dosage, depending on the individual, was one to three pills a day. It was strictly controlled as, despite its success, it did have possible severe side effects of diarrhea, headaches, stiffness, and a number of other ones which as far as I could tell were always in the health warnings of drugs, whether they were anti-cancer, anti-depression, or anti-acid. Two did jump out at me, though—depression and severe mood swings. Enough, I wondered, to kill oneself? And I asked myself, why did Alan have them? Did he have cancer? But hadn't Jackie told me that he was *fighting fit*? I was quickly coming to the conclusion that I had a few things I wanted to raise with her.

I read on, understanding that whisky and a bizarre selection of sweets had prevented Alan from vomiting the drugs up. That raised yet another question of what the stain was. On second thoughts, I did not really want to find out. My helpful and knowledgeable online teacher explained in as accessible terms as it could how the sugar and alcohol had combined to ease the consumption of the Xrenanthol Bulinate. How would Alan have known that? Explainspeak told me that as well; it was in the accompanying notes. There was guidance for overdosing? No, it replied—probably relieved that as a computer function, it had patience inbuilt—it was a fact that some people who took them could not keep them down. Or he might have been told by his specialist (these were prescription-only drugs).

Since coming here, I had unleashed a Pandora's Box of clichés. Not least, that old whodunit chestnut of the intrepid, lone detective—be they private or police—muttering in frustration, "This just provokes more questions than it does answers." Indeed. I decided that this intrepid, lone detective really did need another chat with Jackie. As I deciphered the medical report, I gave her a ring, but despite this morning's assurance that I could reach her at any time, I could not and, instead, only reached her voice mail. I left a brief request to call me.

Getting back to the medical report, it seemed that the large intake of such a drug would have overloaded his heart, causing a massive cardiac arrest. It would have been this, rather than any slower poisoning, which would have killed him. In Asher Joseph's opinion, it would have been pretty quick. Losing consciousness after a few minutes and then probably between five to ten minutes later, his heart all but exploded. This wasn't quite how Asher put it. He provided an extensive description, backed by an obligatory set of graphs and photographs with impressive medical jargon on the effects of an overdose of the drug. I tried to glean as much normal person info as I could. Fixed, dilated eyes and a yellowing of them was an obvious one with the skin changing colour, as both Dave and I had seen. For reasons I once more failed to understand (even with the computerised tutoring) his breath and his urine would have given off a particular smell. Again, as Dave had noticed. The mystery of the stain was also solved. In his death throes, he would have pissed himself. Well, that was nice to know.

That blasted 3-D symbol appeared again, daring me to try it. Against what my heart and head, not to mention my stomach, was telling me, I did my duty and again took the plunge. More close-ups of discoloured skin, tongue, and various other parts of his anatomy fluttered in front of me. I was thankful that Alan did not have a more up-to-date machine because whilst the image would flicker less, the clarity would be greater, and so it would have been even more grotesque. Still, I had a quick look, the emphasis being on the quickness rather than the looking. Despite getting it over as swiftly as I could, the morning's toast was threatening to rise up. Alive, Alan may not have been a matinée idol, but dead, there was no other description but repulsive.

From tests on rigor mortis, which was in the early stages, and the body temperature, Asher estimated that Alan had been dead for between three-and-a-half to five hours. He stated that after he had taken Alan to his laboratory, he could be more precise. He reeled off a whole series of tests which included doing things with stomach contents, blood samples, and whatnot.

The final section of the report was a detailed analysis of muscles, bruising, and skin. Joseph seemed incapable of calling a part of the body by a name I might recognise, so reading was slow. There was also the problem of initials cropping up everywhere, as if they were coalition governments.

Of course, Explainspeak translated these, but the problem with initials is that they often can stand for several reasons. This proved to be unintentionally amusing, as Asher had written that "STD indicated that his body heat was consistent to a trauma." STD, in this case, I discovered, meant Sensory Thermo Diagram and not sexually transmitted disease. It was part of the ESIS, whatever that was, when it was at home. I discovered that that stood for an Electro Sensitivity Impression Scanner, basically a gizmo the size of a cigar packet that showed on a screen various wonderful things, including bruising which might be as a result of pressure. From this, he could tell that Dave had tried to force Alan's heart back to life, but there was no other evidence of any external pressure on the body—none around the wrists, the arms, or the throat. Conclusion: no one had held him down, and no one had forced the pills down his throat.

The laptop was saying that there was still life in its battery, but to be brutally honest, there wasn't any in mine. I felt weary of all this, a little nauseous, and with a stonking headache coming on. There were more pleasant ways to spend a morning—enough of sitting in this room staring at this gore. Morgues weren't my idea of fun palaces, even when they were on-screen. Playing virtual autopsy wasn't ever going to top the games charts.

I got up and turned off the laptop. I needed to settle my stomach, and hopefully a drink and something to eat would do the trick. Especially if it was with the living.

Once more, bravely—heroically, even—resisting the desire to help myself to some of his books, I went downstairs and outside. On my way out, I interrupted what looked like some serious flirting between our friendly red guards. I asked them how long they expected to be here. Hair-gel boy shrugged and mumbled, "No idea." I asked if they knew why they were here in the first place. This time, rifle-girl shrugged. Leaving the two great orators to their quality time, I headed for a café I knew around the corner.

Owned by a Polish family, it had been here for years. Alan and I had come here daily when we were writing our pamphlet together. If memory served me right, he always had a toasted ham and tomato Panini. The owners had expanded their retail empire to include a dry cleaner which I noticed was now closed down, and a corner shop which I could see through the window had nothing, give or take the odd pyramid of tins, but empty shelves.

The café was separated from these outreaches of business by what used to be a bookie's, which was now being squatted. Humorous speech bubbles had been pasted on pictures of past sporting heroes. The televisions that had captivated and enticed punters with horse racing, football, and every other sport you could imagine now sat covered in dust and cobwebs. Next to it was a boarded-up building which I think had been at various times a hairdresser, a newsagent, and a toy shop. Now it was derelict. Times were hard.

I strolled into the café, now the only functioning part of this row of shops. Seeing the camping stoves on the counter, I figured I could get at least something here. Three individuals were already in and seated. Two had their noses hovering above differing types of computer notepads, reading online newspapers. Approaching the counter, I was met by a "Good morning, mate. Sorry, no hot food, but I can do ya sandwiches." I smiled; previously, the owner had called everyone boss. Alan had joked, and I remembered it well because Alan did not often do such a thing, that we'd know revolution was coming when he stopped calling people boss. He had now. The owner had come over to England when he was a young child and, settling into his adopted country, had acquired quite a Bob Hoskins accent. He looked like him, as well. I wondered if the great British actor had spent any time in Warsaw.

I ordered a cheese sandwich and a coffee. Whilst that was being made, I noticed a few hard-copy newspapers in various states of disrepair on the tables, and I grabbed the *Revolutionary Worker* and, for a good dose of concerned Liberalism, the *Guardian*. I'd had my fill of computer screens this morning, so I was happy to stick to reliable, old paper.

Sitting below a picture of the 2028/29 Arsenal squad, I cradled the mug in my hands. I looked around at all the pictures lining the place. The oldest was a black-and-white one of the 1930/31 title winning team. Being a Gooner myself, I had loved all these, but they had left Alan cold. He had just looked at me blankly and went on to talk seemingly for hours about the politics of the British worker's passion for sport.

The food arrived, and I ate it hungrily whilst burying myself in the *Worker*. The front page reported the call from the workers' councils to workers across the world to join in fighting the proposals which were expected to come from today's meeting of the finance ministers in Zurich. Basically, our esteemed ministers were there, begging their Chinese counterparts for cash to bail us out. In return, they were willing to sell, loan, or give anything that the Chinese wanted. Everything was up for sale. The Americans were refusing to help, as they were still in a sulk about the freezing of some of their major companies' assets in Europe. The paper reported on action taken across several countries, including air-traffic-control workers in Italy who were refusing to let their minister even leave the country. In Belgium and France, workers were thinking of doing likewise, so theirs were either going to drive or link up by video conference. The party applauded the action but pointed out that it was symbolic, and what was needed was to remove these people from making the deals in the first place.

The *Guardian* led with the same story but with more hand-wringing. They regretted, again, the position of the US president and argued, as if he would be reading the paper over his muffins, that the European Parliament had been forced to take the action against the US multinationals, in part, because they were draining the former countries of the UK and other countries' economies and in part, because something was needed to satisfy the growing unrest. It hadn't worked, but the president couldn't blame the European nations for doing it. Maybe he should look at the actions of his country's company directors. They went on to call for restraint from the workers' movement across the continent. In a nutshell, theirs was an anti-begging position to China because we should be begging the United States instead, and the rest of us should do as we were told.

And I had to do what I was told. So I looked at the list of phone numbers I'd been given. I knew personally just one of them, Marie Williams. Coincidently enough, sitting here surrounded by the great and good of Arsenal, I knew her husband quite well, as we had spent several seasons watching the Arse at the Emirates. Trying her, though, was unsuccessful, as all I got was her voice mail. I experienced the same result, or lack of, with the other names. Each time, I had to think carefully what I was going to say. With each, I kept it simple—my name and a hope that Jackie had contacted them as I was working for her, or as I actually phrased it, "I, er, am, er, I am kind of working for her."

With the last call, I got success: Kye Toulson. He answered immediately; although, from the disappointed tone of his voice, I guessed that he had been expecting someone else, but still, it was apparent that he had been told to expect a call from me. He agreed to see me with all the enthusiasm you might conjure up if asked to eat a dead rodent pancake, liberally covered with a sauce of horse saliva.

As I was putting the phone away, the owner came over to take the cup and plate. Nodding towards the *Guardian*'s front page, he shook his head and moaned, "I 'ope for goodness' sake they sort it out. I don't know 'ow long I can keep going."

I grunted, not wanting to get into any sort of debate. I asked him if he took council tokens. Being on sickness benefit, I was given a subsidy by the London Workers' Council. He said he didn't, adding that it wasn't real money. So it seemed, "Come on, you reds!" was purely for footballing purposes.

***

I'd been in luck with Kye Toulson, not just because he had answered the phone, but because he had been free, and of every town and city he might have been in, it turned out that he was working not far from Alan's at King's Cross railway station. It took me about half an hour to get there. It was a lovely ride with the trees lining the streets, their branches full with leaves after the long, grim winter. Newington Green, for one, looked great. Blossom was delicately puffing its chest out. The bulbs were leading the way with a stunning carpet of daffodils. Oliver Kilbourn would have been very happy. The sun felt warm, and an invigorating breeze brushed my cheeks as I travelled past what used to be the Emirates Stadium.

I had never met Kye Toulson, but I had heard about him. Most people had. He was assistant general secretary of the Joint Transport Workers' Union. The super-union which had joined all those involved in the transport industry had been one of the first to raise the stakes of industrial unrest. Toulson had ridden the tide of militancy and won his position. Vilified by the press and at times threatened by the government, he had been centrally involved in the national dispute which had ended with total victory. The government, I forget whether it was the second or third coalition, had not imprisoned him but instead had sat opposite and signed the emergency decree to nationalise all train, plane, bus, and tube networks across the country.

I parked on York Way, put the helmet and my lightweight leather gloves under the seat, and walked to the station. Walking past bullet-scarred buildings, I took the nearest entrance, which on its left side showed damage from something obviously larger than handguns. Piles of concrete and buckled steel sat underneath a sagging roof.

A group of rail workers was refusing access to a slightly larger group of police officers. The police required permission to enter areas controlled by the workers' councils, and to the chagrin of this gaggle of law enforcers, this was being denied. Despite having the numbers, they knew full well not push it and had to rely on convincing them. It warmed the cockles of this Socialist's heart.

Sounds bounced all around the huge building, with people darting around like dots on speed. Finding a station worker free of the responsibilities of getting narky with the police, I asked where I could find Kye Toulson and was guided to an office just near where the impressive, white, steel roof swooped downwards. I had always been torn between thinking it was quite a sexual design and thinking that it resembled a sneering mouth. Psychoanalyse that, Mr Freud.

I saw Kye Toulson straightaway, talking to a guy resting on a broom outside the room I'd been directed to. He was probably in his early thirties, and by no stretch of the imagination could he be called fat, but he obviously was not a man who worked out. He had a puffy face which I could see as I approached was decidedly pink. That was accentuated by his shaved head. Not a good look in my opinion for fleshy, pink males. Cool, slim, black guys or young women, maybe, but not for his body type. If coiffure was not his expertise, then neither was dress sense. Baggy, oversized jeans suffocated a yellow shirt which in turn was pinned down by a brown, thin, striped jacket.

He nodded hello, and I made my stilted self-introductions. Saying goodbye to the broom man, he invited me in to what he called his hovel. First impressions were that he was a lot more pleasant in the flesh than his phone demeanour.

"What's that all about?" I asked, pointing to an obviously amateur-made billboard above the door. It featured an enormous face of Elvis Presley looking very angry with the slogan: "Whatever the name, all power to the train!"

He smiled. "King's Cross, *the King's cross*—get it?"

"Oh, yes, very funny," I said, trying to enter the spirit of the thing, whilst worrying what the level of humour was going to be like in this bright new Socialist future.

Noticing that I hadn't fallen down laughing, he elaborated. "Don't you remember when a group of young delegates in the National Workers' Council, students, I think, raised the motion about how many names in London were bourgeois in nature—Hyde Park, Regent Street, Waterloo, and all the rest? They argued that these were tributes to imperialism and should be renamed."

Chuckling at the memory, he opened the door and ushered me into a room the size of a bathroom with no windows but a couple of Flash desks with far-from-matching chairs. The walls had pin boards covered with trade union posters, leaflets, and booklets either side of a computer projector.

"Of course, yes, I remember that; it was in the early days. The eagerness and keenness of youth and surprisingly it was passed! Delightfully bonkers!" I found myself also enjoying the memory.

He positioned himself in a shabby office chair and fiddled with a beaker of pencils. "Well, you couldn't knock their enthusiasm. Obviously, they were in principle correct. But…"

"You couldn't get anywhere because you got lost! Satnavs went into meltdown with dual systems: Pro-Parliament and it is Waterloo Station. Pro-workers and it is Central Station!"

"Everyone thought it had something to do with the Central Line, somewhere near Hanger Lane." He tapped the table in amusement. "And what about Trafalgar Square? How on earth did that become, now what was it, oh yeah, Golden Cross? What's that about?"

I knew that. This was like a pub quiz. "It's from The Golden Cross Hotel which used to be there; it features in *Pickwick Papers*."

"Oh, right," he said mockingly. "Silly me. So it has come to pass that we are electing Dickens scholars. Anyway, we had it here. A young engineer suggested dropping the King's Cross and just having St. Pancras, but then some bright spark," Kye's giggling increased to full laughter, "and come to think of it, he actually *was* an electrician, so he actually was one, pointed out that being named after a saint wasn't much better! Someone else asked whether we knew who Pancras was. So in the middle of the meeting, it gets searched, and it turns out he was some boy from the third century. There was then this big debate on whether that was the type of thing we should be celebrating. Oh, dear, it was funny." He wiped a tear away from his eye.

"It's just birth pangs of a new way of doing things."

He sighed. "Sure, and let's face it, why's it any funnier than naming stations after battles and parks after generals? Got reversed in any case, and we still live with Nelson on his column, well, till they put me up there!"

I shared the joke and smiled.

He patted his stomach. "Though whether the column is big enough might be a problem. I think I am slightly bigger than Horatio."

"Oh, that would be no problem," I replied, trying to enter into the spirit of the banter. "Most of the building trade is in the party. They could do you a good job for a sound price," I mimed, stubbing out a fag. "Oh, and, er, mate, your guttering needs doing. I'll take a shifty and see wot I can do for yer!"

It was probably not PC to stereotype our construction comrades like that, but then, even in a revolution, not everything changes. Judging from how funny he found it, he didn't seem to mind. It must be the way I tell 'em. For the first time, I noticed that there were lights on in the office. "Is the strike over?" I asked.

"Huh?" He pulled himself out of amusing himself over the names. "Oh, no. We have our own power source. The main grid's due back on at 6:30 p.m."

"How do you know that?"

He looked at me as if I was off my head. Did I not know? "Their delegates informed the National Council yesterday. It's to mark their support for the councils."

"Well, that's as may be, but the news hasn't reached everyone. There's quite a bit of panic charging out there."

That seemed to amuse him as well. "There must be at least a day's stored electricity in the substations, and the action is specifically designed to raise a flag, not to inconvenience anyone." Another chuckle. "Although I should add that there's plans afoot to delay the grid coming back on for an extra hour or two for certain areas, such as Kensington, Farnham, and Bath; let the rich really see that ruddy flag."

Then without notice, his tone suddenly changed, keeping his affable manner but becoming more businesslike. "So, Pete, how can I help you?" He sat back in his chair with a genial air and a relaxed demeanour which all but stroked me with a desire to please.

Good question, although I wasn't sure of the answer. I did my best to do so, but it was necessarily vague. He didn't hassle. He had been called by Jackie, and he knew enough to let me stumble around the houses. We shared regrets, and he told me how much he had liked and respected Alan. He asked after

Dave, and I told him I hadn't seen him. "I am not really sure why Jackie gave me these particular names, yours for example. Any ideas?"

"Hmm, I suppose that I've been seeing him quite a lot recently."

"Why?"

"Well, as you know, we are by far the biggest party in the workers' councils, but Alan was keen that we didn't abuse that position."

Intrigued, I asked him how this abuse might manifest itself, and how we could avoid it. For several minutes, we debated revolutionary democracy and the responsibilities to the struggle. When we moved onto the others on the list, he began to sound a little vague. He muttered that they, too, had been working with Alan. That cleared that up, then. I thought they were just sharing recipes.

Before I had a chance to ask what he meant exactly by "working with," he had moved onto giving them glowing references. The males were, to a man, good blokes; all the females were, he paused, thinking of an adequate feminine equivalent to bloke, and settled for guys. He knew what their job was and how long they had been in the party. It all sounded very pally, and they all sounded like one big, happy gang. Funny, considering he had been so dumb about their connection to Alan, he certainly knew a lot about them.

"So how did he seem?" I asked, returning to Alan.

"Fine. Tired. But then, aren't we all?"

"Did he seem preoccupied or worried?"

"No."

Comrade Kye had suddenly become rather tight-lipped. For the first time since meeting him, I was not being treated to the sight of his somewhat neglected teeth in full laugh mode. He looked, instead, rather uncomfortable.

I didn't blame him; I felt pretty much the same, but a man's gotta do, and all that shit. "Did you ever have any thoughts that he might not be all that he seemed?"

"No."

I changed tack. "He was apparently researching something—have you any idea what that might have been?"

He shrugged and twirled a pencil. "Oh, it could have been anything. Pete, he was a Central Committee member. What would someone like me know what they are working on?"

I didn't want to seem rude or disrespectful to him, but I had a real feeling of being fobbed off. "No offence, Kye, but I think that you are being rather evasive. I assume Jackie has told you what Alan claimed in his suicide video. I know it's deeply unpleasant, but I can't see how we can ignore it. Not at this time; it's a far too sensitive time." Hark at me. A few hours on from my morning visit from our glorious leaderene, and I had travelled from couch Leftie to conscience of the revolution.

He didn't take offence but kept the affability meter right there in the congenial zone. "Yeah, I know, but it doesn't stop it being a pile of crap. Look, I know that compared to the likes of you, I barely knew him; I knew him for just over a year, but for me, he was solid. Decent. I found him an interesting and clever bloke, a *very* clever bloke." He veered into composing a eulogy.

I pulled him back. "So as far as you are concerned, then, his suicide was out of the blue."

"Totally."

I was about to speak, but Kye was not used to letting people on the opposite side of the table have an easy ride, and somehow, I had suddenly been moved to the other side. He was chortling, but he was making a point. His approach was still clear of the warning zone, but the needle had dropped a tad. "All I can say, Pete, is that MI5 must have been confident that he'd win all those annual Central Committee elections. You'd have to hand it to them; they certainly chose the right person. I've lost count how many elections I've lost!"

The smile was still there, but so was the seriousness. With humour and an attitude which dared me to disagree, he gave me a look that told me my time was up. And yes, indeed, he got up and with deliberate obviousness looked at his watch. Time *was* up.

We shared a few more jokes about place names, this time coming up with a few ourselves. Mentioning that *regis* was Latin for king kicked off some very juvenile jokes. Bognor Regis became Bognor Commissar. He had now returned to his previous übergenial manner before apologising and saying he had a meeting to attend.

Watching him head off towards the platforms, I thought about what he had said and came up with nothing. So what to do next? I could try the numbers again, arrange to see someone else on Jackie's list, and ask the same lame questions, but I was bushed. I wanted to get back to my day. The day's walk had long been binned. Looking at the time, I calculated that I could swing round to my place, pick up my stuff, and make it to the pool in time. I'd been robbed of my walk, so I could at least swim my one kilometre. Then I could go home, have a nap, and then feed and water myself. Back to sanity.

**

I awoke suddenly to the sound of an incessant and irritating ringing. Flat out, with Red purring on my chest, I felt disoriented. Scrabbling together my brain, I reached across and grabbed the offending phone. Jackie Payne's lightly made-up face appeared on the screen. She was being driven somewhere, as I could see a car seat and rear window screen behind her.

"Oh, hi, Jacks, how are you?" I mumbled, my voice full of sleep.

A rapid "fine" was followed by a trio of questions: Had I been to Alan's? What had I found? Who had I met?

Straightening up and trying to rub the lethargy out of my head, I gave a précis of the day's activities. I did miss out my time in the pool. It was pretty certain that she didn't want to know how my backstroke had gone. Any point she deemed as requiring clarification was promptly sought by her. The questions were more like strident demands. There was little space given for anything other than information to be offered up. She paused to glance at another phone, which gave me a chance.

I asked her, "Did Alan have cancer?"

Simultaneously, while tapping something into the phone that did not have the glory of my mug on the screen, which had caught her attention, and telling the driver to turn left at the next roundabout, she replied that, yes, he had. He had been diagnosed with brain cancer, "about two and half years ago. It was the day of the third banking collapse, you know, the *big one*! Just before…"

I interrupted her. "So he *did* have cancer."

"Yes, yes, he did. He was recovering very well; the big *C* isn't all the threat it once had been. It's more like a medium-sized *C*." She gave a half-smile at the half-joke. "The pills he took the overdose with were having a beneficial effect. His last appointment was very positive. The specialist was of the opinion that he was almost certainly clear of the disease." That was all she thought was necessary to say on the subject as she changed it back to what she wanted to talk about. "So, Pete, you didn't find anything more than Vic did? I was hoping that you would treat this as a priority."

I felt defensive and blurted out that to be fair, out of the list of the great and good, I'd only managed to get hold of Kye Toulson, so what did she expect?

"Fair point. I'll get onto that right away." She didn't sound happy about the situation. I could easily imagine that they were going to get a call *very soon*. She would not shout or even raise her voice; she would simply call them, and they would make damn sure that they answered, and she would tell them what she wanted. They might possibly query or even oppose what she was saying; in which case, she would patiently explain for as long as required until they agreed. And they would.

"It's Marie and Dave I really want to talk to. Have you spoken to Dave since last night? I wondered how he was holding up."

"No, I've tried his mobile and home but no luck. I just keep getting his voice mail. I've left three messages." She sounded very unhappy with that situation. She was certainly not used to being ignored. Quickly, she regained control. "So what's your view on his alleged betrayal?"

Alleged? This morning she was persuading me that it was for real, and now it was alleged? I could have responded by pointing out that according to her new best buds, Vic Cole and Roijin Kemal, the suicide video was genuine, so why would Alan make it up? Instead, I opted for the I-know-what-I'm-doing card. "I did my own test, and the video seemed real, so do you have any grounds for doubting his confession?" My fingers crossed that she wouldn't ask what exactly the test was. She had high regard for the thoughts of Marx and Engels but maybe not so high as to regard shadows on the spines of their books as forensic proof.

"So the question is: *Did* he stop a year ago as he said he had, or has he been passing information to the state's security forces more recently?" She added with an obvious sharpness, "That's what I was hoping you could find out."

"And how can I do that?"

"Pete, you're a researcher. I expected…"

"Jacks, I research, *researched*, art history! I look into the social background of the associates of Leonardo da Vinci or the influence of Catholicism on

Miro's contemporaries, not this sort of bollocks." Feeling tired and aggrieved that she wasn't showing the gratitude for what I had done so far, I snapped at her. "And Jackie, when I'm researching, I am helped greatly if the original sources are available to be looked at! Not much point looking at the brush strokes of J. M. W. Turner if you hide the bloody paintings."

"I don't follow."

I wouldn't have blamed her for that if it was true; it had been a pretty oblique reference. Even by my standards. However, I was not going to let her use it as an excuse. "Yeah, you do. Jackie, all his files were wiped off his computer—*all* his documents. Every record of anything he's done. How can I look at who he's been contacting without that? How can I assess the reasons for the communication without even seeing who and when he contacted? How can I appraise the relevance of it if I can't even bloody see it?"

I had guessed that comrade Vic Cole and chums would not have dared to have done it without her say-so, so she would have had to know about it. Or if she hadn't, then that showed that our friends in blue were still politically that colour after all. Either way, bringing it up now was going to be instructive.

She paused and thought. I could see in her eyes that she was weighing up the logic of my argument against the reason she'd wiped them off in the first place. That answered the question of whether she had known about the erasing—she had. Finally, she'd decided. "OK, you'll get them tomorrow, and you can have his mobile, as well. I'll sort it."

"Good. I wondered why I couldn't find it today," I lied, as in actual fact, I had clean forgot to look for it. Well, maybe not forgot. More like, it had never entered my head.

Then suddenly, "Bye. I'll be in touch." With that, she hung up.

Looking at the blank screen, I thought of the questions I had wanted to ask her, like what was the reason for deleting all his records? What research was Alan doing that was so secretive, it demanded hiding? But it seemed that they would have to wait. I was knackered and felt skanky; with swimming pools not what they used to be, the water wasn't the cleanest. I needed to wash. Then I could return to sleep but in a proper bed. Shower and sleep and get this day over. Then with luck, the whole farce would be over by this time tomorrow.

CHAPTER THREE
Personal and Political Profiles

Surfing the channels, I could see a green light flashing in the corner of the screen telling me that I had a message, but after yesterday, I wasn't in the mood. My intention was to ease myself into the morning. I hadn't slept well; Caroline and Lisa had been bickering in my sub-conscious and had woken me up, and as a result, lethargy was competing with crabby to replace Alexander as my middle name.

Not that the news was a restful experience; whether it was TV, web, or other formats, all were leading on the same story: five people had died in Manchester General Hospital. During yesterday's power strike, the hospital's backup generator had failed, and five patients had died. Three had been on life-support, and two were undergoing operations. The prime minister, health minister, and a host of other leading government figures had been pointing the blame squarely at the workers' councils and with much unoriginality, accused them of having "blood on their hands." The councils had obviously been put on the back foot. To be honest, I thought our response was pretty weak. Jackie's performance on the BBC, especially, was unusually stuttering. Sensing political blood running with the body fluids, the health minister had been particularly aggressive. Set against the facts, he had been effective in his reasoning that the strike had been nothing but pointless posturing that had cost lives.

Backing him all the way was the prime minister, who had popped out of a meeting begging help from the United States, Germany, Turkey, and France to give his mock outrage a run out. Hotfoot from assuring the finance ministers that Britain was not a failed state, he had surely undermined this position by denouncing the "militant criminality" of the action. Wouldn't the great and good of those countries point out that if correct, it only just proved that UK PLC had fallen on hard times? I sympathised with his position; when you are selling something, you want all the cracks and dents hidden.

On every channel you could imagine, whether controlled by news conglomerates, the government, us, or the independent ones, he could be seen calling for national solidarity and the end of the soviets holding the democratically elected NCNC government to ransom. Clichés all, but the deaths had given them an extra oomph of life. His big news was that the finance ministers would be taking his begging bowl to their leaders.

Noticeably, the *Times* was in the newsagents today, having been absent for several weeks because the printers had refused to print it. Obviously, some people had been found to print it, and it was in its paper format, alongside the web edition which had always been unaffected. And the whole issue was apparently focusing on the deaths and a number of other crimes, supposedly of the council's doing. Plus they, alongside other mainstream online news channels, had really gone for the party. Like an old, dearly loved, if threadbare, bath towel, the line about us manipulating the movement was given an airing. The Voice of England site went one step further, saying that our leadership was full of foreigners who were manipulating the stouthearted Englishmen and Englishwomen (this was because we had a Bangladeshi and a Romanian on the Central Committee, and oh, Jackie's parents hailed from St. Kitts). Flicking to other sites made uncomfortable viewing; the Right were having a jamboree. Jesus, even the *Sun* had managed to get a hard copy out, admittedly only with the sports pages (but wasn't that what people claimed they only read, in any case?); but still, it was out!

Taking the tablet from its silver foil, I savoured the calmness it would bring. I really could do with this today. This was crappy news. Finally, as well as chemical help, I sought sanctuary in the weather channel for some respite. Yesterday, there had been record temperatures for this time of the year (ain't they always?). Today was going to be another fine day, though slightly cooler. Now, there was a metaphor waiting to be used. I'd been right to choose my two-button, black suit with thin lapels. I'd chosen a black Fred Perry with twin tipping in purple on the collar which matched the purple loafers.

Comrades Come Rally

Elsewhere, there was talk of law and order problems, which was, again, the fault of the councils. There were also reports of the problem of England's ability to pay for imports because the uncertainty was affecting the fragile credit rating of the country. It seemed open season on us. Even the WWW site, Workers Without Work, the site of the unemployed, was discussing the problem of underrepresentation in the National Workers' Councils. That was our fault, too, as the party was apparently obsessed with workers with jobs and sectarian against those without. There would be a demo soon, it promised.

I had intended to return to my usual morning news appraisal after yesterday's disruption, but it didn't really inspire me to do so. Shit, even Arsenal had lost. It was a barrage of negativity. My head ached. The only good thing was that there was no mention of Alan's death; obviously the party was still managing to keep a lid on it, but that was about the only positive thing about any of it.

And then there was that damned green light flickering. Now, that wasn't going to be a pal ringing to gossip and catch up on things. They had all mostly given up on doing that. It was going to be someone saying something I would do well to hide away from. Red was lying on the sofa, curled up with his paws over his eyes. Yeah, mate, I'm with you. Finally, I gave in and picked up the phone. It was a video message, though not, as I had expected, from Jackie Payne, but from Simon Peary. I pointed the phone at the TV and pressed transmit.

Simon's face and upper body took over the screen. As always, he was casually dressed, this time sporting a yellow cheesecloth shirt that last saw a fashion catwalk in 1971. He flashed his killer smile. He had looked exactly the same for years; he was truly the Peter Pan of the party, the cheeky, unflappable boy next door. There was absolutely no way you'd believe he was my age or thereabouts. Whether he had reached the Big Six Zero, I couldn't tell you, but the simple arithmetic of how long I had known him told me that he was in his late fifties, at least. Not that he looked it. He looked in his thirties. Whatever face cream he was using that gave him his eternal look of youth, I wanted a tub of it.

Simon helped run the party's national office which consisted of fielding communications, acting as a PA for the Central Committee, and trying to organise a highly disorganised, organising organisation. On and off, he'd been doing this for decades. Well, saying that he helped run the office was perhaps an understatement, as that would be like saying Frank Sinatra had been a helper in *The Rat Pack*. Frankly, Simon *was* the office.

He explained that he was contacting me on Jackie's behalf. And there was me, thinking he wanted a chat about the weather. After expressing his pleasure that "I was back in circulation" and saying how pleased he was to hear Jackie report that I had looked well, he got down to business. He was sending over the missing communications both to and from Alan over the past seven days. She hoped these would help me. He had identified as many of the addresses and numbers as he could, but he apologised that Jackie hadn't asked him to do this till late last night, so it was a bit of a rushed job. But, he added, at least it was a start.

He had also arranged meetings for me with all but one on Jackie's list. He would try to rectify that and arrange it so all the illustrious comrades would have the pleasure of meeting me. He also promised to chase up Dave. He promised that over the next two days, I should get to see all the people Alan had been in closest contact with in recent weeks. How kind, Simon. As always, ageless and efficient. No doubt in the previous, sometimes thankless decades, he could have made big money in business, but instead he had slaved for us. His work done, he had signed off with a ciao and a smile.

Did I really want to do this? I got up and decided to get myself another cup of coffee and have a think. Wandering out to the garden with Red following close behind me, I sat myself at the wooden round table and pondered my options. Closing my eyes as the morning sun warmed my face, I came up with two. I could continue with what Jackie had requested and which Simon had dutifully organised and not worry about whether there was any point to it. Was it Bertrand Russell—or was it my uncle—who said that there was much pleasure in finding useless information? So I could grin and do it. Or I could politely decline. It was, after all, a voluntary organisation; I was not compelled to do anything. I had been on long-term sick leave from work for a good reason, so I could just say simply that I was not well enough to do it. She could find someone more competent, someone who knew what they were looking for, or someone more of a mug.

My face felt pleasantly temperate, and I felt calm. This rather contrasted with the issues that occupied my thoughts. Was the suicide message legit? If it was, then surely the question I should face was not one as to why MI5 might have wanted an agent, but why Alan would choose to be one. Absurdly, it was surely the main thing, and yet I hadn't given it much attention. The question was—why would he have started working for the state? This was a complete 360-degree political turn, so what would have caused that?

I thought back on what the party had been back then. Had there been a huge faction fight over perspectives that could have disillusioned him? I could not think of any, and, in any case, what would be so huge as to change him so much? People changing was central to our politics. In our history, we had often had people who got demoralised or shifted their politics, sometimes massively. But it usually took time to do so, and there were many signposts on their journey. Their disagreements were not kept silent but often took the form of heated debates and fiery rhetoric. They weren't usually keeping schtum and signing up to work for the security forces. OK, with his partner and son leaving him, he had been in a fragile state, but heartbreak surely could not act as a recruiting sergeant for the state? When I had felt such, I had turned against myself, not against the party.

So, could they have forced him to? How? How do you force someone to spy on their comrades? That happened in thrillers, but here in the real world, how would they do that? This was all *Alice in Wonderland* surrealism. I could not make head nor tail of it all. Probably, it was best to leave it all alone…Ah, bollocks! I got up and strode back to the lounge.

I opened the list of times and places of these meetings. I groaned. This was going to play havoc with my to-do list. This was Simon's to-do list, and it was going to be a drag. The first was in an hour and a half, at 11:45. Then he had arranged two to follow, the last a double header with two of the list names. The quarter to twelve meeting wasn't even in London—groan. In Watford—double that groan. What would a leading Socialist be doing in Watford, for goodness' sake? It was kilometres away. Watford!

My little scooter might be cool, but it was hardly a speedster, so I would have to leave straightaway. Sighing, I quickly scanned the communications list, which as Simon had promised identified quite a few of the calls. It also identified the type of communication: phone—video or verbal, text, social network (what type of), and so on and so forth. Dates and times were given, as well as duration. What hit me was just how many there were of them. Especially with those six comrades on the list, there were daily, often hourly communications between all of them, including conference calls which often lasted for some time. That was something to ask—what were they spending all that time talking about? I jumped up and searched for my helmet and gloves; it was time to go to wonderful Watford.

***

I'd got caught up in traffic on the way. There were scores of blasted military vehicles travelling north. Buzzing alongside them had been a motley collection of customised vans and lorries, whose purpose was now to threaten rather than transport. Stern-looking comrades could be seen handling machine guns, chewing gum, and eyeing the military convoy with suspicion. Usually having a scooter avoided getting caught up in such things, but it had been bumper to bumper on the A411 through Bushy. A swarm of thirty from the Militant Cyclists Movement, wearing their distinctive yellow jerseys with slogans of Lose Your Chains and sporting a defiant attitude, hadn't helped either. All had refused to let me pass. Bloody Bushy.

Over twenty minutes late, I was running through a shopping mall. I didn't know the area, but Simon had sent the address and directions. The delights of the gaudy, fake gold attempts at retail glamour that had marked the early twenty-first century passed me by as I showed my athletic prowess by racing up the broken escalator. Ten steps up, I was seriously considering the fact that I was going to end my days on a ride past closed burger joints. Quite why Glen Bale had decided to hold a rally at a dilapidated shopping mall, Lord only knew.

I interspersed the huffs with cursing Bale and the puffs with more of the same. Glen Bale, the Bile, Glen Baleful, Glen Fail. He and I had never been what you might call the greatest of chums. Through party stuff, our paths had crossed over the years. Lobbies, demos, marches, pickets, meetings, and rallies, whether half a dozen or half a million, I could bet that I'd turn around and see his condescending face. Beneath a wafer-thin covering of politeness, our conversation would usually consist of three minutes of politics, and then we'd seek asylum with someone else, *anyone* else. If there wasn't anyone else, then we'd settle for a scorpion or a killer shark or a plague-ridden death pit.

Finally, I mounted the summit and looked around for a map. Finding one, I looked for unit 14. This, so Simon had informed me, was an unused department store which had been commandeered by the local workers' council. Great, it was the next floor up. Thankfully though, the next escalator was working. It gave me a chance to get my breath back.

Bale had been in the party for slightly less time than me, but his profile was far higher. OK, recently mine had consisted of being mainly in my own head, but even previously, he had outshone yours truly; many had found something to appreciate in him. His ability had been frequently praised, and I did have to admit that he had shown some skill at heading some serious campaigns and major strike actions. Starting as youthful hacker, he had graduated into lucrative work for ServiceLed, *the* uberquango that had taken over so many public services. Much as I would have loved to say otherwise, he hadn't sold out but had used it as a base to organise a previously difficult group into a cohesive force.

On the down escalator, there was quite a crowd. Obviously, I'd missed the bargains. Then again, I didn't see many bags, so it couldn't have been that great. As I reached the top, I could see that my would-be bargain getters were all streaming out of unit 14. The unit had little of its earlier incarnation left about its entrance. It looked more like Stalin's Grotto. A huge banner proclaimed that here sat Hertfordshire Workers' Council. It hardly sounded like the Petrograd Soviet of the Russian Revolution. But what it lacked in romantic appeal, it made up with less an array and more an explosion of red flags. On either side of the entrance and under the crimson cloudburst stood three enormous guards attired identically in leather jackets, jeans, red armbands, and machine guns. Now, that was more Petrograd.

They were happy to let everyone out but didn't seem too keen to let me in. I was told rather briskly that Glen Bale was busy, as he had just finished speaking at a rally. Seeing their size, I didn't want to be too narky and ask how he could be busy if he had "finished" speaking. Several times I was told that, because of security concerns, access was being restricted to only those accredited to do so. A gruff "Sorry, comrade" told me he considered that there was nothing else to say. I couldn't bring myself to call for Bale to help me out. Instead, I got my phone out and showed him a message Jackie had recorded for me. She was looking straight ahead at the phone-cam and with a clear, authoritative voice, said that I was on important party and workers' council business and should be allowed access to any building and any facility. Evidently, this was sufficient accreditation, and I was instantly waved through.

Entering what must have been the front showroom, women's fashion, I would guess, I could see mannequins circling the room, amusingly dressed as coalition ministers with the faces of each projecting the newsnet, so they appeared to be speaking. Above, hung For Sale signs. A smell of carpet and cheap tea in plastic beakers floated in the air. In the middle were hundreds of chairs. A few were still occupied with people talking, phoning, or on computers. Ahead of them was a makeshift stage with chairs and a couple of tables in front of a screen telling us that this had been a rally of the Southeast ICT Workers' Delegates Caucus. Exciting stuff, I'm sure. Perched on the end of the stage to the left was Bale, busily typing something into his notepad. I strolled up to him in my best, nonchalant, all-the-world's-my-stage manner. "Hi Glen," I said. Keeping the swagger going.

He made a big deal of looking at his watch. Maybe he had only just learnt to tell the time. Where is the big hand, Glen? And now, where is the small hand? Recalling that Toulson had done likewise, I wondered if there was a cadre school that taught comrades to do that. Obviously, he was telling me, silently and with the subtlety of a concrete slab falling on my big toe, that I was late. I felt like telling him to get some manners.

His stoat-like face, which had never even said hello to the sun, let alone get a tan, was reprimanding me: How could I dream of making this great man wait? I ignored it. What passed for cheek bones looked as if someone had pulled them hard behind his head, creating a pointed nose which seemed to be a part of his mouth. When he spoke, although I thought the way he used verbal communication was too slimy to be considered speech, it appeared to have the sole aim of impressing on people his magnificence.

"Rally go well?" I asked.

Very quickly, I wished that I hadn't been so polite, but had instead, risen to the bait and fired off some bitchy barbs, snarling a rebuke at his arrogance. If I had done so, it would have meant an enjoyably childish bout of bickering. Certainly, I shouldn't have asked that, of all questions. I knew what the answer was going to be. I was treated to a five-minute résumé of the ebb and flow of the meeting. He, of course, was simply wonderful throughout. It was worthy stuff, and the type of thing that movements were made of. The struggle wasn't all storming the barricades; usually, it was struggling to get an amendment heard, but I felt as if I was drifting into a coma. Before the life support was ordered, I forced a change of topic.

"I guess that Jackie, or Simon on her behalf, has spoken to you, and so you know why I'm here. Is there somewhere we can talk in private?"

There wasn't the slightest umbrage at the fact that I did not find the subject of how ICT workers could pressurise the government particularly diverting. He never really noticed what interested me. A nod merely indicated that he understood why I was here, and, as amazing as it may seem, it was not to worship him. Looking around, he pointed to a group of chairs corralled into a corner by three clothes racks. Grabbing an attaché case, he led the way. Dressed in jeans and a tight-fitting pullover, he looked trim for a forty-year-old. His was of a healthy, natural slenderness, whereas mine was a rather unintended taking-in-of-the-belt-several-notches variety. But I consoled myself that I had more hair.

We sat down. He placed the case below his chair. Behind him I could see two mannequins, dressed, I think, as the latest defence and education ministers.

I got straight to the point because shooting the breeze with vanilla soul here in an unused department store was not my idea of a wild time, so the quicker I was in, bored senseless, and then out, the better. "OK, first off, what do you think of the idea of Alan Wiltshire being a traitor?"

He shifted on his chair. His face looked as if he had just sucked a very sour piece of fruit. "Actually, Pete, I think you're wasting your time. It's an utterly ridiculous idea, quite preposterous. Alan was loyal to the struggle; there was no way he was working for them. I find the whole idea of it absurd. No offence, Pete, but like I said, I think you're wasting your time; I know Jackie simply wants to dot the i's and cross the t's, but sorry, it's just insane. And what are you going to find out, because there isn't anything to find. And actually, how are you going to do it?" He paused and looked at me with his unblinking eyes. "Still, it's great you're out of retirement…"

Inwardly, I snarled at the jibe but kept quiet.

"No offence, Pete…"

But I was taking one.

"And to be honest, what experience have you in this type of thing? What skills do you bring from your line of work? Clues in the Constables?" He laughed at his own joke.

I wasn't surprised; he was always one to appreciate his own abilities. Lack of self-confidence was never a problem with this man. I just wished I had written it down, as a Bale joke was rare and precious, well, rare, anyway. Oh, he hadn't finished.

"Or look at the hidden clues in the Michelangelos? It's like a rewrite of the *Da Vinci Code*. And you are the, oh, what's his name, the main character; Tom Hanks played him in the old movie…"

OK, that was too far. I was astounded that he had even heard of the book, as it wasn't a party publication. It wasn't imaginable that he would read anything but those. Heavens, whatever next—thinking for himself?

"You didn't think Da Vinci was a programming code, did you, Glen?"

He pulled a face that reminded me of a teacher reproving a naughty child. "Pete, please don't be so touchy. I wasn't trying to be rude."

You always know that someone is being just that when they say they aren't.

"I just don't believe it; actually, I find it somewhat offensive that it can even be suggested."

Much as it pained me to say it, but Baleful had a point. But then I had been given a job to do, so I might as well do it. "I know it's hard to believe, Glen, but are you aware of the video message he recorded?"

"Yeah, Jackie, told me, but that still doesn't convince me. There are a number of things that could explain it. For example, those cancer pills he was on were powerful drugs; we simply don't know how they messed with his head. I am sure I heard somewhere that they had serious side effects, and they could have made him delusional. Or he could have been induced to say it by drugs, or someone could have forced him to do it. Or simply, it's a fake."

It was quite a shopping list of reasons, and what was there to disagree with? I was with him all the way. And yet. And yet, something in me felt compelled to question his certainty. "He didn't *look* drugged or forced. Have you actually seen it?"

Losing a fraction of his assuredness, his speech slowed. "No, I haven't," he answered.

"Watch it," I said, perhaps a little too brutally.

I handed him my phone. He grimaced as he took it which could have been either from the machine's primitiveness or from the thought of watching a suicide message of someone he had known well. I watched him as he watched it. To my surprise, I saw wetness around his eyes and crimson around his cheeks. He possessed feelings. When he had finished, he frowned and remained silent. Greyness spread across his face, colliding with the redness.

"It's terrible," I said simply, because it was.

He still didn't say a word.

"Does it look fake?" I asked, trying to open him up again, something that even in my wildest dreams I would have never imagined wanting to do.

Finally, he spoke. "Pete, it's impossible to tell just by looking at it."

I had a thought. "Surely, you could check it. You must have access to the most advanced technology."

He thought for a second. "That's an idea." He reached down and grabbed his briefcase.

There had been an expectation that he would take it away to some screen-covered office, but yet again, I was *so* out of date. It was in his case! Thoughts of James Bond got rather dashed when, as he opened it, I could see some dog-eared *Revolutionary Worker*s, some pens, an apple, and a half-eaten brown-bread sandwich stuck to an e-book reader.

He took out a rather battered-looking machine which looked to me like a particularly unattractive PC tablet, although with a far smaller screen. He transmitted the message to it. He pressed a few buttons. "I'm using my ISD to check the continuity of the ACHCD, not to be confused with the old ACCHD," he joked.

I wondered if he was speaking English.

"Actually, the MMFs which replaced MPEGs have a certain code that should have a sequential line."

Nope, he wasn't.

As he wittered on, I looked at the clothes hangers. What once had shown fine evening wear now had Day-Glow demo jerkins hanging from them. Maybe it was the timeless appeal of the style of the steward's apparel that always prompted middle-class commentators (the type who overuse the word "narrative" in conversations) to scoff at industrial action as being just "so 1970s, darhhling." We had to find other, more original ways to engage in the narrative of change. Yeah, right; now scamper off and hug your thesis on constructive discourse. Still, truth be told, these jerkins did look like something Dad would have worn. They were even dated when I was on my first demo and lost my political virginity.

Bale looked up. He didn't look happy. "Well, it appears genuine. Everything appears correct…"

He yammered on for several minutes about essentially the fact that the film was as you saw it and had not been tampered with. Once more my Karl Marx volume 5 shadow test had triumphed. And with a whole lot less jargon.

"I still can't believe it, though," he said with a heavy heart.

I asked a stupid question. I couldn't think of a sensible one. "Have you had any suspicions about Alan? Has he ever seemed be anything other than what he was?"

He shook his head. Whether that was to be taken as no, or just a signal that my question did not make sense, I could not tell.

"As far as you know, has he ever had any dealings with the security services?"

He gave me a look.

Yes, even by my standards that was a dumb one. But I was new to this. I changed direction. "You were in contact with him a lot over the last few days. On the Wednesday before, you were in video conference for three sessions, both totalling an hour each—what was that about?"

I could see him pausing; he was debating whether to answer or not, so I reminded him that I was here at Jackie's behest. I hoped that would be our equivalent of reading a suspect his rights.

"We were discussing how to work with other groups in the workers' councils."

I knew that every workers' council had delegates who were answerable to the workplaces or area they represented. Unlike MPs, they were directly accountable and could be replaced at any moment. Some were just individuals, but some, like us, were in parties. Although we were by far the largest, there were several others.

"Yes, Kye mentioned that he is involved in something similar. I didn't realise that there's a problem." He was happy to enlighten me. "The Greens are upset that the workers' movement has not put environmental issues high enough on the agenda and believe—wrongly, as it happens—that we are sidelining them in the cause of good jobs and houses. We are yet to win them to our position that only Socialism can save the planet. It is not one or the other but a synthesis of the issues."

It looked like this was going to be a lengthy explanation.

"The anarchists believe that we have forgotten about the unemployed, and the Democratic Left Party believes that we are ultra-Left and pushing too hard for the final confrontation with Capital. Of course the anarchists believe the opposite." What a crazy, crazy world.

He went on for a good while, deconstructing all the flotsam and jetsam of the movement. Bale was never one to miss an opportunity to lecture someone. The world was there to be one big meeting, to be addressed, by him, Glen Bale. Everything he said was perfectly sensible, and all was correct, but the trouble with Bale was that I always felt as if I was drowning in his verbiage.

"And back to Alan," I said, coming up for air and not wanting him to continue his extensive analysis. Bedding down here for the night was not an attractive idea.

A gloom spread across his face. Guessing it wasn't despondency at having his political rhetoric curtailed, I concluded he obviously found this hard. I hadn't realised that he had been so friendly with him. I hadn't realised he had feelings.

"What I don't understand is," he sighed, "that if, and I say *if*, he was a class traitor, then why would he decide to stop a year ago? Surely, now is exactly the time the state would want to know what we are up to. For the first time in our history, we are a real threat to their existence, a threat to their rule. In the past, we have been at best an irritant, but now—now we have a chance of real power."

Nodding, I agreed. "That's what I've been asking myself."

"And why recruit him in 2010? Why was there a need for a spy on the Central Committee then? If I remember my history, the class struggle wasn't that high then. Actually, it's a bit before my time; I think I was obsessed with playing with my brother's PlayStation back in 2010."

I was happy to enlighten him. "No, nothing stands out. I've been thinking about that. Sure, it was just after the first big banking crisis, but it was nothing like the latter ones. I think it was 'round about that time we had our first coalition, well, the first since World War II." I smiled at a memory that had just popped into my head. "It was the first time I got clumped by a copper, too." Sieving through countless marches, another memory emerged. "It was something to do with tuition fees. I got a good few whacks on the head, Westminster Bridge, I think."

"They should put a red plaque up."

"I'm sure they will," I replied, ignoring the sarcasm.

Bale could not help but give another political lecture. "Of course, with hindsight, we know how over the course of the years, there was a chain of events which have ultimately led to now, but nothing is predetermined. Each time, there would have been an almost infinite set of possible outcomes to given situations. It's the old historical *what if* questions. What if Hitler had been a half-decent painter; what if Trotsky had not been assassinated; what if President Mubarak hadn't been toppled in 2011?"

On he went, giving full vent to his political Tourette's. "I don't believe for a second that they could see that far in advance. Nothing is preordained. The only fate we believe in is the village variety. Even now, we don't know what will happen. There was time a few years ago when it looked like the ruling class would dig itself out of the crisis."

"Still might."

He nodded. "Indeed, the ruling class can escape anything if the working class is willing to pay the price. But there was no warning in 2010 of what was ahead. It was a year when the struggle went up a notch, but they were hardly barricading Buckingham Palace. If memory serves, some paint thrown at Charles was about the limit."

"Not like now." I smirked.

He agreed sombrely.

My attention was briefly distracted by a text going off in my phone. Without thinking (it annoyed me when people did this to me—I found it very rude), I sneaked a look at it. It was from the ever-efficient Simon Peary; he had arranged the last meeting for tomorrow morning. Be still, my beating heart; just how fab was that! He still had no success reaching Dave, though. Turning my attention back to Bale, I apologised. Even he deserved the odd bit of politeness.

To my surprise, he said something that wasn't about politics. "So where do you go with this next?"

I should have welcomed the glimpse of a human being; he had shown an interest in someone else—remarkable! I should have acted my age, replied with an honest answer, and told him that I had no bloody idea. But I was far too used to Bale—the bureaucratic machine—to do that, so I matched his usual self-importance. "I have some meetings that have been arranged for me."

And with that thought, the great detective's questioning came to a halt. I hastily—over hastily—said a curt thank you and left him. I had travelled a long way for absolutely no reason. For the most part, he had lectured me on things I could have told him—only in a shorter, more concise, and with more insight fashion.

***

Untangling myself from Marie William's embrace was a life-saver; otherwise, there was the threat of suffocation from cleavage. Strong arms pressed me close. It was my second or third from her; the first I had received when she met me in the hospital reception had almost put me in a ward myself. I hadn't realised I had been so missed. On the lift up, she had fired dozens of questions at me concerning my present state of affairs. On the fourteenth floor—the Gynecology Ward, where she had worked for years—we had found an empty examination room. Further emotional effusing over seeing me and expressions of concern followed, as I tried keeping the bizarre location and circumstances of our meeting at the furthest reaches of my thoughts. We were perched on the edge of a bed with a variety of medical diagrams above us on the wall, which I avoided looking at, and by a cabinet containing medical instruments, the purpose of which I avoided thinking about.

Once all that was out the way, we covered exactly the same ground as I had done with Kye Toulson and Glen Bale: shocked, check; horrified, check; disbelief, check; pointless discussion over why he would have said it, check; pointless discussion over if he could have done it, check. Our lexicon of stock responses had been interrupted by a pair of nurses and a rather surprised patient. Leaving the poor woman to spend quality time with paper pants and clamps, we gave our apologies and headed up one floor to a nurses' staff room.

It had to be said that from up here, the view from the New Thames Hospital was amazing. It did have an incredible skyline surrounding it. It reminded you, not that anyone needed reminding, how great a city London was, perhaps the greatest on earth. I'd seen this panorama or ones like it of our city all my life, but it still moved me. On my travels I had seen many cities, but with due respect to the likes of Rome, Paris, New York, and Moscow— London is the best.

When it had been announced that a new hospital was to be built on this spot, much had been made of how pleasant the location would be for the patients. Plainly, they had hoped that the panorama diverted attention from how many hospitals were being closed to accommodate it. The New Thames Hospital, or the NTH as it was more commonly known, had been heralded as the best and the most cutting-edge hospital in the western world.

That I could not comment on, but the NTH certainly could boast sweeping views. Near to us was a rooftop bar with lunchtime revellers enjoying the spring air. Solar panels glistened in the sun. Two men were cleaning a large panel straight ahead of me. On the horizon you could see some of the great London landmarks, including as the name suggested, the mighty artery of the City, the Thames. Lapping it all in, I had just caught a glimpse of the dome of St Paul's before Marie once more engulfed me.

She was looking particularly Rossetti-ish today; her huge mop of curly red hair almost had a life of its own. Judging by the way that it was loose and touching her nurse's collar, she wasn't actually on the wards today. When she was, it was bound tightly back. She looked good for a middle-aged woman who found time to work in a hospital, raise three kids, and be a leading party member. Taller than me, with strong features, she was feminine without being girly-girly. Strong was a word you would use with Marie, not just with her face.

Having witnessed many a time her capacity to wolf down numerous courses in any type of restaurant you cared to name, she clearly never gave her waistline a thought. It was annoying that, whilst you could not really call her skinny, she looked trim.

Standing by the kettle and waiting for it to boil, we chatted about various loved ones. We talked about Ashok, her long-term partner who many a time I had celebrated with and commiserated with over Arsenal's fortunes. Whenever I thought of him, I thought of that damn infectious grin and stupid red-and-white felt top hat of his. He was happy and healthy. "You should come over tonight; he would love to see you."

"Perhaps," I said. Her youngest was due to finish university this year. Finish uni? God, that made me feel old.

Marie looked in good spirits. A little weary, maybe, but she pretty much looked all at one with life. For as long as I had known her, she had specialised in women's health as a sister, senior nurse, health supervisor, and whatever her title was now. The thought prompted me to move from strolling down memory lane and get to the point of the visit.

Taking from her a cup of lukewarm coffee, and following her lead by just leaving the spoon on the table, I noted that cleanliness might be king in the wards, but it had slightly lost its crown in here. But to work, I began by asking about something that had been troubling me. "What made Jackie call you and get you to come to Alan's house after Dave had found him? Whatever killed him had nothing to do with dodgy ovaries."

Choking on her drink, she shook her head with amused shock. "Pete, have some respect. You're incorrigible!"

I noted that Marie hadn't answered the question. "So?"

She pointed to one of the orange sofas that passed for comfort in the room. Presuming that she was asking me to sit there rather than showing off the NHS taste in soft furnishings, I sat down. She joined me by my side with rather a clump, and I found myself bouncing up. She was many things, but graceful she wasn't. Hopefully, she was more delicate with her patients. I slid along, slightly uncomfortable at the close proximity. If I was going to question her, then I required distance.

"It's no mystery, really; working in the health services for so long, I do have general knowledge of medicine. I can wrap a bandage."

"But Alan didn't need a bandage," I pointed out.

"I wasn't being literal. I have a working knowledge of medical matters, so Jackie thought I could be of help."

I asked again, "How? For starters he was dead; he needed an undertaker, not a nurse."

Her answer was again far from convincing. "Needs must; you of all people should understand that!"

Now that was another matter. "Whose great idea was it to get me to do this?"

More hair was played with, her left hand unknotting a tangle at the back of her head. "I guess it was a joint one."

Proof, I thought, that two heads were not always better than one.

She could sense my cynicism. "I—actually, both of us—thought you would be ideal…" The reasons given were identical to those given by Jackie; although delivered in a softer, more approachable way, they sounded no saner. She added, "I thought you were well enough to cope with it." Concern and care filled her voice. "You do seem better. Are you?"

I nodded.

"Still taking the medication, I hope. What dosage are you taking now?"

"Down to just a couple of pills a day," I reluctantly answered, not really wanting to go down this path.

She reached across and put her hand on my knee. The tips of her mouth turned downwards. "I know a breakdown like yours takes a while to get over. No one can underestimate its seriousness. We were all really worried about you back then; many thought that you would not pull through. But I had faith in you, and I reckon that you are strong enough to cope with this. I honestly believe that working on this will help you. It will take you out of endless self-obsession and get you to focus on something else."

I let the self-obsession remark pass, but I was glad that she was an expert on feminine medical matters and not psychiatry. "Thanks for that. It's just what I really wanted, a cosy chat with Glen Bale. Always a pleasure."

She gave me her best motherly, caring look of disapproval, as if she'd just caught me smuggling a bottle of lager into her ward. "Ahh, he's OK. You should give him a break, Pete. I think he can be quite sweet sometimes."

I baulked at the concept of Bale being sweet. Some words are never expected to be in the same sentence: sunbathing and Antarctica; docile and rabid dog; Bale and sweet. I swallowed hard so as to keep down the bag of chips I'd had for a rushed lunch and asked about Alan Wiltshire's mood recently. She said, as had Jackie, as had Kye, as had Glen, and as had Old Uncle Tom Cobley and all, that he had been in good spirits. This was going nowhere: same questions and same answers. But with it being her, I felt emboldened to push a little harder.

"I've heard all that, Marie. It's all getting a little bit repetitive, and there are some real questions developing."

She straightened her blue uniform's bib and leant across the back of the sofa. "Such as?" she asked rather too nonchalantly, just a little *too* relaxed, as if she was affecting the impression, rather than it being real. Any second now she would be loudly whistling, swinging a brolly with one hand, with the other draped in her trouser pocket, and carelessly kicking a can to complete the act.

Pushing aside a rather odd image of her in *Singin' in the Rain,* I went on. "Downstairs, you said that you had been in contact with him recently over how we work with other parties in the National Workers' Councils." I paused for agreement. I got it. She nodded.

"The thing is, Marie, that is exactly what Glen Bale and Kye Toulsen said. *Exactly* the same. Now, I haven't heard anything in the news about any unusual friction between us and the other groups. We may not be all loved-up, but appearances seem to suggest that there is a working relationship."

She went back to stroking her hair, finding another hair amongst many that was out of place. "Not everything is reported but—"

I cut in. We went a long way back, and I knew her well, so I could recognise her flannelling when I saw it. "I could believe that, and I could believe that Alan would discuss the issue with other party member delegates in the council, so OK, I can see why he would talk to you. Your profile is high, and you are well respected and liked." Her work over the cancelling of NHS debts to private firms had put her firmly in the movement's eye. "But why Bale?"

Maybe I was imagining it, but I thought she relaxed a little, "Oh, Pete, Glen Bale's a sound—"

"No," I said sharply. "I'm not being petty. I mean, *why* Bale? Why ask him? He's not even a delegate for the National Workers' Council!"

Her shoulders tensed. "True, but you have to say that he's got a high profile in the party."

Pouncing on her reply, I asked, "Why would that matter if the topic of conversation is the NWC? Same goes for the others who have been regulars in these conference calls. Let's face it; Jackie has made it pretty plain that you're all up to something by getting Simon Peary to arrange meetings with you all."

She took a sip of her drink and rolled it over her tongue. As it was the same stuff I was consuming, I knew it was not to savour its flavour. From my knowledge of the writings of the great Val McDermid, I guessed that she was using it as a delaying tactic. Maybe Jackie's notion that, having written a book on crime novelists, I might be useful, wasn't quite so ridiculous after all. Then again, Marie's body language was easy to read, but the trouble was I could not work out *why* she was behaving like this. She had been at least partly responsible for getting me involved in this, and yet, she didn't like it that I was asking the questions. Unless she was sitting on a discarded bed pan, she was visibly uncomfortable at me broaching the subject.

So of course, I continued. "I mean, I'm seeing two comrades next that I've never heard of, Youssef Ali and Olivia Harrison. Kye Toulsen tells me that Olivia Harrison is one of the hotshots from the power workers' union and that Youssef Ali is a comrade who works for the Water and Sanitation Department. For goodness' sake, all faberoo people, I'm sure, but why would Alan want to talk to them about our relationship with other Trots, Greens, ex-Labourites, anarchists, and independents? Harrison, like Bale, is not in the NWC, and Ali, whoever he is, works for the poxy water board. I mean, Marie—why?"

Her tone went up a pitch. "You do know Youssef, Pete; you've met him. You must have done, or at least you've met his boyfriend; he's a great pal of Ashok's. Spurs supporter? They are always winding each other up? I'm sure I remember you joining in on it at one of our parties."

She diverged into a sketch of someone she said that I must know. So reading Ms McDermid hadn't trained me to that great a level; her characters would never have let Marie wander off the subject like I had. In all honesty, I couldn't recall ever having met this Youssef Ali. He sounded like a swell guy but just one that I had never met. Vainly, she tried to get me to remember, hoping that the football connection might help. It didn't. Relaxing, she took a turn somewhere and went from there to question the merits of football, pondering how, even at times like these, so many of us would still be bothered about eleven men kicking a sphere around a patch of grass.

I waited, poised for a chance to drag her back to the subject. As I did, further questions were formulating in my head. I politely would let her finish her familiar thesis on why football continued to be so popular and then ask them. Just then, there was a slight jolt and what sounded like a muffled cannon shot. As I was asking myself whether I even knew what an unmuffled cannon shot would sound like, there was a bigger jerk and a louder noise.

Marie looked surprised. "What was that? With these windows you don't usually hear a thing in here." She got up, causing a ripple of bounces along the sofa, and walked to the window.

The sudden change of expression on her face, her cheeks tightening, and her hand going to her mouth told me that something was up. I didn't have time to be proud of my perceptiveness; instead, I jumped up and joined her. Looking out, I saw what she had seen.

Billowing up from the buildings around St Paul's were great, dirty clouds of smoke, with a separate plume of smoke coming from the cathedral itself. From our position in relationship to it, it must be from the front, rolling down those marvellous stairs. The smoke was quickly growing in intensity.

"My God, Pete, what's happened?"

Before I could answer, I saw red and orange in the black and brown. Flames. I didn't know what had happened, but it was big. Very big. It looked like that 1940 photograph of St Paul's during the World War II Blitz, the iconic one with St Paul's surrounded by destruction. This, however, was in glorious, high-definition colour and was happening right now. Obviously an explosion, possibly two of them, had gone off in or around Christopher Wren's masterpiece.

I looked and saw the drinkers on the roof bar opposite, scrambling out and down the exits. Judging from the way they were holding themselves, some were injured. There was no sign of the two people who had been cleaning the solar panels. The panels themselves were shattered. I hoped that they had just got off them earlier and were now saying how lucky they had been. St Paul's was now completely covered in smoke, and the shops and offices surrounding it were in flames. We were silent. Just watching.

It was the sight of the first ambulance that jolted Marie into action. Her training kicked in. "Pete, I've got to help. Whatever that was, and I would guess that it was a bomb of some kind, there's going to be a large number of casualties, and they'll need every health professional they can find. I need to go and see if there's anything I can do."

She moved away from the window, but I stayed rooted to the spot, staring.

"Pete," she pulled my jacket. "Come on, I have got to go, and you can't stay here. Come on."

I mumbled, "Yeah, of course, sorry."

She led me to the exit before darting off to a back office. In a trance, I walked through the electronic doors and stood outside. You couldn't see the buildings from street level, but as I looked up, the smoke was now rising high. The air was beginning to smell of burnt wood. Surely, that was impossible, as who used wood in those types of buildings? The air felt gritty and dirty. At the end of one of the streets, a ball of bilious smoke was rolling towards me. Coughing, I looked down and saw broken glass everywhere on the pavement.

Stepping back, I pushed myself against one of the bright hospital signs that decorate so many health facilities. I pushed back harder. I wanted to be a part of that sign and go through it and into the wall. A shiver was starting in my ankles and working itself upwards. Stay calm, Pete. Breathe. Breathe deeply. Remember what your shrink, good old Professor Ellis had said: control, Pete; control your breathing, and control your thoughts. I tried to visualise that ruddy designer garden that she had always gone on about. During my sessions I had thought endlessly about every evergreen, bulb, architectural plant, and piece of decking in the sodding place. Now, could I? Thoughts of lawns kept being disrupted by smoke and the approaching sirens of the emergency services. I needed to get away.

I ran around the corner and searched for my bike. People were looking up or heading towards the explosion. For several seconds I could not remember where I had parked it and thought that it might have been blown up, as if my scooter was the next logical target after St Paul's, but finally, there it was, behind an ancient Toyota. I wrenched the helmet from under the seat and started it up. Looking quickly at the power gauge, I guessed I had just enough juice to get me to Camden Lock.

It was silly to drive. I barely took notice of the traffic; only the fire engines, police cars, and ambulances registered in my brain as I sped away, or as speedily as I could. Several times there were near misses and angry car horns as I cut people off, ignored right of ways, and generally tore up the *Highway Code*. It was far from macho; this was no high-speed chase with a leather-clad hero astride a Harley—this was a scared, middle-aged man trying to hide. In my confused head, the only place I could think of to do so was the power substation where it had been arranged I would meet comrades Harrison and Ali.

My hands were shaking as I steered the bike through the traffic, and I tried to get my head back to what passed for normality. My lovely house with Red snoozing on one of the garden chairs was calling me. As I headed north, I knew it would be quicker to get home than to head for Camden. And yet, strangely and for no logical reason, this meeting seemed to be the better option. I felt that it was the correct place to go to. So I rode on.

It was as I skirted Regent's Park that I calmed down. The power substation was just off Chalk Farm Road which, in fact, was not far from King's Cross where I had seen Kye Toulson yesterday. I really did need someone to sort these appointments out. What was required was a PA for this PI. Public Investigator as opposed to private, obviously, me being a Socialist investigator. That was better. Smart-arsed thoughts meant that I was coming out of the panic attack. My normal "teenage humour acting as an outlet" was how Professor Ellis had called it. Not that I was completely back to normal; getting off the bike, I felt distinctly shaky. I straightened up. Breathe deeply, Pete. This, remember, was the final meeting.

Harrison was a power-supply technician and Youssef a water engineer. I presumed that we were meeting here because this was Olivia's place of work. No doubt it would be as useful as all the others. This was turning out to be like a bloody A–Z of careers. Get advice on your professional future by the suicide of a leading comrade. Check out your career options by meeting militants from all walks of life. Still, it could have been worse; we could be meeting at Youssef's workplace and enjoying the sweet smell of sewage disposal. Then again, that might have been more apt.

After taking a mental note of where I had parked, I went to find them. Utilities workers. This was going to be highly interesting, no doubt. Passing the car chargers, which were mostly unused except for two being used by a 4x4 and a Renault, I tried to lose my sea legs.

I had expected to be stopped and asked for ID as I headed past the signs that said Offices and No Access; ducking under the barrier, I still wasn't. Not a soul was about. I could, however, faintly hear the noise of a TV and the murmurs of voices.

Ahead was an open door, which was obviously where the sounds were emanating from. Entering the office, I could see a group of twenty or so men and women watching a large computer image. Ground-level pictures of St Paul's hung in the air, dominating the room, and grabbing every person's attention. I froze. "Breathe deeply, Pete."

The news commentator was telling us in a perfect, media-public-school voice that two explosions had gone off. The first, the largest, was in the shopping precinct next to the cathedral, and the next was in the cathedral itself. The precinct was so severely damaged that no emergency services had yet entered it for fear of the whole place collapsing. Whilst in St Paul's itself, the bomb had gone off in the Chapel of St Michael and St George, completely demolishing it, with the blast reaching out to the knave. The fire services were now in the building, searching for survivors. The emergency services, the commentator said, had been there in minutes. It was too early to say how many had died, but they thought the figure would be high. But after repeating several times that estimates would be difficult, they stated that the designer clothes shop where it was thought the bomb had been left had been full because of a closing-down sale. It was thought that the shop could take up to a hundred people.

Around me were shaking heads and a few tears. Some were asking what murdering bastards could do such a thing. Just then, the side of a building in the background, slightly to the left of St Paul's, collapsed. A woman in front of me jumped as the sound bounced out of the screen.

A colleague sitting near her stroked her back and changed the screen to 2-D. After what seemed an eternity but in reality was probably a matter of seconds of silence, the pictures changed from those of the damaged building to an ashen but still impeccably well-dressed reporter who, judging from the dust-free look of her tailored jacket, was some distance from the scene.

For several minutes the same information was repeated with more shots of smoke blowing down streets and fire raging from the ruins of the shopping mall. Fire fighters and ambulance staff were running in and out of the cathedral. From the height level of the camera shots, it was obviously news drones hovering above the carnage. Every so often someone would either come walking down the steps covered in sheets or being carried on stretchers on the way to hospital. Others were on the way to the morgue.

I felt a shiver start up my leg again. I gently touched an office worker in front of me who was quietly sobbing. "Sorry, is either Youssef Ali or Olivia Harrison here?"

He dabbed his eyes. "Olivia's there, the woman with the striped blouse."

I looked across the desks and saw a woman in her mid-twenties with shoulder-length, bright-blond hair. You knew you were getting older when the cadre was getting younger. She wore a red-and-blue striped top with capped sleeves and black, slim-fit shorts.

"Olivia, someone to see you," he gently called.

She turned, saw me, and nodded. Her fluorescent skin and blinding teeth made her look Scandinavian. Nimbly jumping off the corner of the desk she had been sitting on, she shouted in a voice definitely not Nordic, straight from the south of the river, more Peckham than Swedish. Her bark was directed at a slightly older Asian man who was a few desks away from her. "Kalder's here."

Indicating he had understood, he stood up from his chair. As he did I had a faint memory of a drunken argument with him about the merits of the two North London clubs, but that was all. And then quite possibly it was one that Marie had planted in me. In all honesty, he could have been waving banners, dressed only in banana-yellow boxer shorts, and I would not have noticed him. He had a little weight around the cheeks and waist which the grey suit only partially hid. His short, black hair only emphasised the round face. His whole appearance was of an assistant bank manager.

They both reached me with similarly sombre faces. He spoke first, with politeness, but without formally greeting me. "We can go in here." He pushed open a white door and ushered me in. Harrison followed me and closed it. The room was small, with five seats in front of six large screens which were showing an array of sensors, dials, and graphs. On two sides of the room were floor-to-ceiling, rectangular, large windows that looked out onto some very odd-looking equipment. Equipment that a 1950s comic-book illustrator might have drawn to show what future space travel might look like. The look, though, was of seen-better-days more than future-daze.

The three of us silently sat down, with Harrison and Ali sitting by each other in front of me. Ali puffed out his cheeks as if the effort was draining. Both looked at me, and I could guess that neither wanted to be here, wasting their time. That was hardly an insightful reading of the situation, because frankly, nor did I. What was I going to ask? What was the point? There was no explanation required as to the reason for my visit because Simon would have seen to that, with Jackie's name backing him.

An atmosphere of polite compliance filled the room, along with a touch of Dior perfume. I felt as if they were going to interview me, rather than the other way around. They looked a rather odd pair. Her paleness contrasted with his skin; her slenderness with his slightly plumper physique. He sat smiling whilst she interrogated me with her eyes. They seemed to be scanning me, weighing me up, and trying to decide whether I was friend or foe.

The uncomfortable silence was broken when Olivia spoke first. "Your face and jacket is covered with crap. Were you there?" She didn't need to say where *there* was.

I made futile attempts to clean my face with the back of my hand and shook my head. "No, I was nearby, at the NTH, seeing Marie. We saw it from the window…" I stopped, emotion bubbling up my throat.

They nodded. Silence ruled.

Just then the door swung open, and a middle-aged black guy poked his head around. "Ol' and Youssef, you might wanna switch the TV on; you're going to want to see this." He pointed to the middle monitor.

Olivia looked surprised. One of her blond eyebrows arched, and she seemed to be about to say something, but she chose not to. Instead, she did as he suggested, touching the screen, and it switched from electricity levels to the UKGB News. The report showed the front page of the Anarchist Federation website. All three of us looked at each other in puzzlement.

A media voice told the news in a voice-over. "The Anarchist Federation is claiming responsibility for the double bombing at St Paul's Cathedral in Central London. The reason the website gives is that the rate of progress of what they call 'the revolution' is too slow; it has stalled, and this attack on what they refer to as a symbol of imperial religion and a symbol of capitalist consumption is a sign that this will not be tolerated."

From there, a media type they had found with a Cockney accent read it out. Presumably, they thought the Gor-Blimey voice gave it authenticity. Repeating what had already been said but adding that they did regret the loss of life; however, it was for the greater good that some blood did need to be lost. The puzzlement grew into disbelief. All three of us competed with expressions of incredulity.

"Shit!" muttered Harrison.

Ali articulated her view rather more eloquently. "There's no way the AF would do that. It is simply not their style."

The middle-aged man at the door held up his hands as if to say, "Who knows?" and left the room.

I agreed with her. I had fond memories of demos with young men and women with wild haircuts and large *A*s on their clothes throwing themselves at the police. They were ever the shock troops on any march. It was over two years ago at what was now called the Battle of the Mall where the police, many of them armed, had been forced to flee as their attempt to attack the marchers had been foiled when thousands, rather than just the usual handful, had fought back. The cops had been too afraid to open fire, so finding themselves swamped, they had run. Anarchists had been, as usual, up there with the rest of us. They had outflanked the water cannons and led the charge. Battling with police was their style, not indiscriminate murder. Not to mention that many of the movements in the federation were committed to nonviolence. Occupying deserted factories rather than blowing up shopping malls was their MO.

Youssef was of the same mind. "Some of them are quite capable of individual acts of violence, but it would be government offices or officials, not public places."

"How have they been in the councils?" I asked. "They've certainly been very vocal about how slow the revolution is progressing."

"Indeed, yes, but I cannot see that they would ever imagine that a bomb would speed it up. What do you think, Olivia?"

"No way."

We spoke more about the politics of anarchism, the AF's many criticisms of us and how we were behaving, where we were leading the struggle, and basically everything else they could think of. Both came across as thoughtful and intelligent people. Both were articulate—Olivia Harrison's accent distinctively London and Youssef's, a little plum in it. The conversation was impersonal and breezeless, a political cucumber sandwich—polite but just a little bland. Still, it was nice to talk politics, and I could have easily have done so for a while, but suddenly they stopped.

Exchanging a look, which was impossible to read, Youssef uttered a few inanities, which were basically a well-spoken full stop to the discussion. Turning to my reason for being here, he gently asked, "So?"

"So," I replied, deciding to be direct. "Olivia, what contact do you have with the NWC?"

"Er, some. Mainly through Jackie and, of course, Youssef 'ere."

In other words it was, as I thought, very little. "Because you are not actually a delegate, are you?"

"No, I…"

"So how can you help with the debate on our working relationship with the other political groups in it?"

Her confusion was obvious. She didn't really have an idea what I was talking about. Well then, wasn't that interesting? Such an important matter to discuss which brings these great minds together, and a mention of it draws a blank. I reminded her. "The work you have been doing with Alan Wiltshire. I have been told that it concerned how best we can work with other groupings in the NWC. Is that not right?"

She struggled to regain composure. "Oh, yeah. Sorry, today's news has thrown me."

"What was it that you six were talking about *exactly*?"

"We discussed how it was important not to abuse our position."

A perfect recital and the same as what the others had previously said.

"So what about you?" I asked Youssef. He replied with the familiar, well-rehearsed line. He expanded somewhat, but it was padding. Big and bright, but padding nonetheless. The devil in me wanted to see how much more opulent waffle he could come out with. "And what were these lengthy political debates about? Glen Bale painted a picture that there was a danger that the anarchists were going to jettison their long-standing position of being troublesome younger brothers to the party and decide to leave home and go it alone. Is that right?"

He hesitated, "No, they were more about strategy and tactics."

"Such as?"

He puffed out his cheeks. If there was an Olympic event doing it, he'd be a triple champion, but Olivia had had time to collect her thoughts and came to his rescue by outlining a pretty good description of floating allegiances and drifting accords which conjured up images of icebergs on fast-forward. Maybe she had got the idea from watching late-night nature programmes. Certainly, it wasn't from what was going on in the National Workers' Council.

"So Bale was wrong? I am surprised, because it does seem to fit in with what we have seen," I said nodding to the TV images.

This time, Youssef was smoother. "No, Glen is not incorrect; it would just be inaccurate to imply that there was a substantial issue between us and the anarchists. The united front is holding. There are the usual hotheads, but we had no inkling of events taking this turn."

It sounded plausible but not quite true. I was about to delve deeper when Olivia raised her finger and pointed to the screen. An AF spokesperson was strenuously denying any involvement in the bombing. The Anarchist Federation "totally and without hesitation condemned the criminal and anti-working class act." Their site had been sabotaged, and the claim on it was bogus. A cyber-attack had been responsible for inserting it. It was an outsider's attempt at discrediting them. He placed the blame firmly on the government's shoulders. They were behind this, the young woman said. This was the desperate last throw of the dice from a failing system.

Instantly, the coverage switched to a live feed with the prime minister who had just come out of yet another meeting with the US president, to condemn the outrage and angrily pour scorn on the anarchist accusations. He opened with a barrage of reprobation at the act. His tone sounded genuinely angry at the murder of so many people. Something new was about him; he sounded sincere. His contempt was searing, his manicured silkiness seemingly having been left behind at the office. This was the side of the PM I had never seen before—passionate. His voice all but broke when he promised to bring the cowards to justice for this barbaric and cowardly action.

The journalist interviewing him looked rather surprised himself, with only just a faint glimmer of satisfaction at how this footage would be used around the world. Cyber dollars would be rolling in. Finally there was a pause, allowing another question to be asked. It was one that was guaranteed to further inflame the premier's mood; he asked him about the AF's accusation that this was the government's doing. Judging by the hexagonal red flash that shot across his neck, it achieved the desired effect.

"What government would even contemplate doing that?" he demanded. "What British government would explode two bombs in Central London, aimed at killing so many of its own citizens? This coalition is for the people, not against them. I ask the people watching this—do you think we would be that cowardly? Or even that stupid?" With solemn emphasis he informed us that the latest confirmed death toll was thirty-six, but it was expected to be a lot higher.

"Would they?" I asked. It was funny, but I, this die-hard revolutionary socialist, who had known all about the catalogue of infamy that capitalism was capable of, found this one hard to swallow. I did detect another one of those looks passing between them—a knowing look.

Knowing what? An awful thought suddenly kicked open my consciousness. "Did you know about this beforehand?" I asked with some alarm, thinking that they surely did not; surely they would not just sit back and allow this murder.

Their reaction appeared genuine—genuine and very insulted. Olivia almost spat, "How dare you! Who do you think we are? Who do you think *you* are? Do you honestly think the party would allow this thing to happen? You think we would let something like this happen? Are you actually still in this party?" She lurched forwards, and for a split second, I thought she was going to hit me, but she stopped herself. Yeah, definitely not northern Europe—every Danish and Swedish person I had ever met had been charm and cultivation personified—she was very English. Huffy and humourless. I could see anger seething inside her. I'd overstepped the mark, and she had taken it very personally, *very* personally.

"Of course, comrade. Sorry." I ran my hand over my face. "It's been a long, hard day. I am sorry."

Youssef looked sympathetic, but she was still raging. It didn't take a mind reader to know what she wanted to say next. Only a sense of comradeship and political courtesy prevented her from saying it. It was pointless to continue. What was I going to ask next? I apologised again and decided to leave it at that.

It was time to make a hurried exit. This was becoming quite a habit. I consoled myself that at least I could quickly charge my scooter for free before heading home. I left the staff still glued to the news coverage.

CHAPTER FOUR
Reform and Revolution

Picking up the groceries from the front step, I wedged the box against the wall whilst I opened the door. I suppose one advantage about the shortages was that the food box organised by the Islington Workers' Council was easier to carry. It was also a lot less bother than waiting for hours in queues for the latest bread delivery to deign to arrive.

After giving the meagre contents the once-over, I put them away in all the correct cupboards. I noted that there was no olive oil, which was probably just as well because the price of it was now so extortionate that it would have taken all my tokens and/or my benefits just to get a few drops of the stuff. Times were hell for chefs. Oh well, the pasta would just have to be made without it. Anyway, I had spent enough on the bottle of Merlot. Supplies of that were still just about getting through, but for some reason the workers' councils didn't consider them as essentials, so the price was sky-high. Disagreeing with the council's position, I had braved the cost and got one.

For a few minutes, I was lost in dreaming of heroic wine smugglers risking life and limb for the right grape. No doubt brave and noble, but stocks were running low. Fantasies of vino freedom fighters were interrupted by Red rubbing himself against my leg. It wasn't for love but for feeding.

"Well, Red, at least you're OK—chicken and tuna. Look who is pampered," I said as I stroked him.

Once I had fed him and got my dose of coffee, I headed upstairs pondering the age-old question: bath or shower? I needed one of them, as no matter what technological changes the human mind came up with, getting rid of the smell of swimming pools seemed beyond even the greatest of brains.

Before setting out I had had the forethought to pack my gear in the scooter box because there was no way I could do without my hit of the swim. Surprise had registered in the faces of the lifeguards, and there had been some hammy, theatrical, open-mouthed staring at the sports-centre clocks. It must have been past six by the time I had arrived: this from the 404 man! That's what they called me poolside, because for over six months at dead-on 4:00 p.m., I had got in, swam the front crawl for forty lengths, making my one km, and then got out and gone home. So I was the 404 man. Well, I guess they went for swimming ability rather than quick-witted repartée at the pool. Today, though, it had been a lot later and a lot longer. Firmly in the outside fast lane for 100, 110, 120 lengths and letting no stragglers get in the way, I swam hard. Oh, did I swim hard. The result, however, was the smell. And a few aches.

Checking that the water was on (it was) and likewise the boiler (it was), I chose a shower. The hot water ran all over my face, almost drowning me. It felt good. I lathered up the shower crème and desperately tried to sort the myriad of thoughts swirling around my head. After I had washed and dried myself, I sat down and ate.

With a bowl of pasta and my evening's glass of red wine, I was beginning to feel a bit more human. Perhaps that wasn't the wisest choice of phrase. Today and yesterday I had been feeling all *too* human. I had experienced feelings. As in so many stories, I could say that it all started…It did *all* start with those feelings of anger and surprise I had felt with the news of Alan Wiltshire's death. It had been a novel experience. More so, when along had come frustration, puzzlement, and total shock. Human emotions, indeed, but it had been a while since I had experienced them. The medication I had been on for eighteen months had removed such things. The mind doctors had prescribed them after my breakdown, figuring that by suppressing the emotions, it would give me the space to analyse my feelings. Or to put it another way, I would not get angry at the platitudes the counsellors and psychiatrists showered on me.

The feelings had run deep because, well, I suppose that was when it *really* did all start, when my life had turned upside-down two years ago. But as they say, that was another story. The pills prescribed to me had been new and powerful and wondrous, but still, to begin with, I needed four a day. Three weeks ago I had self-reduced to one. The reduction had presumably created the space for the feelings to re-emerge.

I wasn't sure how I felt about that. I had been happily bobbing through life like a zombie in a Cambridge punt on a sunny afternoon. But I hadn't been happy because being happy would have meant feeling it. I hadn't even been bobbing, as that implied up and down, and there was not any of that—no movement, just stillness. Stillness. So perhaps it would be better to say that I had been like a long-forgotten, narrow boat moored by a quiet bank. A very poetic analogy, I thought, but as I wasn't intending to write any sonnets tonight, I wasn't sure what use it was. It was the desirability or otherwise, of my emotional consciousness which was the point. What other feelings might start to rise was something that could be a worry.

This was all becoming Jean Paul Sartre meets William Wordsworth or pretentious twaddle, depending on one's viewpoint. So I buried myself in the rather (if I say so myself) fine pasta. I took a sip of the red wine and turned on the TV.

As I flicked through the channels, a green light flashed, telling me that there was a message. Wanting to get it out the way, I played it. It was Michael Hughes, the comrade I was due to meet tomorrow. He was ringing to tell me that he had to cancel and would call again to rearrange a time that was good for him. "Anytime, mate," I muttered. Interesting though, Hughes is suddenly too busy to meet me, even with Jackie on his back. Whatever was taking up his time must be serious.

Turning it off, I turned on the tracking list. These alerted me to anything on the net or across the media that referred to my list of target subjects. Arranged in alphabetical order, top of the list was Arsenal—fans attempt once more to take control of club, and at the bottom was Revolutionary Worker—tomorrow's headlines. I opened neither and continued my flicking.

Comedies and, ironically, several cop shows, were playing. One was the new one from the young crime thriller, hot-shot, Brennan Foyle. Something set in Finland. He was a good writer with a nice line in detail, but he was not for me now. The other was an awful remake of the Inspector Frost mysteries. I preferred the original; it was more downbeat, with a better lead character. That actor with the moustache used to be in sitcoms. So I settled on the news. Didn't I always.

The fatalities from the St Paul's bombings had now reached ninety-three. Fourteen had been in the cathedral, with the remainder coming from the mall. It was expected to rise. One hundred and twelve were in hospital, with fifteen critical. They now had footage from inside St Paul's, showing the devastation. The chapel was impassable, but the knave was a scene of smashed stained glass, broken statues, and bloodied floors. The reporter had obviously been reading the same book of florid similes that I had been, as he soared the heavens with mixed metaphor upon mixed metaphor, crossing several centuries and numerous boundaries of naffness.

The shops were still out of bounds, as rescue workers were searching the wreckage for survivors. Watching it was difficult. I kept my breathing regular. Strangely, although it was painful, I felt I *had* to watch. It held my head in its firm grasp.

Pundits gave opinions on the type of bomb that had been used and where it had been placed. Official statements from the police confirmed that the bomb had been left in K Wang's, the high-end fashion outlet. Further discussion was on the effects on the cathedral structure which was repairable, and the shopping precinct which wasn't.

There was more talk on who was behind it and why. The finger was still very much pointed at the anarchists. I had been shocked to see a young AF delegate of the NWC loudly pronouncing that deaths had been regrettable, but he had argued, in a wholly unoriginal way, you couldn't make an omelette without breaking some eggs. The deaths of these people paled into insignificance compared to the murders of millions.

It was only after the footage, several minutes in length, had been shown that the newscaster explained that the delegate was actually referring to the deaths in the Manchester Hospital because of the power failure. It was a pretty disingenuous and wholly shameful deliberate confusion. Despite the clarification, the misinformation had an obvious purpose: to link the deaths at the hospital to those at St Paul's. Certainly, the home secretary had no reluctance in making it, again and again, across several channels; these, he pronounced, were people who didn't care about life. He was far too well-bred to call us murdering bastards, but that was, in effect, what he was calling us.

If the anarchists were the target, we were being hit in the cross fire. Jackie was forced into political contortions, condemning the bombing but stating that we as a party believed the AF denial and did not believe that they had had any involvement whatsoever with it, and at the same time, she seemingly excused the AF delegate for his crass comments about the hospital deaths. Her attempts to explain that she knew him and that he was just a hot-head and should not be taken out of context were twisted to sound like the excuses of an extremist.

Other Central Committee members found themselves fervidly denying that there was any rift within the workers' councils. Each one would find themselves following a heavily edited clip of a heated debate, clearly showing AF demanding the revolution takes the next step. The more moderate, ex-Labour—Democratic Lefts—argued it had gone far enough, and we were somewhere in the middle. That debate, the very nexus of the institutions, was seemingly lost in the muddle of outrage.

The prime minister had been interviewed, wearing his best grey, three-piece suit with matching grey, stern, and statesman face. Positioning himself with a hospital ward behind him acting as a backdrop, he had made sure that his whole being was a statement. He understood why people had been angry at the bankers and world trade system, but those *genuine* concerns had been hijacked by criminals. Now was the time for "getting the work done." Whilst he had endeavoured to obtain further financial aid "so hospitals could do their job and heal the sick," the squabbling soviets were fermenting the crisis for their own ends, resulting in senseless deaths.

Whilst his performance was being telecast, a message ran underneath that the number of fatalities had gone up to ninety-five. The latest was a thirty-five-year-old woman who had been working at the shoe shop next to the retail outlet where the bomb had actually gone off. The tragedy was unfurling quicker than a carpet at a Marrakesh market stall.

I finished the pasta and put it on the coffee table. Red stirred himself from his slumber to sniff it. Turning to other news, I saw that the hard copy of the *Daily Telegraph* was out again and led with the bombings. All news outlets were doing so. The social networks were buzzing. I could see that there was a growing campaign to get the NWC delegates recalled to the workplaces and areas that had elected them so they could be questioned.

A light caught the corner of my eye. A title appeared above the Arsenal Report. It read "Alan Wiltshire—leading member of the United Revolutionary

Socialist Party." It was on an independent news blog. I clicked to read on. In cartoons, a character shows shock when his jaw hits the floor. Mine sped across the walls, up along the ceiling, and then out the window. Unbelievable.

It has emerged that Alan Wiltshire, aged sixty-nine, a long-term Central Committee member of the United Revolutionary Socialist Party (URSP) and well-known figure of the British Left, is dead. He committed suicide with an overdose of one-and-a-half bottles of the cancer drug Xrenanthol Bulinate.

A well-placed source informs us that senior members of the URSP have known about it since Sunday. It is claimed that Jackie Payne, senior delegate of the National Workers' Councils and a fellow URSP Central Committee member, was actually at the scene of his death. She immediately assembled a small team of people, some of whom are serving police officers, to cover up the death.

Our source tells us that Wiltshire was part of a faction in the URSP who is unhappy at the direction the party is taking. Whether this was a reason for him taking his own life is unknown.

Flowery language deserted me. I was gobsmacked. This was not good. The words "assembled," "small team," and "cover-up" were like slaps. "Faction" and "unhappy at the direction" were kicks. Who was this source? And what faction could they be talking about? What direction? What did that final line mean?

I sat cradling the glass. The number next to the Alan Wiltshire—leading member of the United Revolutionary Socialist Party—went from one to three. The story was spreading. Seconds later, it was in double figures. Then it went viral. After only just over a minute, it was in the thousands. It would be hitting every conceivable news organisation, including the giants. The figure was now rocketing. I'd give it five minutes, and some blue-suited news reader would be on TV, announcing that "News has just come in…"

Christ!

Like being drawn to porn, when you know it's wrong, but there's an urge to do so, I looked at them. The first few were innocuous, from URSP members expressing grief and disbelief. Surprise started to creep in, and questions began to be asked about this "party faction." If the comrades were asking questions, then the blogs from other organisations were coming up with all sorts of answers. Many saw this faction as a grouping, demanding that the revolution had gone far enough, and the councils should be disbanded. Others thought the opposite: that this faction wanted to overthrow the government—tomorrow.

Then a sluice of comments started, somehow linking his suicide with the St Paul's bombing. Logic not so much flew out the window, as escaped through every conceivable exit. But as was the way of these things, the arguments and counterarguments mushroomed. Some were now claiming that he had been responsible for the actual planting of the bomb and posted a barrage of reasons why. Others knew why he had killed himself. Others replied that yes, he had planted it, but that was because he wanted the revolution to stop. Two really bizarre sites said he wasn't dead but was living with Michael Jackson.

Then came what looked like a new computer parlour game of Guess-the-Members-of-the-Faction, which had virtually everyone of note in the party (I was aggrieved that I was deemed too insignificant to warrant a single mention—I felt like doing it myself). This was especially galling, as Glen Bale was mentioned in several of them and, what's more, was repeatedly referred to as being "a leading member."

One thing they all did tend to agree on was that this supposed faction included Jackie. Officially, the party was silent, which only fuelled the conspiracy theories. But then, what could we say? Could we give the reason that Alan had given? I could just see Jackie on the news, impeccably dressed and with her best approachable but assertive smile, dismissing the notion of faction-fighting in the party with the comment, "Oh, of course there isn't such a thing; that is just silliness. He was an MI5 spy; that was the reason why he killed himself." I rang her but only got voice mail. Ditto my call to Marie.

There was a nagging question tugging at my head, but it was one I wasn't too happy about answering. Perhaps that was why my thoughts momentarily left Alan and went to the kitchen, for there was that bottle of wine standing and looking very large. My usual routine was always to make it last five days. My glass-a-day. That was the norm, but today wasn't normal, so in I went and poured myself another.

I returned and sat down in front of the screen. I wanted to see the communications Alan had made in the days preceding his suicide. Since Simon had sent them to me, I hadn't had an opportunity to have a really good look at them. Clicking on the names, the first thing that hit me was that the list of whom he had communicated with was just that—a list. I had assumed that each name would link me with the history of the communication. I had thought that all sorts of goodies would emerge. I would see what had been said/spoken and why. At the very least, the written contact would be saved, and, maybe, if the Gods were smiling, they'd be recordings of verbal and visual communications as well. Ah, but we atheists don't have Gods, do we! There was nothing, just a list! Strewth! It was not even an exhaustive one. Of the multitude of ways we could contact each other, this was just a list of phone calls and e-mails! What was this, the twentieth century? This was having a laugh. I tried to remember what I had asked for; yes, I had asked for the list, but I'd assumed I wouldn't just get a *sodding* list! I had expected that more would have come with it. Not just a bloody list! And actually, if Jackie Payne was going to be so bloody literal, she had promised me his mobile phone as well—so where the hell was that?

Facing the simple fact that I had no option but to do so, I made do with the little I had and studied it. Apart from Jackie herself, the main communication had been with the six names Jackie had given me: Marie Williams, Glen Bale, Kye Toulson, Youssef Ali, Olivia Harrison, and the elusive Michael Hughes. Altogether, the list made seven, lucky seven. (Why *was* seven lucky?) But more importantly, what did this particular lucky seven have in common, I wondered? Did seven perhaps make for a faction?

Background checks on them revealed plenty of personal information, from Toulson's siblings, Bale's rather affluent parentage, and Harrison's kids. There was a hell of a lot of fluff. You could find out so much nowadays. I could reel off their hobbies, work records, and even which vets they took their pets to. On the latter, I could see that there was a split in the group between dog and cat owners. Hughes led the former with two Alsatians and Marie the latter with a tortoiseshell by the name of Bart and an albino, Lisa. That I knew from many a pair of trousers being covered by hair, rather than any extensive computer searches. All in all, it was so much info and so little of it of any relevance. I had trivia and a list, a list and poxy trivia.

But assuming this particular magnificent seven weren't engaged in polemics over animal companions, I did wonder what they were up to. They were certainly rather cagey about what they had spent so much time talking about. If I didn't believe it had anything to do with pets, then equally I didn't buy the story about how it was all about our relationship with other parties. Harrison and Ali had barely known what I was talking about.

Reflecting on the meetings, I felt that I couldn't have been more useless; my obtuse questioning had lacked direction and depth. I seemed to have travelled far and got absolutely nowhere (in both senses).

Looking at who else Alan had been in contact with brought up a few mentions of Dave Wiltshire, the party national office, and daily calls to a pizza company who, looking at the times, I presumed had been the supplier of his dinners. Interestingly, there were not many to comrades other than those. One or two had been made to a leading cadre, but it was less than I had expected. There were also several numbers which came up as unknowns. I switched on the identifying search engines to see if I could put names to these addresses and numbers.

Previously, I had cheekily had them, er, co-opted them to, trace the names of private collectors to locate various works of art. This time it was a bit more serious. I had set them up with the help of an IT geek in the party who had somehow linked a variety of Internet and telephone directories together. Using it now, I managed to put names to a few of them, but still some remained anonymous. I was a bit surprised at that. My friendly IT geek had boasted that what he had created would be able to find anyone. Not true, comrade nerd.

What was also mysterious or to be more accurate, concealed, was what Alan had been researching at the time of his death. I was still without a single name of an Internet site which he had visited. Jackie had also not seen fit to supply me those.

I decided that the simple way to find out who the unknown numbers belonged to was to contact them. So I composed a simple message inviting them to a memorial for Alan Wiltshire and e-mailed them. For the phone numbers, I group-called them. Whilst I waited, I would use my time more productively.

Going through all the party sites, blogs, news releases, internal bulletins, and whatever for anything mentioning Alan, I came up with very little. There was a brief article on racism, but he had not written much else. Not even his usual Tuesday column. In the corner of the screen, I could see that my group call was coming up with a number of voice mails and many simply unanswered. Nothing live but plenty of automated replies were whistling back. Returning to my haphazard delving (research was far too grand a name for this clomping about), I did find out that he had cancelled a few meetings, but that was about all. Whatever that research he had been doing, and I was at least certain that his was more focussed than mine, it had shunted all other activity aside.

Thoroughly burying my daily habits, I poured another glass. I had to think. Usually, when researching for work, I would sketch out a centre and draw three possible routes I would explore. I would note down any other possibilities that arose but would try not to veer off until I was certain that my originals had been exhausted. If so, then another three would be tried. This was my method, and it was one that I found over the years had worked well for me both in my professional life and in any writings for the party.

I went back to the names that had been identified by either me or Simon Peary. With each, I looked deeper into their personal histories and basically whatever I could find out about them. This was less a fishing expedition and more a trawling exercise. I wanted to find out as much as I could about each. No European Community fishing quotas for me. Nor, it seemed, any semblance of a logical investigation. My three lines of enquiry were going nowhere; this was more like a Jackson Pollock approach to research: lines going bloody everywhere! Except that is, Pollock usually ended up with a meaningful picture. This was just a mess.

The data piled up, and as it did, my sense of purpose got more and more lost. Finally, I decided enough was enough, because if nothing else, the bottle was nearly finished. The St Paul's fatalities had reached one hundred; the ton had arrived with the tragic death of a pair of twelve-year-old twins.

Feeling tired, I checked the replies I had received from the group call. Some cleared up a few mysteries from people I recognised. Others remained unknown. The one that stood out was the auto-reply from Abby Nite, senior admin officer. She was away from her computer and promised to get back to me. Nice but not so surprising. A thunderous gulp was elicited, though, not resulting from the final sip of the wine, but from who her employers were. It was signed, Abby Nite, senior admin officer, National Police Information Office.

CHAPTER FIVE
The Poverty of Philosophy

Immediately, I had tried to contact Abby Nite but once more had only got the automated reply. Still buzzing with excitement, I had attempted to find out about this National Police Information Office, but despite its name, I couldn't. Or more correctly, I couldn't get access to their site. Not because they were secretive; in fact, it was not actually down to them. That was made clear by the four metre high 3-D pig which popped out of the screen every time I attempted to use the site. The pig oinked and cursed wildly about police violence, finishing it's routine by turning around and showing its rear. The abuse it spouted had all the hallmarks of the militant hackers. Similar things happened whenever I tried other search engines. Obviously, tags had been created to block any contact. Maybe that was why Abby Nite was away from her office. It was all very commendable and no doubt honourable, but it was bloody annoying, all the same. Frustration knocked back the adrenalin.

With little much else to do, I left some more urgent messages on Abby Nite's phone and decided to wait. After that, I returned to the news. The same story dominated. Most had the picture of St Paul's surrounded by fire and smoke. The *Sun* had one word below it: "Bastards." The As it Happens news website had the headline "Fascists Once More Bomb London."

The *Guardian* questioned who had planted it, but whilst appearing to cast doubt on the fact that it really was the Anarchist Federation, it had still nonetheless produced a whole swathe of archived quotes apparently showing that it was a distinct possibility. Pointedly, we were included in the who-said-what roundup. The main evidence being that we were not pacifists and would take action if necessary. This strategy of Liberal hand-wringing preceding finger-pointing was repeated with other news outlets.

The *Times,* however, won the award for the most effective front page. The paper's masthead had been removed, and atop the photograph of a devastated cathedral was one word: "Jerusalem." The next page was all white except for William Blake's poem of the same name. I could easily have quibbled with the Right misappropriating the great poem, but that did not matter as it was highly effective. The message was clear: England, Albion, had suffered enough and was under attack and needed to be defended. "I will not cease from Mental Fight, / Nor shall my Sword sleep in my hand: / Till we have built Jerusalem."

The *Revolutionary Worker* and a couple of the other Socialist news sites all led with an articulate, closely argued article on where we stood on violence—that unlike the hypocrisy of our rulers, we did not rule out the use of it. They would express abhorrence at a few sticks thrown on a demo whilst bombing some Arabic village into oblivion. Ours was to build a better world, a Jerusalem, in fact, as Blake had intended. Our violence would be as little as possible and as much as necessary. However, ours, unlike the ruling class's, was for the benefit of the many and not the rule of the few. Nonetheless, we were against indiscriminate violence and condemned the bombing without reservation. We thought it was more likely to be rogue elements in the ruling class trying to discredit the Left than the AF. The trouble was that such a closely argued position could not compete with the sight of St Paul's.

It was further undermined by the news I had seen just before I had left home. Three known members of the AF had been caught on CCTV entering both the shopping mall and St Paul's ten minutes before the explosions. What made it worse was that there were several witnesses who could verify it, one of whom was a Democratic Left delegate who personally knew them. Arrest warrants had been put out.

Feeling depression seeping in because of the coverage, I sought sanctuary. Leaving the cat purring, I had wrestled with the logistics of ramming my swimming trunks, goggles, shampoo, the final drop of my moisturizer, plus a whopping great towel into the small rucksack which was my carrier of choice. I was determined to keep to my 4:00 p.m. swimming today, despite the fact that, against my better judgment, I was getting rather intrigued in the potboiler Jackie Payne had involved me in. My hope was that I would be able to follow up a few theories and still grab a session in the pool.

***

The elderly couple whose array of news sites I was scanning appeared at the lounge door with the promised tray containing a pot of tea for them, coffee for me, and a plate of digestives.

George picked up the cup of coffee and handed it to me. "Here, lad, have this and help yourself to a biscuit." It had been many years since anyone had thought of me as a lad, but although having been down south for over sixty years, there was still a trace of a Durham accent when he spoke. He wasn't going to break into singing *When the Boat Comes In*, but it was still there.

His wife, Emily, was a couple of years younger and had all but lost hers. She apologized for her rudeness, but she said she was going to take hers upstairs as she had to go out in a few minutes. George dutifully poured and passed a biscuit to her.

As she left, he slowly and carefully sat opposite me. He looked well for his age, which I could only guess at knowing. Some things were just a mystery—George's age was one of them. I had known him for over thirty years, and, frankly, the short-haired, strong-faced man with killer blue eyes had looked pretty much the same since the first time I had seen him. He had that ruddy, slightly unshaven look that white men often get when they reach a certain age, but then, he always had. Also, I could never remember him wearing anything else than the brown casual trousers and beige shirt, with sleeves rolled up to just below the elbow, showing a still firm, muscled body. Rumour had it that George, who cared nothing for fashion, bought his clothes in massive job lots to save money.

I felt a little uncomfortable and not a little overdressed. It was true that I had rushed out this morning and changed only the shirt from yesterday. I was wearing a purple, button-down collar to match the loafers, contrasting well with the black suit. Pretty unspectacular, I thought, but I could imagine how George viewed me—as he always had—a rather overdressed dilettante.

George may have come across as the housebound grandfather, or was it now great-grandfather, but he was rather more than that. George Henry

Armstrong was his full name, but he was usually just affectionately known as the "old man." At a guess, I would say that he was in his late eighties, and along with his longtime partner, companion, and comrade, he had pretty much created the party. In a story much repeated—George was a great one for repeating stories—the party had been formed by the inaugural meeting above a pub of twenty-three like-minded Lefties disillusioned with the existing left-wing groups. The second meeting, a week later in the same pub, it had grown to eighteen. That was a hell of a long time ago. We were now in the hundreds of thousands.

He sipped his tea with obvious joy and looked at me, sizing me up. Behind him were the obligatory masses of books, but there were also four screens, each showing a different news channel. Most of us old-timers keenly followed world events, but George was positively a news addict. That is, if I could be presumptuous enough to call myself an old-timer, sitting there next to someone who had launched the organisation whilst I was learning to walk.

He put down the cup and got to the point. "So, Peter, what do you make of this?" He pointed to one of the screens. He always called me Peter, if, that is, he ever called me anything. We actually had not spoken for over three years, and, let's be honest, we moved in different circles. The phrase "bumped into each other" would be an appropriate way to describe our contact. He, though, remembered me straightaway when I had called. Old age had barely dented his renowned memory.

I huffed and puffed my reply, feeling rather like a dull boy in front of a maths teacher, answering a question which should be quite simple but getting the answer all wrong. Eventually, I was put out of my misery.

"Aye, it goes without saying that still the most obvious culprits are the state, trying to stir it up a bit, but we need to consider the possibility that it might be the AF who was to blame. It fits with their essentially negative view of the working class and their belief that it takes a committed few to jolt them out of their apathy and into action, and then once jolted, they will instantly rise up." A rather brutal view of our allies, I thought, but then George was the straightest of straight talkers.

Holding his large, left-hand palm towards his solid chest, he gently shook it as he spoke. "I think Jackie and the CC need to consider this. What comes first is the future of the revolution. We have to show a clear division between us and the Anarchist Federation. The government will use this to weaken the movement, weaken us. Being muted in blurring the differences is not an option. We should be merciless against whoever did this. Most likely, it's rogue elements from the security services, but we should be prepared to respond to any news that shows it's a splinter group from the AF. Good hearts, them. Weak in the brain department, though."

"That's a bit harsh!" I blurted.

"Ah, you've always been bloody soft," he said without either a smile or any malice but just spoken as fact.

Feeling rather abashed, I did not have a reply, but then he had not finished.

"Fact is, that for all their frequent trumpeting of freedom and the puerile boasting that there is no such thing as the party line in the AF, that just means any minority can take any action they want. That to me is far from democracy."

George was known for taking no prisoners, but I thought even for him, this was too much. Not that I had the bottle to say so, so I put it more gently. "Do you really think it could be them, George?" That was hardly "putting it" at all, but it was the best I could do.

He wasn't put off at all. Indeed, the irony of my timidness was that you could be as hard as you liked with George, and he wouldn't even blink. The old man wasn't one of those who can give it but can't take it. He was tough; there was no doubt about that. Actually, from the intonation of his voice, he was probably rather disappointed with my wimpy tone.

"It's like I said. I think the chances are that it is not them, but we must be prepared for the fact that it *may* be. Our loyalty is to the class, not to a group of anarchists. But whoever it was, the moment of truth is nearly upon us."

"It's been a hard few days," I said. Taking the last bite of the digestive, I hoped that George would ignore the most inane comment I could have made. I was feeling more like a confused schoolboy every minute.

"And we will carry the class with us, or we will die."

I stared at him. It was a black-and-white assessment. "How much have we been hurt by this and the other events, the hospital deaths and…" I stumbled, "the matter of Alan Wiltshire?"

He coughed. "Aye, it's been a difficult week, but we knew it was never going to be easy. We've had worse. Remember, Peter, not so long ago there were armed police on the streets, and the army was ready to take over. We beat them then, because we were rooted in the class. The class rose up and took their chance to clamber onto the stage of history. We were about to be rounded up and put inside jail, but we were too strong. Simple fact is, Peter, if we are embedded in the class, then they will be loyal to us. If not…" he shrugged, "we will fail, and the price of failed revolutionaries is always the same—death."

"So what is your appraisal?" I asked.

"Time will tell." He laughed. He had a loud, generous, hearty laugh. "If in one hundred years, they're building statues of Jackie, then you'll know we have failed, and it's simply romanticizing the past. If they are building a new world—we've won."

"And Alan…?"

"Ah, yes. How did you put it? 'The matter of Alan Wiltshire.' Yes, I heard that's what Jackie has got you doing, looking into his suicide to see if he was a spy for the ruling class."

Surprise must have registered on my face.

"Ah, yes, comrade, I am kept informed. I might be a doddering old fool, but Jackie lets me know what's happening. She told me about Alan and the little job she had you doing. Me, I think there's better things you could be doing than raking up the past. She should get you doing something worthwhile, not farting about with this. Not trying to find out whether or not he was a spy."

"And?"

"That he was a class traitor?" He held up his hands. "Who knows?"

"Doesn't it bother you what's been alleged? You knew him for the best part of his life and spent years on the Central Committee, so do you think it's really possible?"

His reply shouldn't have surprised me, because for all his directness, George was known for his understanding of comrades' foibles. Despite appearances, he was quite capable of being tolerant of other people's weaknesses. "Who can say? We all have weaknesses. Alan certainly did, but what I can say is that anything he did for them was negligible compared to what he did for us. Like I have always said—police spies? Bring 'em all in. They will be the ones doing the hard graft."

I leant forwards. "But why would he? Did you ever doubt his loyalty?"

An affectionate smile spread along his jaw, his eyes twinkling rare nostalgia. "Never. Not for a second, but..." he paused, "if he says he passed on information, then why doubt what he says? Why would he lie? Alan, bless him, was never a modest man, but he's hardly going to be boasting about this. As for why? No idea. That's what you're supposed to be finding out, isn't it?"

"I don't really have any idea what I'm supposed to be doing," I sighed.

He poured another cup of tea for himself and asked if I wanted another coffee. I declined. After taking a rather noisy sip, he told me in his strong, no-nonsense voice, "If you ask me, Jackie's got you doing a bit of box ticking. She needs reassuring, to see if there's something she has not thought of. That's where you come in; you can tick the box where it says, 'Have we been betrayed?'"

His voice left no doubt that he thought whatever the truth of the matter, it was all rather stupid and a waste of time

"What you should be doing," he continued, "if you are determined to waste your time on it, is then upturn a few tables and see what drops." He fixed his eyes on me. "You weren't busy doing other things, were you?"

I replied by simply shaking my head.

Cradling the cup, he smiled, showing a full, if yellowing, set of teeth. "You were a good comrade. I enjoyed your book, *Notes of the Vanguard*, simple but accessible and straightforward history of the party. Your other one, er, *You're Nicked*, a truly awful title but not a bad book. I also used to enjoy your column in the paper, "Culture Wars." Not essential stuff. But there's no harm in a touch of frippery, and you had some interesting ideas on art, music, literature, and the like. I don't know what Jackie hopes you will achieve, but it's good to see you back."

I felt rather proud. I respected the old man more than anyone else alive, and he had just heaped praise on me. Well, what passed for heaping from him. It felt good. That little boy had just received a certificate of appreciation. I would have liked a greater testimonial than the book being "simple" and "straightforward" because I thought it witty, sharp, thoughtful, and inspiring, but I guess I had to settle for what I had got. I pretended I hadn't heard the "frippery" remark.

Trying to remain nonchalant, I told him what the lucky seven, although I didn't call them that, had said and what little I had found out. It was depressingly *very* little. He wasn't aware of their meetings to discuss our relationship with other parties in the workers' councils. But he couldn't see why I would doubt what they had said they had been discussing. He thought it was a good idea to get it just right. At length he discussed how and why we should avoid the twin traps of sectarianism and the over blurring of the boundaries.

I interrupted. "A working relationship, not a love affair or a feud." My rather succinct and witty summation was ignored.

He moved on to how different periods determined different strategies. After several minutes of this and fearing that he might move on to a detailed history of how Lenin had prepared the Bolshevik Party for power and how it was relevant today, I summoned the courage to butt in again. I could listen to the old man for hours, but that was not why I was here.

I asked him if he had any idea who had leaked Alan's death. He just answered in the negative. He also had no idea what was meant by the talk of factions. Evidently he thought both were unimportant. "Frivolous gossip," he muttered.

He was also unimpressed how Jackie had dealt with it. "It was a mistake to keep it quiet in the first place; I told her that right from the start. We are not a secret party; we should be open, aboveboard, and honest at all times. It was going to come out anyway. Did she really think we could keep it secret? I also didn't think much of what she said this morning—rather lame." He growled through some phlegm in his throat. "Saying that we had been waiting for the post-mortem. Pitiful."

He was very gruff this morning. I knew that he rated Jackie as the most gifted comrade we had ever had. One who would go down in history as a truly towering figure. But then again, on second thoughts, George was always gruff.

"She's tired," I said.

Whatever his reply was going to be, it did not come, as at that moment Emily poked her head around the door, saying good-bye and that she'd be back in a few hours.

I sat back in the sofa, unbuttoned my jacket, and ran my hands across my face. "George, I have no idea what to do. You say that I should do as Jackie asked, but what is that? I have no idea, George. No idea whatsoever."

Filed under *S* in George's emotional vocabulary was Socialism and solidarity but certainly not sympathy. He looked straight at me. "Start with what you know. Believe Alan's video. Deal with it. Alan said he started in 2010. What was happening in 2010? You're the party historian, and, well," he chuckled, "I am part of the party history. Let's put our heads together and see if we can come up with something." He went to push himself up. "Peter, give us a hand."

I went over and helped him up. He still had a very strong grip. When he let go, he leant over, picked up the remote control, tossed it over to me, and then went purposely to some shelves behind him to his right. After scanning some titles on the spines, he picked out half a dozen books and put them in front of me. He pointed at the remote. "Look up the back files of the *Revolutionary Worker* and the national papers—see what was happening. Who was saying what and why. Use them." He pointed to the books. "Look in them for backup. One of them is by a comrade by the name of Pete Kalder." He chuckled. "Wonder what ever happened to him?"

Placing the cups and the empty plate back on the tray, he continued his instructions. "I'm going to make us another brew and get some more of those lovely digestives. You start doing your thing. The year 2010 seems a good place to start."

My brain at last started to think. "No, George, 2009. Assuming Alan did start in '10, they would have to have time to set it up, and something must have given them the idea that it was worth having a mole in the party. How big were we then?"

He thought for a second. "Two thousand max. We were small and just one of a number of revolutionary groups, barely a party, more of a sect."

"As I thought—we were miniscule, but something must have happened in 2009 or 2010 to spark MI5's interest. I have a vague recollection of the period, but nothing springs to mind."

He nodded vigorously. "Nor me, either. Perhaps there was something that was seen as minor at the time but made them feel threatened. We should look in the years after '10."

I disagreed. "No, that's hindsight. We should just look at what was known then. You always said, don't overestimate the knowledge of the ruling class. We shouldn't make the mistake of seeing that something happened in 2015 or 2020 and thinking that they could have predicted that."

If George believed you were right, he saw no reason for idle chatter. "You're right. Well, off you go." He disappeared and went to the kitchen.

I made a start at January 2009, scanning the tabloids. I moved through the two years. Most appeared to lead on the trials and tribulations of reality television stars and the flooding of the country by East Europeans, who, it seemed, were becoming multimillionaires on benefits and presumably were all set to get their own reality series.

When I did these sorts of enquiries in my daily work—as it was—I always had to be careful not to get sidetracked. I remembered once in the early days of my professional life doing a brief background search on The Seven Dials, a poor, some might say notorious, area of London in the seventeen and eighteen hundreds. It was for a lecturer who was going to give a talk on the wood engraver Gustave Doré whose 1872 engraving of Dudley Street was going to be the keystone of the lecture. Instead of it being brief enquiry, I had wandered off into a day looking into the history of nineteenth-century London. It got worse when I got engrossed in Charles Dickens's *Sketches of Boz* which featured the engraving, and then from there I started to read Agatha Christie's *The Seven Dials Mystery*. Both were good literature which was my defence in front of my line manager when I was taken to task for missing the lecture.

My line manager of the moment returned with the drinks. I stopped my investigations into long-forgotten D-list celebrities who had appeared on a TV show called *I'm a Celebrity, Get Me Out of Here* and quickly switched to the election of Barack Obama as the forty-fourth president of the United States.

We sat there like a pair of old gits. George watched today's news whilst occasionally commenting on what I was reading. This was a mixed blessing, as it may have kept me from exploring old *Coronation Street* story lines, but he was prone to see a story and say, "And look what happened to him" or "Little did they know" or "Of course, that led to." But I was definite: no hindsight. They didn't have it then, so we shouldn't have it now.

I moved from the tabloids to the broadsheets, not that the tabs were all frivolous nonsense; often there were a lot a politics in there and even on the front pages. In 2009 the news featured the Israeli ground invasion of the Gaza Strip, the growing banking crisis, and the problems of the then-Prime Minister Gordon Brown. It often wasn't my shade of politics but then neither were the broadsheets; they just had longer sentences. Better use of connectives did not make a newspaper great. George would scoff whenever the word "expert" was used.

Every so often I did make the odd, ill-judged attempt at humour over topics ranging from an explosion on a BP oil rig to the death of Michael Jackson (which I pointed out wasn't true according to some websites). My line on the volcanic ash stopping flights was, I thought, particularly amusing and even had a political edge. But it, too, received a blank look. It was a look which very quickly told me to shut the hell up.

He, on the other hand, would give me running reports from today's news: the St Paul's death count had reached 101, with 235 still in hospital. Although, mercifully, none were considered critical, and as the buildings had been searched, it was thought that it would not rise any higher. The AF were still denying involvement and had organised a march of solidarity for those who had died and were injured, or as the AF called them, murder victims of the state. We were supporting it, although both the Greens and Democratic Left weren't.

Back in my past world, I was reading the reports on the horror of the earthquake on Haiti. There was also much on the financial crisis, which was affecting Iceland and Ireland and, by the end of my timeline, was threatening Spain. I could see that it had been regarded as very serious at the time, but, overwhelmingly, the view was that things had stabilised. Indeed, compared to later ones, they had been pretty minor. Would the ruling class have been feeling that threatened? I didn't think so, nor, more importantly, did George. They were cheesed off with the WikiLeaks's exposure of the US foreign policy, but that had nothing to do with us.

In August, 2010, Britain got a coalition headed by David Cameron and Nick Clegg. That set George off into one of his "what happened next" talks, analysing the political situation of that time and what mistakes we might have made. I turned a deaf ear and enjoyed seeing those pictures from the student protests against tuition fees. Oh boy, more than a fire extinguisher had been thrown since then. It made me smile. These were the first demos I'd been on. Back at uni had been when I heard George and Alan speak for the first time. Had the ruling class felt threatened? Again, we felt the answer was a resounding no. Although chuckling, George did recall that he had spoken at some great meetings.

"We weren't a menace to them then," I said. "The intermittent irritant, but that was about it. Who'd foresee that we would grow to this?"

George chose not to launch into a polemic about the possibilities of revolution in any period and instead agreed. Sipping his tea he added, "They would have been worried about the financial situation, but was it worth spying on us? I would have thought they'd have used their resources on the threat from Islamic fundamentalist terrorists—the media was banging on about them enough. Both the Iraq and Afghanistan Wars were still going on and further alienating small sections of Muslim youth…"

He broke off when something more current flashed up on his screen. He was right. The security services seemed more intent on raiding suspected terrorists, and in the United States, especially, a whole number of plots had been uncovered, a lot of which appeared to have had some FBI involvement.

My book lay in front of me, looking pleasantly well-thumbed. I would not have dreamt for a second that years later I would be using it to check up on Alan Wiltshire. It sat there as a remembrance of the past, tugging fondly because it was not just a history of the party but one written at a happy time. There was love in that typeface.

I knew that I was being a soppy git, but I picked it up. What mattered here was not how my life had been then but what might be in there that might help me now. I skimmed past the dedication and saw what insights I had written about the period. The trouble was that, like any history book, I had written with the contemporaneous view back on those years. It had been written fifteen years after the event, and even the language reflected the current events. What might have been seen then at the time of me slaving over a laptop after work as "a sudden growth of membership" would hardly be called that now, when in the previous six months, membership had risen by two hundred thousand. Years after *Vanguard* had been published, the world had changed. We wouldn't see handfuls of recruits as "sudden growth" now; it would be more like a calamity. Write this book now, and this page wouldn't have the exaltation that made it look now rather dated.

With George studying reports from the workers' councils, I changed my viewing to the party website and onto the archive section for *Revolutionary Worker*. The *RW*'s lead articles mirrored much of the mainstream media, although from a far different perspective, and there was nothing on Reality TV. Iraq, Afghanistan, banking crisis, the cuts, and the Gaza were all there. There was coverage of an occupation by the Vestas wind turbine workers on the Isle of Wight and postal, rail, and Ford strikes—all good stuff, but it was hardly a mass strike wave. The most inspiring thing had been the students. The covers of the *RW* were positively orgasmic about them. A bittersweet memory uncovered itself from layers of camouflage; I had met one of those referenced in the dedication through a chance meeting whilst enjoying the hospitality of the Met Police in one of their kettling operations.

George turned back to me. "If memory serves me right…" Of course it does, George; it always does, I thought to myself. "The Irish Republicans start to get active again in 2010, and there was some talk of a resurgence of a terror campaign, which again had bugger all to do with us."

Indeed. I turned the screen off and finished off my coffee. That was me done.

He seemed surprised, asking me whether I had seen enough and what about other media outlets from the period? But I had seen enough; in those days the paper press would cover anything of note wherever it had broken.

"Sorry, lad, you seem to have had a wasted journey."

"Quite the contrary, George. I've followed up one line of thought, and I know of one more I would like to give a run."

There was a hint of a smile on his face. I told him to stay seated, although I had an inkling that he was going to anyway. As I left I heard the TV being turned up.

***

I was stationary on my scooter, trying to get onto Farringdon Street. I had been there for a good ten minutes watching the march pass me. It was a pretty small affair with perhaps a couple thousand people, which was tiny compared to recent ones. But the nature of it and it being pretty much spur-of-the-moment type of thing, I thought was fairly respectable.

Although we were supporting it, there were few party members in it. Usually we swamped the anarchists but not so here. If placards had have been allowed and if we were being honest, then our comrades would be carrying ones proclaiming, "tokenistic support which we are embarrassed to be doing, but you can't choose when to support your allies." But they were deemed inappropriate. Lucky. You wouldn't have been able to fit all that on an A3 piece of card. Not sure we'd be that honest, either.

Chuckling to myself and attracting a few quizzical looks from the marchers, I noted that there was quite a serious workers' council guard present. Clearly identifiable by their red armbands and submachine guns, I could see that they looked nervous. Just as long as they pointed those guns away from me!

I presumed that they feared an attack stemming from the outrage at the bombing. George had mentioned that the Fascists were threatening to come out from under the floorboards and lead a countermarch. There was, as yet, no sign of our goose-stepping, patriot friends. The marchers themselves looked sombre and were your usual anarchist bunch; gone were the white, dreadlocked, combat-trousered youngsters in hoods, and now there was a real cross section of folk. Nowadays, there would be feminists, trade-unionists, independents, radical greens, and basically people who preferred the looser confederation than our Democratic Centralist one. You could even see a few, well-dressed AF members now.

What a difference a year makes. Twelve months ago, millions were on the streets in the world's greatest carnival. The mood had been joyous and celebratory, full of hope and promise. Had it all gone? Before the melancholy started to grow, I was waved on by one of the tiny number of police present. It didn't take long to reach the Harold Pinter Centre. Formerly a conference centre, it had now been commandeered by the East Thames Workers' Council.

It was Byzantine in complexity, the number and interrelation of the workers' councils: local, workplace, regional, and national. You could get elected to some, all, or none; some you had to get elected to, to become a delegate of another. It was the subject of a number of jokes, the latest being: "Why are there so many WC's? Because there's so many motions to be passed" and "What happens if the WC overflows with shits? They'll just get elected to another one." Boom, bloody boom.

This WC was an upmarket one. Walking into the main hall after flashing the Jackie vid to gain me entrance, I could see a cavernous room with rows of semicircular seats, each with their own computer screens. Of the five hundred seats, about 75 percent of them were filled. A petite woman to my right, sporting a hijab, was talking, but her lapel mike was malfunctioning, and I could only hear one word in six.

At the front was a row of tables and seats in front of a huge screen, showing the map of the area covered by the Thames Northeast Workers' Council with streets highlighted in red, green, or blue. My first guess that this indicated the political allegiances of the residents was dispelled when I realised that the subject of the debate was a more bread-and-butter affair. It *literally was* about bread and butter, or to be more accurate, who was receiving it regularly, occasionally, and never. Where was Jesus when you needed him? It was a thought that had come up from time to time when the shops sold out of red wine. It was an important issue, however: the bread distribution, that is, not the second coming. Who was it said that it all came down to bread? I couldn't remember, but I did hope they would find time to deliberate the issue of my olive oil, or rather, lack of.

Thinking of food reminded my stomach that it was well past lunchtime, and apart from two lightly buttered pieces of toast and a few digestives around the old man's, I hadn't eaten. Walking behind the delegates and watching as some young kid fixed the delegate's mike, I reached the refreshment trollies. There wasn't much left, but I did grab myself a poisonous cup of coffee and three limp cheese-and-lettuce sandwiches. Pummelling the coffee with sugar to make it drinkable, I surveyed the projections enclosing the hall. Some showed designs by the young artist Phillip Hallam which slowly changed shape and angle as you looked at them. He was very popular with a lot of the young Turks of the movement. I thought him OK but found his brushwork, if you could use that terminology with e-art, was rather derivative of the Anglo-German artist Frank Auerbach of the 1960s.

Finishing the cardboard which passed for sandwiches, I made my way to find Marie Williams, who George had told me would definitely be here. Poking my head around doors that ringed the hall, I went looking for her. The delegate's computer screen had indicated she was not available to vote which meant that she was in the hall. Hopefully, she was still in the building.

Each room was differently decorated with yet more artwork. I had to say that this was far plusher than the Watford Workers' Council where I had met Glen Bale. There was no huddling by shop mannequins in here, but instead the swish furnishing which, whilst being a little hotel lobbyesque for my taste, did make grassroots democracy more comfortable. And talking of comrade Bale, to my surprise I saw him in a side room sitting beside Marie. I wondered what he was doing here. The pair of them was surrounded by a dozen or so women, who were in various stages of getting up from the comfy, brown-leather armchairs. Strolling into the room, I was assailed by waves of perfumes.

There were several cheek kisses for Marie and nods of good-bye for Bale from the women as they departed. It was a varied bunch of different ages, colour, and levels of makeup. Some had none and others a smattering of lippy and eyeliner, whilst others had depths that would take South American miners to dig out. All totally ignored me as I waited.

Bale and Marie had seen me; she had met me with an affectionate smile, and Bale had offered a scowl. She was dressed in jeans and a blouse that had seen better days (ones when horses pulled carts). Our Marie was not what you called a style icon. Bale matched her in his faded jeans and an ill-fitting, white T-shirt. Both looked in dire need of sleep. Deep lines spanned out from the corners of her eyes. She had attempted to tame the hair and had tied it back tightly behind her head into a ponytail, which accentuated just how weary she looked. The occasional strand was breaking loose which added just a hint of madness to her appearance.

As the last one left, I closed the door and nodded to the departed women as if to say, who were they?

"Sex workers," Marie answered.

"Glen call them, did he? Saw the numbers online?" I joked.

"Grow up, Kalder," he growled, not appreciating my wit.

"Boys," Marie said, trying to settle things down. "Pete, behave; you know why they'd be here."

Yes, I knew. The world and his or her wife/husband/partner (delete where applicable) were now organising themselves, including those previously seen at the margins of society.

I sat down, telling Marie that the old man had told me she would be here which was why I had come. There were a few questions I needed to ask her. I indicated to Bale to stay seated.

"So, Glen," I said, trying to keep the sarcasm out of the voice and the businesslike in. "Marie's here because this is her council, and she, like a number of the delegates, has been recalled to discuss yesterday's bombing, but why, comrade, are you here?"

He wouldn't lower himself to give me a detailed answer. "I needed to talk to Marie."

I wasn't in the mood for small talk, and basically I didn't give a toss why he was here. I wanted answers to other things, so I didn't say anything else on the matter.

"I still have to find out what exactly Alan was researching. Any ideas? Simon Peary, along with other things, neglected to send me any details." I asked bluntly.

They tried to exchange a surreptitious look, but it was as subtle as a piano landing on my head. The look said "simply don't tell him anything." Marie gave me an evasive answer which boiled down to that if Jackie had felt the need to keep the topic a secret, then who were they to disagree? Another piano fell.

I had expected that, and I knew they were not going to budge from their position; they believed it was down to Jackie to answer that one. In all honesty, I agreed. Still, I wasn't going to let them off the hook.

"So you can't tell me if this research had anything to do with the reason why he had felt the need to ring, not once, not twice, but on three separate occasions, someone called Abby Nite, who works at the National Police Information Office?"

That look again. I was getting mightily cheesed off with those falling musical instruments. I pushed harder. "Don't tell me—could she be a comrade? A long-lost pen pal? Why would he contact her? Marie?"

She answered that she had no idea. Bale did likewise when I asked him the same.

"So I can assume that it's either something to do with his research, or he was just touching base with his old spy handlers?"

Bale pulled a face. "Actually, I would have thought that it was GCHQ who would have been doing that."

"Oh, you know, do you?"

He didn't answer. Again, I wasn't that worried about that, because as George had suggested when I told him, the simplest thing was to wait for the woman herself to reply to my call. If she ever did. I could judge for myself what sort of answer she gave. She would probably either tell me to take a hike or lie. How she said either might help me.

I had once more tried to contact Ms Nite just before arriving here, but as appeared to be the pattern recently, I had simply got her voice mail. I was raising the subject of her now to see their reaction. I had expected to meet Marie here, but having Glen Bale as well was a real bonus (something I thought I would never say). I could get two comrades looking uncomfortable and obviously lying, instead of just the one.

"All of you have told me that you were in constant contact with each other because you were discussing how we operate in the councils. These must have been quite some discussions, as there are a quite number of them, and they are lengthy. I must say that I am having difficulty believing that."

Marie went to interrupt and no doubt say something to counter what I was saying, but I didn't allow her to by using the old party trick of just speaking over her. "What was interesting in the little Simon has given me, was who Alan rang after these innocent little chats. The names are not important, but the locations are. Working southwards we get: Glasgow, Edinburgh, Sunderland, Leeds, Manchester, Liverpool, Birmingham, Cardiff, and Southampton. That's quite a list. Was there any reason for Alan being so keen to contact those cities?"

No answer, just a pair of bums shifting weight.

"Maybe they had difficulties with other parties in the workers' councils. What were the difficulties, I wonder? The crap coffee? Stale sarnies?"

In all honesty I wasn't enjoying the obvious discomfort that both Marie and Glen were feeling. I liked Marie, and, well, I guess I could confess the fact that Glen was a good comrade. I couldn't believe that there could be anything dodgy about either of them, but something was wrong. George had said to upturn a few tables, so here I was, lifting furniture.

"Quite a network of people; with Northern Ireland now part of Ireland proper, that makes them run along the spine of Britain." I paused, and then with a deliberately plastic fake innocence, asked, "By the way, did you see the report on the net? About a source describing a faction? What would you call seven committee members, not to mention these further comrades in major cities across the country?"

Bale was going a shade of red similar to a shaving burn, which from the timbre of his voice was from another kind of irritation. "Internet nonsense. We're not a faction. What the hell are you talking about? Is this what you've come for—to accuse us of being antiparty and trying to undermine the revolution? Even by your standards, that's pathetic."

My inflammation levels were beginning to rise, as well. "Really? Marie, tell me, then, why did Alan feel the need to talk to these city organisers every time? Every time, Marie, I should add, after you seven had talked? What exactly were those conversations?"

"Pete, we can't tell you. You need to talk to—"

"Oh yes, I do need to talk to Jackie; believe me, I am going to have a long talk with our leader. I was happy being at home in my little life, but she comes along and says 'Oh, Pete, Alan was a spy, and please look into it' but then hides everything away which might be of any use. Peary would not have been so tardy with the information, unless Jackie had told him to be. I'll ask her why she has made the decision to keep his death so quiet for so long. Have you seen what they are now saying on the net?" I did not let her have the time to answer. "Any ideas who leaked it?"

"Of course not," she replied, leaning forwards to, I think and hoped, put a comforting hand on my knee. "Pete, don't get too worked up; you know you must—"

"Yes." I cut in and moved my knee away from any ameliorating touches. "What about the three musketeers, Vic Cole, Asher Joseph, and Roijin Kemal? Did they have a quiet word with their chums at New Scotland Yard?"

Still in appeasing mode, Marie shook her head. "I would have thought they'd be the last ones to have grassed us up for the simple reason that we would all look at them first. No, definitely not them. The most obvious answer is that wherever they took Alan's body, someone there passed on the information. Party comrades in the police service are still a tiny minority."

"Maybe, or maybe MI5 has a few moles still in the party. Let's face it—why would they put all their apples in one basket? So, Glen, did you leak out the news?" It was a cheap shot and not worthy of him or me. Fun, though.

"Oh, give it a rest!" Bale shook his head as if he was banging a nail into the wall and appeared to be genuinely outraged by the suggestion. It was also apparent that he had had enough of my delightful company, as he rapidly got to his feet.

In contrast to Bale, Marie was gently shaking her head and rubbing her forehead. She got up and followed him as he stormed out. She caught up with him outside, and I could catch snatches of their conversation through the cardboard-thin door. Not surprisingly, it was about me. Bale was certainly not suggesting setting up a fan club. I took the opportunity to achieve some sense of equilibrium. That tingling in my fingers and toes was beginning to grow; I needed to control it. I went back into my mental garden, planning the borders, the shape of the pond, and what to put in the bog section.

It was as the back forest section was being arranged that my breathing started to become more regular, and the tingling began to subside. It was then that Marie came back into the room. She placed herself next to me and unleashed all her medically trained skills of empathy and support. I listened and lapped it up. I was quite happy to go along with it all, as partly the smooth, calm voice was making me feel better, and also partly that I had done all the provoking I wanted to do. What I wanted next was some personal information on Allen.

Smiling in a way I hoped showed acquiescence to her wishes, I gently enquired what Alan had been like in 2010. She replied with a set of platitudes on his abilities and skills as an organiser.

I wasn't here for a tribute and wanted to get a feel of what he had been like. "What was his partner's name?" My mind having gone blank.

"Ruth." Marie pulled a face which made it quite clear that Ruth wasn't someone who was ever top of her best buddy list.

"Yes, of course, Ruth. Ruth took Stuart and left him, didn't she? He must have been pretty upset."

"He was devastated, completely fell apart. Mum and Dad put him up because he obviously couldn't look after himself. He had my room, and I moved into my sister's room. He was a right mess. They were the world to him, and it tore him apart losing them; well…" she stumbled, looking embarrassed.

I motioned her to continue. "He didn't, of course, lose them as such, but he did fear that he would never see his son again. He doted on him, loved him with all his heart."

I was surprised, as party folklore had it that he had neglected his son.

"Eventually, the aptly named Ruth, as in Ruthless, made a deal with him. Hand over half his monthly salary to her, and she would allow the occasional visit. That was the best he could hope for."

"Otherwise?"

She breathed deeply. "From what I overheard in the heated discussions downstairs with Dad, Ruth said she would bring out Alan's drinking habits in court and embarrass the life out of him, and he would see his son even less than what she was proposing."

"Yes, I had heard that Alan had been quite a drinker in his early days. His sessions had been legendary. Of course, all the years I knew him, he was a one hundred percent teetotaller. It was always pure orange juice or, failing that, apple juice."

"Dunno. From what I remember, he was far from being an alcoholic, but, yes, he liked to drink. Occasionally, a bit too much, but then can't that be said of all of us?"

"That must have got worse when Ruth and Stuart left."

She let out a large and generous laugh. "I couldn't say. For some reason he did not invite a schoolgirl along to the pub, but I bet that like many men, he found that several pints, whilst not healing a broken heart, does at least numb it."

"So when did he give up?" I asked.

She sat back in her seat and puckered her lips as she did when she was deep in thought. "Sorry, Pete, I have no idea."

I could hazard a guess.

CHAPTER SIX
Their Morals and Ours

I was able to make it to the pool by 4:00 p.m., but I was not in the mood for any bantering with the attendants, and so I had run in, stripped off, and dived in the pool, barely exchanging a word with anyone. It was blissfully quiet there today: no children bum-diving, no couples canoodling, no speedo-clad racers, and no big lumps bobbing along. Actually, there were a few of the latter, but their painfully slow doggy paddles were where they should be, in the slow lanes. I admit it; I am an aquatics Nazi. Everyone has their place in a pool. I had managed to have a free run in my favourite lane and had just swum. So, free of people and free of lane rage, I could get into a rhythm, leaving the day's stresses back in the changing rooms. Getting the tempo correct, I achieved a uniformity of strokes, turning myself into some swimming cyborg.

This allowed my thoughts to be focussed on what had happened to Alan Wiltshire in the year of 2010; surely, that was the key. It seemed to me that the person I really needed to talk to was Dave, Alan's grandson, and who had become maybe more. In 2010, Alan had all but lost his son, Stuart, when Ruth had left him. In doing so, she had taken his heart and soul. Maybe Dave, the son of the long-lost Stuart, had become a surrogate, a grandson replacing a son, a sort of generational substitution, with Dave coming off the bench. I was profound today.

Before getting in the pool, I had tried his number, and like Ms A. Nite, I only managed to get his voice mail again. What a waste of such erudite thought. But this time, I remembered what George had said: act rather than just react. I rang Dave's employers and explained that I was a friend of the family and needed to get hold of him to discuss the funeral arrangements. They told me that yesterday he had phoned them to request indefinite leave, which, being enlightened employers, or so they informed me, they had agreed to.

There had been a discussion between several of his coworkers of where he might be. One was of the opinion that he had gone up to Scotland to be with his parents; another said that he was at home redecorating as grief therapy, whilst yet another said he had skipped off abroad to somewhere warm.

Turning to complete my twelfth length, I decided that the obvious option was to go around and see for myself. In which case, it would have to be back to just my usual forty lengths. At least that spelt a semblance of normality. Pulling myself out of the pool, I could feel my balance returning. The only slight blot was that it was a shame that after a lovely hot and solitary shower, I only had a rather sweat-stained shirt to put on.

It didn't take long to get to Dave's semidetached in West Finchley. Britain, indeed Europe, was in upheaval, but my world seemed to be centred on the North London sector. A World to Win might be one of our slogans, but it was a world which seemed to be confined to the *N* postcodes. Still, that suited me; I hated long distances on the scooter.

My memory was far from being infallible, but I couldn't recall coming here ever before, and even with the wonders of Satnav, which was at that moment operating, I managed to get lost. Nowadays it was less Satnav and more Occnav—occasional navigation, for when it wasn't being disrupted, corrupted, or hacked. At least I didn't have to resort to a map. How in days like these, we went back into history. At this rate we would be relying on the stars for directions.

All the houses looked the same, with bottoms half-brick and top halves white plaster, giving them the air of thickly iced chocolate cakes. Judging by the preponderance of squares, it would have been a slightly unimaginative one.

Pondering what the proper word for a cake maker was, I opened his iron gate, which was set in the well-shaped high hedge, and strolled up to his front door. Giving it a few rings, I got no answer. I peered through the front, rectangular windows into his front room which looked neat and tidy with little in the way of personality. If, heaven forbid, I was the kind of person for stereotypes, I would say that it looked like the type of home that a solicitor might buy, lacking imagination, but hey, this location had good travel links, and there were good schools nearby. Dave and Yasmin didn't have any children, but it was nice to have high-quality schools in the neighbourhood. I didn't see any stepladders, so if they were redecorating, it wasn't at the front.

Getting the hang of this detective lark, I had the thought that they might be around the back. It wasn't 6:00 p.m. yet, and the sun was still out, giving a lovely spring glow, so perhaps they were gardening or sipping drinks. I pushed on the side gate; it was open, so I walked around the side. They weren't in the garden, drinking or otherwise. The garden itself was neat and, in keeping with the house, very square (as in all meanings of the word).

The room at the back was the kitchen, which looked neat and tidy and empty, except for some cups and plates by the sink. I knocked on the kitchen door but after a few tries got no answer. So, Pete, what next? All your detective heroes would now try the door, but then they would not have to answer to a copper about breaking and entering, would they? But well, I was here, so why not? So I did. To my surprise, it opened. I gingerly went in and called out Dave's name in a rather pathetic, humble voice which if, as I expected him to, he came storming downstairs and caught me in his house, would save me from a scolding.

I slipped off my rucksack and put it on the floor by the washing machine. I noted that the plates were dry. It was a very white kitchen; indeed, with the exception of a few splashes of chrome, it was all white. Everything looked spic and span. Leaving the kitchen, I noticed that I was moving slower than usual, with exaggerated care. This I put down to guilt. I really felt as if I was intruding being here. That strange voice I was using when shouting hello was probably also due to a feeling of wrongdoing, although why the comic and rather camp way I was saying "hall-ow" would in any way compensate for that, I had no idea. But that was how I moved around the house, as an over-the-top sitcom character.

Downstairs, all looked normal, and there was not a sign of a colour chart, let alone any decorating. So what did I think I would find if they had indeed gone up to Scotland or to a sandy beach? It would just be too convenient to find a stray kilt or a bumper pack of sun block sitting on the dining room table with a forwarding number. Then again, did I have any other bright ideas? Answer: no. George said I needed to act, so act I had to do.

I continued my ridiculously exaggerated movement up the stairs, ending very nearly in disaster when my loping stride almost tipped over a large aspidistra in a china pot all over the landing white carpet. I breathed a sigh of relief. How would I explain that away if it had gone all over?

There were three doors, and I made a guess at which one was the main bedroom. Showing my Philip Marlowe brilliance, it turned out to be…the bathroom. A quick scan threw up no kilt, haggis, sporrans, Li-los, or sandcastle design books. Just chrome and white paint with the smell of shower gel. No help there.

Opening the next door, there was a staler, more bedroomy type of smell. The first thing I saw was a waist-high, wicker, dirty laundry basket politely standing next to yet another white wall. As I swung into the room, the dominant colour changed from white to red. Splashes of red ran up the walls and across the ceiling. In front of me on the double bed, there were lakes of red surrounding a body. Dave.

Oh God. Oh my God. Dave! Dave! I ran forwards in an involuntary action to give aid, but a huge hole in his head made it obvious that he was beyond it. He didn't need a doctor; he required a miracle worker.

I steadied myself by holding onto one of the sodden sheets. Suddenly nothing in the room seemed that well-defined. Edges blurred. The blood splatter on the walls seemed to leap out at me, engulfing me, losing me in an eternity of hematic gore. The floor tilted, and the ceiling dropped.

Bile was hurtling up from my stomach, but somehow I needed to look. Despite the nausea, I felt a compulsion to gape at him lying there in blue, torn, boxer shorts and soaked white T-shirt. Or, to be more accurate, the *formerly* blue boxer shorts and white T-shirt, because they were not that colour now. I swallowed the acid taste down hard.

There were wounds on his face, which, only in comparison with the severity of the fatal central one, could have been regarded as being minor. For in his skull, there was an entrance to his brain where none should have been. Nonetheless, the gashes on his face were deep and angry. The reality of death, which was there in front of me, wasn't the kind they describe as looking like a deep sleep. This was not an expression of some poor soul feeling a tad soporific but one of raw brutality. It was obscene. Disgusting. His face was frozen in a mixture of horror and pain, like something from the paintings of Francis Bacon. He was in a perpetual scream. This was not art;

this was pornography of the vilest kind. I could see that his ankles were tied together, and his wrists were in handcuffs. Oh God, Dave! Dave!

It was only now that I could smell the acrid combination of blood, urine, and shit. Why hadn't I noticed that before, I wondered? As if that made any difference!

I couldn't take my eyes off those handcuffs. The blood was smeared along the steel like some macabre installation. I don't know why, but I leant over to touch his hands as if human contact would bring him back to life. No, not human, a human had done this—no, it was an attempt at a *humane* contact.

Gently touching him, something caught my attention. There was another morass of scarlet on the floor, on the other side of the bed. At first glance, it looked like something from a butcher's shop. But this carcass was human.

I scrambled around the bed. Had I seen it move? I leant over it. Quickly, I could see that it plainly hadn't, because there was no way this was a living thing. It was a relic of someone. From the nightdress, I guessed that this must have been Yasmin. Or what was left of her. I once more fought back the sickness. She had been so full of life and had always been the life and soul of the party (both little and big *P*). Not now. Her olive skin was deathly chalky. Her green eyes were red. Her lovely lips were wrapped in mid-howl. She was bound like Dave, and as I gently turned her over, I saw an identical wound in her head. She could boast of having matching ones in her knees. Again, the room threatened to go into a final spin. What monster had done this?

First, I sensed something moving. Then out of the corner of my eye, I saw a movement and then a sound. Fear pulled me to my feet. In one unusually smooth movement, I tried to turn to face whatever it was, but as I did so, a crunching pain crashed through my left shoulder. Quite possibly, my eyes popped as they do in the cartoons from the streaking pain, but I wasn't laughing. I swivelled with the impact, and as I did, I tripped over the body on the floor. This sent me forwards. Bang into another blow, this time slam-dunk on my right cheek.

I fell on the floor, which was by now revolving like some horror show roundabout. Terror, though, was keeping me conscious. I was still on my knees, on all fours. I tried to wrench myself up.

"Move and I shoot," instructed a voice. Call me sexist, but to my surprise, it was a female voice.

I froze. It must be a mare as it felt like I had been kicked by the champion horse of the Grand National. My vision consisted of a red blotch, and two dead bodies lay behind me from gunshot wounds. She said she had a gun. All in all, I didn't see that I had much choice.

She paused. I could sense that she was weighing up the scene. Her judgment could make the difference to life or death—to me. Or worse. Quite obviously, Dave and Yasmin had not died instantly.

"Who are you?" she barked.

Now it was my answer that counted. Say the wrong one, and I lose my life, either quickly or otherwise. I had to guess—was she the killer or the cavalry, or as history showed, one and the same? I took a gamble, thinking that if she was the killer, I would be dead right now. I swallowed hard and mumbled through the pain, "I'm a friend of Dave's."

"Really?" She didn't sound convinced.

There was doubt in her voice. Keeping my head bowed in a deferential manner, I noticed that I had kept my scooter gloves on—the slim, smooth, black ones which now were covered in blood. "Suspicious" was a word that came to mind.

"I've been looking for him. I know his grandfather died, and I wanted to see if he was OK. You see, I knew both Dave and Alan, and I know Stuart, his father, Alan's son." I wittered on in such a vein for several minutes, untangling the web of Wiltshire family ties. If I didn't convince her, then I might bore her into submission.

I stopped before I started to trace his family back to Tudor times and waited for a reply. I didn't get one. I couldn't know for sure, but I sensed that she was still unsure as what to do. If that was so, I said, *prayed*, to myself, that then surely it was a good thing, because it meant that this was the first time she had seen the bodies.

Without anything else coming to mind, I repeated myself. "As I said, his grandfather was Alan Wiltshire. I worked with him, and I was worried about Dave, who I know, I should say—knew—was very close to him."

"Really." She wasn't a great conversationalist, but in this situation she did not really have to be.

"So that's David Wiltshire there? So then who's that on the floor?"

"Yasmin, his wife..." I stuttered. Had they been married or civil partners? The exact nature of their relationship might not have usually mattered, but it did look rather dodgy that I, claiming to be Dave's big, bosom-buddy mate, didn't know that.

My vision was clearing, but the overwhelming feeling of sickness wasn't. With a meek tone, which there was absolutely no need to fabricate because, alongside terror and back pain, meek was exactly what I was feeling, I asked if I could get to my feet. After a pause, she assented, telling me to do so slowly, otherwise she would be forced to fire.

I did as I was told. In front of me was a girl! Well, OK, not a girl; she was probably in her early twenties. Petite and barely above one-and-a-half metres, she could have passed for one. And she was responsible for the agony that was throbbing in my shoulder and face?

She had a small, pale face with just a hint of makeup, ringed by short, blond hair, gelled back. She was dressed in black jeans and pale-green bomber jacket. The most striking part of her apparel was the revolver she held with both hands, pointing at my head. That was a good argument against patronising her.

"You haven't told me your name," she said, looking directly at me and pointing the gun the same way.

"Pete Kalder," I said simply, feeling both very frightened and very sick.

"Prove it!"

The only ID I had was the video message from Jackie. That was risky. It was hardly an impartial rail card, was it? Show her that and I might find out very quickly where her political loyalties lay with a bullet in the brain. But what choice had I? All my other cards were at home—I didn't need my driver's licence—no one got stopped nowadays; they knew me at the pool; the workers' council card—who needed one when you had the vid-message? No, absolutely nothing. I had no bloody choice.

Following her instructions to the letter, I pulled out the phone with my left hand, using only my fingertips, and slid it gently across the floor with the side of my foot. Kneeling carefully, she picked it up and watched it with darting glances to make sure that I wasn't trying to do anything funny. I could have told her that there was no danger of that. I wasn't feeling particularly funny at this moment in time. After she finished she turned her full attention again on my humble self.

A smile flashed across her face, and with one smooth-as-silk action, she shoulder-holstered her gun under her jacket. She stepped forwards and held out her hand. "The name's Victoria Cole, though everyone calls me Vic. It's a pleasure to meet you, Pete."

At that point, a rocket-propelled spew of vomit left my mouth.

***

I sat hugging the toilet, staring at the black-and-white squares on Dave's lino. I had no idea how long I had been here; it could have been easily five minutes or five hours. I had lost any idea of time. Indeed, the key word here was lost; I had certainly lost control over my body. My arms were around the loo because they themselves wanted to be; my brain had sod-all to do with it. I was swallowing hard despite having only air to chew.

Things were slowly improving, though; the earthquakes had passed and now were just your average tingling. My heart, however, was still doing a superb impression of a heart attack. I had tried to create the mental garden to calm myself down, but water features and raised bedding were no match for the sight of two dead bodies. I was turning into a water feature myself as the sheen of perspiration became a flow of cold sweat.

With cerebral gardening having failed, I tried the design of my ideal home. Starting with the inner courtyard surrounded by glass and working outwards, I created my open-plan lounge: all glass, steel, modern art, and terrific views. I had never really found the reason why my psychiatrist was so keen on domestic construction. Maybe her former profession had been as an architect.

I was imagining my personal library when the cop, who I now knew to be Vic Cole, came in. Kneeling and looking concerned, she asked if I was all right. As she did, I smelt the remnants of the lunch I had had which had relocated all over her jacket. There was a huge wet stain where she had obviously tried to wash it off, but the odour still hung in there.

I nodded. I wasn't sure that I had control of my mouth.

"I've looked around," she continued in her calm, assertive voice. "Nothing else to report. There appears to be no sign of a struggle. My initial guess is that they were asleep when the intruder surprised them. From the wounds, I would say they were tortured before being killed. This was no simple robbery. Nothing appears to be missing, either. There's expensive jewellery still on the sideboard and very high-grade home entertainment equipment is untouched downstairs. Can't find any type of computer, though."

She moved closer and looked into my eyes. She seemed to be studying me. "You sure you are OK, Pete? You look rough, which is understandable when you see your first dead body."

Actually it wasn't, but I wasn't going to correct her.

She continued with the concern. "Especially when it's just so horrific. You were acquainted with the family, weren't you?"

Again, I did not answer, but there must have been something in my face, in addition to a deathly white, that caused her to answer my silent question.

"Jackie told me all about you; she said you would be looking into Alan's suicide." Whilst she was speaking, she was getting her phone out in readiness to make a call.

Finally, I forced a few words out from between my lips. "What…are you doing? Who are you ringing? Jackie?" I didn't recognise myself. I sounded like a lost child.

She dismissed the idea. "Good grief, no. The January Accord between the NWC and the Metropolitan Police states that the Met should be notified of all serious crime first, with the NWC notified as courtesy. She jerked her thumb behind her. "I think this constitutes as *serious*." Speaking as if she was reciting it, she explained, "And the Metropolitan Police Service should make every possible attempt to include representatives of the NWC Police Union in a spirit of cooperation.

"We got into all kinds of trouble for not reporting Alan's death to the Met, so this would be dynamite. No, I am calling this in. Jackie will be informed in due course, but she can't be pulled into this. This is heavy. The party needs to keep its distance."

It made sense. I went to get up, wobbled, and immediately felt her arms helping me to my feet. "Then, I have to get out of here," I said, noting my voice was beginning to return to normal.

Amazement was written all over her face. "Run from the scene of a double murder? Are you crazy? It looks like a madman has been in there, and you want to do a runner?"

"Madman, indeed," I muttered. "I need to go."

She shook her head. "No! It's still broad daylight. Anyone could have seen you arrive. I did!"

I was on my feet. As steady as a roller skater on the Titanic, but nonetheless I was up. "So what will it look like when I tell my story about me waltzing straight in here and being the one to find them? How will I explain that? I presume you know *exactly* what Jackie has asked me to look into—would you like me to tell your colleagues in the murder squad that? I'm sure they'd be interested—certainly Special Branch will be, when I am passed over to them. Oh, but it is OK," my tone changed to its default sneer, "because I'll have a cop comrade to look after me." I was obviously getting back to my old self. "I'll be hung out to dry."

Behind her eyes I detected thoughts churning over. I refrained from remarking on how astounding it was to see a police officer thinking. Now wasn't the time, and I still wasn't in total control of my body. She looked at her watch and appeared to be calculating something. She moved from her watch to looking me over, until she decided to speak. It wasn't anything I had expected. "You're right. But we haven't got much time. Take your trousers off and your jacket."

My unspoken question must have been talking loud and clear because she explained, "You're covered in blood. You go out looking like that, and you will raise suspicions. Wash in that sink over there and try to do as little splashing as possible." And after delivering her bathing instructions, she hurried out of the room.

Dumbly, I did as I was bid. I took off the dank clothes, covered in blood and puke, and piled them onto the floor. I lathered the soap and washed with all my strength. Thankfully, I wasn't in Macbeth, although there was certainly a tragedy here, and the blood washed off easily from my neck and hands.

"This yours?" she said, startling me as she rushed back in, holding my rucksack aloft. She was breathing heavily as if she had been running.

Standing there in loafers, socks, and boxer shorts, I must have looked ridiculous, but her only reaction was to hold up a black suit with her other hand. "Put the shirt back on; hopefully, the jacket will cover the dampness, but I could only find whites in his closet, and people will only see the colour. But this suit is fine; it's about your size."

I was being very slow on the uptake.

"You're going to leave looking to any casual observer the same as when you arrived, dressed exactly the same. I don't think the rear of the building is overlooked, so we can hope that no one saw you enter. If anyone saw you at the front or going around the side, then you'll say you came here to find him, and after no one answered the front door, you tried the back, but getting no joy, you left. You saw and heard nothing, and thinking that no one was here, you left. It's flimsy, *very* flimsy, but it's the best I can think of."

I stood there, no doubt looking like a prize prat.

She tried to instil some urgency in me. "Hurry! This all relies on speed. Get a move on, comrade!"

Once more, I followed her instructions. As I did, she bundled my suit into my bag. "You need to burn everything you have been wearing, including Dave's suit, as soon as you can, and then dispose of the ashes as far as you can, away from anywhere even remotely connected to you."

I was looking down at the jacket as I put it on. It fitted OK, but it was just so, well, solicitor's office in style. Would no one notice the style had changed since I had arrived here? What would they think? That I popped in for a quick change of cuffs, pockets, and to add an extra button?

She wasn't that bothered about the cut, though. "It's a bit short in the length around the arms, but it will pass. Now listen carefully. You are going to leave slowly. Slowly, Pete, that's important. You must not, I repeat must not, look as if you are fleeing. In fact, when you go out the front gate, stop. Yes, that's it. Stop and look at the house. Shake your head and look at your phone and then ring here."

Finding my voice, although not my sense, I asked why.

"It will help with the story of you arriving, snooping outside, and then leaving but not going in!"

I was going to ask further questions, but she signalled with her hand to stop. "You have got to go now. I will sort out the details here. Now go, Pete. You have to leave. I'll contact you later. I will call this in when I hear you call here. Comrade, you must leave. Go!"

After running down the stairs, I slowed down and tried my best laconic Robert Mitchum lope to the front. It deserved an Oscar in itself as, whilst calmer than previously, my body still felt like a blancmange in a washing machine.

I looked back at the house, theatrically scratched my head, and phoned. In doing so, I was placing a lot of trust in someone, a police officer, a very *young* police officer, whom I had only met ten minutes ago, but I couldn't think about that. I had to go and get rid of these clothes.

CHAPTER SEVEN
By Any Means Necessary

I flung off my soaking nightwear and ran a bath. The night had been far from restful, with nightmares ripping into my sleep. To be accurate, it had really been just the one nightmare—repeated again and again.

Hopefully, a plunge would help. It would be the third in twelve hours, which, coupled with two showers, had been my attempts to remove all traces of both the murder scene and the lingering smell of smoke stemming from my frantic attempts to burn my clothes.

I had rushed home and into the garden, throwing my clothes into the garden incinerator along with any branches or leaves I could find. It hadn't been what Vic (as Victoria Cole had instructed me to call her) had told me to do, but what had she expected? Whizz off to Epping Forest and casually start a bonfire? Wouldn't Joe Bloggs notice whilst taking his dog for a walk or doing it doggy style in the woods and wonder why a middle-aged man was setting fire to a rather well-cut suit in a public area? My neighbours, on the other hand, were well-used to me using the incinerator on a weekly basis. The standing joke was that my back garden was tidier than most people's living rooms.

Gingerly, I lowered myself into the bath. A massive and very angry bruise had developed where comrade Cole had shown all her police training. I had a lovely diagonal cut and swelling on my cheek to match.

Submerging my head, I fought off an overwhelming sense of self-pity. Instead, I had to think what I was going to do next. The most pressing thing was Dave's murder. Quite obviously, it had something to do with the death of his grandfather. I might have spent my school numeracy lessons daydreaming, but even I had some understanding of the concept of probability, and I would rate the chance of it being a coincidence that a granddaddy tops himself and then a few days later, the grandson gets killed by a homicidal loony as being as near as impossible, without it actually being impossible. They were related, but how? Perhaps Dave had found something out about it, but what the hell could it have been?

There was also the slight detail of my involvement. Cole had been right: running was a singularly stupid thing to do. If anyone cared to look my way, there was a huge neon arrow pointing at me which read, "looks as guilty as sin." However many litres of white spirit I had burned on the clothes or the times I had bathed in precious upmarket shower gel, there was bound to be forensic evidence. Nowadays, they could trace where you last sneezed. If they did look in my direction, then on that line of probability, the label suspect would be at the *highly likely* end.

As for the amounts of me I had left at the scene of the crime, that didn't even bear thinking about. Forget high-tech forensic analysis, you wouldn't need even a magnifying glass, because the scene of crime officers would be tripping over the traces I had left gambolling around the place. The arrow points at "Yep, it's him!"

I pulled myself up above the surface rather too quickly, as pain spread around my shoulder. By leaning heavily on the good one, I tried to make myself as comfortable as possible. Cole might have been correct in her rationale, and as much as being a Marxist makes me believe in the importance of logic, there was no way I was sticking around there. It was like some grisly, horror computer game where rabid animals maul bodies apart. Their bedroom was total carnage. I just *had* to flee.

Resting my arms on the side of the bath, I gazed at the scar tissue. The scars, at least, were not because of Ms *Call-me-Vic* Cole. They were solely down to me. Two years ago, I had found it all too much. My solution to my troubles was to take a sharp, designer kitchen knife and carve great chunks out of both arms. It hadn't been the wisest of moves and one which was not proscribed in self-help books as a way to deal with depression. Blood had hit the walls, resembling a Jackson Pollock. The scene had been similar to the one I had witnessed at Dave's, except that I had preceded my self-assault with the destruction of half the downstairs. At Dave's, the killer hadn't been too interested in destroying every piece of furniture and breakable item they could find. With Dave and Yasmin, it was brutal but controlled, with a clear objective. My episode, as my psychiatrists sometimes had called it, had been brutal but most definitely could not be described as controlled. Sure, it had an objective—to destroy everything I could find. I had been pretty thorough, and sure enough, everything had been trashed—smashed into wreckage with a power I did not know I possessed. I guess that was what guilt and depression could do—give you super powers.

Once achieved, I had turned my policy of annihilation onto myself. I had gone into what remained of the kitchen, picked a knife up off the floor and showed my carving skills. Eventually, I had blacked out, thinking that soon I would see who was correct: we atheists or one of the religions. But I had not encountered the afterlife, or lack of, because Neesha from next door had heard the sound of my self-explosion and had come round. Through the cracked front window, she had seen me slumped on the floor against half a coffee table. She had called an ambulance, and thus Pete Kalder remained breathing on the planet.

Running my finger over them, I could see that they had healed quite well, but there were still large tracks diagonally crossing both arms with little in the way of non-scar tissue between them. I had meant to have plastic surgery, but they'd been on strike when my time for the operation had come round (which had kept me supplied with jokes about scabs for weeks). I had not yet got around to rebooking it.

It was funny, but even in illness the struggle had pursued me. Not only had the surgeons been on strike, but at an earlier time, when I had been sectioned and parcelled off to a residential home, the porters had taken action. One could almost get a complex—another one. Still, on the plus side, the lack of support workers was the reason for my early release.

Marie had not been happy. Maybe, for the first time in her life, she had not been excited by workers taking action. She had felt that I needed more time in there to—in her words—"recover and rebuild myself mentally." In my words, I was surrounded by nutters going even madder from boredom. That had earned me a lengthy rebuke from her for over stigmatising mental illness. She was right, but that said, I was chuffed to leave.

It was gone four in the morning, but I had no wish to return to bed, so grabbing a cup of coffee and some toast, I nestled under the quilt and surfed the news channels. Very quickly Red joined me, using his nose to find his way onto my stomach. Most of the news was dry information on the day's activities of government and the NWC. Top of the tracking list was the word "anarchists," which was limited in its use, only really informing me that those accused of the bombing were still on the run. Predictably, every social network you could think of was talking about it. I looked but did not really watch; it was just images and words, sound and vision.

Alan Wiltshire–Funeral Arrangements appeared above the anarchists. I had been more on the lookout for news concerning his grandson but looked anyway. It was simply, as the title said, the service arrangements for his cremation. The mind boggled at what that was going to be like. The Internet rumours about his suicide would have made it uncomfortable enough, but when news of Dave's murder came to light, it was going to be surreal.

At about 5:30 I fell asleep. I slept for an hour or so, waking whenever I shifted weight onto my bruised shoulder. This was far from ideal, but at least there was no repeat of the dream. I downed a couple of pain-killers, but they didn't seem to do much. Sleep, wake, watch a touch of telly, then sleep. It was like being a student again.

In my moments of playing hunter-news-gatherer, I absorbed all manner of interesting info; it was, I learnt, raining unseasonably hard in Stockholm. Another US baseball team was refusing to tour Britain. Bushfires in Western Australia had finally been extinguished. By ten o'clock, Dave's and Yasmin's murder had been announced. The details were sparse, with not much more than the fact that Dave was the grandson of the leading member of the United Revolutionary Socialist Party who had committed suicide only days before. Dave and Yasmin Wiltshire had been killed by multiple gunshots. I was pleased to hear that it had been reported that they had been found by a police officer who had been detailed to interview them. It was far better than a report detailing how a man had arrived in a stunning, nicely cut, black suit and left in a naff, conservative, three-button one. Of course, when the news went viral, it also went vacuous, with the usual crackpot theories accompanying the meagre facts.

My next wake-up call wasn't courtesy of my shoulder but the phone. Usually, I prefer holding the phone when I talk, but I couldn't be bothered to exert the energy.

"Answer ID: PK1990," I commanded.

The picture changed from TV to vid-phone with Jackie Payne's serious face contrasting sharply with a white blouse whose brightness almost filled the screen like an advertisement for a soap powder.

Seeing me looking not at my best and under the quilt, she remarked, "I can see that you are not feeling that great; got a touch of a cold?" She didn't wait for an answer. "I expect that you have seen the horrific news today about poor Dave and Yas? It's terrible, Pete—first Alan and then those two. Absolutely awful. You must have been as shocked as I was to hear about it."

From the rather obvious and stilted way she was talking, I could guess that she feared that our conversation was being monitored. There was enough wood in her performance to replant a rainforest. But I could also see that she was doing this to spell out what our story was. "I was just ringing you to see how you are, as I know you were great friends of the family. You really do have my condolences, Pete. I am so sorry." She paused for breath, maybe for the first time since she called.

I mumbled agreement and waited for the reason for her call.

Her brown eyes were almost as piercing as her top. She was looking straight at me. "I was called by Detective Victoria Cole, who informed me how she had found them. You won't know, Pete, but Dave's been AWOL since his grandfather's death, so the NWC asked her to try and locate him. She went to his house and felt that there was something wrong, so she broke in at the back and found them."

Jackie was a truly inspirational leader and on a personal note, a lovely person, but as an actress, she stunk. Surely, if Special Branch were watching, they wouldn't be fooled by this! This was nudge, nudge, wink, wink standard.

The end-of-pier variety show continued. "Because of the accord we signed with the Metropolitan Police, I cannot tell you any details, but it was an awful sight. Poor Dave and Yas." This went on for several minutes, with the occasional grunt or mumble from me interrupting the flow of words.

It wasn't until right at the end, when she said what she really wanted me to know. "Detective Cole will be briefing me in greater depth at our national office. You'll be aware that the terms of the accord are that the police will only pass such information to certain named individuals. I am one of those. There will be no one else. The time of the meeting is 3:15 this afternoon. I know that you have a meeting at the same time in the national office, so we could meet up and catch up on old times afterwards."

She finished with a lame joke about supplying the Garibaldi biscuits and signed off. She was as bad a comedian as she was an actress.

I carefully eased myself into my three-button, silver-grey, 1960s-style suit with ticket lapels. Today's choice of shirt was a pink one with matching tie, which leapt out at you so as to give it that extra whizz. Just because my face was now distinctly asymmetrical and my mood was out of sync didn't mean that I still couldn't be looking good. One of the many things that would shame my daughter, Lisa, was my love of dressing up. In her words it was "just so sad for an ancient like you to permanently look like you're going for an interview." I smiled at the memory of our communal laughter, when I had expressed mock outrage at my daughter's comment, not for the "ancient" quip but for suggesting that these were interview suits.

Today, despite the threads, I looked like crap. There was now a large, swollen, pinkish-brown bruise on my cheek which slightly closed my right eye. Due to a broken night's sleep and the stress of finding two butchered people, I wouldn't have looked like an A-list Hollywood heartthrob in any case, but because of our friendly Bolshevik police officer's boot, I looked awful. I guess brutality is just such a hard habit to lose.

I didn't feel great either, and several times I had to get a grip on myself to stop any onset of tremors. I felt distinctly lonely and vulnerable. That was what the suit was all about—camouflage. I was off to a meeting with Jackie and Detective Victoria Cole. There was no way that I was going to give her the satisfaction of me looking like I was on my knees. Not this comrade.

Jackie's subtle-as-a-brick invite to their quarter-past-three meeting meant that it was time to leave. After a long search for the scooter keys, only to find them still in the bike, I left for the national office.

The journey itself did not take too long, and very soon I was swinging into the car park which was in front of the URSP National Office. In reality the car park was a shared one, as for the past three years, the party's national office had been located in this half-deserted trading estate. I think a few hardy firms surviving the economic woes still had a base there, but the warehouse/office building that we had co-opted dominated the site as being the only one in full and active use.

If you had asked me when I had first joined what the national office would be like several decades later in a prerevolutionary Britain, when it was the epicentre of resistance and rebellion, then I don't think I would have guessed it would have looked like this. Being the heart and brain of the insurgency, I think I would have envisaged a towering monolith of steel and glass with robotic, worker militia guards and comrades whizzing about in personal jet packs selling virtual-reality Socialist propaganda. I suppose a vision of Dubai meets Petrograd circa 1917 meets *Blade Runner*.

The reality was somewhat different. The building was a huge, rectangular slab of brick with drab, green garage doors interrupting small, dirty, square, double-glazed windows. Solar panels on the roof were well past their use-by date, unless that is, as an exhibit in the Science Museum. It looked like so many empty, ramshackle symbols of failed capitalism. One of the things that distinguished it from such were the large screens showing not glamorous models selling dreams of sex with whatever commodity they were hawking but a loop of projections of recent workers actions across the globe. As I parked my bike, I guessed that the scenes they were presently showing were last week's huge demonstrations in Helsinki.

The second big difference was the four armoured cars parked in front. By them sat a dozen or so armed red guards variously smoking, reading, and snoozing, who looked less *Star Wars* than Second World War. Ignoring the variety of communication devices and the dominance of women, not to mention a different class composition, this could have been one of those pictures showing Spitfire pilots resting during a brief respite in the Battle of Britain. It was the image of sanguine, relaxed activity, anticipating a call to action. Just slobbing out, in other words.

I flashed my vid-message from Jackie. This time, however, it was not enough to get in, and the huge Sikh male who appeared to be in charge of security rang through to confirm that I was who I said I was and that I had business being here.

Thus confirmed, I walked to reception. This was reception as in what most people would consider a reception: a counter, a few laptops, two hovering 3-D images, several phones lying about, and usually three or four smiling people ready to answer your questions or direct you to where you needed to go. It was where visitors were usually met as opposed to today, in the car park with machine-gun-toting comrades.

Although a constant rotation of people worked in reception, you could usually find the middle-aged married couple of Benjamin and Billie Caplan. Yes, really; Bill and Ben staffed the reception and had heard every Little Weed-type joke and allusion to the vintage TV series that you could think of. Not that it was wise to make any; not if you wanted any help, that is, because whilst Ben was pretty mild-mannered, Billie was an Irish woman you did not cross. Simon Peary was of the opinion that she ran the national office—not him. Jackie reckoned it was Billie who ran the party.

It had been Billie who had vouched for me. In her strong Cork accent, she welcomed me and ordered me to sit on one of the three grey plastic chairs lined up in a row like something you would see outside a head teacher's office. I should then wait for someone to pick me up.

That someone turned out to be Simon. Seeing me, he gave me an affectionate hug. Although slim, he was stronger than you would expect, and my damaged shoulder also decided to say hello to me. He saw me flinch and pulled away.

Now noticing my cheek, he asked, "Hey, what's up, Peter? Did I hurt you there?"

I made up some story about falling off my bike.

He nodded. "'Course, you don't drive, do you?"

"Not now," I replied and tried to change the subject.

Grabbing the first one I could think of, I talked about the news of the prime minister announcing a huge funding package from several major countries. Brazil, China, India, the United States, and Turkey were all going to pump money into our economy.

Simon was always easy to speak to. He chatted away with humour and finesse about how it would affect the situation. He was one of those who had what I think is described as an easy charm. Whatever the topic, whatever the place or the people, he could just schmooze away. He was highly articulate and could call on a large reserve of information to do that articulating with. I often thought that if he had not run the national office, he would have made a superb salesperson. It's not that he had that yucky superficiality you associate with the shiny suit types, but that he had real allure.

He was a good-looking chap as well. With short and always well-cut, blond hair and lovely, clear-blue eyes, on a still-line-free face, he had had his fair share of comrades of both sexes throwing themselves at his feet. His accessible personality matched his face, which always seemed to have a cheeky grin on it.

Suddenly his mood changed, and his look darkened. "Anyway, it's awful about Dave. I've known him since he was a toddler. I can't believe it; I really can't."

I replied by trying to adopt the type of tone and substance of what my reply might have been if I hadn't in reality been rolling about their bedroom in their blood, guts, and flesh. It must have been a believable performance, as we spent a few minutes interspersing commiserations and memories. After a few moments, he said he was aware that I was here to get briefed by Jackie and Vic about the matter. That was Simon, friendly but efficient. I had been given my allocation of bonhomie; now it was time for business.

He led me through several rooms filled with office chairs of eye-burning boldness of primary blues and yellows. They were placed neatly against snow-white tables with unused laptops. Projections filled the walls, watched by no one. After the third room, which had contained enough furniture to house dozens of office workers but seemed to contain only two comrades fast asleep, I asked him about it.

He chuckled. "That's down to me. I found that we could appropriate some office furniture. I've spent far, far too long in the party putting up with crap, low-grade tech in dusty print shops, trying to bang out the newspaper before the computers crash, so I thought we'd smarten up the decor. We managed to get rooms of the stuff because, of course, a lot of firms have people who work from home so they didn't need the office furniture. Trouble is…"

"We do, as well."

"Exactly!" He laughed.

"They're in here," he said, coming to a blue door marked Conference Room. He knocked and left me to it.

Whilst entering the room, my walk became more hunched, and my left arm became limp as if I had suffered a mild stroke; this was no doubt due to the fact that the first person I had seen was Victoria Cole. She had her back to the door and was fiddling with something in the corner. She was in the same jeans and jacket she had been wearing when she had beaten me up.

Jackie smiled. "Pete!" Dressed in body-hugging black trousers with a tailored, white, short-sleeved shirt, she moved smoothly towards me. "Oh, that does look painful!"

At that point, probably at the mention of the word "pain," Cole turned around to face me. Pleasingly, my presence appeared to unsettle her.

I hugged Jackie. "Police brutality," I said simply.

Cole gently laughed as if appreciating a joke. I hadn't made one.

"Good to see you, Jacks. A very cloak-and-dagger invite, I must say."

She apologised and explained that Glen Bale had done wonders with our e-security, but nothing was unassailable. Thankfully, the eulogy to hack-boy did not last too long, and she indicated for me to sit in one of just four chairs in the room. I was about to quip that no wonder the previous occupiers had gone bust if four was the biggest conference they could muster but then figured it was probably down to Simon's attempts at office decor.

Cole had finished her pottering about and gave me her full attention. She had a smile, but something was a bit amiss.

"Good to see you, Pete." She pointed to my cheek. "I am so sorry about that, but I saw the bodies and you hunched over them; well, you can guess what I thought."

"That he had killed them," Jackie said, seemingly accepting this as a plausible reason for thumping one of her old friends.

That old friend didn't feel that accommodating. "The police getting the wrong man—now that's unusual."

She gave a polite laugh, but again she had got it wrong. That was sarcasm, Officer, not a witticism.

I could see that Jackie was now looking a little uncomfortable. She knew her "asm" from her "ism." "Anyway, I'm glad you managed to get here."

Detective Cole also appeared to be far from being a happy bunny. "Er, Jackie, are you sure that it's a sensible course of action to have Pete here? No offence, comrade."

No offence taken, but please don't ever call me comrade again, I thought to myself.

"As it is, we are breaking the terms of the agreement between the NWC and the Met by not having this briefing in a neutral place, because let's face it, the party national office can hardly be regarded as neutral, so having someone present not designated with clearance just overcomplicates things and makes the party vulnerable to the charge of being capricious."

Hmm. A police officer who uses words of longer than three letters *and* says *comrade*—oh, what a lucky find we have made.

Jackie sat down, smoothing down her trousers and pulling a face which indicated that she wasn't bothered about that. But Cole still wasn't happy.

"I'm in enough trouble about not reporting Alan's suicide to the appropriate authorities, so I cannot risk any more. Especially as…" Her voice trailed off.

The poor thing was fretting. I helped out—well, anything for our girls and boys in blue. "I decided that I did not want to be found with their blood all over me. So rather than getting fitted up, I left, leaving Ms Cole to sort things out."

I wasn't going to apologise and especially not to her, so I redirected the conversation. "So, *Detective*, how does it look with regards to that?"

She stood in front of me, but I couldn't read what she was thinking. She looked more like a young woman on the counter of a building society than a copper, or maybe someone from human resources, or a weather girl. But whatever the more worthwhile job to which she should belong, she was a serving police officer, and she was still reluctant to have me here.

I gave her a push. "I think I have a right to know whether I can expect a visit from your colleagues."

She gave Jackie a questioning look and received a nod as a reply. She shrugged. "OK, well, I tried to cover as many bases as possible. I locked the back door and smashed it from the outside, treading the glass upstairs. The idea being that it was locked when you arrived, and it was me who had to break in."

"So how *did* the killer get in?" Jackie asked.

"That's a loose end."

Jackie appeared to take that as an adequate answer. The images of standing in front of an old guy in a silly wig barking "take him down to the cells" indicated that I didn't.

Cole stood, arms folded, clearly used to giving briefings. "I then smothered my jacket with the blood from both bodies and forced myself to vomit, hoping to confuse the forensics."

I tried my best blasé look and avoided any embarrassed shuffling about in the chair.

"Will that be enough?"

"To be honest, Jackie, under normal circumstances I would say most definitely not, but we have three things going for us: firstly, the forensics departments were long ago outsourced to private firms, so their commitment to the police service is fragile. I think they are presently running at sixty-eight percent absenteeism. Plus, a lot of them have been trashed or squatted by various anarchists, so much of their equipment has gone AWOL. Forensically speaking, the police service is back in the dark ages."

Politically speaking as well; evolution-wise, probably nearer the Neolithic Age.

"And the other?" I asked, believing that, being a policewoman, her maths probably did not reach to three.

"We have Asher Joseph, and Asher's good, and he's ours."

Jackie nodded in agreement. "What about CCTV or satellite surveillance?"

"There's no CCTV in the area, and SatSurv is down after the Big Brother Cyber Freedom Fighters attacked police and state surveillance systems. So I think Pete is safe there."

"Which also makes it harder to find who actually did do this," noted Jackie.

"Well, we are conducting house-to-house, good, old-fashioned police work. As we speak, there is a police press conference calling for witnesses."

"OK, good." Jackie smiled, apparently thinking those few sentences were enough to satisfy her, despite the fact that I could be facing a lengthy prison sentence for running from a scene of a crime or an even longer one for being the actual murderer. I, for one, was glad that Ms Payne here was only leading the revolution and wasn't a defence lawyer. To me it all sounded rather amateurish.

Jackie, though, was acquiescent and asked Cole if she could give us details of what the police had found out so far about the killings. Cole agreed and pulled something the size of a lighter out of her pocket and pointed it at the

Comrades Come Rally

corner of the room. Before she did anything else, she paused and asked me if I was going to be OK with this, as the picture definition on police virtual reality was sharp.

My reply was yet again the blasé, nonchalant look which despite my best efforts was probably more Raymond Briggs than Chandler. I turned and asked Jackie if she was going to be OK. She answered yes with a knowing smile. All the while, Cole looked impassively on.

Then the detective clicked, and *that* room appeared in front of us. Dave's manacled feet faced us with a pool of blood formed around the left one. His head could hardly be seen with little more than the shattered forehead in view. We could see Yasmin on the floor by the bed. Her feet were toes-down.

Cole pressed something and slightly changed the perspective so the view tilted as if the bed was at a forty-five-degree angle and Yasmin came into view. We could now see the total horror of the scene. They looked barely human, due not to any lack of prowess of the technology, because that was good, indeed, but because its very excellence had made them look like lumps of flesh on a butcher's table. Basically, because that's what they did look like. However, the basis for this tableau of horror was not a table but a blood-saturated bed.

We sat, and Cole stood, in silence. Whether from shock or from a sense of respect, I couldn't tell you, but for my part it was a combination of both, with a large dollop of nausea. I called on every piece of self-control I could mobilize to sit there looking at this. I suppressed every shiver, bottled down any upwards flow of acid, and strained on every pore of my skin to stay closed. It wasn't easy. Cole was quite correct; it was indeed, impressively high definition.

Even with the best 3-D imaging, you had a slight translucence which gave it a sense of artificiality. This had troubled technicians for quite a few years. Right now, I was exceedingly happy about it. As it was, it was as if I could just reach forwards and hold them.

It was the detective who broke the silence. Speaking in a quiet voice, she said, "It's a terrible scene. I will, if…" she stopped, "if you want…" her eyes were on both of us, but the question was aimed at Jackie alone, "walk you through the evidence we have so far gleaned. I am afraid it's going to be very unsettling."

"Please, Vicky," Jackie quietly replied.

This time she used a vocal command, and the carnage disappeared, and what looked like two sleeping people, husband and wife, lay there in their nightclothes. A yellow arrow appeared, pointing to each of their necks.

"From our initial tests, we think that David and Yasmin were lying in bed asleep. They were first hit by an electric discharge to their necks, enough to simultaneously wake and temporarily paralyse them. From the angle of the burns, we think that both were on their sides facing outwards."

She spoke to the machine, and the yellow arrows disappeared and were replaced by blue.

"Judging by the blood splatters on the handcuffs here," she indicated two of the arrows, "and here on these bindings around the ankles," those were the other two arrows, "I would guess that these were put on first before any of the further injuries. And then…"

The bodies moved to face each other, and Dave's head became propped up by a second pillow.

"What? What happened there?"

"Oh my God," I murmured to myself, fearing what we had just seen. "He's being given a good view of his partner. The bastard wants him to watch her suffer!"

Jackie instinctively put her hand to her mouth to stifle her horror.

"Yes, I am afraid Pete's right. We think, then, this is the sequence of events. Be warned, comrades, it is not pretty."

What we saw was nothing less than a surreal drama of conspicuous barbarism. The faceless computer assassin approached Dave and punched him several times in his face and at various points on his body. He then walked slowly towards Yasmin and did likewise to her. From there, the figure fired a shot into her left kneecap.

I glanced at Jackie and saw her briefly close her eyes, showing a light-blue eye shadow. The pair of us was finding this very difficult.

Cole kept a careful watch on us after pausing the scene. "We think, from the way the sheets lay and the blood trail, that Yasmin must have crawled off the bed," she said, restarting it. "The paralysis would only have been for a short while, so maybe she was trying desperately to escape, or maybe she was dragged off for some reason."

The apparent contradiction of seeing Dave and Yasmin come alive, looking as if they were in some macabre home movie whilst they relived their final moments, made me feel both squeamish and, to my shame, captivated. The identikit killer added the element of a computer game to it. Cole let the recon continue without saying anything. Words weren't really required. Yasmin crawled off the bed and onto the floor.

As I watched, I noted that the animated killer appeared to bizarrely have been based on a former children's television presenter. These IT geeks had a sick sense of humour. I wondered if the man who introduced a five-metre-high pink tortoise to five-year-olds knew that he was the basis of a generic homicidal maniac.

This was far from warm and cuddly, though. He walked around the bed and shot her, first in her right knee and then in the head. The final shot was to Dave's head. There was total stillness in the room, and for what seemed an eternity, the only thing we heard were some distant voices in the building.

Finally, Cole spoke. Her voice was strong but hushed, as if she was speaking to an audience in a public library. "It stops here because we have no forensics to track where he or she went after that. There's an unexplained stain in the corner, away from the bed which we could guess was where he or she changed their clothes."

"You think he reacted like me?" I said in a sentence that was a verbal competition between bad English and bloody obviousness.

The detective didn't react negatively to it; I guess she was well-used to abuse of both the language and the intellect in the police station. "I would think so. He or she would be covered in blood after this carnage. Pete, I should say that Roijin Kemal slightly altered the ICT forensic to cover your, er, contamination of the scene. I guess I should have said earlier; I should have said that we have *four* things in our favour: we have Roijin, and she is brilliant and like Asher loyal to the cause." She gave a weak smile.

Wow, she can count to four.

When Jackie spoke, it was in a voice I barely recognised. It sounded timid, almost broken. "Doesn't tampering also mean that it will make it harder to get the scum who did this?"

Turning the projection off, Vic Cole faced us and simply agreed. I felt complicit in this crime and could not think of a single word to say. I wasn't alone. Jackie, the voice of her class, possibly one of the greatest orators of modern history, was also speechless.

Cole filled the vacuum by explaining that the forensic aspect of the investigation would be led by Asher Joseph. She spoke with almost a hint of smugness. However, as she had mentioned, the police services generally were in total disarray, so it could take some time.

She moved onto some more of the meagre things she did know. "You should be aware that the electric charge and gunshots were from the same weapon—an Alavares Azevedo 12D." Assuming correctly that it would mean nothing to us, she continued without stopping for any questions.

"The Alavares Azevedo 12D is one of the latest models from the new Brazilian armaments company. The AA12D, as it's more commonly known, is a single weapon which is both a high-powered handgun and a Taser, which is light, accurate, reliable, and totally silent. Only a restricted few are available. It is possible to get them on the black market, but it's difficult, and they are not publicly available. They're sold mainly to security agencies—ABIN, the Brazilians, the India's Defence Intelligence Agency, the CIA, and MI5."

"You think MI5 could have done this?" I asked .

She shrugged. "Well, it certainly was not a robbery, as there were valuables all over the house. It also was obviously not a straightforward execution, as they tortured them first and…"

"The easiest way to break Dave was hurt his wife," I said.

"Correct. They wanted something, and this was the best way to go about it."

"But why so…so, utterly brutal?" Jackie asked.

I could guess that. "Total horror, total compliance. I remember one of the Yank wars back in the twentieth-, or maybe it was the early twenty-first-century; anyway, the expression was to use 'shock and awe.' This is it here—only against two people, rather than a population. Face that, and you would do anything."

Cole nodded, and I almost caught a glimpse of appreciation appear across her smooth face. "That's a real possibility. Despite what it looks like, we calculate this was probably all over in twenty minutes. I should say our first estimate is that by the time Pete found them, they had been dead for seven hours."

"What about fingerprints?" Jackie asked.

She sighed. "After the last cyber attacks on the police mainframe, the files are corrupted. Put in a fingerprint now, and you'll as likely get Mickey Mouse or Count Dracula as you are a common and garden-variety real-life person."

For the first time since we had seen the video nasty, Jackie smiled. "I do, of course, see the irony of me asking you if we could be helped by police data systems, and I confess to being disappointed in finding them not being adequate enough."

"The question is then," I said, thinking out loud, "if you just wanted someone eliminated, you would not need this overkill. Two bullets would take less than two seconds—quicker and cleaner. This person wanted information, which Dave was not willing to give."

Jackie turned to me, clearly puzzled. "What information, Pete? Sure, Dave was just a rank and file member; what fantastic secrets would he know?"

"Perhaps it was what he had found out? He had found out something about his grandfather's death and that maybe it wasn't self-inflicted; maybe that, too, was murder?" I suggested.

Cole shook her head vigorously. "No, they did extensive tests back at the lab, and we are pretty sure that it was suicide, *very* sure, actually."

"But," I countered, "you have just told us that everything is a shambles, and you are only marginally better resourced than the Bow Street Runners, so how can you suddenly be sure of this?"

I had expected a fierce rebuttal, but, instead, she looked thoughtful before saying, "You have a point, Pete, but nonetheless I think, *we* think, it was suicide. However, I think that the theory that the suicide of Alan Wiltshire and the slaying of Dave and Yasmin Wiltshire are connected would be worth exploring."

"No."

Both Cole and I looked at Jackie, who repeated it in her more familiar, stronger voice.

"No. I want you, Vicky, to carry on working with Roijin and, er, Asher, is it? Yes, Asher. I want you three to work within the Met and do what you can to find who did this to Dave and Yas, but I want the party at arm's length." Facing me and leaning forwards, I could, for the first time, see remnants of tears in her eyes. "Pete, I do not want you involved any more. You were right in the first place; it was silly of me to get you into this. You said yourself that we do not have the skills for this. And look, because of me you have got hurt and implicated in this horror."

"What?" I said, not fully understanding what she meant.

"I want you to stop looking into poor Alan's suicide."

"Why?" I said, feeling aggrieved at being used and then tossed aside. "There is plainly something fishy about Alan's suicide. This proves it. Jackie, *now* it makes sense to look into it! I don't pretend to be an expert investigator, but I think I was getting somewhere."

Her eyes were drying and her jaw strengthening. "Leave it to the professionals, Pete."

"Pro…professionals!" I spluttered.

She looked hard at me. "I am aware of the enormous irony at play here about what I am suggesting, but I am serious. Pete, I am grateful for your work, but this is for the best."

She rose to her feet; evidently, the red queen was dismissing me. She tried consolation. Her voice softened, and she opened her arms. "Pete, I am really grateful for the work you have done, but no more is required, so go home and get better. There is plenty of proper work for a comrade such as yourself to do. Work you do have skills for, and work that will do good."

I joined her standing up. "What, so I get a beating from your new best friend here and then find myself knee-deep in Dave's guts, and now it's time to go home and stroke the cat? All this so the police can do their job? I thought their job was to keep the working class in place…"

She crossed her arms. Evidently the charm offensive was over. It had been a short one. "I don't need a lecture on Socialism and crime right now, thanks, Pete."

"Actually I think that's exactly what you do need!"

Cole was standing between us, looking somewhat aghast. Being a newly-join, she no doubt worshipped the very air that Jackie breathed and the toilet seat she sat on, but I had been around a whole lot longer. Having done a whole lot more freezing my balls selling *Revolutionary Worker* in the mornings, a whole lot more being bored into oblivion at meetings, being beaten senseless on picket lines, and generally being a sight more of a bloody comrade than her—I was quite happy to see Jackie as a human being. And as one, she made mistakes, and she was making one now, and so I had no problem telling her so.

Jackie was certainly unfazed. She never had a problem with that. However, that was not to say that she was going to change her mind. Put simply, the decision had been made. "I have to go. We have an announcement to make about our response to the financial aid package announced by the government." She looked at Cole. "Vicky, keep me in the loop concerning this. Thanks for your help. I do appreciate and the Central Committee appreciates, how you have been putting yourself out on the limb for us."

Cole nodded thanks. No doubt as soon she could, she would be on the net to all her friends boasting about the great Jackie Payne being nice to her.

Jackie turned to me. "Pete, I know you are angry, but I am right. The correct position, in this circumstance, is to leave the police work to the police and the revolution to the revolutionaries."

I spat my words out. "So Detective Cole and mates are the future, are they? You're launching a new KGB, are you? Jackie's private militia!"

Cole's eyes widened. She had read enough to know that next to calling someone a Fascist, about the worst you could throw at a Trotskyist was to call them as a Stalinist. The rivers of blood between us tended to make us a wee bit touchy like that. Jackie, though, laughed and leant over, placing a hand on each shoulder, and kissed my cheek. "Pete, I would have thought that by asking you to stop investigating, I was doing exactly the opposite."

✸✸✸

When your fictional Yank private eye hits a problem, he goes into a bar, empties a bottle of whisky, and picks up a broad. Our more humble Brit cops in their more provincial novels go to the police station and put up pictures on a board and draw lines in different colours between them. I had always found the US style more romantic, but I didn't much like whisky and had no desire whatsoever to chat up any women. Still, I found a pub about half an hour's drive from the party centre.

Before going in I contacted the police. Cole the Plod had, I had to admit, sensibly suggested that I make the call before they did so to me. It was only a matter of time before they traced the call I had made on leaving Dave's place.

That I phoned them would help with the image of concerned citizen which was going to be our cover story. I had been thanked for my call and told that two officers would be in touch.

The pub itself was called the Highwayman and had a few horsey-type memorabilia. Projections by the drinks showed a shadowy figure armed with musket and duff reproduction of eighteenth-century drawings of the English countryside on the walls to presumably to keep to the concept. On entering it, the enticing aroma of pub grub and warm ciabatta bread reminded me I had not eaten yet. The latter also raised two interesting questions: How did ciabatta bread keep with the old English theme? And who was the black marketeer that the owner knew who could supply it?

The young man serving me tried to keep his eyes off my bruised cheek as he handed me a menu and took my order. As it turned out, it would have probably been quicker to simply tell me what they actually had, as my first three choices turned out to be unavailable because of supply problems. So the black marketeer wasn't that good. Finally, I had to settle for a ploughman's, which I guess did kind of go with the name of the pub. Then feeling the need to treat myself and to hell with how many workers' council tokens and cash it would take, I ordered a fine bottle of Rioja. I joked with the bar man that I could have bought several luxury yachts for the price of the bottle. He didn't laugh.

With bottle and glass in hand, I found a place to sit. There were a few punters in for their early evening/late afternoon midweek drinks. At this time, though, there were more screens than people. A couple were for games, whilst on the other, a cricket match was showing, and the news was on the others. Wanting for once to escape information, whether it was 2-D or 3-D, I found a corner and sat down.

I positioned myself to rest the shoulder, unbuttoned my jacket, loosened my tie, and sipped the wine. Not bad. Still, it should be, as having this probably would mean making the end of the month quite difficult. Financially, some things would have to be reined in.

I thought back on my trip to the centre. I had to say that I had a great deal of time for Jackie and loved the woman; she was possibly one of my closest friends, but she was pissing me off at the moment. *Really* pissing me off. She had sauntered around my house on Monday morning and asked me to get involved, when I hadn't wanted to. Actually, it was less asking me and more instructing me. But now, just a few days on, the scarlet empress turns around and says, "thanks, but no thanks."

So why was I so narked? I had got what I had wanted. I could go back to watching the revolution being televised and Victoria Cole being such invaluable help to her; so all was sorted, and everyone was happy? Well, no, actually. I knew a lot of it was ego-related: I didn't like being told that I wasn't required, and I was a contrary fellow—tell me that the earth is a sphere, and I'll argue that it's a hexagonal prism just for the sake of it. There were, though, a few things puzzling me about the whole thing, and my inquisitiveness (a nice middle-class way of saying being a nosey gossip) had been aroused. I wanted to know why Alan had killed himself, and who had murdered Dave and Yasmin. And what was the link? Taking another sip, I was aware of another question: Why did Jackie suddenly not want me to ask these questions, let alone attempt to answer them?

My consumption of the red grape and pondering of recent events was interrupted by two things. The first was the arrival of the food, which I engulfed with rather impolite haste, with pickle and French loaf scattering everywhere.

The second was a score or so people of varying ages arriving at the bar. I assumed from the fact that all of them appeared to be asking a scruffy, bearded type what he would like to drink, that it was his birthday; probably one of his thirties. He was certainly up for it, as he appeared to say yes to every offer. As it was barely half past five, these must be work colleagues.

I ate my food and watched. I used to enjoy work drink-ups; I liked the feeling of togetherness, of sharing and shedding of work woes, bitching about bosses, and remembering funny episodes. About once a month, we would all pile down to the local, always just for a quick one but always staying the duration. My Caroline was the same; she was a secondary-school teacher, and boy, could those guys put it away. Especially her department—history, which I think was second only to design and technology for having the biggest reputation for partying.

When our daughter, Lisa, reached an age where she, with enough bribery of money, snacks, and the promise of unlimited viewing of the latest US teen show on TV, could be left alone, I would sometimes join them. I would usually be the one nursing the sore head the next day as I foolishly tried to keep up. Happy thoughts. Caroline was good company, the type of partner who was as equally adept whether it was just the pair of us or in company, new or old friends. Whenever we did meet new people, it was always she who took the lead as I took a while to warm up. I was the life and soul of a party when I knew the people. Or so I would like to think. ("In your dreams," I could imagine a smiling Caroline saying).

From what the group was saying as they found a table next to me, I would have hazarded a guess that these were also teachers. From the snippets I could hear, they were of primary level. Either that or fifteen-year-olds had taken up playing in sandpits.

I zoned out from their chatter as they talked of work and who was doing what to whom. Instead, against the backdrop of their laughter and banter, I just savoured the cheddar cheese and thought again over the mad past days. I still could not get my head around what I had seen at Dave's. The savagery of it was something I could not fathom. It was like some psycho had gone berserk, but what made it so chilling was that it had not been random cruelty—it had been thought out. They knew precisely what they were doing and exactly why they were doing it. The trouble was, could we ever find out why they did? Sitting here, sipping the wine slowly, and letting it wash over my taste buds did not help me think any better, but it sure did taste good.

My political ears picked up some familiar phrases from the tables of teachers. They were now discussing the government's announcement of the funding from the World Bank. All agreed that it was a colossal amount. The one I assumed to be the birthday boy, who had an array of pints in front of him, remarked that considering the mammoth amount of investment, there appeared to be little in the way of strings attached.

A much younger woman, barely wearing a yellow top and wearing the tiniest of skirts, disagreed. Her argument was that the requirement to reprivatize the economy, which had only recently been nationalised, was a heavy price tag. Another colleague, of about the same age but more soberly dressed, agreed. He was of the opinion that it was tantamount to reversing all the gains that we had so far won. From his rhetorical phrases, I guessed that both he and the Indian woman in her forties, who interrupted him to agree, were comrades.

She said something I didn't catch but had her table laughing heartily. That seemed to cue the change of subject which like so many work drinks would scatter in all directions like balls on a snooker table. For a connection I could not even begin to speculate about, the summery-dressed female was now regaling the crowd with talk of her run-in with the head teacher that morning.

Could this financial bailout be the reason why Jackie had wanted us to drop any investigation into Alan? Maybe she had more important things to worry about. Perhaps once more, capitalism had found a way to reinvent and save itself. Finishing my rather nice ploughman's (though missing the pickled onions, due I was told because of a shortage), I took out the phone to see what the National Workers' Council was saying about it.

From what I could quickly glean, it was pretty much as our confederates from education were saying: the stipulations amounted to a severe retreat for the revolution. What was of interest was the counterproposal from the NWC. This included a further two hundred companies to be nationalised and most controversially of all, the assets of the wealthy to be systematically commandeered, with action taken against any who tried to move their capital abroad. What presently had been the case was an ad hoc approach to taking over the obscene wealth left by bankers fleeing to their fourth homes in exotic climes.

This had been decried by the prime minister as, "Leading us to a world-command economy where in this brave new world we are all brainlessly servicing one long production line. Communism has been seen to have failed. The idea of one big state is not just wrong but dangerous." He went on to say that the offer from countries such as Brazil, China, and the United States was a generous one, and he rebuked the NWC for talking about fraternity between nations, but when there was an obvious example of such, it was denigrated.

My concentration was broken when suddenly music started to play. It sounded recent and tuneless, so it was no doubt hip with the youngsters. Certainly, it prompted a couple of the teachers to get to their feet and start—what could loosely be called—dancing. The whole group radiated jollity and conviviality.

The dancing continued with dance classics from the 2020s. It was good to watch. When was the last time I had been out with friends? Oh, at first many had tried with invites coming thick and fast, but I had not wanted to really be anywhere but at home. Just me and the cat.

Downing the last of the bottle, I got ready to head for home. The music changed, reaching even further back in soul history. I left the pub to The Temptations telling us that the world was one *Ball of Confusion*. It certainly is.

***

Gratitude was owed to whatever God looked after us atheists for my arrival home in one piece, because drinking a bottle of red wine on an empty stomach whilst buzzing around the roads of London was not the smartest of moves.

Still, I got home (after at least two near misses). And after picking up the grocery delivery from the local workers' council, I opened the door and decided to start to get back into my old routines. Because of both today's meeting with Jackie and Cole and my injuries from the latter, I had not been able to swim, but I could at least catch up on some of the others. Tuesday afternoon had always been downstairs housework time, but due to my short career as a sleuth, I had been unable to do it this week, so I could look forward to that.

After vacuuming, which because of my shoulder was a rather painful chore, I wiped down some of the shelves. Next, I turned my attention towards the books, which *was* useful. I loved delving into my collection, and despite trying to put them back correctly, there would be the occasional lapse, and something would be misfiled. They did appear to be all correct which I supposed was to be expected as I hadn't had much time to read so far this week. That was something I could now remedy. Finally, I checked that the bits and bobs I had accrued over the years on my travels were in their correct place. Jobs done, I poured myself a coffee, lay down on the sofa, and with what I intended to be the last effort of the night, pointed the phone at the screen, chose a suitably non-demanding and nonthreatening film, and settled down to watch.

***

Shaking and shouting, I awoke. Nightmares had again disturbed my sleep. Red had gone flying and had hurtled off to the sanctity behind the door. I got off the sofa, noticing as I did, that the film was three-quarters of the way through and therefore not really worth watching any longer. I turned it off and went to get a glass of water that would help the dryness in my throat and the dull ache in my head. The cause of which could as equally be from daytime vino as it could be from the after-effects of a bad dream.

I felt very alone. Whatever my complaints, Jackie's request had at least occupied me. Reducing the levels of medication had the side effect of decreasing my tolerance of inactivity. Now with it gone, I felt rather lost. Having something and then losing it was the most powerful way of being aware of its importance. I knew all about that. I had once had a lovely family—Caroline, my truly wonderful wife, and Lisa, my clever, beautiful, and yes, sometimes a pain of a daughter. And I had lost both of them.

I was swigging down my second pint of water, hoping to revive my head, if not my soul, when the doorbell went. The thought of not answering did occur to me as, with my shirt half out my trousers, one shirt sleeve rolled up, and the other down with its collar clammy against my neck, I wasn't really dressed for visitors. However, they were certainly persistent, so with the bell being rung again, I opened the door.

I was confronted by a large, broad-shouldered, white man in his forties with cropped, silver-grey hair, wearing a brown, three-button suit with a white shirt and brown tie. Behind him was a familiar face, one Detective Cole. Both were brandishing their police ID tech-cards high in front of them.

His voice was strong and to the point. "Mr Pete Kalder?"

"That is me," I said, launching my charming and totally innocent smile.

"We are from the Metropolitan Police Service. I am Detective Inspector Gerard Martin, and this is Detective Victoria Cole. We are here because you contacted us this morning with information concerning Yasmin and David Wiltshire."

"Of course, please come in." I oozed charm and innocence.

I ushered them into my lounge. They both came in with that confident air that all coppers used to have but had lost of late. I sneaked a look at Cole who was the epitome of professionalism, her face totally impassive. DI Martin paused as he entered the room, waiting for the invite to sit down. All very polite and, of course, it gave him a chance to survey the room. I noted that Cole was doing likewise.

"Please sit down," I told them. Never let anyone say that Mother Kalder hadn't brought her boy up with manners. Even with coppers.

They did so. Martin took my favourite armchair, pulling his trousers up slightly by the knee as he sat. His spine was rigid; his arms rested on both rests. Cole took the sofa and unzipped her jacket, which in doing so, gave me a flash of her black gun holster.

I offered them tea, which they declined. If we carried on with all these courtly manners for much longer, we ran the risk of dancing a Venetian waltz. I sat down in the other chair and immediately felt their eyes on me.

Cole spoke first. "We appreciate you meeting us, Mr Kalder…"

"Call me Pete, Detective, er, Cod, Cold?" I inwardly smiled at that. OK, I'm a kid.

"Cole, Vic Cole, and thank you, Pete; I am sorry that we were unable to give you any prior notice of our visit, but as you can imagine, we are rather busy investigating this. Would you mind if we recorded this? You are not obliged to let us, but it would help."

I agreed. Well, why not?

Coolly, she slid out her phone and pressed something. I presumed that she was filming me. She should have warned me as I would have worn my best clobber.

It was the big man's turn now. "Before we start, I should say that DC Cole is here wearing two caps: both as an investigating officer and as a representative of the Met Police faction of the NWC, which is in line with the agreed protocol between the Met and the NWC."

Wow, had that speech replaced the "You have the right, blah, blah?" It didn't quite have the same ring, but then I guess I am just a traditionalist. My charm slipped a touch. "So that's told me about your colleague's politics, but what about yours?"

He smiled a casual smile, whilst Cole remained tight-lipped. "I won't insult you by saying that I am not political, but I will say that they do not interfere with my ability to do my job, and I do want to find the person who murdered this couple."

I was about to reply when he nodded to my bruise. "That looks quite nasty. How did you do that?"

"One of your colleagues hit me," I replied. My desire to embarrass Cole, however, was unsuccessful. She just looked at me, waiting for me to continue. So did he; so did I. "Only joking. The truthful answer is far more boring; I fell out of the bath yesterday."

Earlier, Cole and I had decided that it was a better story than falling off the scooter which she said could easily be checked simply by looking at it for scratches. Personally, I thought the excuse ranked with the "dog ate my homework" for credibility, but she had pointed out that they had ascertained that both Dave and Yasmin had not fought back in any way, so there would be no incentive to explore how I might have really acquired it.

He nodded slowly as if thinking about it until he used his nose to point out the scars on my one bare arm. "And those?"

I felt a chunk of calmness leave my body. Upper and lower sets of teeth pressed on each other. I met his gaze and smile. "These? These were self-inflicted when I had a mental breakdown. I've got matching ones on my other arm. Look!" For some reason, I pulled up my other sleeve. Normally, I kept them well-hidden, but I felt compelled to almost dare him to make a comment about them.

He glanced at it. "I am sorry to hear that. When was it?"

"Two years ago," I answered, still meeting his look. The dick was not going to shame me.

Cole piped in, probably feeling all red and fluffy, softly and comradely. "You have my sympathy, Mr Kalder."

I bowed my head in acknowledgement.

DI Morgan coughed. "So what time did you get to Dave Wiltshire's house?"

"It belonged to the both of them. It was Dave and Yasmin's," I said, correcting them, as if ascertaining property rights was the most vital thing to be done.

"Of course, my apologies."

I went through the story of how I had arrived at 5:55 p.m. I had knocked at the front door, but getting no answer, I went around the back. Everything was locked, and I could see nothing, so after hanging about a bit, I went home.

The pair of them just sat there listening. "So why did you phone if you knew that there was nobody at home?" he asked.

Shrugging my shoulders, I said, "I don't know why; I just did. Wanted to double-check, I guess."

"Double-check?" Cole queried.

"Yes, I know it sounds weird, but I felt that someone was in the house."

"Did you see anyone?"

"No."

"Are you sure you didn't?"

"Definitely."

"What about hearing anything?"

"Nothing at all. As I said, it was just a feeling."

Morgan didn't pursue the point but asked, "So why did you visit them, and according to our records, attempt to contact them on several previous times?"

Despite having brazenly flaunted them, I did not really want these two people looking at such a private thing as my scars, so I rolled down my sleeves. I told them that I had been asked by Jackie Payne to look into Alan Wiltshire's suicide.

There was a slight questioning glance from Morgan to Cole. It must be bloody confusing to be a police officer nowadays. What was he going to do now? Follow the line of questioning, drop it, or ask Cole herself? After all, he would know that she was involved in the case. Should he ask if we knew each other? If we did, then how could this interview continue? In any event, he chose to ask if I would know why he might kill himself. I told him I didn't.

He swapped Wiltshires. "So Pete, have you any idea who would want to kill Yasmin and Dave?"

"None. He wasn't particularly political. I mean he was a party member, but, frankly, Detective, nowadays you can be a member and not be in anyway political."

I didn't look at Cole but wondered if the barb had cut. A slight look of amusement moved across Morgan's face. Whether or not he knew that I was having a pop, or whether he was enjoying a dart at her himself, I could not say, but he simply replied that he wouldn't know anything about that. No, of course, mate, you are not political.

He then asked where I had been and what I had done in the preceding hours.

Here I had a whole roster of witnesses to vouch for the fact that I was nowhere near the place when I knew, but he did not know that I knew, the murder occurred. I had visited George, and then there was my visit to Thames Northeast Workers' Council. There was that roomful of sex workers who could no doubt testify to that. There was Glen Bale, too, but I wouldn't bet on him doing it. Marie would, though. From there, my—if I remembered my crime-fic vocab correctly—timeline took in my visit to the swimming pool. A least half a dozen would remember the "forty at four man" going well over his usual one-kilometre swim.

Both officers took turns to gently question me, but I could sense that even Morgan didn't think it was me they were looking for—the fabled copper's instinct, no doubt. Or he just couldn't give a damn about several fewer Lefties in the world.

Whatever the reason, the social call was all too brief, and they thanked me for my time, with Morgan saying that he thought he found out enough. As they got up to leave, I resisted quipping to Cole that we should stop meeting like this but instead just said, "Goodnight, Officers."

CHAPTER EIGHT
April Thesis

It was a glorious day, more summer than spring. The garden looked fabulous, with the leaves fresh and green and the peonies looking absolutely stunning in blocks of cerise at angles zigzagging across them.

A quick trip down to the end of the garden had reassured me that my incinerating skills were of top quality, as indeed was my ability at composting, because I could see no sign of the clothes associated with my ghoulish visit to Dave Wiltshire's. Then again, they didn't need great hunks of designer buttons, when a microscopic particle would be enough. No point in worrying, though. I was, after all, innocent. Listen to me, such a touching faith in the British justice system.

Sipping my coffee, I enjoyed the scene and forgot about my forensic problems. I did like it out here. As we had both got older, Caroline and I had started to get into gardening, much to the bemused puzzlement of Lisa. After having another run of the nightmare last night, I had thought that a real-life garden might be more calming than my shrink's imaginary one. It was a lot smaller with a lot less spent on it (OK, that was comparing real with *illusory* money, so did that count? It was so confusing), but it did have the advantage of being genuine and three-dimensional.

There was another positive: the nightmare had returned after several months' absence, but at least it had only come to me just the once last night. At its worst I had been getting it ten to fifteen times a night, basically whenever I closed my eyes. Last night, though, only the once.

Sitting here, tranquillity mixed with emptiness. Feelings of loneliness and hollowness combined with a sense of unfulfillment to produce an almost paralysing sense of lethargy. Only the anger at Jackie's actions provoked any desire to get up and do anything. She had crashed into my life, dragged me into a murderous mess, and then after I had physically and literally found myself in one, had patted my head, told me to be a good boy and trot on home. So here I was—back home, once more compiling to-do lists, once more lonely. I knew full well that the harsh fact was that the culpability for this sense of isolation was all mine. Was it heartache if the ache was self-induced? Almost certainly, it meant that you were not entitled to any sympathy. But then I had no need for anyone to feel sorry for me because I could do that all on my own. It was my stupid fault that my wife and daughter were not here. And it had taken a long time to adjust to the reality that it was a fault that could not be rectified.

So I sat with my to-do list. Looking at my watch, I could see that it was eleven o'clock. For several minutes the idea of simply staying here, immobile, sealed off from the outside world and just observing plants growing was an acutely attractive one. Vegetating could be comforting. The alternative just offered hassle and bother, and yet without consciously deciding on doing so, I got to my feet.

Locking the back door, I washed the cup and fed Red. I changed out of my three-quarter-length, aqua-marine shorts and white, short-sleeve polo shirt and took out something more appropriate. Moving the suits to one side with the back of my right hand until I came across the right one, I took out the black suit with the Nehru collar and nodded, yes, that would be an appropriate choice for today. For the weather it was maybe not a sensible choice, but I thought it apt for the occasion. The paisley lining, after all, would be hidden when buttoned up. As I dressed a memory popped up and made me smile. Looking for such a suit, Caroline had confused her Indian leaders and asked a baffled shop assistant whether they had any Gandhi suits. A stunned shop worker had politely told her that they didn't stock the traditional dhoti and shawl.

Eventually, after Caroline got the collar correct, we had found it. It would be appropriate for today. There was to be a celebration of Alan Wiltshire; the party had insisted that it was not a funeral (there was to be a private cremation later). I was a traditionalist at heart, and dark colours seemed more befitting to the occasion. It looked—with, for once, no pun intended—dead

Comrades Come Rally

good with black winkle pickers and a polka-dot shirt with a small, round, less traditional collar.

The celebration/demonstration/funeral/*whatever* had several feeder marches which all ended up at Hyde Park. And yes, despite the best efforts of our keen chums to rename it due to its imperial reference, it was still called Hyde Park. Anyway, I was sure that most people thought it was named after Dr. Jekyll's alter ego. Countless broadcasts had been made across the media calling on all progressives to show their respect to a lifelong class fighter and to honour his memory in standing up to the bankers who were scheming to overthrow every gain we had made.

All transport workers were to strike for two hours except those carrying people attending. On those, transport was to be free. The power workers would cut off all power to selected areas. (Now there was a good way of getting an idea of what your house price was; if you had your electricity and gas cut, it was in a upmarket area; if you didn't, then sorry, pal, prices were low round your part of town). A host of other workers ranging from road sweeps to theatre actors were also taking action.

My choice of parking space grimly amused me, Baker Street. How appropriate to leave the scooter at the street that was home to the great detective, the Beatles' 1960 boutique, and considering Alan's hidden history, the SOE—Winston Churchill's Secret Army who went behind enemy lines in World War II. Perfect synchronicity.

After parking the bike, I joined the march. My first thought was that, if this was just one of the feeders, then it was looking as if it was going to be huge. This was confirmed when one of the aerial news drones reported that already there were 501,023 on the march. These tiny little flying cameras might get great pictures and could relay news to those marching, but such preciseness did spoil the traditional numbers game where the BBC would claim that there were twenty thousand on a march, the police would say ten thousand, and we would claim a quarter of a million. Now with these drones, you got the exact number. I always wondered, though, how they could be exact. I mean, what if Fred Bloggs was walking his dog; was he counted?

As requested, there were no placards or union banners. People just carried small flags with the red fist. I was one of the few in black. Indeed, I saw only a few pensioners and, appropriately enough, a vicar who were wearing it. Most, though, were in subdued colours; there were, after all, celebrations and celebrations. There were plenty of children, a welcome return to the demos we had before the violent clashes, when protestors had been attacked by armed police and water cannons whilst the army lurked in the wings. That tended to put people off from bringing little Billy and Ria along.

I found myself tagging along with a group of parents and what seemed like hundreds of kids, who were amusing themselves by swinging as quickly as they could round every lamppost they could find. This was quite funny, but it did make them almost as dangerous as a police sergeant with a water cannon as their little legs came hurtling around with frightening speed. My concern was one of those sweet, sandaled feet crashing into my shoulder.

There weren't too many marches I had been alone on. Usually, I would be with a group of people, be it from work, or from the party, or mates, or a combination of all three. It didn't seem to be a problem on this one. Whatever the reason might be for the call to march, there was an air of friendship with people chatting about everything and nothing. Whether they knew you or not did not seem to matter. Within the first quarter of an hour, as we slowly snaked along, I must have spoken to dozens of people. Topics ranged across a broad spectrum of subjects of Alan's life, the state of the country, the changing nature of London, and the quickest way to Oxford Street.

The latter had been from an elderly chap with a cap who had looked at the march in shock because quite obviously he had missed the radio, television, Internet, and newspapers blanket coverage and had been quite alarmed to see thousands marching past when all he wanted to do was to buy a pair of shoes. Jackie had been everywhere, calling on people to support it, for it appeared that she wanted to make this bigger than just merely being a memorial, but she had failed to reach this guy. He wanted brown, size 42 brogues. Despite the concerted publicity, this venerable man had no idea what it was all about. Ah, there was always one. I wondered if he had been counted as one of the demonstrators. Well, that just proved what I had been thinking. If so, make it 501,022.

I had been on many, many marches in my time, and there were different types. There were those where the people cared about the topic but lacked passion, fire, or anger. On these we were at our most English, keeping ourselves to ourselves, with the odd half-hearted chant with someone trying to cope with a malfunctioning megaphone to lead it. I had been on so many of these, the worst being those of three people and a banner outside some civic centre or other, where there would be so few people that everyone could have a chance on the mega-phone to call for a mass fight back! Then there were others where anger and passion was all; youths would have faces covered with scarves and would have slingshots ready. I had a personal reason for having a soft spot for those.

Others lay somewhere in between, where the people had the passion, but it wasn't just a few hotheads but the masses. The emotion could be anger, love, or a mixture of both. On these, people were at the most sociable, with barriers breaking down and people feeling united.

This one was very much the type where you could see and feel the unity and not just hear it on a slogan. As we approached Marble Arch, I got adopted by a pair of women in their early twenties. They remarked on my suit and how cool it looked, which in terms of style was 100 percent correct, but as my armpits could testify, it was not quite so in comfort. The sun was really beginning to cook me.

After praising my attire, they had asked about the bruised face. Thinking to impress them, I did consider telling them the truth that I had beaten by the pigs, by the forces of state oppression, and by the hated police. But then I'd have to say that she also happened to be a comrade. So I went for second-cool and said I had come off my scooter. I thought that lie to be a better one than I slipped in the bath; that had too much of an elderly feel about it. Whether this did impress, or today was adopt-a-fogey day, or simply the mood of the crowd was of togetherness, I don't know, but they certainly chatted ten to the dozen to me.

Very quickly, I learnt a great deal about them, including that they were Zoe and January, had been a couple for just under three years now, and were still very in love. For some reason, maybe because I found their amiability and openness refreshing, I told them about Caroline and Lisa. Li and Li: the best things that had ever happened to me. Zoe touched my arm in sympathy and asked a whole gamut of questions about them. Interestingly, I had no qualms in answering them.

Although some things might change, others did not. Still, for an English march, two things remained important: access to tea and toilets. Both were in plentiful supply, as the local shop and hotel workers who had closed their businesses opened them up for both. This had the crowd murmuring appreciation.

We stopped by a whole convoy of parked refreshment vans, and January queued for drinks and a biscuit each. As we waited, Zoe told me all about how she had met January about two-and-a-half years ago when she had left school and started to work for the Tai-Shan Superstore chain. Both had been involved in the occupations and sit-ins that had kept them open, despite the Chinese owners wanting to pull out of Britain.

"It was an education in itself," she smiled. "Within a few months, I had joined a union, been on strike for the first time, then in occupation, then for my sins got elected on the strike committee, and then joined the party."

She explained that January, or Jan, as she called her, wasn't a member, but she was hopeful that would change. There was a heartening zest about how she spoke. Nothing was bogus about her, and she saw no reason to hide her enthusiasm, which appeared to have no limits. Everything to this young woman was exhilarating. She explained to me what was stopping Jan from joining us; the issue of contention being the structure of a Leninist organisation and how democratic it was. The pair, it seemed, had had many a discussion about it. I suggested that one's partner wasn't always the best person to talk politics with. She disagreed, saying that it was all good-natured, and anyway, she said with obvious pride, whether or not she was officially a member, Jan was as active as she was. A huge, beaming smile accompanied the comment.

Still grinning, she asked me when and how I had joined. My little, red-enamel party badge by my collar signalled that I was a member. When I told her, she whistled and embarked on a tribute.

"That's fantastic. You were the people who built the foundations of the party. Without people like you, we would not be able to be doing all this."

As she continued with the respectful laudation and sincere praise, a few things did pop into my mind in that, despite her genuine niceness, she did make me sound like a revered old piece of furniture. Questions about what it was like *back then* sometimes did prompt me to point out that we did in fact have computers *back then*, and perhaps what she was thinking of was more the nineteenth-century Chartists than when I had joined. We didn't really have to do much in the way of handwriting leaflets. And, yes, we had e-mail, Twitter, and Facebook.

Jan joined us with the refreshments, and hearing about my history, asked if I had known Alan Wiltshire personally. I answered yes and told them about my limited work with him. Both were impressed, making approving nods, especially Zoe who said that she had been to several of his meetings and found him to be a thoughtful and interesting speaker. She remembered one on the French revolutionary Robespierre which he had made relevant to the young audience.

I nodded. "Yes, he rang me for a little bit of help with those. He wanted to know about Jacques-Louis David's painting of the *Death of Marat*. He was going to start with it," I said, explaining why he would have thought of contacting someone as humble as me.

On hearing of my job as an art researcher, they, as many often did, regaled me with their favourite painters. Both surprised me. In their fashionable tartan trainers, three-quarter-length trousers, T-shirts, and punky hair, I would have put them down as being into contemporary e-art. Instead, they said they loved Pre-Raphaelite art, especially Millais. It was an unexpected choice, Victorian and now deemed rather conservative and sentimental. I noted the tone they used in discussing him was similar to the one they had used when talking about us long-term party members. I felt flattered and a little depressed at the same time.

Was I a museum piece? Fact was, for all their kind words, it was these two who were building the movement now. They were trying to change the world; I'd just been watching it go by. It wasn't what you had done, but what you were doing that mattered. And what this pair of young, intelligent, good-humoured women was doing was changing the world.

We moved on and joined another feeder march into the park. The place was heaving but good-natured with the party stewards having to do little in the way of control. The police were nowhere to be seen. Even their drones were absent by request from the NWC, with only the news networks and a few commandeered by us for the occasion, buzzing above our heads. From the other march came the obligatory group of musicians banging the hell out of a variety of percussion instruments from around the world. Then, as I had dreaded, my two new compatriots started skanking to the rhythm. Only one thing was missing, a damned whistle. Oh no, my mistake. A teenager piped up and started blowing tunelessly on one, just several metres from my right ear. I looked on with a sheepish smile. I *really* hated that kind of thing.

Then, as quickly as the two feeder marches had joined together, they dispersed as people broke ranks to walk towards the stage, which was flanked by huge screens. Everywhere there was unity: black, white, yellow, pink and brown; all religions and none; lesbian, gay, straight, bi, transgender or just not sure; able bodied or disabled; old, young or somewhere in between; male and female; white collar, blue collar or button-down; manual workers, office workers, home or office, warehouse or factory, workers with no work or workers unable to work; dressed casually, sensibly or fashionably, and even the occasional immaculately. But all were together. In solidarity. Workers all. Comrades all. Once we had only dreamt of this. But now. Here we were. The reality. It was enough to make you gasp.

Zoe and January stayed with me, but thankfully our musician friends bobbed and swayed in a different direction.

We headed off to hear the speakers. Not being able to get very near to the stage we settled down to watch the nearest screen. My two new pals seemed disappointed that we had missed a few speakers. Zoe asked the people milling about us who had already been on. Ah, to be so keen. They sounded as if they were at a rock concert, asking who had been the support acts.

Amongst a group of speakers, most of whom I had heard of (I noticed that Zoe and January knew *all* of them) was Marie Williams, who apparently had spoken of Alan as a friend. I would have liked to have heard her; Marie was a good speaker, one who was obviously genuine in what she was saying. Her manner was deceptively casual, but she would always have a point. She spoke without notes and from both the heart and mind. Her warmth and intellect combined to make her a powerful orator in an understated way. Rather like her as a person. Our neighbours in the park told us how she had explained Alan's illness and why he had to end his own life. So that was the line: terminally ill, so took an overdose. It sounded thin to me, but I supposed not many here would harbour suspicions of him. She had, we were told, ridiculed rumours of factions of dissatisfaction with the direction the party had taken. He was loyal, she had said. Yes, well, apart from the tiny detail about working with MI5.

She had also spoken warmly about Dave. So much so, we were informed, that there wasn't a dry eye in the park. It had been very emotional, with Marie likening Dave to being like a son. She had urged anyone who had any information on the barbarous act of double murder to come forth (she obviously had one eye on the TV audience watching this).

We turned our attention to the stage where a speaker had just finished and another had been introduced. It was Kye Toulson, who strode on in an ill-fitting brown suit, clutching a wad of paper as if it was a relay baton. He stood behind the mike with legs apart and immediately launched into his speech.

"Brothers! Sisters! Comrades!" he bellowed. "We have come here not to mourn but to organise! Alan spent all his life fighting for the rights of the exploited and oppressed, and now more than ever, that fight must continue."

He continued by outlining how workers in every workplace were now controlling that work. We had moved on from trade unions defending workers to workers' councils taking control. Obviously, he felt it important that we got the full A–Z of how the certainties of old Britain were changing with the new. No doubt they were, but I thought he could have edited it down a little. Maybe I was just suffering from the heat, but he was going on a bit. If he carried on for much longer, I might just feel the need to point out that we'd all been here in the country and didn't really require a lesson on recent history.

He was a passionate, if sometimes a little too loud, speaker. (You hoped that someone would tap him on his shoulder and whisper, "It's OK, comrade, we have amplification, and they can hear you.") They could also ask him to get to the point a little quicker, whilst they were at it. Plainly, he was no mere demagogue; the history of how the struggle in the workplace had changed over the course of Alan's lifetime was nothing if not detailed.

As he spoke, he got pinker and bizarrely seemed to get puffier every minute. Did someone have an air pump stuck up his arse? Could he at any moment float away? I feared that we would have another death to mourn here. Sorry, we weren't mourning, were we; another *death to inspire us to organise*. Sweat dripped off his forehead. Not that I was one to disparage, as it was pretty much the same with me as well. It was just that, although he was obviously a decent bloke and a hard-working activist, my thoughts of the nursery rhyme involving swine and a ravenous wolf were shameless. These screens were so unforgiving!

Trying to get such uncharitable musings out of my head, I looked around. Behind me, people were still coming in, threading their way through the groups who had sat themselves down. In front, the nearer you got to the stage, the more packed it got, whereas the further back, it became more like a picnic than a rally. The spaces got larger and the marchers smaller, as the appearance of children increased in number. And with them came sandwiches and seemingly a whole array of bright beach balls. It was a delightful day. The sky was blue, and the sun was out. What better place to be than in a London park on a glorious spring day. Still.

The good humour slightly jarred with the very real and raw memory of how I had found Dave and Yasmin. Seeing all this camaraderie strangely made me a little cheerless. I hadn't known Dave that well, and I probably had only met his wife on the odd occasion, but even so, it weighed on me. Partly, it was true that it was the first double torture and murder I had seen, but also, well, did anyone deserve to die like that?

Hearing applause, I looked up and saw Kye leaving to loud and affectionate applause which he responded to by turning and clenching his fist. The effect, though, was slightly marred by him strenuously puffing out his cheeks and all but falling over an electric cable. A good man, though probably not one destined to be on posters on students walls. Or to run relay races for that matter.

Well. Well. The next speaker was Michael Hughes. So at last I would meet him. OK, I was with half a million other people, but we met at last. He received polite applause, and a ripple of interest ran across the crowd when they saw his green uniform of the British Army. He marched on in a manner that was obviously military: erect and proud. You couldn't confuse that attitude with that of a postman. *Postman!?* That aged me.

Looking at him did ring a few bells from party websites which told of how members of the military were coming over to us. Dressed in combat fatigues tucked into black boots, with a crisply ironed, green, short-sleeve shirt with a red armband, he looked every bit the military man. His black skin was slightly darker than Jackie's. At a guess, I would place his heritage as West African. His face was longish with a strong jaw. With biceps bulging against his sleeves, he looked like a man you did not mess with.

He launched straight into telling us the latest figures of military defections and mutinies. They received rolling waves of huge applause. This he contrasted with the numerous coalitions that had thought that khaki rather than blue was required to keep the peace. London, Manchester, Newcastle, Bristol, and Wolverhampton had joined Belfast and Derry as cities who could boast of having witnessed troops on their streets. This he expounded at length, sparing us no detail.

My attention wandered, and I aimlessly contemplated the surrounding people who inhabited this part of the park. For the most part, they all looked to be caught up with the Hughes history of squaddies. Not everyone, though, was being so enlightened; there was a group of kids, who I would guess were ten or eleven years of age, who seemed far more interested in pouring fizzy drink down their throats and playing computer games. Idly, I wondered if they were playing war games.

As I looked around, feeling a growing jealousy for those dressed in shorts, I caught Zoe's attention. She was totally mesmerised by Hughes, grinning and energetically nodding, indicating how good she thought he was.

Feeling guilty, I returned to the speech. I truly hoped that he was going to be brief because I was really feeling uncomfortable standing here, sweltering in a suit. I knew that when it was a death of a comrade, we liked to make it political, but did we have to have a lengthy chronicle of the revolution? Judging by what he was saying, I had a feeling that was exactly what we were going to receive. With a strong, authoritative voice, which—thank goodness for small mercies—he was controlling and not shouting down the microphone, he ploughed on.

From time to time, he would ask the crowd a question which he then answered himself. Like a decapitated call and response. The call got no response, because he did not feel the need to have one, so he made the response. Every time such a question was put, his chest would swell out. It would go back when he answered it.

"Would the ruling class allow the fig leaf of political impartiality to remain and the army to stay in their barracks, or would they be ordered out to fire on their own brothers and sisters? On their mothers and fathers? On their sons and daughters?" He stopped short from spreading to nieces and nephews, aunts and uncles, and second cousins once removed.

He expounded on how that question had dominated talk at all ranks across the forces. Was it the army's way to get involved? Was there, indeed, even an option of doing nothing? Or was neutrality, in actual fact, doing *something*—taking sides by deserting Parliament? I followed his logic, even if it was getting rather tangled, but it didn't seem quite in sync with what all this was supposed to be about.

This was supposed to be a celebration of Alan's life, wasn't it? But here he was, carefully explaining the political situation. Clearly, the party was using this for more than just an "Alan was a great guy" event. That would explain why there were such numbers here. Something else was happening.

He spoke of the debates which had gone on at Wolverhampton and on what the army should do. The generals had been on one side, with the privates on the other. These had been historic occasions, not occurring since the English Civil War. Indeed, they were of great significance, but why talk about them now and why here? I didn't think he had actually mentioned Alan's name, and he had been speaking for five minutes. It was also remarkable that on this occasion he had chosen to be so detailed. I had expected some platitudes and some crowd-pleasing, a hearty bout of rabble-rousing, and then off home for a cuppa. But this was closely argued and sometimes rather confusing stuff.

Hughes was a tall man. From the screens you could see that he was no stranger to the gym. They seemed to like focusing on his strong muscles, especially the obligatory tattoo. So far, so predictable, but facially he didn't look like a squaddie. Yes, he had short hair, shaven even, but he was quite a good-looking man with chiselled cheekbones and clear, brown eyes. He looked like the type of soldier that only exists in Hollywood films and usually rides a motorbike. Not that he sounded American, more somewhere like the Midlands area.

Warming to his theme, he asked the question, "So brothers and sisters, is the army neutral?"

This time he did not answer himself, but repeated the question and aimed it at the audience. They responded and replied with a loud "no." But as loud as it was, it wasn't loud enough, so he asked again, "Brothers and sisters, is the army neutral?"

The red panto roared back, "No!"

Satisfied, nodding at the reply, he went on, his tempo increasing. "No, they are not. No, *we* are not! The ruling class might see us as their hired guns, but I tell you, if we are going to be asked to get involved and to take sides, then you know whose side we will be on! The workers! We, the workers in uniform, will not be used to crush the revolution!"

Thunderous applause crashed around the park. Zoe and January were going berserk in ecstasy. I worried about their blood pressure; I knew they were young, but there were always concerns about cholesterol. They were punching the air and yelling approval. No, this certainly was not a funeral. In my experience, audience participation usually did not get past a brief remembrance toast, not this "behind you" stuff. At this rate we'd have two blokes in a donkey costume strolling on.

Catching me looking at them, Zoe beamed a grin and hugged me. "Awesome! Awesome!!" she kept repeating. I smiled back. It was simple but true; we were living in awesome times. Their contact, though, was rather disconcerting as I feared that I was rather clammy. I extricated myself from her. Hopefully, she hadn't taken offence.

Meanwhile, back on the stage, soldier boy had stepped back, soaking up the applause, enthused and genuinely humbled. When it had finally all subsided, he went on to tell the crowd of the growing influence of the army section of the NWC.

"The rank and file of the army will not back any reactionary elements who want to murder this revolution. They cannot rely on the army, but brothers and sisters—you can!"

At that, the park exploded. Zoe and January were virtually in orbit as chants, applause, and spontaneous outbreaks of the "Internationale" rocked the crowd. Even I found my old heart swell and passion rise. I might have to worry about my ticker.

Five minutes later, he marched off the stage to loud cheers, his gait proud and defiant. It had been a powerful speech—closely argued and passionate. But, noticeably, there was not a single mention of Alan, Yasmin, or Dave.

A symptom of middle age was creeping up on me, thankfully not any cardiac palpitations, but I did I have a growing need to go to the loo. I pondered the time it would take to get to the toilets and back with the hassle of elbowing my way through the crowd. It was as I was pondering this great matter that Jackie was announced to tumultuous applause.

She walked on in a bright summer dress, white with huge red roses. Her hair was down, brushing by large silver hoops. She looked as if she was ready to go to a picnic. Jackie certainly was showing how not to wear mourning.

A smile wrapped around her face (you could not say she looked bereaved). "Comrades! They said it would never happen in Britain because we were not like other nations. Whenever it happened in other countries, they would say that we were not a Tunisia. Not the Ukraine. Not Uruguay. Well, comrades, we are not. We are in the British Isles, and it is happening here."

Her tone was not one of heartbreak but rather a triumphant cry of someone getting ready to rouse a summer festival. Hands across the park grew sore from heartfelt clapping; voices sore from cheering. Three comrades dead, and we paaarty!

Prowling the stage and really beginning to look like she was going to start rapping, she did what the previous two speakers hadn't—she mentioned Alan!

"That is what Alan Wiltshire believed in all his life. It was down to him and others doing the often thankless task of attending tiny marches and even smaller meetings so that a small core of people united in wanting a better world would start to grow." Obviously, she had decided, at least for the purpose of this event, to forget the trifling matter of his work for MI5. So, on she went, her passion increasing. "And after years of ridicule from the media, what do we see now? That tiny group of people, vilified and abused, have been proved right! The masses are moving. People are taking control to create a new world. Alan always believed that; Alan always built for that. This movement is a tribute to Alan and to those other early members who sowed the seeds of what we see today!"

More applause. Zoe and Jan looked behind at me and radiated smiles that seemed to say, *you too!* Despite myself, I felt flattered. Old fool.

They turned back to listen to Jackie who was entertaining the crowd with anecdotes from down the years involving Alan and Dave. Finally! Here was at least a semblance of the reason why we were here. I realised that we were in the middle of world-changing events, but individuals should not be forgotten. Especially at what had been billed as a celebration of their lives. Jackie did just that. With her, the mood of the people changed from that of solid revolutionary fervour to that of affectionate laughter and good humour. One story, especially, involving a trip to Dundee, provoked much guffawing. I had heard many of the stories before, some more than once, but they still made me laugh.

What was provoking me was the swelling of my bladder. This old guy would have to make an exit. I leant across to Zoe and Jan and explained that I had to go and that it was great to have met them. They insisted on hugging me again, telling me with enormous grins to, "Have a great revolution, comrade!"

Just then, whilst embracing two strangers and with thoughts of relieving myself, obviously not at the same time, although if they hugged any tighter it might become a distinct possibility, I detected another change of tone in Jackie's speech. There was a greater gravitas. Something inside me told me that this could be a historic moment, and missing it because I was having a pee just wouldn't be right. Nobody missed Martin Luther King Jr.'s "I Have a Dream" because they had to pay the john a visit.

She wasn't raging or bellowing; she was speaking calmly but with force. "And whilst the ruling class dealt with the crisis they had caused through their mismanagement, they tried to make us pay. And to pay *deeply*. Of course, we know that's what they do: the ruling class can get out of any hole if the workers are willing to pay the price. But we would not do so, and we started to take control. I recall what Alan said about the growth of the workers' councils: that Parliament and they could not coexist for long. He said that it was like having the lion-tamer and lion together in the same cage. One would destroy the other. Well, now, sisters and brothers, it is time for the lion to roar and remove that man with the whip."

The huge crowd had gone quiet. She had stopped moving, appearing to be addressing each and every one of them, as if she was in a one-to-one conversation with them all. Thousands of people were listening to her outline the next stage of the revolution. Behind me the noise of the children playing had subsided as parents urgently hushed them. Both Zoe, with her arm around me on one side, and January, on the other, had their mouths open. They weren't alone.

It was quite clear what Jackie was arguing: to protect the progress which the revolution had made so far, it had to be pushed further. Now was the time. *Now* it was time to seize power.

CHAPTER NINE
England's New Chains Discovered

This was becoming a bit of a habit: I see Jackie Payne and travel to Alan Wiltshire's home. And like the first time, when she had asked me to look into the circumstances surrounding his suicide, I wasn't totally confident of my reasons for doing so. Actually, that was a bit of an understatement; I pretty much thought my reasons for going were barmy, but I had just come out of a care home for the mentally ill, so I had my excuses.

Spending too much time on things other than keeping an eye on the traffic, I thought about the memorial rally. Jackie had quite plainly argued for the overthrow of Parliament and the introduction of the network of workers' councils as the governing bodies of the country. That had been the dream of the party and the aim of many, but it had been one spoken of as happening *one day,* as opposed to that day being next Tuesday at 3:15 p.m., after the shopping had been done. True, she hadn't been quite that specific, but the emphasis had switched from *at some point* to *in the very near future.*

This was going to be the big news across the world. The headlines were going to send tsunami-size waves across the globe. Watching the reaction was going to be interesting. Not just of the journalists scampering off to their blogospheres, but the more important reaction to look for was going to be the people on the street and at the workplace. What were they going to think? What were the Smiths, Joneses, Patels, Singhs, McCarthys, or Khans going to make of it? Were the good folk of Glasgow or Norwich or Bristol going to raise a clenched fist in solidarity or their hands up in panic? What was Parliament going to say?

Hurtling around a corner, not giving it the care and attention that I should have, but getting away with it anyway, I drifted onto lesser matters. What were the family of the deceased going to say? The memorial wasn't much of a memorial. Alan got mentioned; Dave, a few kind words, and Yasmin became an afterthought. I truly hoped that mine was going to be a bit more about me (and that someone gave some gentle advice to Kye and Michael about editing speeches).

Stopping at some traffic lights, I returned to what might be the fallout from Jackie's words. Would Parliament send in the troops? Michael had—at length—ruled that out as being impossible, but who really knew? For certain, they would react. I couldn't see a half-deserted session where one skirt-suited, bob-haired MP leans across to her colleague and mutters. "Did you hear what that Payne woman said, James? Tut, tut. The cheek! Oh, dear. Anyway, when's that motion on parking restrictions in Guildford going to be voted on?"

And what of the National Workers' Council? The NWC did have a long-standing policy for taking action if it was threatened, but was that the case now? OK, our cherished PM, his ministers, spin doctors, and the guy who supplied his fake tan hated them and would curse them to the heavens, but were they actually directly threatening them? Jackie had argued that they were, or at least there was an unspecified threat.

How were the delegates going to feel about that? To be sure, some would be in favour; indeed, some would be in the throes of ecstasy, but they would be a minority. A much larger group, in my estimation the majority, would need time to digest the news and hear further arguments. I could be counted in that group. Even after all the years of arguing for the need for revolution, sometimes to a meeting of five in a room above a pub where one of them had had one pint too many and another had to get home early for the kids, I was a bit stunned by it. I was afraid of it. Excited and inspired but, yes, afraid. Certainly, it had made my insides churn.

Maybe that was why before the end of a speech which could one day be seen as more important than Martin Luther King Jr.'s "I have a Dream," Elizabeth I's "Tilbury Speech," Churchill's "Blood, Toil, Tears and Sweat," and Leon Trotsky's "Russian Civil War" speeches all rolled into one, I had to leave early to visit the loo. As the demonstration was singing heartedly the "Internationale," I had been searching for one with a clean seat.

Or maybe I simply hadn't been able to hold on any longer. But whatever the reason, you never saw that in the movies: heroic leader calls for bravery and commitment; troops visit plastic chemical toilet. But as I was in there, I did do some thinking, and, strangely, amongst the earth-shattering implications of what comrade Payne was calling for, I made a little decision for myself. I was not going to stop looking into Alan *and* Dave's *and* Yasmin's deaths. I wanted to do a bit more digging. Some ideas were still nagging away in my head. The main problem of me being wholly unsuitable to the task remained, but I had started it, and I might not be able to finish it, but I could at least go on with it for a bit longer

This meant defying Jackie's direct wishes, but, then again, that was just what they were—wishes. She couldn't order me to stop or punish me if I didn't. I knew it wasn't that simple; I had party discipline in my veins. Cynic I might be, but I had little time for prima donnas who whined on about democracy, when in actual fact, all they wanted was to get their own way, a political version of the teenager's "It's not fair!"

Coming here to Alan's was going against everything I believed in. I respected Jackie, even admired her. It wasn't idle hero worship but an appreciation of her skills as a leader and theoretician. However, for whatever reason or reasons, I thought she was wrong. In a strange sense, she herself had convinced me to take this action. As she had spoken to Hyde Park, she had said that now was the time for people to achieve true freedom in a world where they could make real choices. To do so we should think what we could individually do to help others, to help us all collectively. That for all of capitalism there had been much talk of the power of the individual, but that had just been a sham. What was on offer here was the real liberation of the individual, for her or him to make a difference.

Well, whether you called it respite, early retirement, or on extended sick leave, the effect was the same—I was no longer in the workplace, so I couldn't organise. I hadn't been to my workers' council other than to collect my month's subsistence tokens, and since being released from the home, my days had consisted of watching the news, going for walks, and my four o'clock swim. I didn't think any of them was going to help give birth to a worker's paradise. Something was wrong, and it had led to the deaths of three good comrades, and I decided that I had to find out why. No matter what Jackie had said.

Arriving at Alan's house, I almost had a sense of déjà-vu; for there, as before, sitting as happy as you please, were the two young comrades who had been guarding (and I use the term loosely) it. It looked as if they had been here daily and had set up camp. Both were in the loudest Hawaiian shirts one could imagine, with sandals and pale-blue, three-quarter-length shorts. They each sat on a purple inflatable armchair. In front of them was a table with assorted technical equipment, allowing state-of-the-art access to any possible source of news or entertainment. Bottles of cheap lager and pizza boxes nestled against them. The automatic weapon was still there as a token gesture of security, but that was rather diminished by the fact that they at first did not notice me as they were too busy snogging. Today was obviously the day for me to meet young lovers. I coughed. As they looked up, they greeted me as a long-lost friend with smiles, a handshake, and effusive greetings.

"So you're still here?" I asked, ever keen to state the bleedin' obvious.

"Yep," answered the female comrade. "Nine to five, we are out here, keeping the place secure."

"Aha, and have you spoken to Jackie Payne or anyone from the party National Centre recently?" I asked.

"Oh, no," she replied. "We were just asked to be here."

So everyone had forgotten about you, I thought to myself. Poor bastards. What were they going to say when asked, "Mummy, Daddy, what did you during the British Socialist Revolution?" Answer: "We sat eating triple-cheese pizza and copping off with each other outside of a dead comrade's home." Then again, their flirting had appeared to have gone a step further and seemed to be on a trajectory that could well mean the conception of said child was imminent.

Still, it did mean that the last they had heard was to give me access to the house. I had expected to have to break in, but now they could just let me in.

"Who relieves you at five?" I asked, glancing at my watch and noting that there were twenty-five minutes to go.

This time, the male comrade answered. "Nah, no one, we just go home."

Ah, yes, the-ever efficient party. Secure Alan Wiltshire's home against class enemies but only in office hours. After that, well, no one will break in after then, will they? Oh, no, MI5 have strict rules about overtime, and at 5:00 p.m. they all go home to Esher with their empty sandwich boxes.

They let me in, and I headed straight upstairs. Something had occurred to me when I had been talking to Zoe and January, my buddies for the day. I had told them that I had done some writing with Alan, and as he was known for solitude in his work, it had made me one of only two people who had co-written anything with him. The other writer had died years back in a climbing accident in South America. Thinking about our work together had reminded me of something; I might be an old-fashioned fart, but Alan had been older, more behind the times, and a great deal fartier than me.

I went into his study and took my jacket off, putting it on the back of the chair. I turned his computer on and logged in. Not that I was going to use it at first, although I did try to contact Abby Nite at the Police Centre but received the reply that she was away from her desk. She was never at her bloody desk! What the hell did she actually do? Still, that didn't bother me too much, as it wasn't my reason for being here.

It wasn't even the computer that interested me but the desk it was on. Alan shared with me a love of books and was even more techno-illiterate. He would do much of his research from a hard-copy book in his hand, and he had a system he used when doing so. He would highlight passages in a book using two colours: one for of great interest and one for of possible interest. He had told me that he did this for all his work and had made a great deal of the fact that no one knew this, so I should feel honoured. I hadn't really spent much time pondering this, boasting about it, or getting on the phone to my mum to make her burst with pride. I had distinctly not revelled on how privileged I was. Well, not past thinking it was another example of his ego that he would presume I would feel thus.

But he had said the problem with this method was that he would choose different colours for each major work and then would either forget what colours he had chosen or confuse then with others. So, he would write down the date and the key for the colours, making sure to scribble out the old ones. This would mean his desk was a mess when every so often he would wash the lot away.

I had noticed two things when I came here on my first visit which at the time had not seemed important. The first was just how neat the books and periodicals were in this particular room. All piled in columns on the floor in here. That was very un-Alan. The second was the scribble on the table. I reckoned someone had tidied up here, maybe for the same reason that I had not been given access to what he had been researching on the computer. I doubted, though, they would know about his system.

I scanned the top, and there it was: the date for three weeks ago, with no cross through it, so it was current and showed the key—orange for very important and green for possibly important. Eureka! God bless Alan and his archaic ways!

The next thing was simply to grab every book, magazine, or newspaper that had those colours, and that would at the very least give me an idea of what he was looking at. OK, there may have been a previous occasion when the two colours had been used, but it was well worth a go!

I fairly flew at the piles on the floor. My method was simple: one for those with the colours in them and one for those that didn't. I would have a closer look when I had amassed a decent amount. It took me approximately half an hour to do the floor, and then I moved on to those on the shelves. As I did so, I noticed that there were some very odd ones in here. This was the room where Alan worked, and so he would keep here the most useful literature, including what he was using at the time. Yet in here by the computer desk, the books included several poetry collections, a biography of Mozart, and a natural history book on the life of the polar bear. My guess was that someone had just dumped these in here to hide what he had really been looking at. Rather like my attempt to mix rotting fruit and veg with the clothes I had incinerated after finding Dave. Both attempts at subterfuge were as pathetic as each other.

I had only found five books with the orange/green code in here, so it was obvious I would have to look elsewhere. I went downstairs and cleared every shelf I could find. If it had been a mess before then, it started to look as if an earthquake had hit it. The pile of orange/green was small but growing, whilst the rest piled up in the middle of the room. After I had finished with the dining room, I went into the living room and did exactly the same. We had technology that made your eyes pop, and here I was, scampering about with piles of books! All in all, it had taken me an hour and a half. With sweat making my shirt stick to my back, I ferried them upstairs.

Breathing hard, needing a drink, and beginning to feel hungry, I sat down. Now was not the time to stop. I had a look at what I had found.

The obvious common denominator was major social upheaval. There were books and periodicals containing articles on past revolutions and uprisings across the world, from the French Revolution, the Russian Revolution, and the Portuguese Revolution, to the unrest of the 2010–2020 and 2020–2030 periods. Some I dispensed with, as being obviously from another piece of research (I didn't think that the films of Stephen Spielberg quite fitted with the picture here).

Looking at them, it was quite obvious that the research fitted with what Jackie had been saying earlier: now was the time to seize power. These were all books about past attempts at such. Looking closely to find out in detail why he might feel the need to delve into such a history, I noticed that the highlighting wasn't so much about movements seeking change and what methods they used, but the methods the rulers had used to stop, divert, or crush them. That was a cause for a pause in thought. Such a study could be taken two ways: firstly, to provide valuable information from the past to help us achieve what Jackie was proposing, or secondly, he was forced to do so.

Before all this had happened, the first purpose would have been the scenario I would have opted for. And surely, that had to be the case. I still could not get my head around the idea of Alan working for MI5. What could have caused such a turnabout in his beliefs? If there had been an ideological shift, it must have been seismic. OK, humans were complex creatures, and we were capable of many things, and such changes in beliefs were possible. Historically, people had done so—moved from the Left to the Right. Mussolini and Sir Oswald Mosley came to mind, but surely with either, it hadn't been an overnight thing. Alan would have shown his disagreements. He would not have stayed on the Central Committee, but he had. In any case, his message clearly showed that he had remained a revolutionary, and it had been against what he had been doing.

That, then, must rule out being paid to do so. Looking around the room, it was obvious that Alan may not have lived in abject poverty, but neither did he live in opulence. The man I had known was not interested in material wealth. His clothes were high street, his social life limited, and his car a museum piece, so it couldn't have been for money.

Again, then, it came down to forcing him. How would they have done that? Could they have had a hold on him? That was surely the only thing it could be. Alan had done something wrong, and they had blackmailed him into it. But what the hell could it have been? Alan's idea of a wild time was flicking through Marx's *Kapital*.

However, Alan's admission to having been working for MI5 brought me back to believing it, and so another possibility arose as to why he might be looking up such information, and that was how it could be used to help stop it from occurring.

Every second brought a new idea, so without any firm conclusions, I decided to try Abby Nite again, and again got her out-of-office reply. Did that woman ever work? What the hell was the police force doing? I mean, OK, there had been a spate of police stations being burned down, but should that stop WPC Nite doing what she was paid for? After all, there were plenty still standing.

Still, even that didn't dampen my spirit. I was still feeling chuffed with myself for my successes with Alan's research. Just call me Philip Marvellous Marlowe. I may lack his shoulders but I was getting the hang of this investigating game. OK, it was true that I wasn't certain I had actually found anything. So he had been looking up how the ruling class had crushed revolutions— wasn't that pretty understandable in the circumstances? However, a popping thought was making me think that it did, indeed, mean something more.

So I decided to do a follow-up on the work that the old man and I had been doing. We had looked at what politically was going on in the world then and what might have interested him in the security services but nothing about the people themselves. Conducting an article search on surveillance of protest groups led me to the old-style newspaper articles from the *Guardian*, the *Daily Telegraph*, the *Independent*, the *Daily Mail*, and the *Times*. These supplied a wedge of information. And, I had to admit, a great deal of nostalgia as I veered off and got sidetracked on totally superficial matters I had long forgotten. Too much time was spent on *Coronation Street*. I called on my personal reserve of revolutionary discipline and got back to the task at hand, but it was heavy going understanding it.

There appeared to be a labyrinth of different departments that dealt with snooping on people exercising their democratic right of protest. At a time— well, when is there ever not a time—when the government was obsessed with efficiency and bureaucracy, it was shocking just how many there were of them. Scotland Yard had its own, called CO11; then there was the National Extremism Tactical Coordination Unit, who I gathered kept my world of academia under surveillance. Both were somehow linked with the National Domestic Extremism Team. So that alone was NDET, NETCU, and CO11, but then there was also the NPOIU and TAM who sent officers undercover. It reminded me of us Trots—split and merge, split and merge.

And another thing, this lot was as keen on initials as our coalition governments, and I was beginning to wonder if there had been any coppers actually on the streets, doing such mundane things as catching burglars. Surprisingly, a lot of it seemed to be aimed at the eco-warriors. I had expected it to be all about the Islamic terrorists, but it appeared that the ruling class was more worried about veggies chaining themselves to butchers' chopping blocks than about buses being blown up. It all seemed to have nothing to do with us. We tended to be meat eaters, one and all. But I perhaps scoffed too much; after all, if the ruling class was that worried about them, then they were doing something right.

There was also mention of the anti-capitalist/anti-globalisation demos which we were part of, but then we usually took the role of getting people on them rather than secret plans to wreck a building. Flyposting, not rioting, was more our style, more into mass action than smashing things up.

Noticeably, the later articles appeared to be concerned with these undercover officers sleeping with people in the movement. The whole issue of consent was raised that if the person who the woman who had agreed to have sex with wasn't actually the person they said they were had they indeed consented? Of course the tabloids just enjoyed the salacious gossip with the women variously described as blondes or brunettes. Seems hair colour was a key issue here.

I tried MI5 and got SIS. SIS? Previously, I thought that was a female sibling, but I was informed that it was the Secret Intelligence Service. I wasn't sure whether that was MI5 or that MI5 was a part of it, or it was part of MI5. Then there was Special Branch, which had apparently merged with the Met Police Anti-Terrorist Branch. Then there were the SO12 and SO13 and SO15. It was this gang who did the spook work on the terrorists. Well, someone in the security services was at least looking into people who did horrid things. As for who was GCHQ in relation to the others, I could only guess;

something to do with bugging people and intercepting communications. I know that some time back, they had launched a variety of cyber attacks on the movement but hadn't had much success, in part, because our geeks were better than their geeks.

The articles were interesting but didn't get me far. Too much on the cost of the operations and the morality of the sexual politics, and it all seemed more concerned with police constables in protest movements rather than treacherous members of the organisations themselves, so I saw no help here. Another dead end.

So with my inspiration lying dormant, I tried Abby Nite once more before I left. To my utter shock, a chirpy woman straight from the school of call centres answered. "Abby Nite, National Police Information Centre, Library, and Archive. How may I help you?"

That took me aback. I had not expected her to answer. Now what?

"Good afternoon…er…evening. My name is Peter Kalder. I…er…am the executor for Alan Wiltshire's estate. I…er work for Wells Publishers, and we…er…want to do a final collection of his writings online, and I am just… following up his lines of research, and I know he contacted you."

That sounded *so* lame. It was so flimsy a lie that it had the thickness of a butterfly's membrane. I blushed with how awful it was. Kalder, really, was that the best you could do?

But to my surprise, she replied. "Sure. I read about his death on the net. My condolences." She seemed totally unruffled and calm. "Looking on the screen, I can see that he did contact us on a number of occasions. I can simply send you the list of publications and articles he requested, or if you want, the complete copies."

"What?" I asked, totally dumb struck. I had been expecting a denial or evasion and at best had hoped that I might have learnt something from that. I had been ready to infer any hesitation or motioning to a spy next door listening in or a tape recording to start, one of those large, reel-to-reel ones which became obsolete in the 1950s. You know, standard Harry Palmer stuff. I had *not* expected a polite agreement to send me everything he had asked for.

She sounded amused. "You do know what kind of establishment we are, don't you, Mr Kalder?"

"Er, no, all my enquiries were blocked."

I felt a smile at the other end of the line; though not being linked visually, she could have been flipping a finger for all I knew. "I am sorry about that, Mr Kalder; we have had a problem with security interruptions, although we hope to rectify that in a few days."

I took "security interruptions" to mean hacking.

"We are the national archive of magazines, newspapers, journals, and books related to the subject of policing and criminology," she continued. "We are a public service; think of us as a library. Everything is open access here."

"It has been pretty hard to get hold of you," I said, rather sourly.

It didn't rattle her, and her sweetness stayed. "I apologise for that, Mr Kalder. I am sorry for any inconvenience caused. But now that you have reached me, how can I help you? If we have it, then we can supply it. Of course," she laughed, "all the state secrets are somewhere else. We're not GCHQ!"

I pretended to laugh, too, whilst thinking, so what the hell *was* GCHQ? And what the dickens was the police force doing having a library? I bet their crime-fiction section was a wow. Actually, I was almost tempted to ask if they had my book in stock.

"Of course there are charges," she said, returning to her cool professionalism.

"Eh?" I said dumbly.

Could I hear her smile returning? (I had decided to keep it to voice-only as I figured the facial bruising might put her off, but it did make communications a little more difficult.) "I'm afraid that with the economy as it is, we are forced to charge for our services."

Cuts, hey, what a bummer.

I asked her how much it was for everything Alan had received and nearly choked at the cost. Now I knew why they had a library. Christ Almighty, they could fund an entire divisional police force on that. Meekly, I asked if they took my credit card. She confirmed that my bank was still deemed as solvent, so they would. She took the amount. I was getting really financially screwed now. How I was going to eat next week was fast becoming a more important question than who had decided to declare war on the Wiltshires.

After I stated that the terminal for them to be sent to would be Alan's, she sent them all over. She had been so blissfully uninterested in why I might really want them, she did not even bother to ask why they were to be sent to the very same computer she had previously already sent them to. It did make me wonder what great secret they might contain, if all you had to do to get them was to ring and cough up the dosh.

I got them instantly. She sweetly wished me a good day and hung up. It struck me that she had been a great deal more forthcoming than Jackie. Ah, the great British bobby.

There were 369 in total. Many were extracts from books, theses, periodicals, visuals, and online sites. There were also twenty-three complete police and investigation magazines. Just looking at the titles alone made me wince; there was no way I was going to wade through this lot. I instructed the computer to search them for a common thread, although even I could guess pretty much what it would be, and that was not the cinematography of Stephen Spielberg. The computer agreed with me, and top of the list of ten options was "strategies for dealing with civil unrest". Discussing our relationship with other parties in the councils, my ear. No, they were—in the words of a song of long ago—*Talkin' Bout A Revolution*.

CHAPTER TEN
The Holy Family

Leaving Alan's house, I went straight to his funeral. Or to be more precise, I went to the "post-cremation gathering" that had been arranged. For some reason, despite it being a select group, I had been invited. Would Alan himself actually be mentioned at his own remembrance ceremony, I wondered? Perhaps a nostalgic memory of his foibles or a witty story superficially appearing to throw light on his weaknesses that would in the punch line show him in a positive glow. Or would the party powerful use it to flag up the latest set of perspectives?

By the time I arrived at the party centre, it was early evening. The pleasant spring air retained some if its daytime glow, but there was just a hint of chill floating within it. I had missed—again—my swimming, and again I had missed lunch. My daily routine had gone to pot because of all this nonsense. But then, whilst my heart and stomach shared a distinct feeling of emptiness, missing my familiar life, I knew that I needed to be here.

I was let in and shown to a room, which according to a sign, said it had been the visitors' lounge in the building's previous incarnation. A generous murmuring of conversations could be heard, which indicated that there was a good turnout. No surprise there; Alan was a big figure in the party. That, and no comrade ever refused a free drink. Entering it, I pondered how many visitors the previous occupiers usually entertained, as it was a good-sized room, which on first glance easily took the hundred or so people who were there now.

There had been an attempt to match the mood with huge red flags draped over the walls, which hung alongside posters dating back throughout Alan's life.

They were all here: CND marches, antiwar demos, anti-Nazi protests, uprisings in the Middle East, and such. Along one side of the room, a projection showed clips of the history of the period interlaced with clips of Alan in action and photographs of what passed for his private life. Basically that consisted of a few of his wife Anisha, his son Stuart, plus Yasmin and Dave. Despite all the rousing images of class conflict, I couldn't help thinking that the fact that the pictures of his family were so few and far between made it a wee bit sad.

Despite the best efforts of, I presume, Simon Peary to turn this room of corporate hospitality into something more appropriate (and to be frank I wasn't sure what that was), it still looked like a place where you'd entertain sales reps with soggy sandwiches. The truly ghastly orange armchairs and sofas and spectacularly naff carpet probably made any attempt to change the commercial vibe to anything else as futile. Sometimes décor could not be reformed; it took a revolution. A few red flags wouldn't change this room, especially as they clashed so hideously with the furnishings.

I hesitated to call it a wake, as that conjured up images of wild and big-hearted Irish drink-ups toasting a departed uncle or work buddy. This was more like an awkward birthday party for someone you barely knew, probably back in the 1970s. Put it this way, I was surprised not to see cheese and pineapples on sticks. We Trotskyists might have a better world outlook than religion, but I had to say that this confirmed my view that religions did the biggie celebrations of partnerships, births, and deaths a whole deal better. Despite having been a nonbeliever for most of my long life, I did always feel that secular weddings, baby-naming ceremonies, and deaths were well-meaning, but often, somehow, they came over as being artificial and even sometimes embarrassing. Notwithstanding the fact that I believed them all based on fiction, such occasions in a synagogue, mosque, temple, or church somehow seemed more substantial. Paradoxical, I know, but I guess they just had thousands of years more practice than us. It wasn't the most important thing in the world. Even the prime minister hadn't thrown the fact that we were crap at funerals at us. Maybe he was missing a trick; he should use his Etonian tones to cross the airwaves, saying that we extremists could not be trusted with your dead loved ones.

The sense that I had wandered into a TV drama from the era of early 2-D colour television was reinforced by the sight of Simon Peary circulating with a tray of drinks and crisps. It was an amusing sight—the man in charge of the national office of the party playing waiter. I would imagine he'd be quite good at gliding in and out with his usual quiet efficiency. All charm and snacks. I did smile, though; it looked strange to see him out of his denim uniform and dodgy seventies shirts and instead in a cheap black suit and white shirt. His only concession to his standard, laid-back attitude to fashion was that he wore no tie.

I recognised the majority of the guests as being the representatives of the great and good of the party. I could see that most of the Central Committee was present and looking faintly uncomfortable spending an evening sipping wine and tasting nibbles rather than rousing the masses. Michael Hughes was in deep conversation with George Armstrong. So the old man had made one of his rare forays out of his house. Elsewhere, I could see Kye Toulson, who had de-pinked himself from his overheated appearance at the demonstration and was down to normal size. Looking around, I could see no sign of Stuart or Anisha. I was pretty damned sure that he would have attended his father's funeral and would have wanted to stay in London to find out about his son's murder.

To my surprise, also present was our neighbourhood red copper. In the far corner, Detective Victoria Cole was in deep conversation with a very short man in bleached combat trousers. He kept nervously stroking his atrocious, back-combed, dyed, green hair, seemingly very ill at ease. Why, I could only guess: shame at such shocking hair, boredom at listening to Cole, or grief at being here. From his attire—and shortness—I assumed that he wasn't a colleague of hers, but then, who knew nowadays? And then again, what the hell was Cole herself doing here?

Mingling amongst them, making small talk with some, meeting puzzled looks by a few others, and ignored by most, I helped myself to some rolls and a couple of surprisingly good glasses of red wine. But no, there was no cheese on sticks. I did find out that Stuart and Anisha had attended the small private cremation and had briefly been here, but not being party people, had felt no desire to stay longer than an hour. One comrade told me it was because Stuart was exhausted from both the emotional drain of losing his father, his son, and daughter-in-law in the space of a few days and the long journey down from Scotland. These sounded perfectly sensible reasons, and I thought to myself that it was also quite possibly that he couldn't bear the sight of this carpet for too long. Its burgundy background and blue hexagons was obscene. This place didn't so much need an interior designer as a demolition expert.

I had seen Marie as soon as I came in, but she was talking with obvious emotion to people I did not recognise. Looking at her across the room, I could see that there were large red rings around her eyes, and her skin looked grey. It did not require a degree in grief counselling to know that she was extremely upset. It was confirmation that I was right to come here.

I took yet another roll. Well, I figured this investigation was costing me such a fortune that who knows how much longer I could afford to buy food, so why not stock up here. I suppressed a chuckle—and I call this an investigation? I really had read too many detective novels. In them there was always a logical analysis of the situation and weighing the facts against conjecture; whereas, I was flailing around and eating ham and pickle rolls.

Music was playing in the background, Mozart I think, although I couldn't be sure, as classical music wasn't my forte. The conversations in the room bobbled under and over it with the occasional jarring roar of laughter from a bearded guy in the centre of the room. It all made for an odd symphony of chitchat and clipped jargon set against a horn section.

Drifting along to the odd symphony, I cozied over to a table at the far wall which had a display of all the books Alan had had a hand in writing. Shamelessly, I immediately looked for *A Rebel's Guide to Britain's Trades Unions* which we had written together. Finding it next to his biography of Emile Zola, I picked it up and flicked through the pages. Remembering when we had written it together made me smile, although in all honesty my thoughts were rather more on Caroline and Lisa than on Alan. I seemed to recall Lisa nursing a broken arm at the time because she had fallen out of a tree. Yes, that was right; this was bang in the middle of her obsession for climbing those blasted trees. My trip down memory lane was interrupted by a finger tapping the pamphlet.

A South London accent gave me a snap review. "Good book, hasn't dated at all."

I looked around and saw Olivia Harrison; ah, our young militant from the power workers' union and of course one of the little group of seven Alan had been so much a part of. She was in a slim-fit, green trouser suit, with her hair looking very fashion-shoot in style. Her eyes caught my attention—they looked happy and perfectly normal. No grief there, then.

"When I first joined the party," she continued, "my branch secretary said I should read the *Communist Manifesto*, Elizabeth Gaskell's *North and South*, and your pamphlet. He said that they would give me the perfect introduction to Socialism."

Obviously, she knew how to get in *my* good books; although, whilst the first two were unarguably excellent books, it was a strange combination. Still, I couldn't help feeling rather chuffed being in such exalted company.

Harrison wore a little makeup, and I could smell a slight touch of Chanel. So that wasn't rationed, then. I took a step back as I felt rather awkward being so close and saw that she was wearing apple-green shoes. Evidently, she had listened to the call to make this a positive occasion. I felt very old-fashioned in black.

I smiled. "Thanks, although I think you might be rather flattering me. It's probably rather staid now. Let's face it, when it was written, the world was a different place. That makes it a whole different platform to view the past, present, and future." I laughed nervously. "I sound like the Shangri-Las."

She gave me a puzzled look.

I explained that they were a girl-group (could we say girl-group nowadays?) from the 1960s and that they had had a hit called *Past, Present and Future*. Her puzzlement remained.

"Sang *Leader of the Pack*?" Feeling rather a chump, I gave up and changed the subject to the cremation. She replied that she hadn't gone, although she had been on the Hyde Park march; indeed, she informed me with just a touch of pride that she had been one of the speakers. I asked her what she had thought of the occasion. She had been very impressed, especially with Marie's and Jackie's speeches, but felt that she had been nowhere as good because of suffering from terrible nerves that always led to her stammering her way through public speaking.

I took a sip from my diminishing glass and asked, "Were you surprised how explicitly she had outlined the current position concerning us and Parliament?"

In turn, she took a swig of her half pint (ah, the link between British Socialism and booze—that could be a good basis for a book). "In what way?" she asked, retaining the good humour she had brought to me.

She knew full well what I had meant, but I played along. "I mean that we're at the time where the country could no longer continue with two conflicting forms of government and that one has to win out. Wouldn't you say, comrade, that is a direct call for revolution?"

My analysis did not faze her at all. Smiling, she agreed. "Yeah, did sound like that, didn't it. Well, it comes as no surprise, does it? We've always said that the NWC and Parliament had conflicting class interests. Things can't go on like that forever, so of course there's going to be a power struggle."

Indeed. But we could be in this same position for years. This was no totalitarian regime that holds fast until the last minute and then suddenly crumbles and crashes to the ground in a matter of days.

"True," I replied, studying her reaction. "But as the old man said when the NWC was first formed, we would be entering a period that could last for a long time with both bodies positioning for power. This flux would alternate between struggles in the arenas of industrial, political, and physical confrontation and could last years, decades, even."

She smiled gently. "I remember he talked of nothing else."

I was surprised. "You were a member then? I thought you were a newly… er…"

Another chuckle moved up her body. "A newly-joined?" It found its way out of her mouth, and, laughing, she remarked, "I heard you were a cynic."

I didn't ask from whom she had heard this, but instead, as so many of us Lefties do, I muttered a mangled quote, in this case from Italian Marxist Antonio Gramsci, about pessimism of the intelligence and optimism of the will.

She replied with an apt reply from the same man. What I noted was that it didn't reflect any possibility of her writing the *Great Big Book of Bolshie Quotes* but did show that she was perfectly relaxed about what Jackie had said. It wasn't that I or the other thousands who had heard Jackie speak were necessarily against what she had said or even had not known that we would have to face this situation one day, but we had all been astounded at the fact that she appeared to be arguing that the time was *now*. Harrison, however, was coolly discussing it like you might when someone suggests another round of drinks at the bar. It was as if she had expected Jackie to have said that. But why was she being so coy about it all? She *had* expected it. I would take a guess that it had been the subject of the meetings of the little subcommittee of Bale, Hughes, Williams, Ali, Toulson, Alan, and her good self.

The net gossip that Alan Wiltshire had been forming a faction had stuck in my mind. There had been conflicting rumours concerning this faction. Discarding ones involving aliens or Elvis, it boiled down to basically two. Both had the basis that the members of this highly secretive faction were unhappy with the direction the party was taking, but from there, two completely different accounts were doing the rounds. One said they thought that the party was planning to overthrow Parliament in a coup d'état, and they had formed to oppose it. The other was diametrically opposite, believing that the party was being far too timid and should start the insurgency now.

From what I had heard Jackie say, I wouldn't have used the word "timid." Of course, I might be getting the wrong end of the stick, and I was getting far too overexcited, drunk on the long-suppressed feelings. It might have just been rhetoric, and maybe I had misunderstood her. If so, it wasn't just me, because the huge media storm that had erupted appeared to show that the world at large took her literally. It had been the first item on every news show.

Comrade Harrison here might be taking it in her stride, but whilst I had been at Alan's deliberating about what I had learnt and what to do now, I had surfed the news. Our much-loved and cherished PM had exploded with a fury that was probably usually only aimed at a maid losing his best shirt or the MCC losing a series against Australia. (Loved the game of bat and ball, did our PM: perhaps that was where the coalition got its love of initials—cricket).

The coalition, he had said, was negotiating the crisis. This was no time for extremism. His beloved phrases were familiar, but the tone was more strident than usual. And he had been on every conceivable programme; I was amazed not to find old reruns of *The Simpsons* being spliced with a cartoon PM emerging from under a table and harking on about the middle way.

I asked Harrison what she thought of the prime minister's reaction. "What did you make of his reference to military force?"

Maybe wanting to avoid getting too many laughter lines in her smooth skin, she dropped the smile, but tellingly, she was neither surprised nor overly worried. "Fairly predictable, I would have thought. As Michael said at the rally, the army is promising that it will remain neutral."

"If we can believe that," I muttered. "Let's not forget that it wasn't so long ago that there were tanks in most of the cities, with a good few more standing by at the ready. I remember the Angel; Islington having what they called a light tank (though it looked heavy enough to me) parked by the tube. And it wasn't there to flog the evening paper!"

"True," she conceded, the smile returning after such a brief time away, but added that times had changed.

As Schubert (but then, for all I knew, it was sherbet) replaced Mozart, we chatted about what was the next step for the movement. She appeared to be far better informed than me about events in the councils, but that I guess was to be expected. She, like me, though, was ambiguous in her predictions. Mine at least were from ignorance.

The conversation was guided back to other matters as she pleasantly asked what my personal history was. It was the general small talk you made at soirées, when you bumped into someone you had either never met or met just the once. Our first time had not been an auspicious start to a lifelong friendship, with the backdrop of the St Paul's explosion and a distinct feeling of antagonism she had given off. Recalling that encounter, she briefly chatted about how historically St Paul's had been a place of protest for London radicals, before apologising for her mood when we had met.

I lied and said I hadn't noticed (though her frostiness could have frozen Hades). Nonetheless, she still gave me an apology with excuses to accompany it. She had been, she said, under a great deal of pressure following the deaths in the hospital in Manchester which were still being blamed on the strike by the power workers. It sounded plausible enough, so I told her there was nothing to apologise for. After doing so several times, she nodded and changed the subject.

She appeared a sound-enough person and obviously a very capable comrade. Talking to her, I picked up bits and pieces of info about her private life. She was, in fact, in her thirties (I had put her as being younger, ancient that I am). She had been a member for nine years and had joined when she was living in some London suburb. Joking that whatever happened, she just hoped that her kids' nursery scabbed, as it would play havoc with her union work. From which I also learnt that she had a pair of four-year-old twins.

She asked if I had any children. Obviously she didn't know about Lisa so my answer had rather embarrassed her. She was saved from what she clearly found an uncomfortable situation when Youssef Ali strolled up and with a rather too fraternal arm around her waist, suggested that maybe it was time to go. Jumping far and long in the direction of the wrong conclusion, I wondered if this was a hint of romance before remembering that he had a boyfriend.

I watched them go and turned my attention to people watching. Jackie was talking with two blokes I did not recognise, although from their rapt silence and her volley of words and speed of lips, a better description would be that she was talking *at* them. Marie was still chatting, so I contented myself with keeping an eye on her whilst scanning the books. I played the hindsight game by reading excerpts concerning possible revolution in Britain and assessing how accurate they had been. Then after five minutes, I saw Marie was free. I pounced. Hugging warmly, I got several kisses on my cheek as we locked into each other.

"Steady, Marie. Ashok is a good friend of mine, and in any case I don't think canoodling at a funeral is quite the done thing," I joked feebly.

She laughed. "Oh, he had to go off to do some stuff, so he won't care. He'd love me to have an affair; it might give him some deserved peace." A guffaw started to evolve from the laughing, but she suppressed it by gulping it down. It hadn't been *that* funny; whatever I personally believed, according to Lisa, I was rarely rib-tickling funny. Her amusement was more of a welcome release from tension than from my comic timing.

"Anyway, he could meet you afterwards to chat about the fan take-over of the Arsenal." She pulled away and let me go. "He asked me, now that you appear to be coming out your shell, whether you wanted to go to a pub and watch the game tomorrow?"

"Surely you must know that Jackie has put me back in it. My husk is back surrounding me, so thank him, but no thanks."

It was true; Jackie had forced me out of my self-inflicted confinement, but I was far from desiring sessions of footy and lager, even with such amiable company as Ashok.

She gave me her best mumsy look. "I heard she had told you to stop looking into…er…Alan's situation. You must be pleased about that. You weren't that happy to be given the task in the first place, so it must be a relief to have lost it."

"Of course," I fibbed. "I can get back to my routine."

Changing the subject seemed quite appropriate, so I guided her into talking about her speech which I had heard had been deeply moving and I regretted missing. She modestly protested and downplayed it, saying merely that she had talked about what they had been like as people.

"Which I think was totally appropriate," I commented, whilst noticing that my glass was empty.

She sniffed back a slight wetness around the eyes whilst I poured out another drink and offered her one, which she accepted. Where did they get this alcohol? I asked myself. Had we liberated it from somewhere?

She spoke lovingly of Yasmin, who she called a beautiful person inside and out, and whom she had grown very fond of. I feared more than just a slight wetness in her cornea when she spoke of Dave. She appeared to be trying to use all her strength to hold back more tears.

"You had become very close to Dave, hadn't you?" I asked softly.

She nodded, not trusting herself to speak.

I tried not to sound too interested in the matter because I did not want her thinking that I was still playing detective. "He must have been in a right state when you went around there. It hadn't been too long since he had found Alan, and, of course, I know how much Alan meant to him."

She shook her head, remembering it and describing how Dave had seemed so stunned. There were no hysterics. He was almost emotionless and had what she described as a cold, fixed look to his face.

"Shock can do that," I said, feeling free to play the medical professional about such profound matters. I had a PhD in platitudes.

"He was just so cold, Pete. Ice-like. And yet, he wanted to talk about the most irrelevant of things. He just let forth with a stream of nonsense. He just would not stop talking."

I moved the gears up in my nonchalance saloon. I wanted to look as cool and casual as a Sunday morning golfer in his blue V-neck driving along to the country club with a Tory Voter and Real Ale Drinker sticker on the rear windscreen. "It must have been awful. Still, Marie, you were the prefect person to be there. You had a warm relationship with him." I slipped it into fourth. "So what was he saying?"

"He kept asking me what I thought about Alan, both as a man and as a party member. I guess he'd seen the recording and wanted to know what I thought about it." Her voice dropped in volume, and it was as if she was talking to herself. "Although it was strange that he didn't ask me whether it was genuine or not. He seemed to immediately accept that it was true."

She paused and looking around, asked me if I minded us sitting, as it had been a long day. Finding it a good idea, I got us two chairs and a corner. I didn't push but waited for her to continue.

Her voice was now not much more than a sigh. "He kept wanting to know how he had been when he stayed with us—Mum and Dad and me—after Ruth had left. I told him that I was just a girl back then and could barely remember it, but he still wanted to know. He was quite persistent. I suppose he just wanted to fill in the holes of history of his family, paint in the background."

As one who loved strangling, elongating, and basically murdering a metaphor, I was enjoying what Marie was doing to hers.

"It was difficult to know what to tell him," she continued, leaning forwards as if she didn't want anyone else to hear. "I mean, you don't want to talk ill of the dead, do you? Especially to a relative. But like I said, he was so insistent, so I told him the truth or at least what I did remember—Alan was a total emotional mess when they left him."

A heavy pause, full of meaning, followed. Touching my knee with her hand, she looked into my face with an expression that said that I, of all people, should be able to understand what it was like to lose a partner and a child. Not knowing quite what else to do, I tilted my head thoughtfully and hoped that she would return to the subject of Alan. Empathy over, she did.

"He might have been a cold fish to many, but he loved those two. His whole meaning ended when they walked out on him. Publically, his persona might have been one of dominance and control, but Ruth was the real strength in that relationship; she was the real engine. And, of course, in his own dysfunctional way, he loved Stuart. Whatever else, the birth of his son was one of the best things that had happened to him. Ruth taking him all but destroyed Alan. He took to drinking, big time!"

By now my laid-backness was almost horizontal. "Really?"

"Oh, yes," she asserted. "Now, Dad was one who liked a regular tipple, but he couldn't keep up with him. Virtually every night he would return, smashed out of his brain. I think that's why it sticks in my memory, the smell of beer wafting around the place."

I nodded and tried to mix in an expression of more-tea-vicar-sympathy with casualness. The hope was that it was effective and didn't just make me look constipated. "I'm sure Dave wanted to know everything about his grandfather."

She didn't ask me if I had an upset stomach and went on talking, so I could presume that it was having the desired effect. "I remember my parents talking downstairs—me and my sister would sit on the stairs listening in—about how Alan seemed to have given up and was doing the bare minimum of party work."

In my head I was trying to see where this got me. Obviously, both from the exhaustion of work and party activities, not to mention her obvious distress, Marie hadn't noted the blindingly obvious thing that at the very time Alan was so emotionally devastated, he also started to work for MI5. But where was the link?

When I had lost Caroline and Lisa, I had fallen apart. Caroline had been my mainstay, too, and Lisa had been central to my life. Actually, it was less falling apart and more clawed asunder. I had smashed up my home and cut myself to ribbons with a knife. But I had not rung up Special Branch and asked to go on the payroll. I went into therapy, not into spy school.

"I told Dave that Alan had a rough time but got through it. It was obviously important to him, as he just wanted to dwell on it."

This was risking alerting Marie to why I was so interested in the matter, but I wanted to know about this. I took a sip of wine and tried a sociable look of someone shooting the breeze. "How?"

Marie followed my lead and took a sip, or more precisely a ruddy great gulp, and went into full flow. Grief, not to mention the wine, was loosening her tongue. "Pete, he asked me all sorts of questions about it. Why, for example, had she had left him, which as I told him, I had no idea. Alan wasn't going to tell me, a kid, why his partner had dumped him, was he? He asked me how long he had stayed with us, and I could only guess at that, and I'd put it about ten to twelve months.

"He also asked if I remembered Alan being with someone called Jelena Jacobs. Which I thought was a strange question, but in actual fact I did vaguely remember someone he met a few months after he had moved in. I had reassured him that, just because he had started going out with this woman, it didn't mean that Alan didn't feel loss; he did. Alan was devastated. I would find him crying in the kitchen or hear him in the bathroom, sobbing; he just wanted to find love and consolation. That sometimes happens, doesn't it, Pete? It's the classic rebound."

"Absolutely."

"He just kept asking me questions. I told him that she was just a fling. I didn't mean to be sexist, but she was just someone who made Alan feel good about himself and soothed his broken ego."

"So who was this *Jelena*?" I asked offhandedly, now in award-winning acting mode. Me, interested in all this—nah, what makes you think that? Marie believed it, in any case. She carried on being forthright in her recollection.

"Jelena Jacobs. He asked me all about her."

Marie was keen to let me know again that she had reassured him. "I said that he should not think she was the reason for his grandmother leaving Alan; I made it quite clear that Jelena came after the split. Not that it lasted too long. I think Alan and Jelena separated not long after he moved out of our place." She cradled her glass, and a thoughtful smile spread across her face. "I'd forgotten all about JJ; that's what me and my sister called her, JJ. We thought she was great. As young girls we lapped up visits from a pretty young woman who could teach us all about makeup and clothes. Mum wasn't too keen on those things."

I was now oblivious to anything or anyone in the room. For all I knew or cared, Kye Toulson could now be dressed as a belly dancer and performing erotic dancing with a plastic snake. I was focussed solely on what Marie was saying.

Straining every muscle I had to keep cool and in control, I encouraged her to carry on.

"So what was this JJ like?"

"Oh, like I said, she was an attractive woman, younger than Alan. Slim as anything. She had bright red hair cut into a bob. We loved playing with it. We spent hours doing her hair and trying to talk to her. She was from the same part of the world as George, the Northeast, Sunderland, I think. For months we finished every sentence with 'pet.' She had striking eyes, if I remember correctly which she emphasised with heavy eye-line—"

"White? Black?" I asked.

"White. She had lovely porcelain skin. Perfect, apart, that is, from a diagonal scar above her left eyebrow, but even that made her just look interesting. I think I might have had a crush on her for a while. You know, schoolgirl-type adoration. I had completely forgotten about her until Dave reminded me." Marie's tone changed from fond reminiscing to a more serious and concerned one. "Pete, it was obvious to me that Dave was severely traumatised by finding Alan because he was just obsessing over this woman from decades ago. I've seen this before. Actually, after the St Paul's Cathedral bombing, I met one young pregnant woman who talked excessively about having to get home to feed her dog."

She went on for some minutes about how trauma can affect people. After what I thought was an appropriate time, I steered her back to Dave as much as I dared but didn't get much else. She talked a lot but said very little, not adding much to what she had already told me. Sitting here, I did feel a touch like a fraud. She was someone who cared a great deal for me, and I was just using that to get information.

After I had decided that a great way to cope with emotional pain was to smash to smithereens the family home, it had been she and Ashok who had rallied my friends to tidy, repair, and reassemble, whilst I had my stay in hospital, trying to do the same for my brain. And even whilst I was doing that, I was pretty sure that she was monitoring my progress and doing what she could to help.

She looked like she needed help right this minute. Standing in front of me, she looked pretty strung out. She was, quite simply, exhausted. Emotionally, mentally, and physically, she was near to hitting that wall that we all had learnt to talk about from our American brothers and sisters. I, however, couldn't wait to leave.

After what I believed to be a polite interval, I made my excuses and said that I needed to do something. The best thing I could think of was a blatant lie. "I think I'll write something on the party blog about my experiences working with Alan; the comrades might like that."

Guilt ran through me as she gushed enthusiasm and encouragement and insisted that I go off right now and do it. I got up, and putting down my glass, I asked for the password to the national office computers.

With a loving smile, she beamed. "That's great. I agree. Get cracking straightaway. Superb idea. This week it's 'KayBar.' Pete, this is such good news to hear you're back. I love your writing; it would be so cool to see it again."

After disentangling myself from Marie's embrace, promising to give Ashok a ring, and sending my love to her not-so-young-now kids, I left the room to its buzzing conversations which had increased in volume since I had arrived. No doubt that was due to my sparkling presence.

I searched around for somewhere quiet and with a working computer. After ten minutes or so of wandering around, feeling nauseous at the sight of so much gross office furniture, and apologising for interrupting a handful of comrades working, I eventually found a small office.

I logged on. Marie might explain away Dave's preoccupation with ancient family history as a product of shock, but she was just too knackered to ask the question: How the hell did Dave know this woman's name? His own father was just a child at the time, and yet he knew both her name and that Marie would have met her. Why? Sure, there might be a wholly innocent explanation, but for me, Dave knew because Alan had told him.

If that was the case, then the second and third questions would have been to ask when he might have passed it on and, indeed, why? I couldn't envisage the small talk between grandfather and grandson involving a quick rundown of women the former had shagged. When might that happen? After tea and just before the news? Would it have included one-night stands or quick gropes or only meaningful relationships? I might be Olympian in jumping to conclusions, but my guess was that Alan had told him because it was important. I had no idea why, but obviously Alan had thought it vital to tell Dave about a fleeting affair that had ended years before he was born. Dave understood that, or, indeed, even knew why it was important; that was why he had questioned Marie about this Jelena. Because Marie was too tied up with party activity and paralyzed by the news of Alan, it had not crossed her mind to ask why Dave was so interested in a past fling.

And I figured that if I was taking record-breaking leaps, then go for the long one and guess when that might be. It could have been any time, on any day, in any year. Except that the one thing amongst many that had always bothered me about Alan's death was that, if it was suicide, why was his only good-bye message to the party and not to the human being he loved most on this planet?

Contrary to the right-wing mass media depiction of us, we were not agitational automatons, and Alan would not have thought solely about the movement in his final moments on this mortal coil. He would have left something for Dave. There had to have been a recorded good-bye for his grandson. I was pretty sure that Jackie had not seen it, as otherwise she would have mentioned it, but Dave, I bet, had. He had watched it and thought about it. He had decided on what he was going to do. That was why there had been a thirty-minute delay in calling Jackie. Whatever he had seen and been told about, I bet it had included a mention of Jelena Jacobs. That was why Dave had questioned Marie about her.

And that made me very interested in finding more about Ms Jelena Jacobs. The party membership files for the years 2009, 2010, and 2011 were easy to find. Recruiting all these IT workers had made our filing systems a whole lot better. I entered her name. In the country at large, it was quite possible there was a multitude of Jelena Jacobs; in the population of the party during those years, it was doubtful that there was more than one. And there she was.

Jelena Jacobs, 18 Foot Yard. E8.
Central Hackney Branch.
D.O.B.: 03/05/81. Age 29. Female.
Occupation: Play Worker. Place of Work: Butterfly Play Centre.
Foot Yard. E8 2PB
Union: UNISON. No Union Position held.

I looked at her subscriptions from a bank long since gone belly-up and whistled. The party had levels for the subs which were dependent on your wage. They were a guide only; no one could force you to pay them. No one did, either. And no one actually paid the full rate; no one at all. Except, that is, our budding Rosa Luxembourg here; she paid considerably over the full whack. Looking at that year's fund-raising campaign, she had also been extremely generous. She was a keen comrade, a very keen one, indeed. In my experience, play workers were paid peanuts, so subs like these must have been hard for her to meet.

I had also twigged her branch was the same as Alan's. Not that she had paid them for long: they started January 2010 and finished December the same year, so maybe not that keen. Or something had happened to her that year to make her lose her commitment.

A quick check told me that the Butterfly Play Centre had closed down over a decade ago, and Foot Yard had been demolished and replaced by a leisure centre. Getting nowhere there, I thought about my next course of action, when looking up, I noticed I had a visitor.

Victoria Cole was walking towards me in a tailored, charcoal-grey skirt suit, mid heels, and a buttoned-to-the-neck, canary-yellow shirt. I could see that her hair was slightly gelled to come away from her face. As she approached she gave me a slight smile.

"Good to see you, comrade. What are you doing in here?" she asked, unbuttoning her jacket and sitting smoothly on a chair.

"Nothing," I replied, glad that I had closed the screen and had started dictating a blog but fearing that my face resembled a man caught looking at a porno site. "I was just putting my thoughts down about working with Alan, about his little foibles, and such like." The type of stuff so missing in today's speeches, I thought to myself. "I'm surprised to see you here, Detective Cole; I didn't know that you knew him."

The smile stayed fixed. "Vic, call me Vic, and, no, I didn't, but then, I didn't think that you knew him that well. How long ago was that little pamphlet you wrote together? Ten, fifteen years ago?"

"Jackie invited me," I said, far too defensively.

"Ditto," she replied.

I hated people who said ditto in speech. They were the types to say, or indicated with their hands, punctuation marks, as if they were incapable of giving a nuance to their speech without them.

For a moment she just looked at me, weighing me up. To be honest I was 1.8 metres tall, and she was little over 1.6, but I felt as if she towered over me.

But I was damned if I was going to be intimidated by a cop, especially here at the national office.

"So how's the investigation going into Dave and Yasmin's murders?"

She sighed. "It's progressing, shall we say. We are tracing his movements since leaving Alan's house."

"And?"

"And, Peter, I cannot comment. They're ongoing investigations."

"Is that Detective Inspector Cole or Comrade Vic speaking?"

"Both, and it is Detective *Constable*. I can't speak on an active investigation, and I also recall that Jackie told you that you were no longer to be involved because she wanted all this to be at arm's length from the party. She told you to leave it to us. That's good advice, Pete."

Smug git.

Her right hand gently tapped the desk, as she got to why she had quite obviously been hunting for me. "I thought that you would want to know that your account of your movements on the day of David and Yasmin Wiltshire's murders have checked out. You have pretty solid alibis for the time window of their deaths. My DI, Gerard Martin, is satisfied that you had nothing to do with it, so all the forensic implications won't be looked into. I think you can breathe easy; you're in the clear, Pete."

I muttered halfheartedly, "Thank you. Any idea who it was?" I asked, keenly aware that we both knew it wasn't me, so the key bit of info was—who had killed him?

"Sorry, as I told you before, I can't talk about that."

"I thought we were all comrades together here?" I sneered.

The barb of her reply surprised me. "I am flattered that you consider me a comrade. I didn't think you did. I thought I was just the silly girl playing police officer playing at politics."

"I wouldn't put it in that sexist way, I…"

"Really? So you haven't patronised me, then…*comrade?*" Her voice was quiet, but it sliced through the air like a knife. Her eyes looked straight at me.

She wasn't going to browbeat me. "*If* I have patronised you," I replied, "it is not because of your gender but your job. *Detective*, you are a police officer, and any such person, and I use the term loosely, be they male, female, or one of your sniffer dogs, *is* playing at being a revolutionary!"

If I had expected her to fold, I was disappointed. "So, the fact that I'm a third of your age and have a vagina doesn't bother you?" she calmly replied, with a tone as loaded as a high-velocity rifle with a silencer.

"Actually, I have yet to reach my sixties, so I doubt that I could be triple your age!" Sniffing about my age wasn't the best reply to her comment. I sounded like an aging drag-queen, not a mature, experienced subversive. Still, it might be helping her with her maths.

She smiled. She was in control, and I felt like a snippy twerp.

Trying to get some semblance of self-respect, I adopted my explorative voice. "So, *Detective*, do you believe there is a link between Dave's death and his grandfather's?" That was better. "I hope that wasn't patronising?" No, I just ruined it again there.

Her tapping increased a little, and she kept her eyes straight at me. She was a cool one. Not a muscle moved on her face. Finally, she answered. "I think you are one hundred percent correct. It seems to me, and I should say that DI Martin agrees, that there has to be a link. David Wiltshire found out something about Alan's death, and that cost him his life."

I leant forwards in my chair, feeling like a kid who had just got top marks for a spelling test. "So have you any theories of what that might be?"

I was met by a cool smile. "You know I can't say."

Of course, she was on an active investigation, ya-de-ya! "Could it be an MI5 hit?"

My expectation was that her reply would be some more flannel about me *not* being involved and *her being* involved, so sorry, comrade, etc., etc., but…

"To be honest, I've thought about that." Her face actually started to move, and some emotion began to register. "At a guess, I think I would agree with you, but it strikes me as a strange move. For what possible reason would they kill them? What possible threat could Dave and Yasmin have been?

"And then there's the decision to put DI Gerard Martin in charge. You are not going to wear this, but Martin's a straight-down-the-line copper who believes that the law is there to protect everyone and not to just uphold the powerful." She held up a hand to stop me making any snide comment, but she needn't have because I was listening. I was very much listening.

"He really believes that. *Really* believes. If he finds a security link, then he will flush it out and do his best to bring whoever did this to justice. And, Pete, he is a good cop, a very good cop; if anyone can, he can. There are plenty in the police service who would bury anything, especially if there's a comrade involved, so—"

"Why," I interrupted, "not find someone more 'reliable?'"

"Exactly."

Maybe I was getting soft or had just seen too many of those movies where two people hate each other and end up big buddies, but though I still disliked her because she was still a police officer and most certainly not my best pal, I asked a question I thought I would never have asked. "Do you think it is possible that MI5 have agents in the party now?" I had asked it and to a serving police officer! "And the reason why they were murdered was perhaps to protect them?"

The tapping continued, and her eyes continued to look straight at me intensely. Her young face now looked very serious.

"Comrade, I think that there will be numerous agents from the gamut of security departments in the party. They are there to protect the state, and we are now the greatest threat to that state."

I agreed, and the bile in my gut was not down to her use of the collective personal pronoun.

"Any ideas who?" I asked, trying to sound unconcerned and not tackling her usage of "we."

"I'm just a copper, Pete, and one who's in the party, which you might not like, but my superiors like even less, so I would be the last person they would tell. But it could be anyone, a long-serving comrade who is admired and loved or one you would call a newly-join and seems as keen as mustard. It could be one who has been an active agent for decades or one who has been dormant until now. It could be anyone."

"So you are saying that it could be someone like me?"

She laughed, surprisingly loudly. As she did, she almost looked human.

"No, they would want someone active and high up, and you're neither!"

I just stared, feeling rather insulted, with any benevolent feelings having been purged. But was there any chance of her being intimidated by what I considered to be my fiercest look? Her? She laughed again but indicated that she was closing a delightful chat. My interview was up. Obviously her time was precious. She rose to her feet.

"Anyway, comrade, I thought you would want to hear that you have nothing to worry about any investigation into your involvement in Dave and Yasmin's deaths."

"Poor Yasmin," I thought to myself; she was fast becoming a mere addition. And Yasmin. *And Yasmin.* Not wanting to be too effusive, I nodded my thanks.

As she was leaving, she turned and said, "Stay in touch, comrade; stay in touch."

I watched her leave and then all but jumped on that computer. What the hell did Jelena Jacobs have to do with all this? I searched everything I could think of: electoral register, health service, electricity, gas, and the council records of both Hackney and Sunderland. The most I came up with was that in 2010 she paid her council tax and bills whilst she lived at Foot Yard by direct debit. The same applied to her TV licence. Nothing appeared for Sunderland either before or after a five-year band.

Sitting there in the far-too-bright office, I racked my brains about what to do next. With our IT nerds, you could hack into virtually anything from the national office. Well, obviously nothing like the police, MI5, or Spies-R-Us sites. I went through every London borough I could remember, trying the years 2005–2015 for any record of her paying her council tax. No joy. Then for the same time period for other areas of Northeast England. To my shame, I had to use an atlas to remind me of the places there. But apart from educating myself on places surrounding Durham and Stockton, I found nothing.

Then, mentally listing every bill she might have received, I searched through the two areas again. Despite being separated by the locals' pronunciation of the words "mum" and "path," they were united in giving me sod-all.

What an intriguing person this Ms Jacobs was. Or is? Never was? Whatever Dave had found out, I certainly hadn't. I logged off and decided it was time to risk a ride on my scooter after consuming the equivalent of a bottle of party red.

CHAPTER ELEVEN
Infantile Disorder

Shouting Lisa and Caroline's names or rather what I always called them—Li and Li—I awoke, hugging my pillow closely to my chest. Tears and perspiration drenched my face. It wasn't the only thing that was wet. My T-shirt and boxers were sodden. Needing a gulp of water to steady my nerves, I had leant across to get the glass on my bedside table, but the shakes had been so severe that I had found it impossible to hold it. It had fallen and crashed onto the floor, sending glass, water, and my cat across both me and the bed.

I held onto the quilt, shaking and cursing, more like a child than a man of my age. Every mental trick I knew was employed to try and calm down. Part of my brain was informing me that I was drowning and gasping for breath; the other was reminding me that my trembling body was somewhat sweaty but in no danger of asphyxiating in bed. I knew that it would pass in ten to fifteen minutes. It would feel like much longer.

Self-pity accompanied the fear. Insomnia wasn't an unknown condition to me, but we weren't what you would call friends, more like crotchety neighbours. My shoulder ached and I whined to myself with pathetic triteness. It was healing but still felt rather tender due to emotional wrestling with the pillow. With regard to the deep pain I had been carrying inside me for two years, that was still there. Sure, it had begun as a gut-wrenching agony and had now transformed itself into a dull ache, but I was still very much aware and bothered by it; probably, far more than that of the nightmare. I sounded like a chorus from a country and western song, but perhaps that was only appropriate. In my experience, grieving was wholly unoriginal.

The imaginary garden was, of course, rebuilt. All the old favourites were planted and the hard gardening built. Bizarrely, as often happened, I found myself getting irritated with myself for mistakes in creating it. So, whilst recovering from a panic attack stemming from the grief of the deaths of my wife and daughter, I got annoyed because I couldn't decide on whether to have ferns or hostas in my imaginary shady area in my fantasy garden.

Eventually, I pulled myself together and gingerly stepped over the broken glass and decided that, despite the fact that it was half past four in the morning, I would get up. I made myself some toast and a cup of coffee and sat in the lounge. I decided not to watch the news. I really couldn't bear to see the prime minister drone on again about how Jackie Payne was calling for a revolution. Er, mate, there is a clue in the fact that the word "revolutionary" is in the party's name. OK, those in the Liberal or Labour Party don't live up to their names, but you would have thought he would have guessed by now that we did.

So I grabbed some art books to pore over. It was a pretty random selection, but I noticed that I had picked those whose art contained detail. Obviously, I wanted something to analyse and lose myself in rather than float with. Bellotto or Canaletto was chosen, as opposed to Rothko or Ryman. Hours could be spent in studying the detail.

It worked. I felt myself growing in calmness, and my thoughts strayed onto the book I had always meant to write. I had started it three years ago but had dropped it when personal calamity had struck. The idea for it had been born as Britain experienced the tidal waves of unrest, and I had found it interesting how simultaneously art and music had created new masterpieces whilst at the same time revisiting the classics. My ambition was to show how music from previous generations of past rebels had engaged new ones. Take the 1945 jazz classic of Charlie Parker's "Now's the Time" for one of many examples; in its day it had been a call for black civil rights; at least three generations later, it had been taken up as the theme-tune of one of the anti-government Internet sites. Countless pieces of art from past centuries had been admired anew and often reinvented. This was the grand idea for a book.

My problem had been two-fold: the first was that whilst I could hold my own over most areas of music, I was semiliterate on folk music and pretty much the same on pop music of the last three years. The latter I might have been able to wing with Lisa's help. Worse still, I was totally ignorant of classical. I couldn't tell your Hayden apart from your Holst. That made the book rather lopsided. I couldn't really talk of Beethoven's attitude to Napoleon if it was impossible for me to recognise the fifth from the sixth symphony. Indeed, was there a sixth symphony? A bigger problem was, well, let's face it, saying that people get inspired by other people was hardly the most original thought I ever had.

There weren't any great ideas striking me as I sat here on how to trace the elusive Jelena Jacobs. There was no eureka moment as I admired Belotto's *The Ruins of the Kreuzkirche in Dresden after the Prussian Invasion*; nothing jumped up at me saying, "Of course! The Seven Years' War—why didn't I think of that?"

So leaving painting aside, I went back online and tried every possible avenue I could think of. But despite my enormous self-regard for my abilities, the derestricted Internet, and the little search goodies that I had been given which gave me access to certain, still-restricted areas, I got nowhere. I tried doctors, dentists, libraries—anything. And got—sod-all. There was the bare minimum saying that someone of that name existed back then, but that was all, and I could find nothing before or since.

Even allowing for the ransacking of official records which had gone on over the past few years, it did imply something. The obvious one being that Jacobs was a fake. I could find no record of her before or after, because there was none. Was one of those police infiltrators I had found out about? If she was, then it proved that it hadn't been only the eco-warriors that Special Branch had been worried about. This posed a new question for me. If this was true, then what did that have to do with the deaths of three people decades later? There was also the small point that if Jelena Jacobs was police and got Alan to work for them, then how? I wasn't sure how—I think they were called *honey traps*—worked, but however they did, would it have worked on Alan? Could this Jelena Jacobs have wooed Alan into betraying his class? His party? His beliefs? His life? Become a class traitor for love? Lust? It was difficult to believe. The sex would have had to have been out of this world for that to be the case.

And if I went with the theory that top-class bonking had destroyed his belief in classical Marxism, then why would he have committed suicide years later? What would have caused him to do that? That she was faking it?

213

Of course all this might be flights of fancy from an underused imagination. Maybe she just used another name, went abroad, died, or got married, or was I just crap at tracking down people?

I returned to my bedroom and swept up the broken glass. After emptying the pan into the bin, I made myself a coffee and sat back down with Red. He eyed me with suspicion, as if to say, "Hey, freak, do you reckon you'll be able to keep hold of that cup, or is it going to go the way of the glass?"

Turning to the documents which the very helpful Abby Nite had given me, I searched under Jelena Jacobs and got—again—nothing. It was now approaching six, and I was feeling sleepy, but stubbornness held the greater power, so I settled down to read the theses, articles, extracts, and complete bloody periodicals! All 369 of them.

Hour by hour passed. I dragged myself through tactic after tactic on how to handle strikes, demonstrations, marches, uprisings, mobilisations, and revolutions across the decades, across five continents. I learnt how the Indonesian forces differed from the US, from the Angolan, and from the Chilean, and how they had influenced each other. In doing so I did make some discoveries: the main being just how little an idea these world police forces actually had about the people they policed. Almost to the cop, they plainly had only a very faint grasp of reality. They also had the literary skills of a dead and decomposing sheep. Perhaps Alan had simply taken an overdose rather than read any more of this dross. But if the extracts and theses were dull, then the periodicals were tedious to extremes previously unknown.

Whilst the extracts were in the main international, the complete journals were British. But the themes were the same. Abby Nite had informed me in her efficient, friendly manner that these had to be purchased in their entirety, which, after reading the first three, I put down to gross police brutality. Most of them weren't in-depth articles on anything more important than community policing, donkey farms, or raffles for the local kids' home. Indeed, the sight of coppers behaving "like totally crazy" or "showing how we can laugh at ourselves" or "helping the community out" was more infuriating than reading about how to mount a police charge. I was treated to the sight of coppers across the years and across the country, adopting the headgear or coat of the nearest ethnic group, or smiling happily whilst raising a glass to the camera, or running in a green dinosaur suit in a fun run for charity.

Through my work, I have developed the skill of reading large quantities of detailed information quickly and locating the important information and remembering it, rather like a mental equivalent of Alan's highlighting method. Even so, it was gone ten o'clock when I had finished. I had ascertained more information than I could ever have hoped for about controlling public disorder, charity raising, and just how jolly police officers were. But about anything of use? Our friend "sod-all" was back again.

I was knackered. Despite consuming five cups of coffee, I was feeling the lack of sleep, so I decided to head back to bed. It was as I was slipping off my dressing gown and listening to the forecasted rain when finally an idea occurred to me. *Finally*, inspiration struck. Quite why the rain against the window or me disrobing caused it, I had no idea. But it did.

Whilst going through the utter dirge of what I had just read, a small article came to mind; it had questioned whether or not the safety checks on people who worked with children were rigorous enough. This had followed a tragedy involving a paedophile who worked in a children's home. Back then, checks on a possible criminal history was known as a CRB check. Yes! A CRB check! If she was working at a play centre, then she would have had to have a CRB check, a Criminal Records Bureau check, and it would have to have been kept at the local council. The centre itself had gone and so had the voluntary sector company that ran it, but the council would have kept the CRB. That was back when the word "council" had a whole lot different meaning to what it meant today. Now, it meant elected workers' representatives in the tradition of soviets; then, it meant running utilities and, best of all, keeping records! That was *their* forte.

I dived back online and hacked into the records of Hackney Council. Even though their personal records were confidential and e-protected to a decent degree, my software could bypass them and get in. I looked for Jelena Jacobs, and there she was, but it wasn't the CRB check I had expected. Instead, there was a strange half note/half file:

Jelena Jacobs, Occupation: Play Worker. Pay Scale: SO1.
Place of Work: Butterfly Play Centre, Foot Yard. E8 2PB. D.O.B.: 03/05/81.
Age: 29. Female.

CRB number—not required. Any enquiries refer to Director of Human Resources.
Home Address: 18 Foot Yard, E8 (temporary).
For permanent see 2 Marchland Close. Hartlepool, TS24 6JB.
Correspondence to go to Foot Yard.

Now this was a Eureka moment. Eur-bloody-eka! Marie said that she had an accent like George's; her guess was that she was from the Northeast. And lovely Hartlepool was just from that part of the country!

***

This was all costing me money. After I had noticed the cluster of party badges on the rather large fella at the King's Cross Rail ticket office, I had flashed the vid of Jackie on my phone, dropped Kye Toulson's name, and tapped my small, enamel, red party badge on my black raincoat, all in the hope of a freebie return ticket to Hartlepool. Or even just a discount. Instead, I received a rebuke and a speech on how there should be no favours given. We should be all be treated the same, no matter who we knew. He was right, of course, but my money was getting rather thin. With a few minutes to spare, I boarded the 3:30 p.m. to Sunderland, stopping at Hartlepool.

After trying more online research on the address, I had found very little else. Not even a telephone number. I had discovered a list of occupants from 2008 to the present but no Jelena Jacobs. At the time of the CRB note, one Jenny Underhill was listed as being the owner-occupier. She had moved out ten years ago, which was where I lost her; after that she had disappeared.

Possibly this was all a wild goose chase but I was intrigued with the fact that Jelena Jacobs had lived at the same place and at the same time as Jenny Underhill. It could be that they were merely flat-mates or sisters or lovers but maybe, just maybe, they were one and the same person. Hence both first names beginning with J; you couldn't credit the police with too much imagination.

Details were sketchy. She or one of them or both, might have died or gone abroad, but I could find nothing to suggest either, so feeling screen-weary, I decided to get off my arse and travel there for myself. Problem was, it cost dosh.

The familiar smell of an artificial atmosphere drifted under my nose as I passed along the train. Fellow travellers included several families, a group of middle-aged men, a number of couples, and a ragtag of individuals. I found my seat by the window, facing the direction we were travelling, and made a nest for myself. Packing away my coat and jacket, I had decided to keep with the same suit as yesterday's, as I was just too tired to choose anything else. I did grab a new shirt, a multi-coloured, striped number. With them, I put together an overnight bag, as I figured being this late in the day, I might be spending the night in a northern town. I took out my sandwiches and Coke and shovelled both down me as quickly as I could. With the train pulling out of the station and the buzz of the occupants in my ears, I dropped off to much-desired sleep.

I wasn't awoken by a noise or someone brushing past me as I might have expected or even the train jolting to a stop at a station or a junction; what woke me was the quietness of the carriage. I came to and noticed that there was very little sound around me. Even the children were keeping the noise to a minimum. Opposite, on the other side of the carriage, two passengers who had, I was pretty sure, been sitting apart when I had boarded were now sitting next to each other and were hunched over a laptop. Something about their faces reminded me of a previous time when people had been glued to a screen. I knew something was wrong. Swivelling around, I asked them what was up.

The man nearest to me, in shirt sleeves and burgundy tie, turned and, his face gaunt with horror, replied, "There's been a bomb explosion in Leeds."

I had been right. Looking around the carriage, I saw the same shocked faces watching news unfurl in front of them as I had seen at the electric substation when I had first met Youssef Ali and Olivia Harrison.

He continued, regaling me with the dreadful data. "It's gone off at the British HQ of the Pan European Investment and Finance Bank. It's in the City centre; I went there once for a meeting. Huge, it is. They're saying it's the anarchists again. The latest is that there's up to three hundred and twenty dead. There's not a window left unbroken. Half the roof is missing. All the solar panels are in the street; they reckon the panels themselves killed a couple pedestrians, sliced 'em in half. They fear it's very unstable and about to fall. It's terrible, just terrible."

As he spoke, I switched on the phone to see for myself.

The guy in jeans and polo neck next to him piped in. "Dunno what the AF are playing at. It's exactly the same as St Paul's; they claim responsibility on their website, then deny it."

"Can't deny it now, can they!" snapped Mr Business Man.

"Why?" I asked, seeing the scene for myself—smoke, flames, and smashed bricks at the very heart of Leeds.

"They're holed up in a shop nearby. Gunfire's been heard. There's been shots fired at the ITV news drone. Downed it, apparently. Crashed, boom, right into a bus. The other channels showed that; bet they enjoyed seeing a rival getting hit."

"Good God," I mumbled, as I searched out the news.

My fellow passengers had been correct. Although now it was being said that it could well be at least 364 dead. All employees had to swipe in and out, and that was the number of those registered in the building. I could hear the men across the aisle questioning just why they would do this atrocity. They answered themselves by passionately and bitterly slagging off the anarchists. Jeans and polo said that he was a supporter of the workers' councils, but this was well out of order. Previously, he pointed out, both the anarchists and the URSP had picketed the bank, as this huge multi-national had hoovered up many of the traditional high street banks when they had gone bust. In doing so, jobs had gone with the sweepings.

He was right; we had. They had been the epitome of the greedy few benefiting as the many suffered, but we wouldn't have condoned this. The dead here, as the news *pointedly* explained, were, in the main, low-paid, white-collar workers, not the hideously wealthy. They'd be yachting it somewhere sunny. No, the dead here were just your average women and men, perhaps some of whom were party members.

I switched to the party site and saw Jackie denouncing the bombing in the strongest terms possible. She pulled no punches, and whilst, like me, she was unable to believe that it was the AF, she made it plain that if it were proved to be them, then the party would have to seriously consider its alliance with them. The fact, though, was, as I could hear within the carriage, we were being contaminated with the same Semtex. I would bet with what was left of my month's money that the prime minister and his cronies would be in collective orgasm over this.

I would not have believed it, and yet the news was saying that one of the five leaders of the AF who had been sought for the St Paul's bombing had been shot running away from the explosion, and the other four were trapped in a baker's. It was like some siege from a 1930s comic where anarchists sporting black beards and East European accents do dastardly deeds before Inspector Honest-Englishman traps them and brings them to justice.

My eyelids were heavy, and I desperately needed to get back to sleep, but, news junkie that I was, I couldn't take my eyes off this.

By the time I reached Hartlepool Station, the bank had collapsed, taking the neighbouring supermarket with it. I wrapped my raincoat around me and pulled my cap down hard as the rain lashed down. "A storm's-a-brewing," I muttered, trying so, so hard to be profound.

The station itself was nice enough, if a little soulless, with a smattering of people cowering under the transparent roof as the rain performed a drum roll above their heads. Satnav was up, and it told me that Marchland Close was half an hour's walk away. I pondered finding a bus, which would make sense in this downpour, but that would take up more money (and a cab was well out of the question) so I left the station and headed south—walking. Passing the terraced houses, I tried to figure out what my plan was, because as I dodged the puddles, I had to admit that I did not have a clue. I must have broken the land-speed record for traversing streets, because in no time at all, I was at number two Marchland Close. And voilà! It had stopped raining.

I walked as confidently as I could muster up to the door and rang the bell. A woman in her forties with a toddler in tow opened the door and fixed her gaze on my bruised cheek. "Yes?" she demanded, still looking at it.

I explained that I was trying to locate Jenny Underhill because I was a distant relative from down south who had lost contact with her and was now trying to find her, as I had some important family news, I added for authenticity. There it was again, one of my great cover stories, with as much believability as a fairy tale. No, that was unfair; *Goldilocks and The Three Bears* was a whole lot more realistic than this story. Staring at my bruise, she had coldly informed me that she had only been here for eighteen months and had never heard of her. And with that, she closed the door and shouted at the child.

Gazing at the rather flaky and tacky green paint on the door, I thought to myself how well that had gone. Travel all this way, for all this money, get *this wet*, and get what? Two, three minutes max, of unhelpful hostility. Where was the fabled friendliness of northerners? I hadn't been expecting an offer of a brew and a chat about the Jarrow march, but a smile might have been nice. And she had bugger all idea who Jenny Underhill was. But then, why would she? Who does ever know who lived in the building before them?

Without having any better idea, I decided to go door-to-door with the flimsy story. With some of them, there was no one in, but with most I was met by politeness and a complete inability to help me. Mr and Mrs Crown at number nine remembered her, but apart from saying that in her youth she was a bonny lass, they couldn't add anything else. The distance between the front doors was just a matter of metres, but with each one, my inflated hopes of "cracking the case wide open" got flatter. Thank goodness I had never been a door-to-door salesman because we would have starved! At number thirteen they harangued me about the state of the streets and after spending ten minutes trying to explain that whoever they thought I was, I wasn't, I gave up and said I would have it looked into. Their neighbours took me for a religious type and heaped a rabid atheist rant at me, slamming the door in my face.

Several, though, did suggest talking to Mary at the end house. In fact, it almost became a mantra with the phrase following her name being always the same—she's been here donkey's years. So much so, that it could easily have been her surname: Mary *She'sbeenheredonkey'syears*. I couldn't tell whether it was *Miss She'sbeenheredonkey'syears* or *Mrs She'sbeenheredonkey'syears*. Or maybe Ms.

I rang the front door bell of Mary with the unwieldy and long name and got no answer. I stepped back and thought about what to do. Mary did sound like the woman to meet, but I was weary and beginning to get hot in this coat, as the rain had left us, and the sun had decided to say hello again. So I went online, checked for the nearest bed-and-breakfasts, checked availability, took a virtual tour of those that were, and chose one near the sea.

After a brisk walk, which took me along the coastal wall, I found it. The Tall Ship was a nice, three-story affair that boasted lovely views of passing boats and a hearty breakfast. The boats were probably smugglers and the breakfast a black-market sausage and cold beans, but it sounded ideal to me. The owners turned out to be two white women in their fifties who dealt with me quickly, politely, and professionally.

My room did, indeed, have a lovely view. It was neat and well-furnished with two large prints of eighteenth-century sailing ships. Firstly, as always when I was travelling, I set my things out. I took out my bath stuff and placed them in their order, going left to right on the sink: toothbrush, toothpaste, razor, shaving foam, and aftershave balm. On the nearest shelf went my hair cream and perfume. Next, I hung up tomorrow's shirt and put away tomorrow's boxer shorts and socks. Under my pillow went my bedtime T-shirt. It was an old one bought when I had been on holiday in Milan.

That all done, I sat on the end of the bed and turned on the news. Things had moved at dizzying speed in Leeds. All the anarchists accused of planting the bomb were dead. Shot, the blandly pretty newscaster said, trying to escape the bakery. No police officers had been injured.

But if that was eye-widening, then what else being reported was positively blinding. With the death toll possibly reaching four hundred, a large crowd had formed and attacked the Yorkshire offices of the AF in the centre of the City. Causalities were being reported. Similar scenes were being shown in London, where the main AF office was ablaze, and a mob of a thousand or so was attacking anything connected with them; this included the NWC and us. Bricks were being thrown, and obtaining petrol appeared not to be a problem for this crowd, judging from the litres of the stuff they carried with them. A teenager was shown being grabbed by a group of protesters and being kicked to the ground. People were seen fleeing, holding their heads as blood poured.

I was astounded. We hadn't seen such scenes for quite a while. Put simply, this mob of reactionaries, as well as being politically dumb, were also very stupid about their personal safety. As the reporter was saying, and the news drones was beginning to show, very quickly there would be a counterforce. And the NWC had proved to be very effective in controlling the streets. These pro-Parliament protestors might have it their way for now, but very soon they would be confronted by a much larger and better-organised group. On every channel a blood bath was being predicted. I had to agree with my media friends.

Sitting in a bedroom of a B&B watching pitched battles on multiple channels was hardly an enticing prospect, so I thought I would go out for an early evening stroll, admire the port, perhaps grab a light fish supper, and then see if this Mary was at home.

I had never been here before. I had visited Sunderland and Newcastle for various reasons personal, work-related, and political but never to Hartlepool. Walking around the marina and admiring the boats and listening to the seagulls squawk, I would say that it was my loss. The fresh sea air was invigorating, and the sight of the wind farm a few kilometres out to sea was a pleasing sight. Finding a public bench, I stared out across the water and tried to think about nothing at all. It wasn't easy, as a barrage of thoughts insisted on pushing their way in. As much as the view was a lovely one, I decided to make a move. A thought—no, really, it was a feeling—was bothering me sitting here. Gazing out to that horizon so far away was making me a touch morose so I went in search of a fish and chip shop.

I'm no patriot; well, I wouldn't be, would I? But some things you could be proud of, and fish 'n chips was one of them. I knew a good way to kick the blues: a slab of battered haddock, a pile of chips, two pickled onions, and great oceans of ketchup. Very soon along the front, I found one, made my order, and was experiencing heavenly bliss as I ate it.

A tall, slim, rather gangly man in his twenties, possibly of Pakistani heritage and dressed in a white apron and hat, stood smiling behind the counter. I clocked his Democratic Left badge, he, my party one. Without uttering a word in debate, we silently decided not to discuss politics. He didn't want to lose a possible sale, and I didn't want to lose my grub. On hearing my accent, he decided to ask what brought me here. Refraining from answering that it had been a train, I told him that I had heard his fish 'n chips were the talk of the capital. His smile broadened, and he nodded, understanding that might be so. On realising that neither of us was going to harangue each other, he moved onto that old friend, the weather. Several minutes were spent with me running out tired gags about northerners wearing shorts whatever the cold and him politely laughing, commenting that those from down south considered it cold here. We'd wear an overcoat if the temperature dropped below twenty degrees Celsius. He had a deadpan sense of humour, and it was refreshing to just talk trivia. I could have spent all night in there, but customers were starting to come in, so I said my thanks and headed into town.

Wandering around the streets, I quickly came to the conclusion that it was a pretty town. But I wasn't here to sight-see, so, glancing at the still-working Satnav, I made my way back to Marchland Close.

I rang the bell at number two and found that I was in luck. An elderly woman in her seventies, I would guess, answered, rearranging her headscarf. She looked Somalian to me, although when she spoke she had an accent of pure Northeast. I had to confess to being rather surprised that with a name like Mary, she was of East African descent, but then maybe, Pete Kalder, you have just become so removed from the world that everything surprises you.

"Yes, pet, what can I do for you?" she asked with a friendly smile.

Dressed in brown from head to toe, she gave off a disposition that suggested a positive outlook on life. Her expression was one of joviality, and a huge plus was that she did not stare at my bruise. Both she and the chippie were restoring my faith in northern hospitality. I trotted out my story of being a long-lost relative; trying hard not to flinch at its total and utter flimsiness as I did so, adding that several of her neighbours had recommended her.

"Of course, I knew Jenny. My, she's a popular lass these days. Come on in." She gestured inside, turned, and walked into her home. Either crime prevention was a subject not regularly discussed in these parts, or wound aside, I had an honest face. With the growth of the solidarity, a lot of people had changed; people had begun to see the positive in humanity rather than always seeing the negative. But still. Inviting in a possible mass murderer or burglar, or both, was showing a remarkable amount of trust.

I passed a large gold-and-silver-framed piece of writing in the short corridor, which being in Arabic, I assumed was a quote from the Koran. She ushered me into a small, nicely furnished living room. I could see photographs of what were presumably various family members. On one wall was something I had not expected: a framed blue-and-white-striped football jersey. On closer inspection and forgetting that making myself at home before being invited to do so could easily be construed as rudeness, I noted that it was a signed Hartlepool United football shirt.

Mary beamed with pride. "Bin a fan all me life."

So Hartlepool—pretty, by the sea, does great fish and chips, friendly, and obviously football-crazy—just when could I move here?

We chatted for a while talking about the chippie, how our respective clubs were doing, and what a nice town Hartlepool was. She was an easy talker and happy to pass the time with a complete stranger who sported a face recovering from a copper's boot. I learnt that her parents had come over in the late twentieth century as asylum seekers. She and her two brothers had been born here. Both had moved away with their families. She had mentioned that her eldest was at uni in London, and she pointed to my party badge. "She's one of your lot." That was why, she explained, she had not feared that I might be a serial killer. You don't tend to let them join, she joked. If only you knew what members we did have, I thought to myself.

She went off to make me a tea, which being up north I felt obliged to have instead of my usual coffee, and I settled next to H'Angus, the football club's mascot. Kalder, concentrate on why you are here, I said to myself.

After a few minutes, she returned with a pot and two cups in saucers, all in pretty cream bone china edged with a delicate flower pattern. She said we should let it stand for a while.

Now was the time to dive in. With a commendable disregard to how truly weak this all sounded I asked if Jenny had lived alone. "We, her family down south, heard that she had got a friend to move in." Friend I thought covered all manner of relationships and was slightly more modern than 'female companion'.

"Why no, Jenny bless her, lived alone. Just her and that house."

Not really Mary, not if you have a split identity and go by both Jenny Underhill and Jelena Jacobs – you are never alone.

Something she had first said prompted me to ask her, "You said that Jenny was popular *these* days—why?"

"Oh, I had another one of your family visit here a few days ago."

My heart increased beating by about a million, and I concentrated every muscle I had to stay cool. "Oh?" I said, which was as much as I could muster, feeling this excited.

"'Course, you would know him," she replied, getting up and moving to pick something out of her sideboard. "Oh, what was his name?" As she tried to remember, she gave a very accurate description of Dave Wiltshire. "His wife was with him…er…Yasmin, that was her name! Ah, yes, Dave and Yasmin."

"Cousins, they're my cousins; well, Dave is," I blurted out. I felt that I had to give an explanation, so in a long, meandering speech I attempted to give a reason why both Dave and myself, supposedly relatives, would be looking for her now, at the same time, and yet not know that the other was doing so. It was so weak that it made the original story sound like irrefutable truth.

Mary did not seem to mind. After all, why would I lie? Why, indeed, Mary; why, indeed? Instead, she spent several minutes fondly recalling the conversation she had had with Yasmin about where their respective families came from. She spoke with warmth and told me that Yasmin had promised to keep in touch. "A lovely lass," she smiled. Indeed. It was a shame that she wouldn't be keeping in touch. Feeling uncomfortable, I gently steered her back onto the subject of Jenny Underhill.

She took out a rather ancient-looking computer from under the sofa and started it up. She said there was a file that she was sure that I would be interested in; certainly my cousin Dave had been. The names of other files suggested family events and occasions from the street and locality. Some were marked celebrating past royal events, others, moments in Hartlepool F. C.'s history, and others of fetes, parties, and such like. She opened one marked Misc and scrolled down several pages, until she stopped at one.

"Here she is!" she announced triumphantly.

In front of me was a woman in her twenties, dressed in jeans and a sweater, smiling at the camera whilst holding a dog in her arms. "Our Billy," she explained, "a Staffordshire terrier. And that is Jenny."

And there was the scar in the shape of a tick above her left eye. So Jenny Underhill *was* Jelena Jacobs—they were one and the same! I felt like giving Mary and H'Angus, the toy monkey, a huge hug and kiss but guessed that her hospitality had its limits.

She showed me other photos of Jenny slash Jelena. All the while, telling me what a wonderful woman she was.

"She looks it," I said inanely. Now for the killer punch. "What did she do for a living?"

"Oh, she was in the police. I got a photo somewhere of her in her uniform. She did look grand in it. Ah, here she is. I can't think for the life of me why I took this, but anyhows, here she is."

And there she was, Jelena Jacobs, née Jenny Underhill, in a police officer's uniform. My first reaction was of the jubilation one feels when one has unearthed a fact or point of interest long hidden. Here was the play worker who had joined us, no doubt talking of the unfairness of society and how it had to be changed. Here she was in uniform. The *real* her. Not Jelena but Jenny. Not Jacobs but Underhill. Not a play worker but a copper, the undercover copper. Underhill, underhand, the under the radio… undercover cop.

Suddenly, I felt that this was something I had seen before. The way the uniform cap on her head was set so neatly parallel to her eyebrows contrasted with the scar. She looked the same but somehow different, and it was a difference I had thought I had seen before.

"Yes, she was proud to be an officer. I'd love to meet her now and see what she makes of what's happening nowadays. When we meet, we'll chinwag a bit about Aunt Flo but then end up rowing!" I joked. I kept to myself the fact that we would be doing a lot more than discussing current affairs. I also questioned myself as to where the hell the name Aunt Flo had come from? It was a name straight from the 1950s!

Mary spoke of Jenny Underhill in affectionate terms of how she had been so welcoming to her family and had joined in such celebrations as Eid. "It's sad to say, but it's true, that not everyone was glad to have us here. Most folk were fine, but there were a few who felt uncomfortable having Muslims in their midst. Jenny, mind, had no problem with us."

I sipped my tea and listened to her. Every so often, I would ask a question. Mostly, however, she was unable to help me. She could not say, for example, what exactly Jenny did in the force or even where she worked. Indeed, for someone whom she had known for so long and had such high praise for, she actually knew very little about her.

Finally, I asked my second big question. "So, Mary, how can I get hold of her? Where does she live now?"

"Oh, ten years back, she moved up to Seaham. Got a nice little place there, detached. Has its own pool, no less. Not that I've ever been in it. Sort of lost touch when she left. We exchange birthday cards—hers is in five weeks—and the odd e-mail, but it sort of died. Well, you do, don't you?"

I agreed, and requiring little effort on my part, I got the address. Mary told me that she estimated it would take me half an hour to drive. She said that's how Dave and Yasmin had gone there. I told her that I didn't have a car, so she suggested which bus I could catch. Looking at my watch, I figured that maybe it was a little late to go visiting an undercover cop. I would wait till tomorrow, which would also allow me time to think how I was going to play this and which of my many Shakespearian disguises would I adopt.

I declined another cup, thanked her profusely, and went to leave for my B&B. Before I left, she touched my arm and asked if I would ask Jenny to contact her and to let her know that I had met up with her. I said that I would.

"'Cos I asked Yasmin to, but she never did. Must have slipped her mind."

From there, I travelled from the warmth and friendship of drinking English Breakfast with Mary to rioting in the streets of Leeds, London, Liverpool, and Manchester. The TV images of pro-government demonstrators clashing with ours were chilling to see. Attacks on anything vaguely resembling the AF were spreading across the country. It was reported that a King's Lynn vet called Animal Forum had been trashed by mistake. In retaliation and to counter the aggression, the NWC had mobilised large numbers. As I had expected, they dwarfed the government crowds. Some of the pictures were upsetting, with those previously dishing out the violence now receiving it. Big time. What made it so troubling was the fact that many of the people, who the NWC were fighting with, were not fully paid-up members of the government supporters club. Many neutrals were angry. Normal people were appalled by the bomb carnage. As reports steamed out, the outraged increased.

Social media was full of news that, despite the apparent size of the NWC force, many supporters had refused to come out, sharing the effrontery of the bombs. Not that the government itself was bothered, although they made a real show of pretending to be; there were more crocodile tears than you'd see at a zoo. Basically, though, they merely used it as a large stick to beat us. All this instability and street violence, they argued, was the responsibility of Jackie Payne and her party. She had stirred up the trouble, and she had instigated the volatility of the situation.

CHAPTER TWELVE
Chaos or Community

The next morning I was up, and wishing to escape the reports of street fighting and the sight of the PM revelling in his best statesman role as he pontificated regret and condemnation in equal measure, I fled to the televisual wallpaper of *The Morning World of Dick and Clara* and got dressed. It was wrong to mock, as quite honestly they had to be admired; with the world in flames, this married couple had kept their sofa chat show going with a diet of soap stars and wacky pets. Today, with the death count a confirmed 413 in the Leeds explosion, two buildings collapsed, and most of the major cities wiping the blood off the streets, this pair was leading with the news of the up-and-coming Hollywood marriage.

I checked myself in the mirror, combing my hair. This was more from nerves than conceit. Dave and Yasmin had been tortured to death shortly after visiting the woman, and now I was planning to do the same. I feared that I risked a similar follow-up.

Putting on my jacket, I went over my strategy and comforted myself that Dave and Yasmin had not been killed *whilst* visiting her. Jelena, or should it be Jenny, would not be silly enough to try anything on her own doorstep. I set my phone up to record the visit. I would mention in passing that I had found it difficult to find any parking so she would not know that I had come by public transport. I was proud of that one—good thinking. Back in London, Red and I would decamp to a friend's. I hadn't decided which of the ignored friends was going to have the pleasure of me and the cat, but that would not be difficult.

I had paid my bill, said good-bye, and marched nervously to the bus stop. The extra pill I had taken today was earning its keep. All the mental tricks had been employed and discarded. I hadn't had long to wait before the bus arrived.

Despite an oversized, barking dog at the front and my spine cursing because of the criminal neglect of the nation's infrastructure that appeared to have created a pothole every full rotation of the wheels, the bus journey was an enjoyable one. It afforded me a truly lovely view of the coast. I stared out the window and took in the scenery. I was trying very hard to relax and not think about the possibilities of what might be about to happen. I had ruled out the prospect of Jenny Underhill inviting me in for cream cakes and a trip down espionage memory lane.

I didn't mind admitting it—I was afraid. Very. Even when I had been awoken by the dream, I had lain awake, not dwelling on the past but on the very near future. The appalling images of blood-splattered protestors and mutilated bomb victims hadn't helped. Whenever I saw them, I saw me. They'd been horrific, worrying, and stomach-churning pictures, but the fearful image of Jelena meeting me, pointing her fancy revolver at me, and then pressing the trigger, was holding the power here. Perhaps I should have been ashamed; so many dead and injured and I was worrying about my own neck.

I shook it from my head and concentrated on the dog. How could it bark for so long and so loudly, disturbing everyone on the bus and quite possibly every bus north of Wolverhampton, but the owner who was sitting next to it was blissfully untroubled? I focussed on that great existentialist question of how the dog could be ignored and tried to banish any trivial thoughts of me lying dead in a pool of blood with half my face missing.

Instead, I thought about the meaning of this mystery woman's role in Alan becoming a traitor to the class. I couldn't see him dropping his politics for love or, indeed, lust. She was obviously involved somehow and had played a part snaring him for the state.

My contemplation had to end when my stop arrived. I got up, picked up the bag, rang the bell, and said a fond farewell to my canine friend.

Her house was on the northern edges of the town near the coast, by all accounts a nice part of town. I strode along the road and took the next left. My pace quickened, not from any desire to match my heartbeat, but if this was going to happen, then I better get it over with as quickly as possible. I went over my strategy once more, but who was I kidding—*what* strategy? I just wanted it done and dusted. If she was not in, I was prepared to wait, but that would surely just prolong the agony. Considering what Dave and Yasmin had gone through, that was a bad choice of words.

At the end of the road, passing by a group of teenagers swigging beer, I took a sharp right. I was now just a turning away. The houses were sizeable: new, detached, and with all the new eco-mod cons. Jenny/Jelena had done well for herself. I could imagine why someone like her would do whatever she could to protect her swimming-pool lifestyle and a system which protected her right to live on the high diving- board whilst others dabbled their feet in the urine-soaked gutters.

I turned the corner and stopped. My way was barred. I could not go much further, as a police tape, the yellow-and-black police tape you see festooning numerous cop shows, was draped between a police car and a streetlight. Two armed police officers stood by, bulked up in body armour and with walkie-talkies blaring loudly. I looked past them and saw a large, white, tent-like structure shielding the front of a building. That was another thing I had seen a million times. I slipped out my phone and quickly grabbed a look at the Satnav. It confirmed what had been obvious to me. There were four, large, impressive, white, angular, hi-tech buildings of steel and glass, and one of them was Jenny/Jelena's—the one with the police tent; the one with forensic officers going in and out was hers.

I stood and gawked. Not having a mirror, I wouldn't have known whether my jaw was once more hanging, but it felt it was. Christ Almighty. What was happening? I had come here preparing to meet a class enemy, a murderer, an agent of reaction. I was dreading what she might do, but I felt that I just had to do it. I had seen what someone had done to Yasmin and Dave, and I suspected that she was that someone.

But. *But!* But this was a heavy-duty police presence, and I reckoned that they were not here because her jewellery had been nicked. Here was what looked very much to me like the type of thing you see on the news when there's a murder enquiry. Since getting on the train up here, I had been trembling with the possibility that I would end up under a tent like that. I had not thought for a second that she might beat me into one. I stood for maybe five minutes just staring at the goings-on but taking none of it in.

Suddenly, I realised that I had to leave this place and leave it fast. I should have gone around the area, finding out what I could from the locals. This was obviously linked with what I was looking into, and it was equally obviously big. But I, the great hero, turned and walked rapidly away. Then it dawned on me that I was being silly; I changed my mind, not to stay but to slow down. I didn't want suspicion to fall on me by scrambling away as if I had something to hide. No, slow down. Look cool. Keep moving but keep it normal. This, after all, wasn't the first time I had walked away from murder.

I got to the end of the road. Now, where? Left, right, straight on? I checked the Satnav. It was down! Oh, that was just great. How bloody convenient. Think, man, *think*. OK, use your brain, I said to myself, trying to calm down and think logically. For starters, I had done nothing wrong, and I was no way a threat to whoever was doing this, as quite obviously I had not an inkling as to what was going on.

OK, concentrate. I'll turn left; wasn't it here where the teenagers were? They weren't here now, but maybe they just moved on. No, I was no threat because I didn't have a clue; I mean, I thought Jenny/Jelena was the assassin, but well, if she was, then she'd been assassinated herself.

I looked around to get my bearings; had I gone too far? Where was the bus stop back to Hartlepool? Use the sea, I said to myself. So it was there; so did that make that direction north or was it south? Looking at the horizon, I realised that I couldn't actually see the sea; I was assuming where it was, but maybe it was just the clear skyline by the countryside? I was panicking. Bloody countryside. Give me a city any day. You had bloody street signs for starters!

Again, which way to go was proving to be bloody difficult. My heart rate was increasing, and I was getting clammy and really needed a good stiff drink. There was naff-all chance to imagine poxy gardens right now. I went straight on and then took a left.

Striding forwards and still searching for a bus stop (didn't they have them up here?), I turned again, and, deep in thought, if mental hysteria could be deemed such, I tried to put as much space as I could between me and that white tent. Until, that is, I noted mud beginning to splash up my trouser leg, and there right in front of me was a gate. A bloody gate! What the hell was that doing here? A gate! I stared over it and into a field. A field? Here? How long had I been bloody walking? One thing I could do was to take a shrewd guess that I had taken a wrong turn. Climbing a gate had not featured on the way here. I swung around and started back, taking my phone out to check the Satnav. It was still down.

Then, suddenly, a car turned into what I had now realised was a private road leading to a couple of fields. It cut its speed and slowed right down to walking pace, straight towards me. Lilac with dark-tinted windows, it was a sleek and intimidating machine: one of the new range of electro-Mercedes that boasted that it was both the fastest electric road car and the one that could go the furthest without a charge. It even had a mini, high-specification solar panel which was designed to kick in to get you to an electric substation if you hit trouble. That all made me sound like a motor magazine—very impressive and totally out of touch with what was happening here. It was getting nearer and nearer. Who gave a toss about its 0 to 60 speed or the depth of tread on its wheels, because it was edging towards me!

This car, which was as cool as, well, one that James Bond might drive, was now within fifty metres of me. I could not see into it, but any second it would be in touching distance, so I feared that I would in the very near future, find out who was driving. Getting within metres of me, it turned sharply, blocking the road. I froze, and like a granny facing a mugging, held my overnight bag in front of me. Perhaps I thought that dirty underwear would shield me from what was going to happen. The executioner's bullet would be stopped dead in its tracks by my latest designer socks.

I jerked my head left and right and saw a possibility. There! If I made a run for it, there was a gap in the hedge, and I could go through it into the fields. Whoever it was would have to leave the car. That would give me a slight head start.

Too late. The door swung open, I glimpsed a green leather jacket done up to the neck, and a head bent downwards. "Get in!" it ordered. There in front of me was Victoria Cole, looking worried and sounding urgent but not intimidating. "Get in!" she repeated.

"What on earth are you doing here?" I asked.

"I'm a police officer who is here investigating the double murder of the Wiltshires. What are *you* doing here—visiting yet another homicide scene?"

"I didn't do it," I said more in a whimper than in outrage.

She gave me a look of withering pity. "Of course not. Get in, Kalder, for Christ's sake."

The options flashed up: trudge around the streets of Seaham, looking for a bus stop; hike across the meadows; get myself noticed by the local murder cops; or get in. Cops or countryside—what a choice! I decided to get in.

She swung the wheel and turned the car into the street. She put her foot down, slid it through the gears, and moved away. Now, I didn't want to sound like *Motoring Monthly* again, but it did move quickly.

Glancing at me, she said, "Put the bag in the back, for goodness' sake."

I did as I was told, tossing it behind me into an impeccably spotless back seat and then belted up as she drove along the coastal road. Nothing was said for several minutes. She just drove, and I just looked ahead. When we were clear of any buildings, she stopped.

Turning the engine off, she faced me, elbow on the wheel and her forefingers touching her temple. "Well? What brings you up here and to this address?"

I looked back at her and rubbed my cheek. My good one. I really didn't intend to provoke her. She had, after all, come to my rescue, but I still didn't feel like treating her like my knight in shining armour. She might have come to my aid, but that didn't mean she was my ally. I could account for the coincidence of my being here, but could she?

My silence didn't amuse her. When she did speak, she did from the knowledge of her position of power. "I *know* that you had nothing to do with the murder…" the word was expected, but it was still a jolt, "…of Jelena Jacobs, but would the Northeast murder squad think that? Pete Kalder visits David and Yasmin Wiltshire, and they die; Pete Kalder visits Jelena Jacobs, and she also winds up dead. In both cases you run and flee. You can barely keep your contempt of me from your eyes, yet I'm the one standing between you and all those questions."

She had a point. But what could I say to her? How much was I prepared to tell a serving police officer? Even one with a swish car.

"You need to talk to me, Pete."

I grunted.

She sighed. "Comrade," she almost snarled, "please stop being ridiculous, because there is something very serious happening here, far more serious than your petty prejudices. You *know* there's something serious happening. Use your brain and talk to me."

With an impressive show of imagination, I grunted again.

She slapped the wheel, giving me a start. "You saw the Wiltshires, didn't you? Don't you want to get who did that? Aren't you interested in why they were killed? Or want to know what is happening? Are you so disengaged with the real world that you don't care that somebody might be trying damage the party?" Her irritation grew. "You may hate me, hate what I am, or what you *think* I am, but that is irrelevant because I will tell you, Pete Kalder, I am a comrade. So, tell me, what brings you here? *Why* are you here?"

Before I could repeat a dismissive noise or consciously use my brain, I started to talk. I couldn't stop; I just let it all out. I told her about Alan having a breakdown when his wife and child had left him. Feeling vulnerable he had seemingly found a new love in a keen, intelligent, and attractive comrade called Jelena Jacobs. That was in 2010. That same year after meeting Jelena Jacobs, he started to work for the security forces. She had then just vanished from the face of the earth, but Jenny Underhill hadn't. I explained how I had managed to track her here, and I had expected her to be the killer. I thought she was trying to cover her tracks by removing Dave and Yasmin.

Dave had traced her, too, because he, before me, had found out that this young play worker was, in fact, a police officer by the name of Jenny Underhill. He had known that, because Alan must have left a message for him. It had always struck me as odd that there was a taped good-bye for the party but not for the person he loved most. But the fact was that he must have left one for Dave which Dave had erased so no one else could see.

There was a half-hour delay before Dave contacted Jackie after finding his grandfather, and I now thought that he had spent that time watching the message and trying to work out what to do. I didn't know precisely what was on it, but I could guess that Alan told him that he had found out that Jelena was Jenny and who she was.

For the first time in several minutes, Victoria spoke. Maybe I had imagined it, but had there been a look of respect at what I had found out? Or was that just me wearing ego-goggles? Whether true or not, she didn't heap praise on me when she spoke. All she asked was, "How?"

"I worked out that last night. I saw a photo of Jelena Jacobs in uniform, and it reminded me of another such photo in one of the police magazines which…er…" I paused, not being willing to say quite what Alan was doing, "Alan had been studying. It was in a silly fluff piece they carry, designed to show the coppers…er, no offence, as being such warm human beings. There was a photograph showing a group of police officers celebrating a colleague's long service award. One of them was her. It must have been pure chance that he saw it, and when he did, he realised that he had been duped. He had been betraying the party for a con."

She looked at me without emotion. "But how could she have done that?"

I shrugged and confessed that I had no idea. The options for encouraging, forcing, or tricking him into betrayal were pretty limited. But whatever it was, she was responsible for the corruption of his beliefs and ultimately his suicide. I thought she had also been responsible for Yasmin and David but obviously not.

I urgently needed some air. I unbuckled and got out of the car and stretched my legs, walking towards the edge of the cliffs. I was beat. I was just a silly, middle-aged man, who used to research the historical background of paintings, but who recently had been imagining himself to be Lew Archer. Well, I didn't have a strong, square jaw, and this was definitely not Los Angeles, and I was no slick private eye. Futilely, I swept my hair back as the wind attempted to give me a side parting. Make that a silly, vain, middle-aged man.

Cole walked up behind and stood by me. She had her hands in her pockets and looked thoughtful.

"I was convinced that she was the killer," I whined.

"Well, if she was, then she was killed by her own gun because she was killed by a single bullet to the head by an Alavares Azevedo 12D. Forensic tests confirm it's the same AA12D that was used on David and Yasmin Wiltshire."

"So, any ideas who *it* is, then?" I asked, feeling strangely deflated as if it was an affront to my male pride that she had been killed.

I could feel Cole looking at me as I wallowed in my moroseness, staring out at the waves. "Have you?" she asked.

My reply came out without any prior thought. "Dave must have tracked down this Jelena/ Jenny woman who told him something that had made him a threat to someone. The obvious thought is that there is another infiltrator. You said yourself that MI5 would have us at the top of their to-do list, so my guess is that David must have found out who it was."

She looked at me. "Any candidates?"

I looked back at her. I could see her age in her eyes now; though far from being old (I'd put her at her mid-twenties), she wasn't the woman-girl that I first thought she was. Her smooth, wrinkle-free skin and clear, blue eyes just made her look that way. I guessed that talking to me was like talking to her dad. Maybe that was why she had just asked such a ridiculous question. She had to be joking. What did she expect me to say? Oh, yeah, these Central Committee members are all spies. Here's a list of suspicious types. But then I started to pull myself together. I had just spilled my guts out to her, and she hadn't told me a thing.

"I think I asked you before, but you didn't give me an answer. How come you're here?"

This time she did not hesitate. "We—the police—traced the positioning of his mobile for the last few days, so we tracked him here."

I was astounded. "I thought all that media watching and e-surveillance had been blocked, booted into touch with our geeks out-geeking your geeks?"

"Oh," she smiled, "the geek wars ebb and flow. Sometimes the forces of revolution have the upper hand, and sometimes the forces of reaction do."

"And now?"

"The goodies still are on top, but cracks are appearing, and DI Martin pulled a few strings, and we got the trace."

"Must be confusing, who exactly are the goodies and the baddies, and, indeed, who are the *we*," I said, for once not being *completely* antagonistic.

She brushed it aside by plainly saying that the we, the *important we*, was the party. The police were just her employers, making the point by rhetorically asking whether I ever felt the university I worked for was the *we*. I didn't have time to answer, as she continued with her account.

"He sent me up here to see what I could find out, but when I arrived, three local police officers were setting up a perimeter and launching a murder enquiry. She had been dead for a matter of hours."

"Did you know who she was?"

"Had no idea, although I could make a bloody good guess, when after I barely had enough time to have a chat with the Northeast boys, some very serious-looking, plain-clothed officers arrived, took command, and sent me off with a patronising comment or two. Like yours," she added.

I didn't rise to the bait because I was more interested in other things. "Who were they? MI5?"

"Think so, or one of the other security services; they certainly weren't friends of mine. They snatched the computer pad I had found in the house out of my hands and demanded in a quite threatening way—and I am not easily threatened—if I had looked at it!"

"And had you?"

"Yes. Which I told them. And I also told them quite honestly that, as it was all encrypted, it was total gobbledygook to me."

"Shit."

She grinned. "I didn't tell them, though, that I had copied it all, so I'll see what I can do later. Roijin or Asher might be able to do something with it. Of course, that'll have to be done unofficially, as DI Martin has been told that this murder is strictly out of bounds, and I am to be taken off the Wiltshire enquiry for being politically unreliable."

"I thought that was against the thing-a-majig accord between the National Workers' Council and the Met? I thought the NWC had to be informed of all relevant cases, and a liaison officer is on the case?"

"It is, but, hey, I don't think these fellas care too much for accords."

I thought about what she was saying. "When did you arrive?" I asked.

"Last night, about 9:30. Like I said, I had only enough time to chat to the officers who were here and to the forensic team who was just arriving. The locals had kindly let me have a look around. I didn't find much except the computer pad, which was hidden in her linen basket. I had just found it when our friendly, well-mannered security branch colleagues arrived. That was just before midnight."

"I didn't see anything on the net about it."

"No, you wouldn't. Complete blackout with the story going out locally that it was a missing person's case and anything emerging in the info sphere was getting instantly erased."

"Can they do that?" I asked, astounded that the all-liberating net could be so controlled.

"For a short time and in a restricted field, yes, but it takes a lot of resources, so they must be pretty keen to keep the quiet."

She turned and walked back to her car. I followed her with my eyes, wondering if she was going to speed off, leaving me to converse with the seagulls. Leaning against its sloping bonnet, she pulled out a pack of cigarettes from her jacket. Getting one out, she lit up. Was I being paranoid, or was the fact she hadn't offered me one because she already knew that I didn't smoke?

"So, comrade, what do you make of the period we are in? How do you think the situation is changing?"

"Eh?" I wasn't quite sure what she was asking. Was she asking me how the case was changing?

"The political situation. What do you think about the bombings and the riots which have followed them?" She took a drag of her cigarette.

I hadn't been expecting a political discussion up here. What did she want? An educational on the fluidity of revolutions in developed western capitalist countries? Would she require a reading list? I really did not think that this was quite the time or place.

Still, what the hell. Whatever the reason for her desire to play at politics, I told her straight. It was total bollocks that the anarchists had planted those bombs. *They'd* been planted, more like. The AF just was not into indiscriminate bombings because, if nothing else, they would be savvy enough to know that it would rebound on them. The fact that questions were raised in the councils was hardly a surprise. This was damaging their support. Sure, the pro-government demos had been pretty small and almost suicidal, but people had been disturbed by the deaths and backing for the AF, and, by association, we had been weakened. I didn't know how, but it was my belief that this was a set-up job.

She didn't bat an eyelid and agreed, adding, "And why would some of the most senior members of their organisation do it themselves?" She took another pull on her cigarette. "You know, Pete, for the previous twelve months, absenteeism in the police service has been running at sixty-five percent. Over the last few days, however, there has been a growing number of officers returning to work. Attitudes have changed a touch, too; whilst I have never been popular for my party membership, there has been little open hostility to me because, I guess, they feared the repercussions. Now, though, there's a change; not aggression or abuse, just a decline on the effort expounded in hiding their dislike."

"As if they are growing in confidence?"

Her eyes were looking past me into the horizon. "Yes, not by much. There's still a deliberate cordiality towards the NWC, but I sense something; something's altered. Maybe it's something to do with the bombings?"

For a few seconds, neither of us spoke, both taking in what she had said which made what she next said flabbergasting.

"We—in this case I do mean the police—did manage to find a record of some of the calls David had made and also some of the net-based searches. Now, his and Yasmin's computers weren't at their home. I think they were taken, presumably by the killer, but Roijin managed to map out his usage of the period of time between Alan's death and his own.

"The early use was concentrated on tracking down Jenny Underhill, with searches of census material, tax records, voting register, and the like. There are also searches showing research into how MI5 worked in relation to subversive groups. But after visiting her here in Seaham, the usage changes dramatically. After here, he spent a long time, and I mean up to eight hours at a time, studying—*really* studying. He was carrying out a detailed scrutiny on the backgrounds of certain comrades."

Jesus Christ.

"He looked into several, but his main focus was on a small number: Kye Toulson, Youssef Ali, Marie Williams, Glen Bale, Olivia Harrison, Michael Hughes…"

God.

"And," she exhaled deeply, "Jackie Payne."

I had run out of blasphemies. Poirot I might not be (if for nothing else, I wouldn't be seen dead in a bow tie), but it was crystal clear what that list represented. What shocked me, what really shocked me was how calmly I took it. We both stood in silence with just the usual sound of the coast for company. I didn't shout at her. Abuse her. No threats of violence were made. I didn't rant and rave at her about how long I had known some of those people. Jackie, for goodness' sake, *was* the party! Marie Williams? I had been around when her kids had been born. I was mates with her partner! Even

Bale, odious twerp he might be, had been a loyal party member for decades. I didn't know Harrison, Hughes, Toulson, or Ali that well, so it would be easy to consider them, but they in their different ways had shown total commitment to the cause. And here was this copper, all proud and preening in her new party membership, telling me that these people could be MI5 spies! And yet I did not say a word.

"I am not making any accusations, but quite obviously something is being organised by the state…"

"Another throw of the dice."

"Indeed. They are up to something, and whatever tools they have at their disposal, it is in their interest to use them right now. There might be a perfectly sensible and innocent reason why David would be looking into the background of these comrades, but it is certainly worth asking the question as to why he was. I think we need to find out what this reason could be. Because I think it's bloody strange that following his grandfather's suicide, he spends all his time doing checks on them. Whatever he was looking for brought him up here and then his death."

She was going around the houses. Times were indeed a-changing if coppers were getting shy and retiring. I finished off her thought process. "And the reason could be that after meeting Jenny Underhill, he had found out something that told him of an agent high up in the party. He was seeing if he could find out who that was. Those comrades were his suspects, and while he was investigating them, he found something out or got too close to finding out something, and he was killed for it."

"It's one theory," she said quietly.

I had nothing more to say. What could I say? We stood, or rather I stood, with my back to the North Sea whilst she smoked, leaning against a car probably worth what I had earned in a year. Where to now? We stood like a pair of teenagers on a first date; unsure of how to proceed. Not certain on how much to trust the other or indeed whether they even liked each other.

She was the bolder of the two of us. "I think we both think that the revolution is under attack, and it's up to every comrade to do what they can to defend it. I think we have no choice but to look into this. You know that, too; that's why you ignored Jackie's decision to take you off the investigation. We should act as a team, pool our resources."

"Resources? What resources? What can I do? And who is going to just sit back and let you ask questions about the loyalty of respected, and in some cases, loved comrades? You'll get lynched!"

"Exactly! That's why *you* should do it."

Was she mad?

"Jackie called you a comrade who is fraternal and full of goodwill to all, except other party members; to them, she said you had a reputation of cynicism, sectarianism, and bullheadedness."

Jackie was a fan of mine, then.

"So you stirring up trouble will be seen simply as you being you: Pete Kalder being his bullheaded, obnoxious self; nothing more than a damaged soul playing out his detective fantasies."

Seems Comrade Cole was one, too.

"You see, Jackie was right in the beginning. You can look into areas where I can't, and I can search places where you can't."

"*Please*. Do you really think that we're going to be Starsky and Hutch now?"

"Who?"

"Never mind. I, at least, am one comrade who does not work for the police!"

She fixed her eyes on me. "It doesn't matter what you think of me, although I could point out that if this revolution fails, then the chances are you'll face a short sentence for *past* activity. I, on the other hand, will face the firing squad. But what does matter, is to see if there is any way that we can stop attempts to destabilise the party.

"Somebody once wrote in an agitational pamphlet that it did not matter what you thought of the person standing next to you on the picket line. You could hate every cell of their body, but that was irrelevant because if you could trust that person to fight by your side, for you and others, that was higher than petty feelings—that was solidarity; that was true comradeship. Wise words. I believed them when I first read them, and I believe them now. I wonder where the writer is now?"

Smart arse. She knew full well he was standing in front of her.

CHAPTER THIRTEEN
What Everyone Should Know About State Repression

I unlocked the bedroom door and warily made my way downstairs. It was 8:15 in the morning, and I couldn't put off checking for hidden state enforcers any longer. Fully armed with a camping torch, I was at the ready. Oh, I could mock myself, but I had been deadly serious when I had locked myself and the cat in the bedroom last night. I had brought in his food and water and dug out the litter tray, and he had kept me company as I barricaded myself away for the night. This time, my fitful sleeping had not been due to recurring nightmares of my personal past, but of night noises making me sit up, imagining all manner of comings and goings-on downstairs: masked intruders breaking in and assassins unholstering handguns or unsheathing jagged blades. Images of every horror film, thriller, and chiller TV special came to haunt me. Every creak had been an axe murderer; every owl hooting, a creature from the depths of hell. Descending the stairs, I asked myself why I actually owned a heavy-duty camping torch; I hated camping!

Victoria Cole had assured me that it was highly unlikely that I was in any danger because, as she phrased it, "The state could not kill everyone who knew as little about what was going on as I did," otherwise half the population would be wiped out. Ignorance was safety, apparently.

Sleep hadn't been easy to come by last night as I had lain awake, churning over what Cole and I had discussed. I was self-aware enough to realise that it wasn't just fear that had kept me awake but guilt, too. The previous Sunday,

I had been happy trundling along in my little life. Then Jackie had made an unexpected call. I wasn't trundling anymore.

Finding that all was safe, I edgily made myself breakfast. I had decided against taking one of my pills last night and would not do so this morning, either, as the last thing I wanted to be was numbingly happy. What that did mean, though, was if I kept to my present regime of facing the world head on, pretty soon I'd be grinding my teeth and pacing around in circles. Well, that would make a sniper's job harder, I supposed. How long the abstinence from chemical support would last was open to question; if it was like my past attempts at dieting, then it would be a couple of hours before I would find a secret place and down one. If I did that with chocolate bars, then happy pills would be a real challenge.

On the kitchen radio were tales of woe from both sides in yesterday's battles. For balance, we had a NWC member talking of his kicking and broken ribs, followed by a pro-government supporter and his broken nose.

There were interesting reports concerning the bombing of the Leeds bank. Several journalists were questioning whether there had indeed been any exchange of gunfire between the supposed anarchists and the police. News drones had recorded sounds of guns coming only from the direction of the police. People were demanding an enquiry into the episode. Also, it was pointed out that the postmortem of the five anarchists would be held in secret and performed solely by the police. A request to have a NWC-backed pathologist present had been refused. Despite a painful attempt at impartiality, there was a definite undercurrent of suspicion about the story we were being told.

Foreign leaders had no such doubts; a whole lineup of them was calling it terrorism and called for a return to law and order. The president of the United States was offering to chair talks between the NWC and the government. Sweet. What a wonderful idea to have him as the honest broker; that would be the same president who unleashed state troopers on his own demonstrators. I could see us jumping at that one. I had detected, buried in his rather turbid speech, a slight threat. If Britain was unable to stabilise and "decombust" the situation, then because of "our special relationship," he would offer the government whatever support they needed. I presumed that didn't refer to tourists taking photos of Buck House. It was in the United

States' interests to have a "de-confrontational" UK. He called us the birthplace of democracy. Shucks, if he went on much longer, there would be a tear in my eye.

Today was not going to be, in any sense whatsoever, a fun day, which was made a great more foreboding by the fact that I was far from certain that I had chosen the correct, let alone sensible or easiest, course of action. There was a distinct feeling of unease in my gut. It wasn't indigestion but concern. Trouble was, I didn't have any other ideas, so I was, reluctantly, going to do what we had agreed.

I didn't turn on the TV, as I wanted to leave as soon as possible. I had rung the New Thames Hospital and found out that Marie Williams was on duty till 11:00 a.m. Today was going to be a getting-down-to-business-day, so maybe that was why I had decided upon my three-piece, navy-blue, chalk-stripe suit, with a three-button-down, red shirt and tie. Black, two-button, ankle-high boots, with winkle-picker points and red socks finished the look. I swept back the hair and noted that the bruise had faded considerably; it was pretty much the same, sludgy-green colour as the bags under my eyes. Hmm, nice match.

Grabbing my helmet and gloves, I got on the scooter, noting that it would require charging soon, but I could do that later today. It took me longer to get to the hospital than my previous trip due to largish groups of people milling about in the streets, wielding a variety of weapons ranging from rifles, blocks of wood, and placards to ice lollies. It was a hot day, and Britain hadn't run out of them just yet. There was nowhere near the debris in the roads as there had been in previous street battles, due to the scale being dramatically less than last year's. It had been more after tremors rather than an earthquake.

After a journey that involved much weaving in and out, I got there. As the sliding doors did what sliding doors should do and slid open, I walked up to the receptionist. She was the same woman who had been here on the day of the St Paul's bombing, which made it much easier and then again, a whole lot harder. She smiled at me, delivering that receptionist welcome which they all seemed trained in, presumably at some white-collar academy. As we spoke, she told me she remembered me from that dreadful day. We talked about it and the events since. From the terminology she used, I would have made the guess that she was, if not a member of ours, then a supporter.

I shook my head at the accounts of deaths from the street fighting, feeling just a tinge of guilt about using carnage as a smokescreen but feeling that needs must. "It was awful to see. I know, compared to the Battle of the Mall and the other clashes, the scale of the casualties was comparatively small, but it still shocked me. How many dead were in Bristol—twelve, thirteen?"

Her reply was genuine; her regret real. This was not plastic emotion like mine but honest and substantial. "Oh, I heard it was twenty. My brother lives there; he rang me last night and told me that it was bizarre; the pro-government rioters just attacked the Bristol Workers' Council building for no reason. Completely unprovoked! Madness. They hadn't a chance. One guy was beaten so badly that he died of internal injuries. But, for goodness' sake, they had shot one of the militia guards, so what did they expect?"

"Insane." I temporarily paused, but was eager to leave the subject alone and get to more honest lying. "You had some trouble here, as well, didn't you? I saw on the news a few nasty scuffles down this road after their provocative demo on Friday, outside St Paul's, calling us murderers!" At least this charade had a more legit reason. Or so I kidded myself. "Marie didn't get caught up in it, did she?" I asked, having already established my Marie-is-my-chum credentials. In the space of the first four minutes of my arrival, she had heard about our joint family trip to Bruges and my Arsenal exploits with Ashok. Give me a couple more, and I would be getting out an album of samples of wrapping paper, which she had used on past Christmas presents.

She reassured me, "Oh, no, she was working at home for the last few days—she was well out of it."

A plastic smile pulled my lips. "Good."

Cole and I had shared ideas on what we should do next. She had pointed out that the first thing we should do was to establish where people had been, when the hybrid persona of Jelena and Jenny had been murdered. Remembering the receptionist at the university and even more so, Bill and Ben at the party centre, I suggested that a good person to start with was the woman who was presently amiably chatting away with me. Receptionists knew *everything*.

Marie was at work now. After a quick call, I was informed that she wasn't on the wards but was doing paperwork. I was given instructions on how to get to her office on the third floor. I knew the way, so enjoying the familiar odour of cleaning products, I got in the lift and went to meet her.

Going up, I thought about what I had said at the desk. I *did* have history with Marie. I did remember that trip to Bruges. I think we had started laughing, whilst rallying the kids onto the Eurostar on the outwards journey, and had not stopped until we had arrived back three days later. There were no excuses about what I was doing here, because this was shitty. Absolutely shitty. But then, I had made my decision, and I was someone who liked to keep to a decision once I had made one.

Then again, I said to myself, rehashing my mental argument, I also valued loyalty. I probably valued it above almost everything bar love. And let's face it; you could not have love without loyalty. I had never been unfaithful in any relationship. The thought had not even crossed my mind once I had met Caroline. Well, why would it? When you've met the best…

I had been true to my politics and loyal to the party. Sure, I was a cynical old git and had a reputation for such, but I was a big softie, really. I also thought myself loyal to my friends. I had rather pushed them away of late, but that was not from me being perfidious, just deeply hurt.

I reached her floor and got out, ready to investigate the possibility of her being a treacherous, cold-hearted killer. Yeah, as I said…loyalty. Finding her office fairly easily, I knocked and entered. She had been at her desk working, but once she saw me, she rose, smiling broadly, and warmly kissed me on my cheek. As I returned the affection, I felt that my thirty pieces of silver would not be too long in coming.

Pulling back, she smirked, stroking my jacket collar with the back of her hand. "So whose wedding you off to? Or is it a job interview? You're not going to start working for a living, are you?"

"I always like to look my best, you know that. Especially with those who warrant an office of their own," I replied, faking a smile.

She gave a theatrical grimace. "Shared."

Her hair today was tied back harshly behind her ears, emphasising the lines around her eyes and forehead. Her uniform, though clean, looked old and well-used, adding to the overall impression of a woman severely overworked. This was reinforced by the way it hung from her chest, which I guessed, though I was neither a nutritionist nor a female dress designer, indicated that she had lost some weight recently. She had always been fairly trim, despite having had three children. She always had an active lifestyle—both in terms of running machines and running union activity—which had kept her fit, but now she looked lighter than normal, which, combined with her height, gave her an ungainly stance. You could not imagine Marie sliding across a ballroom to a Viennese Waltz.

She offered me a chair whilst sitting back down on hers. Unbuttoning my jacket, I followed. The unwritten rules of conversation dictated that I first exchange pleasantries, asking after Ashok and the kids, despite asking the same question the previous time we'd met. After that, I would broach the reason for my unannounced arrival. I wasn't quite ready for that right now, so like someone dropping minicab cards through letter boxes, I chose a circuitous route.

"What do you make of all that's going down at the moment? What's been on the news has been sickening. I saw one kid wielding a baseball bat on someone twice his age. I can't believe that the pro-government supporters are being so provocative."

She replied with a noncommittal vagary. There were a few generalisations about capitalism and its death throes but nothing which prompted amazement or wonder. She did not appear to be too interested in getting into a debate about the matter. That didn't really surprise me, as she did have patients to look after; it wasn't all waiting for a passing political discussion. Not getting much after a few attempts, I decided to shift the ground a little and reminisced about how when the latest economic crisis had hit, we had seen hundreds of thousands take to the streets.

Although still rather obviously not inclined to while away the hours chatting, she did join in, recalling how the whole country had been paralysed by a general strike and how the then trade union leaders had appeared powerless. They had stared into TV cameras like rabbits into oncoming car headlights. Here, too, though, she seemed noncommittal, not really that interested, as if there were more pressing matters on her mind. Her whole demeanour was of someone who had something better to do with her or his time.

There was nothing really suspicious about that; her patients wouldn't cure themselves. But with all respect to the women here, I ignored it, because

I wanted to manoeuvre this conversation to a certain point. We drifted along nicely, chatting about recent history and my tiny and her somewhat larger, role in it. I had never been that obsessed with size.

The longer our little tête-à-tête went on, the greater was the thought that it was less from a master plan of sleuthing and more from cowardice to get to the point. I noticed that Marie kept giving a sideways glance at the clock, so I decided that I could not delay much longer and brought it closer to home. "I heard that there were pretty bad clashes around here; near St Paul's it was supposed to have got very nasty. Seems to me that they were going out of their way to aggravate the situation!"

She concurred by simply moving her head and shifted on her chair, which could have been due to its poor ergonomics, or it could have been that this was a conversation she did not feel happy to be having. Or maybe it was just that she had work to do. People did, you know.

Again, I ignored any rival demands on her time. "Must have been a bit hairy round here, though."

"Oh, it wasn't too bad. Most people see us as neutral; just a few broken glass windows." She shifted her weight again. A really crap chair or something more meaningful?

"Good," I replied, trying to look relieved. "So you were OK?"

"Oh, yes, I was perfectly safe."

You were indeed, Marie, at home and nowhere near here.

I needed her to be more explicit, so I probed a bit further: "I was worried that you might be in danger. You are quite the national figure now, so if any of that lot had seen you arriving or leaving for work, you could have been attacked. Or going for some tasty, organic, healthy, low-salt, low-carb sandwiches in the café opposite," I feebly joked, painfully aware that this all sounded excruciatingly artificial.

She replied with a smile. "No, I gave them a miss; I had an equally healthy salad in the canteen, instead."

I couldn't describe what I felt at hearing what she had eaten on that day, or rather, *where* she had eaten. It had become very claustrophobic and stifling in her small nurse's office, surrounded by unintelligible posters and aging computer equipment. Opposite me was someone I felt very close to, someone who had been in the inner circle of my life, but who was now someone I was beginning to harbour doubts about. How could these two feelings coexist?

The next obvious step was to pin her down as to precisely what she, or what she claimed, to have been doing at the time. She was giving the impression of being here, but downstairs, I had found out that she had not been, so where had she been? Now was the time to be more specific and get answers. But I bottled it.

"Any news about Dave's murder?" I asked, changing the subject. "I wondered if that copper, er, whatshername, Cole? Yeah, Detective Victoria Cole, has dug anything up yet? I would just love to know whether or not she had any idea on what had happened to them. It would be nice to think that she had a lead on who had committed that butchery."

Sadness drifted across her face. "To be honest, Pete, I haven't heard anything, though Vic wouldn't report to me, would she? She'll be in close contact with Jackie, not the likes of me."

"Maybe, maybe not. You were, after all, very close to Dave, weren't you? At the funeral, Marie, you looked grief-stricken."

She hung her head, "Yeah, we were close."

I looked at her. I believed her. I knew that she and Dave had been good friends, and either she was an Academy Award-winning actress, or she had been devastated at the funeral. Grief had not been so much written all over her as daubed. But then there was a massive *however* involved. However, I had to now ask some questions which would ignore that; questions she would not like. Feeling like someone might if they were about to admit to their wife that they had been having an office fling with the woman from accounts, I felt a mixture of fear, shame, and worry. I tried to locate my backbone. Pull yourself together, Kalder. I paused and then plunged right on in with it.

First came one of my renowned cover stories. "Well, you're lucky, Marie; I had the privilege of a visit from our comrade cop. Always a pleasure. She grilled me for over an hour. Asking me what I had been doing trying to contact Dave and what I thought it had to do with Alan's suicide. On and on she went. Once a cop, always a cop, I guess; still, if that's what Jackie thinks is for the best." Then without the slightest pause, I slid the question in. "You got any ideas on that front?"

Strewth! Flimsy or what! Surely, she would see through this. I did not know whether to be proud or ashamed at my lack of skill in deception. Did it show that I was the honest type or simply that I was rather dim witted?

"None. I can see how it looks, but I have no idea how they could be linked." She held up her hands.

"Really?" I asked. Marie was a very intelligent woman, a woman not just clever academically but in a common-sense type of way. And yet she did not have any ideas.

She shrugged. "Well, what link could there be?"

What indeed? "Dave didn't give you any clue at what might have pushed Alan into taking his own life?"

Another movement in her chair. "No, none at all; like I told you, when we spoke at Alan's house, he just rambled. It's pretty understandable, isn't it? He had just found his grandfather dead. He was in total shock, he…"

I had stalled for too long. Time to put up or shut up; I decided to be direct. It was time to move up the evolutionary ladder and discover a vertebra. "What about when he rang you afterwards? The day after, wasn't it? Actually, didn't he ring you twice? What *did* he have to say, Marie?"

She looked stunned. I had done it. The boot had gone in, and now as any street thug will tell you, when the right goes in, make sure the left follows quickly.

"What did he talk about with you?"

She must have been asking herself how I might know that and whether she had told me herself, but then she would have instantly told herself that she hadn't. So her response was to deny it. Which she did. "I don't know where you got that idea, Pete, but he didn't. I hadn't spoken to Dave since I met him at Alan's. Didn't he go missing?" Something crossed behind her eyes, but she kept her dismissive attitude going. "No one could get hold of him."

I held my stare straight at her. "That was true for most of us but not for you, was it, Marie? Do you want me to tell you the times he rang? And how long the 10:33 a.m. call lasted? Twenty minutes. Or how long the 3:12 p.m. call lasted? That was longer, by the way—thirty-two minutes."

I was no expert at this. What was the best interview etiquette to gain results? I had chosen the method of asking as many questions as possible and giving the answers at the same time. It made me sound clever but didn't give her much scope of providing her own.

Still, the crudity of the approach had surprised her. "H-h-how do you know?" She looked, for about the first time since I had first known her, vulnerable. Calm, solid, and in-control Marie Williams looked exposed.

I kept my jaw solid and gave her my best I-mean-business look. Think Burt Lancaster's jawline. Not wanting to spoil the effect, I did not tell her that Cole had found this out and told me last night. She'd thrown me the bone, and I was running with it. Keeping quiet on how I knew made me look much more impressive—sleek Alsatian rather than Cole's lapdog. "The thing is, Marie, when I spoke to you after Jackie had assigned me to look into all this, you neglected to mention this fact. Why? Why didn't you tell me that you had talked?"

Her reply was deadpan. "It was personal."

It was a pathetic answer and, in the context of what we were talking about, quite insulting. "So what was the *personal* thing he wanted to talk to you about? As far as I can make out, he was looking into Alan's suicide, but in the middle of that, he feels the need to ring you. Twice. So the question remains: what did he want to talk about?"

She stumbled. "It was family stuff, mainly about *his* family; how his grandmother had left Alan and what that had done to both his grandfather and, in turn, to his own father. How his father had become so isolated—running off to Scotland." She stopped, trying to regain control. It was for only a moment, but it was long enough to regroup.

"Look, Pete, what are you saying?" Her tone had toughened.

Puzzlement had at least temporarily set aside any feelings of discomfort I was feeling at questioning her like this. I continued. "I just want to know why you kept a key piece of information quiet when, as you full well knew, I had been asked—on behalf of the party—to look into it. So what else did he say?"

An internal conflict could be seen on her features; her wish to gain composure and no doubt tell me where to go battled for control with each other. I could not say for sure what it was, but whatever the latter was, it seemed to be unsettling her. It was strong, so I gave another push, then shove, then kick.

"So Dave goes AWOL, contacts you—twice—which for personal reasons you keep a secret, and then he gets found murdered. Any ideas why?"

"Why would I know why he was murdered?"

An interesting misunderstanding. "I meant, *why did he think it was so important to ring you?*"

She exhaled heavily; something which I was sure meant something but as yet, couldn't tell what. Shrugging, she gave in. "OK, OK, so he rang me. As I said, he talked a lot about his family. He talked about how he had heard that Alan had suffered a breakdown. Dave was just trying to get a handle on why Alan might have killed himself."

"Wasn't that why Jackie had wanted me to look into it?"

"Yes, but…"

"So why keep it a secret?"

"His was personal, whereas…"

I didn't let her finish. "Ours just had to do with the party. The revolution. Little things like that. I must say it sounds strange to me, Marie. So he spent almost an hour, over two phone calls, talking about ancient family history?" Any glimmer of sentiment, affection, or closeness had been purged. I silently dared her to hide the truth.

"Well, yes, and he kept talking about people his grandfather knew, his friends, people like me, Jackie…"

"Who *specifically*?"

Her face altered. Surprise at my hardness had momentarily taken her aback, but it was subsiding. "As I said, Pete, it was personal matters. *Very* personal."

Determinedness was replacing hesitancy. She was visibly trying to regain control. Knowing her as I did, I knew that when she had that look, she became truly formidable. Many a manager, or obstructive union official, had found that out to their cost. I knew better than to antagonise her any further; now was a time to retreat and to do so rapidly.

I threw my hands up and shook my head with what I hoped could be regarded as a rueful smile. Then, touching my temples, I exclaimed, "Oh, Marie, I'm sorry. Listen to me, I sound like that Victoria Cole. Please forgive me. It's just all this with Alan, Dave, and Yasmin has really shaken me."

It was basically the same bowing out I had used with Youssef and Olivia. Play dumb after the event and run. The advantage of such a course of action was that looking dumb did not seem to be a stretch for me, although I was aware that I sounded rather camp and theatrical when I did. There was enough ham in my performance to stock an upmarket deli. Her eyes did not signify any clemency but rather a desire to go to war.

I reached across and gently touched her arm, in what I hoped appeared to indicate a desire for support. "To tell you the truth, all this has brought back feelings I have been rather trying to bury, alongside thoughts I don't want to have again. I don't need to explain, do I, Marie?" Brazenly, using every emotional bit of currency I had to spend, I even found myself stroking the underside of my arms where the scars from self-inflicted wounds were. Classy.

Shamelessly, I ploughed on. "And to make things worse, I'm out of my pills. Oh Christ, what a mess! Sorry, Marie, it's just when that Cole said that, I don't know; I flipped. I *am so* sorry. Please accept the apologies of an idiot."

Despite her anger being vivid in her eyes, her body relaxed a little. She had too much regard for me to think that this was anything other than a friend apologising for a histrionic outburst, because he was feeling pain from emotional wounds reopening after being in proximity to the sad deaths of people he knew. She laid her hand on mine, which was still on my arm.

"You have nothing to feel sorry for, Pete. I understand; I really do. Jackie should never have asked you to look into this—it was just unfair. And, well, you are right; I should have told you that Dave had phoned. That was my fault."

She gave me an understanding look, and the chagrin was waning, but I sensed that there was something else there as well. She might be all-forgiving, but I had hit a nerve. It wasn't just annoyance at being accused of complicity or her being spoken to like that, but she was uncomfortable at the position she had found herself in. I wasn't the only one playacting here. That was perhaps why she again apologised but added rather too quickly that she had much work to do, so she had better get on with it. She was bringing this unfortunate meeting to a close, in an oh-so-friendly, compassionate manner, but one that did not countenance any opposition. The hand waving you off at the station with a tear and a hanky was one gloved in chain mail.

I left her office with a whole mixture of conflicting thoughts in my head. All were troubling. This had been far from pleasant, and the day had only just begun. Leaving the hospital, I tried Michael Hughes again but once more only got through to his sodding voice mail. I was in better luck with my next call—Youssef Ali; obviously your water worker wasn't as busy as your squaddie.

Still, as I scootered past clean-up crews, the thought of what might await me did trouble me a little. He was, after all, in the water cleaning and waste-disposal business, and that to me meant sewage. So telling me to meet him at his place of work did conjure up images of being knee-deep in shit, wading through the excrement of our fair city, clad in rubber galoshes and yellow fluorescent tops, and assailed by a total, nerve-killing stench.

He had said that midmorning the management committee was meeting to discuss the priorities of the next few days. Discuss priorities of the next few days? Didn't they stay the same? Making sure our loos flushed and the taps ran? What was there to debate? How much chilli was in Mr Blogg's ten-inch floater or to worry about the turds from the WC1 area?

Trying to banish the thought of my suit being covered in crap, I increased my speed. Once on the Edgware Road, I made good time. I had been given the address, which did not sound like a sewage pool, not that I was too sure what name such a place would possibly have. It would hardly be 1 Turd Avenue. In any case, arriving there about an hour after I had left Marie, I confirmed that it was a medium-sized block of offices. I parked, put my helmet under the seat, and went in.

My fears proved to be unfounded. At the reception, which had an exciting backdrop of large action shots of overflow points, treatment centres, and tunnels, they gave me a pass rather than wellies and pointed to a lift, telling me where the meeting was being held.

The meeting itself was in (pun intended) full flow as I let myself in to what looked like any conference room in any office in any industry. There were approximately twenty in the room; all sat around an oval table with the obligatory smattering of laptops, pencils, and irony of ironies, mineral water. I felt a childish disappointment at the same cross section of smart, smart-casual, and casual that you'd find in any organisation. No heavy waders or safety jackets, just skirts, trousers, shirts, blouses, and jackets. Dull.

Youssef nodded hello as I entered and indicated a spare seat in the corner. No one looked up; probably, dressed as I was, they took me as another manager, and so a corner seat was where I deserved to be put. After a few minutes of listening, I gathered that the two guys sitting opposite me, both in navy-blue suits, actually were senior management. I guessed this by incredible deduction, when several of the others kept directing comments such as "management needs to" or "we instruct the management team" in their direction. They would sometimes acquiesce and sometimes oppose what was being said, but the impression was clearly given that it was out of politeness that they were here at all. The topic of the discussion was desalination and contained much jargon, which meant nothing to me, being such a dope about such matters.

All of a sudden, I felt something vibrate in my trousers, and it was certainly not excitement at the topic of the meeting. Slipping out my phone, I saw that I had received a text from Victoria Cole which read simply: "Michael Hughes @ New Scot Yard demo. 4:00." Later I could ponder how she knew this and what the meaning of her knowing it was. Right now, I was here to ask Youssef a few questions, and that meant sitting and waiting.

He didn't seem to be in too good a mood at the moment. His face shouted irritation, and every time one particular person spoke, he jumped down her throat, even for comments which I considered quite sensible. But then what seemed logical in English could well be bonkers in water-supply speak. But certainly whenever the woman with the heavy earrings spoke, he became very dismissive.

I did, though, experience a flutter of excitement when, as I listened to one speaker referring to his brother and sister from the pumping stations, I saw a large bag by his feet, containing what I was certain were waders.

Youssef himself was in a brown, striped, summer jacket over a pale-yellow T-shirt. He had had a haircut since I had last seen him and now wore a severe crew cut. It did show something I hadn't noticed before and that was he had very pretty eyes with feminine, long eyelashes. As the Comrade Earrings began to match his irritation, I noticed his mouth, as it turned up at the end into a false supercilious smile, was also rather petite.

Strewth, did Lenin ever have to sit in meetings listening to arguments over the effectiveness of water purification? Or be so bored that he passed the time studying the mouths of comrades? Did he sit there thinking, hmm, Nikolai Bukharin, great economist, but don't trust him; his lips are too thin?

My attention was grabbed when he barked at her. "Are you going to oppose everything I say, comrade? We try to work as a team here!"

She met his stare. The two managers smirked. One of those with the waders coughed. "Brothers, sisters, let's keep this fraternal here…"

I had never realised that water and sewage could get so heated. Hot shit, indeed!

It was proposed that they move onto the next agenda item. I wondered how long this would go on for and whether my reason for living was decreasing. I went back to thinking how bizarrely he reminded me of a pouting teenager. The mention of the question of the drought issues in central Africa, however, did briefly prick my interest. How Cricklewood could tackle global warming could be an interesting topic, but sadly it was deferred.

So back to the living coma. What was making this even worse was that sitting here, mentally mocking, was all very good, but I wasn't that obtuse to understand the all-too-obvious irony that whilst they were discussing sewage systems, I was waiting to try my hand at a form of muck raking. It would have made me feel better to report that I was racked with guilt or churning with self-doubt, but I wasn't. Yes, I didn't feel proud being here, but I felt fewer qualms about meeting Ali than I had had whilst questioning Marie. She was worth a million of him, and I had agreed to sacrifice loyalty to her. Should I worry how easily I had moved to mistrusting her?

The windmills of cheap self-analysis were interrupted when I heard mention of defending the utilities from attack. My expectation of where the direction of the threat was coming from was way off target.

Youssef led the discussion. "We've all seen the call on the social networks to turn the anarchist methods against them."

All nodded. I didn't. I hadn't. What did he mean? *Using* the anarchist methods? Not the anarchists themselves?

"It's been circulating for a couple of days now, and I fear it's growing in strength. We cannot tell who had originated the call, but it is clear that what is being proposed is a terror campaign against buildings either associated with, or under the jurisdiction of, the workers' councils. We don't know who is instigating this; Parliament has, for what it's worth, denounced it, and publically, at least, distanced themselves from the call…"

Around the table there were a few, "Yeah rights".

"And," he continued, "it may be all hot air from a few Fascists trying to prod Parliament into action or gain revenge, but then it could also be real. They specifically mention several buildings that are used for meeting and organisational purposes, but we cannot rule out a possibility that we are a target. Let's face it, the Capital's water and drainage systems are of great importance."

Heads nodded alongside murmurs of agreement, including Ms Earrings. Even management concurred.

"I have taken the liberty of contacting the local workers' council and requested militia protection. I hope that is acceptable."

It was, with the only quibble arising from management about how quickly they would be here, because time was of the essence. Youssef gave details on how many would be allocated and when they would arrive. He suggested where they could be deployed. There was a brief discussion about how they would be fed, before getting into the details of which tunnel or pumping station should get priority. The thought of fleeing crossed my mind as even talk of explosive devices turned into dull rambling minutia of waterworks.

Finally, however, management saved me! One of them suggested continuing the discussion after tea. To my eternal relief, it was agreed that there would be a half-hour's break. They all filed out of the room, no doubt to pour themselves hot beverages, locate a biscuit or even two, and to chat amiably about fluoridation. After the last one had left, Youssef rose to his feet and plonked himself down next to me. He didn't bother with any niceties.

Breathing out wearily he said, "So you said that you were doing a series of profiles on comrades for the party blog."

Hearing him say it didn't improve my confidence at my abilities at dissimulation. The idea of pretending that I was writing party blogs had been my idea as a way to answer questions without arousing suspicion. Cole had not been impressed but had not been able to come up with a better one. I gamely explained how it was just an attempt to add a more human face to comrades who were the backbone of the party; to show that we were not as the media portrayed us, as soul-less automatons. My fingers were crossed in the hope that he would not wonder why the masses would be interested in the life of a drainage man. I needn't have had any worries. After all, the passion I had just witnessed could have easily convinced me that there existed a hydration sect fervently worshipping pipes, and because of which, any piece on one of the great priests of water could lead masses of conversions. Who would not want to know about him! Well, there would be no problem with baptisms; that was for sure. Or, in other words, he could spare me ten minutes.

I had to confess that his tone tended to suggest that he thought he was humouring a comrade who hadn't anything better to do. Before starting, I asked him about sister earrings. What was her story? Why was he so antagonistic towards her?

He looked guilty. "Was I that bad?"

I broke it to him that he was pretty hostile. Was she a class enemy? Traitor? Steal all the biscuits? Worse than that—dissed the pipes?

He shook his head, "No, Helen's OK, really; a bit obstructive sometimes, but she's not bad. It's just me. I've been working too hard, I guess. I'll apologise when she comes back in. She means well, and I don't think she deserves what you said I was like."

Whether making your witness feel bad about himself or herself was in the *Miss Marple Book of Clue Hunting*, I could not tell you, but I decided to change the subject and asked if he minded me recording this, as my memory was terrible. With an ill-disguised indifference, he said that it was OK by him.

I kicked off by asking about his family background.

He told me how his mother had come over from Mumbai and his father from Izmir in Turkey at around the same time, at the turn of the century. They had settled in Birmingham, and within the first few months of arriving, both had signed up to an evening class to improve their English; they met, shared the absurdities of the language, and the rest was history.

"I get my looks from my mother and my love of raki from my father." He smiled for the first time since I had arrived.

"Was it a political household? Having parents from different parts of the world must have made for an interesting home life."

His smiled remained. "Interesting, yes. Loving, yes." The smile widened, puffing out his cheeks a little. "And very loud. I have four siblings, and I can tell you that, separately, Indian and Turkish cultures are shall we say, extrovert. Put them together, and that does make for a din!"

"And was it political?" I asked again.

"No, not really. Neither Mum or Dad were."

"At all?"

"No."

His bad humour had returned. He wasn't as affable as when I had first met him with Olivia Harrison. He had been like this through the meeting, so I could at least feel reassured that it was not my questions that were giving him the hump.

"So what did they do for a living?" I asked, explaining that I was trying to describe the background of his life.

"Mum was a housing officer and Dad, a train driver."

He pretty much closed shop over any further details concerning his parents, apart from noting that both were still alive and doting on his eldest sister's children. He was somewhat more forthcoming concerning his two brothers and two sisters, telling me what they did for a living and their political allegiances. The latter breaking down to: one brother, party member; one sister, a fellow traveller; one brother, fiercely pro-government; and one sister, totally uninterested. He appeared to be on good terms with them all and spoke with a warmth that managed to put aside what was irritating him for at least for a moment.

That did not survive my next question. "What do your parents think about your sexuality? Was there a problem?"

"Why?" he asked, obviously unhappy at some perceived subtext to the question. "They're both from third world countries and Muslim, so therefore they must be 'backward' and homophobic?"

I assured him that I didn't mean that at all and knew full well that both tolerance and prejudice weren't confined to one religion or geographic location. I just thought that it was a legitimate question. It wasn't; it was a clumsy one, but then all this was to hide my genuine concerns, so I had not given them much thought.

"Both Mum and Dad have been cool about my being gay. Both love my partner Nevin dearly."

"Really?" I exclaimed in exaggerated surprise. "But he supports Tottenham Hotspur!"

His frown dropped, and a small laugh arrived. "Just shows how Liberal they are, I guess!"

Nice save. Having got back into his good books, I wanted to stay there for as long as possible, because that would make all this a whole lot easier. "So you joined the party—three years ago?"

"Nearly four. It was after I had come down to London and started working in what was then a privatised utility. I met some comrades who were already active in the union. They took me to a joint meeting by Jackie and the old man, and that was it! Bang! I joined on the spot!"

"So it was all pretty sudden. You didn't spend time attending meetings or reading the *Revolutionary Worker*?"

"No, it just made sense then and there."

We spent a little time talking about how it took people different amounts of time to decide that joining was the right thing to do. It was an interesting discussion, but I was acutely aware that in a few minutes' time, a group of water-cleansing professionals would be returning. I did not have the stomach to have to sit through that again. Robespierre may have reputedly faced the guillotine face up, but even he would have baulked at the thought.

"What with your professional work, party work, and work for the NWC, you must be busy in the extreme?"

He confirmed what I knew. "I'm not actually a delegate to the NWC. But, yes, things are hectic at the moment, especially since the threat to disrupt the water supply."

"Do you think it is a serious one?"

"Possibly. You don't know what the state will do to stay in power."

No, indeed, you did not.

"Did the bombings surprise you?"

He looked at me sideways. "Yes. Yes, they did. I cannot believe it was them."

"So you'd put it down to the state?"

He shuffled in his seat. "Yes, I believe it was." So the seats here at the water board were as crap as at the NHS. He seemed to be as uncomfortable as Marie had been. Memo to the new workers' state—build better chairs!

I agreed; I, too, pinned the bombings on the ruling class, but the difference was that I wasn't so strangely uncomfortable about saying so. He became evasive when I asked him what made him think that and why. After a few attempts at prodding a substantial answer out of him, I could tell that the bad humour was returning so I switched subjects, or rather returned to a previous one.

"Anyway, give me an account of your average day."

He did so at length, informing me how it was a balancing act between his duties on the management committee I had just seen and his outside political activity. I found it very easy to make sympathetic noises about the severe calls on his time—especially with regard to the former.

"Take, for example," I continued, "the last few days; what would be the breakdown of the activities of Youssef Ali?" I gave my toothiest smile.

His account of today was full and detailed and boring in the extreme. That changed when he got to telling me about the previous days when it got very sketchy, not in a Leonardo sense but very crude, vague outlines. Indeed, he had to be encouraged to say anything at all about them. I wanted to know where he had been at the time of Jenny Underhill's death. Of course, despite being a novice at this game of disloyally suspecting comrades, I did not say this out loud, but I feared that the dryness of my mouth and my rather stagey insouciance made it bloody obvious.

His reply was that he had been visiting comrades across the industry, building up support for both the party and the NWC. The Greens, he explained were very strong in his sector. They would be, I mumbled in sympathy. I probed further and got some details as to which particular comrades he had met and where they were working.

He did not seem too happy at my proposal of *A Week in the Life* profile. Not that it really said anything in itself because there were many reasons why that might be, and most of them were positive ones. Still, where I was now, I saw everything as suspicious. I did ask myself why he was modestly shunning publicity. I would have liked to explore why he was keen to hide his light under a bushel, but I was thwarted by the return of the management committee. He did not seem to be too disturbed by their interruption. I might even have guessed that there was relief at seeing them.

I realised that it was time for me to leave and silently said sorry to comrade earrings who, I feared, despite Youssef's promise to play nicely, was going to face an even rougher ride than she had previously experienced.

Quickly thanking him and leaving, I made my way to the lift. As I did, a familiar vibration caused me to stop. Taking out the phone, I saw it was once more Detective Cole. I rolled my eyes. At this rate we would be moving in together. I looked to find out what she wanted. It was a text. It read: "Turn on Ch6Net News. Nothing on wall when I was there."

Having no idea what she meant but feeling totally intrigued, I found a corner near a water cooler (well, there just had to be one here, didn't there!) and turned on the suggested Internet channel. A reporter was talking over a familiar scene. It was the home of Jenny Underhill, complete with the white police tent covering the entrance. The reporter was telling the news anchor about the murder of a retired police officer. The details did not fit with Cole's story. Here, the reporter spoke of several bullet wounds in her, whereas Cole had told me it had been just the one to the forehead. Here it was from a Heckler and Koch machine gun, which, the reporter commented with heavy emphasis, was freely available on the streets and that "coincidently" many of the NWC militia carried them. He couldn't have given it more weight than if he had strapped blocks of iron to it.

"So what do we make of the graffiti found on the wall of her living room?" asked the anchor.

With that the pictures changed from the outside to the interior, focussing on several sentences sprayed in red: "When one makes a revolution, one cannot mark time. One must always go forwards—or go back."

It was a very familiar quote, and one many would know. It was perhaps Jackie's most used quotation from Vladimir Lenin. Sure, many could make claim to it. I think even a past prime minister had used it, but the fact was that most people seeing it would think of us. What Cole was saying in the text was that this had been sprayed post murder. That was not what was being said here. Although being very careful not to point the finger directly at the party, there was a strong implication that the quote showed that the murder had been political and aimed at a former member of the police service by an angry member of a Left organisation. Obviously someone thought we had marked time for long enough, and it was time to make a move.

***

Numbers were growing on the streets. Being on the bike made it difficult to judge the mood, but from the faces I could see, it was more grim determination that celebratory. Most of them were supporters of the workers' councils of one type or another. Standing aside, often literally and figuratively on the opposite side of the street, were much smaller groups of pro-government supporters. Both eyed each other with wary suspicion. It all felt as if the tension was physically slowing me down.

I arrived at New Scotland Yard at just past three. On leaving our sanitation comrade, I had received several more texts from Cole who appeared to be setting herself up to be my leader/mother/ commander/ commissar. She informed me that Hughes was overseeing operations at the demo. It wasn't one of ours, but we were stewarding it and had organised a small-scale affair to counter it. He would be here from 2:00 p.m., liaising between the two sides.

The building towered above with its bottom five stories sheathed in dented buckled steel and decorated in antiestablishment slogans. Standing there reading them was like an exhibition of recent history. Behind them stood an obstinate refusal to bow down to pressure: smashed windows and burnt, hollowed-out wrecks of offices. But the tanks and troops stationed in front of the building were not here to defend a symbol, because the upper floors were still operational, still upholding the government, and still opposing the workers' councils. The effect of huge sheets of metal thrusting upwards and topped by glass had once been described as a battleship carrying a Kew Gardens greenhouse. Hardly Thomas Hardy imagery, but it was pretty accurate.

I could see Hughes across the street talking to one of the police officers. From the copper's uniform, I would think that Hughes was negotiating with a senior police officer. He was busily pointing towards Westminster Abbey, which was where the demo was going to end. In her many missives, Cole had informed me that this demo had been called by the police under the banner of Reclaim Our Streets. Publically, the demand was that both the government and the NWC were ignoring law and order and what was required was that the two of them should sit together and talk. The subtext was somewhat different: the NWC were allowing criminality to run amok in the anarchy of the times; anarchy that had been caused by them.

Hughes shook Top Cop's hand, turned with stiff military precision, and walked back. I had positioned myself by one of the many party vans parked along the route. My scooter was on the opposite side to The Yard and was parked outside the row of boarded-up shops that had long since tired of the violence connected with this part of town.

Many of the vans were the types in which the back came down to create a small stage. They had often been used in carnivals or festivals to carry musicians or to act as kid's floats. Comrades were busy decorating them with red bunting, balloons, and giant red fists.

Hughes didn't notice me, but instead he marched past (did this man ever lope anywhere, or was the parade ground in his genes?) to a group of a dozen or so soldiers. They were rather different in look to the other comrades who were congregating. The group he was talking to were all muscular, tattooed, and uniformed. This was in contrast to the many who were dressed in hats of varying sizes and colours and wearing masks of a multitude of comic characters with a good few modelling primary-coloured balloons floating on strings from their wrists. It was a bizarre sight.

It might be over-egging it a tad, but I would have sworn that they stood to attention when he addressed them. Certainly, there was a formality emanating from them which could not be said of many others on our side of the street. Their only concession to casualness was the coffee they were all drinking, courtesy of the Venezuelan international chain of coffee shops that had boomed in these days of street protests. Tea might be the drink for shock, but coffee was the marching brew. Whoever owned the company must have a fleet of Rolls Royces courtesy of us. Certainly, one could wonder how they almost uniquely could get the stuff into the country.

Out of the latest incarnation of New Scotland Yard, which had been opened with fanfare and a minor royal but now looked worse for wear, and passing the smashed remnants of the world-famous sign, a long line of smartly dressed police officers streamed out onto the pavement. They conducted the most orderly march I had ever seen. Smoothly moving along the road, they took their positions. I stood watching them minute after minute, and there appeared to be hundreds of them. All had their plastic buttons looking shiny, and their boots all spic and span. Who exactly was keeping our wondrous city safe from the forces of anarchy?

Joining them appeared a few people in wigs—not drag queens but judges! I was fascinated by the sight. Would the protocol of marches apply to this one? Would there be the anarchists in dreads playing bongos? Or for them would it be Swansea CID on tambourines? Would there be young paper sellers with their organisation's publication pressed lovingly against their chests chanting "Jackie, Jackie, Out! Out!" To my disappointment it did not appear to be the case. They just filed out, politely and without fuss.

On our side were…jugglers! In front of me, twenty young men and women in clown's trousers were tossing balls, skittles, and soft toys merrily up into the air. Hughes had left the soldiers and was now talking to them. They were joined quickly by several comrades in full fancy dress. He waved over other comrades who, like those already here, seemed more in kids' party attire than confronting the cops' street garb. I couldn't help smiling to see—now a distinctly less comfortable—Hughes giving instructions to children's entertainers.

Above me, on the platform of the van, a young woman was trying out the PA by telling a number of rather well-worn jokes. More comrades were now appearing, but we were very much smaller in number than the coppers who were now becoming a substantial body of people.

Walking through the thin line of space now separating the police and our side, several clumps of journalists were moving, microphones and cameras in hands and sincere looks on their faces. They would stop now and then and ask a constable a question and, for news impartiality and to show balance, pose a question to a steward making giraffes out of orange balloons. Above us, news drones captured the whole glorious battiness of the occasion.

I was going to join Hughes and the circus of communards when he turned and walked over to me. I was disappointed, as I had experienced a sudden desire to hear what type of instructions this military man would be giving to them. Keep the noses red? Skittles high and the joke flowers well stocked with water? To be more precise, he didn't come to me but came over to talk to the comedian on the platform. He checked with her that everything was OK and wheeled around to attend to the next van.

Taking my opportunity, I introduced myself. "Hi. Michael Hughes, my name's Pete Kalder…"

A look of total incomprehension showed on his face. My fame had not reached him, then.

Shaking his hand, which my fingers could testify had a very firm grip, I gave him the story I had spun to Youssef Ali. Recognition finally flashed across his strong features, when I mentioned that I had been the one who was to talk to him about Alan Wiltshire until Jackie had taken me off the investigation. I said that I was now writing profiles of leading comrades. I faked a laugh about how she was desperate to get me to do something useful. He didn't crack a smile but just looked at me with a face that silently commanded that I get to the point. Because of just that, I did exactly the opposite and asked him what was happening here.

For a second he relaxed, and with a resigned look he answered, "The police have been planning this for a while. It's been all over the social networks—they have pulled out all the stops—calling officers from across London and from all the local forces. They're using the 'safety in the streets' stick to beat us with. The latest murder of that retired policewoman from up north has given them an extra zest." He pointed to several officers carrying large placards of a head-and-shoulders photo of a woman in uniform; a woman with a tick scar above her eye—our friend Jelena Jacobs/Jenny Underhill, cop and pretend comrade, Alan's lover and spy. I laughed at the irony.

Hughes looked at me with a surprised expression, but I couldn't explain. A woman working in the shadows, whose job, whose very life, was kept in the darkness, was now being paraded along the streets of London on two-metre, square placards. Someone might also be demanding to know whose cock-up this was. I couldn't believe for a second that MI5 had wanted this.

"So, please, comrade, explain what the hell is going on here?" I asked.

He sighed. "We decided that the latest street battles don't help us. We are well past that now. That period is well and truly over. I mean, who do they benefit? The workers' councils have to prove to the waverers that they can be a viable source of government. So this is to be a peaceful protest with no weapons on our side, and the police have agreed that there will be none on theirs." He poked a finger at the large number of police, judges, and magistrates opposite us. And it was true that there was a lack of body armour and what looked like a lack of weapons; the huddle of pro-government soldiers was plainly unarmed. Even the two tanks had their turrets facing downwards.

It was just like Christmas at the Somme! We'd be playing football on no-man's-land at this rate!

He turned his attention to our numbers that were also growing, though in far smaller, but it had to be said, brighter numbers. "We decided that, rather than have a large opposition demo, we would have a smaller number to steward it and one which would…" He sighed again, but heavier than before, "counter it, by poking fun at it. Instead of speakers we have stand-up comedians, and instead of militia we have members of the Entertainers and Workers Group."

"Superb!" I chuckled; it was quite deliriously daft and yet gloriously inspired. "So the world sees a demonstration by the police and the judiciary, which is itself policed by clowns and judged by jugglers!" It was Dadaist in its brilliance. "The best way to pierce pomposity was by taking the piss!"

Judging from the unhappy and puzzled look on comrade Hughes's firm jaw, he did not share that view. For a second, I took time to admire it; now that was what you called a firm jaw!

I was tempted to explore whether or not the decision to choose a comrade with a rifle for a spine and the stiffness of a flag pole to supervise this festival of the absurd was itself part of the joke. Above me, the comic was telling the one about the police car and the farm. Knowing the punch line, I ignored it and guided Hughes to more important questions.

I explained that I had much of his background already, but if he could spare me a few minutes, then I would appreciate it. My expectation was that I was going to receive a curt brush-off and a lecture about how busy he was, but instead there was almost a murmur of relief as he agreed.

Indeed, he embarked on a brief roundup of his personal history before I had a chance to turn my phone on **record**, let alone ask a question. He had joined the army at the age of fifteen through the Sign Up To Serve campaign which sought to lower the ever-growing employment numbers by putting them in uniform. He had trained as an infantryman and had served in several hot spots across the globe, fighting for the flag. He expounded his beliefs at the time of joining in a tone of amusement at his naïveté (now he was such a political sophisticate).

"What sort of things were you asked to do as a private in the British Army?"

He gave me a knowing look, and even a hint of amusement flirted with his face. "Oh, nothing at all that could be regarded as a war crime. I was only ever part of something that could be regarded as being within the rules of war, but, of course, as we are only too aware, the very rules of war are the rules of the ruling class who ultimately use war against us."

"Yes, indeed, comrade." We lived in times where people only seemed to converse in political speeches. "But what *exactly* was your role in the army?"

He did not flinch at the question, but took me on a very long and detailed tour of his duties. Very, *very* long. I had to confess that at times I drifted off and zoned into a meandering story involving a judge, a dying Fidel Castro, and a horse thief, which the comic was rehearsing for no particular reason. After all - who was going to listen to her? I returned my attention back to Hughes.

"So what was the moment when you came to the big questions of why you were doing this? Why were you being expected to risk your life for what someone had said was your country? What or who were you fighting for?"

"Oh, I'm sorry to disappoint you, comrade, but there was no huge flash of inspiration; there was no momentous occasion when I saw the light. I did not witness any atrocity which led me to doubt my role in the armed forces. It was quite simply that when I returned from NATO tours and saw former comrades thrown on the dump, it disturbed me. Oh, sure, we have the psych support and the housing aid but in reality? Returning soldiers were being treated as they had always been—cannon fodder. That's when I started to question things.

"Then one rainy February night, I sneaked into a meeting about someone I had never heard of—it was Frederick Engels, by someone I had never heard of—it was Jackie. There were near on a thousand people there talking about an obscure Victorian gentleman, and to my surprise, I found it thought-provoking. And, well, I kept asking questions and kept getting answers."

"And you chose to stay in the army rather than leave; that's an incredible position to take. Even today after the politicisation of the forces, it is still not the norm, but when you took the decision—you were one of the first. You could have been drummed out of the army or thrown into prison."

Modestly, he stroked away the compliment. "Comrade, you make it sound grander than it was. Maybe at other times I would have resigned.

Actually, there's no maybe about it. At most times, I *would* have resigned, but remember this was when society in general was getting politicised. I was not alone; there were thousands, millions doing so. They were asking the questions; they were coming up with the answers. I was just listening to them. I had the confidence to do it because I felt that it wasn't just me."

We talked of the situation now, of how all the armed forces had faced internal debates: to intervene or not, and whose side? There was now an uneasy agreement that no member of the armed services would use lethal force on the streets of Britain. There was, however, an allowance for them to show support and assistance. Hence, even here in this magic mushroom of a demo, there were Her Majesty's forces facing each other.

He stopped for a second and took a call on his phone, which, judging from what he said, was from comrades further up the marching route. Time was short. I had to get to the main question pretty quickly, as despite his obvious preference for making political speeches rather than supervising someone performing magic tricks, I could tell that he would have to go soon because it appeared that the police were preparing to move. Our comics were approaching the mikes; the counter demo was bracing itself with mimes, balloon animals, and itching powder. From the sneers on the faces of the officers by me, our approach was antagonising them more than any punch-up would.

His call finished, I got to my point. "So what does a comrade in the army do now? What are his or her responsibilities? I guess I mean, what are you expected to do on a daily basis? Who do you report to?"

He responded to the final question with a long, twisted, and tortuous explanation of his chain of command, which included the usual military procedure but what now had to also include the military representatives of the NWC. I nodded, trying to look interested.

Just as I had asked Youssef, I asked him what his usual day would be like. He replied, with his attention more and more drawn to the march. It was about to get going. Much of his days appeared to be visiting barracks and talking to other soldiers, explaining what our vision of the future was.

"Take the last few days," I said, thinking that, from his meaningful looks at the soldiers who were splitting up to join the stewards, I did not have much time left. "What have you been doing over the past few days? What is the average day for comrade Michael Hughes? For example, what about yesterday and the day before? What's been the itinerary for the previous two days?"

He answered without much thought and seemingly without a single muscle being used in his face. Even when talking, he retained a strange, small, fixed smile. It was perfectly horizontal, so much so that brickies could use it to check the levelness of their walls. As he spoke the image of a ventriloquist came to mind. "Oh, I have been doing the usual, party work, you know. Yesterday, I was at Aldershot and then Portsmouth. And, ah, the days before? Mainly clerical stuff; even the revolution has its paper work." His attention was not on me but the front row of the police demonstration.

I turned to see what was so interesting and could see that it was at that shuffling, impatient phase when you know it will be starting soon. Then, from one of the windows of the coffee shop, there was a flash. It was followed by the sound similar to a whip crack. For a microsecond I thought it was one of the circus entertainers, but then behind me there was a scream. I turned to see that at about twenty metres from where we stood, there was a disruption in the crowd. People were fanning out. A second bang quickly came. It was a gunshot. Voices of panic were being raised as people were rushing for cover, heads bowed, arms covering their heads. One policewoman shoved me aside, diving down, yelling, "We're under fire! They're firing!"

Hughes was loudly shouting at his phone. Seconds later, there were more shots. This time, they were coming from the upper levels of New Scotland Yard. The comedian above us had hit the floor of the flat-back lorry, with her head level with my chest, her face distorted with fear. I followed the trend and dropped down. Windscreens shattered. I was covered with glass as I fell to my knees. There was blood on my hands. My mind registered glass—glass and blood. And then total blackness.

CHAPTER FOURTEEN
Rebel Girl

I lay back with my feet on the coffee table and took another sip of the rather average red wine I had purchased from the corner shop and gave a silent prayer to the French workers who had defied the UN embargo and got it here. We might be running out of many of the essentials in this country, and the sight of empty shelves was becoming commonplace, but, hey, our alcohol needs were being looked after. Maybe that was what kept the government in power. In 1917 the slogan had been one of land, bread, and peace; we lived in a much more sophisticated time, and it was now latte, ciabatta, and Pinot Noir.

Not that I had felt very sophisticated at New Scotland Yard. I had come to, with a worried-looking Michael Hughes and female stand-up comedian in attendance. To my embarrassment, it had turned out that I had fainted, and other than my pride, I was unhurt. The blood on my hands had turned out to be just red dye from one of balloons that had been filled with such to add to the carnival atmosphere. Yes, it had sure done that.

My next worry was what might account for the wetness on my lower stomach. That, though, only heightened the humiliation when I realised that it, too, was not blood from a mortal wound inflicted on me by some wretched class enemy, with his heart full of hate and his soul a dead, selfish lump of oppression, but had resulted from the fact that on passing out, I had wet myself. Although the colour of my trousers and my jacket hid it from public view, I had been extremely keen to get out of the place.

From Michael Hughes's demeanour, it was apparent that I was not the only one who felt abashed there. He had been charged to keep order, and there had been a reasonable impersonation of *Gun Fight at the O.K. Corral*. He assured us that, despite his phone failing, he had gained control of the situation quickly and had contacted his opposite number to prevent an even more serious breach of the peace. The Met commander was furious and demanded to know why someone had opened fire on the march in an unprovoked attack. Hughes himself had been outraged at the charge, saying that the first shots had come from the seventh floor of the New Scotland Yard.

Militia were arriving fast to facilitate a withdrawal because, though the exchange of gunfire had only lasted five minutes, it had still left one police sergeant dead with three further officers seriously injured. Their colleagues were getting ever-vocal in their desire for revenge. Tension was seriously rising. All of a sudden, street entertainers didn't seem quite such a good idea.

I had got to my feet and fled home as soon as I could. No way in the universe was I going to stay there, taking on a raging bunch of a thousand coppers, spitting bloodlust with only clowns as my comrades and a wet patch around the crotch.

So I sat in dry, green, tonic sta-press trousers and purple polo shirt. Casual was required here, sitting, downing wine, and wallowing in self-pity. I had been happy with my routines and to-do lists. Sure, it got a bit lonely sometimes, but it had been loneliness of my own choosing. I had felt safe and secure in it. Could I say that of the present? Just how many days was I going to get involved in violence? I was meeting people; some of them were dead, and others were being shot at. I also had a brand new bezzie-mate in Victoria Cole, and who had never wanted a cop as a pal?

I could see the future: nights in, supping cocoa with something like Coldplay as the soundtrack, whilst she reminisced on beatings she had administered in the cells. She was certainly one who appeared to have an urgent need to contact me right now; I had ignored numerous phone calls from her.

More importantly, I had ignored my pills, which was at least something I could feel proud of. During the early days of the breakdown, I had suffered several fainting fits brought on by, well, even after several tests and checks, they hadn't known why. So emotional stress was blamed. Wasn't it always? But I had decided to give up the pills, and no matter what mess I had found myself in, I was going to stick to that. What courage that showed. Or at least that's what I told myself, as the feeling of being a little boy caught short in front of his eldest, sternest, and most Edwardian of aunties returned to cower me. Sure, I pissed myself in front of clowns and police officers, but pal, I stood tall in the saddle and refused the temptation of medical support. I would face this alone. John—bloody—Wayne!

The phone went. Surely it wasn't Cole again! I looked. It wasn't. It was Jackie. Reluctantly, I picked it up but kept it to voice only.

"Pete? It's Jackie. Is it you? Why is this on voice?"

Because I wanted it to be. "Yes, Jackie, it's me. How are you?"

"Not good. We need to meet. What are you doing right now?"

Enjoying dry trousers. "Not a lot. I decided to have a quiet night in after my four o'clock swim—you know I can't do without that. It's part of my rehabilitation to have exercise and a schedule." I wondered if that sounded as false to her as it did to me.

"Right," she said with an undercurrent of disbelief that answered my silent question. "Well, I need you to come to the centre because we need to talk."

"Er, sorry, Jackie, but I can't right now. I'm kind of busy, maybe tomorrow. And anyway, the charge is all but gone in the bike, so I am not sure how I could get over and…"

She was not having any opposition from me. No was not a possibility for her. Ms Payne had given a command, and little old me was expected to obey. "You can charge it at the substation by the centre. I'm sure you have enough to get that far. Pete, we need to talk. This is important. I'll see you within the hour. Agreed?"

My brain had replied with one thing, but my voice had said something different. "OK, I'll be there." With that she hung up, and I faced Red and asked him why the hell had I agreed to go?

***

I had been there within the hour. Basically, I did as I had been instructed. Now I sat with my hands, if not physically, then figuratively between my knees, waiting for Jackie to finish her meeting.

It was no exaggeration to say I had that feeling you experience when you're waiting outside the head teacher's office, expecting a bollocking for your behaviour in the geography lesson. My adoption of the cavalier lounging pose was as transparent here as it had been back then. The difference now, though, apart from being a lot slower and having developed an interest in geography, was that I was in a small office surrounded by 3-D printers rather than an overheated corridor. The people who saw me were photocopying placards, rather than harassed teachers hurrying to their next class. But it was still rather galling being here. If I didn't know better, and to be frank, I didn't, I would say that the delay was deliberate. I sat, feeling guilty, although I was not too sure what I had to feel guilty about.

The appearance of a smiling Simon Peary gave some respite. Dressed in double denims and with a leather rucksack slung over his right shoulder, he bounded into the room, beaming pleasantness. Friendship always seemed to follow Simon. Seeing me, he smiled and gave me a gentle and playful slap on my shoulder. "Hi, Pete! Nice Harrington. No suit and tie today?"

He slipped something onto the copiers and proceeded to tell me that he was off to speak at some meeting called by local residents concerning the party's attitude to young offenders. He pulled a face of mock horror, but I knew whatever the meeting was, he'd be great. He knew that, too; Simon had that confidence which empowered him rather than overpowered others, assured but not brash.

He didn't fear this meeting; he just wasn't excited by it. Simon did not do routine. In that way he was quite the opposite of me. Oh, I loved revolts and the like, as much as the next Bolshie, but I also enjoyed the drunken debates in pubs about all and nothing. Simon wasn't like that; he thrived on activity. Downturns in the class struggle bored him, and often as not, off he would go, cycling around Eastern Europe or Central America. Then, back he'd come, tanned with rippling calf muscles and his eternal bonhomie.

After photocopying something that looked like a miner's lamp, he grabbed a chair and sat by me. His baby-blue eyes flashed sympathy. They reminded me of the look a friendly literacy teacher would give me every time she saw me sitting outside the head's office. She had known I was in for a telling-off, and so did he.

"What mood is she in?" I asked, travelling back in time to a North London school.

He scratched his head and tried his best not-as-bad-as-you-think look. "Listen, mate; you have got to understand that Jackie's under a great deal of pressure at the moment. These last few days have been hard on her. All this shit that's been going on: the riots, the bombings—today's fiasco, it's all landing on her head. The media loves her—she's articulate, calm, well-presented, and always there to give a voice and a face to the movement. Now we're going through a rough patch, she's up there to be brought down."

Momentarily forgetting my reason for being here, I asked, "Is it just a 'rough patch' or something more damaging?"

He gently kissed his teeth. "I don't believe for one moment that it will do us any lasting harm, but we're getting hurt by it. No doubt about it; we are facing a concerted attack in the councils. The Greens and the Democratic Left have made gains at our expense. Our line on the bombings has raised questions about our integrity. We have stood by the anarchists, but every day there seems to be more proof it was them. A substantial number of the class don't believe the government would do such a thing, and with the anarchists seen at St Paul's and actually being trapped at Leeds, then you can understand why people ask—'if they are innocent why were they there?'" He paused, and sat thinking about the implications of it all. Stretching back, he sighed and rested his hands behind the back of his head. "Then the question arises, if they were responsible, then why are we standing by a bunch of homicidal nut-jobs?"

"How do you see the wind blowing?"

He gently shook his head. "The AF has had a quarter of their delegates withdrawn and instant elections called. Of those, the majority has gone to the Democratic Lefts and the Greens. As for us, well it's had a much smaller effect. We've lost fourteen percent—mainly in the Southeast, but we have to bear in mind that this is the first time in two years where our support has gone down. Previously, the worst that's happened is that it's stayed level. Now it's dropped, and the feeling here, and judging from the talk in the chat rooms elsewhere as well, is that it will get worse before it gets better."

I was intrigued. "What talk?"

"Oh, that we are getting impatient, and that the party is planning a coup d'état, and that's what the events of the last week have been all about; they're the opening salvo of a seizure of power. Nonsense, of course." He paused again and gave me a rueful smile. "But people are asking questions, and you see, the responsibility of answering them is falling on Jackie's shoulders. She's exhausted; I bet, at best, she's getting four hours sleep a night, and she's eating utter crap. Usually junk food and a cup of tea on the way to her next appointment. To tell you the truth, Pete, I'm worried about her. She needs to keep up her strength."

It was a troubling picture he was painting, and one that had me included as a detail. Maybe it said something about me that whilst Simon in his laid-back way had indicated that the party and Jackie were facing difficulties, my focus had remained on my own skin. Bad conscience, real or perceived, was making me feel worried, so I did what I always do when that happens—I acted cool. "So, Simon, have you any ideas why she's so keen to see me? She doesn't want me to do some of the media work, does she? Field a few interviews?"

Politely, my lame quip received a smile. I just didn't have the natural charisma that Simon seemed to possess. "I'm just saying that we are all a bit thin-skinned at the moment, maybe quicker than normal to take things the wrong way..."

I was digesting the warning he was giving me when at that moment her office door opened, and Glen Bale appeared, half-turning, saying his farewells to Jackie who was following him. I caught his eye, and he gave me a fixed look. Simultaneously, Simon rose from his chair and tapped my arm.

"I suppose I should be getting on and letting the good residents of Clerkenwell know what the Socialist utopia neighbourhood watch is going to look like. Take care, Pete. Nice to see you again." He grinned and gave me a wink.

Bale followed him out without saying a word to me. I didn't get a wink, either.

Jackie stood and stared straight at me. "You better come in, Pete." Yes, indeed, just like my headmaster. The feeling that I had caused offence increased.

Walking in, however, was where the similarities ended. And it wasn't that when I used to follow Mr Richards, his arse would almost cause a total eclipse of the sun, but with Jackie it barely cast a shadow. Or that his grey suit trousers would flap like sails, but hers hung as true as plumb lines. No, the office was very different. Hers was a third of the size and did not smell of pine. Instead, a smell of chilli and chicken pervaded the room.

Nor were there drawings from years eight and nine up on the wall. Instead, there were six screens. Two were set on news channels, with the other four indicating that there had been recently been communication with Paris, Istanbul, Berlin, and New York. All great cities and obviously ones she liked to have conference calls with. All read: Communication Ceased at 7:18 p.m. GMT. I glanced at my watch; it was twenty to eight.

She swung behind her blue tubular mini-desk, indicating for me to sit. Doing just that, I felt a slight disappointment that the whole supreme controller vibe was spoilt somewhat with every conceivable square centimetre of the floor covered in paper and her highly desirable desk boasting four empty pizza boxes. With such insightful detection worthy of P.D James' Commander Dalgliesh, I would guess that they were sweet chilli and chicken. Also, an executive power base would not have screens that had substantial amounts of plaster tape keeping them together. Rather hesitantly, I sat opposite her.

She moved the boxes to the floor, but it was too late; the image was just ruined. Not that it seemed to affect her a great deal. She sat with her carefully manicured fingernails formed into an arch. I had expected her words to be along the lines of, "so, Mr Bond, we meet at last." However, what she actually said was, "You were at today's police demo, weren't you, Pete?"

"Yes, I was passing and—"

She cut me short. "You were there when the shooting started?"

"Er...yes, I was talking to Michael Hughes when it all kicked off."

Tired she might be, but her eyes were still sharp and bored deep into my head. Obviously, she did not have the time to waste on social niceties, so she got straight to the point. "Who in your opinion fired the first shot?"

Now there was a question that even in my somewhat rough school, you would not expect from the head teacher, and it wasn't what I had expected here. But I took a deep breath and quietly told her. "From where I was, Jackie, well, I have to say it looked like it came from our side. I could be wrong but..."

She asked if I was certain. I said that, yes, I thought I was. Although I knew the implications of what she was asking were large, I was relieved that we weren't talking about why I had been there or why I was still poking my nose into Alan's death. My reply had disturbed her, and she sat silently, eyes closed, mulling over the implications. Her eye shadow showed signs of the need of a touch-up. Signs, indeed, that she was working hard. Jackie was someone you would usually expect to look like a fashion shoot even if down a mine shaft. After a few seconds, she asked me if I knew who had fired.

Beginning to resemble a weight-lifter about to make his final lift, I took another deep breath. "Well, I saw a flash from the coffee house where a few minutes earlier, a group of party-affiliated soldiers had been standing outside it." I had not answered the question, but the implication was crystal clear.

She saw it; disheartened but not overly surprised, she commented sadly, "The news is saying much the same."

"Who were the squaddies? Newly-join mates of Hughes?"

She swept aside an imaginary speck of dust, or maybe it was a lump of pizza. She did not reply; evidently, she wanted only my opinion and had no wish to enter into any discussion on the matter. I was not here to offer my thoughts on street violence. The topic was closed, and as it changed, so did her manner. Any element of friendliness, and there had been very little of it in the first place, suddenly dissipated. "So, Pete, you were there asking Michael questions about his life and what he had been doing over the last two days." Her eyes widened with the eyelashes wiping the air. "He told me that you are starting a blog for the party about the lives of some comrades. It sounds a fun idea, but which blog would that be, Pete? I'm not aware of it, and neither is Glen, and he's our IT lead."

So I had not got away with it. Here came trouble. It was not that her tone was either aggressive or antagonistic but more like a lawyer cross-examining a witness. Her spine had straightened, and she was looking intently at me, waiting for my answer. Despite the fact that we went way back, and I probably could take more liberties with Jackie than most, I still could feel a little in awe of her. She was never one for airs and graces, but just the force of her personality set you back a little. And it had to be admitted that, as the times had changed with her role becoming so dominant, it was as if history itself was being absorbed by her. As if she herself represented what was happening to the country.

Be that as it may, she was still Jacks. In any case, I was not in the mood to be intimidated, so I gave a solid reply. "I am doing one off my own back.

There's no problem, is there? I thought that I would start to get active again, and this would be a good, gentle introduction." I gave a toothy, cheesy smile.

There was a twinkle in her eyes, which I guessed meant that she was not wholly convinced by my story. "Is that why you asked Youssef the same questions? And, of course, you paid Marie a visit, too." A smile flickered across her face. "Oh, come on, Pete, writing a blog to raise the profile of other comrades is simply not your style. I simply cannot see you doing something so…" she grappled for the word, "humble."

I could have taken offence at that. I could do humble, but I was feeling uneasy at this whole thing. I was not totally sure what was going on. She was behaving oddly. Quite obviously, she considered this to be important enough to warrant her time, but whilst she was concerned, she was not what you could describe as being angry. There was affection present but not pleasure. All in all, I could not say what was going on in her head.

This was especially the case when the smile disappeared as quickly as a rainbow between the sun and the rain. "Not to mention the fact—" she continued, "and please, Pete, do not tell me it was a coincidence, because," her voice lowered somewhat, "that would *really* piss me off, and believe me, I really am trying to see the lighter side of this so I don't get annoyed—that these are three of the comrades you were to talk to concerning Alan's suicide. I have too much on my plate to have my time wasted. You have ignored me and carried on investigating, haven't you?"

Her tone really did sound like my old headmaster. Not that he swore. But then I had never conducted any investigating at school. Apart from seeing what smoking a fag felt like. Such idle thoughts were swiftly shoved aside by a desire to snap back that she was getting rather above herself if she thought she could be driving around doling out edicts, which the proles should obey. She had not shouted or ranted or threatened, but there was the strength of struggle in her voice. I kept silent, realising that now was the time to make a decision. Should I tell her and risk her wrath? Wouldn't she stop me dead in my tracks? And what if—even no matter how unlikely—she was personally involved? I could not believe that, but even so, I did feel trapped. So, feeling that I had no other option, I decided to tell the truth. Wasn't it Mark Twain who said that, "when in doubt, tell the truth," or was it my uncle? Anyway, truth it was.

"Yes." I returned her look. Certainly not with interest or even with the same power, but I at least did not shrivel.

OK, Jackie, do your worst.

Surprisingly, she relaxed. When she next spoke, it was in a softer and friendlier tone. "Thank you for not lying to me. Can I ask why you have, and what's so important about the last few days? Marie, Youssef, and Michael have all said that you were really interested in them."

So much for my cover story; it had been so poor that I blushed at the thought of it, so I might as well continue with honesty; after all, I did have the advantage of knowing more of the story than she did.

"Can you put on the news report of the police demo?"

She looked puzzled, but even so, she turned to face the TV and crisply instructed it to find and locate today's TV report. The media options came up, and she asked me whether there was a particular one I wanted. I just told her that the first would do as long as it showed the beginning of the march, prior to the gunshots.

With an expression of complete bafflement, she told it to go to the BBC and freeze on the first frame of the demonstration. In front of us was a picture of a middle-aged man holding a mike in front of rows of gleaming police officers.

"Zoom into the march itself and focus on those placards they are carrying, the ones of the murdered retired policewoman from up north."

She did as I asked, until the large screen was filled with the picture of the police officer on a banner proclaiming her as a victim of red terror. Jackie looked at me, questioning me as to what on earth I was doing.

"That is Jenny Underhill. She was murdered," I said, pointing to the crystal-clear image of a young policewoman. "That's a very old picture of her. I would guess that it's twenty-odd-years old. I suppose some bright media hack in charge of the Police PR hoped that a picture of a pretty young woman, full of life, vigour, and opportunity ahead of her, would have a greater emotional pull than a middle-aged woman who may have lost her looks. Even with these enlightened days of p c PCs, it appears that sexism and ageism are still a part of their makeup. It is almost quaint in how much out of date it is. Anyway, this is the woman who was murdered at home in the Northeast, and the police are accusing us of being the killers."

Time for a dramatic pause, waiting for her to exclaim surprise, acknowledge my brilliance, and shower me with honours, but, instead, she just looked at me. I hadn't told her anything new, so she sat waiting for me to continue. Ignoring my feeling of disappointment, I found that it would have been difficult not to. Warming to my theme and to my shame, somewhat enjoying it, I explained, "The irony is that by using such an old photo it helped me recognise her."

"You recognised her?" Jackie said, finally showing some interest.

"Oh, yes, though I never met her. Marie did, and I am sure George Armstrong did, too. Although they would not know her as Jenny Underhill; they'd know her as Jelena Jacobs. Jelena Jacobs—a young, keen activist who not only decided to take our membership card but Alan Wiltshire into her bed. He found solace in sex with her after Ruth had left with Stuart in 2010. She had a relationship with Alan in the same year Alan said he first started passing information to the state. Alan and the other comrades no doubt saw her as an intelligent young woman convinced by our politics and full of a desire to be active in campaigns, but in reality she was a police officer. She was sent into the party to keep tabs on us, and in doing so, she got her claws into Alan. Indeed, Jacks, I would even guess that was why she was sent in: her mission was to trap Alan. I don't know how she managed it, but she's the reason why he betrayed the party. As soon as he was hooked, she left."

I paused again. Surely after all that, they would be designing squares to name after me and erecting statues. None were offered. Maybe she wanted time to ask questions. But she asked none and just indicated that I continue.

"In Alan's research…" I looked to see if she was willing to tell me here and now what this research was, but again, she made it obvious that I was the one who was intended to talk. In which case, I continued, "he saw a photograph of her in her police uniform and realised that he had been duped. That was why he killed himself—on the possible eve of the successful conclusion of what he believed in, it had become plain that he had sold his soul for something false and corrupt when a world of decency and truth was looming."

Jackie gently rubbed the back of one of her hands and closed her eyes as regret spread across her face.

From scolded boy to excitable youth, I poured it out quickly. "Somehow, Alan told Dave this, and Dave tracked her down. I went up there, and people identified Dave. He met and spoke to her, and within days of doing so, Dave and Yasmin were themselves both dead after being brutally tortured. The question is, Jackie, who did that and why? And then days after their murder, almost as regular as clockwork, she herself gets killed. The question is again, who killed her and why?"

She silently folded her hands again into a steeple and rested her petite nose. I now had her full attention. "MI5?"

"Quite probably or someone like them. I have no idea how they operate, but, Jackie, it probably was, *has to be,* someone like them, but we should ask *why* kill them?"

My question confused her. "What do you mean, why?"

I explained. "Why was it so important to kill this Jelena/Jenny? She had not been involved with us for decades—so why was there a need to kill her? And Dave and Yasmin—they were tortured by someone trying to extract information, but what possibly could they have found out?"

"To cover their tracks?" she suggested. "They figure that the flow of history is running our way, and if they don't find a lifeboat, they will drown."

"Nice purple prose, quite the flowery imagery, Jacks."

A suggestion of a grin flicked her lips. "Must be the company I'm keeping. So if this is true, then it is truly appalling, but in all honesty I am not sure what the NWC or the party can do about it, let alone what you can do on your own."

Now in my stride, any reticence had flown out the open window. I all but shouted at her in excitement, "But again, I ask you, Jackie, why would they kill them? So Dave finds out that Jelena was an undercover cop—so what? What are we going to do about it? Why would they feel the need to kill Dave and Yasmin? How could they hurt the intelligence community? Two solicitors who specialised in representing asylum seekers unearth the fact that the state sometimes used underhand methods against Lefties—wow! And then we announce that the earth is round! They would not bother about them! Maybe at other times they might be an embarrassment, but frankly they have got bigger things to worry about right now! So I repeat, they think history is ours, and they fear the consequences.

"I believe that there is truth in that, but I think that such decisive and brutal action can only be explained if someone feared that these three people were a threat and could expose them, but expose them as what? Surely with all what's going on, they don't have the manpower to waste on tidying up the past? And anyway, Jacks, they have done far worse things than keep tabs on us. No, I think the only exposure that would warrant these killings would be if the killer was an undercover agent in the party *right at this moment*. What if they were active now, and through Jenny/Jelena, Dave had uncovered them."

"Active?"

"I mean, active as in working for us *and* British Intelligence—right now, right this minute."

"Good God," she murmured.

After several moments pondering what I had said, an expression of understanding crossed her face. Her hands dropped, and slowly she spelt out her thoughts. "So she was killed two days ago. *That policewoman was killed two days ago!* And you have been asking Marie, Youssef, and Michael what they have been doing over the past two days. Christ!" Distress and outrage filled her voice as realisation cut into her. "God! Pete—you're bloody insane. It's a disgusting idea. Obscene! You were asking Marie, Youssef, and Michael where they were because you suspect them—you were asking for an alibi. Bloody hell, Pete, even by your standards, that is derisive!"

I did not back down; it was too late for that, and strangely, I was emboldened by her anger. "Is it any more sick than knowing that Alan Wiltshire worked for them?" I demanded. "That every time the Central Committee met, he was passing on his notes to his handlers? Not many people knew what Alan was doing—he had locked out the world for a week. Only a select few had any contact with him. Same goes for the fact that only a small number of people knew that Dave had gone AWOL. Most of the party had no idea. And think about it, Jacks, who would MI5 want in the party? They are not going to have some rank-and-file member who can tell them no more than they can find out on the net; they are going to have someone high up, a leading comrade. They would want someone who is in the know and who is privy to the upper workings of the revolution."

"That's bit of a thin basis to start questioning comrades and doubting their loyalty! For goodness' sake, Pete, Marie's supposed to be a friend of yours!"

"As George Armstrong always says, there's no place for sentimentality in revolutions."

She swatted the air. "Ah, never mind him; you know as well as I do that the old man's a hard nose. Surely you don't believe that?"

"As you have just said, I am seen as a cynic, so here I am—being cynical!"

She didn't buy my offhand remark. "Oh, but Pete, you are a special type of a cynic, and that's a sentimental one. You cannot suspect Marie? Anyway, on that basis, then, I should be on your list." She let out a small, amused, if horrified, laugh.

"You were, but I discounted you for two reasons. The first is that, put quite simply, I am not that bad a judge of character to have recruited an MI5 spy to the party—that cannot be possible. And secondly, if you are a spy, then we are finished anyway."

The slight tone of macabre amusement persisted. "Well, you shower me with praise—I am important to the cause, and to top it all, I am not a spy." But then her mood changed radically. Leaning forwards she almost dared me to articulate my position. "So what *exactly are you* suggesting?"

"That I'm simply looking into it. You started me on this, and I think you should let me continue. What harm is it going to do? The worst that will happen is that I cheese off a few comrades, and what's new about that? And there is the possibility, OK, I admit it's a slim one, that I can find out who it is."

"And is that *really* the worst thing that can happen? You think that Glen Bale's dislike of you turning to contempt is the only thing you are risking? What about undermining the party? Causing divisions? And have you considered the possibility that if you are right, then the same person who killed Dave and Yasmin will do the same to you to keep you quiet?"

I am not a hero. Things scare me as much as they do anyone else; more so, probably. I have never been one to put myself at risk for no reason, or at least for the vast majority of my life, that has been true. That's why the nearest I ever get to dangerous sports is to dive into the pool, and then that is never, ever off a board, just by the side and not from the deep end;

parachuting, bungee jumping, white water rafting—all pointless, as I could see. I did not want to risk any more danger than I would face when crossing the road (and then I make sure to look both ways). Nor had that changed now. I did not want to die and end it all in a blaze of glory with a huge funeral decked in red flags and the order of Lenin. That might sound strange coming from someone who only two years back had taken a state-of-the-art Japanese kitchen-carving knife from a set of them costing the equivalent of a city break to Berlin, and ripped his arms to shreds. But because of that, I knew that I did not want to die. It was true that for a long time I have not particularly wanted to live either, but apathy does not make for suicidal tendencies. Not anymore.

I did know, however, that it was something I had to do even if I wasn't sure I could explain why it was so. Being such a long-in-the-tooth Socialist, I had a huge bank of quotes I could call on to support a point of view. We had spent our lives bringing them out at appropriate times to strengthen an argument or to refute another. All the past's great radicals and rebels were there at my disposal. Trotsky, he was always good for one. His final days isolated in his Mexican exile surrounded by cacti and rabbits, with an ever-diminishing group of supporters, meant that he could be relied on to have something to say about almost anything. Then there were the artists, those such as Picasso or Warhol who liked a witty turn of phrase. Or maybe from popular culture I could be terribly post-modern and ironic. They were all there, and yet all I could say was, "I have to look into this, Jacks. It's important."

The memory of the savaged corpses of two decent people who had worked to try and help others could have been used to give reason to such a foolish notion. Me? Take on the MI5? Ridiculous. But. *But* Dave and Yasmin were sound. They were people I knew. I liked Dave. I could have described the look on what remained of his face which was pure, undiluted pain and anguish or the sight of his lifelong partner drenched in blood on the floor beside him.

I could have raged how the powers that supported this murderous scum had corrupted Alan's life and so many others. They were not the heroes of the books I loved to read. They were people who supported a world where people got fat and rich whilst people starved. That was no lecture. No hectoring: just the plain, barbaric truth.

And that was why I had spent most of my adult life trying to do my little bit in furthering the fight against it. To give my weedy support to any cause, trying to defend those oppressed or exploited by it. And here we were, in Britain today: if we succeeded, then we were quite possibly on the beginning to a new dawn, but if we failed, it would be the start of a long, dark night. I did not really know any more how to help or if there was, indeed, any help I could give, so perhaps this was just one way of doing it. I could have said all that, but instead, I just said, "Trust me."

She looked at me. For a few seconds, who she was and what I had become was lost, and we simply saw each other as the same two people who would go flyposting together, with Jackie sploshing up the paste and me on lookout. Then it would be off to the pub to talk about, well, about everything. Whenever she would go into thought, she would get this strange, distant look in her eyes. It would not usually last that long before she would come to a decision. And it wasn't so this time, either.

"I have to face facts here, don't I, Pete? You are going to carry on playing the amateur sleuth whatever I say, aren't you?"

I smiled. "What sort of revolution is it if you can't tell your leaders to piss off once in a while?"

She nodded. "Right. Sit there and put an amused look on your face."

I had no idea what she was talking about but tried to do so.

She instructed the screen to call G. Bale. Within seconds he appeared, regaled in a capped T-shirt and wet hair. It was not a sexy look.

"Jackie—hi. What's up?"

"'Fraid I cocked up, Glen. Pete's here and has reminded me that yes, I did think a few pieces on the party site about comrades would be a good idea." She was as smooth as silk. "Just frivolous stuff, but there'd be no harm in it, and it might convince a few that we don't intend to send their babies down the salt mines. They're called *Ordinary Lives in Extraordinary Times*—sort of a-day-in-the-life type of thing."

I enjoyed the look on his face. It was total disappointment at a missed chance for my humiliation. My mood lightened.

Jackie played it straight and sounded businesslike. "I'd clean forgotten about it, what with everything else that's going on and all. So, Glen, if I send you the stuff tomorrow, could you load it on?"

"Yeah, sure, Jackie. How many are there?"

"He's done half a dozen so far, but I'm looking to double that and then have them on rotation. Could you set up some artwork and a byline?"

"Yeah, no probs."

She thanked him, and he beamed satisfaction at being of service.

The screen went blank, and she returned to face me.

"Very smooth, Jacks. *Ordinary Lives in Extraordinary Times*—snappy title. So much for never lying to the class, although I guess lying to Bale doesn't count."

Wagging her finger, she rebuked me. "Don't be smart. You need to write something up, make it witty and lightweight, you know the thing. Write a piece on Youssef, Marie, and Michael and have it ready by 8:00 a.m. tomorrow. I'll give you some stuff about me, and I'll get you some on George so you can do one on him and…"

"The old man? What's his day going to be like? Got up, watched the news, watched some more…"

"Should be pretty easy to churn out, then, as you can relate to that."

Ouch.

"Pete, now's not the time for jokes because I may be going along with this, but I don't find it very funny or indeed very pleasant. So leave the comedy routine at home. I'll back you up, but you need to know that if there is any chance that you will damage the party or go around upsetting people too much, then I will tell every comrade I can to have nothing to do with you; I'll make sure that your cat is the only living thing you'll ever talk to—understand?"

"Totally." There had been nothing ambiguous in her warning.

"As I was saying, I could get some notes from Jerome, and you could write a piece on him."

I tried to lighten the mood, as I found her tone somewhat intimidating. "You two still together? I thought you had separated?"

"…Er, yes, we did, but we got back together about eighteen months ago. Although we pretty much just pass each other in the hall at the moment; I can't remember having more than ten minutes with him alone, anyway…" She seemed slightly off-put by the reference to her private life but regained her aura of command when she returned to her default setting of organisation.

"He could give you some stuff about the engineers' union. To keep you safe, this needs to be halfway believable, so you can't just include those you are interested in, as that may draw suspicion. It mustn't look quite so bloody obvious. I'll organise a circle of comrades you can interview. I am right that you have told no one else about this, aren't I?"

"It's just me Jacks," I lied.

"Good, keep it that way, and you will report back to me. Now, you need to get writing, and I need to get off to a rally in Woking."

With that, I was dismissed and left the office with mixed emotions. I had succeeded in convincing Jackie that I should continue, but was that necessarily a good thing? Did I want to wade in this crap? And it had to be said that Jackie's attitude was confusing. I had expected her to be outraged at the thought that I was investigating comrades she worked closely with, and so she had been, but it had only been briefly, *very* briefly, and then she had agreed to it. It seemed that George Armstrong was not the only one who dismissed sentimentality.

CHAPTER FIFTEEN
A Vindication of the Rights of Woman

As I entered the Soul Shack, I immediately noticed that there had been a few changes since I had last been in. For starters, the wall by the bar used to feature a floor-to-ceiling still, taken from the 1979 film *Quadrophenia*, featuring dozens of antique scooters. Fictional, youthful rebellion had made way for the real, and Brighton had been replaced by Paris because a blown-up photograph from the 1968 student uprising had taken its place. I smiled; nice touch. Good old Maurice, keeping in touch with both the theme of his bar and the tremors of the times.

Maurice was the owner of this establishment. He also ran the vintage music shop next door and a coffee bar down in deepest South London. He was also the coolest guy I knew. A tall, slim man in his thirties, his preference was green-eye-inducing, immaculately cut suits, always with high-collared shirts. His family hailed originally from Ghana, but he, like his father, was a Camden man. With a smooth, micro shaved head and a long face boasting cheekbones of a model, it was a wonder that I liked the guy. Indeed, his looks and the fact that he was a Chelsea supporter made it positively miraculous. Politically, it was more difficult to place him. Probably, vaguely left-of-centre would have been my guess, but any conversation veering that way was usually jovially manoeuvred into safer territory.

He was explaining to two young women that it was extremely difficult to get fresh oranges at the moment. He could only offer blackcurrant cordial as a substitute. I patiently waited and scanned the bar. There was a good crowd in here tonight. There usually was; even in these confrontational days, people had fun. *Needed* fun. Wasn't that true of any era? What Maurice had done here was to cater for the demand, using the shortages of the new to his advantage by recycling the old, or rather to be more accurate, recycling the already recycled. People enjoyed the friendly but chic atmosphere, all done out in a combination of retro and *retro*-retro 1960s and 1970s décor. Few of the assorted things that stood or hung in the place were actually from the era. There were some, however: a few prized pictures of such musicians as John Lennon, Dusty Springfield, and Georgie Fame competed for space with pop memorabilia on the walls. Two 1968 Lambretta scooters stood on a two-tone stand at the centre of the bar. Northern soul boomed out of the sound system to complete the swingin' motif of the place.

It had to be said, and, being rather a pop obsessive, I was the one to say it, that some of it actually did not match the era. To his amused indulgence, I would point out that the album cover which adorned the wall to the right of the Gents, The Who's *You Betta You Bet*, couldn't be placed in either decade. But he would always simply reply that it was the vibe of the bar and not a religion. Of course he had a point; the e-soundscapes he played on Monday nights were hardly of the era, either.

He turned, getting a drink for the pair who had finally decided on which nonalcoholic beverage they were to have, when I caught his eye. A smile lit his face. "Hey, Anna," he said to a bored-looking barmaid lurking behind him. "Could you get these people lemonade and ice and half a Coke—we still have some of the domestic stuff left—with a packet of salt and vinegar crisps. Cheers."

Anna nodded but informed him in a tired tone that they were out of the crisps. He apologised to the customers before turning his attention to me.

"Pete!" He leaned across the bar and grabbed my arms with compassion and strength. "It's great to see you, man! I am so sorry about Caroline and Lisa—I know you went through a rough time. Sorry." He spoke smoothly but quickly, with many of the words sounding as if they were joined together into one long one.

I nodded. I had no real wish to talk to him about them.

Like all good bar staff, he could feel the mood, so did not press. "How are you doing?"

I held his arms with a little less pressure and admired the quality of the cloth. "I'm fine. Well, you know. I'm getting there."

Pouting as a way of solidarity, he did not say anything; instead, he insisted on buying whatever I wanted as a drink, including any bottle that took my fancy. "Consider it as a present, a kind of welcome back to the world. The place has missed the elder statesman of style." He grinned. "What about this; it's my finest red." He picked a delicious-looking bottle of Merlot from under the counter.

Ironically, I had just cadged a nice sum from Jackie as a reimbursement for services already tendered and for those about to come, so I was comparatively flush. However, I knew an expensive wine when I saw one, and at today's prices I'd need a wheelbarrow of cash to afford it. So having sold my soul, I might as well do the same for my liver, and I accepted his kind offer.

As he opened the bottle and located some nibbles (he explained that a shipment of nuts had come in, but he was out of olives, and, as he had just found out, crisps, too). Images drawn from old newsreels of food supplies came to mind, with foreign workers heroically loading ships with emergency cargoes of pub nibbles as aid to the workers of England, Scotland, and Wales. My thoughts were interrupted when he asked me if I had seen today's match. I confessed that I had not, and, indeed, I wasn't even sure which one he meant.

He looked shocked. "You played us today at half one."

"Of course it was today, wasn't it? What was the score?"

His smirk gave me a sense of foreboding. "We walloped you 3–1!" The cork popped—my heart did not. There was a feeling of sickness in my gut. Whatever other crap life could throw at you, football still had the power to bring you down that little bit more.

"Well, we've been hit hard by the decision of some countries recalling their nationals. That's devastated us; I mean, we've lost Chen, Yang, and Liu—that's half our midfield."

Maurice wasn't having any excuses. "Liu's been in the reserves all season, so you can't use that one, and come on, we've been just as hit as you have. Remember, we have lost both our goalie and centre forward!"

The sound of the wine pouring somewhat softened my dejection. He came around the bar with the tray. "Not that I'm one to gloat, though; it's hard times all around for us footie fans right now. Anyway, let's take this to your seat." He pointed to a table in the corner. It was where we had always sat, just under a magnificent photograph of Charlie George celebrating scoring the winner in the 1971 FA Cup final against Liverpool. A thought suddenly occurred to him. His eyes lowered. "If that's OK? If it brings back some feelings you'd rather not have, then the place is all yours, man—just point out the seat, and it shall be done."

"That would be fine, Maurice. Cheers. Oh, and actually someone's coming in, so perhaps a second glass would be sensible."

He raised his eyebrows.

"Purely party business, Maurice, party business, so don't get any foolish ideas."

He shrugged, although with an impish grin indicating that he didn't quite believe me, but he didn't argue and just went off to get me another glass before attending to a group of punters who had just arrived.

Caressing my glass I thought about Jackie. She had most definitely been strange back there. I had expected explosions on the scale of New Year celebrations, of the type before the economic collapse, but, instead, after the briefest outburst, she had quickly accepted the concept of me snooping on friends of hers. Maybe it showed my irrelevance, or then again, maybe she suspected something.

My pointless ponderings were interrupted when Victoria Cole came striding into the bar. As she entered I could see her eyes surveying the scene. She spotted me instantly and walked purposely over. "Hi!" she nodded and slipped off her green leather jacket and threw, rather than hanging, it over the chair. Again, as she moved, she was taking everything in. "Nice place; very old school." She smoothed down her tailored, white shirt over her slim waist, which her pleated grey slacks emphasised, and sat opposite me.

I asked her if she fancied joining me in a glass. She thought for a second, weighing up a glass of wine with the possibility of a pint or something totally non-alcoholic (she'd be lucky on that score). Finally, she went for the wine. "Just the one, though; I'm driving."

We spent the next few minutes in a painfully polite discussion concerning the bar's interior. She spoke as if we were in the Egyptian Hall of the British Museum. Accompanying the desperate attempt to gloss over our differences and create an illusion of unity was an overwhelming incomprehension of any of my explanations of what was on the walls or even playing on the sound system. She thought Mary Love was a porn star on the net rather than a long-gone soul singer presently purring out "You Turned My Bitter into Sweet." Behind me, Maurice was flashing me looks that would be worthy of a *Carry On* film.

Rapidly tiring of my summaries of Mod, Glam, Soul, and Punk, she took a sip of her drink, indicated her approval, and then said in a tone resembling more of an accusation than a statement of fact, "I've been trying to contact you all day—what have you been doing?"

Her attitude made me go straight on the defensive. "I've been busy. Why, what's the urgency? Have you found out something?" Sniffy, snapping, short sentences—I sounded as if I was thirteen again, back-chatting my dad.

"Not really, no," she sighed. "I just thought we should go over again our strategy and maybe give it another thought. I have a few concerns about what we decided."

So we had a strategy, had we? There was me thinking we were just making this up as we went along. "Why, are you having second thoughts?" I asked, as if I was still talking to my father.

Her mask of coolness slipped a little, and she sounded concerned. "No, well, yes, I suppose I have a little. It's just that I think we ought to be careful not to harm the party, especially as it is all just pure guesswork. I mean, we don't actually *know* anything. Even if we are correct and the state has their people in the party, it could be anybody. The last thing the movement needs in these difficult times is for us blundering around, accusing good, solid comrades. That would be both reactionary and counterproductive."

There spoke a *newji*; only a newly-joined to the party would consider these difficult times. The largest organisation in the workers' councils and workers' councils that were one half of the dual power running this country, and these were difficult times? I could tell her about difficult times—giving out sodden leaflets to bored shoppers in torrential rain on a Sunday morning with five other suffering comrades (constituting half the local branch)—now *those* were difficult times. The likes of me would call these exciting times.

"I don't like it that we are going behind Jackie's back because—"

I stopped her. "She knows."

She sat bolt upright in a manner straight out of CGT casting. "What?"

"She knows. I told her before ringing you. I told her what I had been doing today and why."

Her relief was obvious, even to blowing out her cheeks and exhaling air heavily; I was beginning to feel that I had walked into an animation where everything was exaggerated. But she looked sincere. Obviously, she was worried about upsetting Mummy. "Thank goodness. I cannot believe we even gave it a thought not to tell her of our suspicions. I mean, Jackie Payne!" She gave a false laugh. "Fancy us suspecting that Jackie could be anything but true Marxist. Betray the revolution? No way! Oh, you do not know how much better that makes me feel. So what did she say about what we had discussed?"

For reasons I could not explain, I found her breathless jubilation that Jackie Payne was backing us rather annoying. Cole might now be a party member, but she was still one to follow orders and respect her seniors. Yes, ma'am; no, ma'am; can I get you a cup of tea, *ma'am*?

I decided to spike her relief. "She wasn't happy, and frankly, I don't think she believes any of it, but she would rather be safe than sorry. Jackie weighed up the balance of possibilities and thought it was worth going for. She obviously has a lower opinion of me than you do..." (Was that a dig at myself, her, or Jackie? Or all three of us?) "She does not think there is a possibility of me doing harm to the party, whatever questions I ask. Oh, she gave me the warning that if I did, I would face expulsion and a life-term of social Siberia, but I doubt if she thinks there is any real risk of that happening, as otherwise she would have blocked me. Jackie doesn't usually do ambiguity."

Nothing I had said had dented her joy. Gushing continued, unabated. "That's as may be, comrade, but it's nonetheless taken a load off my mind. I have been thinking about nothing else all day. Comrade, you were right to tell her about us; we need her backing to legitimise any investigations we will be making. Besides, I owe everything to her. It's not too much to say that she changed my life—because of that woman, I am a new person. I could not bear to think of betraying her."

Oh, pass the sick bucket! This outpouring of effusive verbiage was making me queasy, so it was with some happiness that I broke the news to her. "I don't think you are quite clear on what I said. I told her what *I* was doing, but I did not tell her about you, or that we were working together. As far as

Jackie is concerned, I still would rather work with a wild, hungry, and irritated Philippine cobra than with you."

It said a lot about her admiration for Jackie that she didn't so much as make a murmur about the allusion to a reptile but instead was mortified about the fact that, contrary to what she had thought, I had not gone into the confession box and told all. "Why the hell didn't you tell her everything? What's the idea of keeping her in the dark about me?" Her tone had abruptly gone from relief to anger. PC Cole did not like to be left out.

"Because," I explained, "whilst I have no wish to hurt the party, I don't want to be ineffectual. This may seem strange to such a *committed comrade* as yourself, but I haven't spent most of my adult life playing this game just to blow our chances when we are so near to hitting the jackpot. However, I want to find this person. I *really* want to find this person, this murderous scum, and to my sincere regret, there is more of a chance of doing that working with you than doing it on my own, as I seem to recall you yourself suggested.

"Remember that it was Jackie herself who created the division of labour for the pair of us. It was she who wanted you to do the police work and for me to talk to the comrades. It was she who saw a difference between the two—I never did; I just saw the pair of us being narcs. But whatever: if that's what Jackie thinks and wants, then so be it, and that's just what we are doing. I didn't tell her about you because you are still only doing what she asked for. You are looking into the double murders of the Wiltshires. The only difference is that I have carried on investigating and have the occasional contact with you. She now knows about the former but not the latter. So what? I don't tell her about every person I chat to. She's the leader of the party, not my mother. I also seem to remember, whilst being up in the wilds of Northern England, you being the keenest one to do this. To be honest with you, if there is someone in the party killing their way to anonymity, then the fewer people who know about what we are doing, the better."

I had finished my lengthy speech and took a big gulp of the rather fine alcoholic tonic and then another of oxygen, because I appeared to have neglected to breathe whilst lecturing Comrade Cop here. I waited for a sharp rebuke. I was fully aware that my own tone had moved into the vexed zone. Normally, I did not talk so harshly to police officers, not unless I was in a large, baying crowd, that is, and never previously whilst sharing a bottle of wine.

She remained silent. Thinking as she sipped her drink and picking it up with her right hand, she rolled one of her gelled hair strands with the other. Having always held the opinion that coppers thinking was a highly dangerous proposition, I asked her if she had found out anything, the idea being that if her gendarme switch was flicked on, I would be spared more lectures on party loyalty.

It worked. She left the hurt outrage behind and moved onto outlining what our present position was. "We have got nowhere at all with David and Yasmin Wiltshire's murders. So far we have found no useful forensic traces at all in the house. Of course, without the police database in operation, even if we did find something, with nothing to compare it with, it is pretty meaningless. We have interviewed the neighbours but have drawn a complete blank. No one saw or heard a thing. Considering what went on in there, it is pretty surprising that no noise could be heard. We also had no luck with the CCTV, as so far we have not found any that were operational, so we have drawn a complete zero. And I mean a COMPLETE ZERO!"

She sipped her drink and oozed frustration. I almost felt a sense of sympathy but consoled myself that was due to the fact that the failure of her and DI Martin to find anything out at all also greatly hampered my attempt to find out what was going on. I asked her if there was anything else.

A small, almost silent sigh, preceded her reply. "We have been trying to work out what the pair of them was doing between him finding Alan's suicide to the time of their own deaths. We know that just over an hour after leaving David's grandfather's house, both he and Yasmin rang several people in police forces across the country. It seems they knew the officers from their legal work. We, in turn, contacted them to find out what the calls had been for. Basically, it surrounded the sole question of whether they knew the woman in the picture. With most it was a negative, except for one, a retired detective sergeant, Russell Fox. He told Yasmin who she was and where she could be found. It sounds bizarre, but they, DS Fox and Jenny Underhill, met each other at police training, had an affair, became friends, and er…kept in touch through their mutual interest in philately."

"Stamp collecting?" Philately was a big word, and I wasn't sure that she knew what it meant.

"Seems so." She did! "This DS Fox gave her the address, and they drove up there. We can place them at Jenny's Underhill's house on the day before they were murdered. I managed to get hold of one of the local force, and they have a neighbour who saw them arrive at midday. And from credit card receipts, we know that they charged their car at Middlesbrough at 2:12 p.m., so whatever she told them, it did not take long to say, and after hearing it, they felt no need to stay up there. They went; they talked; they went home."

"That's a long way to go and then just turn around and come back."

"This says to me that they were desperate to get back. We also know that she was driving."

"How do you know that? CCTV?"

"No, I managed to convince someone at the communication's union that I was a good guy, and he agreed to tell me who David had been in contact with for our time period. David also rang several journalists who are regarded as experts on security matters; so obviously it was Yasmin doing the driving."

I was going to ask how who was driving helped us but didn't have to; obviously she was showing off her deductive reasoning skills. Instead, I concentrated on Dave. "Let me guess, he was asking them about the role of British intelligence and their surveillance of the British Left?"

"Correct. Although, if these two are what pass for serious investigative journalists, then there would have been nothing to disturb the beauty sleep of the spies."

"Pretty mundane stuff, was it?"

"Yeah, and of no help to us. It helps fills the gaps in Roijin's data, but that's about all."

We both drank the wine. I finished mine and poured myself another one. I offered to top hers up. She prevaricated, thinking about driving home. Behind her, I caught Maurice's eye. If his theatrics continued much longer, I would seriously reconsider the fly-guy image I had of him. I tried to flash an amused but dismissive look back at him, but I probably just looked tipsy. The wine was mounting up, with this bottle adding to the glasses I had drunk at home. Finally, she graciously allowed me to top hers up, saying that she would risk it. Oh, what had this country come to? Oh, the anarchy.

"So, what did they do when they got back? It must have been something quite substantial, as for days they were nowhere to be seen."

"I am working on that; so far I've drawn a blank, but I'll keep looking into it."

For a moment or two, we sat in silence. What was this mystery research they were doing? It was certainly a risky job to do as both they and Alan had died from doing it! It seemed scrutinising computerised files had a higher occupational death toll than construction work. Did they provide hard hats for it?

Suddenly, I remembered something. "Did you have any luck with the computer files you copied from Jenny Underhill's computer pad? They were encrypted, but you reckoned that you could get that sorted."

Sighing, she shook her head. "Roijin did manage to crack the code; it turns out that it was a pretty simple one, but there was nothing there to help us, as they all related to her stamp collecting."

"What?"

Code cracking? Had I just walked into a *Monty Python* sketch? A dead spy has encrypted computer files, and they are about ruddy stamp collecting? Not secret codes but watermarks!

Cole explained. "Seems our Jenny had a sideline—the illegal import of rare stamps. There were files documenting contacts for the buying and selling of them; how much she paid and how much she got for selling them. There was also a catalogue of the stamps she owned—she had quite a collection. She was, at the time of her death, greatly excited by a transaction involving a large amount of money for a Red Mercury and an Inverted Swan—rare stamps, apparently. I contacted DS Fox, and he was horrified. He confirmed that all the files concern black-market philately; he's going to ask a colleague he knows in customs to look into it, but it has nothing to do with us."

"So we have busted wide-open an international postage-stamp conspiracy! Just great! Just bloody wonderful!"

Options to laugh or cry were presenting themselves to me. The laughter won out. What on earth was happening to this world? With everything going on and with capitalism facing its greatest threat, there are people smuggling stamps! Why, of all the things you might smuggle in or out of Britain, would you choose stamps? This was surreal! Maurice looked over to see what the fuss was about. He smiled.

Cole chuckled. "And so the Penny Black dropped."

"That was one truly terrible joke," I groaned, but noticing that her hissy fit over not being Jackie's blue-eyed girl had totally disappeared, I welcomed the change in attitude.

Pulling herself together, she removed the temporary show of humanity and asked, "How about you—any luck?"

Inwardly, another groan. This one, though, was very different in character to the previous. "I talked to Marie, and she was very evasive about the phone calls she received from Dave; she said that they were about family history."

"Did she go into specifics?"

"No, she was pretty vague."

"Did you push her?"

"If you mean did I take a rubber truncheon to her and clap her in handcuffs, then, no, Detective, I didn't!" My hackles rose. I slurped a drink and tried to talk myself into calming down. She just looked at me, seemingly unfazed by my comments. Getting myself together, I continued. "She did lie to me, though. She told me that she was working at the hospital, but that wasn't true."

Behind her eyes, I thought I could see that she was mentally taking notes. I felt like a grass, a sneak, someone running to teacher to tell tales. But that was what I had decided to be: assistant to the head girl here. So, in for a penny, in for a pound. "Actually, both Youssef and Michael were also rather sketchy as to where they were over the past few days."

"Where did they say they were?"

"They didn't really—once more, all I got were vague outlines."

"Did you ask?"

I was getting a little pissed off with her attitude. "Yes, but I had forgotten my handcuffs!"

She replied with a somewhat puzzled look of someone rather bemused at another's irritation and with a very annoyingly casual voice. She sounded as if she was talking to a naughty schoolboy. "You've used that one already; try to get some new material." Barb delivered, she thought for a second. "I will see what I can find. What about Youssef; did he mention what we had found out about his father's job?"

"No. According to Youssef, his family was completely apolitical. Which is strange, as we have found out that his father is a police officer in the Turkish secret police, which have been linked with multiple human rights abuses against political dissidents, but that is not political." Rather like you British bobbies, I thought to myself. "Of course, it isn't something you would want to broadcast, so it might not mean anything. And just because his dad was no good and worked for the state's intelligence community doesn't mean that he does. My dad was an electrician, but I have difficulty rewiring a plug."

"How closely did you question him?"

I was beginning to feel out of breath as I battled valiantly to stay civil. She was confusing the fact that, for my sins, I had decided to do this, but I wasn't doing it because I had seen this as a smart career move into the detection business.

Eddie Holman's "I Surrender" came on, and I tried to use his sweet voice as a soothing balm. It didn't work. Great tune, but totally inadequate for anger management. "Come to think of it," I sneered, "I did not come straight out and ask him whether being a part of the repressive state apparatus was a family tradition, and would Papa be proud of his productivity this month? 'Dad, three murders; is that a record?' No, Victoria, I did not. He's a comrade."

She shook her head, telling me off. "Kalder, if you are going to do this, then you are going to have to do it properly."

That was a mistake. I hated—with a passion—people who called me by my surname. Rude wankers did that. I sneered, "I intend to, and I refuse to be lectured on etiquette and professionalism from a serving police officer. The fact that you can rule out Jackie because you hero-worship her doesn't exactly impress me. Unlike you, I have known many of these people for a good time, and I am trying not to let personal feelings get in the way. So leave the police academy lectures at home! And don't call me by my surname to my face, as it's very public school and obnoxious. Behind my back is fine; I do that all the time to other people. But the name is Pete when talking to me!"

I had hit a nerve. So coppers had them! Her response was abrupt. "I ruled Jackie out because she did not kill either the Wiltshires or Jenny Underhill."

"And that's based on the fact that she can recite, word for word, *The Communist Manifesto?*"

Her jaw straightened. "No, it is based on the fact that because of the media's almost obsessive coverage of her, I can create a timeline which accounts for virtually every second of her life for the previous month. Usually, when you're making one, you are lucky to be able to account for an hour or two. She was seen at the mass rally at Derby at the time of the Wiltshires' murders, and there is a host of meetings she attended with hundreds, no, make that thousands, of witnesses at the period of time when Underhill was killed. I know, because I checked. I may have found it deeply unpleasant and regrettable, but I know how to do my duty, *Pete*."

I snorted. It was a fine impression of an uppity kid. I slugged back a mouthful of the wine to at least give the impression of having passed puberty.

Obviously it worked, as she spoke to me like you would to a truculent teenager. "As I explained to you, if David Wiltshire found the need to look into the personal history of seven comrades after visiting an undercover police officer, then the obvious step is to see if these seven can account for their movements at the time of their murders. That was what you were *supposed* to be doing. I monitored the media coverage of their movements. All of them are in the public eye and spending much of their time in well-publicised meetings, so I did some online accounting.

"Kye Toulson was pretty much taken up with meetings with his French and Spanish rail union counterparts and can be seen getting irate with some inane questioning from a net reporter on a platform in Dover at about the same time as I was arriving at Jenny Underhill's house, so he has a solid alibi. That cannot be said of the others. For Ali, Williams, Harrison, Hughes, and Bale, despite having seriously packed diaries for the previous six months, they go remarkably silent for the period of Underhill's murder."

"Meaning?"

"Quite possibly nothing at all, but it is one avenue worth pursuing."

"Jackie's going to arrange meetings for tomorrow at the national office with Brown, Harrison, and Bale."

"Really? What has she said the meetings are for?"

I told her about the pretence of *Ordinary Lives in Extraordinary Times* site and how she was going to include several other comrades so it would not look too obvious. From the rather strained smile, I surmised that she wasn't quite as impressed with the story as I had been. Not that she said that, because that might be regarded as criticising Jackie. Indeed, she told me that it was an interesting idea but in a tone that a parent might use when confronted with a paper of green and red smudges and told that it was a picture of a pony.

"So what else should we be doing?" I asked, trying to ignore a nagging unease, which only the red grape was suppressing.

"I think you need to look for yourself at the histories of these comrades and see if anything pops up. Nothing does to me, but you might see something that appears to be unusual for a comrade. I think you should also be asking around. Police work is often just asking endless questions."

Inwardly, I shuddered at the situation that I had found myself in, sitting here receiving advice on how to be a good cop.

Cole was probably enjoying all this, and on she went. "I will contact some people I met from the Seaham local police. Almost certainly they won't be happy at being pushed aside by the spooks, so they might be willing to talk to me. See if they have picked up anything. Maybe they had a chance to interview a few locals who may have seen someone visiting Underhill. 'Course, I'll have to do it before Tuesday morning." She grinned.

I was at a loss to know what was amusing.

"You haven't heard? Starting 9:00 a.m. Tuesday morning, all police officers are to withdraw from active duty for forty-eight hours to protest against the killing of Jenny Underhill and today's incident at the demo."

I was astonished. "A police strike? Christ! But I thought that the Police Federation has always been dead against them because it would play into our hands. Give law and order to the workers' councils, and you run the risk of the biggest question being asked—whose police force are they? Who do they keep order for?"

It was her time to take a sip of her drink and think for a second. "And from what I hear, they have the full support of the government. As you say, with the situation so volatile, it seems a high-risk strategy to go down this path. This suggests to me that they are planning something, probably to show that the councils can't keep order."

"What was the reaction of your...um...er...colleagues over the sniper fire?"

"Puzzlement, mainly. Many cannot see why the party would publically go for non-confrontation and choose the strategy of ridicule, only to open fire. They're not stupid." She paused, daring me to make a comment, but I was too interested in what she was saying to do so. For once I resisted. "They can see the sense of Jackie's denial of responsibility but baulk at the thought of an agent provocateur. They do not buy the idea of the government—the government who has maintained their standard of living whilst others have crashed—*their* government would open fire on them."

"So what is the general belief as to who did it?"

"At a guess, I would say that whilst officers do not totally believe that it could be a premeditated action, it's evenly split between those who think it was a party member who lost his head, those who think it was someone with mental problems who has been inspired by us, and those who put it simply down to the madness of the times. *Inspired* by us. So even after the confusion, it's still coming down on us."

A pumping tune was turned up by Maurice after what looked like a request from a group of customers at the bar. It was, I thought, Major Lance, but I wasn't too familiar with it.

Perhaps it was the wine, but a scary sense of, if not benevolence, then at least the temporary suspension of hostilities, overcame me. "What's the attitude to you been like?"

Her reply was composed. "Oh, there've been a few words expressed; a few voices have been raised. When I was leaving the station to come here, I was spat at. You haven't a brother in the police force, have you, Pete?"

I laughed, genuinely finding it amusing. Funny and self-effacing, the woman had talents! Perhaps that was why, to my surprise, a small, a very small, concern showed itself. "Are you OK?" I asked.

Her indifference to her own situation remained. "It's nothing I can't handle. I might even prefer it to the fake friendliness, and you could argue that if hostility to the party is growing, then we are certainly doing something right."

"Indeed." I replied, feeling both totally unable to untangle that knot of logic and an unexpected support for her.

I poured what remained of the bottle into my glass, not bothering to offer her anything, as I couldn't bear the thoughtful pout and calculating eyes it would be met with. So I made the decision: you're driving, so, no, you shouldn't have another one.

She looked at my glass and then the bottle. Without saying anything, she got up and went to the bar. I looked into the bottom of the glass but got no answers, only a slight feeling of appearing like a prat. Looking across, I could see her deep in conversation with Maurice. Cole jerked her head back and laughed. Obviously, he was working his charm. I dreaded what they were saying, especially with the furtive looks in my direction.

She returned with another bottle of the same Merlot. How the hell had he managed to get two bottles? Obviously, Maurice had some friends with transport links to the Continent. She sat down and poured herself another glass. "Nice bloke, your mate Maurice; gave us this bottle gratis. Well, I thought I could cope with another one—let's face it, even if I get stopped, the paperwork will get lost in the strike."

I hadn't really planned on having that much more and, indeed, wasn't even sure if I could. I also hadn't thought that we would be in here for that period of time. Comrade cop, though, obviously did.

"He says that you and your partner were regulars here and that you have been coming off and on for the last five years."

"Yes, we both liked it here." Like some cancerous growth, a fear started to swell inside me that she was going to go all fuzzy and warm and offer sympathetic words. Thankfully, I was spared that, as she changed the subject onto someone far more important to her than the likes of Caroline.

"So you recruited Jackie? I presume that's why she feels so fond about you. Whenever she talks about you, she always has an indulgent smile and an attitude of affectionate tolerance. It reminds me of how I feel towards my sister. She's a great woman, but she's as mouthy as hell—I love my sister, but she infuriates the life out of me!"

"And you're the quiet one?" I asked doubtfully.

"No," she said taking a sip. "Just one who can listen." She edged slightly forwards in her seat. "So what made you join the party?"

It was ancient history, and I had no wish to start chatting nostalgically about the good old days, reminiscing about my most cherished moments of building the vanguard. I was not going to sit here and be treated like some museum exhibit. Wow, comrade, what was it like way back when? Look—he has a 2016 membership card. Gee, how whizzo! I shrugged and mumbled a bland reply along the lines of being convinced about the party's politics. Judging by the fact that she did not question me further on the matter, it was obvious that she was not that interested in my political development. Strangely, I felt a little insulted by that.

"Was it then that you first met Caroline?"

Oh, we were back to her. I had the distinct impression that Cole might be preparing to manoeuvre me into some kind of bonding session to facilitate a team-building exercise. I had no intention of talking about either Caroline or Lisa. I didn't to friends, so I was damned if I was going to do so with her. I could sense, though, that she was itching to get under my skin and find out about my life with them. They were hovering above us, a subject I had no desire to address. Not here, not with her. I had only recently been able to do so myself, let alone attempt to do so with a stranger. I mumbled another response.

Apparently, nondescript, noncommittal replies did not dishearten her, and she asked further about our life together. Did this woman not get hints? Once a nosy cop, always a nosy cop. The wine was mellowing my mood, not least because in this day and age, I was unaccustomed to the luxury of two such fine ones, so I wanted to avoid any confrontation. I felt tired and a little tipsy and was reluctant to get into a fight. But if she carried on snooping, then I was going to tell her where to go. So, I again decided to change the subject, but this time, a move onto current events. Safer all round if we kept to finishing the wine, slagging off the prime minister, and debating the strength of the movement abroad. Then I could get home. Thoughts of Caroline and Lisa were best kept there.

CHAPTER SIXTEEN
Make Way for the Winged Eros

His temper fraying under the oppressive heat, he sweats despair and anguish. How many times does he have to tell this story? This must be the umpteenth time, so please stop reaching back.

The road winds with teasing glimpses of the blue ocean, flirting between lush green hills and steep cliffs with hard grey rocks, all underneath blue skies. Villages pop up, and beaches laze along, looking so pretty, just like a Raoul Dufy painting. Not that anyone is appreciating the wonders of the coastline. He is dividing his time between watching the unfamiliar roads and arguing. The beauty of nature has been totally lost in the cramped, sweaty, and aggravated cage of the car.

He had said it did not matter that the air-con did not work. It had. He had said that they would get a cool, natural breeze from having the windows open. They hadn't.

It's been a sweltering, tiring, and long day, and being English, no one has enjoyed the break from the cold and the rain. It's too hot with not enough breeze. With the humid evening giving no respite and the tyranny of the holiday schedule ruling their lives, any holiday fun has been left at the last apartment. They are now hurtling along in a rented vehicle full of dissatisfaction and niggles. In the back sits Lisa, in one of her moods. Nothing has been right today, and simply everything has been just *such* a bore. With every chance she has had, she has opposed, complained, and ridiculed. She has done so by resembling the eighteenth-century European powers in her swiftness in switching alliances: with him against her mother, in solitary battles, in one to ones, or her taking on the pair of them together, and as at present, in concord with her mother against him. The cause of the struggle this time is the seat belts.

"Did we go on holiday to wear seat belts?" she demands as if it is one of life's great hardships.

Listening to her music, rapping crashing in her ears as she studiously ignores the stunning scenery and tries to ignore her father, unless of course, that is, to rebuke him, she moans about his shirts, his shorts, his history lessons on Pompeii, and his constant going on about art.

"Caroline, please stop reaching back. There are some pretty sharp corners here."

Li!

Her slightly tanned face and jet black hair make her look so beautiful. He can't—isn't—appreciating that right now. She, too, has no seat belt. Her alliance with Lisa has been formed, and she is reaching back. He can smell the sea and the sun lotion on her as she brushes past him, leaning back. There's redness on her shoulder where she's caught the sun. Her arms show signs of too much sun from the orange summer dress that's she's been wearing. The one she bought in Portsmouth when they were visiting relatives. She's reaching back, her body at strange angles. He can see that she has lost one of the pair of buttons from her left shoulder strap.

"Please, Lisa, put that belt on."

"Give it a rest, Dad."

He looks in his rear window and sees his daughter: his dear, stroppy, lovely, fifteen-year-old daughter. Fifteen years going on thirty, going on five; in short, a fifteen-year-old. Her hair is tied back like her mother's. Hers is a slightly rounder face. More brown with less pink. Not that she is totally without the telltale signs of too much sun. He can see blotches on her nose and chin. Too much sun; not enough lotion; he had told her to wear more cream. Too much attitude and not enough appreciation of how lucky she is.

"Give it a rest, Pete."

"Give it a rest, Dad."

She's in her yellow T-shirt and white, very short, shorts. And those headphones; he can hear the thump, thump, thumping from the driver's seat.

Lisa's refusing to pass her mum's bag over. Caroline wants a bottle of water. This relentless Italian sun is dehydrating them all. Lisa is pretending not to hear and is concentrating hard on her music. Caroline's not angry though, and instead of an irritated scowl, there is a bewitching smile, indulgent at her daughter's small defiance. She always did, *does,* and would forevermore tell him that if they were in favour of people rebelling, then they could hardly complain when they faced one of their own. She's reaching back, almost frozen in time.

A small realisation, a small consciousness occurs. It always happens now: just as he catches sight of the pair of them—Li and Li, exchanging a knowing glance, a glance at his expense. It happens now.

A large, black dog runs in front of the car.

The seat belts, Lisa and Caroline.

Li and Li!

He swerves to miss it but loses control of the steering wheel. There's a moment when Caroline turns and looks first at the fast-disappearing road and then at him. The car crashes down the steep banks. They roll. Then roll again. The car is back on what remains of the wheels. They hit something big and crash to a halt. Caroline is propelled through the screen. Her body is prone in front of the car, slashed with cuts, drowning in blood. Lisa is wedged behind his seat, with her head at an angle it was never intended to be. Music is still coming from her headphones. Thump, thump.

***

It is then that I wake up.

It was *always* at this point that I woke up. Trembling, sweating, and crying as I always was when I woke, I tried to pull myself together. I hadn't had the full dream for at least six months; recently, they had been ill-defined images, but usually during the night, Li and Li made an appearance in some form or another.

I sat up in bed, trying to steady my nerves. If only it was a bad dream. But it wasn't. It's a memory, a memory of what happened. My whole body shook with grief, which despite being two years old, felt harsh and brutal.

We had been on holiday on the Amalfi coast. It was meant as a break from the recent upturn in militancy. We needed to recharge our batteries as the pair of us were exhausted from combining activism, work, and playing emotional Ping-Pong with our only daughter. We had always loved travelling; that was why we had Lisa so late in life.

The dream was an almost perfect reproduction of what happened that awful day, with the exception of the black dog. I never actually saw it that closely to know its colour or size. It had been the driver of an oncoming tourist coach who had seen it. It was he who said that it was big and black. It was never found, this big black dog, and we never knew if it came from one of the local vineyards or farms, or if it belonged to a passing tourist. However or wherever it came from, it ended up by starring in my blockbuster nightmare.

The Italian authorities took the driver's testimony, and I was quickly dispatched back to London, with the corpses of the two people I loved most in the world.

I didn't have a scratch on me.

So I relived that split second that ended their lives and might as well have ended mine. It was always the same, and it was always as if I was a passive observer in what happened. I did not even see me. It was only when I woke that I remembered the shocked frenzy with which I had tried to get the blood, their blood, off my T-shirt. I could even remember the T-shirt I was wearing—one of a recent exhibition of Fernand Léger. I had not tried to move them or save them. They were obviously both dead. I had stroked Lisa's hair and held Caroline in my arms.

But they were dead.

I had killed them—as good as killed them. My attention should have been on the road and not on point-scoring.

I had been found sitting in the road, unable to say anything of sense; not from a language barrier—by all accounts, the rescue services were pretty fluent in English; it was just that I hadn't been. Staring at the twisted, lifeless body of my beloved Caroline, repeating over and over again that one of her eyes was not in the socket. Not where it should be.

But in the dream, it is as if I play no part in the accident. If only. My part is not to control the car, to be too busy squabbling with Caroline and Lisa that I lose control of the car. The Italian police might have seen me as innocent and not guilty of anything, but they were wrong. I was guilty. As guilty as hell.

I had their blood on my hands.

Dragging myself out of the bed, I flung off my soaking nightwear and ran a bath. Shower, when you want invigoration; bath if you want to send memories into, if not into oblivion or even hiding, then to a place where they can be controlled. I closed my eyes and tried to construct my virtual garden. Mentally, starting at the back door, I moved backwards, laying out the borders, planting the shrubs, and thinking of the ground cover. On I went with this horticultural therapy.

Slowly, it began to work, as my heart went from impersonating a bass to a snare drum. My breathing also started to cease the resemblance to a tuba solo. Submerging my head I felt some relief; I hated, I mean, really hated, tubas. An overwhelming sense of self-pity always seemed to be part of the garden design, and as customary it was growing in me. Usually, that was the sign that the ugly, aggressive, and violent self-reproach had passed, but that wasn't quite the situation now. It had certainly lessened, but it was still there. I asked myself whether I should I take one of my pills. Sure, they numbed my senses, but that was something I could do with right now.

I went under again. For the briefest moment, I wondered what it would be like to stay under, but I rejected it. I might not be on a perfect keel, but for over six months, I had passed that stage of thought. On surfacing, my head decided to join in the orchestra of pain, which my body appeared to have become, and start up a beat of its own. Just what I needed, another member of the percussion section! From the dryness of my mouth, it appeared that this particular ailment had a more mundane reason than the death of Caroline and Lisa; this, I guessed, was from that last glass of wine.

Leaning against the back of the bath, I decided that, at least for now, my trip to the medicine cabinet would be for the head rather than the heart. With exaggerated care I pulled myself out and dried myself off, grabbed something for my dehydrated brain, and noticing that it was barely past 3:00 a.m., headed, with not a little trepidation, back to bed. The choice wasn't a fabulous one, between a hung-over semi slumber and a troubled sleep being tormented and bullied by a nightmare.

CHAPTER SEVENTEEN
One Step Forward Two Steps Back

Sir Edmund Hillary must have felt like this when he finally scaled the peak of Mount Everest: every inch of his body aching, head throbbing, and his mouth without any hint of moisture. Ditto for me. True, the difference was that the great New Zealander's aches and pains were due to immense physical exertion, stress, and altitude; mine was down to too little sleep, too much self-condemnation, and a little too much red wine.

I did not feel that good. Crashing around my head, the size of a tennis ball, was what was left of my brain. My eyelids were turtle shells slapped on my eyes.

At least, once I had crawled back into bed, I had not had a repeat of *the dream*. I was not once more plunged into watching Caroline and Lisa bickering to their death. Not that it had been an undisturbed night's rest; not with a banging headache, a dry mouth, and a deep feeling of unease. As a result, I felt like crap.

Blame Cole for that. She had convinced me to have another and had spent a couple of hours chatting about subjects ranging from the structure of the workers' councils to future changes in architecture, basically, anything that didn't fall into the categories of her personal life or mine, or what she now had begun to call *The Wiltshire Case*. I, on the other hand, had been happy to discuss the latter but most certainly not the former. Sharing grape did not suddenly make us colleagues. I could not say what she thought about that, as I hadn't given her the opportunity to say. Or at least I thought I hadn't.

She had insisted on driving me back, saying that I was in no fit state to ride. This was true. This had been the first time that I had been out for an evening since Caroline and Lisa's funeral.

At 7:00 a.m. on the dot, I had received a painfully cheerful call from Jackie, who reminded me that I had several profiles to write for my *Ordinary Lives in Extraordinary Times* blog. Dragging myself out of bed, I had used every remaining brain cell that I possessed to do so. Calculating that they numbered in the region of half a dozen cells, it was pretty damned heroic that I had managed to send the pieces to her in just over an hour later. She had immediately returned the call, telling me that she had organised morning meetings at the national office with Harrison, Bale, and Toulson. For good measure, she had also added two Central Committee members and Simon Peary just so as not to attract any suspicions.

In turn she had asked me if I knew of anyone I could call on to interview, who in her words "weren't party hacks or old lags, but real people." I don't know why, perhaps it was the hangover, but I couldn't really think of anybody. I certainly did not want to contact any of my friends. I had solidly refused all contact with them for two years, and I was not going to suddenly ring them up now and say, "Hi. Been avoiding you for twenty-four months, but can I interview you?" Work colleagues? Well, the same applied. My political activity had been rather restricted of late; restricted, that is, to chatting to the lifeguards at the pool and to the guy at the corner shop. Oh, and let's not forget shouting at the television. Through my brain muzz, I tried hard to think of someone else so as to avoid looking like a total Billy No Mates. Anyone; perhaps someone I had recently met? I wasn't going to interview Cole, so who else?

For some inexplicable reason, my first thought was of the comrades guarding Alan's house. Could they still be there? Completely forgotten about and by now probably all loved up in a makeshift shelter in front of his front door. They would add colour, but then what could I write about them? What would their average day be? Woke up, kissed, went on duty, door still there, snoozed. Kissed, got lunch, snoozed, left for home, door still there.

Luckily, before the pause became an embarrassing silence, I had a brainwave. Though, with my head feeling the way it was, a better description would be that I had a brain ripple. Something Jackie had said had prompted a memory. She had said the same thing at Alan's remembrance rally at Hyde Park: that great ideas had the power to raise people above personal misery. Zoe and January had loved the quote. Zoe was definitely a member, and quite possibly January was, too, by now. Giving her what details I could, I put both their names forwards.

I wasn't looking that fabulous; sure, the bruise on my cheek had almost gone, but the greenness around the gills would have covered it even had it hadn't. Not feeling in a condition to prat around in prêt-à-porter, I just grabbed a thin-lapelled, black suit, white shirt with a red slim Jim tie and matching socks, and forced myself to make the arduous journey to Soul Shack to pick up the scooter.

The bus journey had been painfully drawn-out, with the loud conversations and bustling travellers jarring my head, and each brush or sound blitzkrieging my personal space. It wasn't that long a journey, but it felt like a historical epoch. The relative peace of the walk from the bus stop to my bike did not last because, whilst putting my helmet on, a strolling Maurice had passed. He was wearing a different suit from the previous night, but the interest in me and Cole remained the same. The fact that I felt the thought of physical contact ridiculous, and not a little repulsive, so soon after Caroline's death, made it miraculous that I kept my temper and dismissed his joshing in fake good humour. I made my escape before my weakened state caused a slackening of self-control and I told him where to go. He didn't deserve that, so I went. I also hoped for his sake that he didn't make any such remarks to her. I had felt her kick; I knew what she was capable of.

The ride had loosened the iron vice on my skull a few notches, and I had arrived feeling a little better. It was immediately noticeable that there was increased security surrounding the party centre. Five armoured cars and assorted makeshift steel-clad vans stood threateningly by, with dozens of comrades milling about, seemingly with no purpose. The aim, no doubt, was to create an atmosphere of tension and apprehension, but there was a vibe more associated with a summer picnic. The comrades who presumably were supposed to be guarding our nerve centre were lolling around, looking as if they were waiting to be photographed. Most sure did look good, but with regard to protection, I thought they were sorely lacking. As we had always been a Socialist organisation and not a military one, this was hardly surprising, but in light of the radio news of a Coventry organiser of ours receiving a near-fatal shooting, then perhaps it could be said to be regrettable.

After walking around, past, and in one case, over, what was presumably the guard, I was eventually let in and directed to a huge space. The past incarnations of this area had included a shop floor buzzing with forklifts of a DIY superstore and a storage depot piled with container boxes.

Now it was a space used for a variety of uses, ranging from the storage of propaganda paraphernalia, parking, and, on this occasion, mass meetings. The plastic seats were out, and the projectors were purring in front of them. Combined, it made for both a real and virtual meeting.

Looking around, I estimated that there must be three hundred actually here. Scattered along the several projections were two hundred or so more. Just the first few faces I saw told me that this was one hell of a meeting. Whether you could actually touch them or not, sitting here were the leading members of the party. All the Central Committee were present, alongside every one of the great and good that I knew of. I stood and played Bolshevik Bingo and could call house within about three seconds. This was a heavy-duty affair.

I stood at the back, leaning against a huge steel shelving unit and just gawked. One comrade in the room, whom I vaguely recognised, was closely arguing that he felt the motion was rather conservative in character and that more was required, but nonetheless he would, however, support it. The speaker who followed him, who we were told was speaking from Manchester, announced that she also would be supporting it but felt that the motion had it just about right. I was intrigued as to what it actually was about. The following speaker, just in front of me, enlightened me with her opposition to it. She felt that whilst she had sympathy with its objective of showing the government that we still had the power, the idea of a general strike was a step back. We had passed this stage, she argued. She spoke at length and with great articulation. Not so the spotty youth speaking from Carlisle, who, what he lacked in coherence, made up for in passion and animation. He resembled somebody having an epileptic fit. It was a relief that he was in 3-D image only and not physically present in the room, as we'd all be sheltering from his saliva. He, too, opposed it.

The next speaker rose unsteadily to his feet. It was George Armstrong—the old man—a venerated leader and comrade. Seeing him I wondered if I required a seat. He was a long way from your Fidel Castro all-day speeches, but he was still very capable of speaking for quite a time. Every face was turned to him, ready to listen to his views and consider their position in regard to them. And every bum was being shuffled in its seat to locate a comfy position.

He coughed and spoke slowly but deliberately. "Now listen to me: the two comrades before me are quite correct that we have moved past the period where general strikes are our main weapon of choice. However, it is obvious that over the past few days, we have been on the back foot, and the initiative has—even if temporarily—slipped from us. Its bin like plodging through the clarts…"

Younger members frantically looked around; hoping for a simultaneous translation such is used with non-English speakers. However, whilst it might be operated for German, it obviously wasn't for Geordie. I'd heard him use the expression several times before and knew it meant wading through mud. Armstrong though didn't explain so they remained in ignorance. Forever wandering if they had missed a historic quote. Possibly in Latin.

"Because of this, I believe that the tactic of a general strike is the right one to employ for three reasons. Firstly, collective action makes us feel our strength, and thus it will give us confidence. Secondly, it will show the spineless lackeys of the ruling class that we are still the power, and lastly, it will act as a forceful rebuttal of the slander thrown at us over the recent days.

"Anyway, I believe we have talked enough; this debate has gone on for over an hour. Let's vote now. Vote to raise the demand for general strike in the National Workers' Council. We should stop this shilly-shallying around and *vote!*"

He sat down. It had been short and sweet. There were murmurings of support and mutterings calling for a vote. Bottoms around the hall gave a silent thank you. A comrade at the front, who I guessed was the chairperson, asked if there was agreement and, getting the answer, put the motion to the vote. After their voting buttons were pressed, the total flashed up: for—325; against—131 with five abstentions. The latter annoyed George no end, as he grumbled that revolutionaries never abstained. "Me mam brought me up to make a decision."

As the details were being arranged as to how it would be raised, I searched for the people I would be talking to. I did not have to look too far, as, waving wildly enough to attract low-orbiting satellites, January and Zoe quickly drew my attention. I nodded acknowledgement and walked towards them. Seeing me, their waves were reduced to those employed on aircraft carriers to direct jets.

Both were clad in jeans, T-shirts, and boots, and both sported beaming smiles. With arms lowered, we exchanged hugs, and to my chagrin, January immediately noticed that I was not my usual glamorous self.

"Been on the town, Pete? You look a bit worse for wear!" They both smirked.

I admitted that it was the case of one too many but avoided any details. Not that I had any time to, as breezing towards me was Jackie.

Not bothering with any kind of welcome, she told me a brief outline of what was going to happen today. "You're in Simon's office; there's a timetable in there. I've given you half an hour for each. I'm afraid that will have to do, as these are busy people."

"Good, that will be fine," I replied, not taking any offence at her brisk manner, because I guessed that you didn't need to charm your personal sniffer dog, and that was pretty much what I was becoming. I introduced Jan and Zoe, Jan adding, "January, as in the month."

I added that these weren't old lags or hacks. They laughed but looked rather puzzled. Jackie smiled and chatted to them. Obviously, friendliness was a commodity she felt that she could spend on these two. Zoe appeared almost ready to explode as she asked her questions about what the party's plans were for the industries that were being occupied. Despite her phone ringing continuously, Jackie explained what our position was. Each question fired was met by a detailed answer. This wasn't surprising; Jackie had not gained her profile by just sound bites and photo opportunities; she knew the importance of individual comrades. Time was short, however, when there were millions to consider, so she apologised and said that she had to leave.

Before she did, she turned her attention back to me. "So is there anything else I can do, Pete?"

There was; it was something that had occurred to me on the way here. I thought I would do a good deed today, so as a good boy scout, I told her, "You asked two comrades to keep an eye on Alan's house after his suicide. I think maybe they have done their stint and need to be relieved."

Momentarily, she looked discombobulated, but a sign of recognition appeared. "Oh, I remember, yes. Are they still doing it? I thought it was only going to be for forty-eight hours."

"Nope. They're still there."

"Poor bastards," she muttered. "OK, right, I'll get onto it."

And with that, she waved good-bye, and I heard her make a call, asking to be put through to the comrades guarding Alan Wiltshire's house.

I smiled; they'd appreciate that. Now for my bob-a-job.

The three of us made our way to Simon's office, which was on the top floor of the left-hand side of the building. It was somehow apt that it was next to Jackie's. With just the minimum of furniture and accessories, it was humble rather than extravagant. Its purpose was work rather than luxury. Two screens were bolted to the walls, which were flanked by framed revolutionary posters from the Spanish Civil War, being the only concession to style. In front of them was a steel desk, on top of which was a sleek, cream computer. Several pens and a notepad sat geometrically close to it. I sat down. They did likewise. I set the pens out parallel to the paper, which I straightened. Next to those, I placed my phone and pressed **record**.

The whole room whispered neatness and efficiency with everything in its correct place. Not that there was a great deal to the place. The only furniture in the room, apart from the desk, was a small, perfunctory bookcase with each shelf half-full. It was a misleading sight, as whilst Peary may well have been the engine of the party national office, he was no mere office manager. He was widely read and had contributed quite a few articles to party publications. For such a man who thrived on activity, his passion was strangely devoted to linguistics and the politics of language. Many of the titles on the shelves reflected this, with writers such as Raymond Williams and Terry Eagleton liberally being represented. His e-library had many more.

Not that I could study them. I didn't have much time. Jackie had set me a tight schedule. Turning my attention to Jan and Zoe, I started some preliminaries. It transpired that the former had joined the party yesterday, radiating joy at the happy event, with her partner beaming pride like a parent at the birth of their first born. Had I ever felt like that, I wondered? Joy at belonging. A passion of commitment. Or was it all greeting cards' schlock? I still believed, but was it from the brain and not from the heart? Maybe, back in the mists of time, when dinosaurs had roamed the earth, it had been from both. Would I ever get it back?

Shoving such thoughts aside, I asked her what had convinced her.

"Nothing really explosive. I just thought that I had equivocated for long enough, and I should just do it. So, comrade, I did." She grinned and fished out a membership card from her inside jacket pocket and held it up with her right hand and made a jokey fist with her other one.

"The recent riots and violence didn't put you off, then?"

She scoffed. "Nah, 'course not. I don't buy the line that we have been stirring up the violence—I mean, why would we? It's totally counterproductive. No, I think seeing how quickly and enthusiastically the government has jumped onto the bandwagon, I would look to them first."

"And would you say that is a view held by many?"

"I think so, although there are a few who are getting worried."

Zoe spoke for the first time since entering the office. Maybe she was getting her breath back after meeting with Jackie. "Well, I think it's probably more than just a few. Look at the disagreements we've been facing within the Tai-Shan Superstore collective. We only just won the vote of confidence."

For several minutes they discussed the political situation at their workplace and how some new company created by a conglomerate of ex-cabinet ministers, businessmen, and bankers was seeking to take over swathes of the British retail industry. Going by the name of Rushton & Colleagues, it appeared to be a major threat, and perhaps at any other time, I would have been greatly interested in learning more, but I was acutely aware that time was restricted. As much as their company was pleasant, the fact was that they were here to give truth to the lie: the lie being the blog; they, being the truth.

I steered them back to describing how they came to Socialist politics. Zoe, especially, gave an elegant account of her political trajectory. I would use it verbatim for the blog.

Next, they spoke of what they had been doing for the past few days, which was somewhat less riveting. They ran through their work in retail, which they were at pains to point out should be noted because it showed that they did a day's work in addition to party and NWC activities. They were also actually on the committee that co-managed the chain.

I was also educated into the intricacies on the exchange rate between currency and workers' tokens, followed by negotiations with sister organisations on the Continent. After getting enough for the site, not to mention growing numb at the detail, I swiftly ended the interview as I had to fit in three more fakes, as well as talk to Harrison, Toulson, and Bale.

They left, thanking me for thinking of them and saying that they were looking forward to reading it. Passing them on the way was another fake. Simon Peary breezed into his own office and sat down. Like any good host of any note, he checked that his guest had everything he or she required. This, in my case, consisted of some chairs, a table, and the coffee and pastry, the latter having just been kindly brought in by him.

He sat cross-legged, his hand resting on his top knee, and wore white flannels, blue shirt, and matching plimsolls without socks. He reminded me of someone who had just left their yacht at the marina. His manner was equally relaxed. He positively oozed chillness.

He flashed his cheeky grin; in doing so, the action pinched his cheeks and slanted his eyes. "Peter, so how's it going?"

"Fine," I answered, whilst taking a life-saving gulp of the coffee and a first mouthful of pastry, although I managed to deposit most of it onto my lap.

Affability and effortless charm just drifted from him. He seemed genuinely enthused by the idea of the blog. "It's a great idea to do these pieces. I've always loved your writing; it always reflects your sardonic style, which I have to admit that I do like. Although, mate, I am afraid my story is going to be pretty boring. It's just organisational management and alike. It's mostly pure hackdom, Pete—write that up, and you'll send the comrades to sleep." He chuckled.

"Every revolution needs organisation." I smiled, placing my cup to the left of the computer. I tried to think how quickly I could get this and the next one out the way. My target was a total of fifteen minutes for the pair, and then I could spend more time on Olivia Harrison. Not much effort was required with Simon. The process was simple: ask a question and get a smooth reply for a couple of minutes. He had been around long enough to know what was required and managed to include a sound bite to even the most mundane of chores.

In all honesty, the only thing remotely interesting was his recollection of his youthful experiences as an antiwar campaigner during the BBC years of Blair, Brown, and Cameron, which had led him to our door, but even that was a familiar story for many people. Indeed, it was noticeable that for the highest levels of class struggle Simon had been there. He had efficiently but quietly oiled the wheels of the often creaking party machine through general strikes, wars and economic collapses. It was just that it was all rather back-room stuff. Worthy stuff, smoothly explained but dull.

After efficiently dispatching Simon Peary, in came a Central Committee member I had never met and indeed had only heard speak a few times, and then only on news programmes. Jonathon O'Leary hadn't been on the CC for long. In his late twenties, with a slight tan to his clear white skin, he sported a small, well-cut beard. Dressed in his usual baggy, green trousers and tight, olive shirt, he looked like an elf. Not that he was in the mood to discuss his wardrobe. Or what the class struggle was like in Middle-earth.

He was not the happiest of people to have here. Clearly seeing this as a total waste of his time, he had marched in, sat down, and told me so in no uncertain terms. He announced that, as a member of the NWC, he would have to be building for this evening's vote on tomorrow's proposed general strike, so sitting here, "chatting about how I spend my days and what I read" was and is "utterly pointless and totally inane." I agreed. Especially, I thought, as he was mere window dressing. Not that any window would have had him. I doubted if he would actually be even considered to decorate a shop front. Not even in the past, desperate days of the marketplace when stores were almost paying customers to take the products away, might he face that particular call-up.

However, I played my part and patiently explained its intended purpose. It did mean, however, that we conducted it in superfast speed. I asked my "pointless" and "inane" questions, which he replied to curtly, as I pondered if he had pointed ears under that hair.

Mercifully, it was soon over. I looked at my watch: O'Leary and Peary in and out in seventeen minutes—not bad at all. I might even have achieved the quarter of an hour if the former had not have spent several minutes repeating his opinion that I was wasting his time. If there was an Olympic sport for this type of thing, then hang that gold medal around my neck. Then again, I wasn't too sure what exactly was this type of thing. Sitting here, lying to good party members just so I could investigate others—surely it wasn't a gold medal but thirty pieces of silver that should be hung around my neck.

Finishing my cold coffee, I did not have long to wait for my next patient. This was beginning to feel distinctly like a doctor's surgery, a view reinforced by the information from Olivia Harrison that I was acquiring quite a queue in the copying room. Already waiting was Glen Bale. He was not, she informed me, a happy Bolshie. He, too, had better things to do than wait for me to see him. Judging from the broad smile on her face, she either knew of my opinion of the good comrade Bale or that he had been educating her on his of me. Or both. We may have swelled considerably in numbers in recent years, but the party still sometimes resembled a gossip-ridden village.

She looked all set for summer in her short, lemon skirt and magnolia blouse. Her blond hair was blonder than I remembered, and I could see the first telltale signs of freckles. Despite the smile, the pure blue eyes, and the relaxed personality, she was projecting; I sensed that something was not right about her. Quite possibly it was my own state of mind that was yearning for a good few hours' sleep, but as I saved the last interview, set the script editing software in motion, and pressed **record**, I sensed a cloud cross her face.

I asked her if she understood what she was here for. She nodded and without comment told me it was for a series of blogs I was writing. Unusually, I noticed her eyes. I am not an eye person. In passing, I might note their colour, but that's about as far as it goes, but with hers, they stood out. There was a distant, almost frozen, look to them. Was she on something?

Feeling that a question on the possibility of her being a druggie was not a good opener, I asked instead if she could go into detail about the reasons for her joining. As she did so, I was pleased that once more my humble pamphlet received a name-check. She spoke clearly and without the evident antagonism of my previous interviewee, but it was in a passionless politeness. She told me how she had got involved at school by becoming concerned about the state of the planet and from there, got involved in broad-based, green activism. During that work she had come in contact with the party, and after what she termed "question and answer sessions," she joined, adding "well, I thought, why not? What else was there?" Whilst she spoke I got no sense of any emotion whatsoever for her decision.

I had considered asking her whether she saw any contradiction between her concerns for the environment with being a power worker. Being a delegate for the power workers meant that she represented nuclear power workers, but nuclear was a mode of power that she was against. However, I decided that it could be an interesting debate for another time.

Instead, I asked her more general questions about her work in the power workers' union. Here, too, it was detailed whilst keeping to the point, and yet it seemed to lack any soul. Even sitting in the chair, she sat almost frozen with her left leg crossed over her right and her hands folded in her lap. Throughout the twenty minutes she was in the room, she remained in that pose. I knew that if it had been me, I would have recrossed my legs, scratched, or coughed. She did none of these but just answered my questions. It was like conversing with a mannequin. The whole atmosphere of the room was cold, not from hostility but from numbness.

Every time I met her, there was a different Olivia Harrison. The first, soon after the St Paul's explosion had been quite arsy and antagonistic. She had appeared to be not far away from throwing a punch at me. Whilst at Alan's funeral reception, she was all pally, and I was close to being nominated top of her birthday invite list. Now she was the ice-cool professional. I was beginning to come to the conclusion that she was a rather odd person. Would the real Olivia Harrison please stand up? Again, I refrained from asking the question. I was new at this game and wasn't sure how I would ask her why she had such mood swings. Or whether she was on drugs. Instead, I remained patient (after all, the longer she took—the longer Bale had to wait) and just listened for anything which might be of use.

Her opinion on the chances of winning the power workers to taking strike action was instructive. "It's certainly not going to be an easy position to win. You'll remember after the last one, we were blamed for the deaths in a Manchester hospital, which had quite an effect on people. There was quite a barny about that. Let's face it; no worker wants innocent deaths on their hands.

"Winning the workforce over to the workers' councils had been pretty difficult in the first place. With the recent events causing so many casualties, it has weakened us further. We're still the majority, and the policy of support for the NWC remains, but only *just*.

"Now there's the added problem that part of the deal which the prime minister has made with the foreign powers would include a fifteen percent pay increase for all essential workers, which would include us, plus job security for five years which is tempting to some, but the price of that is to sign a no-strike clause."

I flicked a pencil against my knuckles to give the impression that I was a thoughtful chap; plus, it provided some movement in this office, because the stillness was beginning to become rather oppressive. She had spoken about important challenges facing her, and yet she had done so without a flicker of emotion: no irritation, frustration, or concern. It was as if she was reading out a shopping list.

"Will you win it?" I asked.

"Possibly, yeah, I think we probably will, but there'll only be a few votes in it. After this, I have called a meeting of all the delegates to discuss the matter."

So now I knew. Fascinating, but nothing to do with what I wanted to know. I decided that now was the time to use the "describe a typical week" storyline to find out where she was, or at least claimed to be, at the time of Jenny Underhill's murder.

She did, without hesitation or dissent, describing in tight, almost mechanical detail, the three days in question: how she had spent the mornings working and the afternoons attending meetings. I was given further minutia of what her work involved and what had been the main topic of conversation at the meetings, the latter boiling down basically to the government's offer and the explosions in Leeds and St Paul's.

Every so often, I would question her on a particular point or ask her to elaborate on something. Eventually, I had run out of things to ask. She sat, pursed her lips, and waited. Feeling rather awkward, I mined my rich seam of platitudes, said my thanks, and bid her good-bye. Her time in here had probably reached the limit of half an hour.

On her leaving, my plan had been to make a few calls, catch up on the latest net gossip on Arsenal, and keep Bale waiting a bit longer. A nap to sleep off this thick head would be pushing it. However, I didn't have the chance, as no sooner had the door closed, than it swung open, and there he was, as badly dressed as always. Underneath the suede jacket was a T-shirt shouting some slogan or other. I could have sworn his pointed nose twitched as he came in. Perhaps he was seeing if he could smell the odour of normality. The only thing you could smell in here, Bale, is your bullshit.

Oozing affability from every orifice, I welcomed him. "Morning, Glen. Soooo sorry if I've kept you waiting, but it's a busy, busy day today." I was deeply proud of my obnoxious politeness.

He huffed and sat down. Legs wide apart. Indeed, if there was such a thing, one could say that it was power sitting.

He didn't intimidate me. Even sitting like that. I tried to impersonate Simon Peary—all foppish charm. "I am running a few pieces on leading comrades—on why they joined, what they think of the period now, and their daily life."

A supercilious smile slid across his face. "I presume seeing me was Jackie's idea."

"Why?"

"Because if it was yours, I would not be one of the comrades being interviewed."

There was cold, solid, cast-iron logic to what he had said, and it was in my interest to agree with him, despite such a thing being pretty much antagonistic to my very soul. I would just love to have told him to sod off and that the sum total of his knowledge could be put on a postage stamp. He was old enough to remember them. But then that would have led to me attempting to explain why I had chosen a dick-squirt, and someone the world knew that I considered to be a dick-squirt, to write about. I certainly would have to have dredged up every particle of my damaged cerebrum, to justify why the hell I would consider dick-squirt to be a leading member.

So I said, "Yes, it was."

His smile moved further along the horizontal plane. He was feeling good that Jackie thought him such a worthy comrade and one of such standing that the world would be interested in him. I swallowed my pride and basically everything else that could be swallowed and said that she was sincerely hoping that he would help. The smile stayed. My smugness monitor hit danger levels.

Right then and there, I could have done with a month's supply of my pills, a few bottles of Burgundy, forty lengths of the pool, and an hour of imagining the garden, because being pleasant to him was a real strain, and it was going to get worse. Historically, revolutionaries had to suffer prisons, gulags, exile, and torture for their beliefs. I suffered Bale. Still, it had to be done, and actually lying to him was going to be a lot easier than to the others.

We kicked off, as I had done with everyone else, on how he had joined the party. He had done so thirty-two years ago. He had been an Internet activist and explained his political history. "I was very much into the idea of individual action and felt that the net had superseded the old forms of struggle. The virtual struggle was going to be the key area, social networking as opposed to Socialism. Hackism was going to be the way forwards."

That made sense. This social cretin could organise without actually having to meet anyone. But I kept my thoughts to myself. "What changed your view?" I asked innocently.

"Actually, it was rubbish!" He laughed. His laugh was like a horse. I guessed he had just made a joke, but for the life of me, I had no idea what it was. He explained, "There was a dispute on the bins. The refuse collectors were on strike against their company—pay cuts, I think, or was it pensions? Anyway, for one reason or another, I got involved. Sure, the net was ideal for spreading information and aiding debate, but it was totally useless at stopping the scabs driving the lorries out."

He elaborated; he had worked alongside comrades and finally had decided that there was life outside the virtual. He had been a member ever since.

I couldn't help myself. "Yes, Glen, I cannot recall you ever disagreeing with the Central Committee." It was said with the greatest of Hollywood smiles, but he knew it was a dig. To be in the party for so long and not on occasion disagree with the party line was unusual. I myself had done so countless times. Not our Bale, though. He was a good old hack. And not just in computer terms.

He didn't rise to the bait but just reeled off times when he had indeed done so. But because of party discipline, he had stopped his disagreement.

Pompously, he expounded on how if the difference had been of such a magnitude, then he would have left the party. I was outflanked, as it was a view I agreed with, although when I articulated it, it was without the pomposity and self-righteousness. To make his point a little more strongly, he added, "They were mainly about strategy. I've never been as concerned with minor points…as you have."

Nice attempt at a dig, pal, but I let it pass. Taking a deep breath, I started. "So, Glen, tell us in detail what you have been doing for the past few days. A part of the blog is a sort of a daily life, so what I would like is for you to describe what you've been up to."

"Actually, I haven't been *up to* anything, but let me see. Well, yesterday, I was here sorting out the systems. They're getting on a bit and need constant care and attention. I must have been here for the best part of twelve hours. Most of it was spent improving our security, as there is a possibility that some of our protection has been corrupted."

"Meaning?" I asked, hastening to add, "in terms I can understand."

"Basically, we think people, probably in the government's pay, have managed to get past two of our outer screens. There's nothing too sensitive there, so we should not worry too much. Nonetheless, we need to make sure that it goes no further."

With a sincere wish that he would not bludgeon me with jargon, I asked him to elaborate. What I got was more computer babble. I feigned understanding. "Aha, and what about the previous few days?"

"Well, the day before that, I was on a rare day off. So that's going to be really boring for your *little* article. In the morning I caught up on household chores, and in the afternoon our daughter Jane came around with her new partner. They stayed for something to eat, and then we all went off to the pub."

Questioning him on the details, I could see that he was surprised at my interest in his domestic life. With surprise sliding towards suspicion, I changed the topic, so I was unable to get the precise timings of his dull life.

"And the day before?" I asked, faking a smile.

"The day before?" he pondered, as if such complexities of the calendar were too much for him. "Oh, of course that was Friday; that was all party business, visiting various workplaces, listening to the mood of the class. I was called in by the comrades who worked there and…"

"Which workplaces?" I asked, rather too bluntly. Subtlety has never been a great strength of mine, didactic being more my style. In any case, I was using what tact I possessed on being civil to him. Feeling as washed-out as I did, it was an even harder job than it might have been. Still, he didn't question why I might want to know.

"In the morning I was at Kroner International, at their main offices at Canary Wharf. I must have addressed everyone in the building, except the directors, that is. They're still allowed in the building, but we kept them and their coterie out of the meetings. At most of them, there was concern at the direction the revolution was going. The debates were lively but fraternal. Where did I go next?" he paused, obviously enjoying himself talking about his favourite subject. Himself. "Oh, yes, I drove to Constant Constance Industries at Hounslow. That was pretty hard with the Democratic Left there in large numbers. The anarchists have lost all their delegates in the local workers' councils and the DL has taken them. Again, the debate was fraternal, although again, there were quite a few questions asked about how stable things are, and what is going to be the next step. I would say that it's pretty level pegging between us and the DL in the area, but I think they were interested in what I had to say.

"On Thursday I was in Guildford and Godalming. I don't know if you are aware or not—I am not really sure how acquainted you are with current affairs at the moment, what with the call on your time for these articles and such like—but there has been a week-long strike by the Telecom workers in Godalming. Actually, it went well; I think they liked what I had to say."

He gave a brief sketch of the political debates and who was arguing what and for what reason. Having been in the party for so long, he was adept at succinct analysis of political differences. He was also good at positioning what he had argued and how it had gone down at the centre of his narrative. Finishing, he waited for the next question, but I had asked all I wanted, and so I gave a plastic smile and thanked him. All in a tone I hope said, you are now dismissed. Pillock.

He nodded, and as he was rising to leave, suggested a few comrades who were union reps at the Constant and Kroner who would make ideal candidates for the blog.

The door closed and instantly opened, and Emelia Dias ambled in with a frown and the smell of cheap perfume accompanying her and lowered herself onto the chair. She was in her late sixties and as round as a beach ball. Great shocks of grey hair flopped over her wrinkled face which she spent her whole life battling against. She had been a Central Committee member for decades. Only the old man—who, it was rumoured, had once had a thing with her—was higher in the aged comrade's league table than her. For we, like many other cultures, respected our older members.

I felt uber-guilty for her being here. She had served the cause well for a generation and deserved better than to be used cynically as a mirror to deflect anyone wanting to pry into what I was doing. Of course, it had been Jackie who had arranged this; I would never have dared to ask Emelia Deas to submit to petty questioning, but if Jackie had no qualms about wasting the time of this well-respected member, then perhaps nor should I. But I did. With a large measure of respect, I went through the charade. With each question she replied in a voice that was muslin in both its thinness and strength. Each word sounded as if it would be her last, with air flowing around it, and with each, another was woven into her speech.

Interesting though her answers were and though I admired her, in truth I was only half-listening. That is, until near the end, when she dramatically changed the topic of the conversation. "You were the one who was trying to find out about Alan's death, weren't you?"

I admitted that, yes, it was me.

She looked straight at me, as if trying to get into my head which was not an advisable thing to attempt, as it was pretty cloudy in there. "What is your opinion about the talk that he had systematically betrayed Socialism for most of his adult life?"

Stumbling, I replied with something along the lines that I hadn't been given much time to form an opinion. She remained silent but looked at me intently. I had thought she might offer an opinion on the matter, a fierce and passionate denial that such a thing could be considered, or a bitter denunciation of his abandoning his principles, or at least a philosophical reflection on the matter in the manner of George Armstrong. But she said nothing and just looked.

Finally, she spoke about something she clearly felt was important. "I was thinking about the matter the other day. I remembered that in 2011 he dropped out totally. He just went into himself. He withdrew from activity and became locked up in his house. I went to see him, and he was quite a mess. Oh, he was never vain, not in a physical sense—intellectually yes, but not physically." She gently laughed. "But even by his standards, he was in disarray. His home was a shambles, and he looked like a tramp. He was obviously suffering depression."

"Did he say why?" I asked, my interest very much aroused.

She shook her head. A tuft of hair flopped over her left eye. Pushing it back, she said that he had refused to discuss it at all. "I assumed at the time that it was over his personal troubles. To be honest, I forgot all about it fairly quickly and had paid it no mind for years. But a few days ago, I was doing something and noticed some of his books on file, and for some reason they reminded me of it. I have no idea why." Another quiet laugh came from her throat.

"How long was he like that for?"

"I suppose it was only about three months, but I think it started about the time of the UN involvement in Libya—you remember when the uprisings in the Middle East had spread from Egypt and Tunisia and into rebellion against Gaddafi, so whenever that was, that was the time he had a breakdown."

She did not expand on what she meant or why she thought it was important to tell me, or what conclusions I could draw from it, but she quite plainly thought I should know. She also believed that she had nothing else to say. Once she had delivered the memory, she pulled herself up with obvious effort, thanked me, said with a chortle that she was looking forward to seeing her name up in lights, and left.

Right there and then, I could have folded my arms, rested my head on them, closed my eyes, and put this cacophony in my head to sleep, but, alas, I knew there one was more person to see. Although we had confirmed that Kye Toulson was nowhere near where Jenny Underhill had been killed, I still had to see him so as not to arouse suspicion. I sighed heavily, feeling very sorry for myself; you never saw TV cops having to interview people just as a ploy. I got up and looked into my waiting room, or the copying room, as most people called it. Kye was on the phone in some conference, discussing tomorrow's action. He nodded and indicated that he would be five minutes. OK, comrade, I only wanted you to unknowingly be used in this subterfuge that was growing more ridiculous the longer it went on.

I went in and waited, staring at one of the vintage Spanish posters featuring a drawing of a bowlegged peasant hard at work, hacking away at the most deceased-looking plant ever to have been produced by a pencil. There was a slogan beneath her but because right now, with my mind in a mush, I could barely translate my own name I didn't really know what it was saying. So I stared and tried to keep my spine from dissolving.

After the promised five minutes, he came in smiling. Indeed, he looked positively jovial as he entered. Chortling, he apologised for the delay. He was wearing a grey baggy suit and shirt which gave the impression that ironing was considered to be reactionary, as was having the said shirt tucked in properly or his blue tie properly tied around his neck. The whole look was one of a sixth-form student bunking off afternoon lectures.

He sat down heavily, putting his brown-leather, battered briefcase by his feet. He opened his hands and chortled, "So I have fame at last! Do I need a media consultant with me or maybe a lawyer?"

"Oh, don't worry, comrade. I have promised Jackie that we shall skirt around all the many sordid details of your personal life."

"Oh, I wish there were some sordid details to skirt around! I don't have time to say hello to me girlfriend, let alone get up to anything else. Comrade, let me tell you, revolution and sex do not mix!"

"Well, that gives me a great sound bite, Kye, even if it might not serve our interests greatly."

And so our conversation ambled light-heartedly along. I asked him the same questions as the others, even though Cole had established his itinerary for those days with cast-iron certainty. He was a warm and generous man and seemed happy to indulge in this frivolousness for ten minutes or so, despite the minor call on his time to organise the bringing of the country's transport structure to halt tomorrow. Trains, buses, planes, helicopters, trams, and electric bikes: all had to be stopped.

Spending time with him was a pleasant experience. He had a very listenable voice, and judging by how relaxed he seemed, I thought he was enjoying it, too. He probably appreciated having a few moments away from the hustle and bustle of his life. Sitting here chewing the fat was probably a minibreak for him. After just under twenty minutes, we had wrapped it all up, and he left waving, already with a phone pressed in front of his face.

Finished. Now I had some pressing matters to see to. All through these interviews, a copy had been sent directly to Cole. I wanted to know what she thought of it all and what she proposed would be our next move. I also was keen to tell her of the idea I had had during these sessions. Like most things it was pretty simple, but I was sure that it would clear up at least one mystery.

As only her head and shoulders were visible, I could only have guessed where she was. But as I wasn't really that bothered whether she was at home, at work, or in Santa's workshop, I did not hazard to make one. She was sporting an indigo-and-cream blouse. "Hello, comrade, and how are you today?" Her tone was polite but lacked warmth.

I plunged in—half as a demand and half with enthusiasm. "What do you make of what Emelia Dias said?"

"Emelia Dias, the Central Committee member?"

No, Emelia Dias, the synchronised swimmer. "Yes! Dias, the CC member! Have you not listened to this morning's interviews?"

"No. I've been rather busy this morning."

Great. No hurry, then, Officer. We're tracking down a suspected MI5 agent, and you get sidetracked into counting paper clips.

I would guess that she could see my surprise, because she immediately explained. "It's been one hell of a time. Other comrades and I have been arguing on why I should be allowed into the union meetings. We were proposing to turn tomorrow's police strike into one supporting the NWC general strike which, if we win tonight's vote, will be on the same day. We knew that we had no chance of winning, because party members are a tiny minority in the service, but it was a chance to raise an argument. But we weren't allowed to even attend the meeting. Outrageous! A total ban on all officers known to be pro-NWC! Even those who have expressed some sympathy with the councils were barred from going in! It was a sham of democracy."

Yes, indeed. My idea that the Metropolitan Police was the cradle of democracy was cruelly crushed. "Isn't there some agreement or protocol of some kind that insists that you are party—no pun intended—to any police federation meetings? It seems strange that there's one demanding that the police notify the NWC of relevant investigations, but not one for letting police officers go to meetings for the police."

Visibly, her muscles tightened around her lips. "There is—rule TG306. But in light of the shooting, I don't think there is going to be much attention paid to it for a good while. We were physically stopped from entering the hall, and those of us who did managed to smuggle ourselves in were dragged out. And…"

"Sorry, did you say you were *dragged* out?"

Despite my attempt at being very mature and fraternal and sensible and acting my age, she could tell that I was amused at the thought, because her face became a concrete mask. "Yes, a pair of comrades and I from south of the river were frog-marched out. It got quite ugly with the three of us trading punches with a dozen of them."

The vision of feds brawling with each other, helmets flying off, truncheons being waved, and cries of "you're nicked, my son" was one that succeeded in at least temporarily shunting my hangover over to one side. Whilst my skills at diplomacy would never have won me the Nobel Peace Prize—then again, bearing in mind the war criminals who had won it in the past, I would still have been a more deserving candidate—I knew better than to allow that full-facial smirk to surface. I focussed back on my headache to pull the appropriate sombre look as she continued.

"We made a complaint to the senior officer in charge of liaison, but he just was not interested. Instead, he called my superior officer, who informed me that I was being reassigned to road safety. I will be spending my time telling seven-year-olds to look both ways and to use the zebra crossing."

"Well, not tomorrow you won't; they'll be closed because of the general strike call."

Was I imagining it, or did a smile almost see the light of day on her face?

"So, basically, the days of pronouncements telling us of how the force—sorry, *service*—of how 'the service is politically indifferent to who is in power, and that the political views of the officers are purely personal' is over? That's a shame. I particularly liked the comment a few years back from the cop spin doctor, 'we're a broad church; only we wear blue, not black.'"

I chuckled.

Cole did not. My career in discretion had not started well. Her face bore all the emotion of an Easter Island Moari. Only the jaw wasn't quite as square.

"So what *did* you call about?" she curtly asked.

"Oh, yes. Emelia Dias told me that in 2011 Alan Wiltshire had some kind of breakdown. That must be linked with the events surrounding Jenny Underhill. Whatever happened, it caused this reaction."

"So?"

"So we should contact Stuart Wiltshire, his son, and Dave's father. He might remember something about it. I know he was just a kid, but he might have talked about it in later years. At the same time, we could ask whether he had any recent contact with Dave and perhaps have some idea of what his son was up to. It's so obvious, I don't know why I didn't think of it before!"

If I had expected thunderous applause, then I was disappointed.

"I can't tell you why you didn't, but I can tell you that DI Martin and I *did*. We interviewed him on the day of Alan's funeral. He was all but estranged from his father. After his mother moved out, it was almost ten years before they had any meaningful contact. He had no idea what Alan was doing during that time. Ruth, it seems, painted such an unappealing portrait of his father that he was in no hurry to meet him. And I have to say that Alan did not seem in any great hurry to meet him, in any case. Seems fraternal feelings of comradeship do not always extend to those you are in relationships with.

"After that it was just birthday and Christmas phone calls, usually a few days after the actual date. He wasn't that much closer to David. He had not talked to him for months. He did not even ring him after Alan's suicide. His son finds his father dead, and he does not contact him—I think that tells you something."

I wasn't going to be put off. "No offence, Victoria, but maybe he did not want to talk to two serving police officers."

"Maybe, but from what I saw, Stuart Wiltshire was a rare person nowadays—lacking any political views whatsoever. Living up in the Highlands seems to be a deliberate move to isolate himself from the outside world and avoid having an opinion on anything to do with it. I saw him as being totally apolitical. He even took David's body up to Scotland, so as to avoid any politicisation of his funeral. He tolerated the memorial rally for Alan, but he made it quite plain that he did not want the same for David."

"Dave's body has been released?"

"Yesterday morning. The forensic officers have done as much as they can, so DI Martin signed it off. The important point is that I think Stuart is not really interested in politics and so would have no reason to lie to us. So much so, that I could only think of one other person like that, and that's DI Martin himself. Who, I should say, did some digging and confirmed what he had been saying."

My big idea had ascended at the speed of sound and had then been hit by a few laser-guided sentences, crashing in flames at the speed of light.

Not that she was having any more luck. "Sorry to say, Pete, but we have hit a brick wall with our investigation into the double homicide of David and Yasmin Wiltshire."

We were at least united in using impact metaphors.

She continued elaborating on how paralysed the police force had become. What had previously been a joy to behold was now proving to be irritating. "Forensics, the two officers who have been at work, that is, have come up with nothing. To be honest, with the police databases so corrupted, that's not much of a surprise. The DNA and blood databases are useless. Basically, they just found what we saw—lots of blood, puke, and other bodily fluids with obvious torture. They did find that the back door had been opened by a GHJ7."

Before I had a chance to enquire what one of those might be, she further educated me in the ways of police detection.

"That's a piece of a kit that certain departments have to open locked doors without the need for a battering ram. I am sure I needn't tell you who gets a GHJ7 as standard.

"I have also been persevering with what traffic and security CCT had been working in the area—which, frankly, wasn't that many but drew a blank there, too. None of the recognition software registered any vehicle belonging to any of our suspects."

She did not flinch at the use of such terminology with reference to senior members of the party both of us belonged to, but I did. But I, the spineless accomplice, said nothing.

"With so many officers on the sick, it has slowed the investigation down to a snail's pace. I think we should concentrate on the murder of Jenny Underhill. With her, our killer had to leave his comfort zone and travel the length of Britain to do it. In doing so, he, or, of course, she, had to find where Underhill lived, find her home, and then return back to his or her own. If you ask me, in doing that they will have left tracks."

"So how are we to trace these tracks?"

"Do as we had decided. Check the alibis of those we are interested in. You need to chase up Williams, Ali, and Hughes and get more details of where they say they were. Now you've got Jackie's backing, you can push a bit harder. I've got a few things to chase up. I'll do that and listen to your tapes. We'll contact each other if we find anything. Good luck, comrade. I have to go now." And with that I was dismissed. I did not even have time to wish her luck with the road safety.

CHAPTER EIGHTEEN
Up and Down Stream

My head plopped onto my knuckles. Anyone coming in and seeing me with my head bowed and hands grasped together might presume that I was deep in prayer or in some otherworldly meditation. Tempting as it might have been to appeal to a higher being for aid, the pitiful truth was that I was only summoning up my strength for the rest of the day. Somehow and from somewhere I managed to.

Switching the phone to go through the screen, I wondered if my deathly pallor might add a sense of gravitas to my snooping. I called Marie Williams first but only got her rather unimaginative answering message. Many people had created mini-movies starring themselves over a thumping soundtrack to announce that they were unable to take the call. Marie's simply had a photograph of her and the family with an instrumental version of the old Disco number, "We are Family."

Michael Hughes's wasn't much more exciting. True, we were treated to a montage of action footage of the recent turbulent months, but it was sadly lacking any musical background. The important thing, though, was that he, too, was busy. With him, like Marie, I left a message sounding exceedingly pompous and dropping Jackie's name, saying that it was crucial that he ring back ASAP.

It was third time lucky phoning Youssef Ali, because he answered almost immediately, sounding rather out of breath. Judging from the sounds of the cars and the general hubbub in the background, he was walking in the street. Being on voice-only, it was only a guess. I told him I was ringing to follow up our meeting, to flesh out what he had already told me so I could make the blog more three-dimensional. To really get an idea of what his life was like as a party member, activist and…er…water engineer. Blah, blah, blah.

I could hear a car alarm going off nearby him. His voice remained amicable, so it couldn't be taken as any kind of sign of his mood. "Sorry, Pete, did you say that you want to know more details about my last week?" Clearly, he was puzzled at the absurdity of the request. "I cannot see that is particularly important or indeed interesting, but I guess why not, so…er…yeah…sure…could you hold on a second?"

The phone went on mute for a minute or so, before coming back online. "Sorry about that, Pete, I was just finding somewhere quiet. I've stepped into a shop; so, yes, you want to know the rundown of my week. Okeydokey."

He went on to do as I asked, giving an itemized account of the past few days. Mentally, I calculated as to how verifiable it all was. I figured it pretty well was, and despite there being a few gaps, it was something to work on. I didn't have a clue where he had learned to say "okeydokey," though.

The call had not taken long, which now left me wondering what to do next. For a few seconds, I drummed the table with my fingers, artfully showing that I had no sense of rhythm, before coming to the conclusion that I should do as Cole had said—start to check these comrades' stories. And where better to start than with my old chum, Glen Bale.

I grabbed a sandwich and a can of some ghastly, fizzy, gaseous sugar-water, which was still easily available, presumably because the international ruling class wanted us to suffer. Taking a gulp and a bite, I left the national office. There were considerably fewer comrades outside than when I had first arrived. Those who were left were now in varying stages of undress, enjoying the spring sun that was totally unencumbered by clouds. The temperature, according to my bike, was twenty-one degrees Celsius. A glorious day to go for a ride.

As I hovered around the one-hundred-kilometres-an-hour mark speeding, or what passed for speeding on my scooter, along the A roads, the wind swirling around my open-faced helmet revealed itself to be rather effective in tackling the effects of the night before. Going through Stoke Newington on the A10, I did have to cut the speed by some when I passed the police station. It looked deserted, but you couldn't be sure that some keenie cop wasn't whiling away his day, monitoring the traffic drone cameras. After all, Cole had told me that over recent days there had been a steady return to work of the force. Such a sharply dressed rider would surely attract attention. Dutifully keeping to the speed limit and even attempting an air of respectability, lest they sense just how much alcohol was still in my bloodstream, I continued.

My enjoyment of weaving in and out of the traffic had the effect of improving my sense of being. It was times like these when two wheels really came into their own, making up for the winter months when often the time taken to wrap yourself up in layers of warm but lightweight clothes could take as long as the journey itself. Then, of course, you had to strip off at the other end. I had been using a scooter for over twenty years but had been using it as my sole way of private transport since the accident. And in all those years, I had still to master the art of taking off bike trousers with any sense of style or dignity. Often I would rather just get wet than face that palaver.

Since that moment in Italy, I had never driven a car, never again wanting the responsibility of having a passenger. The thinking being, if I crashed, let me die, no one else. When I had returned to the UK, the first thing I had done was to sell our car. I would never, ever put my hands on a steering wheel, ever again, even if it meant riding in rain and wind. Better that than kill by driving.

Through Whitechapel, I passed closed and boarded-up units that had once housed coffee or wine bars and rooms that had not been rooms but spaces for the local artists to explore the human condition. Ah, the good old *human condition*. Now there was a term of its day; a day when these units were open and buzzing to talk of the human condition or the *narrative* of the installation. That was about the time when Alan Wiltshire's narrative was becoming a lot more complex than it previously had been.

Heading up Commercial Road, or as some wag had rechristened with a spray can, Cooperative Street, I was getting close to the main offices of Kroner International. Kroner had become quite a beast on the world's economic arena. Through gobbling up swathes of former public sector services every time a government announced its latest reform, it had grown from merely a private company providing cleaning services to, at times, the de facto local government, the NHS, and everything else you could think of. It had not been satisfied with bidding for new contracts but had bypassed any notional idea of competition providing value for service by just hoovering up the companies who already held them. Through a ruthless attitude to wages and conditions and a critical eye on what constituted providing a service, it had spread its influence nationally and then across Europe.

So far, big profits, but Kroner had had problems of late which had begun when the trade unions had grown from a foothold in the workplaces to a firm, controlling grip. In the fight against redundancies or for better pay, party members had gained influence, and so when the upsurge occurred, Kroner had found itself being locked out of many of its own workplaces. These were now controlled by the workers' councils.

Finding the huge tower block which held their head offices, you might not have guessed that recent estimates had it that 65 percent of its "service provision" was now out of their hands. It looked in the rudest of health—all thrusting concrete, steel, and glass. I couldn't remember the nickname of this particular skyscraper. Probably an ironic one from a kitchen or bathroom utensil; the people of Britain might have always been portrayed as being less voluble than their European sisters and brothers, but we had always had a sly view of big business.

A bull-necked, red-faced security guard, wearing the obligatory macho accessory of wrap-around shades, came marching over as I dismounted from the bike. It seemed that for "security reasons" nothing could be parked in front of the building. Obviously, he feared that hidden in my headlamp was a missile launcher. More likely, they feared squatters moving into the empty offices that flanked the square. To be fair, the fact that they hadn't done so already must be a tribute to their effectiveness. The Squatters' Alliance had become highly adept in converting empty properties into homes. Not these, though.

He looked fierce, and this, I knew, was enemy territory, so whatever the reason, I mumbled "sorry" and moved it.

I took a left into a side road which had a small row of shops, including a bar that was draped in a large banner proclaiming it to be a politics-free zone: "Come here to enjoy the prime wine, not to whine about the prime minister." It was neutral, so the owner supported the government then, as did its punters. Below was a sign regretting that they were out of white wines "due to the political situation." The Reds were depriving the poor darlings of white. It was a tough life.

Strolling past the guard, I walked into the cavernous reception as confidently as I could. It was a huge area, dominated by a palm tree in the centre, surrounded by a white-leather, circular sofa. The effect was more of an upmarket Moroccan hotel than an internationally renowned business. The reception desk echoed the feel, with three identikit women wearing Venetian-Red lipstick and black, bobbed hair. I approached the one in the middle, who asked, without seemingly moving her lips, how she could help me. I refrained from requesting a room with air-con and a sea-view and instead asked to see Johan Sanders. Bale had informed me that Sanders was the union rep here, and he was a party member.

"Can I ask you, sir, what the nature of your business is with Mr Sanders?" she asked in a trained monotone, her lips still not moving.

I puffed out my chest. "National Workers' Council business," I said curtly.

She looked down at a screen on her desk and, using a tapered forefinger, swiped the image controls flickering in front of her. "I'm sorry, sir, but Mr Sanders has been granted five hours a week on union business, and he has already used that up."

I smiled back. "It really isn't my concern how much facility time he has been *granted*. I am on NWC business and have personally been asked by Jackie Payne to see him."

"I'm sorry, sir; we do not wish to interfere in his trade union rights, but he has other responsibilities." She gave me an air-stewardess smile. Although, as the cabin crews were one of the first to declare for the NWC, that was perhaps a slanderous comparison.

"I really am not that bothered about his 'other responsibilities.'" I took out my phone and played Jackie's video message. Backing it up, I added as she watched, "Ask your supervisors what they would prefer: to let him take a five-minute break from his 'other responsibilities,' or I make a call to comrade Payne and get her to organise a squad of two hundred militia to come and set up a lively and very committed picket outside your lovely offices? Ask them whether your security could handle that." I finished with what I hoped was a menacing smile, but catching sight of it in one of the mirrors, thought it looked more *Dennis the Menace*.

"Please, wait one minute, sir," she replied, still admirably cool. Turning away so I could not hear, she made a call. Whoever it was obviously balanced the two and found in favour of me. I was to be "granted" time with him, she said, out of consideration of having a smooth working relationship with the National Workers' Councils.

Yeah, right. I sat by the palm tree for a few minutes before a grey-suited man in his thirties, with almost bleached features and shoulder-length hair, appeared from one of the lifts and introduced himself as Johan Sanders. He indicated outside so we left the trio of made-up mannequins and sat on a bench.

I introduced myself and explained why I was here, using the excuse that I wanted to add some colour to my profile of leading comrade Glen Bale, who, I understood, had spoken to a number of meetings here last Thursday. This continued demand of paying respects to Baleful was really beginning to strain. Heroically, I managed to keep down my lunch.

He explained why they had been held. "Yeah, I wanted to both raise the profile of the party and to explain how we see the future. There have been questions here about recent events and people asking whether the revolution has run out of steam."

"These were well-attended meetings?" I asked.

He smiled ruefully. "No, I wouldn't say that. There are only two party members in the building, actually only about ten percent of people in the offices are supporters of the NWC. We were allowed to hold them in the building because of the influence of the councils in the country rather than in the building itself."

It was not quite the mass meeting defying the evil bosses that Bale had depicted.

"Glen spoke well; he patiently went through how the councils had sprung up, following in the traditions of former such organisations but argued that we should not stand still because our enemies would not; they would be planning a counteroffensive."

"What was the attitude about the supposed anarchist bombings?"

"There were some pointed questions, but he answered them well. He simply asked who benefitted from these bombings? Was it the party? The NWC?

The Anarchist Federation? It is claimed that it was the AF who planted them, and predictably by doing so, their support has been damaged, so who was the most likely to have planted them? Who historically had the most blood on their hands—their class or ours? I thought he was very convincing. Certainly, he received a warm round of applause for the points he made."

"Aha, and what time were these meetings?"

"Er, floors one to seven were the first, and I think that was about half past nine. The final one was at just before lunchtime."

That ruled out him travelling up north in the morning. Something struck me. "Why, in particular, did you invite Bale?" I tried not to show any antagonism because, for once, truly none was intended; I merely wondered what the connection was.

Shrugging, he told me that there was no great mystery. "I just rang the national office and asked for a big-name speaker, and they sent Glen, which I was pleased about because he has a high profile and is a very good speaker. He made a real effort here which I appreciate. We are rather a bastion of reaction, so any help is appreciated. After the meetings he stayed and walked around the building." He smiled. "He had his sandwich box out, taking bites out of his cheese rolls as he went round talking to people who hadn't attended the meeting, which I thought was good of him."

"Had you met him before?" I asked, thinking that all this praise made it a real possibility that it might not be him, though the thought of anyone wanting to be Bale made the mind boggle. That a person might suffer that much vanished when he told me that, yes, he had met him previously at IT events. It seemed comrade Sanders here was an IT engineer himself.

I asked some fake questions to make the cover story sound realistic and was preparing to depart, when he changed the subject and told me how he had held quick-fire meetings about the possible general strike tomorrow. The mood, he said, was favourable, and he reckoned that the NWC supporters in the office block would follow the call, which everyone expected would be made when the NWC discussed the party motion, predicted by the net to happen at around 6:15 tonight. Of course the majority here would work, but they would have to do so without technical, admin, and even refreshment support. This was because of, he told me, where the majority of the members were. We discussed what tomorrow might be like for a few minutes. Basically, it sounded like there might be *accidental* sabotage to the company intranet and perhaps more importantly, no tea. I made my apologies, thanked him, and said good-bye. He wandered back to the palace of privatisation to carry on the good fight. I wished him luck.

Next stop was Hounslow, and if that proved to support Bale's claim, then it would surely rule him out, unless with his IT skills, he had created a time machine and had managed to both address meetings here and kill a former cop up in South Shields at the same time. It seemed a criminal waste of the space-time continuum, but you could never tell, could you?

Crossing Tower Bridge was a joy, with the panorama of the City either side of me, looking absolutely stunning. Was there a better view anywhere in the world? Behind me were the towers of cash registers of Canary Wharf and ahead, that cathedral of past art, Tate Modern. Every time I saw the skyline of London, I ran the risk of collapsing into sentimental prose about the city of Charles Dickens, William Morris, and J L Turner, or pontificating on how streets could act as links in time between the centuries. Or if I was in one of my baser moods—who we could bang up in the tower after the revolution; perhaps organising groups of American tourists to busily take photos of the prime minster trussed up like a turkey at Traitor's Gate. Or if we really wanted him to suffer—put him behind the till of the gift shop and unleash three classes of seven-year-olds on a school trip.

After crossing the Thames the second time and once more indulging myself in flowery imaginings, I cruised along the side of the river and into the posh wasteland of West Kensington. That put a smile on my face. Out-of-work headhunters dragging their contact numbers behind them alongside investor bankers grieving about having sod-all investments to bank, begging for direct debit contributions to help with the upkeep of their domestic servants—oh, yes, they do not want to add to the multitudes of the unemployed by losing their cleaner or the poor prat who puts their socks away. OK, I did not actually see any down-and-out toffs, but I as sure as hell hoped that they were wondering, fearing, what their future was.

Finally, after having to slow down considerably through Isleworth because of road works (some things don't even change for a revolution), I got to Hounslow. Constant Constance Industries was by the Heath, in a series of low-level offices. Unlike Kroner, they were confident enough, or at least they used to be, in their profile not to have a thrusting phallus. Certainly, as I parked the bike—as well as noticing the absence of security guards—I saw just how lacking this company building was in corporate machismo. I had never heard of CCI before looking them up on the net, but apparently they had made their money providing data for other companies; in other words, a basically pointless organisation.

Here, the receptionist appeared to have no problem with my request to see the union official and just asked me to wait whilst she called her. Madini Patel was a very tall woman, who kept her whole body perfectly vertical as she came over and shook my hand. Dressed in white jeans and a white, polo-neck shirt with a denim waistcoat over it, she looked like anyone you might meet at a bar—a young person's bar, as I would estimate that she was in her twenties. A small, enamel badge with the letters DL was on her left breast.

Because she was a member of the Democratic Left, I wasn't sure what reception I would receive. The two parties worked together over specific projects, and there was no doubt they had some decent members; some of them, however—indeed, more than just some of them, saw us as antidemocratic and too dogmatic. It was difficult to read what category she fell into as she smiled at my introduction of myself, but it was a polite smile that could cover a multitude of views. Bale had said that his reception here had been fraternal, but I could not rely on that too much.

She took me into a front office, which could just about cope with the table and four chairs in it. The walls were totally bare, except for the ubiquitous screen on the one opposite the door.

"So you want to know about Glen Bale's meetings here for a blog you are doing? Excuse me, comrade, but it doesn't sound like it's going to be much of a thrilling read."

I grinned and attempted a joke. "We've taken to heart the DF's accusations that we are adventurers, so we are slowing the pace down."

No guffaw followed, but she did smile. "Comrade, meetings in Hounslow certainly can't be called adventurous. I fear the URSP are getting soft. So what do you want to know?"

"Pretty much everything; give me a flavour of the meetings."

Obviously, she saw no harm in doing so, as without any further comment, she said, "OK, well, if that's what you want. I arranged a joint meeting of CCI and the nearby industries; they all tend to be IT around here, although the garage for the LMW is at the end of the street…" She saw my puzzlement as I tried to wonder what the initials stood for; we seemed to live in a world where words had been replaced by letters. "Local Municipal Works, LMW." She further explained, "It's the people who repair the roads."

I nodded, understanding now that we had used morphemes.

"Anyway, I called it to discuss the situation in the country. This trading estate sends about ten delegates to the Hounslow and Twickenham Workers' Council."

"Why was Bale invited?"

"I've bumped into Glen on countless occasions. We meet. Sometimes support each other's motions, sometimes not. Then he tells me that I am a relic of a ruptured Labour Party, caught between reform and revolution, and I tell him that he is a well-meaning Trot who is bound and gagged by the party line and belongs to a tradition that is a threat to democracy. We then swap papers and go our separate ways."

"I can promise that I won't be telling you that you are a relic; this well-meaning Trot is here in the spirit of friendship. And anyway, I'm pretty much a relic myself."

The polite smile returned. "Oh, Glen is, too. He feels it's his duty to recruit me, and when that fails, it's his duty to insult me, but he's OK. That's why I called him here. There's not many of you here, so it was good of him to come."

"Really? I thought you and we had equal members here?"

That amused her more than any of my attempts at wit. "Oh, that must be Glen's famous 'optimism of the will' that he is always banging on about. No, you have a dozen members in the LMW and a few elsewhere, but we hold sway here. There were a couple of anarchist delegates, but they were recalled, and we won the election to replace them both. I think Glen would like to think that everyone who is not formally a member of a party is a follower of yours. Which sometimes they are, and sometimes they are not."

She chuckled. I had the feeling that much of the humour was at our expense as opposed to anything intrinsically funny, but in any case it did not last long before she gave a brief resumé of the meetings in, I had to admit, a very fair and balanced way. Whilst she would occasionally insert a pointed political point, it was, though, on the whole, fraternal and nonsectarian. Actually, "fraternal and nonsectarian" was the phrase she used to describe Bale and which, I had to admit, prompted a slight grinding of my teeth. The key point was not her rose-tinted view of him, but that in the middle of this tribute, she backed up the times Bale had been here. As they said on TV, his alibi checked out.

Still, for appearances' sake, I had to wade through more of her recount, which when you cut through all the detail, boiled down to the fact that half the workforce here had concerns about how far the revolution would go, and basically it was better to digest the gains made by the movement, rather than push any further and risk losing them—basically, the line of the Democratic Left.

Finally she stopped, and tilting her head to one side, gave me a quizzical look. "I am still surprised that you came all the way here; after all, you could have just phoned. This blog, what's it called again?"

"*Ordinary Lives in Extraordinary Times,*" I replied sheepishly, as I was really beginning to dislike the twee title.

"Yeah, you come out to leafy Hounslow for something we could have easily just talked about? Surely there's more than just wanting a description of a pretty bog-standard meeting that brings you here?"

I felt my buttocks clench.

"It's not to sound me out about the action tomorrow? The net's full of it. I thought that was the real reason for your being here."

My bottom relaxed. I assured her that my role in this seismic moment in history was nothing so grand, but as there was at least an element of the revolutionary still in me, I did take the opportunity to ask her for her views. She was, it turned out, broadly in favour, as it appeared were the DL, which meant that with their and the remaining anarchists' support, we would easily get the motion passed, even if all the independents voted against it, which she said was unlikely. It appeared that it was a popular idea amongst the NWC.

"To be honest, I think the vote is a formality—it's going to happen in any case. We have just held one here, and it was unanimous. There are a lot of brothers and sisters who are unhappy at the rise of violence and dark mutterings. I presume you have heard about Leicester?"

Assuming that she didn't mean its cheese or football team, I confessed that I hadn't.

Accompanied with a heavy sigh and a look of regret, she told me of the morning's news of a pitched battle around the central police station. Fourteen were confirmed dead, with scores injured. The police were blaming the party, whilst we were pointing at rogue members of the armed forces who were ignoring the NWC/government accord to refrain from using them in civil disturbances. Smaller such conflicts were being reported in places as far apart as Ipswich and Manchester.

"I must say that I'm really concerned at this turn of events. I thought we had left the violent street battles behind us months ago. Your party's phrase that we are in a 'war of manoeuvre' might be literal. What we need to get away from is the idea that senseless killings are going to promote Socialism. Gang warfare will only lead to Fascism or a society run by gangs, which let's face it, is pretty much the same thing. The URSP and the police shouldn't play gangsters."

She looked at me, daring me to disagree, but I wasn't here for that, and in any case I wasn't sure that I did. I had got what I wanted so I just looked amicable and understanding. This rather surprised her. Her eyebrows arched with the novelty of a party member resisting the invitation for a political ding-dong. We were known for our passion for arguing the toss over any subject from global warming to how to make the best pancake. Not today, though. I nodded, thanked her for her time, and left.

As I was leaving the building, making the transition from frosty air conditioning to a by now blazing sun, my phone went. Answering it, I saw Marie all decked in her nurse's uniform. My detective skills were now becoming impressive, so I was able to use this fact, alongside her hair being tightly tied behind her scalp and the presence of a sign behind her indicating the direction of A&E, to ascertain that she was in a hospital.

She was, she said wearily, replying to my call. It showed her renowned efficiency that at a time when she would be building for tomorrow's mass strike, alongside a small matter of doing her job and being a mum, she still would return phone messages. That was Marie, though; she never left something for later; she would always do what was required. Reliable should have been her middle name (I think it was, in actual fact, Rose, but there you go) which just piled that guilt on me further.

I explained that I needed some detail on what she had been doing over the last few days for the blog. Her face betrayed a slight irritation with the request or perhaps a disinclination to answer. Still, after a momentary pause and subtle sigh, she went through what she had been doing. Was it my imagination, or did she rather hurry her account of Thursday? She certainly maintained that she had been at work. I asked what she had been doing there. She answered that it had been a day on the wards. That was what she had told me before, and that was what the receptionist at her hospital had told me was not the case.

The widespread use of visual phones had made lying on the telephone so much more difficult. Undoubtedly, this had hit cold-callers trying to flog you the latest telecom innovation and, obviously, pervy heavy-breathers the hardest, but it also wasn't doing us any favours either. I could see in her face that she was lying, and I was damn sure that she could see in mine that I *knew* that she was. Maybe I was just tired or being plain old soppy, but I could feel my eyes watering up. I swiftly thanked her and cut the call.

"Shit!" I said to no one in particular. I needed time to think about this. The warmth of the day prompted memories of barbecues around hers and Ashok's; adults necking bottles of Brazilian beer; kids playing with any ball they could find and in doing so, smashing their garden to smithereens; laughter and the smell of sausages and cooking veggie burgers filling the air.

Wandering aimlessly, I found myself entering the Heath. It did look wondrous in its early spring splendour. There was a particularly fantastic bed full of dahlias, daffodils, and hyacinths, creating a kaleidoscope of colours and textures. Ahead of me, I could see two, large, flat-top vans with people sitting and standing on top of them. In front there were a hundred or so people. Wanting to banish the thought of Marie and tiring of trying to find innocent reasons why she might lie to me, I headed for the group.

It was certainly a varied group. Sitting on the vans were, in the main, men of differing ages, all dressed in hideous green overalls. In stark contrast was a group of women, all corporate and correct, standing in front of them to their left who, judging by their constant examination of their shoes, were deeply concerned about their stilettos getting stuck in the grass. Around them was a variety of people sitting on the grass in differing states of undress, ranging from T-shirts and shorts to shirt sleeves and jackets on the ground. Nearby, a couple of city types were standing, looking enviously at those occupying the deck chairs that were grouped to the right of the vans.

I was somewhat disconcerted when a young black man, on seeing me, jumped up and offered me his chair. Despite my thinking of myself as a young, middle-aged type, this guy considered me of an age to put his seat at my disposal. I swallowed my pride and accepted his offer. Well, vanity was one thing, and a comfy chair was another.

As I sat down, one of the women in high heels was speaking. It was a multiracial bunch, black Caribbean, black African, and Asian. White people appeared to have been replaced by a race of orange. All had eyelashes that were big enough to keep the early evening flies away, makeup which was several millimetres deep, and slapped-on fake tans.

The woman speaking was wearing a black pencil skirt and white, short-sleeve blouse and was one of the orange people. She spoke in a South London accent. "We think it's about time something was done by the councils. Where we work, the management has been getting rather cocky of late. This is just what we need to do to let them know that there's no going back to the old ways. No chance, mate. Strike tomorrow and show 'em who's boss!"

So they were discussing the strike. (I really now could rival the finest of fictional detectives). Judging by the nods and murmurs of approval from the women around her, whatever workplace they were from was up for it.

Immediately after she had finished, two men who had been sitting on the grass, one an elderly African guy with white hair and spectacles and the other a bare-chested, carrot-top who I thought should be careful showing that much flesh to the sun, started to speak at the same time.

From one of the flat-top vans, an Indian woman who was possibly wider than she was tall, with jet-black bobbed hair, interrupted. "Comrades, can we have hands up for when we want to speak?"

I noted that she, too, was in green overalls which, it had to be said, did not really suit her. Noting the logo on her colleagues, I could see that our green-dressed friends worked in the parks.

Both would-be speakers apologised, and Ginger made way for the older guy. Obviously, it was be-nice-to-the-oldies-day today.

He spoke in a very slow, well-pronounced manner, which, whilst not posh, did sound like he was somebody who valued every syllable of speech. "Thank you, sister. I was merely going to say that I agree wholeheartedly with the sister from Lamis Brothers. Indeed, I don't know if you had the disagreeable misfortune to see Lamis on the television a few nights ago, but he was on the news with that toothy, slimy, patronising, snobbish drone he has, and he was attempting to say that Britain needed to restore order if it wanted financial support from the United States. I know we should be eternally grateful that he had dragged himself from the tennis courts to impart this pearl of wisdom."

A few of the women snarled obscenities at the mention of their boss's name, but he continued.

"Well, I would suggest that Mr Lamis worry about what is happening in his own city of New York and not what is happening here. And, incidentally, the United States can keep its money."

There was widespread applause for the sentiments. Especially from the women who obviously worked in one of his department stores. Lamis had been closing down branches across Europe due to financial problems and had been threatening to pull out of the UK entirely. Looking at their attire, one would have guessed they were either from makeup or perfume but certainly not the sports counters.

The red-haired lad, who must have been still in his teens, shouted, "All out tomorrow!" He was met with cheers as well as a couple of well-meaning heckles from his mates lying next to him. "Yeah, and it's going to be twenty-four degrees Celsius, so get the beers in!"

The crowd laughed.

The woman standing on the van pointed to an unshaven white guy who, like her, was wearing the ill-fitting park attendant's uniform, and who was standing on the other vehicle. "Jim, you wanted to speak."

He cleared his throat and, with a somewhat nervous look around him, gently shook his head. "I'm sorry, brothers and sisters, but I disagree. Going on strike tomorrow is foolish, and I see it as just band standing. I mean, what are we going to achieve? I don't see the point. I really don't."

"Piss off!" shouted someone from the front.

Ignoring him, he continued. "It is just posturing with people losing a day's pay for nothing more than to make Jackie Payne look good. I—"

A man in his twenties, sporting a bandana, jumped to his feet. "Shut the fuck up—scab. Why don't you go back to your mates in the government!"

"Please be quiet, and let Jim speak. We are all friends here."

"He fucking ain't!" the Bolshevik Bandana retorted, pointing at Jim.

A ripple of dissatisfaction went through the crowd, with a few telling the hothead to cool it and let the man speak.

The women on the back of the van again asked for some decorum.

Jim nodded his appreciation. "Thanks, Bhavani. Look, I know I am in a minority here, but let's just take a second to look at what we have achieved in the last few years: unemployment has been stopped from what looked like an irresistible rise; plans are being made to provide homes for the homeless; Britain has pulled out of NATO; we have a fully democratic government for the first time in history. OK, there are shortages, but that's because of the embargo. Now if we…"

This was too much for Bandana. "Who the hell is this idiot? Somebody shut him up!"

Bhavani, the woman on the van, shot him a dark look but spoke in a calm and quiet voice. "No, comrade—could *you* please keep it quiet. This is a civilised discussion here. The key word being—civil!"

The makeup sisters cheered their approval. They were backed by deeper and slightly more threatening growls from the green-clad workers up front.

"Actually, this is a meeting for the park attendants, of which Jim is a member. We have allowed sisters and brothers from other workplaces, such as yourself, to be here out of a sense of fraternity, but if it comes down to who has the most right to speak, then I am afraid he is far higher up than you are! Jim, please finish. Then the brother over there in the pin-stripe suit is next."

"That's it, really. I was going to point out the planned new schools and hospitals. I know it's not perfect, but the strike will only hurt us. Who will suffer if we come out again?"

Again he was heckled. This time, though, it was from one of his colleagues and in a humorous tone. "Jim's just scared he won't get his bacon butty tomorrow!"

Through the laughter, which even Jim joined in with, a second heckler, raising himself slightly from his wheelchair in mock-jubilation, added, "So that's beer and bacon sandwiches for tomorrow!"

"And sunscreen!" added another.

"We can provide that!" yelled a tall woman from Lamis Brothers. "Self-tanning or normal?"

Bhavani waited a few minutes to let the jollity subside before allowing the standing gentleman in the pin-stripe suit to speak. In an accent I could not place, but sounding supremely confident, he said, "This country cannot afford these well-meaning but costly handouts that have brought this country the biggest debt..."

Bandana boy was back. "Oh, fuck off, prick. You—"

"I have asked you before, and now I am telling you in more direct terms—shut up!" shouted Bhavani, who evidently had thrown the *How to Chair a Good Meeting* book away, or at least had given up on the chapter on patience being important. She had lost it with this man. "I see from the badge that you, like me, are a member of the URSP." She did not wait for a reply but drove on with growing outrage. "In which case, you will know that, for starters, we encourage debate: that, *comrade*, is what workers' democracy is all about. Shouting down people who we disagree with is not Socialism—it is Fascism!"

Applause met her comments, including from yours truly. But she had not finished.

"Secondly, please refrain from using bad language. Leon Trotsky wrote how revolution should refine language and not debase it like you have." Her irritation turned a little sour, sneering, "And if you have never heard of Trotsky, then I would suggest you read comrade Peary's comments on the subject. He is quite forthright on the matter. If you continue with your interruptions, I will have you thrown out!"

I smirked. How very English. So that was becoming key text for the British Revolution—how to talk properly and the art of good manners. I was sure that Simon, when he had written those articles on how capitalism had corrupted language, of how swearing was a symptom of the alienation and isolation of the working class, hadn't dreamt that it would be quoted in public meetings.

The chair was still admonishing the heckler, who by now was the size of your average garden gnome. After she had lectured him further on democracy, the party's image, beliefs, and politics, and some more on the use of appropriate language at meetings, she indicated that the next speaker was a middle-aged woman with short, blond, spikey hair, in a patterned knee-length skirt and green, short-sleeved blouse. Speaking about Britain's debt crisis, she spoke in favour of the general strike tomorrow. Several speakers followed in the same vein until it got to that part in a meeting where you know that nothing new will be said, and all the arguments have been raised. From now on it would just be people wanting to hear their own voices. The chairperson realised it, too, and now had to make the decision as how the vote would be taken.

Jim suggested three votes: one for and only by the park attendants; a second for and by the other workplaces represented in numbers here—Lamis Brothers, and, finally, a vote by all. This decision was debated by the meeting for about half an hour. Democracy could be very time-consuming! Finally, it was agreed by all, with the chairperson staring darkly at comrade Bandana, daring him to oppose it. He didn't. Wise boy. Volunteers came forwards to act as tellers and count the votes.

The tellers were voted in. The way the votes were going to be carried out was itself then voted on and unanimously carried. Then, *at last*, came the actual vote. The park attendants voted first, and with a majority of twenty-five to six, it was carried. With a blow to my obvious stereotyping, I was somewhat taken aback when the workers from Lamis Brothers voted nineteen to zero in favour. Red wasn't just the colour of blusher, then! Or the colour of Bandana Bolshevik's embarrassed face. Finally the rag-taggle of all of us voted. That went through, seventy-five to twenty. Cheers echoed around the Heath, and once more a wag questioned who was going to be delegated to bring the picnic hamper for tomorrow.

I sat back in my deck chair and watched the meeting disperse. Some of them went home, whilst others stayed to enjoy the glorious April evening. The sound of chatter was accompanied by the twittering of birds. Hoping the creaking was the canvas and wood of the chair, I took off my jacket, unbuttoned my shirt, and relaxed. I knew that at some point I should contact Cole and tell her about Marie sticking to her story about being at work, but that could wait.

I also needed to look into what Olivia Harrison had been doing that day. There was something odd about comrade H. It had been as if I had met three different people on the three different occasions our paths had crossed. There was also something not quite right about what she had told me. It wasn't that she had been vague like Marie about what she had been doing; quite the opposite, she had been very precise with times. It was as if she had been expecting the question. I know that I could not have been so precise about what I had been doing a few days ago. Probably not that precise about what I had been doing today.

I snuggled back to think, my eyelids getting heavy. Heavy.

***

Caroline, please stop reaching back.

He is in the car, the steering wheel passing under his hands, as he drives around curves of the Amalfi coast. Caroline is asking for her water. It has been a hot and sunny day, and she is gasping, she says. It's in her bag. Lisa, pass it to her, please. But Lisa is refusing to do anything for either me or her mother. He, but I know it is me, is getting irritated. I am hot and tired and fed up of Lisa's stroppy, unhelpful stance. She should be grateful that she is here enjoying a marvellous holiday. Just give your mother her water.

Caroline, please stop reaching back. There are some pretty sharp corners here. Lisa, do as you're told. She is being a right pain. Caroline, she can't hear you above the noise she's listening to. Oh, for God's sake, just get it, will you? I don't like you leaning back; it's distracting. It will be quicker if you take the seat belt off.

Take your seat belt off.

She does.

The black dog runs in front of the car.

The young man wearing a bandana appears.

That's new.

He wasn't there, and he had never appeared before in this. There is blood on his face and soaking the bandana which has become a bandage. He looks at me and whispers, "Fuck."

***

I woke with a jolt and found myself alone in the Heath. The deck chairs had all been left facing the empty space where the park maintenance vans had been parked when they'd been acting as a makeshift stage. I looked around, hoping that I hadn't screamed out, and if I had, that no one had heard me. I could see several couples a few hundred metres away, but they were more interested in cuddling and drinking from a bottle than anything I might have said or done.

For a moment or two, I thought about the implication of the appearance of the loudmouth from the meeting into my nightmare. For some reason, it felt like a violation. It was my horror, and one which had a set, organised, and predetermined timetable. And that did not include Bandana Boy.

My phone said it was a quarter past seven. Checking the news, I could see that the NWC had voted overwhelmingly to call a general strike tomorrow. It would begin at one minute past midnight. Jackie was widely quoted, giving the reasons for the action, alongside assurances that all emergency measures would be taken to ensure health and safety.

As expected, the prime minister was shown condemning the move, denouncing it as being destabilising at a time when he had just arranged a bailout from foreign powers. Which, he said, bubbling with all the enthusiasm of a boy buying the new season's football kit, would be coming online very soon. His face then reverted to the sombre, funereal, statesman look, and he predicted dire consequences for the country.

It was as I was watching him warn of Armageddon that a call from Victoria Cole came through. She was sitting in her car with sunglasses pushed to the top of her head. Her eyes looked around me to see where I was.

Chuckling, she asked, "Where are you, Pete? You look like you are in a park!"

I explained where I was and why (missing out the part of me falling asleep in the chair). She didn't enquire any further because it was obvious that she had something she felt was important to tell me.

"I've been looking into the past of our suspects." Noticeably, calling such comrades suspects did not disturb her, but it made me flinch. Apparently, being a die-hard party member did not prevent her from being an out-and-out police officer. "Including," she continued, "whether or not they have any form—a police record," she needlessly explained. "There's minor stuff like illegal flyposting, or like Glen Bale being done for trespass during student occupations, but I did find something interesting about Marie Williams."

She paused, which, if the purpose of it was to get my attention, was a success.

"Ten years ago she was arrested for grievous bodily harm at a demo, but all the charges were dropped."

I remembered it. "Yeah, the police were trying to remove some squatters, and things got heavy. The protest went on for only a few hours. Through Twitter and what-not, people heard about it and came to the area and supported the squatters. Then, as I recall, the riot police went in hard, and as well as busting heads, they made dozens of arrests."

"And Marie was facing a serious jail term, but the charges were dropped."

Moving forwards in the deck chair and trying not to get wedged in it (as I was wont to do), I explained, because judging from her excited look, she thought this was a telling fact. "We mounted a huge campaign. Marie has always been a well-known and respected activist in the NHS, so we won support straightaway from the health unions and from there, other unions. We had celebrities and MPs on board, too. It was a textbook example of the use of a united front, and the police backed down."

She looked far from impressed. Moving her glasses back a touch, she swept my account to one side. "Maybe, maybe not. The fact is, though, I looked at her file, and there is a terse message which read," she looked down at a piece of paper, "'Stop and desist from the prosecution of Ms Marie Williams. *A*Block* with immediate effect.' I have never come across the term 'A*Block' and had no idea what it is, so I asked around.

"It seems it is a message that is sent from the security services when they wish to stop any investigation, prosecution, or legal proceedings against an individual. It can prevent action of any nature. It is done so in the name of national security. The old-timer I asked, who's been in the police for over twenty years, says he has only ever heard about them; he has never actually seen one. They are regarded almost as some mythical beast like a griffin or unicorn, but it exists and can stop any judicial action, without appeal. They send it, and the police stop everything they are doing in regard to the named individual."

I had nothing to say. I was stunned. She seemed not unduly surprised by my response and continued on with her cool professionalism. "I got the name and address of the detective who led the investigation and have arranged to meet him tomorrow morning. I will pick you up at 9:00 a.m., and we can see what he has to say. What about you? Have you found anything?"

Her eyes darted around the screen, looking at my position. Lying on a deck chair with just-awoken eyes in a park, was not the look you might have expected from someone throwing everything they had into finding out who could be selling out the revolution.

Ignoring the silent but none-too-subtle question as to what I was doing, I slowly and with a heart full of regret told her about Marie lying about where she was on Thursday. She did not say anything when I had finished, but it was painfully obvious that she thought we needed to take a good look at who Marie actually might be. It was dawning on me that it would not be too long before we both would have to talk to her. Jackie might not be happy about it. Let's face it, Marie was a highly liked and admired woman—*I liked and admired her*—but we could not just question the people we didn't like. Otherwise, Bale would have been water boarded and electrocuted by now. What Cole had discovered was disconcerting, and we owed it to people, not least to Dave Wiltshire, to explore all the possibilities. In all honesty, though, I wasn't sure what possibilities there could have been for the police to have been instructed to stop action against Marie.

There was also the fact that Jackie was under the impression that I was working solo, because, well, basically I had lied to her. But then I might as well be hanged for a sheep as for a lamb. Whatever that might mean.

Cole was keen to stress that we did not solely look at Marie and ignore the others. I told her that Bale's alibi checked out (keeping any tone of regret out of my voice) and that I was planning to start looking into Olivia Harrison's and Youssef Ali's tonight.

That appeared to be sufficient for her, and I was beginning to note that Cole was not one for long phone calls. She acknowledged my words and then simply said good-bye. "See you tomorrow morning." Maybe she feared the bills, or perhaps being such a simple cop, she was like people in the past who, when photographs had been taken, feared that this action meant that their soul would be taken, too. Perhaps she feared lengthy visual calls would do the same to her. Assuming, that is, she had a soul.

I walked back to my scooter with my jacket buttoned up. The temperature was dropping, just to remind us all that summer was not here quite yet. The ride back was pleasant with the gentle breeze brushing my face, and, making good time, I was feeling invigorated by the nap that had almost banished the sore head. Some people were already putting up banners and flags in preparation for tomorrow, and the mood appeared to be one of celebration.

The day was giving way to night by the time I returned and picked up the groceries. Or what there was of them; a note written in green felt tip apologised for the slim pickings but said that the embargo had been particularly effective in the last few days. Well, it looked like tomorrow was going to be a hungry day with everything closed.

I pushed open the door and took the box into the kitchen. Grabbing a coffee and some chunks of cheese with some rather stale crackers (I was out of bread, and none had been delivered), I went into the lounge. Red lifted one eye and gave me a cursory look as he dozed on the sofa. I sat down in my chair and gobbled down the food. I turned the television on, and a news flash was coming in. Jackie Payne had been shot.

CHAPTER NINETEEN
The Mass Strike

It had not been the evening I had expected. My original plan had been to eat, catch some news, and then head to bed for an early night. I had intended to have contact with only two living things—the cat and Youssef Ali: the former, to stroke; the latter, to question about his alibi for the time of the shooting of Jenny Underhill. The cat was fed, and the news watched. However, it had been a pretty late night. Getting to bed well past midnight, my two phone conversations with Ali did not concern Underhill but the shooting of Jackie Payne.

Within milliseconds the news had gone global. Jackie Payne, the leader, the guiding force, *the face* of the British Revolution, had been shot whilst leaving the meeting of the National Workers' Council, following the vote for a twenty-four hour general strike. Also shot had been Bob Scales, deputy leader of the Democratic Left. Both had been killed by sniper bullets.

In the short time it had taken the labyrinth of news agencies to prepare their reactions, some of their viewers had begun to take action of their own. People had swarmed onto the streets, wanting to vent their anger and their grief. Images of crowds were shown, growing spontaneously and without direction in major towns and cities across the country, unfocussed and almost dazed, unsure of where to go or what to do. That is, until news came in that the sniper had been apprehended and was a member of the security forces.

Without any instruction to do so and without any communication other than that ancient and low-tech partnership of word-of-mouth and shared feelings, the crowds started assailing any symbol of the old order. Police stations, local government offices, and banks were attacked first. Then came the biggies: members of the NWC militia surrounded the army encamped around Parliament, as they did Buckingham Palace and the Bank of England. First, windows were broken, and then the fires began. This acted like a clarion call, bringing people in cars to add to the pressure. The numbers grew. Drone TV picked out the faces of the government troops metamorphosing from cool confidence to contempt, to concern, and, finally, to definite signs of fear.

But it was not just supporters of the workers' councils who were feeling the urge to occupy the streets. To everyone's—well, certainly my—surprise, government supporters also streamed out. Within the same amount of time a football match would take place, the familiar sights and sounds of the initial skirmishes of street battles were being acted out—Bristol, South and West London, Manchester Central, and east Liverpool. To begin with, it was sticks and stones and a lot of words, but no one had any doubt that someone, somewhere, in some city or other, was running to fetch his or her, concealed weapon. A lot worse than broken bones was being predicted.

Everyone wanted to be outside, and the reason was not to enjoy the early evening. I, too, felt the pull and might have joined them, until I saw the news posted that the earlier report of the death of Jackie Payne had been mistaken. She had been shot in the shoulder and was undergoing surgery. She was wounded but not dead. A huge sigh of relief shook my body. Relief and even gratitude swept through me, almost giving me a sense of euphoria. She was going to be OK.

Ten minutes later, a rather bizarre alliance of party Central Committee members, police commanders, surgeons, and even the prime minister himself assured everyone that her wound was not life-threatening, and that all would be well. The gunman was denounced by all across the political spectrum as a lone loony, and calm was called for. Bob Scales, deputy leader of the Democratic Left, they added, was also still alive, although more seriously hurt. It was thought that he, too, would survive.

The prime minister made a point of thanking God and saying that whilst he had serious political differences with Bob and Jackie (note the use of first names—what a guy!), he held no ill-will towards them and political violence was not the British way. So he probably thought the tanks parked by Big Ben for the last eighteen months were just there to let the kids climb over? Who was he kidding?

The emphasis was obvious; it was an appeal *to us* to calm the situation. It was funny, but we were the ones who were always being labelled control-freaks or quasi-Stalinists who sought to control the population, and yet here was our gloriously *democratic* government calling on us to do just that—control the masses. Damned if they think we do, and damned if we fail to do.

Judging by the news footage, it was somewhat too late for such a call. Across the country crowds were growing and attacking anything that resembled the state's authority.

Reports were coming in from Leicester that someone had found their weapon, and shots had been fired. What was going on in Leicester! Didn't they have problems earlier? People had scattered, sheltering behind cars, but the reporter said that the early signs were that no one had been hit. Yet.

With one eye on people fleeing into the cathedral, I rang around comrades to see how Jackie was doing. It was then, after half a dozen calls with no luck, that I got through to Youssef Ali, who answered promptly with a polite smile.

"Pete, hi. How are you? I expect you've rung about Jackie."

I was pleased that he didn't think I had hit the limits of redundancy and was calling at such a time to go over a minor detail in his biography for the blog. Despite being a busy man, he found time to fill me in on what had happened. Firstly, he told me that she was expected out of surgery at any moment. He assured me that it was considered in no way being life-threatening. It was strange, he said, why the report of her death had been so quickly put out, and it had taken some effort to correct the mistake. Bob Scales, he added, might not be so lucky, as he had been hit in the chest. Old Scales, a decent-enough chap—a former trade unionist and what in my youth might have been called a Labour Left—now seemed to be condemned to be secondary to Jackie.

Ali was actually at the hospital where Jackie was being treated, so our conversation was interrupted by him issuing instructions to party members. He was controlled and efficient, dealing with each problem with calm authority. From the snippets I heard and occasionally saw, they ranged from security issues concerning possible further attacks, public announcements, arranging getting her belongings there, and how to respond to events on the streets. I would never have guessed that a water company worker could be so decisive.

He told me that she had been leaving Workers' Hall and was in conversation with Scales about tomorrow's general strike and how to coordinate action between the two parties. Around her was a small group of comrades who were to have a follow-up meeting in a minibus in the car park. Buzzing around them were reporters who were firing off questions, statements, and demands when three shots were heard.

He explained, "I was just behind her, but I had no idea what was happening. The first thing I heard was the shattering of the glass when one of the nearby car windows shattered with what later we found out to be the third shot. The actual shots themselves were almost inaudible. It was a sound I had never heard before, like a burst of wind coming out a pipe. I'm told that is the sound of that particular brand of high-powered rifle. I didn't know that at the time. All I knew was the glass shattered, and then suddenly Jackie dropped to the ground. A second later, Scales followed."

Even in the shooting itself, Scales took a second place behind Jackie.

As Ali turned to deal with a question, I pondered how lucky we had been. It could have been so easily the case that the early news of her death was true. That would have been an interesting question: how much would it have harmed us? Would it or could it have stopped the movement? Would it have slowed it or maybe even quickened the pace?

I did not have time to think for very long because Ali returned to more concrete matters. "We all hit the ground, and her bodyguards covered her body, whilst some militia people went to where they figured the shots had come from. They must have moved quickly, as they managed to grab him as he was ducking out of one of the nearby office buildings."

"Do we know who he is?"

Ali could only tell me what the news had been saying.

Once he had hung up, I sat watching the action unfold like a voyeur poring over agitational porn. One thing did strike me and that was, whilst it had been our supporters who had hit the streets first and had, so to speak, thrown the first stone, the government supporters had come out en masse and had quickly outnumbered us. That was surprising. In the previous major street battles, we had always had the upper hand, and so they had learnt that it was foolish to take us on. And yet, here they were—out in force and upping the ante. Quite clearly, it was they who were taking the initiative. Very

Comrades Come Rally

strange, indeed. After all, it was Jackie who had been shot—our leader, our inspiration, *our* Jackie. It was understandable that our supporters would take to the streets, but what could explain the pro-government supporters swarming out, quicker and sometimes in greater numbers?

Youssef rang me back some time later and told me that Jackie was out of surgery and that they were hopeful there would not be any long-term damage. "As soon as the drugs have worn off, she wants to make a TV statement, hopefully within the hour."

"What?"

"She's worried about what's happening," he explained. This was not disciplined action but a dangerous reaction lacking any focus.

After he had passed on the medical update, I returned to watching a variety of city centres turning into mobs of people running forwards and backwards, ducking down, and springing up. By now the hidden weapons had been found, and exchanges were being reported. They certainly weren't hidden now.

I tried to contact a few more friends and people I knew, but all were engaged. Seems that they were all talking to each other, and I was unable to break into the ring. One person did ring me, and that was comrade Cole. I wasn't quite sure why she had. She said that she had wanted to discuss whether this shooting was related to what we were looking into. As we both agreed very quickly that that was highly unlikely, I did not understand the need for the call.

Our scumbag was trying his hardest to stay hidden and cover his tracks. This scumbag leant out a window and shot two of the country's leaders—on prime-time TV. Plus, he had a high-powered rifle. Ours used a pistol. Not him, then, or her—let's not be gender-specific about scumbags. It was sorted, in just less than two minutes. She was obviously feeling lonesome, as I couldn't get rid of her. Her previous calls had been to the point, but this one went on and on.

Presumably, the shooting had disturbed her. One effect was that at last she seemed to appreciate my genius, asking me a whole gamut of questions, from how the case was progressing, to the significance of such numbers of government supporters on the streets, to anything else she could think of. She was talking to me through her television, so I could see her sitting on a white sofa in leggings and sweatshirt with her feet tucked under her. She looked like a student watching *Breakfast at Tiffany's* on a rainy Sunday afternoon, the day after her lover had chucked her. Perhaps the shop shelves were empty of chocolate digestives or ginger cookies, so she had rung me instead. It slightly disconcerted me.

Whilst parting with pearls of wisdom, I took the opportunity to see what I could of her place. It all looked very well-chosen and classy and bloody expensive. How much were these coppers on! Fancy car and plush pad! Jesus, no wonder they were fighting to hold on to their way of life! Beating the crap out of student protestors whenever they wished, expensive technology, designer home, and wheels of pure cool—who the hell would want a fairer society? And let us not forget that she was no commander or inspector but merely a detective. Shame she didn't use some of her loot to invest in some shelves and pictures, as I really disliked minimalism. It smacked of someone trying just a little too hard to look trendy. Or they were just an unimaginative bastard. I favoured the last one in her case. With the trendiness of her flat burning into my retinas, and figuring that whatever her personal problem was, Audrey Hepburn was a better bet than me, I said good-bye and hung up.

It was worth considering what my life had come to, when at the same time that people were organising with complete strangers, acting in unison, regardless of gender, race, sexual orientation, or religion, I was having a phone conversation with an officer of the law. As far as I was concerned, they did not really have a race or gender, except that they were police. Unable to reach a single person I knew, I had to make do with Detective V. Cole. And it was undoubtedly the longest phone conversation I had had in years.

I settled down and spent the rest of the evening surfing the news. As the night wore on, the balance of class forces changed on the streets, with our side quickly swamping the government's. Not that their side backed off. There seemed a demented, even heroic, determination to take us on. Despite the majority of the militarised supporters remaining in camp and the big artillery kept muzzled, the death count soared.

As if the TV wanted to stoke up the carnage, the footage showing Jackie's shooting was played every twenty minutes on every channel. As Youssef had told me, I could clearly see him walking behind her and Scales. I could also see on his right a joking Kye Toulson, sharing something funny with Michael Hughes.

I had only really seen Hughes looking stiff and important, or even more stiff and important. Here he was evidently seeing Toulson as the life and soul of the party. His lips were apart! He was not only smiling but actually grinning. The second thing that interested me as I froze the report was—who else was there? Ali had said that she was being followed by a group of comrades she was about to have a meeting with. And who else was there but Marie Williams, Glen Bale, and Olivia Harrison! All the gang were there. Now what was that meeting they were off to, *going to be about?*

***

Next day, nine o'clock prompt to the second, and I was opening the front door to my seemingly bestest phone buddy, who was today's first—and no doubt last—visitor. Dressed in three-quarter-length black trousers, blue trainers with a burgundy chevron that matched her canvas jacket of the same colour, and with beige cap tilted back in a cock-sure manner, she looked very spring-like.

She smiled, said good morning, and walked straight past me, remarking as she went into the lounge on how much better I looked this morning, "'Cos you looked shit last night."

"Cheers. Come in."

I followed her to see her sweeping the room with her gaze, hoovering up everything she could see. First were my pictures on the wall. I suppressed the temptation to explain them to her, or even why we humans might like to have attractive or thought-provoking images up on the wall. After surveying those, she moved to suck in the wall of compact discs, picking out Horace Silver's *Song for My Father*. Good choice. Jazz classic. She looked at the cover and opened it with the interest of an archaeologist examining an unearthed artefact.

I felt the need to justify such an outmoded piece of technology. "A CD, compact disc. I prefer them. You get the album as it was intended, with track listings and artwork, keeping its artistic integrity."

"Yeah, my mother still has them. All boxed up in the shed. She was big on Jay Z and Kanye West—you've heard of them, I suppose?"

I didn't have time to respond, as she was off to look at the photograph on the fireplace. I took out the CD from where she had put it, replaced it in its proper position, and followed her. Why did I feel so subservient? In my own home! She didn't touch the photo but just looked. It was of us—me, Caroline, and Lisa—Christmas 2020, by the tackiest Christmas tree we could find. We were laughing, partly because of the bottle of wine we had consumed on an empty stomach at breakfast and partly because I had just tried on the new swimming trunks Caroline had given me and found them rather too tight. All the essentials had been crushed. It had been a good Christmas. But then I sensed that Cole knew that already.

Finally, after a visual sweep of the books, she sat down. Had I passed, I wondered? Too much stuff, no doubt, for her taste. Ah, but Your Honour, they are all in order. All neat and tidy. I could also plead mitigation that this was a lot less than there used to be. Oh yes, that night, *that* night, when, as an appetizer, I had smashed up my home just shortly before carving up my arms for the main course.

I brought in her tea but no biscuits. Chance would be a fine thing. And then I noticed her bringing out a half-packet of digestives from her jacket pocket. Obviously, she had contacts for such luxuries. Helping myself to one, I asked her if she'd seen Jackie's late-night press conference.

Slurping her tea, she nodded. "Mmm, yes, she was superb. Straight to the point. No holds barred. When she said that the prime minister may not have been the one actually pulling the trigger, he was the one who took aim—I thought that was brilliant."

I agreed. "She looked rough, though."

"Yes, she looked…er…grey. But then none of us look our best after an emergency op' to remove a bullet. We all thought she had been killed, so let's be thankful for small mercies." She took a hefty bite of the biscuit. I noticed crumbs falling to the floor. I'd clean them up later. "Do you think she will be able to cool things down? She seemed very keen to defuse things; there was a real sense of urgency about her; 'course it might have been the shock and the medication. But I have never heard her be so uncompromising in opposing violence."

"Like she said, the government supporters appeared to be the most eager to get stuck in, and you need to ask yourself why. There's no way they can muster the same size forces as we can. Oh, they can throw the first punch or Molotov cocktail, but that's about it."

She agreed. "In the station there were officers I haven't seen for ages. It was busier than it has been for ages. And there was something strange in the air, a feeling of resignation, but also of hope. Weird."

"Hope?"

"Yeah, they were getting psyched up, but along with the fear, I don't know, there was a belief."

Were they thinking about attacking protestors today? "How were they to you?" I asked.

She shrugged and swatted away an invisible fly. "Oh, fine. I'm their pet Leftie. I may be a party member, but in their eyes I am still in the Force."

She finished her tea. "Anyway, we need to get going." In one movement, she put the cup on the table and got to her feet.

I had been given my instructions and like a good boy, padded after her. What was happening to me? Finding my jacket and locking the front door, I saw that she was already in the car. The hoods over the front lights were closing as the windows began to tint.

I noticed a red pennant flying on the back aerial, and to make doubly sure that no one could mistake her allegiance, there was a red fist stuck on the rear side window. It looked rather incongruous—such a straightforward sign of solidarity on such a sleek, expensive machine. Champagne Socialists, Bollinger Bolsheviks, and here was the Sports Car Communist. Actually, with both the environment and the economy being in such a mess, having such a car, even a 'green' one, was considered by many nowadays as tacky. Curse me for being impressed.

Buckling up, I asked her who we were going to see and where.

She instructed the ignition to recognise her voice and to start. It did so, with the engine purring into action as we drove off at speed. "Acesto Savas. He was the officer in charge of the case against Marie Williams. He's retired now. Moved out to Norfolk a few years back."

Despite being told by the authoritative car computer that she was clear to turn right, she stopped momentarily to double-check for oncoming traffic.

"I don't know him personally, but DCI Martin used to work with him—rates him as a decent copper," she paused. "Don't start, Pete, you know what I mean."

I hadn't intended on saying anything, which perhaps was a sign of the *Alice in Wonderland* world I now lived in that I could take such a comment as being perfectly logical, despite its multiple meanings. I was in some sort of post-modernist hell.

She continued. "Martin gave me his number, and though obviously I did not tell him why I wanted to meet him, he rang him to say that I was OK."

I sat and watched North London go past. There weren't many people on the streets at this time; the marching and meetings would be later. Now it was just people out strolling and chatting. A few were hanging red flags out of their windows. The fighting last night appeared to be over, once we had mobilised all our supporters. When you have such overwhelming numbers, then the other side usually returns home to mourn the good ole' days in the comfort and security of the lounge. The evidence of the fighting was a few burnt-out cars and the odd burnt-out building.

The mood now appeared, as much as I could guess—speeding along in this luxurious and well-engineered but nonetheless status-symbol machine— to be agreeable, without being that of a carnival. There weren't really the numbers out to create one, and after all, quite a few people had died last night. There was no tearing up of pavements or pulling down streetlights. Quite the opposite—people were clearing up the night before. Passing through Loughton, there were visible signs of blood, which the locals were energetically washing down.

Cole had used all her energies up in the conversation department last night because she drove in silence. I didn't say anything, either, and just people-watched. It was strange that nothing was really moving. Obviously, there were no buses or trains. Every type of workplace you could imagine was closed. Not one that we passed was open. What was odd was that there did not seem to be many cars on the road; it was as if the strike included driving. What it did mean was that we made good time. The M11 looked like one of those old photographs of when motorways first opened, and there were so few cars on the road.

"So where in Norfolk does PC Acesto Savas live?" I asked, getting bored of looking at empty lanes.

"Chief Inspector, Chief Inspector Savas. He lives in Swaffham." She could see that I hadn't the faintest idea where that was, so she explained. "It's a nice little market town between King's Lynn and Norwich."

None the wiser, I asked about the man himself. "Acesto Savas, where's that name from?"

"Acesto, it's Acesto Savas. It's Greek." She giggled. "Although Martin calls him Ace."

Wow, how hip and happening.

"He was in the service for the best part of two decades. He retired five or six years ago. He's a w…widower."

I noticed a slight pause followed by a rapid blink before she said the dreaded word. She would make a really crap poker player.

"He's pro-Parliament, but Martin says he will be cool with us visiting. I think DI Martin used his charm on him, and he'll be OK."

More silence continued. We came off the motorway and onto the dual carriageway. Silence continued, pressing down on us. Feeling it too, she put some music on. I only had a vague recognition of it until a few minutes in and then realised that it was Wiseman. Popular amongst the younger comrades, but to my ears unlistenable. Now we had his drone to see us on our way. My lip couldn't help itself but curled up. She flashed me a look. "You must love his "For What It's Worth." That chorus, "Stop children, what's that sound?" is just brilliant. You have heard it, haven't you?"

"I've heard it. It's OK, but it's not his. It's a cover. The original was back in 1967, by a band called Buffalo Springfield. Theirs was a whole lot better."

"I stand corrected," she mumbled.

That was the last of the conversation until we got to Swaffham. The suburbs had made way for the country, green and blue replacing the concrete and red. Passing through the town, it was noticeable that whilst most of the shops were shut, some defiantly were open. It was one of those places where you just knew that somewhere there would be a cricket match, with someone bowling a googly. Not that I had any idea of what the hell a googly was. Turning left at the Fry Centre, we parked outside a small, detached house.

Acesto Savas answered the door before we even had had a chance to use the huge, wrought-iron, fake Victorian knocker on his pastel-yellow front door. Looking around at the ever-so-English niceness of the area, I guessed that this passed for excitement in these parts. Oh, they'd be talking about it for weeks: "Just think, Ms Jones, not just one visitor but two; one of each sex. Oh, how exciting. How lucky is Mr Savas. Oh, and one of them wore a lovely, two-piece, summer blue suit: the jacket with a single button and two pockets, with a mustard Fred Perry. Oh, how lucky he is, that Mr Savas."

The lucky man let us into a neat, if small, well-furnished home which had pretentions of being an Edwardian cottage but plainly wasn't. When we had parked, Cole had presumed to instruct me on how we were going to play this one. Basically, I would keep my trap shut and not, in her words, launch into a lecture on the role of policing in the capitalist system. I was there as liaison from the NWC. She was going to allow me to speak if he said something that did not match my recollection of the event. But she said, just before Savas opened his door to the main excitement of the month, to keep it civil and polite. We *need* him.

During the opening minutes, I did just as she told me to. I sat there nursing a cup of coffee and looking around. It was a nice-enough place, neat and tidy, with nothing out of the ordinary. The furniture was the striped-cotton-with-wooden-elbow-rest variety, set against beige décor. The walls were pretty plain with just two water pastels of undetermined artists.

She told him that we—the party—intended to wipe the slate clean of any past conflicts between the police and the protestors, so in the spirit of reconciliation, we were just looking back over the last decade to find out the facts and put the story to bed. Whether it was the presence of so many clichés or the just the plain silliness of it, he obviously thought it was a fairy story and did not believe a word. Not that he seemed to care; he readily agreed that it was a great idea, and he would do whatever he could to help. The pair of them then cop-bonded over fond stories of what a great guy this DI Martin was and the hoots they had had together.

Savas was a man probably in his late fifties, early sixties; in other words, we shared the same generation. He, though, had a lot less hair than me, with a dome of shiny skin which was edged with white hair on either side. His triangular moustache, which sat above the length of his mouth, was of a similar colour, although a few black hairs were putting up a valiant rear-guard action against the aging process. It was a rather drawn, long face which, when not smiling, could have passed for an undertaker's. He did, however, smile a lot, which lent him the air of a respected uncle.

Despite focusing on Cole, he did cast me the occasional glance to check me out, to make sure that I was not making a barricade of his comfy cushions. On our arrival, as he firmly shook my hand, he had made the point of telling me that he was not a supporter of ours. Although not considering himself political (I had forced myself not to smile, seeing Cole's eyes demanding me not to), at a push, he said that he was a critical friend of the government.

He had joked on how smart I looked, compared to how scruffy he did, and did this show that when revolutionaries started wearing suits, you knew that they had won and were preparing for power?

I sat wondering what this veneer of conviviality hid. What was behind that charm? He was in shorts and a skin-tight sweat shirt, which made it obvious that in his day he had been a fit guy. No bags of doughnuts for him. How did he keep fit? What, or who, did he use his strength on?

Finally, Cole indicated a change of subject by shifting her weight slightly on the sofa and got to the point of why we were here.

He leant across to the occasional table by his chair and put his cup down. As he did, he instructed the TV to come on and change to computer mode. He swiftly muttered a code, and the screen changed to one with a police logo and the title Ms Marie Williams File.

Out of the corner of my eye, I could see Cole was, as they say, somewhat astounded. Just me guessing here, but Ace Stavas shouldn't have these kinds of files at home to look at when there was bugger all on telly. He could see that an explanation was required. "I've got a hold of copies of any of the cases that might prove to be a problem when you lot come to power," he said, nodding to me in his best uncle look. "Just in case there are any questions about what I did as a serving police officer."

So he thought there would be hourly firing squads and a reign of terror. Sadly, Cole's story was nearer the mark than that particular view. The party had repeatedly said that we would look to the future and would embrace anyone who did so, too, regardless of their past. Shame. Piccadilly Circus would be ideal for a guillotine.

He opened up the file. Scanning down the page, he read out, "Marie Williams was arrested for grievous harm against a police officer, a PC Wilson, who had just finished training; both were on an anti-cuts demonstration in North London. It was a smallish affair, a few thousand. Started off OK, but things then turned violent. To be honest, I think we have to hold our hands up and say that we were rather provocative that day, a few months before we'd got a kicking on another demo, and this was revenge time." He took a look at his notes, although I had a shrewd idea that he didn't need to, because he had been revising them before we had arrived. "Yes, that's right; it was a Monday evening. Tottenham, the High Road."

Something seemed to excite Cole. "I remember it. I was preparing to go to uni. My parents lived near the High Road, where Tottenham meets the Edmonton boundary. My Dad came home and suggested that it would be better stay in." She grinned. "So, needless to say, my big sister and I had to go for a look!"

She must have seen my surprise. "Didn't you know that I'm a North London girl? Tottenham—born and bred."

Actually, it was the fact that she had been to university that had surprised me, but I didn't say anything.

Twitching her head my way, she continued. "Both Pete and I are North Londoners, though he hails from the home of the other, more upmarket, but lesser, North London team—Arsenal. He's the posh one."

Savas chortled with her. Queasiness swirled in my stomach, from the potent brew of observing cop-love and the bombshell that she supported Spurs. But I was here for a purpose, and I had to keep my mind focussed, so I said nothing on the matter. Professional, hard-boiled private eye attitude couldn't, however, achieve miracles, and I couldn't let the middle-class jibe pass without comment: "My family lived in a three-bed council flat on the Packington Estate; my father repaired the street lighting, and my mum was a TA in a school. Not what you call the aristocracy!"

I could sense a little embarrassment in the room at what many might have described as an outburst, so I attempted to lighten the mood. "And don't even get me started on her supporting the Spurs! Police officer, I can just about cope with, but Tottenham Hotspur fan?" It might have been a save from an over serious response, but it wasn't anything that would get me into the comedy hall of fame.

Savas smiled. Probably calculating that it was politic to do so. He continued, "She attacked him with a piece of scaffolding, which she had picked up from a restoration site. He received injuries to his face and neck; he had lost his helmet in an earlier melee and a broken ankle. Poor bloke, it was his first fisticuff demo—you never forget your first time being hit." He laughed.

Cole joined in. So did I, but with a good lacing of sarcasm and venom. "I definitely do."

The laughter subsided. Now he had a forced smile that matched mine.

So, treating contrariness as being next to Leninism, I dropped the smile. It wasn't a snarl I spoke with, but it wasn't too far from it. "It was a setup. Marie is one of the sweetest people I know. She is a carer—that's why she has worked in the NHS all her life. There's no way she would have done that."

His face remained immobile. "She was clearly identified by CCTV footage." He got the menu up and clicked. "She was arrested at her home two days later. She was held and questioned and then released when supporters put up bail." He stopped and looked at the both of us.

I remembered. They had come at five in the morning, terrifying the kids and dragging her out of bed. Ashok had phoned us straightaway. Caroline in turn had contacted a lawyer she knew and sent her to the police station. That first call was the start of the Free Williams Campaign. We had then got a hold of the more wealthy to raise her bail, her very substantial bail.

"No way. Marie is simply not the aggressive type."

He didn't say anything but just pointed.

We saw a high-definition image of a woman being chased up a side street, followed by a bare-headed police officer. Finding herself in a cul-de-sac, she turned and appeared to be shouting at the officer. He moved forwards. As he got closer, you could see her frantically looking around until she saw something. As he appeared to be grabbing her, she picked up a steel tube and hit him across the skull and across his spine and, as he cowered, his leg.

Savas pressed a button, and the frame first froze and then zoomed in. Not that he needed to; very clearly, it was Marie, face distorted. It was a look I had never seen before on her. It was one of pure rage, undiluted anger, and outright aggression.

I could not accept this. "Sorry, but this is fabricated. Let's face it; the police have never been too shy of covering their backs by faking evidence.

You are not going to tell me that the police have never attacked a demo and then pleaded victimhood to the press, ignoring the substantial injuries to those pursuing their rightful duty to protest, and complaining of a few cuts and bruises themselves?"

I avoided looking at Cole, as I knew she would not like this. This was not the plan; I was not keeping my gob shut. This was exactly what she did not want.

Savas himself did not seem to be phased by my outburst. Being so very polite, all was politeness in the parlour; class warfare in the streets but tea and cupcakes indoors. They'd be calling this the green tea revolution in the history books. Reasonableness personified, he sipped his tea and nodded. "I will not disagree with you that there is a sad history of certain of my former colleagues getting too involved in the action and taking it too personally and using disproportionate force whilst carrying out their duties."

Feeling aghast at his reaction, I did not let it be. "Which is always excused by us being told that the police have a difficult job to do! Funny, but teachers have difficult jobs to do, but they are not allowed to beat people with riot sticks!"

"Which is quite true, and as I freely admit, we have committed wrongs in the past..."

Cole moved forwards to become a physical barrier between us, correctly fearing that his sweetness was making me very sour. She tried to find the middle ground. "And it has to be said, sometimes at the behest of those in political power."

He was happy to meet her there. "Absolutely, Vic." His demeanour changed, and he grew in seriousness. "But I do not think so in this particular case. As I said, I think the riot police were indeed looking for a fight, but Marie Williams was guilty as charged. I took over the investigation. Not only did we have the CCTV, but we had the testimony of Wilson himself and two fellow officers. Of course, they could have easily been dismissed, but we also had eyewitness reports from passers-by, shopkeepers. Look, we even had two from the march itself."

He moved away from the CCTV and showed us pages of written statements. "You're welcome to look at this at your leisure when you leave. It's all here because, I'm sorry, my friend, but this was not a fit-up. We did everything by the book, honestly, and aboveboard. We had enough evidence to put her away for a long time. It's all in here."

Cole told him her number. He pressed **send**, and she confirmed she had received it. Looking thoughtful, she then decided to ask the big question. "Tell us about what stopped you from prosecuting. Tell us about the message: 'Stop and desist from the prosecution of Ms Marie Williams. *A*Block* with immediate effect.'"

He pressed a button, and there it was—in glorious 12-point Times New Roman. It was signed, Charles Hutchinson.

The memory appeared to excite him as he told us what happened. "So there we were. As far as we were concerned, the case was all wrapped up and ready to go to court when my governor comes down with this shambolic figure. I tell you, he was no James Bond. He was," Savas adopted a snooty, public school English accent, "Charles Hutchinson and he had with him an 'A*Block.' I'd never heard such a thing. My governor had. In the cause of 'national security,' they were going to throw the whole investigation into the bin."

"Do, did, they have the kind of power?" I asked.

"Oh yes. If or when you come to power, it's those characters you want to investigate. They do it very rarely; usually it's terrorist-related. Whoever happens to be the big bogeyman of the day—Irish, Islamic fundamentalists, Rumanians, you name 'em. It's not usually nurses."

"Did he say why?" Cole asked.

"No. Didn't need to. Only that it was important for national security that we drop it. The ironic thing was that Williams was actually in the station at the time. Can't remember for the life of me why she was; she was on bail, and we had all that we needed, but whatever the reason, Hutchinson, as bold as brass, walked into the interview room, with me trailing behind him, and he announces that we are dropping all charges because of lack of evidence."

His affable charm slipped a second, and he chortled, until realising that maybe it wasn't the most diplomatic thing to do. "She must have been surprised because she knew we had her. Hutchinson was good. He certainly knew the case. I stood there as he demolished the witness's credibility and the CCTV footage. He even took a pop at us. Not that I remember her asking why he was there or what he was doing. She just sat and listened as he took us apart."

Cole suggested a possibility. "Maybe she thought that the campaign had scared the prosecution off?"

"We certainly thought that!" I spluttered.

"Maybe, but I doubt it."

I could believe that. The campaign had been effective and had gained widespread support but not enough to get the cops to back off from avenging an attack on one of their own. I wanted to know about this Mister Hutchinson. "Where was he from? Special Branch?"

"Something like that. They never told us. The governor just flashed his 'don't ask' look, and we didn't. We knew nothing about him other than his name and that when he said jump, we said how high?"

Cole was disbelieving. "And was that it? Hutchinson comes down from on high and says stop, and it stops with no questions?"

"Oh, we wanted to ask some questions, but how could we? All of us, including PC Wilson, were instructed to sign the Official Secrets Act. He made sure of that before he left, and we were threatened with dire consequences if we broke it. I was fuming; mark you, that's nothing compared to how Wilson felt. He left the service soon afterwards. But what could we do?" He looked straight at me. "As I said, it's them you have to look at; not us poor coppers who were just doing our best to keep the cities safe."

Very moving.

"I don't know what Williams thought about it all. I don't remember what she said, if, that is, she said anything at all—you'd have to ask her. Once he had delivered his hatchet job, he sent us out, turned off the mikes, and closed the observation window. He was in there for about ten minutes. Whatever he said, she left afterwards, and that was that."

"Any idea what was said?" I asked.

"None."

Cole cleared her throat. "Was there any canteen gossip about it? This must have caused eruptions at the station!"

That was the code we had agreed on, or rather she had told me before we had got there, that if she said "canteen gossip," I was to make excuses and go to the loo to leave her alone to hold handcuffs with him. So I did. He told me it was up the stairs on the landing. So up I went.

To give her time, after washing my hands, I nosed around upstairs. With just two bedrooms, it wasn't going to take me long. I poked around the first door and didn't see much: a bed, a wardrobe, an armchair, and two watercolours. This place had all the finesse of a provincial B&B.

My snout then went round the second door. Aha, the master bedroom; that had two armchairs and a bedside cabinet. What I did notice was a large photograph in a gold frame on the bedside cabinet. I stepped into the room a couple of metres to take a closer look. It was a head-and-shoulders shot of a slim woman in her fifties with long, black hair. His wife, I presumed. Yes, obviously it was his wife. The frame was tilted towards the bed, so every morning when he awoke, the first thing he saw was her. It was also the last thing he saw at night. It was pointless, really; he had no need of prompts, of things to remind him of her. She was always in the middle of his brain. She always would be. I had killed enough time and went downstairs. At the door I could hear them talking.

"Things must be hairy for you at the station at the moment."

I heard Cole sigh. "That would be an understatement. It's been tense for some time, but over the past few weeks, it has got far worse. I'm used to the anonymous notes on the computer screen, the silence when I enter the room, and all those games—you get the idea, but it's moved onto a different level now. The abuse has grown. I've had slashed tyres and a few broken windows at home."

Savas was mumbling something sympathetic which I couldn't catch, and then I did hear him ask, "Any threats?"

A bigger sigh. "Well, it's gone from threats to real stuff. I got cornered in the loos a few days back. Three of them—Christ, I trained with one of them—and I had, shall we say, a dance with them. Just cuts and bruises, but they've promised more. Of course, I got no sympathy from anyone else. Just grins."

More talk from Savas, which I could not hear.

"To be honest, Acesto, I'm not worried. They won't ambush me again, I can tell you, and I will bide my time, because, to be brutally honest, time is on our side and not theirs. But in the meantime, I will be more alert, and they will never, never corner me again."

With those stirring words and before she called out the Red Guard Brass Band, I went back in. In doing so, it appeared to act as the cue for the meeting to be over, with Cole taking her cap off her lap and putting it back on her head, angled at just the right number of degrees. Rising to her feet, she thanked him for all his help. Savas offered us more tea and biscuits, but my partner had made her mind up and said we had to go.

He seemed to be sad to see us leave, offering us again the chance for further refreshment. Again, she declined. Just as we were leaving, he smiled weakly. "I do hope that was of help. I know we don't see eye to eye, but I've never meant to do anything other than my job."

I looked at him, and, declining to give the obvious answer, which I would have expected myself to say, I instead said, "Acesto, you really have no need to worry. When we do come to power, we have no intention of witch-hunting former officers of the police service." Smiling, I held out my hand, which he took and shook. One of Cole's eyebrows was raised. He watched us drive off.

"So?" Cole asked, heavy with implication.

"So," I replied.

She swung the car into the main road and towards the Green. "So do you believe him?" she repeated.

I shrugged. "Why would he lie? He's too afraid of soviet tanks rolling along his road to lie. He struck me as bending over backwards to wipe the slate clean, and this is him doing just that. What do you think?"

"I think he was credible."

For a few minutes, we sat in silence to contemplate what that might mean. "So what did you kids talk about when I went out of the room?" I asked.

We passed a row of cottages with pristine hedges. "Not much, really. He could not tell me any more about the visit, not any hard facts, anyway. He did say that the theory doing the rounds in the station was that the reason why the charges were dropped was that either she was an MI5 agent who had, and these are his words, not mine, 'gone native,' or she was about to be groomed by the agency. But there was no proof to back up either theory. I had to say that they do sound plausible."

"So what do we do next? What would you do normally?"

She scoffed. "There's not really anything you can call normal nowadays! But if you mean what we would do if we had the resources, then I think we'd put some people on checking with both people who had been involved in the campaign and the officers involved in the police enquiry; we would try to track down this Charles Hutchinson and, of course, talk to Marie herself."

The Green passed us, and I saw a small group setting up a couple of fold-away tables with red balloons and a home-produced banner that read URSP. One comrade was getting books and what looked like cakes out of a box.

I thought about what she had just said. "Well, there's just the pair of us, so we have to prioritise, and I would say that means talking to Marie herself. No going round the houses this time; we have no choice but to ask her some very direct and very uncomfortable questions."

She flashed me a look. "Meaning?" We turned onto the A road, and she put her foot down.

"Meaning just what I said—question her." I could not see how I had been at all vague. "*Really* question her as you would do if the police were officially involved."

"OK, but we are not. She'll just brush you off."

"Possibly, but it won't be just me. It will be you, as well, and you have not forgot, have you, you are a serving police officer; we will both meet her and question her. If she won't cooperate, then you have the power to arrest her."

That caught her attention. She shot me a look. "Are you joking? Arrest Marie Williams? Apart from the fact that she is a leading member and a close friend of Jackie's, she is, or I thought she was, a close friend of yours!"

Rather than gaping at me, I would have rather Cole kept her eyes on the road, especially at the speed we were going.

I knew what I was saying. I knew that I sounded like an iron-fisted Bolshevik. Inside, my internal organs had turned into whipped cream. "Something's happening in the country; the situation is changing and getting much more fluid and unpredictable. This means that we are approaching one of those times when the class struggle could go either way; the slightest thing could tip it one way or the other, and that surely is when an agent of the state, deep within the revolutionary party, would be very useful. Indeed, crucial. This is too big for niceties, so yes, I think we should do whatever it takes."

"And if we are wrong?" she asked simply.

"Then the only living thing that will want to call me a comrade is my cat. And even he will have doubts."

"Apart from me; I'll be a leper, too." She grinned. "Are we allowed to use that term?"

I had no idea. What constituted politically correct language had left my head at the hideous thought of me and Cole living out our days tending her collection of thumbscrews, hated by everyone. I returned to my line of argument. "I think the reaction is mobilising; they are hoping to destabilise the country. By turning the tables on those who usually do the destabilising, they can seize the initiative."

She nodded. "Savas advised me to keep away from the Return to Law March today." She smiled, appreciating the irony. "It has been called a peaceful march on behalf of all law and order workers—that's the police to you, comrade—but he reckons a small, hard-core element is going to try to hijack it and turn it violent. He reckons it is going to really kick off."

Neither of us spoke for several minutes. She drove, and I watched the countryside become more suburban.

Finally, she spoke. "OK, agreed. Any idea where we can find her?"

"Of course. There's a strike on. She'll be at the hospital on a picket line!"

"OK, but we cannot interview her on a picket line!"

"No, we will take her to your police station."

"What!" Worryingly, her eyes left the road again and stared at me. I really should stop saying surprising things, as it could get us both killed. Now, that would be a brutal irony.

"The police are taking their own action, so the station will be empty, won't it?"

"Er, yes, but…"

"And you can get us in?"

"Of course, but take Marie Williams to a police station?" She adopted a sing-song, nonsense voice. "But of course, if you are going to arrest her, you need a police station." Her eyes were now dangerously focussed almost entirely at me. Anger snapped the sarcasm out of the reckoning. "Are you serious?"

"Totally. We need to take her by surprise; it's about all we have going for us. She does not know we are working together, and she will not expect to be arrested and taken to a cop shop."

She could hardly believe what I had said. I could not, either.

"But wouldn't it be crossing a picket line; I mean, there will not actually be one there, but the principle, I mean? I am on strike, and you want me to go into work. It would be scabbing!"

I shrugged. "It's a reactionary strike; it's against the NWC. So who cares?"

"But the comrades within the service are taking the action to *support* the General Strike, not the reactionary one. If my colleagues know I have been working, then any connection I might have with them will be lost."

"You're working now."

Was this woman for real? Discussing principles and the philosophical gymnastics facing her and full of concern for the solidarity of her comrades in the police force. Then again, what classed as real here? I was arguing that she break it so as to arrest a long-standing friend of mine. Now that was a handstand.

She countered in this game of twisted logic. "Well, no, but we are not on official police business."

"And we won't be when we are in the police station?"

"Well, yes, but as I said, I will be seen as a scab."

I remembered what I had overheard. "I'm sure you are already seen as worse."

Increasing our speed, she thought about what I had said.

As did I. Guilt took a hold. The source of it not being from the possible incarceration of Marie but from the comment of how she must be seen as worse than a scab. It could easily be seen as a cheap shot. For once, I had not meant it to be. Whether she took it to be one or not, I couldn't read, but suddenly she spoke. Not to me but to the car's Satnav. The address she gave was Marie's hospital. For a second or two, nothing happened, and then it woke up; the route appeared.

CHAPTER TWENTY
The Social Contract

Returning to London, it was obvious that here was a town about to be painted red. The colour was ubiquitous—flags, banners, pennants, and foam fists. Even flowers in window boxes were the colour. Every closed workplace, it seemed, had the banner proclaiming the slogan for the action: Theirs Is the Real Violence. A large part of the electronic advertising had been hacked into and programmed to say the same. People were congregating in jovial huddles in readiness to attend their local events to mark the day. Others could be seen sporting red armbands or entering the few workplaces that were open, presumably to persuade those working to stop. Everything was local, so there was little traffic on the roads.

The NWC had called on this day to be the day we turned our streets into social centres. There were to be the obligatory marches and speeches, but the idea was to have much more than that: roads were to be pedestrianized to allow children's events. Some were to have sports days; others were putting on ad hoc arts and craft workshops. One road we passed appeared to be in readiness for a bike race. People had organised open-air seminars on topics ranging from flower arranging to the history of Marxism; from debates on the next steps for the revolution to the drama of David Edgar. The atmosphere was one of a carnival and fun. The edginess of last night appeared, at least through our windscreen, to have been left behind. All very commendable, but it did play havoc with our Satnav which was not quite in tune with all this street activity.

Looking at the car's computer screen, the lead stories included reaction to today's strike. This could be summed up as: the government and the established media, against it; we, the anarchists and the Democratic Front, pro; and the online community seeing both sides of the argument. Nothing, then, that could be said to be particularly stunning or surprising about anyone's positions.

The *Daily Mail*'s net coverage did focus on how it was, in their words, "sick"—no, actually they said it was—"**sick**"—for there to be strikes and a planned demonstration close to St Paul's so soon after the "**outrage** of the **murder** of **innocent tourists** by **anarchists.**" Ray Montag, their highly trained investigative journalist, had uncovered the shocking (sorry, the "**shocking**") fact that some of those involved in this demo would be members of the Anarchist Federation. Scoop Montag had achieved this by the forensic analysis of, er, the anarchist Internet site which said that they would be. This was the same organisation accused of the "**outrage**," he protested. It should be "**banned**," he demanded which, considering the police were crippled, was code for bring in the army.

What he didn't say—couldn't say—was that this yearning collided with the central problem that at present the army might not be crippled, but it could be described as being anaesthetised. Who did he want on the streets? Would its readers want Michael Hughes's faction out supporting the NWC? Sure, there was an opposing group, one who tended to have more pips on their shoulders, who would heed the call, but what about the vast majority who had made plain their unwillingness to get involved in civilian matters on the streets of Britain?

With my head far from dizzy from such revelations, I looked at the other news and saw that several world leaders had joined our PM in denouncing today's action. Here, the *Guardian* site asked simply what effect would a strike in Britain against a British government have on the governments of Turkey or the United States or France? Our PM did seem to be cuddling up to certain foreign leaders. It wasn't only our side who could show international solidarity; so could theirs. It called on both sides to show restraint and negotiate.

Cole was deep in thought as she drove. Probably meditating over what we were about to do which was simply that we were going to interrogate a leading party member in the middle of a general strike. The contradictions for us personally in doing so no doubt occupied and troubled her. I was busy trying to evade them.

I looked at the images the news was showing around the area of Marie's hospital. It seemed that they were preparing a long chain of people draped in red, linking the different workplaces in the area. It was meant to be symbolic, but I thought it looked twee. When the camera swept along it, I was relieved not to see Marie's face amongst them.

We were now close enough to the hospital to see the demonstrators themselves. Cole parked the car and unbuckled. Turning around in her seat to face me, she gently asked, "Ready?"

I returned the look and sighing heavily, replied, "Yes, come on, let's find her."

"And then what, Pete?"

The question surprised me. "What do you mean?"

"I mean, you would like me to arrest Marie Williams, but how the hell do you expect us to get her to the station? Do you think she is just going to get into the car and take a ride to check whether the police strike is holding? You don't think comrade Williams might ask if I am on strike? If I am, then how can I arrest her? And if I am not—then *why* not? The party line is that I should be taking strike action and in doing so, be engaged in active propaganda to undermine the police service as a viable anti-revolutionary force. And yet I would be arresting a senior party member."

I wasn't going to be lectured by a newly-joined on Marxist ethics, and on top of that, guilt- tripped by someone who had known Marie for a fraction of a second, so I took it upon myself to explain the blindingly obvious. "Which we would not be doing, unless we felt that we had to." My temper strained against its fetters. "I thought we had already had this discussion! She has questions to answer, and we have to ask them. I've known Marie since before you were born, and as you pointed out, I regard her as a friend, but this is bigger than friendship or personal loyalty, so please don't get 'more redder than thou' with me."

Plainly, I was getting angry; nonetheless, she kept on. "We *think* she has questions to answer, and we should try to encourage her to answer them, but all the evidence points to the fact that actually, for decades she has been a loyal and—"

OK, that was enough. "Spare me the convert's sermon!" I snapped. "You really do not have to preach to me about good comradeship. By putting aside personal feelings, I am trying to be one."

Noticeably, she was keeping her cool, whilst I lost mine, a fact which only inflamed my mood more. She repeated the central flaw in what could only loosely be termed a plan. "I ask again, how will we get her in the car? Snatch her? Kidnap her? Overpower her? *How*, comrade?"

She was infuriating, mainly because she was right. It was not a viable option, but I had blinded myself to the obstacles, because the less looking I did, the less I would notice the truly objectionable thing I thought we had to do. I was suggesting—no, I was arguing—that I betray a good friend. Luckily, I did not have time to decide whether or not to answer her by once more pompously analysing the political situation for a justification, or loftily reminding her of what we had found out about Marie, or even of using my old fallback in times of difficulty—throwing a strop, because she pointed and shouted, "Look, there she is! It's Marie."

With great effort, she was getting out of a black people carrier. She had been in the driver's seat, but others were flowing out of the other doors. There must have been a dozen in total getting out of it, all with red armbands, beaming smiles, and good humour. Marie appeared to be equally in a positive frame of mind. She looked the epitome of spring joy—a broad grin, chatter, and relaxed-looking, dressed in pale-blue trousers and cream, short-sleeve blouse, her ginger hair bouncing off her shoulders.

I looked at her and sighed: all those memories, all our shared history. There had been a time when Marie's family and mine had been very close, more like one extended family than friends. Sitting here in remembrance of a closeness we once had, I valiantly fought the doubts ripping me apart. I might be able to construct a believable mask of ruthlessness for Cole, but even if I could fool her, I couldn't do so with myself. Not fool, but certainly confuse. I hadn't been lying; it *did* make sense to challenge Marie, and what was at stake was bigger than personal feelings. Seeing her now, however, reminded me that putting aside friendship was harder than it sounded. She looked so full of life, buzzing around, organising, and talking in equal measure. I had no doubt that she was popular at work because everyone liked Marie—actually, most loved her.

My thoughts were interrupted by Cole: "I'm sure that's not her car. I thought she had a mini, a silver mini, registration…er…"

What was she wittering on about? Ruminations of loyalty, friendship, comradeship, the political, and the personal were abruptly halted by Cole blithering on about cars. What was she going to do—challenge her for an out-of-date tax disc or take her name for her brake light not working?

"It's not. That's one of the party cars." I said, unable to resist answering her, but managing to do so without the sarcasm. "I would guess it's from the car pool."

"The car pool?"

She looked confused. Probably, she had visions of BMWs swimming front crawl or Toyotas diving. Naughty, naughty, must keep it nice. "We keep a pool of cars at the National Centre for comrades to borrow," I explained.

An idea flashed across her small face. "Of course, yes. The car pool. Idiot! Why didn't I think of that?" She leant across and gave a few instructions to the PC, and the screen changed from scenes of protests to that of the National Police Network screen saver. Once in, she rapidly typed in several passwords and negotiated her way through a number of menus until she got to CCTV Coverage of the A1. I had no idea what she was getting hyped-up about. Road safety must be a real priority for her.

She recited the car's reg. "Some of the cameras are still working, only a few, mind, but there's enough. I searched for cars known to the people we are interested in, but I did not figure on the car pool. Why, I have no idea. It's an obvious thing to check. I mean, we might not..." She stopped, as a car's image came on-screen; a black people carrier, driving north, just south of Doncaster at 9:35 a.m. It had been filmed on the day Jenny Underhill was murdered. She zoomed in, but the tinted windows meant any recognition was impossible. But what we did know was that Marie was, right this minute, getting cardboard boxes out of the same car.

She looked at me. If she was expecting applause, then she was going to be disappointed. After all, if it was that easy, then why hadn't she done it in the first place! Even so, I swallowed my pride and told her what I thought we should do. "This makes it even more crucial that we talk to Marie because she needs to explain a few things. But yes, you are right—we have no right to arrest her." Mentally, I shouted a hooray to that. I think fears of super spies had got me over excited. Still, I tried to sound as if I had a grip on what we were doing. "I do think we need to question her as closely as we can and then report back to Jackie and see what she wants us to do next."

She agreed. A sneaking feeling tugged my cerebral cortex that this was exactly what she had always had in mind for us to do. The cortex muttered, "So ain't she a clever Fed."

Leaving the car we went over to her. I felt distinctly uncomfortable and not a little nervous. We caught up with Marie as she was opening up the boxes and handing out plastic cups of coffee and tea. "Supplies for the front line!" she was cheerfully shouting.

Several people from the local offices took a cup and raised a toast to the revolution. They all appeared to know her name and, from what they were saying, knew that she was both a nurse and a leading party comrade. We hung back, watching.

She hadn't seen us and, after delivering the refreshments, started to walk towards the crowd gathered outside of her hospital. We followed behind, with me, for one, feeling more like a criminal contemplating an unlawful act than somebody attempting to stop some unidentified regressive action. We watched as she took a few phone calls.

Cole told me, "We need to stop her from reaching those people."

She went off in a trot. This one followed.

"Marie!" she yelled, catching her up and positioning herself so Marie had no option but to stop.

Catching up and trying not to breathe too heavily, I added, "Marie, we need to talk. It's important. *Very* important."

She looked surprised, and her attention darted between the two of us. Something in our manner, our tone, and the very fact that we were together at all, made her pause for thought. Telling the caller that she would ring them back, she put the phone in her trouser pocket and gave us her full attention.

"You know Victoria Cole, I presume," I said, starting with the social niceties.

She indicated that she did. I could tell from her expression that the sight of the pair of us together was one she had not expected to see. Revolution might make strange bedfellows, but quite obviously, Marie had never thought she would see the day when I was sharing time with a copper. The grin that had been stuck to her face since getting out of the car faded from her face.

"What's up, Pete?"

"We need to talk urgently. Is there anywhere for us to talk in private, Marie?"

Pausing for a second, obviously trying to guess what brought us here, she finally agreed. "OK, this way. I'm afraid I haven't got long, but if it's that important." She pointed to a couple of unopened boxes on the pavement. "You can make yourselves useful and carry them for me."

We bent down and took one each. I was a little disturbed that it was quite an effort for me to pick it up. I felt my muscles tightening and my lungs expanding to take in air; my cheeks were growing in temperature. Cole looked totally unperturbed, breezy, and having no effort with hers. She asked Marie in total innocence, "Just as well you have a big car to fit all this in." She nodded towards the people carrier.

"Oh, that's not mine. My old dear gave up the ghost a few weeks ago; I've been using that from the party car pool."

"Useful," Cole replied after finding out exactly what she had wanted.

I concentrated on trying not to drop the thing. "What's in them?" I asked, between breaths.

"Coffee, tea, milk, sugar, and some sweeteners, too; seems we still have to watch the calories even in days like these!" She chuckled to herself, remembering previous conversations about the tea order. "There's a café up here which the owner is letting us use as a local strike refreshment centre. That's where we can talk, and you two can tell me what all this mystery is about!"

She strode on, exchanging pleasantries and banter with the growing number of people who were appearing on the street. Some of them wore hospital clothes of nurses, doctors, and porters, but many did not. Whatever they were wearing, however, there were a fair few who knew her by name. It took us ten minutes to travel twenty or thirty metres as we weaved our way through the throng. The final few were hard, as the box now weighed the equivalent of a blacksmith's forge. I was relieved to arrive at the café and see a huge banner in the shape of a menu:

*The Striker's Lunch: tea/coffee with two rounds of sandwiches (a choice of fillings)—**Free***

The Emergency Cover Worker's Lunch—the same as above, for 2 NWC tokens

*The Scab's Lunch—**Starve!***

On entering we were met with the smell of fried food (so much for decades of healthy eating campaigns) and the sounds of incessant and excited chatter. There were thirty-odd people of all shapes and sizes crammed around tables.

The woman behind the counter welcomed Marie with obvious warmth and affection. After reciprocal cheek-kissing, Marie asked, or rather told, Cole and me to put the boxes on the counter.

Marie looked around the tables for somewhere to sit, but Cole read her mind and quickly suggested that we go somewhere more private and quiet. The café owner heard her and offered us the office at the back. Thanking her, Marie told her that we wouldn't be there for long and headed for the door next to the toilet marked Staff Only.

We walked through a corridor so narrow that my shoulders brushed the walls, which meant it was very narrow, as sadly I am no muscled beef cake (and padded shoulders are just not me). We passed a staff loo that appeared to double up as a storage depot for bundles of paper rolls, pushed a glazed door, and went into the office.

The office was a small room that looked as if it had been constructed to exemplify the word "poky." If ever there grew up an interior design style of Poky Deco, then this would be the template for it. Just about big enough to house the three of us, there were three wooden garden chairs, a small table badly painted blue, and a hand basin in the far corner, with the smell of bleach and the naked light bulb adding to the feeling of solitary confinement. Strangely for such a warm day, it was rather chilly in there. Just to add that extra touch of class, I guess. It was probably a damn sight more oppressive than anything they were allowed back at the police station. I couldn't really see many international deals being settled in here.

Marie seemed not unduly upset not to be met with a fully functioning office with technical and admin support and a pot plant on a filing cabinet. She marched in and slumped onto one of the chairs. "Well, what's all the mystery, then?" Her manner was a hybrid of intrigue, puzzlement, a hint of slight irritation, and a dash of amusement, or maybe that should be bemusement.

I sat on one of the chairs opposite her. My manner was one of shitting myself. Cole chose not to sit but instead leant against the door. It may have been done with a leisurely nonchalance, but, nonetheless, she *was* against the door, as in, barring it.

"Jackie has asked Victoria and me to work together to look into Alan and Dave's deaths. She thought it was dividing our resources to be working separately, so here we are—partners." I flashed my ironic smile. "And there's something you might be able to help us with."

She looked first at me and then at Cole. "I must say I was rather taken aback seeing you two together," she said, obviously amused at the concept.

Cole smiled, joining her in appreciation of the ludicrousness of the whole situation.

Mine had lasted three seconds. I simply muttered, "Indeed."

She got down to business; this room did not really encourage anything else. "So how can I help?"

I crossed my arms, steadied myself, and then dived in. "Marie, you remember ten years ago when you were being done for GBH, attacking a police constable on a Tottenham cuts demo?"

Her facial muscles tightened. "Of course. I'll never forget it; it was a terrible time for me. I thought I was going to prison, unable to see my kids for years, and losing my job. It was hell! I still sometimes have nightmares about it, even years later. Quite possibly, apart from when Mum died, that was the worst time of my life."

Despite the location and the reason we were here, or perhaps because of it, I still could not resist the urge to make a naff joke. "You would have thought you'd get a medal for lamping him—not a prison sentence!"

Marie smiled slightly. I did not look to see what Cole was doing.

"Except, of course, I was not guilty."

We would get onto that in a minute. "It was an effective campaign, wasn't it? We had a number of the major unions, a dozen or so MPs, several investigative journalists, and a whopping great marquée of celebs. How many signatures did we have—ten, twenty thousand names? It was a textbook united front campaign!"

"It was, although you say so yourself. You and Caroline were brilliant running it." The memory amused her. "Poor old Lisa, she was so hoping to move into the bigger room, but you commandeered it for the campaign. I think she was as happy as I was when they stopped the case. She got her room, and I got my freedom. I appreciate it, Pete, I really do. I wouldn't have lasted two minutes inside. It was bad enough being in prison awaiting bail. I will always be grateful."

Despite the reason for our trip down memory lane, it was nice to remember it. "It was good to win one for a change, especially with the state in the middle of their periodic clampdowns on protest. I have to say that I was very surprised that they backed down. I've always thought that it was unusual. They hadn't in the previous cases, and there was a hell of a lot more evidence against you than the others."

I looked at her for signs of guilt or embarrassment, but I could not really see any. She looked relaxed and appeared to have no problem in talking about it. "Like you said, it was the strength of the campaign. They balanced the flak they'd received for putting a nurse behind bars with the gain of taking out a union militant, and they figured it wasn't worth the hassle."

"That's what I thought." And it was. Until that is, our visit to the Norfolk retirement home for pigs had come up with an interesting alternative. "Thing is, though, why would they back off after one of their own had been attacked with a piece of tubular steel?"

"Except I didn't attack him with any such thing. It was a frame-up!" she said indignantly.

For the first time since entering our cubbyhole, Cole spoke. Her voice was cool, calm, and almost gentle. "Well, you wouldn't have been the first person to have that done to them. Except…" She moved away from the door and put her phone on the table. Sliding it to face Marie, she pressed **play**.

Puzzlement made way for deeply uncomfortable shock as she watched the footage of herself grabbing a length of scaffolding and, after pushing the policeman off, hitting him repeatedly with it. Watching this, any thought of nurses being gentle agents of care took as much hammering as the copper did. Timing it to perfection, Cole finished her sentence the second the film stopped. "You actually *did* attack the officer."

Marie did not say a word. She just looked at the phone.

"Would you like to see it again?" Cole asked. "We can zoom it and get a better shot of your face."

After a moment of embarrassed silence, Marie tried to shrug it off. "OK, so I hit him. After the violence they had poured on us, what's wrong with one of them tasting a little of their own medicine?"

"I can relate to that, but why weren't you honest to us back then? Credibility was everything for such campaigns!"

She didn't answer but instead asked us a question. "Where did you get this, and what's the reason for showing it now? It's ancient history. What possible relevance is it to the present?"

"It's indirectly linked with what we have been looking into," I replied.

"How, what—"

Cole interrupted. "Who told you that your case was being dropped, that the charge of assaulting a police officer was not going to be pursued?"

"The guy who was running the case…er…Savvidis…no, Savas was his name, I think; Greek fella. He told me that there was not enough evidence. What is this?

"Did he say why, Marie? Believe me, it is important."

"As I said: not enough evidence."

"But they did have," protested Cole, whilst keeping the politeness. "More than enough!" Her tone changed a shade, with it hardening a notch more. Not that she had been anything but boating-lake smooth so far. "You were in the police station, weren't you?"

"That's right; there was some problem with my probation. Then out of the blue, he comes in and tells me that I am off the hook."

I could see Cole was ready to question Marie further on what had happened in the station—after all, that was why we were here—but I needed to get something off my chest. I still wasn't happy that we had been lied to, way back then. "But you *did* hit him! You *did* do it."

She momentarily looked at the phone. "Yes," she said defiantly. "I did hit him, but it was self-defence. He had been going berserk on the demo. He had previously been pulling and shoving anyone he could find. He had shoved Ashok to the floor with his baton. He was out for trouble. I heard afterwards that on a previous march, he had been criticised for not being strong enough, so he was making up for it on this one. He was ready to blow!"

"So why didn't you tell us?"

She shrugged. "Would it have mattered? I was provoked!"

"Of course, it would have mattered!" I spluttered with outrage. "We have always had to be honest and straight up in campaigning. One deliberately false campaign over a miscarriage of justice would smear every other. The state can lie and lie again; if we do once, we get harmed. They have had their law and order, and we have had honesty and integrity. Damage that, and you damage us. If they can discredit one campaign, they will use it against others. If it was self-defence, then we could have used that. For goodness' sake, Marie, they could have had a field day with us on this! You should have told us!"

Cole ignored, or wasn't bothered about, the politics of it. "Did you know about the film?" she asked.

"They had told me the week before." She looked at me with regret. "I had been wondering how I would tell you but—"

"But? But—"

My indignation was nipped in the bud by Cole asking her to explain how she had been provoked. This made Marie think for a moment. She was weighing something up in her mind. Folding her arms she replied, "He'd molested me. He had groped me earlier." Her eyes, for a moment, looked at the ground.

"Groped you," Cole repeated, mulling over her answer.

I was not in mulling mode. "So why not tell us that? We could have used it in our defence!"

Marie had no answer. She just looked embarrassed. I felt a very different emotion. Once more, though, Cole positioned herself between my angry disbelief and Marie. It looked very much as if she was not particularly interested in the details of the case but more in what happened after. "So was anyone with Savas when he told you?"

"My solicitor, James."

"And on the police side? Anyone with DI Savas?"

"Oh, I can't remember. I think he was alone. Why? Does it matter? I really do not want to think about it. It was a very painful and stressful time, and I see no point in raking it up again."

"It's the person he was with that interests us. You do not remember a Charles Hutchinson turning up?"

"Er, um, no…"

"Marie, please think. This is important."

"Well…maybe…yes…I recall him. He didn't really say much."

Cole turned on a friendly smile. "*Really*, comrade? He didn't have a private talk with you?"

Marie's embarrassment gauge moved up a scale. She pulled her folded arms closer into her stomach. "Er, yes, that's right; he did talk to me after Savas had left."

"Ah, so you do remember him!" I snapped. "So what did he say?"

For a brief moment, Cole's mask of polite interest slipped, and I saw irritation. It was aimed at me. It was just for a second, though. Sliding back into place the professional cool, she asked Marie where her solicitor was for this.

"James left the room with Savas. This Hutchinson guy hung back and spoke to me after they had left. James was furious; he wanted to know what had been said."

Cole almost purred the next question. "So what *did* Charles Hutchinson say?"

She breathed out. "He warned me that any attempt to sue the police or make any political capital out of this would mean repercussions for me and my family. He said that he would ensure the prosecution restarted, and then after he had made sure that I spent the next decade inside, he would use everything at his disposal to go after Ashok and the kids. I believed him!"

Sensing that I had something to say on the matter, Cole's mask slipped again. It was obvious that I was tugging at it quite forcibly. She flashed a look at me, demanding that I calm down and let her do the talking. "Did he say why he was doing this?"

"No."

"Did he say who he was and who he worked for?"

"No."

"Didn't you wonder?"

"I just figured that he was a senior police officer. To be honest, Vic, I didn't care. All I was concerned with was that it was over."

Her hands gently tapped each other. "Of course, Marie. But let us be totally clear. Hutchinson did not say who or what he was?"

"As I said, no." Marie's voice was now sounding vexed.

Cole marched on, regardless. "Did he ask for anything in return for this let-off?"

I could see something stirring behind Marie's eyes. She unfolded her arms and stroked the arms of the chair. "No. Why? What are you implying?"

Umbrage shot up me, like a wave starting at my feet and travelling towards my head. It didn't have time to reach my brain, as my gob was there before it. "I guess we are asking why an MI5 agent makes the effort to demand that the police drop all charges against you, charges of attacking one of their beloved, and one that they can prove beyond reasonable doubt. But MI5 decided to stop them. Why? Why, Marie, would MI5 care so much about you? What—did you do, deliver a baby Bond for them?"

She tried to mutter something, but I was getting tired of this charade. "What did you offer them in return, Marie? Did you tell them how close you are to the senior comrades in the party, or did you actually describe yourself as one? Did you tell them that you could pass valuable information to them, Marie? Oh, maybe not all the time, just when the situation gets so dire for them that they need some extra special help."

She was torn between laughing, sneering, and shouting. "Are you accusing me of working for MI5? I can't believe that you are! Me? A spy?"

I was aware that I was now leaning forwards, gritting my teeth. I am not a particularly aggressive man, but that was what I was appearing to be right now. "Simple question then, Marie—why would MI5 help you out?"

Belligerence was met with belligerence. "He didn't say. For the most part, he was just threatening me—rather like you are right now. He just said it was my lucky day, and somebody must like me a lot."

"Yeah, the head of MI5 or Special Branch or whatever the spook agency was."

"Or maybe it was how we thought, Pete: that convicting me was deemed more trouble than it was worth. Why, Pete, have you given up faith in the power of struggle?"

"Bollocks!" I spat. "It was an effective campaign; it was not a bloody uprising! They wouldn't have given up the prize so easily. Tell us the truth. Why do you think they stopped?"

"I *am* telling the truth!"

"You sure? Because you have told a few porkies to us so far, haven't you, Marie? Let's see, now. Firstly," I raised my right thumb, "for years you have insisted that you did not hit that officer, but now we know you did." I raised my forefinger as I counted off her duplicity with my fingers. "You failed to tell us about the CCTV, which I grant you is understandable, as it rather undercuts your Snow White innocence. You told us that you never met Hutchinson, but then, oh, yes, you did. He did not talk to you—but, yes, he did." Triumphantly, I held up three fingers. "Now that's the hat trick. Oh, you can pass this off as ancient history, but, Marie, don't we as good Marxists learn from history? Well, I have to say that I think there is quite a lot to learn from what happened in that police station."

The room was heavy with tension you would need more than a knife to cut. A chainsaw might have been more appropriate.

I carried on, though. "But let us not stop there, Marie. You told me that last Friday you were at work, but you were not!"

"Of course I was!"

I showed my clenched fist. At this rate, with so much use of my hands, I would be able to make a few shadow puppets with them. "And repeating that lie makes it five. I checked at your work, and Victoria checked your hospital's logging records, and you were off that day! Funny, this," I nodded to my fist, "usually symbolises solidarity, but with you it symbolises the growing habit of yours not to tell the truth." Theatrics were increasing alongside the sneering. "Oh, I'm sorry. That's not quite right, is it? I forgot: you also neglected to tell me that Dave had contacted you after his grandfather's suicide. So that makes six downright lies!"

I was almost breathless from the stress of my accusations. And with all this hand movement, I risked straining something. Whilst I sat drained, Cole stood impassively as Marie and I clenched in a verbal struggle. Marie herself seemed to have no difficulty in summoning up energy. Outrage was pumping her up. She sharply turned to face Cole. "You hacked into our computer? What right have you to do that? How dare you!"

I answered for her. "Because Jackie gave it to us. So, tell us—where were you?"

One of Marie's large hands swatted away such an idea. Maybe she wanted to play shadow puppets, too. She could be the hare. "I don't believe Jackie gave you the authority to do this. That is just crap. I was doing party business—*important* party business. You remember doing things like that, Pete?"

I would be the hounds. "In the people carrier, I suppose?"

For a moment her anger subsided, and she looked confused. "What?"

"You were caught on camera travelling north on the A1. On the same day that Jenny Underhill was killed in Seaham. Can you explain that?"

"Who? Who on earth is Jenny Underhill?" For a second or two, she did give the impression that she had no idea who Jenny Underhill was. Then the penny dropped. "Oh, her!" She appeared genuinely surprised. "The undercover officer? Surely you are not trying to link me with her death as well! Christ, Pete, do you take me for some kind of serial killer! Why would I want to hurt her? When I knew her as Jelena Jacobs, I was just a kid. The first I knew that she wasn't who she said she was when her picture appeared on the news. I was astonished. But if you think I hooked up her when I was watching *The Simpsons* then you're mad, Pete, stark, raving mad!"

Now that wasn't a very politically enlightened way of referring to mental illness. And she being a nurse!

"So where were you on that day" I continued, "and how come the very car you are driving today was seen travelling in the same direction of her murder? Explain that, Marie!"

We were now so close that we were almost exchanging bodily fluids. Marie's eyes now matched her hair, but this was not some revolutionary red—this was fury, flame-throwing fury.

"You've lost it, Pete." She snarled. "You have spent too long moping around and feeling sorry for yourself. Take some more pills and have a lie-down. Caroline would be disgusted at what you've become!"

I felt an urge to lunge at her, but Cole's hand lightly touched my back, acting as an effective restraint. Marie jumped to her feet in a rage that, in all the years I had known her, I had never seen. Looking at her, you could see just why the geographical features of a volcano were often employed in writing to describe extreme anger. And it was worryingly obvious that I wasn't the only one who was quelling an urge for a physical confrontation. Cole, standing by me, subtly changed her position from that of placater to that of defender, and for a few seconds, I sensed that Cole was bracing for an attack, but none came. Instead, rather than throwing punches, Marie hurled insults at me, barged past Cole, and slammed the door behind her.

I thumped my fist onto the table. Too hard; it hurt. Aggravation was making me tremble. I took in deep breaths and calmed myself down.

Cole moved and sat on the chair previously inhabited by Marie.

I snapped at her. "Yes, I know; you don't need to say a thing. We were to take it softly, softly because we have no standing and could not her force to do—or say—anything, and I didn't."

She did not say a thing but just sat there all Zen-like.

Frankly, I didn't give a toss about how I had fared in the *Apprentice Interrogator* show; it was not my lack of technique that was so upsetting me. It was the strange, contradictory feeling that was tearing into me. In one instance it was as if my heart was about to implode, and I was going to have a cardiac arrest, and yet I also felt heavy and lifeless. Guilt fought with anger, with no clear battle lines, and no clear sense of objective. So what took precedence? A woman I would trust with my life with the fact that she had been caught out lying? And what did it make me that I had so quickly jettisoned a lifelong friendship for an image of me hoisting the revolutionary banner, no matter what the cost?

Now, in this crappy storeroom with Cole sitting there looking all bloody knowing and thoughtful was not the time to debate my actions, so I took a deep breath and asked, "What did you think about her answers?"

"I don't know," she mused. "She did not really answer any of the things we asked her. Something is definitely a bit strange about it all. She cannot explain any of the things we put to her. On the other hand, I would have expected her to be able to. I mean that if she has something to hide she would have been prepared with a story that could explain it. Surely, she would have anticipated being asked these kinds of questions and would have a set of answers, but she didn't. She appeared genuinely surprised and startled by them. As l said, I am not sure."

It made me sick at how I was desperate to pin culpability to her so as to absolve me of any possible wrongful actions towards her. "Perhaps she thought that she was in the clear, with the political situation as it is? She got blasé."

"Perhaps."

For a moment or two, there was complete silence in the room. It was not a situation I wanted to last long. I did not want to think too much; we needed to act. "I think we need to follow up a few things before she can come up with a story. Firstly, I think I should pop into the party national office and see who was borrowing that car. No offence, Victoria, but I think it would be better if I did that rather than you. I am not the only one who has issues with comrades in the police force."

She smiled.

"What?" I asked, thinking that I had offended her. For once, I had not intended to, as after our recent meeting with Marie, I guessed that I could do with some allies.

"I think that's the first time you have called me comrade."

I grunted. "Yes, well, but, Victoria, do you agree?"

Luckily, she didn't get all warm and fuzzy and ask for a hug. Instead, she kept it professional. "Absolutely, and I will do something you cannot. I'll give Roijin Kemal a call and see if we cannot find out something more about our friend Charles Hutchinson. As you said yourself, I am in a unique position, so I should not worry too much about scabbing, and there will be nobody about in the station so we can have some peace to do some rooting about."

She was flying. Did she get off on this sort of thing? On she went. "Roijin is an expert at getting into systems that she shouldn't be able to. And we could also see if we can find anything more on that people carrier. After all, if it's a communal vehicle, it does not mean that only Marie was driving it. Maybe we might get lucky and see if there is any coverage of the driver getting out of it at a charging station or for a coffee and a visit to the loo."

She stopped, presumably hoping for some applause, but I didn't feel like clapping. I guess my hands were all worn out. Suddenly and without warning, what I had been suppressing exploded and doubt blurted out of my mouth. "Are we right to look at Marie?" The interview with her had shaken me more than I had expected. I had gone in wrapped in Socialist self-sacrifice and full of my revolutionary duty, but confronting the reality of accusing Marie of treachery and murder, I had been knocked back—hard. "Is there really anything which links her with any of this?"

Cole stroked her face; although it was smooth and apparently hairless, it was in the manner a man might stroke his five-o'clock shadow. "To be honest,

Pete, yes I do. It's all pretty tenuous, I know, but it's still very strange. I think we have no choice but to try and find answers. I realise that it's tough for you, but we have to do it. But if you still think the situation is like you previously thought it was, then there's a whole lot more at stake than personal feelings."

Or loyalty, I said to myself. In which case, if I was setting myself up as a latter-day Stalinist henchman, I might as well go the whole way. "We should also look at the others," I said, believing that I had nothing to lose but antagonising another comrade. "For example, there's something very odd about Olivia Harrison's behaviour. She appears to be a different person every time I meet her."

Cole was still stroking her cheek with her thumb. Was it the norm for maverick cops to do so much with their hands? I was making bunnies with mine, whilst she was all but caressing her face with hers. "Yes, I suppose we should, although I am not sure that we can do all this by ourselves."

"You've got Roijin Kemal, the fabled ICT forensic scientist, whatever that is, and you've also got this Asher Joseph, whatever he does. Can't you use him as well?"

"True, but even with Roijin, it hardly makes us a police force. And as for Asher, he would do it in a flash, but he's a forensic scientist; he checks prints, hairs, skin traces."

"He can use a phone, though, can't he?"

She grinned sarcastically. "Yes, Pete, there's a three-week course at Hendon on using the telephone, but—"

"Good, well, then you have the tapes of what Harrison, and Ali for that matter, told me, so they can check up on them and see if their alibis hold up. That is the expression, isn't it?"

She confirmed it was—in cheap Yank crime downloads.

It was a measure perhaps of how corrupted and degraded I had become, that I did not flinch when suggesting that two police officers should investigate two leading members. I had no doubts, though—it just had to be done. No matter how distasteful it might seem, it was the right thing to do. Maybe that was why Jackie had given me backing; she somehow thought so, too.

Cole did not seemed put out by the idea, either, except for the practicalities. "But, we come back to the old problem: the fact that comrades are not going to take too kindly to cops investigating them."

The point was still valid, but with comradeship and solidarity appearing to be principles that were under siege, I had an easy way out. "Understood, but Joseph and Kemal can lie. They can simply say that they are researching for the blog. They don't have to say that they are police, unless it is useful to do so. Seems to me your political ambiguity can be used to work for us: a copper when it helps; a comrade when that helps. Any comrade can contact me to verify it, and remember I have Jackie's backing. Let's face it, the truth is so ridiculous, who is going to believe that over the lie?"

She agreed with my suggestion, and we arranged to meet up later. Thus, having uttered sentences I never thought I would ever have uttered, we left the café. Marie had long gone, and she and the people carrier were nowhere to be seen. For self-preservation's sake, I purged any analysis of what had happened in that café, but I knew, as humble as the place might seem, I had changed in there. Whether it was for better or worse, I had no wish to think about.

CHAPTER TWENTY-ONE
What Next?

The journey back had been a strange one. Cole had been fairly happy to talk, but I resembled a sulky teenager, all angst and introspection. For the most part, I had just gazed at the marches we had passed. They had been pretty schizophrenic in character, simultaneously containing both a spirit of carnival with face paints and entertainers and the more serious side of revolution with striking workers, fists raised, and voices out loud. But whatever the aspect, they were usually beside someone on stilts.

It was all turning into a surreal outpouring of resentment and rebellion. We'd had the standard parts you'd expect in any off-the-shelf-ready-to-use revolution: mass strikes, occupations, workers' council, and the like. Predictable components. And didn't you always get hurt putting it all together? The hammer on the thumb? Ours had been a little more serious with them, predictably resulting in fatalities. Seemingly, the ruling class were only fans of Gandhi or Martin Luther King when there was a bank holiday to be had, or an excuse to condemn street violence. They weren't mentioned over much when they sent in the paratroopers.

But on assembling this uprising of ours, it had been surprising how much culture had become part of it. Having been a Leftie for so long, I knew off by heart the stories of Leon Trotsky and his civil war train containing poets and painters, but that had been in a semi-feudal society where the majority had been denied access to education. That could hardly be said to be true in twenty-first-century Britain. Sure, the later European revolutions had had their share of culture, but, hey, you expected that of the likes of the French, didn't you? They couldn't go to the loo without a bit of culture. But here?

And yet, leaving my house, I had had to walk my scooter down the street because it had been blocked off. Ten-metre-high projections were showing the local youth's e-art accompanied by the sounds of local boy-made-good musician with the moniker, KLCalibrations and his brand of music which the teenagers lapped up.

A neighbour with a fashionable haircut and shirt had stood amazed that I was leaving all this. There were to be drum and poetry workshops on the Green, even perhaps a combination of the two, he had breathlessly told me. Yes, I know, I thought to myself. I had had the privilege to hear the constant chatter and practice recitals all through the night. There was also to be an impromptu performance by some striking actors of a few scenes of the plays of Sean O'Casey. I had offered my apologies and tried to escape, but he had dragged me to one of the projections by house numbers eighty-six to ninety to show off his work. He informed me that he valued my opinion as he knew that I was a professor of art.

I had smiled and neglected to mention that I was only a humble researcher (retired, through ill-health). I also had searched for diplomatic ways to say that whilst politically I was all in favour of seeing the barriers of bourgeois art being broken, that didn't mean that all the art was good art, and his was… well…shite. Instead, I said it was interesting, and I saw it as a mixture of Marc Chagall and Frieda Kahlo, their later periods. Later, I silently added, as in, if their dead, rotting carcases had lifted a brush.

Escaping his beaming, proud face, I had encountered another oddity of this revolution. One neighbour was organising the litter-clearing posse. Now, politeness, good manners, and community spirit, which for decades had been the catch-phrases of the right, had been taken over by us. They had been forever bemoaning the lack of it with the youth or modern society, yet now both the youth and modern society were proclaiming them.

But there was no cuddly fuzzy companionship here outside the party centre. People looked tense and unsmiling. You could breathe the apprehension. Previously, the groups who had been providing the security had been conspicuous by the distinct lack of supplying anything like it. Tans had been topped up, and sleep had been caught up on, and if the British Nazis had been summoned from their neglected sulking slumber and had attacked, they wouldn't have met much opposition. Not today, though.

Comrades Come Rally

The comrades lurking by the first-floor windows had been noted. The silhouettes were holding what looked like long sticks. Too chunky to be sticks. And even to this novice, sticks obviously weren't much use poking out of windows. I would hazard a guess that those sticks also had triggers. And the highway maintenance lorries parked in a V shape at the entrance of the trading estate looked very useful to create a makeshift barricade. All the deck chairs had been stashed, the TVs and PCs put away, and the mobiles back in their pockets. Instead, there was a motley collection of vehicles. Next to two armoured cars and a tank, stood a vigilant group of heavily armed young men and women who were eyeing the horizon with suspicion. The hardware had large red fists painted on them, but they still looked foreboding. I was watched closely as I approached.

Two young, white women dressed in black berets, polo necks, and knee-length leather coats flagged me down. They had obviously been reading the history of the Black Panthers, so when they asked me my name, I was tempted to reply Bobby Searle, but the sight of the machine gunner on top of the nearest Land Rover pointing straight at me, dissuaded me from any pithy comments. Timing was everything, and now wasn't the time. We had come a long way from attending marches with leaflets, a copy of the *Revolutionary Worker*, and a bottle of mineral water in case the cops penned us in. Now we resembled an army and not a metaphorical one.

There was much huffing and puffing as the two guards found little in what I was saying to make them feel obliged to let me through. I felt a growing desire to shriek "I was a comrade before you were" or "Don't you know who I am?" But they were steadfast in their refusal to let me get any further. Luckily, any hysterical shouting was prevented when Simon Peary nonchalantly strolled out the building, pulling out a packet of cigarettes.

I called out his name in a strange voice that was distinctly at the camp end of the spectrum. Somewhere deep in my consciousness, I had obviously thought that talking like a drag queen was going to stop me from being shot. As that thought crossed my mind, a man in a dress and blond wig did actually appear from the centre and headed for one of the cars. For a split second, I asked myself whether he had heard me and thought it was a trans-gender convention. Or that I was dreaming all this. No, I said to myself, my dreams of late were nothing like this. This had a comic edge to it, and there was no blood. This was no dream.

A very real Simon, one not dressed in stereotypical female clothing, called over to the pair of erstwhile defenders of the proletariat to let me through. With a shrug, they did so. Parking the bike and turning the engine off, I walked over to him. He was breathing in his first fix of nicotine when I got to him.

"This all looks a bit heavy, Simon."

"Yeah, we got some info that whilst the Reclaim Our Country March is supposed to be a peaceful one, there might be elements who want to make it more proactive and take a more aggressive stance. We are just taking a few precautions." He exhaled. "So what brings you here again, Peter? You're becoming quite a regular."

I gave some vague around-the-houses answer about doing a spot of research for Jackie. His eyes were scanning the people in front of us. His mind was not on my exciting travels but was focussed on what was happening here, and so in way of a reply, he merely muttered something unintelligible beginning with an *H*.

After delivering a variety of inane excuses, I headed to reception. Not that I got that far, because on entering the building, to my surprise, I was met with a body scanner, the type you associate with airports. This was new. A grinning comrade apologised and told me that we had 'acquired it' from Heathrow. He also told me that we had been warned that we could be targeted by a suicide bomber. Walking through, I refrained from pointing out that having this device within metres of the reception door meant that if I was such a bomber, then I could just let it off now and take half the building with me.

The music of Pete Seeger was playing as I entered. As usual, Billie and Benjamin were doing the work of half a dozen people with every limb seemingly doing some job or other. Truly, the king and queen of multi-tasking. It was as if there was a pair of octopuses in here. In one hand was a computer, whilst with the other Billie was tapping some type of keyboard. Her mouth was occupied with telling some poor sod off for daring to want something. For a second, I didn't see Ben until the shiny dome of his head appeared from behind a photocopier, which frankly could have been outside with the tank standing guard. What century did that hail from? Judging from the ink smears on his hands, it was that age-old problem of jammed paper that had haunted offices throughout human history. Get that particular trial of capitalism sorted, and we would have even the most die-hard monarchist on our side.

"Hi…er…" he thought for a second, trying to recall my name, "Pete, what can we do for you? If you have come to see anyone, then most people are out."

I waved my hand. "No, no. I'm on an errand for Marie Williams. She left a bag of quite important party stuff in one of the pool cars and was wondering if anything has been handed in?"

He called over to Billie, asking her what was in lost property. She didn't answer, didn't need to, because the look she flashed him quite clearly told him to look for himself because she was busy. He smiled weakly and, lifting the counter, went behind and looked. Kneeling down, he ran off a list of items ranging from a phone to, rather surprisingly, a trashy 1970s novel, but no bag. I feigned surprise and disappointment.

"Hmm, has she had the same car? She can't remember because she says they all look the same. I can give you the reg of the one she has now."

Rising to his feet, he looked apologetic. "She should have rung rather than ask you to come all the way here. I could have told you that the days of keeping track on who has what car are long gone." He pointed to a square piece of plastic with hooks, most of which were empty. "We are just too busy here. I keep telling Simon that we need help."

"Not that he listens," Billie interrupted, despite still being on the phone. "Expects us to do everything but cuts our staffing. Used to have five working here, we did; now look at us, me and Ben, whatever use he is. I told him that you can't have a working office run on a skeleton staff. Of course, you can't!" Her Irish accent was usually very noticeable despite living in England for the last forty years, but when she got agitated, it went a whole degree stronger. It was that way now.

Still, rant over, she returned to her call. Ben continued with his explanation. "We used to have a logging in and out procedure, but now it's just the case of if you need a car and we have one—then take the key."

"You don't have any kind of monitoring procedure or a priority list?"

"Well, it is supposed to be for those who really need it, but we don't check up on that. We trust comrades not to abuse the system."

I was feeling frustration crawl up my throat. "So, for example, you could not tell me who had a certain car on a certain day?"

"Sorry, Pete, no idea."

"Oh, not, say, on, Friday last? That's when she thinks she lost it."

"Sorry, I could not tell you whether it was here or on loan and if so by whom."

Frustration moved up an inch. "Marie says she's been using the car-pool cars for quite a while now. What with her workload and everything, she has rather lost track of time. Can you remember whether she has been in since Friday? Because it would make sense that if she hasn't, then she must have used that car on that day."

He didn't have time as Billie piped in again. "Oh, Marie's always in and out. She's usually in at least once a day."

"Does she keep the same car?" I persisted.

He shrugged and looked at Billie who answered by giving me another long lecture on how overworked and understaffed they were, and comrades did not appreciate that. "They just come in and demand help, and we are supposed to drop everything and run after them. How do we know who is driving what car? Often they just come in, leave the keys on the counter, can't even be bothered to hang them up, and grab another set. It saves them the bother of recharging the engines. I spent most of yesterday charging up four cars that had been dumped here. Ridiculous it is—ridiculous!"

Facing a pained expression because of Ben's inability to be of help, I tried to come up with another idea. Looking out at the armed security gave me an idea. "What about CCTV? The centre is surrounded by it. Let me have a look, and I will be able to get the car reg, and so we could trace the car."

It was a brilliant idea. I was a ruddy genius. Except. Except that he told me that the CCTV had been down for three and a half weeks. Breathtaking, just bloody breathtaking! Fearing an attack from our political foes, and we line up bloody tanks, but something as simple as CCTV and we don't bother.

"Couldn't we have got it fixed?" I asked, astounded at the fact. "Ask Bale or his hordes of IT geeks or Simon, for that matter; he's quite handy with that sort of thing!"

Ben just shrugged a nothing-to-do-with me reply.

With technology being of no use, I was about to rely on that greatest of computer—the human brain and specifically the memory—and ask whether they had any idea of what Marie was doing that day, when the entire office shook with an earsplitting noise. It was not a bomb going off, not, at least, a real one. It wasn't, either, that someone had decided to put some rock music from this century on the music system, because we were still very much in late twentieth-century folk with Christy Moore now taking his turn—no, it was a roar booming from deep within Billie's soul. Moore's gentle burr at the injustices of the world was completely overwhelmed by hers. Her outburst had sent my stomach into orbit as I jumped from the sudden eruption.

Ben, though, appeared to be used to this type of thing. After enquiring as to what the cause of this upset was, we learnt that the Internet had crashed.

"I thought the net was one of the things we were maintaining today? It was seen as an essential service."

Billie's reply was almost spat at him. "Well, I think we can guess that this is the government's doing, don't you? It fits with the other reports we've been getting. The areas we have maintained a power supply to have been sabotaged and now have stopped. All gas and electricity are now blocked. Hence," she pointed to a dim bulb above her, "us being on back-up generator!"

"They've crashed the whole net?" I asked.

She swung the screen to show me, and it merely had a message saying that everything was offline due to today's illegal general-strike action. So they were blaming us and moving the control of the action away from us and if not to them, then into the hands of someone who might be friendly to their cause—chaos.

Ben nodded, obviously reading my thoughts. "We've heard that most of the street lighting went off during the night, when the power workers had agreed that domestic roads in all areas, except the affluent, would remain on until 8:00 a.m."

"The power was on down my way and up to full capacity; a neighbour showed me his e-art, and that takes a few bits of oomph to get going."

For some reason Ben decided to give me a detailed account on the state of the cyber world. "I doubt whether that's the case now. Then again, our members in the power industries have been trying to ensure that the agreed supplies have been forthcoming. Thing is, all it takes is one engineer to sneak a program override or to flick a switch, and the power stops. We have a team running checks on the grid, but it is not easy. It is like a swarm of annoying wasps. As soon as we swat one of them, anther one appears."

"Trying to bugger us up," I muttered to no one in particular and hoping that my disinterest would dissuade him from furthering the political lecture. I mean, sure we were living in political times, but did everything have to have a polemic attached to it?

He agreed, adding more tales of woe. "There has been a sustained effort to enforce the blockade and to regain control of food supplies routes so as to bring them into the strike action, despite being another area with an exemption."

Seems they did. Interesting though. They were indeed trying to stretch the general strike, so it would bring the country to a halt and make everyone suffer. The bosses being more militant than the militants would make it look as if any action taken by the NWC was against, rather than for, the people.

The three of us were pondering how the day was turning out when the door slammed open, and a six-year-old boy came charging into reception from the warehouse, wearing game-goggles. I had no idea what particular game he was playing, but it involved a gun of some sort, as he was pointing his fingers at the pair behind the reception desk. Ben faked being hit whilst Billie shot him back a look that stopped him in his tracks. She was not in play mode.

Following him in was Michael Hughes. In shorts and beige V-neck pullover stretched over his muscular black chest, he was smart-casual with power. His demeanour was none of those things. He looked sweaty and almost fearful, as he saw Billie glaring at the child.

"Al, I told you not to run off. I am *so* sorry, Billie. I really am." His voice was only slightly below the begging level.

She all but barked back at him. "We are not a baby-sitting service here! I've told you, Michael, he should not be here. This is no place for a child!"

Grabbing the boy's arm from the obvious fear that Billie was about to rip it off and eat it, he hurried an explanation. "Naomi's on strike, and so is the nursery. She's got the older two, and I said I would have him."

Billie didn't answer. She didn't need to; she had said quite enough.

It was as he was reeling from her look, that he first noticed moi standing there. Instantly, he straightened, and every muscle—and he had a few—tensed.

Showing fear was acceptable and understandable when confronted by Billie, but in front of me, then our brave soldier-comrade, hero of the red force, needed to show just how tough he was.

He silently nodded. His son pointed his virtual gun at me. We stood in an awkward silence for a second or two until we were saved by Simon's arrival. He strolled in and mimed shooting Michael's son. Billie tutted disapproval.

He oozed mock charm. "Just protecting you, Billie; the class can't do without you."

Her head bobbed up, and she chuckled. "Get away with you!" Oh, the smoothness of this man. He could even calm the fevered Billie—something not to be dismissed lightly. With just a few words, Prince Charming had turned the dragon at the mouth of the cave to the bashful princess. Not that the girlish mood lasted long. Embarking very quickly on a long tale of the problems she was facing in trying to keep everything running, words like inferior, substandard, and amateur came thick and fast. Like whiplash, she added that there were also too many children here, which, she reiterated, was not the place for them.

Michael himself looked like a naughty boy. Simon didn't help matters when he told her that the water supply had just been cut off. This prompted more dark mutterings in an accent so thick, *thankfully* so thick, that we could barely understand her.

Simon looked at Michael, and he looked at me. I looked at my shoes. Finally, sensing that good news might lighten the mood, Simon told Michael that he had found someone to look after his son for a few hours. The party had organised several crèches for comrades in the area, and he would organise a lift for the child to get him there.

Stiffly, Hughes thanked him and asked him how the picture was looking across the country.

Simon sighed and considered the irony of the situation we found ourselves in. "Virtually everything's at a standstill—everything! We have even heard that pro-government engineers have vandalised local emergency back-up power supplies. We reckon they are trying to do a repeat of the Manchester hospital incident. The flak we received when one didn't come on and several patients died would be multiplied with this sabotage. The Thames Barrier is completely without juice. Naturally, the PM is denying it's them, but they have blown our emergency cover right out of the water—quite possibly literally, with regard to the barrier."

"I'll get some people over there. Where else?"

He ran through a long list of workplaces in London where the strike had been hijacked. Every so often, he would loftily volunteer to help, but each time, Simon patiently outlined what we were doing. I stood, listening in discomfort to a situation which confirmed the view that there was a determined effort to lever control from our fingers.

Outside, former secretaries, street cleaners, cameramen, and cooks were running about, trying to create an armed guard, the fear being that there might be a more concerted effort to over-throw the councils. I was no military expert, but it all looked rather disorganised to me. I doubt if this could be ranked alongside great defensive operations. The Duke of Wellington could rest in peace.

The music changed, and Irish English changed to Chilean Spanish. "Well, comrades, I sincerely hope that there is no profound meaning for having this playing at this moment in time," I pointed upwards, indicating the smooth folk sounds and deliberately aiming the remark at Hughes, who was just about to try and catch up with his son, as he prepared to take on some unidentifiable enemy back in the warehouse.

He turned and looked puzzled.

"Victor Jara," I explained. "He was a Chilean Socialist folk singer. Murdered in 1973 during a military coup overthrowing a Socialist-Democratic government. The military held power for over twenty bloody years."

An affectionate smile crossed Simon's lips.

"What?" I asked. "Isn't it?"

He patted my shoulder. "Of course it is, Pete, and you are never one to hide what you know, are you? If you got it, flaunt it! Wear it on your sleeve, hey, Peter!" He laughed.

Hughes didn't; he just sniffed and fled with his son into the warehouse. Watching him leave, I muttered, "Well, I'm sorry, Simon, but Hughes is such a pompous ass, it brings out the worst in me. Jesus, the man sees himself as the saviour of the revolution!"

That just encouraged him more. Between laughs he replied, "But, Peter, you think *everyone* is pompous!"

I joined him, although with slightly less volume. He had, after all, a point. The amusement ended when Billie interrupted him to demand what he was going to do about having no water here. "We can't be expected to use the toilet without having any," she said. He considered the matter. I just stood, looking on, rather at a loss to know what to do next.

My mental drifting was halted when Michael came striding back in, son firmly in tow in one strong hand, with the other taking a call. Out of the corner of my eye, I caught sight of a familiar bunch of red curly hair on the phone screen. He did not mention her by name, but I knew it was her. The call was brief, and his response appeared to be merely agreeing to instructions.

It must have lasted no longer than a minute, but it galvanised Hughes. Turning on his heels, he knelt by his son and tenderly apologised that he was going to have to leave him for a few hours but that *Uncle Simon* was going to arrange for him to play with some other children. Simon smiled benevolently at the mention of his name. The boy appeared unfazed and was more concerned with adjusting his goggles and complaining that the colours were wrong. Simon knelt by him and said that he would sort that out for him, too.

After a kiss on the boy's head, followed by a ruffling of his hair, Hughes curtly said good-bye and marched outside. That guy was straight out of the 1950s. I just expected him to take out a Lucky Strike, have a smoke, and chew over how Joe DiMaggio's season was going.

Simon was by now looking through the goggles and adjusting the translucent control. I looked at Hughes's erect back striding towards a Land Rover and came to a decision. If Hughes was meeting Marie, then I wanted to know where. Don't ask me why, because I couldn't tell you, but something was urging me to follow. Call it intuition or gut instinct or the fact that I had nothing else to do, but I hastily said good-bye and left.

By the time I had reached the bike, he was already driving off. I turned the engine on and discovered that Satnav was offline. Well, of course, it was. I was going to have to follow him and guess where he was going. That was not going to be easy, as a red scooter, ridden by a man in a sharp, two-tone, blue, five-button suit was going to be damn conspicuous. Something in my head, though, said that it was worth the risk.

I pulled away and kept my distance, seeing him turn right. He was heading north. I knew the road well enough to know that for several kilometres there were no turnoffs. The road was pretty deserted, so I could see him gaining speed. It also meant that by following him I would be as plain as a boil on your arse.

Out of the trading estate, there was only left or right. So I went straight across, right up over the pavement, by a row of shut shops, the foot-rests scraping badly on the ground. I drove along the pavement for a few metres before darting down an alleyway. Passing an elderly couple, I received a volley of abuse and demands that I get on the road and that pavements were for walking and not mopeds. Moped! Piss off! It was a bloody scooter! And I had every intention of getting back on a road. I knew that parallel to the A-road was a series of double-backs. I hoped I could shadow Hughes by being on those.

Hitting the street hard and jarring my spine, I finally came off the pavement. This bike was not designed for off-roading. I looked ahead and saw a road to my right. Approaching it, I saw a problem: blocking it off were tables laden with food. Poxy, annoying street parties! I slowed down and weaved in between two which appeared to be salad tables. I was now in the road, but I could see obstacles ahead consisting of people standing about eating, drinking, and chatting. That soon changed, as despite giving dozens of apologies, the conversation changed to criticism. A few cheese rolls flew past my ear. Seeing a gap in the crowd, I twisted the accelerator, only to be confronted by a couple sitting on stools drinking from a bottle. Breaking hard, I turned and went around them. I now had to ride diagonally across the street to avoid yet more tables. How much bloody food did they have in this street? I thought there were soddin' shortages! Something squashy hit my back; looking down, I saw the remains of sandwich passing under my wheels. Great! It wasn't like this for Steve McQueen in *The Great Escape*!

Finally, I could see the end of the road. I said a silent prayer that this was not a cul-de-sac and that this end of the road was taken up with a small bouncy castle. Avoiding mowing down excited children, I squeezed past. I just hoped that not all the roads around here were like this, as I would soon lose Hughes. Again, I got some luck—ahead I could see the next road was clear.

I turned up the speed. As much as I could, that is. McQueen had ridden a Triumph TR Trophy motorbike; I most certainly didn't.

Negotiating the backstreets, laid out like an asymmetrical, chequered tablecloth, I went as fast as I could and didn't worry too much about the rules of the road. The trouble was that, whilst I was having to turn left and then right again and then left again to travel in a northerly direction, Hughes was travelling on a straight road in a vehicle whose heater had more power than this scooter. There was a real danger that he would very soon be pulling away from me. Without the Satnav I had to rely on my memory and hope it was correct, that coming up was a slip road. And there it was!

Using it to rejoin the A road, I scanned in front of me and couldn't see any sign of a Land Rover. I feared that I had lost him until ahead I saw the tail of a traffic jam. For once it was a welcome sight.

Stopping behind a blue van, using it as cover, I searched for the Land Rover. Sitting there, I could not see any sign of him, but I did hear that many of the cars had their horns on repeat. A minute or two passed as we sat there, with the sound rising in volume. Despite the lights still being on red, the traffic ahead of us started to move. Obviously, the lights were broken or tampered with. Whatever the reason, as we set off, a lorry ahead moved, and I saw in the fast lane the Land Rover. I weaved in and out to get closer until I could ride with the lorry between Hughes and me.

In the centre of the junction, all directions on the move created bedlam. I had to have my wits about me as I watched for cars all crossing at once, whilst keeping Hughes at a distance that meant that he would neither lose nor see me.

Once we were clear, things were safer, but as the traffic thinned out, two things became troubling: firstly, with less traffic I was once more in danger of being easily spotted, and second, I was going to have trouble keeping up with him.

The bike was shaking as I pushed it to its limit, making it sound like a demented bumblebee. Ahead, I could see Hughes, but if we stayed on this road for too long, that would not be the case. The signs indicated that there was a roundabout approaching. He reached it only less than a minute before me, but I couldn't see which turning he had taken.

That remained true until I was actually on the roundabout and saw that it was the second left. Turning rapidly and without having time to indicate, I crossed lanes just as a silver rust-heap of a 4x4 missed me by millimetres.

Hughes was slowing down, which gave me time to catch up to him. Congestion by another set of lights and running through green, amber, and red in rapid procession again and again slowed him further. He turned left and headed for a residential area.

I did likewise but frantically searched for a road I could travel down in parallel to him. The only thing in his rearview mirror would be me until I could find a way to get out of his line of vision. After forty-five long—*very long*—seconds, I eventually found one and took it. He went straight on whilst I turned. And found myself bang in front of a group of people standing listening to a speaker, pontificating on a dining chair. Breaking hard, attracting turned heads but not actually hitting anyone, I wobbled badly and narrowly missed a rubbish bin. You never saw this in the movies. Unless it was slapstick.

Turning again, I again traversed the back roads as he went straight. I had to be at each junction of the residential ladder first so as to make sure that I could see him pass. This meant again praying to the God of the roads that no toddlers were crossing, as they risked being an accessory on my headlights.

After three of them, I stopped and looked. This time I saw him heading straight for me up the joining road. Crap!

Without looking anywhere else, I swung the bike and did a U-turn into someone's driveway. That did not endear me to an elderly chap who was spending the general strike trimming his hedge. I mumbled apologies and sped off in pursuit of Hughes. I could see him taking a right. I followed, trying not to get too close. Then after a minute or two, he stopped in front of a house. Passing him, I found a place behind a parked ice cream van.

I noted the car Hughes had parked behind—the same car from the pool which Marie was using. So she was here before him, no doubt warming the kettle on a bonfire because the grid was down. Sliding up my visor, I kept my eye on Hughes, who was getting a large sports bag out of the passenger side.

I phoned Marie's hospital and asked the receptionist how I could contact her. She explained that Sister Williams was on strike, and within the hospital was emergency cover only. I told her that I understood that, but I needed to get in contact with her in regard to workers' council business. She replied that she could not give me her number because I could be anyone. This was as I had expected. Whilst I went through the charade, I observed Hughes walk up to the front door and knock. And who should answer it but the lovely Glen Bale.

"I understand, that's quite right of you, there are enemies of the revolution everywhere," I purred down the phone. "Could you tell me, however, where she is at the moment so I can meet her?"

This she could do, she replied. Sister Williams had said that she would be on trade union duties all day for the local activities.

"So she is in the vicinity of the hospital?" I asked.

"Well," came the reply, "I cannot see her right this minute, but she said that she would be within five minutes of the hospital from midmorning onwards."

I thanked her and watched another car arrive and park by the Land Rover. It was another blacked-out car from the national office. Youssef emerged from the driver's seat. From the passenger's, Olivia Harrison climbed out, clutching a briefcase. Well, wasn't this lovely and sweet. A national general strike, and these leading members of the party have a meeting out here in suburbia, the land of kid's trampolines and magnolias. Around these parts the hot topics would be hose-pipe bans or parking zones. Is that what brought this top cadre here—to fret about the politics of residential life? Tea and biscuits when they should be working out the problems we were facing today? Weren't we without both power and water today? And yet here were the reps of those important services meeting here. Jackie had told me that this little group of theirs was set up to discuss our working relationship with other parties. Sure, and I sing like Frank Sinatra. This bunch was up to something. They were not meeting secretly in this anonymous and commonplace house to chat about voting tactics.

I rang Cole, but nothing happened. Glancing down from watching Ali and Harrison join the others inside the house, I read a message telling me that the network was down. I would guess that it had been pulled down. By whom I didn't know, but it meant that I was here behind this ice cream van all on my own.

CHAPTER TWENTY-TWO
From the Old Family to the New

Soul Shack was heaving. Open since midnight, it was rammed with strikers of all ages excitedly talking about the day's events. Opinions flew everywhere, with some hailing it as a success, others bemoaning it as a step backwards. A sizeable and vociferous few were arguing in assorted cubbyholes that the revolution had stagnated and needed a boost. The violence in Central London was another favourite topic for debate, with accusations and conspiracy theories abounding. It was only going to be a matter of time before Elvis was found to be behind the use of water cannons. I'd give it a few more pints.

I sat by my usual table where Maurice had deposited me after clearing it of youth. He had been quite sweet, apologising for upsetting me for his wind-ups about Victoria Cole, which he said had been meant in jest and from a friend who was just pleased with the sight of me apparently back on my feet. Decently, he admitted that it had been childish and cack-handed. I had told him that he had not upset me at all. He had, but that was down to me and nothing he had said. I didn't want to be wrapped up in cotton wool. Not least, because the fluff would be hell to get off my threads.

Once it was clear that diplomatic relations hadn't been broken, he had hovered over the table, mulling over the latest reports that, due to the growing instability, it was likely that the football season would be again suspended. If so, this one could last two years. Not that I had really listened.

Luckily, my phone was fully up and running by the time I had got here. Out of anything other than money banked on the phone, I breathed a sigh of relief as I pressed it against the bar pad. Lucky also that Maurice had slashed the prices for anyone involved in the action. I hadn't been, but I got the discount in any case.

In fact, my phone, according to the missed calls, had ceased to be bound and gagged at tenish. Not that everyone had been suffering from the enforced silence. After about half an hour watching the house where I had seen Hughes, Ali, and Harrison enter, I had observed Kye Toulson arrive, talking into his. His was working fine. He was laughing. He always was, it seemed. This time no doubt amused at the fact that his cronies could meet in secret but still have access to the outside world. Unlike the rest of us.

That had been the only excitement I had enjoyed, standing and watching the house. On the telly, the cops can sit in their cars, munching chips and be as happy as Larry spending hours on surveillance. I got bored after fifteen minutes. I had stuck it out for another hour until the call of nature had proved irresistible. Something you rarely saw on such shows. Maybe it's because they haven't reached the time of life where the call is so strong. Dutifully, I had returned to my position afterwards. Until that is, I received a different call from my body. I hadn't eaten for ages.

Figuring that an hour would be neither here nor there, I had ridden off to find a street party. By chance one was nearby, where, after parking, I had casually strolled in, giving off the air of a local enjoying the liberation of collective action, and helped myself to some bread and cold meat. People had seen me and been totally unconcerned that I was a stranger there, blagging some grub, and had merely apologised for the paucity of the food. Once I had eaten, had a much-needed cup of coffee, and used a comrade's loo, I had returned to my vigil.

Seeing movement in the lounge, I had known that someone was still in there (just call me Eagle Eyes Kalder) but I could not say who. All nature's needs had been met, so, apart from boredom, I saw no reason why I could not stay for a while.

That was why what had happened had been so startling. I have no idea what started it. I remembered feeling hot and bothered in my suit, which I put down to the fact that, despite new record temperatures, I was still wearing a jacket. I never liked baring my arms, as the scarred skin always attracted not-so-subtle stares. Or perhaps it was the embarrassment as to why I had them that made it too difficult to show them. And then there were the questions, endless bloody questions. I found the sight of the scars disgustingly ugly, so Lord knows what others would think of them. The price of vanity was feeling occasionally rather overheated.

Sitting here in the bar, I tried to piece together what had happened. I had felt sweaty and bored, but then what? Maybe standing there, staring at the outside of a common and garden outer-London house, my thoughts had wandered. Perhaps it was the repercussions from not taking my pills. Whatever the reason, being there, doing nothing, I had turned in on myself.

Vaguely, I could remember questioning myself as to what they were doing. But that couldn't explain the overburdening weight that had crushed my soul. Images of Caroline and Lisa had stamped it even harder. The next thing, I was on the floor with a cut forehead and dusty pavement pressing on my nose. Turning to face the house, I had hoped that none of them had seen me faint. Fainting wasn't really in the surveillance manual. I *think* I had thought that. Then blank.

Logically, I must have blacked out. How I got from a side road by the house to an empty car park by a shopping mall, I couldn't say. Confusion had swiftly turned to relief. The journey there must have been achieved in a daze. Something which was not conducive to safe riding. It was a miracle I had not had an accident. I could have been killed. But I had not. Sitting on the ground with my back to the bike, I felt my chest vibrating.

It had been the phone, Victoria to be precise, and she was calling to arrange a meeting to discuss what we had found out today. In obvious good humour, she appeared to be amused at my failure to answer her previous calls, and I was treated to a view of her tonsils as she laughed at possible reasons as to what I might be doing to make me miss them. In truth, her suggestions had been a lot more exciting than the reality. Dumbly, I had apologised and agreed to meet. Then looked around.

I had never been in the car park before. It held no romantic links or any connection whatsoever to my wife or daughter. Indeed, until I looked at the Satnav, (thank the topographical Gods it was operational) I hadn't the foggiest idea where I was. Turned out it was Pinner. That meant nothing to me. But whatever the reason, the time was five to eleven at night, and I was sitting with my back against the front wheel of my scooter—in Pinner. I could not explain why.

Why I had suffered the episode was an interesting question. Of course, I had experienced them before but not for a good while now. Surely I was healing? Now I was pill-free and able to think on other matters than the accident. No longer did it rule my life. It hadn't disappeared, but it wasn't so large and all-consuming. And yet I had found myself in Pinner, on the floor. Alone. At eleven. Nothing suggested a trigger. One minute I was counting the tiles on a terraced house, and the next there I was—in Pinner. Nothing I could think of could explain it. There had been no screeching of wheels as a car sped past the house (all the traffic had obeyed the speed limit, and there were no near-misses). I had seen no blood—there was not even much in the way of red here, be it paint, fists, or banners. A distinctly middle-of-the-road road, then. No dogs had crossed. There had not even been a passing Italian.

Finally, I had tidied up my head enough to ride to Soul Shack. Attempts at further trying to unravel my subconscious were interrupted by the sight of Cole weaving her way towards me. She appeared to be the epitome of jolliness. Armed with a pint, she was sporting a beaming smile and would even occasionally chat to someone. The life and soul of the party, it seemed.

Dressed in jeans and a T-shirt featuring the words A World to Win! and with only a touch of makeup and severely swept-back hair, she could have been mistaken for a student celebrating finishing her exams.

She sat down with legs apart and took a swig of her drink, licking her lips and nodding in appreciation. I half-expected her to close one eye and growl, "aha, Jim, lad!"

Instead, she grinned. "What a day! The caucus for the police comrades was on fire today. I had thought it might be a bit flat after the past few days, but the atmosphere was so positive! It was probably the best I have been to. I tell you, Pete, it was invigorating; I think I'm still buzzing. After it finished we all went to the Green Park rally. It's still going on now. After the speeches, it turned into one big party." She took a sip of her drink before returning to said caucus and rally, going further into detail after joyous detail.

As for me, I wasn't in the best of moods—blackouts tending to dampen one's spirits. A smile was too much to manage. Instead, I studiously finished half the glass and asked, "So did you actually have a chance to do any of what you were supposed to be doing? Did you manage to trace Charles Hutchinson? Did you even *try*?"

Her face straightened and grew in seriousness. "No luck at all, comrade. For most of the day, the police network's been down. I did manage to spend forty-odd minutes or so, but got nowhere. Then again, every time I got anywhere near anything interesting, security codes stopped me, and to be honest I don't have the IT skills to get around them."

"What about your colleagues, Asher and Roijin—I thought they were supposed to be good at that sort of thing?"

She took another sip. "They couldn't do it. Asher refused outright because it was a strike day. He wanted to go to some happening in his district and said he would see what he could do tomorrow as he felt that doing any police work, even if it was for the party, would be scabbing. Roijin, on the other hand, had intended to help and did actually briefly come into the station, but after she heard my conversation with Asher, she changed her mind. She agreed that it would be strike-breaking, and so she left."

Animosity returned, and I stared at her. So I was screwing up my mental health whilst she twiddled her fingers, discussing the morals of strikes. Was it "a world to win" or a world that had been turned upside down? "How principled of them," I sneered. "Did you have any luck with *anything*? Except of course, the bonding session?"

She let the comment slide, but her mood had altered, taking a more businesslike approach. My sullen vibes must have been having an effect. "Using the car-reg software, I checked as much of the CCTV of the surrounding area of Jenny Underhill's house as I could. Not surprisingly, most of the cameras have been trashed, and those which are still in use were hit by the network crashing. Still," she paused as her lips turned up a little in a satisfied smile, "I did find a camera in operation on an electric substation where the party car is filmed recharging. It is a five-minute drive from Underhill's. You cannot see who the driver is, but it would appear to confirm our belief that the killer was driving that particular car."

She stopped and took a drink. If she was waiting for applause, then she was disappointed.

"Anything else?"

"No, I'm afraid that's it. What about you?"

I told her about the cosy meeting in the outer reaches of what was classed as London of our merry band of leading members. She didn't seem unduly surprised, just a touch politically and professionally interested. That exasperated me. Surely, she wanted to know why these comrades seemed to be unable to go half a day without meeting each other and wanted to sneak off from a general strike to meet in the suburbs. Judging by Hughes's reaction to the call, it hadn't been expected, so what could it have been about? I could not imagine it being about how the cucumber sandwiches were going down at the street parties.

My thoughts were interrupted. "What about the carpool?" she asked

I frowned. "No real joy there. Basically, any comrade can pick them up. There's no logging in or out. No tracking of the loans. They knew Marie had borrowed one, but whether the one she is driving now is the one she had on the day of Underhill's murder, they couldn't tell me. It's the case of if a comrade needs a car and there's one free, they can have it."

"Are they only for some comrades, Central Committee members, or other top cadre? Can those doing meetings or have far to go borrow them? Or is it literally that anyone can take them out?" she asked.

"Technically, it's anyone, but I don't think Billie on reception would actually let any old comrade do so. I am pretty sure that I wouldn't be able to waltz in and take one out for a spin."

"How confident are you of that?"

"Pretty. Billie takes no prisoners; she runs the national office, and nothing happens without her say-so. I think she would only let the senior comrades use them."

We sat in silence, processing where this took us. Or rather, we sat without speaking. I could hear a female loudly moaning about the lack of toilet paper in the loos, ranting at length at how luxuries could get through the blockade, yet essentials were in short supply. I didn't catch what Maurice's reply had been because Dubstep, circa 2004, suddenly thundered out of the system. The pub's cacophony of conversations surrendered to the bass.

"So what do you want to do next?" she asked, raising her voice and nudging me back to the point of us being here.

Her question was unexpected. "You're the expert!" I replied, jerking my glass in her direction.

"But I think this is your call. What do *you* want to do?"

Where she had got the idea that I had any clue of what was going on, I had no notion. Why was it my call? I threw it back at her. "Well, if it was an official police matter, what would *you* do? What would be normal procedure?"

She decided that it was a sensible thing to ask, despite, she said and had said before, that it had been a good while since anything had resembled normality. And even then when it had been, she added, every force worked in a different way. "Still, we would have a force working on the Wiltshire murders, which would look at the forensic evidence, any witnesses, and for people connected with the victims who might have a motive. Of course that's what we, or rather now just DI Martin has been trying to do, but with forensics in chaos, that's all been crippled. The force doesn't have the numbers, let alone the respect or authority, to question witnesses or people connected with the case. Martin has told me that it's just him and a few old-timers hitting brick wall after brick wall. People either tell him to take a hike or give him the barest of cooperation."

Not knowing how long this tragic tale was going to take, I cut to the chase. "So he's found sod-all?"

"The official statement would say that the investigations are ongoing; saying that he had 'found sod-all' is pretty accurate. Anyway, if things were not quite so…" she searched for the word, "complicated, then we would be in close contact with the Seaham force, who in turn would be going through a similar procedure with Jenny Underhill's murder. One obvious avenue to explore would be what linked Alan and Jenny, which we know, and see who else might have a connection with the pair of them. Obviously, that's not happening, as Special Branch has closed it and sealed off any involvement of the regular police. From what I hear, they seem more intent on blocking any interest in the matter rather than finding who killed her."

I asked her what she meant by connections.

"Connections: for example, was there somebody who knew both Alan and Jenny…"

"Marie did."

"True," she replied, sounding unconvinced, "though she was fairly young at the time."

"She still might have discovered something!"

For a moment, she didn't reply but pouted and nodded. The impression was that she was humouring this old goat and didn't take any of what I was saying seriously. "So why kill David and Yasmin?"

I didn't have an answer for that. A snarling irritation was growing at the circles we were travelling in. "So, I repeat, what do you think we should do?"

She jumped straight in. We had finished playing the polite game of *what do you think,* and now she was going to tell me what needed to be done. "Your gut instinct was that there is something fishy about this committee and the work Alan was doing…"

"Fishy? Gut instinct? That doesn't sound very scientific."

"It's not. But that's all we have."

"We need to find out what this committee actually met about?"

She hesitated. "Yes."

That was up to me to find out. What she could do was to find out who this Charles Hutchinson was and where he was now.

She agreed. "Finding him is a priority, and that's what we will be doing when Asher and Roijin return to work tomorrow." She looked at her watch. "Or should I say, today."

I thought for a moment or two. "And I need to take a deeper look at these senior comrades, but I can't do that alone. I'm going to need help. I need to get some comrades to help."

She scoffed at the idea. "Comrades? Who's going to help you snoop on members of the ilk of Bale and Williams?"

I brushed aside her doubts. "Oh, no worries. I have a couple of women in mind that can be relied upon."

Disbelief was evident in her face, but she didn't say anything. Again, we sat and drank, feeling our calf muscles vibrate from the music. For the remainder of the time, we arranged practicalities. I left her there, ordering another pint and chatting to Maurice. I went home to Red.

CHAPTER TWENTY-THREE
Friends and False Friends of the Working Class

Ringing Zoe and January at 1:00 a.m. was perhaps not the most fraternal of things to do, but then again, I was not contacting them for particularly fraternal reasons. January had answered though, and judging by the somewhat inebriated revellers who could be seen around them, they were due to be up for a few hours more. They were obviously energised by the day and had jabbered away about what they had been doing.

It was with a slight sense of guilt that I had asked them if they could spend tomorrow, or to be more precise, later today, on party business. Zoe had joined us, wearing a bandana, which was sliding down the front of her face. With a tipsy smirk, she had hailed me as a long-lost pal and asked me what was up. What was required, I told them, was that we were going to expand the *Ordinary Lives* blog into a vehicle to show how rooted in the working class we were. This required further details of certain comrades and how they spent their days. This was the lie I was using to hook them into both checking the alibis for our suspects on the day of Jenny Underhill's murder and to see what they had told people they were doing that day to see if they matched.

Their response deepened my sense of shame. They had not been keen on the idea, not from any sense of how slight the logic of the request was because they did not, could not, even dream that I would be misusing comradeship so much. They were not naïve, and they were not stupid, in fact quite the opposite, but they considered the point of being comrades was to trust and work with each other, and so the possibility that I might be duping them was one that did not have any connection with their view of reality. Before all this, I believed the same.

The problem was that they were keen to be at work to build on today's events and felt that my request was rather bureaucratic. Despite an alcohol-induced speech impediment, January's mental facilities were still fully operational. She felt that I was asking them to pen-push, when there was activity to be had. I just grabbed that pen, and pushed and pushed, debasing any sense of comradeship I might have, by stressing its importance and the fact that it was what Jackie wanted. That had worked. January had finally agreed and then convinced Zoe, saying that a day would be neither here nor there at work, and that this might help temper the propaganda doing the net at the moment that we were crazed, closet anarchists intent on continuing the bombing.

This I had been unaware of, and was surprised to hear the gossip that Westminster Abbey was top of our target list for the next bombing. This in its small way, January had said, or rather slurred, might be a neat way to undercut the media bollocks, or as she put it, *the mejia bolloksh*.

Finally, they had both agreed. I gave them the comrades' names and the two dates I was interested in and where I thought they had been. To cover myself, I did say that it could be quite possible that these were wrong. In some petty, self-deluding belief that it would help in the subterfuge, I had also given them a couple of quite innocent names. Just as they were ringing off, I had added that the people concerned were not to know, as it was meant as a little surprise for them. The fact that they did not question this said a great deal of the separation of their morality from my motives.

The truth was that my hand-wringing was minimal. When I had been awoken by the morning's huge thunderstorm and had laid there with Red, listening to the rain, I had not in all honesty felt that much guilt, because anytime such an emotion had crept up, then the image of Dave and Yasmin butchered in their bedroom appeared to batter it down. The memory of their dead bodies, fixed in their final writhing from a brutal torture before their deaths, was quite an argument against worrying too much about lying to fellow comrades. It was not seeing the actual torn and ripped wounds that so disturbed me, but imagining the agony the pair of them had gone through.

It was the thought of that unbelievable hell, which justified my using Zoe and January's decency, because, quite frankly, the total attack on Dave and Yasmin's was in another world.

It might be pompous, but I did honestly believe that I was doing it for them. Perhaps the thought of a mole undermining the revolution was the headline in the story, but really the substance of it was what had happened to a couple of decent people. This was no abstract concept, but flesh and a lot of blood.

Playing the part of the hero, I should have been pensively pacing up and down whilst gazing at pictures of the suspects with arrows and annotations in thick black marker pen. Even the huge advancements in IT had not killed off the marker pen. So I did the same.

Finding the only wall not covered with either books, music, or pictures in the house had led me to my bathroom. I took down the long silver mirror. Then up went photographs of Youssef Ali, Olivia Harrison, Glen Bale, Kye Toulson, Michael Hughes, and Marie Williams. And what a motley crew they were. I had found a picture of Ali in a midstream rant down a megaphone, looking for all the world as of he was straining out a constipated crap. Diagonally downwards was a photograph of Harrison from a social network, in long, blue dress and matching huge hat. Where the hell it had been taken, who knew, because she looked as if she had come straight from Ascot. Bale obviously looked rat-like and intense. You *can* tell a book from its cover. The one of Toulson was from the huge transport strike of two years ago and had him wrestling with a large banner and, yes, sporting a huge grin. Out of the group of photographs, the one of Hughes was the odd one out, as it was pre-party, in uniform, receiving a medal of gallantry. He looked young, stiff, and extremely proud. Since then, he had been radicalised and had become older, stiffer, and prouder.

Then there was Williams, playing with her children and husband. I had chosen that one deliberately because I had taken it on a picnic by Kenwood House, ten years ago, celebrating her case being dropped. I had picked it because I needed to be clear about what I was doing. No hiding the reality of what my actions meant; I wanted it staring in my face.

Considering that the research department here in the homemade police force consisted of me and a rubber duck, it was self-evident that I had to narrow this down; so my first scribbles were the locations of where Toulson and Bale were on the day of Underhill's murder. These had been confirmed, so whilst I still had questions concerning the pair of them, I put them to one side.

Instead, sitting on the loo with the laptop, listening to the rain crashing against the window, gaining revenge for the hot spell, I tried to find out news clips, videos, blogs, and every type of communication you could think of that I could access. If the Bristol town crier had been bellowing a rhyming couplet, then I would have tried to record it. Despite the cyber struggle having taken its toll on police powers of snooping, Cole's mate Roijin had sent me the software to get into areas usually out of bounds to the rest of us. That, though, just created a bigger problem. I got library-size files of information, but what was of use, and what was junk? So I could find thousands of words written about her arrest and prosecution and the collapse of the case, but did that help me any? I had learnt, for example, which journalists had supported her and which had not and of the cast of a certain, short-lived soap series who had publicized it, but so what? A well-known theatre actress who played the show's tart-with-a-heart was on the campaign committee; very good, very interesting. Big Deal; didn't help me much here. In actual fact, I had worked with her and found her to be committed and generally a good sort, but did that help me with the reason as to why the case was dropped?

With Roijin's technical goody box, I had accessed Marie's bank files and found that she spent little of her salary on much besides the essentials of bed and board. I wrote up B&B and then next to it in capitals—BUT SO WHAT? Did that prove that she was not on the state's payroll? I could only see the NHS monthly salary. But then maybe she had another account, or maybe she was doing it out of principle? Did she feel so strongly about supporting parliamentary democracy that she had worked for them out of ideology? There was so much information but not a great deal of knowledge. I did get up and write comments and arrows around her picture. The wall started to fill and look impressive, beginning to look like one of those case-history walls. That is, if you ignored the fake Victorian bath opposite. I stood in front of it and looked thoughtful. They did that in TV cop shows.

How much help it was to me was still not apparent. Whilst the police had recovered a little of their power, there were still areas that were out of their reach, areas that might be useful to me right now. Some time ago, those interested in the class struggle of the information community had made an addition to their strategy of mounting attacks on the state and had created their own walls of defence for the people to stop the forces of repression from having the capacity to carry out any surveillance on them. That meant that I was protected from MI5 finding out about my interest in Picasso fansites, but then it also meant that I could not find out if there were any e-mails from Marie to an M type person. Of course it might also be the state itself protecting her. Or both. The infobahn was a bloody confusing place to drive.

I could, however, access her public blogs which did supply one useful piece of information, which was an amusing passage that told of how, on such a massive general strike, she had spent the day making coffee and handing out biscuits but suggesting that the role of snacks was a sadly neglected historical area of past revolutions and that she hoped scholars of the future would rectify this. It was classic Marie, self-deprecating and amusing, and showed her not as a woman who felt the need to boast of her achievements and her hard work. She was the opposite of Bale; he'd organise a fire-works display spelling out what he had done. Marie, in contrast, felt no need to aggrandise herself. The trouble was, the times she said she was doing this were exactly the times when she was in the house. Yes, Marie, who would write the history of lying to the class?

Feeling uncomfortable and also rather silly, I adjourned to my bedroom along the corridor. My bed was now my desk. Then without thinking of its importance, I picked out a compact disc and pressed **play**. I had done so without thinking, and it was only when the first few notes appeared that I realised what I had done. It had been many a month since music had been heard in the house, but now was not the time to analyse why I had broken the self-imposed music-embargo. It was Miles Davis, circa 1950, so perhaps it had been chosen to create the musical backdrop; some cool jazz might counter how far I was from being Chandleresque, perched there on my bed, fighting the cat from getting on the computer, and from time to time, running to the bathroom to stick printouts onto the wall or write part sentences.

I left the reasons for this change in circumstances behind and instead turned my attention to Olivia Harrison. She had struck me as a strange fish, a woman of many moods. Looking at the coverage of her in the party sites and paper where she was a frequent visitor, it was obvious that she was highly regarded both within our organisation and the wider movement. I watched several newscasts. She was an articulate performer, if not a particularly inspiring one. She expounded a position well and covered all the points but lacked any passion. Still, I guess the subject of power supply is one which is pretty difficult to make interesting. Having said that, there was a clip of her talking passionately about how a future Socialist society would make green energy a priority, a real priority, and not just a priority for successive governments to say that it is.

She was twenty-nine-years old, and despite her accent, which had led me to believe that she hailed from a semi in Essex, she came from white-collar stock of a family of teachers. Not that I could find anything about her family, only that both her parents and elder brother worked in secondary schools. Interestingly, purely from a love of the surreal rather than any importance to the case, I found out that she had wanted to be a dancer and had attended a minor drama school. I wondered if that accounted for her mood swings. Maybe, it was a case of the old diva gene—all strops and hurling vases. Maybe, but then again, she worked at an electric substation; hardly the Sydney Opera House.

In her old student's file, there was a still photograph of her apparently in the ballet fifth position. I had no idea what the fourth or sixth were. There was also a short clip of her jazz dancing, exemplifying toe rise, it said. I watched and wondered how many of the leading Bolsheviks had been able to turn a few moves. Was Bukharin a whiz at the tango or Zinoviev a wow at the fox-trot? No, I guess that would have been Leon who would have been the keen fox-trotter. I giggled at my joke. All this wasn't improving my wit. Obviously, spending so much time writing on bathroom walls was sending me mad or madder.

I was busy writing geography next to her mother's name when the phone went. It was back in the bedroom, so it took me a second or two to get there. It was Zoe, so it took a little longer to find somewhere that looked a suitable backdrop. Private detectives traditionally split their time between the streets and whisky joints; I was half in the loo and half in the bedroom, surfing the net and scribbling on walls. I decided the best I could do was the landing in front of the small bookcase. The books were actually collections of humorous writing, but Zoe hopefully would not notice.

"Hi!" I said, finally answering.

"Hi, Pete, where are you? It looks like someone's house."

"Oh, no, I'm doing some…er…research. Have you had any luck?" I could see that she was at what looked like a bus shelter.

"Well, we have got some great quotes from Marie William's colleagues; we've spoken to quite a few, both in the hospital and in the local workers' council. Pete, I only hope that the people I work with are as effusive in their praise about me as they were of her. She is so respected, loved even. There was this time…" Zoe went on to recount an episode which typified what a comrade of quality she was. Judging from how she looked and sounded, the night's fun had had no dire consequences. She sounded clear and energised. "I think you could use that in the blog. We did have some problem, though, with some of the dates you gave us, as they were a little wrong; no one could remember her being there, so you need to recheck them."

I agreed, thanked her for her work, and asked her who she was going to tackle next. I saw no reason to spend more time on this. It was confirmed, then; Marie Williams was not at the hospital when Jenny Underhill was murdered.

"Jan's gone to get some footage for talking heads for Michael Hughes, and I think I will travel to Youssef Ali's workplace. I have to say, Pete, that it feels rather silly not being able to let the people involved know what we are doing. It's not like we are arranging a birthday party for them. I felt a right clot telling the hospital staff not to say a word to Williams. It's just a bit childish."

I gave my most comradely smile and said that it possibly was, but, hey, can't we be a bit childish now and again?

"OK, well, it's just…is that a book about Charlie Chaplin behind you? What sort of research are you doing, Pete?" She laughed.

"No, it's that, this library, er, has a history of film section. Anyway, I must be off. Thanks for contacting me. Buzz over what you have, and ring again when you have more. Cheers, comrade." I hastily rang off. And felt crappy.

Now was time for some coffee and toast. Grabbing them, I adjourned to the lounge and moved Red off my chair. He really did have the ability to be everywhere at once. I should enlist him in this little police force of ours.

By chance, the TV was set to a US channel. It was probably the only thing I could get last night. The picture was of a silver-haired, middle-aged guy, wrapped in a beige raincoat, sheltering under an umbrella with the houses of Parliament neatly positioned behind him. He was pontificating about the English weather and extending it as a metaphor: perhaps following the night's events, Britain's Revolutionary Spring might be suffering a dampening of spirits. Perhaps the clouds were gathering but for whom, he asked. And on the allusion went. On and on. And on. As one who had a sneaking love of such things, initially I quite enjoyed the cheesiness of it, but then it did start to grate. I wanted to know what exactly he was referring to, what "events"? The general strike had been a success, hadn't it?

With the weather allegory finally ending, we switched to a suited prime minister standing by a bust of Clement Attlee. He looked serious. He had a serious tie. It was not going to be one of his "now listen, guys"-type chats. This was statesmanship. He was scathing in his condemnation of the "mindless murder and lawlessness of yesterday and the barbaric tragedies of the night." He looked straight into the camera and announced that "so far" the death toll was ninety-eight. This, he repeated, just in case some of us could not manage two-digit numbers. This, he feared, could rise to three digits. His tone indicated that we might have to reach for our abacuses. I still did not know what he was talking about. I had been far too focussed on particular times and places to notice any of the days'—or nights'—news. Considering the way he was talking, it must have been huge, but I had not registered anything, yet it must be all over the net.

He turned up his sincerity switch and launched into a speech. "We have arranged a bailout of billions from our friends abroad, which will help this country get back on its feet and allow people, *the* people, to enjoy the life they deserve. I believe that people are not interested in a civil war driven by outdated dogma. I believe that people are more interested in a fair society, where no one is too rich or too poor and where people have …"

Ahh, it was a variation of one of his "people" speeches.

"This will give people the chance to achieve their full potential. The United Revolutionary Socialist Party, with its anarchist storm troopers, is intent on foisting a Communist state on us. I understand that within the soviets there are well-meaning people, but I say to them, especially to those people in the Democratic Left, look at what happened yesterday in Dundee, Swansea, and York. Is that left-wing democracy? Or has democracy been left behind and been replaced by Fascism? Extremism is not the British way. And, yes, I say, British, for the governments of Scotland, Wales, and England are united in finding a way, a peaceful way, out of this crisis. Trust us!"

It was nothing particularly new, except his earnestness might be up a notch or two. But he had still not said what had specifically happened yesterday. Something noteworthy did come next, though.

"The coalition has arranged financial aid to this country, so we can get our financial institutions up, our hospitals operating twenty-four hours a day, our schools back to five days a week, and our trains running on time. But they are not going to just hand over such large sums if we cannot show order and stability. This we have to achieve. They are willing to help us achieve this, and we should welcome their support. The United Revolutionary Socialist Party harks incessantly about international solidarity. Well, whilst they preach it, we practice it."

It appeared that our American TV hacks did not really do much in the way of questioning, because after what amounted to a lengthy party political broadcast for ailing capitalism, we were switched to Jackie Payne outside a closed train station. Judging by the clear skies, it had been recorded yesterday.

Dressed in grey, baggy trousers, with a matching two-button, large-lapel waistcoat that partially covered a lighter shirt, and her arm strapped across her chest, she actually looked quite corporate. She had straightened her hair and had pushed a pair of sunglasses over it.

Her voice had lost some of its stridency. Not that she had become a mouse, but she sounded weary, and her skin didn't quite have the colour it usually had. "I think we can all read into the prime minister's remarks that he is threatening us that if we do not do what his cobbled-together group of Labour, Tory, and Liberal careerists want us to do, he will use force to crush democracy. We have no desire for confrontation on the streets, but then again, we will not flinch from defending ourselves."

In a passing, almost inaudible, comment, as we were returned to the news anchor, it was stated that Jackie's comments had been made before the night's events. And, yes, he did make a joke encompassing ships' anchors, the English weather, and England's naval history. I was just about to switch to the

Internet to find what these events, in fact, were, when our punning anchorman introduced the channel's reporter in Swansea, which, for his American viewers he explained, was a city in Wales, who he said had witnessed pro-National Workers' Council's troops opening fire on pro-government supporters. What?

"Dervla, you are embedded in the NWC militia. What can you tell us about last night?"

"Well, Ted, as you can see, behind me they are still tidying up from the night before."

The camera swept the area, showing a parked ambulance and people clearing up debris. It lingered on large blood splatters on the pavement.

"The handful of official police who were here, alongside a couple of forensic experts, have just left the area. As of yet they have not given us an official statement. As you may be able to see, the streets are being tidied up. This suggests that they have collected as much evidence as they require. As to what happened here last night, that is hotly contested. The pro-government supporters claim that whilst they were holding a peaceful unarmed protest outside the Welsh National Workers' Council, several shots were fired. We have a clip here."

Jerky footage was shown of the reporter, resplendent in flak jacket with press on her back and front, interviewing a young man when shots were clearly heard. The camera moved away to show people diving to the ground and a group of soldiers, hooded but with red armbands, visibly firing into the protest. Zooming in, you could just about hear anti-coalition slogans being shouted as the soldiers were firing.

Back live with Dervla, she told us that twenty-three had been confirmed killed in Swansea. Reports were coming in, which she pointed out could not be verified, that the soldiers were from a local army camp that had been one of the first to swear allegiance to the NWC. "This is what protestors say happened."

A smooth-looking, executive-appearing man appeared, with the name, Robert Thompson, and job title, advertising executive, under his image. The word "eyewitness" followed. "It was the most horrific thing I have ever seen. I was with the protest; it was a peaceful one; we had decided to make it last through the night to show our opposition to the policies of the NWC and

Comrades Come Rally

to show our support for the prime minister. We had sought and obtained permission from both the police and Swansea Workers' Council, and we had settled down for the night, when at about 4:30 a.m. a group of men emerged from the council building and just started firing. We all scattered. My wife and I hid behind a car. Its windscreen was smashed by a spray of bullets. I was hit by the flying glass…" he pointed to several raw but small cuts. "I just thank God that that's all we suffered. It was carnage. Horrible!"

We returned to Dervla, who said that this report was echoed by others on the demonstration. "This is what Michael Hughes, a military spokesperson for the National Workers' Council and leading member of the URSP, had to say about the matter."

Hughes appeared in a black, padded combat jacket, buttoned to his muscular neck. The small enamel party badge shone in the camera's lights. He spoke with determination and defiance. "Firstly, our sympathies go out to the families of the bereaved, but what I would also like to say is that we refute any suggestion that those who opened fire were supporters of the NWC.

"Our position has always been one of condemnation of mindless violence. We support the right of peaceful protest. We have checked at the base, and no members of the armed forces, let alone NWC supporters, left the perimeter. As our accord with the Welsh Parliament clearly states—no members of the armed forces should be seen or used on the streets unless there has been signed permission by both sides. Neither side gave such permission. And I repeat—no troops were out of barracks.

"We believe that these were outside agitators, imposters, agent provocateurs, who were pretending to be from our side. Any fool can put on a red armband."

A voice from behind the camera asked him about the fact that witnesses had seen them come out of the workers' council building.

His reply was quick. "Then they are mistaken!"

We were once more reunited with the sombre-looking Dervla, who had become internationally famous for reporting anywhere it was dangerous or was suffering from a natural or man-made disaster. If it was a hairy situation, then Dervla would arrive. You knew it was *really* bad if Dervla was there. I could only imagine what the neighbours might think if they saw Dervla come around for dinner. House prices would collapse. People would flee with all their worldly possessions.

"We cannot verify either claim, as neither the news drones nor the surveillance satellites were in operation, but whether it was the NWC or groups pretending to be from the NWC who were responsible for the firing, what we do know is that twenty-one people lost their lives due to sustained machine gun fire. This is Dervla Gorman from Swansea, Wales."

I was shocked. There had been violence before, but this was not clashes on the street; this was gangsterism. We did not do this. We were for peace. Sure, we were not pacifists and would use force when necessary but only when necessary, really necessary. We would not open fire on unarmed protestors!

But then a report came in from Dundee that was virtually a carbon copy of Swansea. The accents were different, and only—"only," indeed—fourteen had died, but everything else was the same: a nighttime protest outside an opposition building, although this time, it was a party meeting house; at roughly the same time, a group of masked soldiers opened fire. Witnesses confirmed that they were shouting anti-government slogans and wearing party insignia and came from the building. The voice-over stated that we also denied being any part of this.

If that was bad, then the report from York was appalling. A bomb had gone off in a police station near the streets known as Snickleways. Forty-two were dead, ten of them cops, and the rest were people living nearby. The toll had been made higher by the fact that the emergency services had difficulty getting there because the traffic system had been paralysed by the strike. Interspersed with witnesses talking whilst nursing wounds were flashbacks on the previous day's bombings. We were even treated to previously unseen footage from inside St Paul's just after the explosion there. Numbness crept along my veins watching it. That turned a lot colder when it was reported that a well-known United Revolutionary Socialist Party activist was seen hurrying from the scene.

I left my unfinished toast and coffee as the anchor discussed with some cloned expert as to why we might do this. The expert was of the opinion that a sizeable contingent in the party felt that the pace of the revolution had slowed too much and was using terrorist outrages to kick-start the momentum.

It showed just how depressing the news was that I went upstairs to seek sanctuary in narking on comrades in the party. Ali was next. Miles Davis had finished, so I replaced him with some free jazz because I badly needed to get some oomph. Otherwise, I feared that I would just might hide under the quilt.

He had made quite an impression in the world of water and sanitation, our comrade Youssef Deniz Ali. From the combined records of the company and the trade union, I found out that he had started work as an apprentice at the age of sixteen and had become a fully qualified engineer a few years later. By the age of nineteen, he had been elected workplace union representative. At twenty he had led his first strike. He appeared to have joined the party ten years later. There was no sign that previously his politics had extended any further than being an active trade unionist. The clips showed him to be a sound speaker who could connect with the crowd.

Since he had joined us, he appeared regularly in internal bulletins about organising in the workplace. He was elected to various union positions before becoming a delegate to the National Workers' Council. So far, nothing exceptional, except one small matter: a couple of years ago, he had been a member of the faction inside the party arguing for more direct action. There were only a few pieces by the faction, and it had disbanded after losing the vote at the national conference. Interestingly, one of the names supporting them was Marie Williams. But I guess it was no big deal, nothing too outrageous, just part of an internal debate.

The next hour was spent trawling through his work in sanitation and many apt analogies from his work came to mind as I did so. No joy; really, *no* joy at all. The same could be said of his public blog which did nothing to dispel the view that working in the utilities was worthy but dull.

I accessed his bank records, wondering how it was that I could get into these but not his communications; I guess it was just the case that banks always let you down. Now there was something eye-catching, not his subs to the party which were somewhat higher than usual, but the rather large monthly amounts that came in two days after his salary. What did he do to earn that amount of dosh, I wondered? Checked people's drains? Weekend work clearing gutters? I marked it up thickly with a huge circle around it. Sitting on the toilet, I looked at it pensively. It was from a bank that was obviously Turkish; even with my limited knowledge of geography, I knew Izmir was a city somewhere in the Southwest of Turkey. I clicked on the name and just got the bank account and a name, Diyanat Deniz Ali. A relative, no doubt.

Despite suffering from a sore arse from sitting on a toilet seat, sore eyes from staring at the screen, a growing boredom, and not to mention a ruined bathroom wall, I ploughed on. Perhaps it was the glamour of it all, or maybe it kept my mind off the nightmarish events of last night, or it was just that I was a Goddamn hero, but I moved onto Hughes.

Outside, the rain was reaching biblical proportions, with Noah expected at any moment. I scooped up masses of info about our soldier Mike. Much of it was from our appallingly titled Comrades in Khaki site, featuring him talking to soldiers, sailors, and pilots. Interestingly, unlike the others there was a huge amount of net chatter about him. This ran the full gamut of views, from appreciation and admiration to death-threatening vile abuse, some of which was physically impossible. It was pretty obvious that he attracted such extreme views on account of his being in the army. Worryingly for him, it included threats against his children and his partner, indeed, even to his parents; this included their address, indicating that they now lived near Stoke. His bank account looked pretty normal, suitably stretched and distressed for our present hard times.

As I was wading through the net, I received a missive from January who had found some, as she called it, "human interest stuff," on the very man I was reading about. The file contained photos, two video interviews, and some typed notes.

Both videos were from fellow party members in the military, recounting how it was due to Michael that they had joined. What interested me was the story one comrade soldier told about how last Friday the pair of them had toured various naval establishments on the south coast and the friendly reception they had received. That was the day of Underhill's murder, so, if true, it meant that Hughes had an alibi.

However, looking closely at the material, it did seem contradictory. Something was still not right. For starters, there was something strange about yesterday. January had been unable to ascertain *exactly* what he had been doing or indeed where he had been. She herself had been puzzled by this and had wondered why the secrecy. She said that several different comrades had vaguely mentioned to her that he had been in Scotland, doing something ill-defined, but then at least one comrade had said he had been in Bristol. Another said that he'd been in the Midlands. I told her not to worry about it (but neglected to tell her that I thought it was certainly well-worth looking at).

I was considering my next move and not really listening to her, as she finished her call, complaining that it would have been a whole lot easier if she could have just gone straight to Hughes himself and echoed Zoe's opinion that it was all a wee bit silly. It was a lot of things, but it was not silly.

As soon as she was off, I sprinted onto the computer to check the party sites to see if anything confirmed soldier boy's movements either last Friday or yesterday. None were of any help. Everything looked either old or non-time-specific. Numerous messages had been posted on those days, but none mentioned locations. Indeed, they were pretty general and nonspecific, unusual maybe, but not especially suspicious.

I looked again at the interview, but the camera was too close to his muscular frame to see anything in the background. Sadly, the home-camera app, which allowed the viewer to point the recording anywhere they liked, had been turned off, so any chance of moving it away from his face to where he was standing was denied me.

Whether this meant anything, I wasn't sure. I was feeling extremely weary. I looked at the time and saw that it was coming up to twenty past two. I had been doing this for just over five hours. I needed a break. So whatever Hughes had been doing would have to wait. It was just another thing that needed investigating.

Quickly, I updated the *Ordinary Lives in Extraordinary Times* blog. Well, it might all be a front, but there was no harm, after judicially editing and cherry-picking the info, in actually using it. And if I said so myself, it looked quite a pro job.

Smoothing out the creases made on the quilt cover and putting the CDs back in their correct alphabetical order in the bedroom rack, I quickly tidied up, putting everything in order. It felt faintly daft, fannying around making sure everything was precise when my bathroom looked like some circa 1990 art school attempt at an art installation.

Grabbing some bread and cheese, I stood staring out the kitchen window at the garden as it shrunk in the onslaught of the weather. Huge puddles were appearing, and flowers were pushed towards the ground as the drops became less and less rain and more a barrage of missiles.

I don't know how long I was there hypnotised by the view, but by the time I had washed up and had returned to my computer, I saw that I had a message from Zoe. She was not a happy person, as she moaned that once more my information had been incorrect. Just like in the case of Marie, she had been unable to find out what Olivia was doing yesterday. She hoped that this was not a wild-goose chase and a waste of her time, as she had better things to do than chase shadows.

She was barely finishing the rebuke, as I was unearthing my waterproofs and preparing to brave the elements on my scooter.

CHAPTER TWENTY-FOUR
State and Revolution

It was less riding and more sailing down Upper Street, as I headed to where I knew Jackie would be. The news had been full of the fact that the National Workers' Council was having an emergency meeting about the night's events. There wasn't anywhere she would be other than there.

I just hoped that I would be able to get there. The wind and rain continually pushed the bike to the centre of the road, and it was a battle to keep it on the correct side. Turning was a life or death struggle. With the tiny tyres, grip was a problem, and the uncleaned roads awash with rain made it a slippery experience. Then there was the utter joy of having an open-face helmet with a swing-down visor. Great in hot weather, with the sun in your face, looking cool, but in rain—you all but drowned. The rain hit the visor and then somehow defied gravity by going under it and then upwards smack-bang into your face. Gasping for breath under the continual downpour, I spluttered as I rode. My eyes were red, my lips blue. Not so cool.

And finally, I looked such a chump dressed in waterproofs. On a scooter there was a thin line between cool and nerd, a line that got narrower the older one got. And with nylon trousers and jacket hauled over a suit, that line was well and truly crossed. Leathers were out—not my style, too rockist, looked good on a macho motorbike but not a scooter. Too ott. But then. But then, these nylons were hardly modernist.

Through Holborn I was treated to a number of showers from lorries ploughing past me—reactionary bastards. This trial by deluge went on for a quarter of an hour until, thankfully, the skies started to clear as I headed towards Central London. The rain stopped, and the sun came out. Dampness appeared under the waterproofs as I sweated. It seemed like a historical epoch before I got to the place the NWC used as its centre.

Parking my bike, I tried to remember the quote about revolution and imagination, something along the lines of revolution freeing the imagination. True, but that wasn't quite the case here, with the building used as the centre for the National Workers' Council boasting the name The Centre for the National Workers' Council. When it had been taken over by those of us favouring a different type of government from the parliamentary system, there had been days of discussion as to what it should be named. Every time someone suggested one, there had been a counterargument saying that it excluded some group or other, or that it sounded too like one of the parties involved. The interminable debate had sapped the soul with its nit-picking and navel-gazing (could you have both? I guess you could, if personal hygiene wasn't high on the agenda—no doubt, delegates would have debated that as well). Finally, tired of wasting such a large amount of time on a comparatively trivial matter, someone had proposed naming it just what it was. So it became the CfNWC. Not that such a mundane name really caught on because pretty soon, everyone started calling it simply Workers' Hall, an ironic reference to its original title—the Royal Albert Hall. It was even tagged as that on my Satnav (when it was working).

Actually, having been brought up knowing it as the hall of the royal German spouse, nine times out of ten, I myself called it the Royal Albert Hall. The circular exterior of the building was now draped in red, green, black, and purple flags, and slogans and heroic pictures of the British people in struggle. These hung from the frieze which had always ringed the hall, portraying the triumph of science and arts. There had also been a debate on what kind of triumphs these actually were. In the end, for what it was worth, it was left uncovered. It had to be said that whilst I could appreciate and even applaud the young workers' enthusiasm, passion, and good intentions of neutralising an imperial architecture, I did feel that the effect was of turning it into an enormous multi-coloured yurt.

I pulled off the waterproof trousers with as much dignity as I could but with little success, finding myself hopping around for several minutes, impersonating a stork playing hopscotch. Eventually, I sorted myself out, pulling down the jacket and straightening the collar. Everyone looked too busy getting on with their daily lives to notice a prat bouncing about by a scooter.

I navigated my way through the first few rings of security by showing Jackie's vid-message but not so the inner one. A couple of Democratic Left guys, sporting DL badges and large armbands, waved rifles under my nose and barked that only delegates and observers were allowed in today. "This was no longer a tourist attraction." I smiled, guessing that particular line was a favourite of theirs. I tried to explain that I was working for Jackie but had no luck. Because of the unrest, safety precautions had been tightened up. Those on security detail certainly were. As a spring.

I feared that I would be stuck there, squelching in sodden socks, staring at the building, and contemplating the influence of amphitheatres on the architecture until by chance, another militia guard joined them. Luckily, although a member of the Greens, he knew me personally. Like me, he was an Islington lad, and after a brief, if somewhat uncomfortable, conversation encompassing the loss of Caroline and Lisa, which he said he had only heard about six months ago, followed by a stilted discussion about what I was doing now, he vouched for me. I was then let through.

Circling the building were stalls run by a variety of organisations. Some were there to recruit members whilst others hoped to influence delegates. There were the big three: us—the URSP, the depleted anarchists, and the confident Democratic Lefts, plus groups ranging from Women Workers at Home, Islamic Socialists, and even BEAR—Be a Revolutionary—the children's rights group. Then there was a collection of animal rights, environmental pressure groups, and various Greens. The whole place had the feel of a market. Quite how secure that made it, I could only guess. Did they all have acquaintances from Islington to vouch for them?

I bypassed the hawkers selling food and drink (how on earth did they get through security?). The smells changed as the food did. Doughnuts made way for veggie burgers. Then skirting the posse of delegates catching a fag, I braved the corridor of propagandists. Death by slogan. By the time I was walking through the large, glass entrance doors, my pockets were bulging with leaflets and even a souvenir key-pad holder from a recycling pressure group.

The foyer was equally heaving, with huddles of groups discussing, gossiping, or just catching a breath. Despite its constant use, the interior still looked grand. The delegates generally kept it clean, feeling that the architecture should be respected. It helped that the interior curtains, seats, and carpets were red. The delegates felt right at home.

The arena was out of bounds to non-delegates, with or without mates from North London, so I headed to the stalls where NWC supporters who were accredited observers sat. I wasn't one but tried to look as if I was. I affected a serious but confident air as I looked for a seat. A row of upturned umbrellas dripped rain onto the lush carpet. Very English: Bolshies with brollies.

In the middle row, there were a few seats vacant, so I chose one next to an elderly man sporting a yellow rainproof and enjoying his lunch of tea in a flask and what smelt like tuna sandwiches. He nodded and mumbled, "Hello comrade," as I sat down. Yep, from his breath, it was most definitely tuna.

Above me, the mushrooms that were sound-diffusing discs (or something or other) changed colour at regular intervals. This had been the compromise in the discussion of what colour they should be to replace the Tory blue. The Greens, for example, felt that too much red was biased towards the Socialists. To keep everyone happy, there were now different colours.

I turned on the screen in front of me, which, from previous visits, I knew could provide a wealth of information, from details of who was sitting where, to film of delegates speaking from elsewhere in the country. I could use it to look at the personal history and voting record of the delegates. The effect was to put those in the arena under close scrutiny.

That could not be said of the Circle which was for the public. Here, people could come in, nameless if they wished, and watch grassroots democracy in action. Not today, though; because of the security restrictions, no one had been allowed in.

That was not the case with the Boxes, where the media sat. The place was heaving with representatives from the ladies and gentlemen of the media in the hall. You could have fun finding out which news outlet called it the Royal Albert Hall, The Workers' Hall, The Centre for the National Workers' Council, or as one online news site called it, "The building formerly known as the Royal Albert Hall but popularly known as Workers' Hall but officially called The Centre for the National Workers' Council." An accurate description, but not one conducive for snappy headlines. Personally, I had a secret admiration for the *Sun* who called it "The Prince Albert, The Hall of Pricks." Nasty and anti-working class but guiltily amusing.

The hacks (the media type) were lapping up the debate on last night's violence. Even from this distance, you saw their eyes sparkling and heard the collective licking of lips at the prospect of some juicy confrontations.

Judging from the raised voices, they were certainly getting what they wanted. I looked at one of the observer's monitors and saw that the person doing most of the shouting was a Midlands speaker from the Democratic Lefts.

When the hall had transferred its use from opera to operatics, we had stripped the arena and stage and refurbished it for the delegates. It was considered appropriate that the people look down on them; symbolic positioning to prevent any belief that they were above the working class they represented.

If memory served me correctly, a committee of museum and music delegates oversaw this, ensuring that no damage was done and anything that was moved was done so carefully and then stored. And again, this being the NWC, this in itself had to be debated—at length, and being the NWC, that of course had led to other debates, motions, and counter-proposals. The main issue had been that old chestnut commonly known as the Buck House Question.

Now the Buck House Question had basically grown out of the renaming debates of a few years back. It was one thing to want to rename Victoria Park, People Park, but what about buildings whose very existence represented class rule? Buckingham Palace, for example? What would happen to it after the revolution?

Rather like the question of renaming, the party or, to be more accurate, the older members of the party, initially had not taken the issue too seriously and indeed had rather taken the piss, pointing out that we should not get ahead of ourselves—the revolution hadn't actually happened yet. I had been one such older member.

We had misgauged the mood, though, and our newer recruits had argued that we take it seriously. The anarchists were demanding that such buildings as Buck House, Windsor Castle, Chequers, et al. should be either blown up or, at best, gutted and converted into flats. This was a call that many of our fresher-faced activists found attractive.

Finally, those of us with a fair few campaigns behind us had finally woken up and taken it seriously. These buildings were ours—built and paid for by us, and we should not destroy them simply because there had been squatters there for a few hundred years. We should preserve them as works of art for the new workers' Britain; their use as museums, education centres, or even, yes, homes, could be determined later.

The debate had become slightly less abstract when the home of the Lord Mayor of London, Mansion House, had been squatted. The people inside had decided that whilst the Flemish paintings on the walls were not to their taste, they should be preserved. I had been called in, and in a surreal twenty-four hours, I, along with a platoon of red militia, had supervised Mansion House's toffy art curators in cataloguing and packing the paintings carefully to be kept for prosperity. Meanwhile, as I had discussed the finer points of the artist Hendrick Avercamp, the anarchists and a good number of the party's teenage membership had been excitedly planning how they would storm the Bank of England.

The compromise had been agreed by the NWC, although this only prompted our heritage activists to question the future of the memorial statues that cover British cities. Are they tributes to class enemies or works of art? I could not for the life of me remember how that particular issue had been resolved, as even I, with an interest in such matters, felt the life being pulled out of me by such an arcane squabble. In any case, with a lot of them the question had been answered by locals just pulling them down and re-using them. I had heard that with one particular statue of the Duke of Wellington that it had been pulled down using a tractor and was now in bits, being used as a rockery at an OAP home. His Waterloo had been horticulture.

The hall's historic grand pipe organ was now encased in a protective case behind the huge screen which was running footage from York. Where the choir used to sit was now home to various secretaries. My friend in the next chair had by now finished his sandwiches and was crunching his way through smoky bacon crisps, appearing to be treating his visit as one might the cinema. No doubt, popcorn would be the next thing to be shovelled down his throat, sure to be followed by spraying bits across his lap and onto the floor for good measure. Obviously, food shortages didn't affect this man.

In front of the delegates sat the officials, including Jackie, as president of the NWC. She was the recipient of all the ill-will being spat out by the Brummie on the floor. This place wasn't going to be high up on her list of fun places to visit, what with her last one resulting in being shot at and this one being shouted at.

Not that she was receiving any sympathy from the speaker, who, I saw from the screen, was called Tyrese Don and was a train driver. He was not a happy train-driving Brummie. His bile seemed unending as he threw all kinds of accusations at her and the party, although basically they all boiled down to the fact that the party was positioning itself to lead a coup d'état.

His speech lasted about five minutes, ending with an ominous list of the party comrades who had been recalled to either the workplace or locality to account for the violence. "Will they return?" he bellowed. Then, just as he was finishing, his voice theatrically dropped to a whisper. With the microphones barely catching it, he looked at Jackie and said, "Will you continue to be the Sister President?"

Applause and heckles responded in equal measure. Personally, I found him to be rather hammy, but there was no doubt that he had electrified the hall.

The next speaker was a wheelchair-bound and very Aryan-looking woman by the name of Anna Azrenka who, the screen informed us, had been a delegate for Dorset for three months and was an independent. She was far less abusive and spoke directly to the motion, which helpfully was also screened up for all to see what exactly the argy-bargy was about.

It argued for a suspension of "all direct action, physical and cyber, which was in outright opposition to the government" because, it explained at length, it would "create a space to reopen a dialogue with the Parliamentary authorities." She had an eloquent if mousey voice, politely setting out the reasons why it was a sensible option to take a pause. Her manner was less of addressing the masses and more of discussing what stitching to use in her embroidery. It was, she said, neither a retreat nor a sign of weakness in the movement.

The procession of speakers who followed her, did so against film of recent riot scenes from Sunderland. Mark you, for the quantities of tear gas being used, it could have equally been the Battle of the Somme. The speaker from the Greens, who was reading from notes, assured us that it was indeed the City on the river Wear, from which he hailed.

After he had finished, others followed. Some were in favour, some against; a minority just wanted to yell. Some were party members, and some were not. As they went on, I checked out who was here. As well as Jackie, Youssef Ali, Marie Williams, and Michael Hughes were all present. I looked down at the places where they had been logged in and saw nothing but empty leather seats. Then, I had an idea. I did occasionally. It might be that a delegate's history of attendance record could be checked on the screen; if so, I could see whether Ali had indeed been here on the afternoon of last Friday, Jenny Underhill's death. He had told me that he had. I checked. You could see the register of attendance. And according to this - he hadn't.

Well, well, it seemed all the rage to lie to me; positively the vogue to misinform yours-truly. First Marie, then Harrison, and now Ali. So where had they all been? Playing a polite game of Liverpool Rummy in the conservatory whilst sipping a cold white wine spritzer? Maybe not.

My attention was drawn to a familiar voice. The media in the box sparked into action. Sausage rolls, cups of stale tea, and expense sheets went flying as they suddenly decided to take notice of what was happening. This was going to be good. This was news. Whatever she said would be added spice for the headlines already written; most of them were not going to be rave reviews. Jackie had been called. To no one's surprise, she announced that she wanted to speak to oppose the motion.

As usual, she began her speech by slowly outlining the political background to the situation we found ourselves in, including the twists and turns of our journey here. It was in this section where the humour, usually laced with barbed wit and aimed at our foes, was the most heavily loaded. This was setting the scene for her to argue what she believed should be the next course of action.

Her arm was still in a sling, and she was dressed in the three-piece number I had seen her in previously. Being someone who used her arms widely to express a point, this rather unbalanced the look, with one hand cutting, punching, pointing, and waving and the other just painfully bouncing on its support.

One-armed she might have been, but she pulled no punches. She ravaged the motion as "a seemingly innocuous platitude for peace, but in reality, it was a call for us to drop to our knees and wait there with our head on the block for the axe to fall." Her passion filled the hall, anger propelling her words. Her message was not far from the one she had delivered at Alan's remembrance march, but it was up a notch in intensity and urgency.

All around me, the observers stopped everything and focussed on her. Even the picnicker next to me halted his munching. Some looked directly at her, some alternated between her and the screens, but no one solely looked at the reproduced visual image. She might appear tiny down on the floor, but you felt that you had to see her in the flesh. Her words demanded personal attention. The real thing, not the pixelated reproduction. Distractions stopped. You sat and listened, and even if you had not uttered a word, it felt as if the pair of you was in an intense conversation.

She dismissed the accusation of a putsch with a swish of her strapped arm. We had never, she said, hidden our belief that the state was not neutral but was one of class dominance. It was hardly a secret; look at our blog, first line, first paragraph of *What We Believe* and read it there. But the final round of the revolution would be when the majority of the working people had decided that Parliament no longer served its needs. That was when we would take total control. "And that will be with the backing of the class and the backing of the National Workers' Council, and it will not be a coup—it will be an insurrection!" Cue thunderous applause and lightning heckles.

She reminded the listeners that we had been one of the first groups to help set up the workers' councils which the Democratic Lefts could not equally claim. They had still been hopeful of using Parliament as a vehicle of Socialism. "And we welcomed your change of heart and your embrace of the new system of governance, but don't then accuse us of not being Democrats. We were building these assemblies of working-class power when your party was still passing laws on school assemblies at Westminster!" Cue laughter. Cue some boos. She pointed the finger of blame at elements of the coalition who were hoping to destabilise the situation.

A heckler yelled, "Why would they want that? Destabilisation only helps us."

Few people dared individually heckle Jackie for good reason. She was very adept at using it to build her speech around. And so it was here. She repeated the heckle, using it as the foundation of her position, explaining why it was in their interest to destabilise the situation: by doing so and blaming us, they could use that as an excuse to bring in measures to suppress us. Enthusiastic applause drowned out the isolated cries of "Rubbish!"

As the hubbub continued, I noticed a figure moving to a seat near the back, on the right. He wasn't of much interest, but the man next to him was—Youssef Ali. He was leaning down and picking up a black leather suitcase from under his seat. Turning, he quietly walked past Jackie. Was I imagining it, but did for a millisecond she shoot him a look of surprise?

I jumped up, almost knocking a snack bar out of the luncher's hand, and headed towards the exits. Leaving the thought that perhaps our food shortages were all down to that one man, I descended some stairs. Keeping my back to the wall, I peered around a corner to where the delegates left the arena. I wanted to see where Mr Ali was off to and was trying to keep hidden. My attempt at discreteness, however, looked more like I was playing hide-and-seek. At any moment I might jump out and say, "Boo!"

For a second or two, I lost him, so I could not say which exit he had used. Being as likely as any other, I took the first but could not see him anywhere. Scanning the scene in front of me, all I saw was the bedlam of guards and stalls.

It hadn't taken me too long to leave my seat, so he would not have time to get far. That meant that either he had got into a car that had permission to be within the security circle, or he had used another exit. I ran around the circumference of the building, avoiding comrades on cleaning duty, armed with brooms and buckets; a small group of teenagers doing things with computers; assorted groups handing out leaflets; an elderly couple selling T-shirts; and even bizarrely, by the second exit, a leotard-clad mime group. What the hell were they doing here? I couldn't help myself, but I turned for a moment just to try to guess what they were doing. One had his arm pointing to something bouncing up and down, whilst the others knelt. No clues there, then.

Turning in time to avoid falling head over arse by colliding with a paper seller, I saw him. He was standing by a people carrier, talking to Glen Bale. I

Comrades Come Rally

stepped back, hid behind a stall from a small sectarian group, and watched. Both looked serious and were looking around. I stepped further back and positioned myself behind a display of the groups' manifesto. It was then that Marie appeared, looking flustered and as if she was apologising. Whatever her excuses, they appeared to be enough, as she was met with nods, and they all got in.

So it seemed that here was another day, and here was another away-day for this group. It seemed they were meeting more often than your average lady of leisure with her home-counties coffee mornings. I was right to come here because it was bloody obvious that it was important, no make that *essential*, that I talk to Jackie.

***

I had been back in my seat in the hall for an hour, waiting for a chance to talk to Jackie, but had been out of luck. She had not even popped out to visit the loo, and although she had not spoken again, she had stayed, listening intently and occasionally making notes. We had narrowly defeated the motion, and the council was now onto a discussion about food distribution. Ironically, my compatriot, the keen lunch-packer, was now nowhere to be seen. Maybe he was going to get called as an expert advisor.

The people carrier had sped off too quickly to give me any chance of following it. Anyway, not being Jason Bourne, one car chase a week was enough for me, so I had come back in to bide my time and seek some answers. As we approached the second hour, I was beginning to admire her constitution. I needed the lavatory. And the discomfort in the pit of my stomach was either due to the desire for something to eat or dissatisfaction and frustration at the situation I found myself in. Or both.

I had received a text from Zoe who had said that she had been unable to get much in the way of information on Youssef Ali because much of the info I had given her was wrong. Yes, indeedy, Zoe, like him claiming to be here last Friday when in truth he had not been. I detected a note of unhappiness in her message which informed me that both she and January felt they had done enough and were going home. If you can have a subtext in a text, the one here was, "we hav wastd enuff time on this!"

Fearing that if I did not soon go, I would wet myself and also needing to stretch my legs, I got up and made my way to the main entrance where huddles of delegates indulged in the holy trinity of refreshment-break activities: munching on snacks; drinking cold, insipid tea; and/or speaking into phones. Be they selling vacuum cleaners or a new world order, delegates could be counted on to be doing at least two of those three prior to or after a visit to the toilet. Conference fatigue was a great leveller. I, though, was on a higher mission: I dumbly walked up and down, mulling over thoughts and debating what to do, what was happening in the country, and *what the hell I was doing*.

My mind wasn't quite the articulate discussion that the NWC could rise to. Mine was more akin to a bar-room brawl with mouthy drunks hurling abuse at each other and the occasional chair getting thrown.

It was whilst I was trying to bring in a mental sheriff that a ripple seemed to disturb the atmosphere of the lobby. The cause of the change in temperature was Jackie striding rapidly through the throng. She moved like you see film stars move, eyes ahead but slightly down so as not to catch anyone's attention. And quickly. Before you could say, well, anything really, the back of Jackie was all that could be seen as she left the building.

By the time I turned and wrestled past representatives of the movement who were munching, drinking, or talking, she was heading towards her 4x4. A phalanx of party militia swung behind her. People separated for her. I was not so privileged. She marched. I dodged. The assorted human accompaniment to the Workers' Hall made progress difficult. Despite a valiant effort to keep up with her, I only had enough time to see her slide into the back of her car and speed off. Shit! What was it about people flying off and leaving me behind! I could get a complex at this rate.

The pub-slanging match in my head got a whole lot more anti-social. I did not so much walk into the gents (and boy, did they have a mega row over whether it was a remnant of class bias for men's loos to be known as that!) as crash through the doors. Finding a cubicle, I rammed the lock shut, unzipped my fly, and relieved my physical distress. Unfortunately, dealing with my head wasn't quite so easy.

The shouting match between my ears was raging, and I found my lips mouthing the different parts of it. Punching their way into the scrap were now the heavyweights of grievance and disappointment, but even these mighty beasts were being outfought by the super-heavyweight of self-pity. I zipped up and sat on the lavatory and could hear my breathing increasing. As if to echo my head, I was snorting and clenching my fists. Muscles throughout my body clenched and unclenched. My teeth ground fillings away, and my blood pressure was going into orbit. In the movies this was where doctor whats-his-name turned into the Incredible Hulk. Here, though, within the rage, a small voice was dodging the blows, hoping that none of the delegates here were psychotherapists. If they saw this performance, they'd section me. Had the NWC its own mental hospitals? If so, then I could think of a fair few comrades I would like to send there. But enough of Glen Bale. The thought made me smile and had the effect of beginning the cool-off.

My breathing was moving to regular when my phone went. The main concern was now to quickly get control of myself. I closed my eyes and tried to banish the B-movie melodrama and get back to normal. Back to normal. Deep breaths. Cool the temperature. Swallow gently. With the final ring, I flicked it on.

"Yeah?" I panted, still not totally in charge of breathing.

The screen showed a somewhat puzzled Victoria Cole.

"Where…what the hell is happening?"

Damn. I forgot that the video was still on.

"I'm…er…at Workers' Hall."

"You look like you're in a public toilet!" I could see the thought of me panting in a men's loo was throwing up all sorts of images in her head. None of them were pretty. Nevertheless, it did not stop her from telling me that I was to stay there, and she would pick me up because she had finally tracked down Charles Hutchinson.

Grab something to eat, she had told me, because it was going to be a long drive.

CHAPTER TWENTY-FIVE
Beware of Spies!

We were heading west at speed, seemingly in an endless procession of overtaking. Technically we were still in the wonderful metropolis of London, but as far as I was concerned, there was little of London about where we were, and instead it was just part of the sprawl collectively known as suburbia. I had always believed that this was the place where you could enjoy the drawbacks of the capital with none of the benefits. You got the litter, crowding, and poverty but none of the culture, vibrancy, or buzz. You gained a few trees, but the only real countryside you enjoyed was the narrow-mindedness. I wouldn't be moving here too soon. My ashes would be spread across the City.

We were on our jolly jaunt because Cole had found out that Charles Hutchinson was now a resident living near Taunton in Somerset and heading to cider-land. Now that was real countryside. Not that I could honestly say that was a good thing. A simple rule of thumb was the more trees there were, the less likely a Socialist would receive a friendly welcome. Still, this might be a shit job snooping on the party, but it did mean that you got to travel. Norfolk, Durham, and now Somerset, this was turning into all the points of the compass journey of discovery. Maybe I could settle down after this and write one of those travel books where some bloke wanders around, usually by some wacky form of transport—steam engine, push-bike, or roller skates, making pithy comments and needling out sweet eccentricities from the locals. Cole's sports car was less zany and more rubber-burning, speed-kicking. Or perhaps it was just the way she drove it. We hadn't really met any eccentric locals as of yet, but you never knew, my luck might change. In Somerset I might find some druid collective; wasn't Glastonbury around there? I seemed to remember something about King Arthur supposedly being a former resident. Then, again, we were off to visit a former MI5 agent, not some mythical monarch.

As Cole attempted to impress me with her advanced driving skills, I was trying to impress her with my advanced detective skills. The former, I feared, had far more substance than the latter. It was as I was doing a fairly feeble attempt to explain the rather embarrassing fact that I had been wandering around the Workers' Hall lobby like a zombie when Jackie had left, when a song on Cole's car music system caught my attention. Till then it had been a random selection of tunes from the previous decade, but this was one I had heard of. It was such an oldie as to be regarded as positively ancient.

"This is The Raincoats!" I said, doubly relieved at hearing a decent song and being able to leave the Jackie cock-up behind. "It's 'No One's Little Girl'! I love that song; it reminds me of an aunt. She was a great fan of the band. I sorta grew up with them. How come you've got it? It's from the 1980s, no, it must be the late 1970s? I'm certain that it predates me."

Doing a fair impression of a Formula 1, the car pulled away from the lights. "Yeah, I saw some of their CDs in your collection and thought they had a cool name, so I checked them out and discovered it. I liked the sentiment."

I felt rather uneasy at what she had said and what other snooping about she had conducted on my life. Had she noted that, out of thousands of CDs, only four of them were classical? What about my books? Had they been analysed? Her interest in me was flattering, or *something*. No, it was definitely more of the something, and it was a little spooky something. Perhaps it was an overreaction, but I really did hope that the rest of the music was hers and not mine.

I coughed. "So what about you?"

The question had been asked approaching Hounslow, but I seriously feared that by the time we got to Bristol, she still would not have finished. She expanded at length, at how disappointing, frustrating, and simply upsetting her day had been. This was where I should have been supportive. Should have been. Instead, I had to stifle a giggle when she recounted the story about her smart card being blocked, causing her to be unable to get into the police station. Her sidekick, the mysterious Roijin, had come to the rescue and used her own to gain access. Her troubles had not ended there, though, because both of them had been denied computer access. Everyone had refused to help. They could not even get a drink, as the drinks machine refused to accept their ID. That was probably just as well because both had found that they were also barred from the toilets.

I swear that the only reason why I did not crack up laughing was from concern of what her possible reaction would be. Not from any fear of her, but from the vision of her losing concentration at such speed, spinning off the M4, and in my final seconds on this mortal coil, hearing Cole whining about life in the force. Car accidents are not very pleasant. I was at least an expert on those.

So I kept my gob shut and took in *Police Story*. Their knight in shiny armour was good ole' DI Martin who rode in, brandishing passcodes and swipe cards, and with a puff of—dragon smoke, the magical cave of all the facilities of the modern police station opened up for them. That was great for Roijin and Cole but not so much for my travel comfort, because at least her griping had been humorous, but now I was regaled with the lengthy cyber-orienteering as she had tried to get a location for Hutchinson. Her terminology lost me for great chunks of the story with anti-phish, anti-bot, anti-this and anti-that. Anti, auntie; it sounded like a meeting of female relatives. Then there were flags and blocks and cul-de-sacs and a whole slew of other jargon. Drifting in and out of her speech, I managed to fathom, that basically it all came down to the fact that it had not been easy to find out what had happened to him.

"So how *did* you manage to trace him?" I asked, wanting desperately for her to get to the point. Why couldn't she speak like she drove?

She answered with relish, "A row about an overhanging tree."

OK, she had my attention now. I at least had the grace to give her the luxury of a pregnant pause before she explained.

"In the end we simply searched the police databases, what's left of them, to see if there were any other mentions of a Charles Hutchinson whether as victim, witness, or criminal. Frankly, it was grasping at straws.

"We had failed to get anywhere with any security route and equally drew a blank with the more mundane civil arena: birth, death, social security, and so on. It was the only thing we could think of. So we brought up any and every mention of anyone called Charles Hutchinson. Of course, Pete, we didn't even know if that was his real name. Anyway, we trawled up piles of possible mentions. I was surprised, even with the system so corrupted, you have no idea how many times a Charles Hutchinson has been involved in a police report."

She was correct—I didn't. Not that I had given it much thought.

"Then," she continued with her discovery, "I came across a six-year-old file of a dispute between two neighbours concerning an overhanging tree. One wanted it cut, and the other felt that, as it had been there since before either had been born, it had a right to be there. There were some fisticuffs, and Hutchinson was arrested, but his name had initiated a flag, just as had happened with Marie Williams. And just like with her, no action was to be taken. The code indicated that in some way he was, or had been, connected with the security services. Ironically, it was this flagging which kept it on the system. A by-product of such flagging is that it has extra cyber protection because of its importance. So whilst under cyber attack Mr Average Charles Hutchinson of Nowheresville would lose his police records, this one of our Mr Hutchinson stayed."

She looked at me, perhaps waiting for applause. I thought I better respond quickly as we were speeding at one hundred and fifty kilometres per hour and overtaking an army truck, so I wanted those eyes focussed on the road. However, I did not answer in quite the way she hoped. "Of course," I sniffed. "It might not be the same Charles Hutchinson."

My lack of admiration did not seem to faze her. Her answer was Sahara dry. "Sure, there may well be another Charles Hutchinson connected with MI5. And that is why we are travelling to see this one to find out."

And with that, we lapsed into our preferred mode of operating together—silence. I stared out the side window, admiring the early evening whizz past as we ourselves passed anything we encountered, whilst Cole imagined she was driving in a Grand Prix.

I must have dropped off, as I found myself lifting my eyelids up, noticing the sun was almost down, and the headlights were on. Seeing the sign for Bristol, it confirmed that I had been asleep for a time. Sheepishly, I looked across at Cole who I was sure had a slight smirk on her face. "We'll be there in half an hour."

We came off the motorway, but that didn't appear to necessitate any lowering of our speed. Indeed, even as the roads became narrower and expanses of space became filled by houses, she just kept her foot down. The Satnav was down, and I wondered if she knew where we were going. I thought we had come off the main road far too soon, but Cole informed me that Hutchinson didn't actually live in Taunton but in some village on the outskirts of the town.

Despite her cool authority, I noticed that when we reached a junction, she looked in all directions, including behind; taking far more of an interest in the road signs than you might normally do. Either she was checking the area for a holiday home, or she was indeed lost. Thankfully, the act did not go on for too long, and we pulled over. Putting on the hand brake, she turned and reached behind to get something off the back seat.

Well, well, a road atlas—a *paper* road atlas! Call the British Library; we have a museum artefact here! And call BBC News, because a cop can use it! There was almost a look of pride when she told me that she had bought it a few weeks back. Scanning the index, she found the page with her finger and traced a route from where we were to where we needed to be. Sometimes, the old ways are the better ways.

Moments later, off we were, with impressive wheel-spinning on the road, and turning sharply to the left. As we drove on, I had to own up to a feeling of disappointment with the number of houses there were. I had never been to this part of the country before and had expected fields and meadows with good, honest country folk chewing straw and pushing ploughs, but, instead, there seemed to be endless driveways and expensive front gardens. True, both were growing in size, and the separation from the neighbours was increasing in distance, but it was still hardly the rural idyll here.

Glancing at the map, she slowed and turned into a lane that had only recently evolved from a dirt track. We had not turned into arcadia. Judging by the make of cars sitting in the carefully constructed rustic drives, this was more the land of professional getaway than pastoral graft. About half the way down, we pulled up on a finely cut verge and stopped.

"Here we are," she announced, pointing to a house opposite. "Meadow Cottage, home of Charles Hutchinson."

I looked across at the grey stone building with a large chimney running up the end. Two state-of-the-art windmills spun rapidly in the evening wind. "Cottage? Looks more like a bloody stately home to me!" The conservatory alone looked the size of my ground floor. "How many bedrooms has it? Must be seven or eight. Probably got a swimming pool, too! Seems that public sector cuts in pay and pensions did not quite affect everyone."

"No, it hasn't a pool. And it looks…" she was leaning forwards, fiddling with the car computer screen, "like only three bedrooms. Hmm, it's deceptively modest; more brickwork than space."

"What the hell are you looking at? You got Estateagent.com as a favourite? Checking out your retirement home?"

"Surveillance: there's an infrared camera fitted to the roof of the car."

I looked at what was interesting her. It looked like the love child of an x-ray and a computer game. I realised that it was the inside of Hutchinson's home. "Impressive," I muttered, torn between mockery and childlike excitement. "We really are going hi tech!"

"Hardly," she said coolly. "It's been standard kit for years. Actually, it's pretty old hat. Our American friends are well beyond this, but it has its uses." A sardonic grin crossed her lips. "Apart from being able to tell you how many bathrooms it has—two, by the way—I can tell you that Mr Hutchinson is not home at the moment, and there are no cameras installed. In fact, I cannot see any security at all, not even a burglar alarm."

"So what are we going to do?" I asked, watching the screen give us a guided tour around his kitchen. It was pretty basic, the image that is, not his kitchen; you couldn't tell from this what it actually was like, but you did see the furniture and the power points. Whether he was a fan of green peppers or what cornflakes he liked was out of its capabilities. No doubt the Yanks could do that.

"Do? We are going to wait here for him to come home."

"What if he's out for the night?"

"Then you and I are going to spend a long night in here; a *very* long night."

That did not sound fun. Stuck here for hours, with what passed for conversation, did not sound the most wonderful time to spend in the country. I wondered to myself whether we should go for a hike or go bird-watching or whatever you were supposed to do in the countryside.

Thinking of something more substantial, I asked, "Shouldn't we be talking to the neighbours? Doing house-to-house?"

That provoked an unexpected reaction. She laughed. "House-to-house? And what, comrade, would we be seeking to ascertain by doing so? Whether he had let it drop over a pint that he used to work for the security services? Maybe one of them had seen him executing a terrorist in his garage. No, I don't really see any point in doing that."

I hated sarcasm, especially when directed against me (naturally, when I was the instigator, that was a different matter). I grew defensive. "We could find out when he moved in or whether he is away much."

The amusement was still plain to see on her face, and with her arms folded, it just added to the antagonism that she was provoking. The tone of her reply didn't help either. "He purchased the cottage back in 2023, but from what I could glean from the bills, he moved in properly seven years ago."

Not wanting to show how she had managed to irritate me, I made a great play of closing the window. Never had pressing a button been given so much attention. I had been feeling a bit chilly from the evening, proving that we still had a way to go to balmy summer nights, but the reality was—doing it gave me something to do.

Maybe she felt the same, because she announced that if we were going to be sitting here, we could do with some music, and she would see if she could find something to my liking. Within seconds, a percussive beat heavily referencing Afro-beat started, quickly followed by a gentle suburban voice singing over them. It was instantly recognisable as "Horchata," the opening track off Vampire Weekend's classic Contra album. I had spent an entire year getting drunk to it whilst at uni. From such a fleeting visit to my house, she had certainly picked up my taste in music. It was rather unnerving, eerie even, and I thought about the fact that I might be sitting next to a stalker.

Still, it was good to hear it again, and it saved me from any more showing off from little Ms comrade-know-it-all. Without asking if it bothered me, she took out a cigarette and lit up. She alternated taking puffs and flicking the ash out the window.

It was surprising, then, when she broke the silence, not with a boast but a confession of incomprehension. "I must confess that I still do not see the link with Alan's suicide, the double homicide of David and Yasmin, and the killing of Jenny Underhill. The time frame does not quite make sense."

Without waiting for a request to do so, she ran through what we were facing. "We have presumed that Alan was recruited to MI5 by Jenny Underhill, then known as Jelena Jacobs in 2011. Decades later, Alan commits suicide when he finds out her double identity. Then David and Yasmin play amateur sleuths and get themselves killed, presumably because they found something out about the death of Alan, but what? And why kill Jenny? Does that mean that our killer was also working for MI5 and has been since 2011? In which case, most of our suspects can be ruled out, including Marie Williams, who was, as she pointed out to us, just a child then. And if they had someone in the party, then why would they need another? Why hook into Alan? And if they are post-2011, then what links them with Alan and Jenny's relationship? It all seems so disjointed."

I agreed that it did not make for a smooth chain of historical linkages. There appeared to be breaks in it; no continuity. "Unless," I volunteered, "that we are dealing with more than one spy."

She looked thoughtful. "A conspiracy? You think that there may be a group of people who are trying to undermine the party? Hmm, that's a possibility." Silence was allowed to settle as she pondered the question. "So is that your thinking on this liaison committee? You've been plain enough how you don't believe that they are working with other parties; what could they *really* be up to?"

I had an idea about that, but I kept it to myself. Instead, I felt myself transported back into Dave's bedroom, staring at his distorted torso, frozen in his final agony. On the floor lay Yasmin, lying like a mound of blood and flesh; the memory of her lively personality and sharp brain blurred by the overbearing carnage of the room. I felt vomit creep itself up my throat, but a determination to avenge their deaths kept it in check. Cole was right; none of it made sense. Nothing seemed to fit, but Hutchinson would at least help sort the pieces. I don't know why, but I *knew* that. He may not have been in the room or even have known of their existence, but he had helped put those manacles on them. That brought up an interesting point: in knowing that, or believing that I did, it suggested that I had faith in Cole's judgment. I believed that this Charles Hutchinson was the same man who had come from MI5 to release Marie all those years ago.

Did Cole find corpses taking up valuable head space, I wondered? Was her brain full of the stabbed, shot, and hanged doing nothing but just being there dead? It wasn't as if David and Yasmin were haunting me. They weren't chasing or trying to hurt me or demanding that I find their killer by dropping obscure clues. They were just there. They were passive victims. I did not have the room in my head to have any more. The other two were more active. They were the ones pursuing me, accusing me of, at best, negligence and maybe even more. It was more than the literal meaning that the blood of Caroline and Lisa had been on my hands. I believed that, no matter how many times well-meaning people would say otherwise.

Any temptation to bond over a mutual horror was dispelled when a two-note low noise emanated from her throat. I looked into the wing mirror and saw a man dressed in a mustard-coloured jacket and blue denim jeans ambling up the lane. On his head was a straw trilby, and in his hand was a plastic shopping bag. He paused as he opened his gate, and there was just a slight turn of his head in our direction. It had been only a very tiny tilt, but I had seen it. He had checked us out. Cole had seen it, too.

"We'll give him a few minutes and then go in." She leant across and opened the glove compartment; reaching in, she took out a matte-black gun. She switched something on, flicked something else back, and then looked down the barrel. It was Hollywood, and I had not the faintest what she was doing. She unzipped her jacket (she was wearing her green-leather, high-zip number today) and slid it into an inside pocket.

We made eye contact, and I could see an idea pop into her head. "You can have this," she said, going deeper into the glove compartment and pulling out a smaller version of the gun she had just holstered. She had a right little armoury in there. I had to say that I was somewhat taken aback at the suggestion.

"He's a former member of the security services, possibly still is, and he could be dangerous. Often as not, they're not much more than clerks, but there's a few who are the type of people you do not really want to cross."

"No," I said simply. I was not going to play cops and robbers, not for her and not for that ruling class enforcer. I had never touched a gun in my life and was not going to do so now in some phoney attempt at fooling someone that I was dangerous. Quite obviously, such a man would be able to spot the fact that I had never touched a gun before in the blink of an eye.

She moved in closer to me, presumably thinking that it was such a stylish accessory I would not be able to resist it. "No," I repeated.

It did not seem to worry her. "OK," she said, "then…" She returned the gun and searched about the glove compartment again. This time she did not bring out a gun but a book—Karl Marx's *Das Kapital* volume 2. "Have this."

I stared at her. "What am I going to do with *that*? Hurl quotes about surplus value at him?"

She smiled. "No, put it under your jacket, and it will at least put a seed of doubt in his mind whether you are armed or not." She handed it to me, and I did as she suggested.

"Why not. I'm more Karl than Koch!" I quipped. Against my better judgment, I appreciated the style of the idea.

However, my humour did not impress her very much. "It's Heckler and Koch; the gun makers are Heckler and Koch." She was once more looking in the glove compartment. What else was in there? Was she going to bring out a ground-to-air missile? She didn't; instead, it was something more mundane, because this time she took out a police ID card.

"Here, this is a spare; it used to be. Well, it doesn't matter, but you need to be wearing this. We need to be legitimate in his eyes or else he will refuse to help us."

I was mortified. This was worse than being offered a gun. I had not spent too many years being herded around backstreets, charged on picket lines, shoved aside by riot shields, hit by truncheons, and flayed by water cannons to now be pretending to be one of the bastards who had been meting it out. What was it with her and her desire to have me act the policeman? What was next—a plastic truncheon and toy handcuffs? And again she seemed to believe that Charles Hutchinson would fall for it, whereas I didn't believe that he would be so gullible. And if he was, then he must be a right twit. And a really crap spy.

I waived it aside. "No chance. Listen, the days of cowering in front of the likes of him are long gone. We are cleaning his type off the streets. I am damned if he'll intimidate me! No, for too long his public school ilk have ruled; he is no longer the master of us. No, we go and tell him who exactly we are and what we want him to tell us."

A fine speech, I thought, worthy of a salute or two. Instead, Cole snipped a reply. "So why should he help us?"

"Because," I replied, "he serves rulers, and if he is any judge of events, then he will know who are about to become the new rulers."

At this rate I would have a tear in my eye. Cole, though, just shrugged in agreement, evidently not having a desire to argue the matter, and got out of the car. I followed, and standing by the car, pulled my jacket down and straightened myself out. I had chosen the three-button black suit today, with Chelsea boots and a triple-stripe shirt. I was pleased that I had decided to wear a tie, as it added gravitas. Looking at Cole, she still looked like a student to me in green jacket and beige capri pants with slip-on casuals. I did note that she had kept her jacket partially open, giving Hutchinson a chance to grab a quick peek of her gun. She, too, was sending a message.

I waited for her to walk around to me and followed her as she crossed the lane towards his house. "Wouldn't have put you down as a book person," I commented, patting my chest.

"They're the new thing—books are back. The written page is the new app."

Before I could control myself, I chuckled. It was just a short one, but nonetheless I killed it off as quickly as I could. I had no wish for either Hutchinson or Cole to think I was an easy touch. Cool, stylish, and professional was the vibe, not giggling merriment.

Cole rang the bell and held up in her right hand both a police and party ID. I just looked directly at the door. I wanted to look mean.

There was just the one lock to be opened, and it was noticeably done so quickly. He had been obviously expecting us. Judging by the fact he opened it with nothing more lethal than an ironic expression, he felt that he had no reason to fear us.

Cole summoned up all her assertiveness training. "Mr Charles Hutchinson?"

He gave a slight bow to answer in the affirmative.

"Detective Victoria Cole, on National Workers' Council business and this is Peter Kalder, on assignment to Jackie Payne personally."

As she spoke, his eyes flashed from her ID, to logging the fact that I had not deigned to show any, to glimpsing the handle of Cole's revolver and clocking the bulge in my well-tailored jacket. You could tell that in less than a second, he was sizing up the situation.

Not that he looked in much shape to jump to any dramatic action. I did not expect any rooftop escapes from the man who stood before us and for whom the word "ramshackle" could have been written. His belly flopped over his belt. He was almost hanging off the door frame with a half-smoked fag and glass of whisky in his right hand. You could add nonchalance to his description.

"Ahh, I noticed the car's plates, so I knew you were from our glorious constabulary, but I have to admit that I had not expected purps."

He spoke with that slow lounge style which many public school boys did, as if everything was faintly amusing, and nothing was worth taking seriously. Cole all but bristled at the "purps" barb. Purps was short for purple, a right-wing term of abuse for police who were members of left-wing organisations; purple being the mix of blue and red. It was an innocuous term that was surprising in its power to offend, but then words were just labels for meaning, and behind "purple" was pure hatred.

Not that he seemed that snarling; indeed, he seemed almost convivial, adding, "So what can I do for you both? I would not have expected the likes of you to be this far out in the country. Collecting for the cause, are we?"

Cole replied, putting her ID away and in doing so, unzipped her jacket a little further. The tease of that gun had just gone up a notch. "We need to talk to you. May we come in, please?"

He took a drag of his cigarette and smiled. "Glad to see politeness is still an important aspect of the police service. And please forgive me if I say that I am flattered to be visited by someone so young and attractive."

I was bored of this bollocks. Hopefully, my bark hid my nervousness. "Well, I'm no purp, and I ain't young or pretty; more crimson, middle-aged, and not bothered what you think of my cheekbones. Please move!"

As I finished, Cole had entered in one gliding movement, somehow pushing him into his house and done so in such a way that it was totally lacking in aggression or confrontation; judging by the smirk on his chops, it did not concern him over much. I was close behind her, and within no time we found ourselves straightaway in his lounge.

The first thing that hit us was the all-powerful smell of tobacco. Even Cole, a partaker of the cancer stick, noticed it, with her nostrils visibly twitching. It hit you like a smack to the gut, irritating your eyes and making you fear that it would bring on heart disease at any second. Maybe this was his home security: break in and suffer cardiovascular disease.

The second thing which hit me was the oak bookcases lining every part of the walls. I was rather proud of my collection, but his swamped it. There was no space for music or paintings or photographs or even walls. From the fake velvet carpet to the cracked ceiling were shelves.

"Please do come in," he chuckled.

"Thank you," Cole snarled, visibly getting more irritated with the man.

"What can I get you? A whisky? Perhaps vodka would be more appropriate? Or don't our brave defenders of the proletariat drink on duty? So maybe tea or coffee?" He rattled the ice in his drink, took a hefty gulp, and waited for an answer.

I, for one, felt rather awkward. What do we do next? We had forced our way in, but he had reacted not by fighting or abusing us but by offering refreshment. I felt rather silly staring at him. I was unsure what to do with my arms which just hung lifelessly by my sides, and I heroically tried to suppress an almost sexual urge to check out what was on his bookshelves.

Despite drinking something which plainly was not carrot juice and wearing a shirt which had last seen an iron when Neville Chamberlain had proclaimed "Peace in Our Time" (and I noted was seriously misbuttoned), I did not think for a second that he was drunk, let alone *a drunk*, or even tipsy. This was theatre, and he was acting this way to show that he did not give a damn who we were or why we were here.

His performance interested me, as I had only ever really encountered this type of person in espionage novels. Cole, though, was not intrigued. "We're fine," she snapped. "Just please sit, and let us ask you a few questions." Bless. Despite being pissed off, her police academy training politeness was still there. Always the copper.

He nodded and held out a hand indicating for us to sit on the green- and orange-striped, four-seater sofa which looked to me as if it was worth a few bob. For all his dishevelled personal appearance, his home was impeccably clean, well-kept, and full of quality furniture. He was no burnt-out wreck, a casualty of the class war, just seeing out his days in a bored coma. His home might stink, but there was care here. The décor was deliberately tasteful and complementary. This was a home of relaxation and happiness, lived in by a man content with his lot. The overwhelming style was of, ironically, a smoking room at St. James. Not just from the smell of cigarettes and cigars but the lush furnishings in deep colours.

Looking around, I compared his place to mine. The similarities were obvious—books and neat furniture, but mine was more modern, less crammed. I like to think of my home style as being concentrated but not cluttered. The titles that could be seen from where I was standing appeared to be, in the main, classical philosophy. Books by and about Socrates and Plato stood out.

We turned to sit. As we did, he stepped sideways and stubbed out what was left of his cigarette in a glass ashtray which sat at a convenient distance on a side cabinet. His arm moved again, and rather than actually seeing him, I sensed him stretching his hand towards a drawer. Stealthily, he began to open it. Cole spun around, pulling out her gun as she did.

She pointed it at his temple, commanding him. "Don't even think about it!"

He froze, except for a grin wrapping his mouth.

"Just getting another packet out, *comrade*," he replied, drawing out the syllables of the last word with obvious irony. "Can't the condemned man have his last cigarette? I thought that was the etiquette?"

"And why…c-o-m-r-a-d-e…" Cole said, matching his stretched pronunciation, "why would you think you are condemned?"

The tense atmosphere in the room told me that there was not much sense of solidarity between these two members of law and order. There was me thinking they were all one happy family, and I find this. These two were very much estranged.

He was still in his exaggerated frozen pose, which was his way to tell her where to go. He was not intimidated, worried, or even a little concerned. He rattled his glass, slopping the ice around the liquor. His voice lowered. "Just joking, just joking." His grin oozed contempt. "I know full well that you are not here to execute me for my past sins, as even as new as you are to the levers of power, you would not have parked your rather fancy, and if I dare say so, rather bourgeois, sports car, in full view in front of my humble cottage. And," he added, warming to his theme and thoroughly enjoying the situation, "and, did not your leader, *Miss* Jacqueline Payne, say in her delightful Swansea speech, that the National Workers' Council guaranteed that there would be no blood revenge? What were her words? Ah yes, 'We will wipe the slate clean so we can all feast on tomorrow's banquet.' Rather affected in my view, if not pompous, but that's just my personal opinion but—"

Cole was not impressed with his performance. "Shut up and move your hand away from the drawer!" she told him.

He did as he was ordered.

Holding her gun in her right hand with iron steadiness, she opened the drawer with her left until it was fully open. I moved behind her and saw the deadly contents of a spy's kit: a pack of playing cards, a multitude of felt-tip pens, a crossword book, several elastic bands, a couple of paperclips, a roll of sticky tape, and two packets of cigarettes. Collectively, this was known in the espionage world as clutter.

"May I?" he asked, unable to keep his grin from widening.

She nodded curtly and reluctantly lowered the gun to her side.

With great appreciation, he took the wrapping off the packet and took out a cigarette. Sliding it into his mouth, he struck a match and lit it.

Cole wasn't finding it erotic. "Have you any weapons in the house?" she demanded.

He exhaled. "No, not even a penknife," he explained with a candour, which if true was surprising. "I presume that the reason I owe the pleasure of your visit is because of my former employment. In which case, you should know that I am knowledgeable enough to consider that it is pointless to possess one. If someone considers me such a threat as to be worth eliminating, then a hidden pistol is not going to be of much use. It would be more embarrassing than anything else."

He spoke with one of those toff intellectual voices where every sentence was uttered at half the speed that someone else might. I always thought it was affectation to make them sound clever. In my experience they were usually as thick as shit, but that slow Oxbridge drawl meant reciting a limerick sounded like an epic poem.

Maybe it was that which made her believe him, because novice that I was, I personally could not ascertain the basis for this trust. Was this modern police work? She's out on the beat and meets a man in a mask, with a sawn-off shotgun and a swag bag, who, when asked if he had robbed the bank, says no. OK, then, she says. Whatever the reason for her trust, she holstered her gun.

He pointed his fag at her, holding it between two fingers, making it look rather like a sign a boy might make when playing war but not having a toy gun to hand. He really was taking the piss. And was Cole ever being wound up by him. "Time for tea," he said, aiming his fingers at her. "You might not want one, but I do, and I think we *all* could do some cooling off."

The "all" was Victoria Cole, but after the drive, I was gasping, so I didn't quibble. "Coffee for me," I replied.

She did not look at me, so I could not see her expression, but I sensed that she considered my answer had been the wrong one. "I'll come with you," she growled.

"Fine, the kitchen's through there. Meanwhile, Mr Kalder, you can avail yourself of my library." He pointed with his free hand to the far corner, by a large, floor-standing lamp. "You might want to search out some volumes of Russian literature. I am especially proud of my Dostoevskys and Tolstoys.

"Come on in; you can choose which tea. I guess Earl Grey. Not got any Russian tea, I'm afraid." He laughed at his own joke. "What shall I call you? Detective? Comrade? Miss? Ms Cole?" He wandered off, winding her up like a Victorian toy. She followed, silently fulminating and squeezing out replies.

With disgraceful haste I trotted off to look at said novels. There I spent several minutes, admiring his collection of 1971 and 1973 Penguin editions. I all but fondled his copy of Tolstoy's *The Cossacks* with its drawn pictures of suitably Russian-bearded fellows on its cover. It was in quite good condition but had obviously been read a few times. And judging by the nicotine odour emanating from its pages, he had been the reader.

My admiration was ended by their arrival back in the room. He was carrying a tray with a teapot, two cups, a mug of coffee, and most impressively of all—a plate of sliced melon. Where the hell had he got melon? I put Gogol's *Dead Souls* back in its place. He gave me an appreciative smile; Cole rolled her eyes. Her mood had now moved to F for foul.

"So you must have been one of the first 'purps.' Miss Payne must love you for that."

The answer was a sharp rebuke. "Please don't call me purple; I find it quite insulting!"

His face moved to mock sympathy. "Of course, of course, quite gross of me. I must mind my manners. A thousand apologies."

We all sat down, and he announced that he would be mother as he would not want to stereotype "Detective Comrade Cole." His comment corrected my earlier thought; no, she was on E for explosive. Sipping my coffee, I marvelled at both his ability to obtain fresh melon and the lovely fresh coffee I was enjoying, and on top of all that—his ability to so utterly irritate her. He was having a far greater success than I had had.

"I have explained to Mr Hutchinson why we are here," she informed me. "And he has agreed to answer some of our questions."

I took a bite of the melon, which tasted good. "Why?" I asked, between sucking the juices and trying to avoid getting any on my trousers.

He spoke as he was pouring. "As I told Detective Comrade Cole, any information I have will long be out of date and will not hurt the security services. I have done my bit, and whilst I will not tell you anything I think will endanger any 'live' operatives, I see no reason not to talk about old history. The feeble politicians have got us into this God-awful mess, and they can try to get us out."

He took a sip of tea, followed by a bite of melon and a drag on his fag. Then to add to the delightful cocktail, he took a sip of his whisky; so much for the upper classes knowing about fine dining.

"As I also told your colleague, my area of concern was mainly not in the field. Oh, of course, I had done my bit, undercover and all that sort of thing, but that was mainly in eco-activism, not your sort of thing, and that was decades ago. You can't really go hairy and scale barbed-wire fences at nuclear power stations when you're some old fogey carrying this." He patted his stomach. "Recently, the years before I retired, were spent running the office—again, though, more eco-stuff. You know: save the planet, electro-pollution, etc. etc."

Cole brought out her phone and pointed it at his laptop, which was perched on the corner of the coffee table. "I want you to have a look at a few things. May I transfer?" Her look made it more of a demand than a request.

"Sure, go ahead, it's on." A sly thought had occurred to him. "Are you not afraid that I could use the connection to plant spyware into your files?" he goaded, sliding his machine towards him.

For the first time since we had encountered Hutchinson, she smiled. It was a fake, unfriendly, aggressive, and defiant smile, but beggars couldn't be choosers. "I have first-rate security, and if you even try to do so, I will arrest you. All you will get from it is what I want you to. Anyway, I thought you were retired?"

"Yes, of course, just asking."

Sweeping his wayward hair back over his head, he looked at the screen and saw the picture of Marie Williams. Cole told him who she was and then showed him the documents relating to her arrest and investigation. He leant forwards and first studied the photograph and then read the files.

Even so, Cole ran through the details, outlining her arrest for attacking a police constable and stating that plainly there had been sufficient evidence to pursue a successful prosecution, but Detective Savas had noticed a security flag appear on her file. He was to desist. After seeing it, and in the time he could take a bite out of a doughnut, he had received a visit from our friend Hutchinson here.

"Why was that? Why did you visit her?" she asked.

He took a drag on his fag, ash falling on the screen, which he brushed off into the cup of his hand, depositing it into the ashtray. It must have been at least six seconds since the last one. His reply was vague. "It was a long time ago. To be honest, I don't remember it. The old grey matter is not quite as astute as it used to be. As I said, it wasn't my area..."

"So to repeat—why did you visit the station and talk to her?" I asked. His raconteur affectation was beginning to lose its amusing aspect.

He took a sip of his tea, with, yes of course, his little pinkie up. I could see tobacco stains under his nails. "Well," he drawled, "because of just that. If it was required to halt the investigation, then head office would not send someone directly involved in it. The intelligence community is a strange fish—we love our traditions and etiquette. And the etiquette would be for the department head to contact another and request an *immediate desist*. Let's see, back then it would have been Department NA, who would have been running left-wing cadre—they would not want to send one of their operatives along in case he was identified. It sounds like a messenger job. They'd send someone along, me in this case, to tell the local bobbies to cease their interest."

I pondered who would call a department NA. It sounded like the beginning of some 1960s chorus, *nan a na hey*, or was it the office that liked to say no?

Cole had no such idle thoughts; she simply asked, "So why talk to her? What did you say to her?"

"As I said, I can't even remember the visit. Listen, *comrades*, it would have lasted an hour or two—tops. You seriously don't think I can remember a two-hour visit that happened ten years ago. Could you?" He sighed, resigned to having to explain the obvious to two proles. "I would have got a call—told to pop along and chat to plod and then to the Leftie and then leave. As for what I might have said to her—I can't remember."

"Could you have been talking spy to spy?"

"Maybe," he shrugged, smiling, clearly amused at Cole's way of putting it. "But I wouldn't have thought so, because if it was the case that the agency wanted to talk directly to one of its own, then I think they would have sent someone from the relevant department—most probably, in the words of many a movie—her direct handler. Not some messenger from another office. We were quite territorial back then—each to their own."

Cole was not giving up. "But we return to the very simple fact that a clear-cut case was blocked. Her file was flagged, and it prompted a visit from you. Why would that be? What could be so important about her that a senior MI5 agent visits her?"

He shrugged. "I am flattered that you considered me to be a senior agent; really, I was far more humble…"

I tried. "Are you sure you do not remember, or are you just faking amnesia because of who we are? Would you tell us if you knew something?"

"Mr Kalder," he smiled. "We live in interesting times; the future hangs in the balance: will you finally take the final push, or should I say putsch," he chuckled, amused at his wordplay. "Sorry." He straightened up and made a face of apology as if we had been mortally wounded by his petty barb. "And take power, or, on the other hand, will our friends in the establishment seize back the initiative. But that is why I am not being more enlightening. I should make it plain, in case you are drafting up any conspiracy theories, that

I am telling the truth when I say that I cannot remember. I really, honestly, cannot."

My expression obviously was not one of belief.

"But you are correct; I would not tell you something if it might aid you to such an extent that it injured our side—and, yes, there are things I would not dream of telling you, but, and no offence, I would tell you that outright. No, I really cannot recall this visit. It was not that important to me."

Cole persisted. "So I ask again, why visit her?"

He sipped his tea, savouring it at length, and flicked back to her photograph. "Well, I concede that if she was an agent, then perhaps the department who was working her would have wanted to keep her at arm's length and sent me. But as I said, that's unlikely because of my involvement. I had nothing to do with workplace militants, but the detail is irrelevant. You, I mean your organisation, would only be interested in any involvement of the secret state. You would have been suspicious about any contact with the security services; I doubt if you would have given a hoot which particular department we were. Agencies of state repression are agencies of state repression to you lot. No, my guess is that it's more indirect than that."

"Meaning?" I asked.

He sighed again, keeping the world-weary philosopher act going. "Meaning anything, really. It could have been the first step in grooming her..." He saw me flinch. "I know it's an unfortunate term, isn't it, what with its paedophile connotations and all...but then from your political perspective, it might indeed be appropriate." Seeing that we had not given any response to his waffling, he continued. "Or that she had unknowingly crossed the path of a person who was of interest to us—"

Cole interrupted and asked what he meant.

"That someone in the course of the arrest and charging was, directly or indirectly, connected with us. It did not necessarily have to be this Marie Williams."

"The police constable?" I asked.

Cole looked doubtful, but Hutchinson seemed less opposed. "Maybe, or another agent had requested it. Or we had wanted her to continue whatever she was doing because we were monitoring her. Honestly, it could have been anything!"

Our illustrious police comrade looked him straight in the eyes. "I don't believe that you don't remember. Tell us what the private talk in the police station was about."

"As I said, I don't remember. I really don't! But if it helps, then I can say that it could have been a number of things: a message passed on, a threat to desist in political activity, a cover story to hide the real reason for the halting of the prosecution, or quite possibly I had to deliver her a threat to keep her mouth shut."

For a split second, my attention wandered off what he was saying and onto savouring this truly delicious coffee. Would I, I asked myself, have the power to requisition it in the name of the workers' councils? It was very, indeed *very*, nice. Going back to what he was saying, it was blindingly obvious that he was doing a lot of talking but not actually saying anything of any meaning. All we were getting were lists of possibilities, which we could have come up with ourselves.

"How would you go about making sure that she did not talk?" asked Cole.

He waved his non-fag hand about, as if he was just dismissing a petty idea. Then he smiled. Took a smoke and then just smiled again. He was telling us that he was not going to answer that. Cole tried her best, but he just smiled and dead-ended us.

My partner in detection realised that we were not getting anywhere and changed the direction of her questioning. "Was it standard practice to try and bribe, blackmail, or convince long-standing members in left-wing organisations to work for you or would you place your own people?"

This time the tea was left, and he sipped his whisky. There must be quite a mixture in his stomach. I expected another stone wall, but to my surprise he answered. "It would depend on the situation and what we were hoping to achieve. The goal of intervention would determine what actions we would have taken. Budget allowing, that is; we, like everyone else, have to count the pennies. So at certain times we might just make use of assets, whilst at others we might plant our own people in. It would be all to do with the contours of the class struggle, *comrade*."

"And presumably the law?" I asked. "You needed to stay legal."

His look suggested that he considered that one of the silliest questions he had ever heard. A blush advertised my naïvety, so I quickly asked another—hopefully a more sensible—question. "And what about now? What would the priorities be at this time?"

He laughed. "Oh, for the last few years I would imagine that everyone from the night-shift cleaner upwards has been focussed on your organisation!"

"Can you offer us any names?" I asked, tongue firmly in cheek.

Superficially, his humour increased, but he spoke with a frosty antagonism. "Suspect anyone with a pulse."

Cole was not joining in and went back over his visit to the police station. Who had instructed him to visit Williams? Why had they allowed the investigation to continue for so long and not just stop it right at the beginning? Could he not think of anything he had said or done? All her questions were met with fake bonhomie, from which it was impossible to tell whether he was telling the truth or not.

She finally changed tack and asked him if he could negotiate his way around the IT security blocks that she had encountered surrounding the arrest of Marie Williams. She had only been able to get to a limited amount of the information. If she could enter those files, then she might be able to follow the chain of data back to something more useful. However, the blocks were plainly MI5-created and ones she could not crack. I guessed that her explanation was more for me than him. He would know that.

My expectation of what he was going to reply was again wrong. I had thought we would receive some friendly, jokey reply, masking a dry, acerbic answer which amounted to him saying bog off! But instead, he simply muttered, "Why not? It is ancient history. Everyone's long gone. Probably the codes have been all changed but why not? Anything to help with the new world order."

Taking the obligatory drag on his cigarette followed by a sip of his whisky, he paused for a second. Then his fingers worked rapidly over the screen. Occasionally he would mutter a command. The air of lovable but dilapidated dilettante vanished, and he looked the efficient pro. I doubt if even Cole had any idea what he was doing, but we hoped that he was trying to see who had flagged up Marie Williams's file. Of course, he might just be on SpiesReunited and touching base with old friends.

I sat pondering, not only why he was doing this thing in particular, but the fact that he had not asked some very simple questions. Specifically, why had he not asked us for the reason why we wanted to know this? Wouldn't his inquisitive mind have wanted to know why we were interested in events a decade ago? It seemed to me these were the first things he would have asked. I would have done so, but he had not. I decided to ask Cole later if he had done so during their quality time in the kitchen.

He gave a low, interested grunt and keyed in a few more numbers and letters, and the grunt became a harrumph. He faced us. "I can get past the security block, but all the links and files have been deleted. Nothing exists." It was a pretty simple fact he had discovered, but he thought we simple folk needed further explanation. "Think about being able to unlock a door, entering a room, and finding that it has been cleared out. They were pretty thorough. Someone really wanted to protect this Miss Williams."

"Why would they want to delete the information?" I asked.

From her expression it was clear that Cole knew the answer to that and did not have to ask it but was interested instead to know. "When was it done?"

Hutchinson also did not appear to think my question was worth answering but replied to Cole, simply saying, "Last Sunday, 8:34 a.m."

The timing was interesting; I wondered what had happened for them to have taken such action.

"Can you say from which computer they were deleted?" she asked.

"Sorry, Detective; they," he gave a deep laugh, "listen to me—*they*—I should be saying we!" He pulled himself together. "As I was saying, whoever deleted the data is far too clever for that and, I have to say, using far more high-tech gear than I possess. I can tell you that it was from a moveable machine, probably a phone, so I would guess it was not from any agency building. But who it was…Jesus!"

We both jumped and shouted, "What?" He surely wasn't suggesting it had been him! If it was, then we were seriously out of our depth!

Hutchinson explained, removing any thought that we were dealing with a mystery of biblical proportions. "You have a Popov and a bloody nifty one. The bugger is managing to bypass my security and get into mine! Boy, is this one good!"

He frantically began typing and repeating words like "halt," "desist," or "bypass!"

"What's a Popov?" I asked, none the wiser.

Cole looked both surprised and worried. Looking at her phone and his laptop, she explained. "It's a piece of spyware which can be sent into a computer to monitor usage and communications. Obviously, someone has put one in my machine. Furthermore, it will travel to other machines if it regards them as an appropriate destination. It has an intelligence to decide that. So if I chat to my mother, it won't bother, but obviously it regards Charles as a useful place to go, so it is invading his files. The thing is—I thought I had security to stop anyone planting one—all police officers are issued with it."

"It had no chance to stop this one," he mumbled, in a tone switching between awe and concern.

"Can you tell when it was installed?" she asked, with a voice betraying apprehension.

He did not answer for a moment or two, but when he did, he stunned the pair of us. "Er…yes, two Saturdays ago at 10:10 p.m."

We both sat in total silence. At approximately the same time Victoria Cole was being contacted by Jackie Payne to look into the suicide of Alan Wiltshire, someone was installing this Popov thing. How about that for timing. My astonishment was side-shunted when a thought occurred to me. I took my own phone out and handed it to him. "Could you see if there's one on mine."

His disdain increased, as did his horror that I was using such an archaic piece of technology. He probably did not even consider it as being technology. Quickly, he did a few things I had no understanding of. He still might be on SpiesReunited or, indeed, signing me up to it. To be honest, I had expected what his answer was going to be, but maybe not the explanation.

"Yes, I am afraid that you, too, have one. You might, of course, have been infected when she had contacted you."

"What time did I get this little goody?"

"Well, it was a few hours after Detective Cole."

Both Cole and I knew what the importance of that was. We had not yet had the pleasure of meeting each other—cyber or otherwise. So I had not been infected from Cole's phone, because at that time I blissfully had not even an inkling of her existence.

Whilst the pair of us was individually lost in thought, Hutchinson visibly relaxed and gave a "hurrah" you might have heard at Henley Regatta. He explained that he had beaten off the Popov. He spoke about it with admiration you might have done for a genius nephew. I was thinking that someone had found out very quickly about Alan Wiltshire's suicide and had instantly perceived a threat to their identity. Was it a coincidence that one of the first people Jackie had contacted had been Marie Williams? Was I seeing links where there were none, or was I beginning to have it confirmed that Marie was somehow involved in all this?

"That was the day that Alan Wiltshire committed suicide," I said, having decided to see if I could use Hutchinson's special expertise to solve something that had been, dare I say it, bugging me. Cole looked at me in amazement. She did not think I should be talking about the matter to him, but as I saw it, we had not much to lose. "He was a senior member of the United Revolutionary Socialist Party, and in his suicide video, he claimed to have been an informer for the security services. Have you heard of him?"

He said that he hadn't, because, as he repeated, he had been involved in the militant green movement. I wasn't sure that I believed him but didn't push the matter. I was more interested in the process of recruiting spies. "How did you go about enrolling spies? I mean, those who are already members of an organisation you want to infiltrate, whatever the type, and who you want to turn traitor?"

He stubbed out an old cigarette and took out a replacement. Cole had touched upon this question earlier and met with a complete rebuff, but maybe this Popov had unnerved him, because this time he answered. "Oh, there are lots of ways. Sometimes they come to us because they have had an ideological epiphany, and they have changed their views. I have heard that it has happened, but I think it is pretty rare. Occasionally, we can use a financial inducement because of debts, which are often gambling, although to be honest that's rare with the likes of you on the Left. Your mob tends to help each other out with money problems.

"With the Far Right, it's more usually—money and sex. Sexual naughties—adultery, an unusual sexuality, and whatnot—are popular weaknesses. They cannot go around preaching God-fearing morality, hell, and damnation for orgasms and then be caught with their thongs down. Once again, it is an area that, too, does not apply to you lot. You're rutting mad. If it moves, bonk it, and then try to recruit it." He laughed at his own joke.

We didn't.

He continued with his outline of MI5's charms. "No, usually it is blackmail of a different sort. Perhaps they have a link with a dodgy businessman, or they have shares in some polluting big business." He thought for a moment. "Or we might offer to get you off a serious crime. It could—"

I jumped in. "Is that what you spoke about with Marie Williams?" I asked.

He smiled and shrugged. "Nice try, *comrade*, but as I told you, I honestly have no recollection of that visit, but I will say that the usual procedure was that contact would be limited to one officer who is often referred to in the movies as a handler. If there was a conversation to be had about turning her, then I would have only been involved if she had been a green activist. Was she?"

I shook my head. He knew she wasn't.

"Well, in that case I would not have been used."

I returned to how they might have got Alan to work for them, as not for a nanosecond did I think he had changed his political views. He had died a revolutionary. "Have you any ideas how they—your side—might have turned Alan Wiltshire?"

"Ruling out a change of mind and him seeing that capitalism is not responsible for all the world's ills and that it's the least bad system we have? Well, then I would guess that we would frame him, tie him in legal knots, and then pull."

He grinned and slowly inhaled his cigarette with obvious delight. I was beginning to see why he so irritated Victoria. I asked him what kind of knots, but he simply muttered something about the flesh being weak and poured himself another whisky.

He had got bored with the game of chatting with the Bolshies. All further questions from us were batted away like flies annoying him during an afternoon drink. Eventually he announced that he had things to do, and with artificial politeness, asked that if we were done, could we leave.

As we did so, I turned and saw him grinning like the proverbial Cheshire cat. Only with a fag between his smug lips and a glass in his right hand. He raised it in salute. I resisted the temptation to raise my middle finger.

CHAPTER TWENTY-SIX
Through What Stage Are We Passing?

Driving back from Hutchinson's, Cole was in reflective mode, pondering what we were to do next. So far we only had vague hints and circumstantial evidence to go on, but it was still pretty obvious that we needed to do some background checking on Marie. Cole's voice was weighed down with such gravitas that it was amazing the words did not fall to earth. It wasn't just her tone which made it so grating; the way she was talking to me made me feel like looking in the back seat to see if we had a small kid in the car. We had to check this, check that, speak to him, speak to her. On she went, spelling it out ever so slowly and stage by stage. And in doing so, she made sure she used language that the imaginary child in the back would understand.

On the radio, reports were flooding in about riots across the country. Kensington was ablaze, and shots had been fired at various empty homes of long-fled businessmen. It had spread to Chelsea and Fulham. News was coming in about similar arson attacks on wealthy areas of Bristol, Brighton, and Bath. Various pundits were analysing why there had been a return to such violence, which had not been seen for some time. But it was so much talk with so little actually said.

Cole had noticed the fact that my attention had wandered off her and onto the radio. "Whilst we were in the kitchen, Hutchinson said that we would soon be facing the 'moment of truth.' He seemed to be trying to give the impression that something was about to happen, which would mean big changes in Britain, something he knew about and we did not. I wonder if he had some idea that this might be going to happen."

"Big changes in Britain? Well, proof, if proof is required, of what a truly distinctive intellect Charles Hutchinson is: the possibility of big changes in a time of revolutionary upheaval. Whatever next? When apples fall, they hit the ground?" I was equally as dismissive of him having some insider knowledge of the riots. "How could he?" I asked. "It pretty much sounds uncoordinated. I am sure the government will try and pin this on us, though why anyone would think we would bother with this petty rioting is another matter. The only idea he has of something happening is that when he finishes one bottle of booze, there will be another stashed in a cupboard."

She didn't say anything but concentrated on trying to break land-speed records.

Her silence brought an element of guilt at my sneering. "You think he still has contacts in MI5?" I asked, attempting to sound cordial if not fraternal.

She shrugged.

Personally, I did not assign much importance to the disturbances. For the life of me, and with the tautest stretch of my imagination, I could not see this being a "moment of truth." Despite the hyperventilating of those in the television and Internet stations, the rioting seemed rather old-fashioned. Quaint, almost. I mean, Elvis swinging his hips and flicking his quiff was daring and challenging in 1956. But by 1962? That was just square, Daddy-O.

As we overtook three cars at once, she continued musing on what Hutchinson had said and particularly what he had *not* said. She was of the opinion that he knew far more than he was letting on. Whether that was about Marie or the broader political situation, she did not say.

I wasn't that impressed with agent Hutchinson. He appeared to me like someone playing a game. There he was, rolling out the burnt-out, gin-sodden, ex-spook clichés, when, in fact, he was just a bored public-school twit who spoke slowly. He tried hard to sound philosophical, but he was just a dim-witted has-been who had read Voltaire once for an essay and over lengthened his vowels when he spoke.

Enough of all this crap, I said to myself: Hutchinson playing George bloody Smiley and Cole coming over all police-procedural. Taking out my phone, I checked on chat rooms and saw that the riots were the main talking point. A discussion was raging between those people condemning it as mindless violence and those arguing that it was a sign of people frustrated at the slow speed of progress of the revolution. This, they said, was proof that people wanted the NWC to up the ante. At other times, that would all be very interesting, and I would have joined in, but not now. I checked up on news of Marie. Someone of standing usually had some sort of diary available for people to see. Finding none, I looked at the party blog and got more success. Maybe this wasn't a moment of truth, but it was time to stop this farting about.

"How quickly can you get us to Camden?" I asked.

"Camden? North London?"

And she thinks I stereotype cops! Strewth! I sneered at her dumbness. "No, Camden, New Jersey; yeah, North London."

Ignoring the sarcasm, she worked out the journey. "Well, we are just passing Reading, so, an hour and a quarter?"

"Can you make it in an hour?"

"Yeah, sure, if I put my foot down."

I didn't want to think about how much faster that would be, but needs must, and my personal safety took a second place here.

Worryingly, taking her eyes off the road, she gave me a look. "Comrade—why?"

My reply was more passionate and full of heat than I had imagined that it would be. "Because I am tired of piss-balling around, and I think we don't have much time to do much more of it. Whether the Somerset spook does or does not know about 'a moment of truth,' it is pretty clear that the situation is volatile, and the party can ill-afford a comrade working for the other side who could be passing on information. What's more," I added with the image of the blood-soaked bedroom in my mind, "if we just continue fannying about, then the scum who killed Dave and Yasmin will get away in the smoke of revolution, and I am stuffed if I am going to let that happen. Marie is speaking at a public meeting there, and I think we should have a chat with her and get her to speak to us. I mean *really* speak to us. This time, we need to force her to answer the questions." I took a deep breath. It had been quite a speech.

She wasn't impressed. With barely a glance at the road, she questioned what I expected to happen. "And say what exactly, Pete? She's not going to cough up and confess, is she? Not with what little we have. I don't even think she will want to talk to us full stop."

"Stop" was barely out of her lightly made-up lips when I jumped in, mimicking her voice. "So, *Detective*, what *are* the alternatives? As you have been saying for the previous dozens…*and dozens*…of kilometres, our options are pretty limited. We can't get into the security service files 'cos the spooks have blocked them and not given you plod the codes. So what shall we do? House-to-house? Evenin' all—who's the grass? I could ring Zoe and January and have them round up every party member in Western Europe and imprison them in what sodding remains of St Paul's!"

I was now in full ranting flow. "You've made it plain that the powers-that-be have sealed off the investigation to Jenny Underhill's death, so that is sod-all help to us. And by all accounts, your pals in uniform are hardly straining themselves to solve the torture and brutal murder of the Wiltshires. You've been shunted off to road safety and can't find anything about that— *so what shall we* do, *Detective?*"

Finally, I finished and stared at her, daring her to argue with me. Her reply was simple. She pressed the accelerator and overtook a food convoy on the inside. I nodded, giving the indication that I recognised the fact that she had seen the sense and the cast-iron logic of my argument. Silently, I knew that I was grasping at straws and had the sneaking suspicion that she thought so, too. There was also another feeling, one of hope that Cole had attended *all* her advanced-driving skills courses as we were now giving a very good impression of a virtual-reality racing car in some death-race futuristic game. I knew that whenever I played one of Lisa's such games, I always spun off into flames. Her skill on the wheel better be a sight more skilled than mine on a console. Or at driving.

***

We arrived at the school in just over the hour, which she was at pains to explain to me, was solely due to the fact that I was a really crap map reader. She prayed for the restoration of Satnav. Otherwise, she asserted, we would have been here in less than fifty. I didn't argue; I was still recovering from the replication she had created of the Indy 500. I unclenched my hands from the map book, ignoring the claw marks in the paper. Approaching the building, I tried to get my heart, breathing, and various other general bodily functions approaching normality.

The time was 11:35 p.m., and according to the net, Marie Williams was to have finished addressing a meeting over the structure of health provision in a Socialist society at 10:45 p.m. I wasn't overly worried that we were late, as I knew Marie well. She always spent at least half an hour after a meeting going over what she had said, what others had said, questions asked, questions answered, points raised, points ignored, and often as not, why the IT had not worked. Plus, meetings always overran with comrades from rival grouplets keen to score points off us.

We swung into the front playground of the Bainbridge Primary School. Apart from a pair of goalposts (one broken) and a handful of cars parked at the far side, by the red brick wall of the school building, it was empty. Either this had been a very poorly attended meeting, with the good folk of Camden not caring—revolutionary or otherwise—about how clinics were going to be run in utopia, or they had all gone home. I wondered who the remaining cars belonged to. Cole parked parallel to the end one, a rather flash one, rather too flash for your usual party groupie hack.

I saw a middle-aged man slowly get up from a park bench by what I guessed was the entrance. And that was what it said above the door. He ambled towards us, belly flopping over ironed jeans. He certainly did not walk like she drove. Despite the distance between his original sitting position and the car being not much further than twenty metres, we had enough time to turn the engine off, unbuckle, and get out of the car. I even had enough time, despite being a lifelong atheist—to offer a silent prayer to the God of safe journeys (or should it be a saint—Saint Christopher? No, at that speed, a fully paid-up and professional God is required). If this was security, then we had some way to go before we caught up with the presidential bodyguards.

He turned out to be the site manager who was waiting for the meeting to end. That surprised me. To end? How many were in the meeting—a dozen, or did they all walk? He explained in a gentle, amused manner that the main meeting had indeed finished, but she was having a follow-up.

Cole gave him a big solidarity smile and told him that we were due to have a chat with her ourselves. He didn't ask why; he obviously wasn't that bothered.

"Who is she meeting?" Cole asked.

He shrugged. "Damned if I know. All I do know is that whatever it said on the blog, the health meeting was always due to end at 9:30 p.m. This morning I got a call to keep it open a little longer, also, if one of the classrooms could be opened for them. The main meeting, the one on health, was in the hall. Well-attended, actually; we can seat eight hundred, and all the chairs were taken, and there must have been a couple of hundred standing on top of that."

After telling us where to find this little gathering, we left him returning to his bench. He hadn't even asked our names. Passing the reception desk, we entered the hall, which still had the chairs out and the usual residue from meetings—leaflets, papers, coffee mugs, and the odd bottle of water—and took a hard left, passing several storerooms and the medical room, and headed upstairs. We had not discussed how we were going to play this. Cole obviously thought I had some master plan. She was wrong, but I was not going to correct her. I was just not ready for another one of her seminars about our possible options.

The school smelt like a school. We were hoping to change many things in this world, but could we ever get rid of the cocktail of disinfectant, sweat, and paint which schools always smelt of? Could we ever get years five, six, and seven to wash and years eight and nine to go easy on the cheap deodorant? Or was that just asking too much? We passed PE kits hanging off coat pegs and coat pegs hanging off paint, which was hanging off walls barely hanging on.

Children's displays of pictures, poems, and stories of how a new world might look were packed onto impeccably put-up backing paper. Judging by the pictures, the future would be one of lots of bright food, happy dogs, and people with large round heads and no eyebrows.

The site manager had said that they were meeting in Class 5F, which was at the end of the corridor. We were a few classes away when we heard a class door rustily open. A voice was heard before a body was seen, saying goodbye and promising to ring her later. It was a voice I recognised. I grabbed the nearest door handle. In the movies they are always unlocked, allowing the hero or heroine (let's not be sexiest, even when there was about to be an embarrassing and possibly dangerous collision) to find an escape hatch. This one—thank the great scriptwriter in the sky—was, too. But I resisted the temptation to thank God, *a* God or saint, of convenient bolt-holes, as time was short, so I merely opened it and ran in. Cole followed, looking a little puzzled. Maybe she thought I was popping in to catch up on some marking. I silently shut the door and knelt down. Showing puzzlement mixing with amusement, she did likewise.

Seconds later, a group of three voices passed us. The loudest and the one I had originally heard was the pompous snivel that Glen Bale called speech. He was discussing his plans for tomorrow, which he grandly informed his companions involved a trip to Watford. The response he received was not the applause he no doubt craved but a stiff reply matching him in self-regard from Michael Hughes. His step was steady and confident. I heard Aldershot mentioned but nothing else. I could not tell who the third was until they were nearly at the end of the corridor, and then I heard the laugh. So the third musketeer was Kye Toulson. Their voices and his merriment travelled past the debris of the school day and walked downstairs.

Like some cheap 2030s sitcom on an obscure satellite channel, still on my knees, I opened the door and peered around to see if the coast was clear. It was. I beckoned Cole to follow. I had hoped to swagger and confront; instead, it was turning into pantomime. She looked at me with a raised eyebrow. I tried to brass it out. "We can see to them later, but I want her to be alone."

"Of course," she replied in a tone which I could not decide if it showed trust in my strategy or merely mirth at the cloak-and-dagger of it all. I would not have blamed her if it had been the latter. Brushing dozens of tiny bits of cut paper off my knees, I tried to reassemble an image of competent but laconic purpose.

We entered the classroom and saw Marie with her back to us by the window, peering at something in her hands. She was dressed in a dull, shapeless, blue dress and black rubber-soled shoes, which, even knowing her lack of interest in clothes, I could guess was health-service vogue.

Between her and us, on one of the tables, were a few sheets of paper and a top-of-the-range computer. It was on and mid program. Hearing us, she turned, her face changing from surprise to distaste. Her mouth opened to say, no doubt, something far from complimentary. After our last meeting, I did not expect a warm embrace, a kiss on the cheek, and a compliment on the suit. So I got in first. "Well, Marie, we meet again." Why I wanted to sound like a Bond villain, I had no idea, but as I had no pure white cat to stroke, I tried to adopt a more normal voice. "And here you are, once more meeting with our friends on this *secret subcommittee*. What was it about this time—discussing the standard of food provided for the children? Governments might change, but that never does, hey?"

I spoke quickly, with authority and heavy sarcasm borne of a sense of urgency and fear. As I did, I swung the computer around. Behind me, I could hear Cole dragging a chair to sit down, in front of the door.

Marie barked, "What the hell do you think you're doing?"

Obviously, there was little of our friendship remaining. How quickly it had been lost, but now was not the time to mourn it. I kept my reply strong but casual. In my mind this was the fictional PIs of Marlowe, Spade, or Archer. "Seeing what you scamps are up to." I looked down at the hovering screen. "Maybe you've been deciding on a new menu for the infants or… what the…"

In front of me was a kaleidoscope of data—graphs, maps, and virtual imagery. It was hard to make sense of. One appeared to be a diagram of the country's power grid, with arrows and circles. Elsewhere, there was a graph showing something called transmission levels. Both were running with what looked like a simulation of soldiers attacking buildings and telecommunication masts.

"I said leave it alone, Pete; this is not your business!" She started to walk towards me, not a dive or a vault, just a movement, but it was still a little too quick for Cole's liking. She jumped to her feet and shouted for Marie to stay where she was.

It didn't impress Marie. "Piss off!" she snarled and reached for the computer.

A blur was all I saw of Cole as she launched herself at Marie, grabbed her arm, and swung her around 180 degrees. Marie, though, was not one of your cowered victims who just meekly accepted a cuffing from a copper—not after years of battling them on the Cities' streets; that and the experience of dealing with uppity NHS patients meant she was going to do one thing—put up a fight. And she did—with a smart back kick that caught Cole on top of the thigh. She groaned, let go of Marie, and fell on one knee. Obviously, she had missed a few of the hospital brawling twilight sessions, because she was unable to press the advantage; she crashed into a desk, sending rulers and pencils scattering in all directions. A palm PC fell to the floor, bouncing under the table. It must have been what she had been looking at when we entered.

Unsure of what to do, I stepped forwards. It was pretty lame, but I didn't know quite what the correct course of action should be. Here was an old friend—OK, in all probability an ex-friend—fighting a member of the police service, but it was the latter whom I had come with. So who do I come to the aid of? Do I tackle Marie? Tackle Cole? Stand there spread-eagled to separate them? To my way of thinking, I wasn't capable of any of them. Neither were damsels in distress. In any case, Cole was much quicker than my thoughts. In one movement she got back on both feet and aimed a fierce karate chop to the back of Marie's neck. Marie howled in pain. Cole positioned herself to one side, clear of any further kicks, yanked Marie around, and threw her onto a chair. Landing heavily, Marie fell back, rocking it on its base. As she pitched forwards, Cole gave her a backhanded slap across her right cheek, and in a single movement, which had obviously been learnt at cop school, she pulled out of her trousers what looked like blue nylon tags and snapped them around both wrists, binding Marie to the chair.

I stared with a mixture of disbelief and confusion. Revulsion battled with a sense of need. I had known Marie for so long as a friend and comrade, and here I was, witnessing her get beaten up by a police officer. And yet, if what I thought was happening turned out to be true, then it was justified.

Marie sat stunned. Her red hair, which had previously been harshly clipped back, had come unmoored and had flopped over her ears. Cole was searching her pockets and patting her down. She took out a wallet and a phone. Turning around, her professionalism slipped a bit, her voice betraying concern, and she growled, "It better be important what you've got there!"

Glancing at the screen, which had now changed, and at the papers on the tables, I mumbled, mainly to myself rather than to her. "I think so; these are diagrams of the air routes over the country and the airports and aerodromes and these…these…are the roads linking them." This was interesting stuff, and it was my guess that the comrades had not been planning their hols. One box had popped up, showing virtual yellow arrows pointing to sections of the city maps with a dizzying array of pie charts springing up all over the shop. It was all moving at speed, but if I couldn't understand the details, I was getting the broad sweep of it all.

Leaning across Marie, Cole fished out something black and showed it to me. It was a small, very neat, black gun. "NHS issue, do you think?"

"Piss off!" was the articulate reply. Marie had, it seemed, come out of her daze. Her eyes had lost their glaze and were now focussed on Cole. "It's protection against attacks from the likes of you!" She let out a stream of bile and abuse, focussed mainly at me, but taking in Cole as well, which, as she did not know her personally very well, was more generic than individual. Actually, some of her comments about police officers and the sincerity of those who had switched to our side were ones I had much sympathy with. Not so true were the ones aimed at me. They were rather harsh and personal, *very* personal.

"Christ, Pete! I know you've had a breakdown, but that does not excuse this shit. You feel guilty about killing your wife and child—well, that's understandable; frankly, you should. You always were a crap driver, but what is this trash?" She tugged at the tags binding her. Her venom deepened to match her bruised cheek. From personal experience I knew that it would turn several lovely shades of purple and green. Cole was an artist with her blows. The air was also turning blue; here was a comrade who did not go along with comrade Peary's ideal of a world of civilised conversations—she was exploding with fury.

I ignored her and went through the files. She had obviously been using them with Toulson, Hughes, and Bale because they were open and completely unprotected. Judging from the detailed and knowledgeable comments alongside the pictures, I would guess that those esteemed radicals had played a major part in creating them. Cole was standing behind me and watching. With many of them, we could only guess what they were, appearing to be whole reams of IT jargon, but others were more obvious with an extensive amount devoted to transport and communications.

Marie had stopped denouncing the role of the police in our society and my mental stability and was just watching us. She spoke quietly. "You should not be looking at that. You do not know what it means."

Our eyes met. Oh, I knew. I knew very well what it meant. All those secret meetings with the others—I knew what they were about.

I straightened up. "Marie, can you explain why you were one of the first people Jackie told about Alan's suicide?"

For a moment she looked confused. "What? I don't know; she trusts me, I suppose, unlike you, who seems to think he's in the middle of a John Buchan novel." She turned and sneered at Cole. "He'll explain who he was, *Officer.*"

Despite myself, I grinned.

With a voice so cold it would have frozen Venus, Cole asked, "And is it explained in *The Thirty-Nine Steps,* why and how, at the same time as you were being informed of Alan Wiltshire's suicide, my phone and computer were being bugged?"

"Good God, the insanity is spreading. Officer...*comrade*... Victoria...why the hell would I do that? Or indeed know how to! Do you really believe his," she nodded in my direction, "absurd idea that I work for the ruling class!"

The three of us looked at each other in total silence. I could feel my heart pumping against my rib cage. My throat was constricting with unbearable dryness. Christ! In front of me was a woman I had known for the majority of my adult life. Her husband is, *was,* one of my closest friends. Lisa had played with her children, and Caroline had got drunk with her. I looked deep into her eyes and then down to the computer. It was showing a film of travelling along the Channel Tunnel.

We could not give up. Personal feelings were not important here. Not with what was here. "So how come you cannot account for last Friday? The day Jenny Underhill was murdered? You were not where you said you were, and you know, Marie, I cannot think why you would lie to me. So, where the hell were you, Marie?"

"None of your business. It is not your concern. Now untie me—*untie me now!*"

I almost choked on the words. "I'm sorry; we can't do that. This is too important."

"Important? You pompous ass! You self-obsessed egomaniac. Important? More like fantastical!"

Looking up at her, I forced the words out. "Marie, if it is so fantastical, then how come after we accused you of being a traitor, you didn't react? You didn't report me to Jackie or to the Central Committee or to the Internal Democracy Commission." The words were choking me, but it had to be said. "Why did you take no action, Marie? If that had happened to me, I would have had you hounded out of the party, but you did nothing. I would have smeared you as being uncomradely and a Stalinist scumbag, but you did nothing. Why, Marie? Why didn't you do anything? Why the hell not?"

"You are off your head, Pete, off your head! You're not making any sense. I didn't, because there are more important things going on right now than your illusions." She turned her head to look at Cole. "Victoria, I know you are doing what you think is right, but this is madness. Surely, you cannot attach any credence to Pete's fantasies. Untie me. For heaven's sake, believe me. It wasn't me who bugged your phone or killed Dave. If Pete was thinking clearly and wasn't befuddled by grief, he wouldn't for a second think I could do that to him." Her self-control had been only temporary, and once more it was breaking, or she wanted to give the appearance of it doing so. She yanked at the bindings and tried to stand. She screamed, "I virtually grew up with Dave, for goodness' sake. I could not have done that to him! It was not me!"

"No, I think it probably wasn't."

I spun around and stared at Cole. What had she said? Had she really said what I thought she had?

CHAPTER TWENTY-SEVEN
In Defence of Marxism

Oh, Li, what have I done? Like a pair of naughty kids whose game had got out of hand and had ended up exchanging blows, Cole and I sat at a desk, awaiting the head. She sat, arms crossed, whilst I fiddled with a pencil sharpener. I couldn't speak for her, but I knew that I had a real sense of unease at what was going to be said. My excuses were to hand, and blame was ready to be thrown, because I had more than a feeling that this was not going to be pleasant. It had not been the nicest of things we had decided to do, but at least we had had good reason. But that was before Cole's volte-face.

After ushering me out of the class and away from Marie's fuming incendiary stare, she had followed me into the adjacent classroom and had leant against a wall, the amateur shrink in me surmising that she was using it for support because she felt vulnerable. Her comment had been a cold slap, like a haddock across your cheeks on a freezing-cold Aberdeen morning. "Comrade, I don't think she is the one." Her voice was deliberate because she was iron-solid in the belief that we had made an almighty screw-up.

Not wanting to even consider that a long-standing friend and leading member had been assaulted, bound, and accused of murder and betrayal for sweet FA, I had demanded to know what she had meant. What on God's earth did she mean that she believed her? I was outraged; we had done all that, and we were wrong! I wanted to—*needed* to—believe that we were right. If we were, then perhaps, maybe, double-perhaps, we could say that we had been justified in doing it.

"You asked her why she had not reported you after you had accused her," she had explained, noticeably using the singular and, in particular, the singular about the singularly yours truly. "Any innocent member would have done so. But that's the wrong way of looking at it. Think about it, Pete. What can we say about the killer? We can say that he or she is ruthless in self-protection and will act decisively to do so. Any hint of danger and the killer would move to neutralise it. And yet, despite accusing her face-to-face, she did nothing—*against* us. If she was the one who planted the listening bugs, then she would have known that we were trying to build a case against her. If so, why did she not eliminate us? Why did she not either discredit or even kill us?"

I hadn't an answer. I merely punched the wall. Or rather, I did a fake, pathetic, quasi-macho punch. The killer knew what we were doing and had taken no action because, put simply, we were doing the wrong thing. We were focusing on Marie and not him or her. There was no need to kill us when laughing was all that was required.

Oh, Li, what have I done?

I had been the one who had rung Jackie and informed her of our actions. She, as it happened, was in town, having just finished appearing on a late-night London news programme discussing the riots with the home secretary. It would be fair to say that my call had managed to piss her off far more than the minister possibly could have.

We were in the class next to 5F, probably for our own safety. It was very much like the one we had been in—all number squares and examples of the children's writing. Not that we were admiring the sweet kiddies' work; we were sitting there, crapping ourselves. Marie was now untied, and despite these classes being made of solid Victorian brickwork designed to muffle the noisiest of classes, we had heard her telling Jackie what had happened and what should happen to us, mainly to me. I was thankful that the revolution had no immediate plans for firing squads because, otherwise, Marie would have been commanding one right now. And she would insist that I not be allowed a blindfold. It could best be said that Marie was not a happy bunny at the moment.

Outside, four large, heavily armed guards, Jackie's increased protection, stood chatting. All we needed was one of them to be a relative of Marie's or the spouse of a former patient of hers, and that firing squad could well become a reality.

Comrades Come Rally

After twenty minutes the noise from next door subdued. They were obviously now talking in standard volumes. Or to be more precise, Marie now was. We had been unable to hear Jackie because she had been listening and speaking as you might expect a human being to do. We had heard Marie because she had been raging and yelling, like a wounded bear might do.

I heard class 5F's door open and saw one of the guards move, presumably summoned by Jackie whose sling I could just see through the glass. Straining to hear what was being said, I only caught that he was to drive her home after she was *done*. As he left, our door opened and Jackie came in. We were about to be done.

She was wearing black- and white-checked, sharply pressed trousers, flat shoes, and a neat, tight-fitting cream shirt. A small, leather, black briefcase hung over one shoulder whilst the other supported her right arm hanging at ninety degrees in a white sling. Her fingernails, like her lipstick, were a gentle lilac. That was not the colour of her mood. Ridiculously, considering the human effluence we were in, I caught myself wondering whether or not you could actually have a lilac mood. But whatever—Jackie was most definitely not in one!

Marching in, she gave me a look, which in books might have been described as being withering, but that would not have done it justice. It was far, far harsher than that. It was a look that could have caused mammals to self-combust.

With her one good hand, she pulled out a chair and sat before us, took a phone out of her trouser pocket, and turned it off. Laying her bag on the desk, she opened it, took another two of them out, and turned them off, too. Yet another one was taken out, a battered relic of several decades ago, but this one was turned to silent. This was not looking good. Finally, out came a packet of cigarettes and a lighter. I was surprised; I thought she had given up years ago, but I did not say anything. Now really was not the time to discuss health issues or will-power. Our situation was cigarettes and incommunicado—not good.

Silently, she offered Cole one, who declined. It was the first clue that she might be feeling as nervous as I was. I could see her tighten her arms and guessed that she was dying for a fag but did not trust her hands to hold it. Cole—a human being in shock!

Jackie lit up, took a few drags, and then, not even looking at me but at a display of planets, simply said, "Explain."

And so I did. Most of it she already knew, but she seemed to want to hear the whole debacle from the beginning again. Noticeably, it was me who went through it. Cole just sat there, arms crossed, looking ready to be punished. I explained that it was our opinion that whilst Alan had been researching, he had seen a picture of someone he had once known as a comrade but had discovered that she was a policewoman. She had been known in the party as Jelena Jacobs, but her real name was Jenny Underhill. He even had had a brief romantic thing with her. I stumbled over why the hell I would call anything a "romantic thing," but I continued.

"My guess,"—actually it was *our* guess, but I was the one who seemed to have been nominated to be the fall guy, so I might as well take what microscopic glory there was to be had—"is that she was the trap to get Alan hooked. We don't know how they managed it, or what it was, but it was something bad enough to make him feel that the shame and fear of the party's reaction was worse than working for the state."

Saying the words out loud did not give them any more substance. When it was in my brain, it sounded plausible, but hearing it did quite the opposite. But I had committed myself to telling it, so I persevered. "How much he told them over the years, we have no idea. He could have given them nothing, a little, or everything he knew; we cannot say. We also have no idea whether he recruited anyone else to work for MI5.

"Perhaps that was what Dave found out when he visited Jenny Underhill and found out that she was Jelena Jacobs. Maybe she informed him of one person he had turned. Or maybe Alan had a minder in the party. Whatever it was, our guess is that Dave had found out about another agent in the party. That was why he and Yasmin had been killed—to silence them. After, that is, they had been tortured to find out if anyone else knew their secret."

The more I spoke, the more it all sounded so trite. Maybe, possibly, probably—all had the substance of sand. The hope was that Jackie would not ask what proof we had for all this because I would have to whistle and change the subject. I couldn't see that she would be impressed by my rendition of *Strangers in the Night* and a discussion about the best plants to put by a pond. But the plain truth was that this was all built on pretty flimsy evidence. No, that wasn't fair; there was not much in the way of evidence. It was guesswork which was holding it all up.

I had a desperate urge to pull at my collar as I felt my body temperature rising. The room suddenly felt very small, with it almost sticking to us, like a large ball of cling film which had developed a mind of its own.

My unease slightly lessened when Jackie waved away some smoke; blowing it to one side, she injected some light relief to the moment. "Taylor, the caretaker, sorry...*site manager*, will have my guts if he knows I'm smoking in here." She put the cigarette under the table whilst looking around for the smoke detectors. Smiling, she mumbled to herself, "A fugitive from bylaws."

The respite was far too brief, as, for the first time, Cole spoke. "The senior officer, who was working with me on the Wiltshire case—Detective Inspector Martin, reckoned the murders of David and Yasmin were coolly and efficiently done. It was not some random act of savagery but one of deliberate cruelty."

The smile disappeared, and a shudder visibly crossed Jackie's shoulders as she continued listening and smoking, whilst returning to study the orbits of the planets in the solar system.

"And this person," Cole continued, "was so fearful of being caught that they sent a virus to my computer so they could monitor what I was doing. The same happened to Pete's when you contacted him."

I pointed out how the timings coincided with Marie's involvement.

Then there was the issue of her arrest for assault on a police officer which had been mysteriously dropped.

"After a long and successful campaign to defend her," Jackie stated, with a little annoyance.

"After the intervention of a member of the security services by the name of Charles Hutchinson," I replied, proceeding to tell her about the fact that her file had been flagged by MI5 as not to continue with any prosecution.

She did not look impressed. "So far, you have not really given me much. So tell me, Pete," she bowed her head a little in Cole's direction, "and Vic, what was it that specifically prompted you to come here and terrorise Marie… and what made you stop?"

Cole perked up once more. She wanted credit for the last bit. She explained how she had realised that if Marie was the killer, she would have already taken action against us. If we were correct in our hypothesis, then whoever was the mole was prepared to do anything to conceal the fact. What was done to David and Yasmin was proof of that. A bug had already been inserted in our computers that would have been monitoring every communication we made, and the mole would have known exactly what we were doing. So if it was her, then why hadn't she acted against us?

With her good arm still below the table, using it to shield the cigarette, Jackie asked what Cole could do to trace who might have placed the bug. Cole unfolded her arms and went all keenie on us, explaining in depth the collapse of the police force and all their systems. I wasn't sure whether she was telling Jackie all this to boast about the power of class in the struggle, to bemoan how hampered we'd been, or to remind Jackie what a wow newly-join she was. Whatever the reason, Jackie lifted the fingers of the slung arm to show that she got the message.

"Maybe Glen Bale could do something," she suggested.

Just great, Bale comes riding over the horizon to save us all.

Putting aside such a calamitous thought, I asked, "I'm still troubled, though," still thinking that there was something important being missed here, "about the fact that she made no complaint against us when we challenged her. That shows some evidence of guilt to me".

I was sounding pitiful now. Trying to accuse her of anything just to justify my actions. Nicking next door's recycling bins was going to be next on my list.

Jackie turned and faced us. Looking at her, I could see how drained she looked. Her hair, bobbed today, had lost its usual TV ad shine. She looked tired. Knackered. I wondered when was the last time she had had anywhere approaching a decent night's sleep. Not to mention the effect a bullet has on one's health.

"She did complain, Pete—to me. She wanted you expelled for uncomradely and anti-democratic behaviour. She *certainly does so now*, and more, besides. I really would not expect any future invites to barbecues around Williams's house anytime soon. What you did to Marie is unforgivable. You two have behaved in a bullying and violent manner, which is not becoming to a party member. When news of you assaulting and imprisoning Marie goes public, you are going to face demands for sanctions against you that I will not be able to protect you from, and, to be honest, I not sure that I would want to. She wants your—"

Passive had never been my thing, and just sitting here having my hand slapped was not my style. I had an urge to slap back. "So, Jackie, why did you stop her from doing so? Seems to me that if she is so pure and innocent, then she should have been allowed to take any action she thought was reasonable. Why did you deny her that right?"

I leant forwards, hostility rising in my voice. "And why, Jackie, have you been so keen for us to continue? It's all very well, us sitting here having to defend ourselves, but we have just been doing exactly what you wanted us to do. What is this, Jacks? We do the dirty work—*your* dirty work—and you stay blameless? Why have you been so keen to give me the space to look into the matter? If the party wants to investigate my actions, then let them do so, because they can also investigate your role in all of it. You knew what you were doing and what you had asked me to do. So I repeat, why have you given me such freedom?"

Cole looked wide-eyed at my threat to make sure that the great Goddess Payne would share in the fallout to come. In her recently acquired revolutionary fervour, she had perhaps become a little love-struck, but she underestimated her leader.

Jackie herself was unperturbed and flicked some ash away. After thinking for a moment, she came to a decision, and with coolness personified she told us why. "Because I have no doubt that we have been infiltrated by the security services. Various, shall we say, party 'initiatives,' have been predicted by the government, and," she waved her sling, "it was not planned for me to be at the meeting when I got this. I was actually due to fly to Paris to discuss the international situation with our European comrades. But the CC felt that in light of the recent troubles, it was important that I stay here and address it. It was pretty much a last-minute decision—so how did the sniper know I was going to be there?"

"So you harboured a few vague doubts and decided it would be a whizz to get us to go around kicking over stones."

"I'm not sure about your terminology, Pete, but yes, that's about right."

We were in class, but I was in no mood to be given lessons on literacy. "It wasn't exactly hard to guess that you'd be there, Jacks…Jackie; I would have expected you to be. You must have other reasons for thinking that they have people in the party. And, anyway, your shooting came well after you had dragged—and let's not forget, Jackie, that yes, *you dragged*—*me* into all this. It can surely not be a surprise that the state security forces would be taking an interest in us, but why are you so bothered about it at this present moment in time?"

She replied with some bland waffle about wanting to clean the crap of the past off our shoes. Did she have an answer, I wondered, as to why, if Marie was such an innocent, did she lie to us as to what she was doing the day Jennifer Underhill was murdered? My tone was one of a challenge.

Undisturbed, she looked at me and met it. "She was with me, Pete. We were working together on something. I can vouch for her. She was nowhere near the North. Unless you count a comrade's flat in Enfield as the North, that is, but she has an alibi. I am it."

My partner-in-the-shit just sat there and accepted the reply as being perfectly reasonable, but as I had said on the way here, I was tired of piss-balling about.

"She was with you," I repeated. "And you did not think to mention that incy-wincy fact to us?"

"I had my reasons."

"Did these reasons have anything to do with that little secret subcommittee of yours?"

She didn't answer but just blew out some smoke and then frantically waved it down. I guess that's why I had always wanted to smoke—you looked so cool, it helped keep the weight off, and you could use it to buy time.

"You don't need to be coy," I said, wanting an answer. "It's been bloody obvious from the beginning that this cosy committee is more than just liaising with other groups in the workers' councils. The people on it are too important and meet too often for that to be the reason. And it is suspicious to say the least, how many times one of them says they were somewhere, when in fact they weren't. That suggests that there are secret meetings going on. Which, let's face it, you would not have to do if the only thing you are discussing is how to work with the Democratic Lefts or the Anarchist Federation. What would you be frightened of? That they might steal your chocolate digestives?"

I swallowed hard and took the decision that it was time for me to tell her that I knew what was going on. "Alan was researching the methods of policing insurrections. Then, right here we have half the committee looking at the infrastructure of the country. You might want to ask yourself why they would be doing that. So let's look at the committee's membership itself because it is pretty instructive. We have you—leading member and the political heavyweight; Marie—leading trade union comrade and works in health; Toulson—trade union and transport; Bale—IT; Harrison—power; Ali—water; and of course Hughes—the country's face of the army council. It reads like an A–Z of careers. Or, to put it another way, the kind of comrades you'd want if you were planning the insurrection. How am I doing, *comrade?*"

There was a faint smile on her lips which were resting on the cigarette. Glancing at Cole, I imagined that she was wishing she had taken one herself. She was looking at me, with lips apart and with a face that said, "What the?"

I was so glad that I had impressed my friend here. But I hadn't finished. "Now what I have not been able to figure out is whether you are working with the support of the Central Committee or not. You see, Jackie, I trust you with my life. You are the most honourable person that I have ever met, that anyone has ever met. I cannot imagine that you would organise a coup, because that is what it would be, well, a coup. Without authorisation from the NWC or the Central Committee, the party, let alone the working class as a whole, it would be a putsch with no legitimacy. The net is full of such thoughts. There is a distinct group who believes that either the party as a whole, or a secretive cabal within the party, is about to do just that. We have never shied away from the fact that the ruling class would not passively hand over power but would have to be forced to do so. Meaning that armed action might have to be taken, but the understanding has always been that this would only be considered when the majority of the class demands that course of action. For all our positive thinking, that is not the case now."

Pausing, I waited for a reaction. Neither woman spoke. Indeed, Jackie showed no response; not a facial muscle twitched. She just sat there watching me. As for Cole, she was sporting an expression Edward Munch would have been proud of.

Not receiving any astounded gasps of wonder, I continued my Poirotesque explanation (although perhaps he was unlikely ever to have elucidated on the seizing of state power). "We have the majority of the delegates in the workers' councils, but as you have said on countless occasions, that does not automatically equate to supporting revolution. There has been no mobilisation for such a call and no political campaign to build the foundation for one. This is not our politics. It would be an adventure by minority, not a working-class revolution. But I think the net gossip for once has a point that needs addressing. So, Jacks, are you planning a coup?"

She looked around the table and seeing what she wanted, reached across and got something shiny. It was a pencil sharpener, which she used to stub out her cigarette. Then she gave me her full attention. "And what is your opinion, Pete?"

I met her gaze. "Jackie, there is no one I look up to more than you—personally and politically, but I am not going to give some dumb speech praising you. But, well, if you have organised a coup, then get one of your boys out there, and get them to put a bullet in my brain."

Flattery rarely had any effect on her and overblown statements less so. Coolly, she asked, "And if it has been authorised by the Central Committee?"

"Then," I sighed, "unless the great and the good on the CC have good reasons—and they would have to be bloody good ones—the party has just lost a member."

This was a big moment for me. I felt the room crushing my skull. Cole looked like the proverbial rabbit caught in front of a car at night. Jackie, though, did not seem that tense. A broad grin appeared, and with her good arm, she reached across and patted my hands. "Oh, Pete, ever the Democrat, and ever the drama queen," she chuckled. "I don't want to besmirch your intellect or question your political analysis, but perhaps there is a third alternative. What if I am not the one organising a coup, nor is the CC, nor is even the party, but someone else? Did you consider that possibility?"

Cole blurted out, "The anarchists? The Democratic Lefts?"

I looked at her. Idiot. Who else was she going to suggest—the neighbourhood watch? It wasn't them, but I realised *who* Jackie meant. It was unbelievable.

"The government," I said, almost in a trance. "The government itself is planning a military coup to regain a hold on the situation."

She pulled her hand back and tapped the table in way of applause.

But why? How? She read my unspoken questions and explained. "They have tried squeezing the working class to pay for the crisis, but when the class refused to pay any more, they have been in a quandary, flitting between the carrot and the stick. With the economy in its present mess, buying off the opposition has become a non-starter. That leaves the stick. They tried using armed force to suppress the movement two years ago, but that was a disaster. Every time they escalated the suppression, it escalated the struggle. Using water cannons and rubber bullets all merely inflamed the situation and made things worse for themselves. The riot police could not cope, so they called in the army. That, as we all well know, just pushed the doubters over to our side. Calling a state of emergency only poured petrol on the flames. Soldiers refused to fire on their brothers and sisters, and splits appeared. That's when Hughes joined us, creating the party caucus within the army."

Cole piped up. "And the police fell apart. They're weaker than they were back then. They failed then; why would they succeed now? The army would not follow such orders."

Good God. "Unless…" The air routes, the Channel Tunnel, and the ports—it was dawning on me.

Jackie and I looked at each other. It was as if Cole wasn't there.

"Unless," I continued, finally getting it, "unless the government is not relying on British troops to take power but are planning to bring in foreign ones. The British government is going to call foreign troops to be used against British workers?"

She dipped her head. "Why not? We believe in international solidarity; why be surprised that they do? The British ruling class has never been timid about doing so. George III used German troops to try to quell the American War of Independence, as indeed did George II at the Battle of Culloden against the Scots."

Then all those international meetings with generous offers of cash bailouts had strings attached. The strings being that the British Spring had to be brought to an end. They wanted summer cancelled and to call in winter. And within all those seasonal references came a stark reality: the money from the other countries alongside their troops would be sent over to bring order back to the country.

Of course, even in the last century, countries had called in foreign powers to aid a crippled ruling class—the old Soviet Bloc or NATO, or the latest coalition of stooges to support whatever Washington wanted, but somehow this seemed a totally different matter. The idea was just too extreme to be believed. How could it work? I could conceive the concept of the prime minister authorising such action, because I would not put anything past him, but surely other members of Parliament would not countenance such action.

"But would they be able to control a whole country? Could they hope to suppress a seething and hostile population, one that has become politicised and one that has become ever more confident in its own strength?"

Jackie didn't answer; instead she let the questions hang there, as if daring me to answer them myself.

Who knew what Cole was thinking, or even if such a novel experience was an uncomfortable thing for her. Certainly, she didn't answer, but—and perhaps predictably—she was more concerned with what the state itself would do in response to such a blatant attack on its sovereignty. With her hands gesticulating wildly, she heatedly questioned the possibility. "But surely British troops would not tolerate foreign troops patrolling the streets of London, Manchester, and Leeds? Surely they are not going to sit idly by as US hit squads marched into their own home towns? I don't believe that they are going to stay confined to barracks if NATO, EU, UN, or whoever are rounding up British civilians. It would mean street fighting between professional armies on an unprecedented scale!"

Jackie replied in a tone and manner you would use if describing a method to construct a wardrobe. "The idea is to mobilise what troops are loyal to the government; they estimate that accounts for approximately forty percent presently on British soil and up to sixty percent abroad. The latter, they presume, are more reliable, because they haven't been 'infected' and so can be trusted. They will be flown, shipped, and driven to swiftly subdue—and you can guess what that may mean—those army elements that are loyal to us and then pen in the others. They'll do the same with the air force and navy. In addition, they hope to call on over half of the police for active participation."

Cole was outraged as someone might be, once they found that the ruling class was not all cricket-loving ladies and gentlemen who played by the rules and helped old ladies cross the road. "Under what pretext could they impose such…such…an invasion?"

Of course. It all made sense. And I was a complete prat. "They have been destabilising the situation, so they can move to a point where they can use the supposed anarchy to justify calling in the army to bring order. The troops they can rely on plus armies from 'friendly brother nations' are to be portrayed as heroes defending the weak. The St Paul's and the Leeds bombings and the other so-called anarchist acts of terrorism have been the government's work to ferment discord!"

She nodded. "Absolutely, as are tonight's riots. Not to mention all the things that have been going on over the past few days. Remember how news was pumped out that I was dead so as to provoke a reaction. Then there were the seemingly senseless and almost suicidal attacks on our supporters. That's just part of the whole destabilisation process. It will be stepped up, and eventually they will call in the army to restore order."

Even if my brain might be feeling ready to explode from the horror of what she was suggesting, it was at the same time working clearly, perhaps for the first time in quite a while. "It can't be the whole government, as that would mean too many people were in on the plan, and, in any case, not all MPs would be in favour of bringing in foreign powers. I don't for a second have any illusions about the suits who sit under Big Ben, but I cannot think that even your average Tory backbencher from the shires would go for this. Smithers-Smythe might support the restoration of the death penalty, but not if Johnny foreigner is flicking the switch; army on the streets—yes, but the Coldstream Guards, not French paratroopers."

With both of us leaning forwards, Jackie somewhat askew because of her slung arm, we could have been mistaken for a pair of lovers. "Actually, it's *nations*, not just one nation; several are preparing troops, including the United States, Turkey, and even China. But you were right—there *is* a small cabal organising an insurrection, only it's around the prime minister—not me. It includes some of the cabinet, several generals, major industrialists, and even a remote royal exiled in Canada.

"Once the situation is deemed appropriate, the PM will call a state of emergency, but unlike the previous times, a further—top secret—procedure will be enacted: Parliament will be suspended, with direct political control passing to the PM and other allotted officials. The cabinet is aware of its existence, but what they do not know is that it will then go onto a whole new level. Any MP seen as unreliable will be arrested. As will any other member of the ruling class; judges, for example, who really believe in fair trials will face imprisonment without one. They'll be the lucky ones, because at the same time, pro-government troops will descend on the leadership of the party, the NWC, and other 'anti-British' organisations. We will not be arrested, just shot. The idea being that such decisive action will behead the movement, and after it is at least momentarily stunned, the foreign troops will be brought in.

"The mass arrests and executions will follow with the hope that within twenty-four hours, we will be once more a land fit for capitalism. That will be the basis for the huge financial bailout that he has arranged with other countries."

Cole came out with a neat sound bite. "The price of economic stability is blood?" Silence answered her. All that could be heard was the gentle, deep chuckling of the guards outside in the corridor.

Jackie continued. "Simultaneously, whilst they are purging unreliable elements, if key areas of the infrastructure cannot be taken over, they will be removed or sidelined. If necessary, because they lack the manpower to replace them, they will simply destroy what's there. That could plunge the country into darkness, with power stations down, the rail paralysed, and the net down. But they consider it a worthwhile action to remove us..."

I was hypnotised by what she said, but exasperation interrupted us. "But why," Cole demanded, "don't you announce this? People would not agree to this state-sponsored vandalism, not even those loyal to Parliament. By making it public, you would stop it dead in its tracks! I think we could get the prime minister indicted for treason. You have to go public! Remember, during the first crisis, when the far-right was campaigning for British action against the united Irish republic, public outrage stopped it. The same could happen here."

And then we all go home happy, get some hot milk and jam on toast, and watch *The Sound of Music*. Still, it was a fair point and one I might have made. And yet hearing it gave me the answer. "Because," I said, "we have been warning the world that the ruling class will resort to violence to protect its interests for as long as we have been in existence. Let's face it—it's the basis of our politics, so few will see it as an emergency unless we can give details and provide specifics of the counter-revolution. And I presume that we do not have those?"

Jackie shook her head. "We have our sources, people who, whilst not supporters of the workers' councils, equally have no wish to see us become a military dictatorship, but they have only been able to tell us so much. We do not know exactly when it is planned, but we have been informed that it will be within the fortnight, and as for where they concentrate their forces, we can only guess…"

So they were guessing—hence the simulations on Marie's computer. They were not to start the revolution or a counterrevolution—they were to prevent one. I felt foolish in the extreme, and, I had to admit, very ashamed. As if I needed the humiliation to be public, I said what I thought this committee had really been doing—the *defence* of the revolution.

"Indeed, Pete, indeed. You were right about how they all hold key posts. Kye has intimate knowledge of the transport system and Harrison the power. These are two important areas we have to control. The government may have the majority of the weaponry, but that does not run trains or power stations. The same applies to the computer network and the water system. All of us, including Marie and me, have some standing in the movement, and faced with such an attack, we could mobilise thousands, hopefully millions, into the defence of the revolution. With Michael providing the armed support, we *might* just win."

Never had Jackie's agreement sounded so sour to these ears. And there was me rampaging around, trampling on everything and everyone. What had I done?

Cole again spoke out. "Why don't we pre-empt them and seize power for ourselves?"

"Because, Vicky, without proof of the government's plans, it would appear to the class exactly how Pete said—that we had seized power in a coup. We might well be able to take power, but whether we could retain it and how we would be forced to keep it, would be another question. Ironically, in doing so, we would in fact weaken ourselves and make us even more vulnerable to attack. It is the Central Committee's view that we wait and prepare, wait and prepare."

Silence returned. I followed Jackie's gaze to the four Galilean moons orbiting Jupiter.

Just then, a faint vibrating noise was heard on one of her phones. She apologised. "Sorry, comrades, I need to get this." She answered it with a noticeable edge to her voice. "Yes, Simon, what's up?"

We heard Simon Peary give her the news of what was happening. Despite keeping his usual urbane calm manner, you could hear, even from across the table, worry in his voice. Jackie herself looked grave, a look that turned even more serious when he informed her that there were concerns being voiced from Michael Hughes about the situation. Bale, it seemed, was in agreement with him.

"What about Olivia and Youssef?" she asked.

"I don't know. I can't reach them at present."

"Find them! And get all the committee to my place as soon as possible. No—make that, at once!" She closed the phone and rubbed her head. It seemed waiting and preparing was becoming a risky strategy.

CHAPTER TWENTY-EIGHT
In Search of a Method

It was gone three in the morning, and I was halfway putting back a mountain of Miles Davis CDs onto a shelf. The original idea had been to rearrange the music and shelve them by genre, but the same old problem arose. What if the band or musician crossed genres? Separate them or keep them together and undermine the concept? And what if the genre, say Mod or Britpop, covered different decades—do I keep the original with the next generation—was retro Britpop the same as Britpop? So I returned to the old, dependable, if mundane, alphabetical order.

After our meeting with Jackie, Cole had dropped me off at Workers' Hall. I had tried to insist on her letting me get there under my own steam, but she had pointed out that, due to the rioting in Central London, all public transport had stopped. Whilst doing an accurate impersonation of spoilt brat in a huff, I had all but stamped my feet and said, "Well, OK then, I'll walk." The idea had been waived away, and she had told me to get in the car.

It had seemed essential for me to pick up my scooter. A lifetime ago I had parked it outside the hall, and it had been a long, long day, and I needed everything at home with me, in its correct place.

The need was great, but it was not the easiest of places to reach, because of the substantial numbers of workers' militia surrounding it. Old Prince Albert would have found it somewhat ironic that the hall Queen Vic had dedicated to his memory contained pesky peasants who were armed to the teeth because of the fear of an attack from those of the higher orders who would like a return to something his Queen might have approved of.

My very own Queen Victoria had dropped me off in, appropriately enough, Victoria Road, which was the closest she could get me. From there, I had to negotiate numerous roadblocks and armed militia along the A315.

Opposite, in Kensington Gardens, which usually contained campsites of people lobbying the NWC, demonstrating against it or supporting it, or people just camping there because they had nowhere else to stay, it was unusually quiet. Only a few tents remained with a few DIY totem poles, but as for people, I could not see any. I had the distinct impression that the area had been cleared because of security issues.

It took seemingly forever to move forwards. Still, after numerous displays of Jackie's video message, I had reached it. Plumes of smoke had billowed up in curls with flames rampaging through many of the surrounding buildings.

A further irony was not lost on me when I heard fire engines emblazoned with party insignia rushing to put out the fires, which the PM claimed had been started by political criminals inspired by class hatred, i.e., us—the party. But of course I now knew that yes, they had indeed been started by such people, but from the other side, *pretending* to be us.

I had got home safe and sound and found that Singh's, my local corner shop, was still open. He had been kind enough to let me have two bottles of wine on tick (even if they were truly foul and worthy only of cleaning the drains), and after gulping down two glassfuls, I had embarked on music classification. I hadn't played any of them; the brief return to wanting to had vanished once more, and I had returned to the sound of silence. But it was nice to feel them again, looking at their cover art, remembering the music, when I had bought them, and what Caroline and Lisa had thought of them. Usually it was Caroline, smiling and humouring me, and Lisa, rolling her eyes and muttering, *Oh, Dad.*

Dozens of news channels kept me company as they reported, in near orgasmic tones, the violence. These were interspersed with talking heads from the party, with a procession of the Central Committee members pointing the finger at agent provocateurs whilst sombre, badly dressed experts discussed the "internal dynamics of civil disturbances." You almost had to admire the front of the prime minister with his plastic outrage and phoney concern at the danger to "lives and property." This, he said, was no time for extremism; the country had to find the middle way. Yeah, like a military dictatorship. Following him, other robots from National Coalition for Negotiating the Crisis Coalition were wheeled out to spew similar platitudes. I played "who's in the know and who's going to get arrested" game as each made an appearance.

Other news was that it was becoming even more likely that the football season was to be cancelled due to the riots. This was a shame, the sports commentator said, because it had been just getting interesting. Especially, he chatted on, as there was news that three of the clubs who had previously folded because of the stock-market collapse were hoping to begin playing again as cooperatives. Personally, as one of them had been an Arsenal bogey team, I was glad they had gone belly-up. His fellow studio expert, who had the personality of a glass door, had nodded and said that, even in these political times, people needed entertainment, something to distract them from their troubles. Never mind, mate, maybe the Chinese infantry had a team. They could start playing after they had marched up Pall Mall. That would distract us from our troubles.

I was bushed, and after sliding Miles's *Siesta* back onto the shelf, I joined Red on the sofa. He was fast asleep, purring away in front of the weather forecast, which said it would be a warm but cloudy day with a top temperature of twenty-two degrees Celsius. The first bottle had been finished off, so I opened the second. It wasn't the greatest of tastes, and my throat felt like a razor had been taken to it, but then in days like these, I shouldn't complain. It was a distraction, after all.

The TV was getting on my nerves, so I turned it off. Plastic friendliness and faked knowledge from the presenters and bullshit from the politicians could be extremely irritating. So I sat and drank. Sat, drank, and stroked the cat.

Oh, Li Li, what the hell happened?

I rolled up my sleeve and saw the white scars where I had sliced off my tattoo with glass. It had once read "Caroline & Lisa" and had gone from my elbow to my wrist on the underside of my arm. I remembered getting it done the month after Lisa had been born at a small tattoo parlour not far from Stoke Newington. Funny how you remembered silly things; so long ago but I could clearly recall standing there in my finest threads behind two young women having sleeves of roses tattooed onto their arms. Mine had been rather simple compared to their artwork. I hadn't even gone for fancy lettering: just Ariel Black, two centimetres high.

Despite having lots of sessions with shrinks, that night, which seemed so long ago, was still a bit of a mystery to me. Of course, I knew the facts; I had smashed up my home and slashed at my arm, but why had it happened just then? Who knew? Why had it been so important to cut out "Caro ne & sa"? Li and Li were my nicknames for them, pronounced Lie and Lee, but why had it mattered so much that I was just left with li and li? No one had explained that to me. Caroline and Lisa were their names, after all, but something in my brain had objected to them. No idea why, but for some reason it was important to me. I just had to have li and li on my arms—not Caroline and Lisa.

Not that you could see them at first, not with the blood and flaps of skin. Then came the bandages. And here I now was. Li, this was one big screw-up.

I traced the lines of the letters with my finger. Yes, one big screw-up. Crap. Now was the time to discuss this with Caroline; she would have known what to do. I looked across to the pills on the table. Not from any desire to end it all; I was past that stage. I hoped. No, from the possibility that perhaps one would lighten the mood, even the keel, get me thinking, blah, blah. How long had it been since I had taken one of them? All things considering, I had done well without them. All this shit and I had held it together—without the happy pills. Well, Li, at least I had done that.

My finger went down the vertical and across the horizontal of the L. I looked down. My vision blurred, and the wetness came. Then sobs tore into me.

***

Cradling my arms, I sloped into the bar. I don't know why I had chosen it. With its spotlessly white walls, eye-burningly bright lights and huge, curved, glass window, it was not what you could call cosy or atmospheric. Still, it looked like the only living thing on the street. I sat on a stool, and the blood poured like a river onto the floor. Glen Bale served me, dressed as an ice-cream man. Obviously posing as Mr Whippy was the look for hacks this spring.

"Look at the mess you're in," he sneered. "Mind the floor, we've had comrades working hard making this spic and span, and then you come in;

suddenly it looks like an abattoir! Whose blood is it? Yours? Caroline's? Lisa's? Dave's? Yasmin's? So much to choose from, isn't there, but you've just let it all wash past, haven't you, Kalder. Never had any depth, did you? And isn't it funny how Yasmin only exists as an afterthought after Dave. She was quite a woman in her time, but you hardly give her a moment's thought. I can really recommend a selection of books dealing with women's oppression."

"Please be quiet, Bale," I mumbled through frozen lips. "I need a drink."

"A red wine, no doubt. Nothing common like a lager, I suppose."

The woman in a red dress looked up from her drink and snarled. I realised that it was Marie. She had lost her muscular frame and looked supermodel thin. She always had had large eyes, but the weight loss and the blue eye shadow had made them almost look like saucers tonight. Suddenly they grew angle-sharp and hard with pure anger, almost taking on the fire of a dragon. "You betrayed me, Peter. You betrayed Caroline, and you betrayed Lisa. You are finished. I will devote my life to destroying you!"

Bale sneered. I could swear that he had whiskers. I had always thought he was a stoat. "You are scum, Kalder. You are all alone! Marie—solid, dependable, working class, loyal Marie—and you accuse her! Her, so dependable!"

"Dependable," she nodded. Dependable.

I was still without a drink and occupied my time by getting a serviette to mop up the blood, but there was too much, and no matter how much I tried it, I couldn't stem the flow.

"The main arteries have been cut. There is no going back," she said, showing a diagram of the arm on her laptop. "We could laser them to close them, but this type of joint wouldn't have that type of equipment here. Oh dear, Pete, what shall you do?"

Marie slid her right hand and touched the hand of the man who was sitting next to her. Dressed in an angular grey suit with a Humphrey Bogart trilby, I hadn't noticed him when I had entered the bar. At first, I thought it was her husband, Ashok, but it was, in fact, Jackie. Both arms, I could now see, were perfectly OK. The sling had been slung. She gave Marie an affectionate pat on her knuckles to reassure her.

With her other hand, Jackie put a cigarette to her lips and asked me, "Now what, Pete? What are you going to do now? Go back to watching the news, going for walks, and having your regular swim? I bet they have missed you at the pool." I could not decide whether her tone was friendly, angry, concerned, or sarcastic.

Agitation shook me. I mopped harder. The blood just would not go. The more I mopped, the more pools appeared on the counter. "This is just so unoriginal!" I shouted. "This must be your doing, Bale? This is cheesy enough to be from you—cheesy, and totally without any hint of original thought! Blood that will not wash. Oh, how very Shakespearian. No, it was just too corny to be that. Trouble is, if it was, it is not me who is the Lady Macbeth!"

"He always likes to show us how much he knows, doesn't he," Bale said, as he wiped the counter. What pissed me off more was that he appeared to be having greater success at cleaning it than I did. His jaw was becoming more angular, and yes, definitely, he had whiskers, which were growing.

Marie agreed, her eyes dark in betrayal. "Oh yes, Glen. Ever since I have known him, he always wants to show us how cultured he is, and how much he knows about music and art. He does so love to strut his learning."

"Art!" Realisation dawned. "Wait!" I shouted—again through sealed lips. "I know this place!" I looked around. I *did* know this bar, even to the mustard door that was now opening.

"See what I mean!" jeered Bale.

"It is not a bar—it's a diner, based on one in Greenwich Village, New York. This is *Nighthawk*s by Edward Hopper! It was painted in 1942, and many people think it's about loneliness."

Bale was not impressed. "Off he goes." Behind him I sensed nodding blank faces.

"But I don't even like this painting—it is too familiar; it's on place mats and cigarette lighters; it's on the wall of every student who feels a little alienated. It's become a cliché in itself. Why am I here?"

Youssef Ali was standing behind Marie, dressed exactly like Jackie, as if they had come hotfoot from the cast of *Guys and Dolls*. "Pompous ass. The painting's popular, so he doesn't like it!"

"What are you doing here?" I demanded. "You shouldn't be here!"

"Why shouldn't I? Do I not fit in here, comrade? What is it that you are saying? You barely notice me; obviously I am not important enough to register in your mind. You have all but forgotten about me, haven't you?"

I tried to protest, but no words came out. I wanted to say that in the painting there was somebody serving a couple and another customer with his back to the viewer, and so there should not be a customer standing, but I was unable to. The look Ali gave me was an accusation. Why did he think that I was ignoring him? I felt a sick feeling, broaching on fear, that he was accusing me of something.

He was joined by Olivia Harrison who appeared in jeans, then changed into a short skirt, and then a trouser suit. It was like some old-fashioned drawn cartoon where the boy with a crew cut flicks the pages of paper quickly so as to obtain movement. As her attire changed, so did her hair—from flowing downwards, to clipped up, to cut close; Mohawk to bob to braids. Her mood seemed to change, too; anger to hysterical laughter to tears to contentment.

"Darlin'," she purred, holding Ali close, "it ain't just you. He barely notices me, either."

Then I found my voice. "You can't be together! Ali's gay! I've met his boyfriend—he supports Spurs!"

"That's me—Asian-posh-gay-Youssef!"

Bale leant on the counter. "Oh, comrade, surely you understand that sexuality is fluid. What are labels? Can't we be all things? Is sexuality predetermined or socially constructed? Is a woman who has had relationships with other women for twenty-five years and then has an affair with a man still a lesbian? Or is she straight? If so, can a few months counterbalance twenty-five years? There are some great articles in back copies of *Revolutionary Worker* I could recommend to you."

Just then Red's claws dug into my arm. For a second or two, I was disturbed enough for my mind to briefly register that this was a dream.

"Why this painting?" I shouted, although whether I did so in the dream or in my bed, I couldn't say.

Hughes marched in—dressed in full combat gear. "Why—what would you prefer? A Picasso or a Miro? What a snob!"

Sitting behind Bale I glimpsed the old man, nursing a pint. "Aye, he always was that. Good comrade in his day, mind."

Panic gripped me.

Standing to attention by Jackie, Hughes barked a reply as if on the parade ground. "Still playing the detective, Kalder! Have you not noticed that there is a revolution on! We want to change the world, and you want to play detective!"

"And not a very smart one, either!" growled Harrison, whilst simultaneously smiling.

Ali now appeared to be some distance from Harrison and had changed from his 1930s gangster look to *High Society* top hat and tails. "Maybe he can go back to looking at paintings and reading. Jackie, dear, will there be a position for an armchair Socialist in our new society?"

My lips might be unable to move, but that didn't mean that I had to take all this crap. "Piss off, wanker!"

Simon Peary affectionately stroked my back. He was dressed like Bale in a white jacket and hat but also had football shorts and wore trainers. "Language, Peter! Let's be civilised now." He disappeared along with the old man, talking about football and whether it would survive in the new society.

"I think Kalder would be ideal in such a position!" bellowed Hughes. My head sunk into my shoulders from the sheer volume of his voice. Did he really have to shout? "In an armchair," he continued at top decibels, "pontificating about culture. Who would be better than Kalder at doing that?"

I heard laughter and saw Kye Toulson at the other end of the bar, bulging out of his jacket with his trilby cocked back, looking for all the world like a 1940s cockney spiv. He was pointing at me with a sausage roll, laughing. As he did, Marie joined him, then Bale, and then the whole bar. Thousands were pointing and laughing, jeering and sneering.

A familiar voice whispered in my ear. I could smell a familiar perfume and knew the touch on my arm.

"Oh, Pete."

I leant into her. "I miss you, Li."

***

I awoke on the sofa to find Red's arse in my face, warm dribble coming down my chin, shirt glued by sweat to my back, and my face soaked with a sheen of tears. For the moment, though, I wasn't concerned with how I might look. I gulped down air and tried to calm down and figure out what had happened.

Obviously, I had fallen asleep. I remembered having the usual dream of us driving along the Sorrento coast, the arguments with Lisa, the seat belts, and then the crash. But then I had found myself in the bar.

I got off the sofa and cleaned myself up with a flannel, grabbed a coffee, and tried to decode the dream, because perhaps my subconscious was trying to tell me something.

Half an hour was wasted trying to figure out what the meaning was of me being in *Nighthawks*. Each new theory got more intricate and farfetched. So I left that and tried to remember as much of it as I could. I could remember all of it; well, I thought I could, as there was no way to really tell, was there? If I had forgotten it, I would not know I had dreamt it.

All the people I had encountered in this farce had been there, and it was obvious as to why Marie had appeared so angry and Bale a dick—because both were. Quite what it said about my opinion of the others didn't bear thinking about, with Michael Hughes barking orders like some 1950s sergeant major, Olivia Harrison dropping her *h's* like a Victorian flower girl, and Youssef Ali articulating like a member of the royal family.

When I had become semi-awake, I had tried to control the dream, but of course that was futile. Trying to have a grip on real life was hard enough, let alone in a fantasy world. If I had managed to, then maybe there would not have been scores of soap stars—past and present—there, joining in with the mass ridicule of me. It didn't take Sigmund Freud or Carl Jung to understand why there had been ranks of the party taunting me—I felt alone and isolated after accusing a good friend of treachery. But soap stars? How did the suicidal single mother, who had previously appeared in *Dr Who*, alone in her northern bed-sit or the adulterous husband with the pet Alsatian fit in? It probably just showed how pointless all this was. What had Glen Bale asked when I had first met him in my role of Bolshie snoop; was I going to do a *Da Vinci Code* and find clues in paintings? He had been mocking, but now look—here I was trying to decipher not just a painting but a painting I dreamt about.

Going online and also scooping up every art book I possessed wasn't much help. I did background research on Hooper, US art of the period, and the world events at the time of its painting. All it confirmed was that in the dream I had got the essential facts correct about the painting. That was pretty impressive, but it didn't really help me here. I then sat there, racking my brains to see if there was any connection between the painting and me or the painting and any of the comrades in it. With every great idea, I drew a blank. So much for the Hopper code.

The time was almost 7:00 a.m., and there was still time to get some sleep. Getting ready for bed, I went over the dream again. The smooching between Harrison and Ali was intriguing and worth a question or two. That is, if Jackie had not instructed us to stop the investigation. As for now, I needed proper sleep.

***

I managed to get another four hours before the sunlight woke me. I got up, shaved, showered, and ironed a shirt. I had chosen a loud, deck-chair-blue-stripe shirt. To go with it, I eventually plumbed for a blue slim Jim and the double-breasted, four-button, black jacket suit. Despite it being lunchtime, I grabbed two slices of toast and pondered what I was going to do today. As my dream-time companions had so articulately put it, it was back to keeping the armchair safe with left-wing politics. It was strange, but although it had only been a fortnight since Jackie had dragged me into all this, I felt empty. It was no longer comforting but suffocating in its isolation.

After washing the plate and sweeping the crumbs off the table, I planned out my day. For sure, it would be the pool at 4:00 p.m., but what to do for the hours before? I made myself another coffee, and then, well, and then I just swore. I could not go back to my old life. Not now. The armchair would have to do without me. I sat in front of the TV and switched it to phone.

Cole was clearly taken aback to see me, sporting a huge, beaming smile—the biggest I could force on myself—and holding a large bowl of crisps and an (empty as it happened) bottle of crap wine. "Hey, Victoria, how'ya doing? I thought to celebrate getting off this bullshit job, we could party around here. I mean OK, we wasted two weeks and pissed off some comrades, but at least I got a friendship out of it."

"Er…yes…Pete…"

I had hoped that such bonhomie, so unmistakably not me, would flag up to her that something was up. I meant it as a code to indicate that I wanted us to continue, but of course Cole was a cop, so subtlety was not her thing. So it was time to ladle it on thicker.

"Although, let's be honest; I can't see Marie being any kind of friend of mine for a good time, but she'll come around soon enough. I mean, *comrade*," I slopped it on, "we were only doing what Jackie asked us to do. But come over, and let's party, with a small *p*."

I hoped that she wasn't a vegetarian with all this ham about. Still, two things were achieved: I didn't throw up after saying it, and she got it. I could be on daytime TV with these skills.

"Er...great idea...I'll be around straightaway. Er...*save* the crisps for me."

After she hung up, I realised that I had no clue as to where she lived and so had no idea how long it would take for her to get here. Actually, come to think about it, I didn't know much about her at all.

Judging by the wallpaper behind her, she favoured the modern style of home décor, assuming it was still in vogue, because the myriad of style sites, blogs, and magazines had declined into almost a coma of late. For a while, they had made game attempts to be current by running features on revolutionary design, but you can only have so many articles on situationist ties and constructivist bedspreads, or how with the popularity of the works of Lenin, whether the waistcoat would make a comeback. The party comrades had scoffed, and I had secretly rather enjoyed them; most importantly, people had ignored them.

I didn't have that long to ponder the state of interior design as she was here in less than half an hour. Apparently, she lived nearby; then again, with her driving, who knew? On opening the door, I was treated to some rare Cole wit when she apologised for forgetting the wine and asked whether my formal attire suggested that we were going out for a meal.

My response was a polite smile, and I let her in. As I did, I explained why I had suggested a drink, because to come straight out and say that we should not give up would have been seen by our opponent, who no doubt was still monitoring our communications. Her wry smile indicated that, yes, she had gathered that, and, no, she was not expecting booming dance music and gyrating youths. Covering my clumsiness, I asked what she had been doing. She was dressed in her usual straight jeans and leather jacket so there were no clues there. She had, she replied, been staring at the walls, wondering what to do next.

Around cups of coffee, I told her of my dream. Seeing her face, I hastily explained why I was telling her this, which was not that I believed there were any great insights to be gleaned from it (I did not mention that I had spent a good amount of my time trying to find some), but that I had dreamt was the important part. "Because it shows that I will not be able to let this rest. If I dreamt it once, then I can guess that I will do so again. I have some knowledge of repetitive dreams, and this won't be a one-off. Nothing in it is telling me anything, but the fact that I had it is telling me that I will not—cannot—forget this. I am damned if I am going to let it lie. I know Jackie said that we should…"

"Her exact words were that we were doing more damage than any spy could do."

"She was being funny." (I hoped). "As I was saying, she said to stop, but we can't—too much is at stake. So, OK, Marie is probably not the spy; certainly she did not kill Jenny Underhill—unless of course Jackie is lying, but that is not to say that Marie is not working for the other side; she didn't, if you noticed, explain why MI5 intervened in her prosecution. But other comrades still have a few questions to answer. Why for example is Ali regularly receiving money in his account? What's he doing, saving for a rainy day? And what about his side-kick, Olivia Harrison? They seem very close. And what of her moods? Something is troubling her!"

"So you propose to put every comrade under suspicion? Have you ruled me out, then, Pete?"

Her grin subsided when I gave my rather blunt but quite honest answer. "Of course. You'd be useless. Jackie might sweet-talk you, but most comrades don't trust you—certainly not enough to pass on anything important to you. No, it would be somebody who could make a difference, so I say we stick with the group we have been looking at."

She took a thoughtful gulp of her coffee and then succinctly outlined what were the minor problems in my position. "So without any tangible evidence or proof or, in fact, any real ideas, we are going to go around the party, pointing the finger at anyone and everyone, and in doing so possibly undermine the efforts of the committee and quite probably getting ourselves expelled."

"Yes."

"Christ, Pete, you would never have made a detective!"

"Thank you."

A smile tickled the edge of her mouth. "You are saying, then, that we continue the investigation?"

"I think it is our duty."

I don't know what I had expected her reply was going to be. It was obvious that last night had hit Cole hard. When you invest so heavily in someone, it hurts when they turn against you. Not that Jackie had, but that was how Cole had taken it. She had taken it very personally when Jackie had dismissed what we had been doing. Of course there had been no emotional outbursts from either of them. To be sure, Jackie had been angry and had let that been known in the course of our long session in the classroom, but there hadn't been any flying furniture, and Cole had not fallen to her knees and wept, but Jackie's words had undoubtedly upset her. She had sat there with a concrete mask for a face. Rather similar to the one she was sporting right now.

I suspected that comrade Cole idolised Jackie, and her hero had just told her that she was crap. Not nice. In all honesty I did not particularly enjoy it myself, but the fact was, the first few times you get a bollocking in the party, it does hurt, but you get used to it. She would learn. If she remained in the party, she would have to. So the thing was, what was going to be her reaction to having her halo slightly tarnished? Sulk? Get depressed? Or as we Trots were wont to do, set up a rival party and moan about the party's internal democracy? Had she decided that she going to take the criticism on board and do as Jackie had told her?

Or was she going to say, "Stuff this! Jackie got us started on this, and we need to finish it?" That perhaps if the great leader had told us about the committee and the plans for a military coup by the government it might have helped us! That to give up now was to admit that we had wasted two weeks on a wild-goose chase asking comrades dumb questions.

"So what do you suggest?" she replied.

Good. She had more bottle than I had first thought. Maybe one day she would make a half-decent comrade.

Now came the part where I had to make a suggestion as to what should be our future course of action. It was funny, but I had been giving that a lot of thought and had come up with a clutch of ideas, but something she had said prompted me to jettison most of them and move forwards on something that had been lurking in the back of my skull since we had found out about Hutchinson's intervention in Marie's prosecution. "In the past, what stopped the police from stomping around the party and interfering with the activities of Special Branch or MI5?"

"Comrades who were of interest to them—either as moles or informers or if they were under surveillance —would have been flagged like Marie was."

It was simple, bloody simple, and so bloody obvious. "So what if you could get us into the police files, and we look to see which comrades were flagged? We know that our ability to find any further info is damn right impossible, but we wouldn't need to. If comrade X has been flagged, then that would say to me that it is worth looking into comrade X, especially if they happen to be one of those who have already come to our attention."

She thought for a second. "Except the files are somewhat corrupted, many are missing, and if they are still there, then it is quite possible that the flag itself has been removed." She paused, as an idea occurred to her. "But that would still tell us something, because we would still be able to see the date when such a flag had been removed."

"The case of the dog not barking, rather than barking," I said.

"Huh?"

Never mind; now was not the time to explain literary references to Sherlock Holmes. Instead, I asked, "So it's an idea?"

"It is. Come on, we need to go to my workplace. We can't access such files remotely."

She got up, full of vim and vigour; a look of concern, though, crossed her face and held the emotions in check. "It's not going to be easy, Pete. I don't even know if I will be able to get in the building or what sort of reception I am going to get, let alone you."

I got to my feet, joining her, and walked to the bookcase by the window and took down something. I turned around and waved Marx's *Kapital* volume 2 at her before slipping it into my inside pocket. "Ready and armed, comrade."

Although she was smiling, she spoke with a warning. "We might need more than that to protect us." She unzipped her jacket; the handle of a gun peeked above the leather.

"No, this is enough; like I told you, guns aren't really me. Let's hope the old slogan of 'Words are weapons' holds true."

***

The big copmance/comrademance didn't last very long. By the time we arrived, I was heartily tired of her giving me advice on how to act when we arrived. She told me how to stand, how to move, and to avoid provoking any officer there. She then once more outlined the political situation in the police force. Then I was given instructions on what we were actually going to do when we got there. The eternal tutelage, plus the fact that she referred to the police station as "her workplace," as if it was some normal office, depot, or centre, had put an end to the temporary chumminess. Oh, and she was still calling it a service; it wasn't—it was a force: the police *force*.

The outside of her workplace certainly did not look ordinary—even during this period. Two burnt-out panda cars were the first sign that we had arrived. The police station itself looked more like the setting of a futuristic thriller than somewhere you might go to report a missing cat. Great sheets of metal covered the front, which, due to a chemical covering, meant that would-be graffiti artists and fly-posters had been unable to attach any political commentary to it. Instead, the bare steel said it all.

Just before we got out, Cole once more asked if I wanted a gun. Frankly, I thought it would be a good idea if I had one; my bravado had subsided once getting here, but there was no way that I was going to succumb to her lording it over me. Sure, pride should not come before a bullet, but there you go, that was me. I declined.

Following orders, I let her walk in first. The reception, both as a noun and a verb, was one of a cold defensive vibe. The reception room was a dirty, cream, concrete cube with four plastic chairs. It stunk of urine and fear. There was no counter or office but a black camera screen you looked into. Next to it was a grey, rusty metal door which had a card swipe to its right.

Cole tried hers on it but did not appear surprised when it did not work. She addressed the camera screen. "Come on, not this again. Let me in. I am still a serving police officer."

She got no reply. So she repeated it, adding her rank and police number. This time, she received a curt, "Piss off, bitch!"

Obviously the customer-care courses had been cancelled. Shouldn't that have been piss off, police constable bitch? Not that she looked upset by it. Her reply was friendly. "So you're on today, Josh. Come on, you remember what DI Martin said, that politics should not interfere with the running of the station. Let me in. Christ's sake, Josh, we used to work together on patrol. I don't want to have to remind you of the times I helped you out—remember the chemists? Let me in."

She was met with silence.

She tried a different approach. "Well, at least do me the courtesy of opening the two-way, or don't you even have the courage to be seen?"

Seconds ticked. She stared defiantly at the screen. The mind boggled at what might have happened to the chemist. Had he been too nervous to buy condoms? Had he been caught with itchy balls cream?

Finally, it went transparent, and standing there was a callow youth, probably in his early twenties but looking younger. He even made Cole look old. Maybe he was just a kid, and Cole had bought him some strawberry-flavoured condoms?

Her voice softened. "Thanks, Josh. Look, I need to get in so I can access the computer. I am not stupid, Josh; I know what the guys think. Let's face it; they have made it perfectly plain what they think. Toby and Govey have never been subtle, have they? But as DI Martin said, I have every right to be here, and I need to get to my PC."

He didn't look convinced and did that teenager thing of looking at his shoes.

She persevered. "Come on, Josh. You're not like them—you've got a brain; so come on, Josh, be a pal, and let us in. Anyway, who's in charge today?"

"Klamm. She's in her office if you want me to give her a ring."

From the way her voice changed, I suspected that this inspector, chief inspector, or Indian chief—whatever rank she was—was not one of Cole's best friends. "Just flick the switch, and let us in. We will be in and out in a matter of minutes."

"Sorry, Vic, I would really like to do that, but it's difficult."

I was bored of this. I had had enough of spotty plods to put up with this one. "Excuse me," I muttered as I gently moved to her one side. She looked a little taken aback but didn't protest.

My smile then changed into a snarl. "Now, *Josh*, listen very carefully to what I have got to say. I will keep it simple so you can understand—there will be no long words or anything. You will be aware that there were disturbances last night. Attacks were made on buildings, which were deemed to be reactionary. We are tired of being patient and waiting our turn. You know what, *Josh*, last night we started to take what is ours!"

I hoped my tone was threatening enough. My strategy was simple; a nobody like him was not to know that it wasn't us who had started the riots; he would have just read the reports, understanding most of the words, sounding out the others, and believed that we were on the rampage. In which case—use the fear.

"You, I am sure, will be fully aware that two police stations were firebombed. Thirteen dead, I believe, at the Central London one. Shame, should have been more."

That got a reaction. He glared at me with hatred. That'll do for starters, and now for the follow-up. "Well, *Officer*, I must apologise. Apologise, that is, for being rather vague on the numbers, because I was there. No, actually, Officer, I am being rather modest because I *led* it."

I flashed him the Jackie video on my phone. She had forgotten to erase it; perhaps she was getting royalties for the number of times I was using it. "We asked for help, and they took a rather negative attitude, and so we replied—forcefully. Come to think of it, it was an attitude rather similar to the one you are taking now. Now, *PC Josh*, you have a choice here: you have the numbers—in bodies, if not brains—to give us a hard time, but I would not advise it because I will have the North London militia here before you can say 'I want my mummy!' and have this place in ruins. The smell of roasted pig will be in the air for months. Sometimes we need to be decisive. And, Josh, I *will be* decisive. Now make the right decision, and open this door up. Now!"

The glare I gave was one of defiance and power, hiding, I hoped, the dread that he would call my bluff and have his mates give me an exhibition of how to use a riot stick.

The click of the door opening was my reply. He turned and shuffled some papers. I indicated for Cole to go in first. She did so, giving me a questioning look. I shrugged. "Too many Hollywood movies."

The back of her head shook, and I heard her mumble, "Roast pig, indeed."

We marched down the corridor, passing empty offices and locked doors. There appeared to be a real need for some sickness monitoring in this place. Despite the macho posturing, I was crapping my pants being here and so was deeply appreciative of the lack of police officers. A ghost town was exactly what I hoped for.

Coming to one door, she tried the handle and then walked in. It was a small office, walled with screens—many just saying Connection Failed. There were five desks. Four were as you would expect: computer, phone, light, paper, pens, brown files, and photos of the respective families. One wasn't, though. Oh, sure, there were elements of the usual, but in parts. The computer was smashed ; the pens snapped in half and with great imagination, the word "bitch" had written on every piece of paper. Finishing it all off; I noticed the desk itself had one leg missing.

"Yours, I presume?"

"Used to be. We can go in here."

We passed into another, much smaller office, which said it was Martin's. How exciting, the inner sanctum. Two of the walls had large, rectangular computer screens, with the third a large map of London. The final wall was made of glass, so he could spy on the minions, no doubt. Cole pressed something, and the glass turned opaque. Neat.

She opened the computer and said the passwords. She explained what she was doing. "When I looked before, I was just checking their files. There are two ways of marking files: The first and the most obvious and the most widely used, is the Instant Flag. How that works is that when anyone looks at it, it will notify you of the message immediately. So social services might put a child-at-risk flag or a kid at school might have one for asthma. That's all I looked for. The other type is the Discrete Flag, where it will notify another agency, but you might not notice it yourself. Neither Asher, Roijin, nor I knew how to access those, but watching Hutchinson I think I do now."

"So do it, then," I said, so she didn't feel the need to explain any more. I got it—wasn't I the one who had suggested that we look at comrades' files to see if any flags had been removed?

Cole nodded. "So shall we start with Ali, Toulson, and the, er…committee? I'm not sure what name to give it."

Ah, yes, that jolly little gang of theirs. I didn't know what it called itself, either. "The CoC—the Counter offensive Committee? DoRC—Defence of the Revolution Committee? PRiC—the Party Running rings around us Idiots Committee?" Note to self: lighten up; your fangs are showing. Let's not show your bitterness here. "Yes, but look further and wider. Search the net, not on your phone but on the PC, the top hundred comrades and then start with them."

"But how exactly do we judge who the 'top hundred comrades' are? Is there a league table for that? Is there promotion and relegation battles?"

Flippancy was my domain, so, I ignored it.

"Anyway, aren't we all equal?" she added.

Once more I held back; this time refraining from dredging up the *Animal Farm* quote. "Yeah sure," I muttered. "Just find the comrades who have the most hits on the net; but as I said, make sure the no-name committee members are included."

"OK, it shouldn't take too long."

Looking up at the screen linked to the PC, I could see that I knew most of them. One particular name made me think. "Kaela Suleiman is based in Aberdeen, too far away. I think our one is based in London. Try the top hundred hits for comrades in London and the South east, and include mentions in party publications. A comrade can be important but not necessarily in the mainstream news. Not all our cadre are sought out by the TV news."

"OK, here we go."

The list went up. Not surprisingly, I wasn't one of them. I wondered which number I actually was. Did it go that low? Linking those with the police files, you could see that some comrades had no files at all.

This would suggest that they had never been arrested, but then again, it could simply be that the agit-hackers had wiped them.

She then swept the files of the names given for any that had been Instant Flagged by the security agencies. I tried to think of a time when the word "flag" merely meant the Stars and Stripes and the Union Jack (in any of its variations). As she did, I looked at what offences they had committed. Most were predictable: trespass because of occupations, disturbance charges because of demos, public nuisance, battery of various types, etc., etc. I did note that one leading member had been done for throwing a lavatory out the window of his first-floor flat. I was intrigued to read more about that, but Cole was focussed on looking for the Instant Flags. None were.

This was what we had expected, so she went straight to the Discrete Flags. No anthems played.

"As you can see," she changed the screen to something that said Arrest File Index, "the AFI has been screwed with. According to this, Jerry the mouse was sentenced for GBH against Tom the cat, and look, here's Thor prosecuted for climate damage. So it's plain that it's unreliable."

"We knew that already."

"Also, of course, this is just the list of people who have had some contact with the police; our guy might not have. They might have been kept clear of any problems."

"Possibly, but they would want our person to be high profile—up front and taking a lead in the struggle, and that would run the risk of contact with the police. Keep low and safe, and you would get nowhere in the party—safe but useless. No, he or she will have had conflict with the police; it would have been worn like a medal."

"OK, then, let's see if there were any flags removed."

She went back to the list and scanned it. It whizzed through the names like a sweep through the class struggle of the Capital. Militants, trade-unionists, campaigners, community activists, strikers, marchers, theorists, historians: they were all there. The old and the new; young and old; black and white; men and women; gay and straight; able-bodied and disabled—and we, the equal-opportunity marshals, just stood there ready to judge one of them. Not on what they had achieved but solely on a computerised attachment. Or rather, the lack of one. That's progress.

Decades passed in seconds until it stopped at one. And there it was, a name with a file, telling us that at 5:03 p.m. thirteen days ago, a Discrete Flag had been removed by an off-site computer.

We stood staring up at the name. After a moment of attempting to take in what we had seen, we looked at the date it had been first put on. Oh, Christ. This was totally unbelievable. I felt a multitude of emotions looking at it. They started to stack up a like a pile of pallets—shock, surprise, disbelief, nausea. The list would have continued, but I only got as far as feeling sick and could not even contemplate trying to make sense of them, because just then, a shout caught our attention.

"Right, you two pieces of shit—put your hands up, and get out of there! Don't even think of doing something silly, because there is a machine gun pointing at you!"

CHAPTER TWENTY-NINE
How History Is Written

It was extremely funny now, sharing a good laugh about it all and patting ourselves on our backs on how well we had done; but when it was all kicking off, it wasn't the child's play we were now portraying it as. Nor, despite what we were making out now, were we feeling quite so unbothered. No. When three armed coppers had come in, hurling abuse and threats in equal measure, we had been big-time bothered.

It had not felt like playtime when two Neanderthals, who I was informed actually did have Homo sapiens names of Toby and Govey, stormed in, wielding large machine guns and acting out poses gleaned from various action movies. Josh stood awkwardly behind them, with a smaller automatic weapon strapped high under his chin, reminding me of the old photos of John Lennon with his guitar. Not that young Josh did any singing; he wasn't imagining a brotherhood of man. Not including Victoria and me anyway. He didn't actually say a word the whole time. He just stood there, embarrassed.

Toby, or was it Govey, whoever it was from this double act of cartoon bullying, had threatened to blow out the glass wall if we did not come out. We had done so. Obviously, they were fans of US gangster movies. Cole, I have to admit, had been impressive. She had coolly turned the computer off after wiping our search history and had gone out first. Thankfully, it hadn't been like the ending of *Butch Cassidy and the Sundance Kid* where they come out shooting to certain death. She had come out slowly and with her pistol in full view, held tightly with both hands. Her aim had alternated between the two (she plainly deemed Josh not to be a threat). I nervously followed behind with my hand close to the bulging inside pocket, ready to whip out the "gun" at any moment. Truth was, just then I was sincerely wishing that I had taken up her offer of having one. I do not want to sound like some wet liberal, but Karl Marx was just not enough at that moment: fabulous for understanding capitalism but not quite so, for shoot outs.

The goons had barked that they wanted Cole out and me in the cells. They did so, interlacing the demand with obscenities, references to her presumed sexuality, what would happen to me, and a general sketch of their view on left-wingers. They were not positive. What particularly upset them was not any discussion of the legitimacy of NWC, or the viability of Socialism, or even the fact that Cole was here, or the seeming importance of her sexual inclinations, but that I had threatened to organise an attack on their station.

Oh yes, we were laughing about it now, but when they were quoting what I had said, I had been rather regretting being quite so forthright in my imagination. In the movies the hero always gets away with it. That wasn't the feeling I had then. They were miffed—*really* miffed. For some reason, the "roast pig" comment seemed to be rather hurtful to them. It had looked very much as if the choice was going to be either being riddled with bullets or being hosed down in the basement (or words to that effect). Cole had stood firm, too preoccupied with a pair of machine guns pointing at her to rebuke me for either what I had said or what I had neglected to arm myself with.

Luckily for us, the cavalry arrived. It was the first time in my life I had been so pleased to see two senior police officers. In had strode DI Martin and Inspector Klamm, the latter being a tall, severe-looking woman in uniform, grey hair, and a sour look. They had demanded to know what was going on. Our new friends, Toby and Govey, had told her that they were arresting a terrorist intent on destroying the place. From their tone they had expected support, congratulations, and quite possibly a parade.

It was here, though, that Cole had really come into her own. To my consternation, she had laughed and holstered her gun. Shaking her head, she had said that "good old Josh" had got the wrong end of the stick, and we were here just to do police/party liaison work to *stop* such a thing from happening. Would Pete have come in a three-piece suit and with a tie, for goodness' sake, if he was leading a mob? And would he have come unarmed? Then came the masterstroke—she asked me to bring out the book. As they watched— warily—I produced *Kapital*; as I did, Cole recommended that they read it.

Despite the fact that it *was* quite possible that I would have worn a suit and come with a book if I had been leading a mob, it had worked. Though being unhappy that we were there, Martin and Klamm led us out—to our relief and to the fury of Toby, Govey, and their pet poodle, Josh. Murder or incarceration had been avoided. That particular fact had been such an important one, that it had temporarily obscured the very important one we had found out at the station.

But temporary it was, and it did not last long. Even sitting here, listening to vintage Paul Weller (once more, Cole seemed to know what I liked) and indulging ourselves in amused reminiscing, the name was whirling around my head. Cole had pointed out that it was not proof in itself, as Marie had also been flagged, but even so, certain things did fit.

Suddenly, all the jollity stopped. And so did we. After the non-Gunfight at the OK Corral, she had said it would look better if we walked purposefully to the car and drive off. So we did, not going off in any particular direction, but it was with purpose. Well, we made it look as if we had a purpose, but plainly that was not the case, ending up in a half-empty supermarket car park. Immediately after screeching into a space, she had turned and asked me what we were going to do. By the trolley cage we talked, discussing what the bloody hell that purpose could be.

The basic, cold facts were that we thought Alan had committed suicide, but perhaps we could never be 100 percent certain; we could guess why Dave and Yasmin had been murdered, but the police had been unable to find any clues as to who might have done it—from what Cole said, they simply had no idea and had given up. Then there was Jennifer Underhill's death; security services had shut that down, and our idea of finding out who had an alibi for that time had been shown to be pointless. We had a name, but then so what? What were we going to do, write a letter to *Revolutionary Worker*? As Cole put it—we needed cast-iron proof, and we had no way of getting it.

I am not sure that you could grace our decision with the name "a plan;" it was more of a cobbling together of desperation, stubbornness, and a lack of any other alternatives. It also would not be quite accurate to say that it had been a joint decision. Cole had pretty much thought it was dangerous and ill-thought out, or in police jargon—"stark-raving bonkers!" But then, she basically did not have an alternative.

We drove out of the car park after leaving Cole's phone hidden in one of the trollies, taped under the child seat. Then it was time for stage one.

She was a little confused when she looked up at the sign at the top of the building which was just about readable: East London's Finest Upholsterers. I explained, giving a brief history. "They were the previous owners, a family firm who ran it for over one hundred years; they went bust, and several families of rodents took over occupation. The party purchased it in 1990. In fact, it was the party centre when I first joined. We kept the sign up, if only to give visitors a chance to make jokes about armchair Socialists."

I looked at the large padlock securing the two huge iron gates. I had the key at home, so it looked like we were going to have to do a spot of climbing. Then I looked at my suit. No chance.

"Detective, could you do the honours, please."

I had dreamt of doing this. She took out her gun and told me to stand back whilst she aimed and fired several times into the padlock. After the third, she managed to tug it open. Feeling rather cool, I pushed the gate open and strolled in. The next barrier was going to be easier. The visitor's door was locked by a PIN number.

I punched in 551818, "Karl Marx's birthday. It has not been changed, as the party still uses it to store things. There's a wealth of history in there, which is worth preserving. I've used it in many of my writings."

There was no swooning from Cole.

The power was kept on for us occasional users, but the dust and cobwebs were signs that the key word here was—occasional. I heard, or thought I could hear, confirmation that small, four-legged animals had reclaimed the building for their home. We walked past the long-dead printing presses, which were usually seen in museums, and headed to the offices. The smell was one of damp and disuse.

I stopped by the far wall, which stretched up two floors, and looked up at the vast collage of photographs of demonstrations surrounding an enormous red fist. The placards read like a history of the first two decades of the century—anti-cuts, anti-Nazi, antiwar, anti-climate change, anti, anti, anti. Here was a sign of how things had changed—now we were pro-workers' power, pro-NWC, pro-redistribution of wealth. Pro, pro, pro. I walked to the right of it and wiped the layer of grease covering a photograph roughly half actual size.

There in the front was a woman in her twenties, twenty-three years old to be precise, dressed in three-quarter-length combat trousers, a T-shirt, and a leather jacket. Her clothing, like her shoulder-length hair, was jet black. The only colour that could be seen was the white fronts of her Converse trainers and her pale, clear, sublime skin. She looked young, slim, and happy. I tapped it to show Cole.

"Who's that?"

I half-joked, "I'm surprised you don't know because you seem to know everything else about me, including what music I like. It's Caroline, my partner. I am not sure that either of us would have considered her to be that back then, as we had not been going out for that long."

She smiled. "Oh, the music's easy; you're rather unusual in being so out of sync for your age, but when you adjust to that, you are pretty predictable. But I don't think I've seen a photo of Caroline so young."

"That was when she was in the Black Bloc."

She gave me a look of incomprehension.

"Militant anarchists."

She looked closer. "She was beautiful, Pete. She looks like a lovely woman."

"She was, and she got lovelier and more beautiful as she got older."

There was silence. I sensed that Cole was being sensitive to the moment and did not want to intrude on my thoughts. Well, for a second or two.

"Is that? No, it can't be!" she yelped and pointed to the figure behind Caroline. "Is that you?" She burst into gales of laughter.

I gave her butterfly eyes and confirmed that it was. On reflection, my dandy tendencies probably had been, even by my standards, OTT on that march with my slim-fitting, bright—very bright—blue, two-button suit with a shocking-yellow shirt, matching socks, and brown brogues.

"Shit, Pete! You even wore a suit in your twenties! Even when you were on marches!"

I shrugged.

She was trying to control her amusement. "Were you a couple when this was taken?"

I confirmed that we had been.

She was still trying to control it. "You two look so different, Pete! Caroline looks so, well, like an urban warrior, and you look like you've come through a time tunnel from 1960s Carnaby Street!" Mirth once more gained the upper hand over control.

Personally, I didn't think it was *that* funny. I hadn't either, when the print workers who used to work here had hooted with similar amusement whenever they saw me. I thought I looked nifty strolling along in a blinding suit, with a placard casually resting on my right shoulder. A thought struck me that after all this was over, I would take a copy of this and show Maurice at the Soul Shack. It would look rather glorious behind the bar.

"She's not how I imagined her to be."

I didn't answer but just shrugged again. It seemed an obtuse comment to make. What had Cole expected, Li in a beehive and miniskirt? Do you only fall in love with people who dress the same? I could have done the obvious and simply replied that opposites attract, but that would just be too hackneyed. Even for me.

Cole, though, held no fear of the banal. "I suppose that opposites attract."

"Indeed," I mumbled.

Silence returned. The humour was our way of hiding the blatant fact that what we were planning was dangerous and risky. Exchanging banter about the past obscured the present—which was terrifying. In the stillness here, the reality encroached with the force of an iron fist.

You would not have guessed from the echo-ridden atmosphere of now, how bustling this place had once been. We might have been little more than a splinter group then, but this was an energetic and thriving place when I had joined. People rushing about, getting things sorted or discussing a problem in places I had never visited, or sometimes, even heard of. It had been a vital place, full of enthusiasm, passion, and commitment. On my first visit here, I had both been intimidated by it all and at the same time excited by it. Whilst the party was based here in the upholsterers, I don't think that ever really changed. The buzz was ever-present. Oh, yeah, back then, our group was small enough to fit in a village church, but there was a real belief and passion.

Not that I ever thought, even in my drunken imagination, we would really be the size and the position that we now found ourselves in.

But time was ticking, and the absence of any sound was growing too oppressive. "Let's go," I said.

The first room we entered was where the journalists worked; usually there were just three working here at any one time. Lining the walls were framed front pages from the *Revolutionary Worker*. I glanced at the first few: the No War for Oil on the first day of the 1991 Gulf War; our reaction to the first election of Tony Blair: The Tories are Out: Now Build an Alternative; The Bankers are the Real Looters, dated 2011, but then that could have been at any time.

Memories flooded back to earnest, scruffy comrades busily writing articles on bulky PCs, chasing a story, or desperately trying to magnify an incident into a major struggle. The names escaped me of the people who had sweated in here or what had become of them.

I left Cole to study the headlines and learn something of the days when the only contact that the likes of her would have had with the party was to kettle us. My first job was to turn the CCTV on. Despite it rightly belonging as an exhibit in the Science Museum, it still worked. Reaching around and twiddling the wires at the back of the screens, I got them working. Not all the cameras were still operative, and one obviously needed adjusting, as it was looking straight upwards into the clouds. The pictures were black and white and primitive, but they would suffice. In truth, coverage, whilst not being comprehensive, wasn't too bad, which was due mainly to the constant threats from neo-Nazi organisations. I also turned the alarms on, too. Later, I would turn them off, but I did not want any unexpected visitors until we were ready for our special one.

Whilst still reading the front pages, Cole lifted her right arm and tapped her watch—it wasn't to show me how flash it was—but to indicate it was time to make the call. She was right. I got my phone out of my pocket and called Cole's. Not surprisingly, she didn't answer, as it was still strapped to the supermarket trolley, so I got her chirpy answering message.

I spoke as calmly and as naturally as I could. "Hi, it's me. I was right when I said that I would be able to find out more from him. He was very talkative, and he confirmed what I had suspected. I knew that we were stupid to get diverted to Marie. OK, I know that you will point out that I should have let you into my suspicions earlier, but, like I said, you do not accuse a comrade of treachery easily.

"The bottom line is that I have solid proof of which comrade is the MI5 agent. As I said before, I haven't told anyone, and as I promised, you are the first to know. Or rather you will be; sorry, Victoria, I'm rambling here; I hate these things. I am not going to tell you who it is over the phone, especially not to an answering machine! Meet me at the old centre, the *old* old one, you know the one in the East End, at…" I looked at my watch. It said half past four. In front of me, Cole had turned and was watching me. "Yeah, sorry, see you there at eight. *Come alone* as I just want to keep it only us two for the while. We'll probably arrive at the same time, but if I arrive first, I'll leave the visitor's door open. We'll meet and see how we are going to bring this to the party. It isn't going to be easy, especially after the disaster with Marie, but we will think of something. OK, well, see you at eight."

I hung up. If I said so myself, I thought that had been pretty damned magnificent. They'd be polishing an Oscar for that performance.

This was not the time for acceptance speeches, and Cole said simply and with ice-cold precision, "And now *you* are the bait."

I understood; indeed, I was the one who had suggested it, but I did not really need it to be spelled out; my heart was already racing as fast as it could. Any quicker and I'd have a heart attack.

She went to the centre landline—the type last seen on the History Channel—and called Asher Joseph and told him to contact Roijin and be here at 7:00 p.m. She emphasized that she wanted the pair of them to be armed. According to her, Asher did not ask why but just said that he'd be here. Certainly, the fact that she was on the phone for so little time was a strong indication that there had not been much of a conversation.

That was not the case with my call. Once she hung up, I rang January and asked for her and Zoe to be here at the same time. Oh, for comrades just to follow orders. There were times when you could understand why Russians had preferred the straightforward world of Stalin, where you did as you were told or face the Gulag, to the endless debates of Trotsky. I was on the phone for ages, trying to explain why I wanted two young comrades to visit a deserted print shop in East London. She was puzzled and wanted to know the reasons. I was not sure whether I should feel insulted or flattered that a possible reason for wanting them here was a dishonourable one did not occur to her. She just thought I was nuts. Still—eventually—I convinced her. My painting a picture of how gloriously magical sieving through historical archives did the trick, that—and my grovelling. Boy, was I going to owe them big time.

But that would come later. Right now, we had set the trap. Three armed coppers and two independent party witnesses were to be waiting to see if our name would turn up.

We had figured that as we were being listened to, then why not use that fact? Our name would be hearing a story of how, with superior intellect and through a dynamic investigation, we had unmasked the traitor. It was baloney, but would that person take that chance? The traitor had not with Dave or Yasmin or Jenny. Our calculation was that our suspect would not do so in this instance, either.

It was a desperate chance we were taking. If our con worked, then we would be welcoming a determined murderer to visit us. If it didn't, we were no nearer to unmasking the MI5 agent. Admittedly, it was not a sophisticated plan, but we had tried to think of ways to, if not make it believable, then sow the seed of doubt in the killer's mind. Although Cole had assured me that satellite surveillance was still jammed, we had not even taken any chance that the position of her phone could be traced, by leaving hers behind at the supermarket.

As far as the killer was concerned, it would be a meeting of the two of us at 8:00 p.m. But, in fact, he or she would be meeting half a dozen of us. We would see how well the suspect coped with that. Unlike Yasmin, we would not just be lying there, unarmed and vulnerable, unprotected against a cowardly attack.

Now to lay it on thicker. Going back to my mobile and remembering to switch video off, I phoned the party's centre, the present one that is, and got through to Billie Caplan, who answered in her usual distinct way of sounding simultaneously both singsong happy and aggressive. We exchanged pleasantries, and then I got to work asking her questions. They involved the use of the centre's cars and the comings and goings of comrades at the time of

Dave's murder. It could have been my imagination, but as the conversation continued, I was sure that she tensed a little. She answered everything I asked, but the answers were short and with as little explanation as she could give. That was unusual for Billie; normally it was the case of stop her talking if you can. Maybe she was busy, or more likely, she had heard from the gossip network about what had happened last night.

I knew full well that at best it would be circumstantial, but that was not the point—with a few pointed questions, I would add to the belief that we knew who it was. We were using the killer's paranoia and the knowledge that, given the slightest hint that they were known, they would act decisively.

Cole glanced at her watch and announced that she was going to look around and check on the building. We wanted only the entrance to be useable so we could control the situation. She smoothly pulled out her gun and went to look around, declining my half-hearted offer of company.

I gave George Armstrong a ring. With several televisions in the background blaring news reports, I asked the old man some questions. They were inconsequential in themselves, but as well as giving the eavesdropper further nerves, they would help me get the whole picture. I still couldn't quite believe what we thought. He was his usual bluff self. It was obvious that he was only half listening—if that. Most of his attention was aimed at the TV. The fact that he did not mention the previous night showed that he was not aware of it. Yet. If he had been, he would have taken me apart at the seams for acting on so little a basis. I could not wait for his thoughts on what we were doing here!

Cole was still on patrol. The CCTV was only for the outside, so I couldn't see her, but I could hear her pottering about, rattling doors and windows, and moving furniture about. Meanwhile, I checked out a few things on the centre's network. This really was going back in time, not only in what I was looking up but how basic the machines were back then. It was a wonder that you didn't have to shovel in coal. I searched the party records for the branches and the history of members.

Cole returned, announcing that all was well—doors and windows bolted. We had forty minutes before Asher and the others arrived. So to kill time—bad choice of words—*waste* time, she pottered around the adjoining office, rifling through old, yellowing copies of *Revolutionary Worker*. I was doing likewise on the computer. The system here was too ancient to be online, so I was just delving into the documents in the old format in the shared system. It wasn't much faster than Cole's method.

After a quarter of an hour, Cole reappeared with grimy hands and a bored look on her face. She checked on the CCTV screens.

"Nothing happening," I said, whilst reading a piece on world debt.

"Good," she said, in a tone which seemed to imply that she wasn't too impressed with how I was preparing for the big showdown. Not that she enlightened me on what exactly I should be doing. Instead, she told me that she was going to once more check the place out and evaluate where she would want our guests to be positioned.

"Hmm," I said, not really listening, as I had got distracted by an old article of my own. She unholstered her gun again and went out. "See ya, Clint," I muttered, wincing at the naïve style of my writing.

It wasn't a bad piece; it was a bit earnest and a tad self-important, but it said most of the right things in the right way. It concerned how successive governments had deprived working-class, indeed even lower middle-class, families of the few chances they ever had of getting into higher education.

Not that it was what I was supposed to be looking for. Self-criticism wasn't the purpose of us being holed up in here. I went back to searching back copies of the paper, looking for clues, something, *anything*. Then the computer crashed. Christ, I remember the days when these things happened. I laboriously rebooted. It seemed to take ages; entire historical epochs came and went whilst I waited. Did we really use these things? Whilst waiting, I looked at the CCTV screens. They showed nothing but the same views of walls and backyards.

This was the hardest time because just sitting there made me think of what we were going to do, and I did not want to do that. I had no desire to dwell on what we were risking, and so my strategy had been to throw myself into what I was good at—losing myself in research. Immerse myself on the minutia of the party's history rather than the very real possibility that someone could get hurt.

Finally! Finally, life returned to the machine, and I continued my searches, but it was useless. In my heart, I knew full well that there would be nothing here, but I had to look. Whilst looking at the report back from the party's annual conference, a thought struck me. I tried the internal bulletins. These were the circulars the party sent itself, which could be informing the comrades on thirty *Revolutionary Worker*s sold on the high street or how the strike at the biscuit factory was going. It could also give hints on internal problems.

I was nosing through an update on the air steward's strike when I heard a thump from the print shop. Comrade Cole was building a barricade. Marvellous; she'd obviously read *Les Miserables* too many times. No doubt she'd be breaking into "I Dreamed a Dream" at any second.

"Cole!" I yelled. "Victoria, what are you up to? Now is really not the time to be tidying up the place."

Dumb cop! I got up and went into the print shop. I called again and heard a muffled reply. It hadn't been very loud, but I guessed it was from the far side of the building, near the toilets. I wandered over, dreading what I was going to walk into. In just under two hours, I was going to confront a state-trained killer; the last thing I needed right now was a view of Cole having a crap.

Then again, she was probably moving those great, hunking, iron shelves. They had once contained paper, but now there were just old rotting wooden pallets. If that was what she was doing, then she could count me out. I had almost done my back in, moving them when I'd been a healthy, well—healthy-ish student in my twenties. I got to the toilets, but she wasn't there. That was a relief. I headed down to the back of the shelving.

"Come on, Victoria, where the hell are you?"

It was then I saw her. She was lying face down on the floor. Her right leg was at an odd angle, high by her waist. Her arms were above her.

They say that at times of great stress, time appears to move at a different speed—either all at once or in slow motion. At my greatest time of such stress, that had been true, or at least my memory of it told me it was true. As my car had spun out of control, I sometimes remembered it in slow motion and sometimes as if it had been fast-forwarded. Because I had rerun that moment so often, I could not tell you what it was like at the time of it happening because memory had a way of rewriting history. Here, though, it was clear—everything moved very quickly.

I ran to her with a multitude of thoughts in my head. Had she slipped? Had something fallen on her? There were still piles of junk on some of this racking, and whilst we might be shit-hot at organising in the workplace, we were pretty slapdash at organising a workplace. Had the killer got here early and killed her? As questions tumbled around my head, I felt both concern and fear. Running to her, I looked around; I could see no object that would have fallen and more importantly, no assassin. Her gun was a few metres away. And she was moving, so my instant guess was that she had slipped. The sound she was making was a gentle moan, akin to one I might make after too many red wines the night before.

"Victoria?" I stroked the back of her shoulder. "Victoria, you OK?"

She moaned again. This time, though, it sounded worse than a hangover. A *lot* worse. Then I felt dampness in my knees and saw red liquid.

"Victoria, no, for Christ's sake, no!"

I gently turned her over. Her moans grew in anguish. Holding her, I saw a hole in her jacket on the left-hand side of her stomach. Blood was now visibly pouring out. Her face was so pale as to be virtually translucent. Her eyes stared past me up at the lights. Her lips were fading and set ajar.

"Vic!" I yelled, holding her tight.

Something stirred in her mind, and as she seemed to come to, her right hand gripped my arm. Again, they say that in times of stressful danger your mind goes clear. Mine didn't. I held her, watching the blood soak my jacket. It ran down my arms and onto my trousers. Blood everywhere.

"Vic. No. Vic. Don't die. Vic."

My paralysis was only broken when she strained to warn me. "Pete… run, he's…"

Finally, my brain started to work. Still holding her, I tenderly reassured her that everything was going to be OK and that I was going to ring for an ambulance. Laying her back on the floor as carefully as I could, I told her that I was going to get my phone out. I reached into my inside pocket and drew out the pistol. This time I had taken up her offer. Marx did not seem quite enough at this juncture.

Still bending down, I spun on toes, winding up to get to a standing position, holding the gun out in front of me with both hands. It was, I hoped, exactly what I had seen countless times in the movies and more importantly, how Cole had taught me in the supermarket car park, the latter to the consternation of passing shoppers. It was a quick and smooth and well—please let it not be a pun—executed move. Or I hoped it was.

In front of me, smiling, stood Simon Peary. Smiling and aiming his gun straight at my head.

CHAPTER THIRTY
The Revolution Betrayed

"Nice stance, Peter. Vic teach you that, did she?" He gently mocked. "Yes, legs in a good position, gun nicely held. Aim's a bit off, though." He pursed his lips to show sadness; feigned sympathy seeped out of him: poor old, dear, Pete Kalder. He sighed. "That would be my only criticism; you're presently aiming at the lights behind me. Aim at the head is the preferred choice of the professional, but let's not run before we can walk. A body shot would be safer." His tone was his usual, jovial, friend-of-everyone that had charmed many a listener, but it had to be said that it was not exactly having the same effect on me right this minute. His smile was in all probability sincere; I could bet that here was a man who enjoyed his work, but it was distinctly *un*charming; menacing would have been a far better description.

Luckily, he hadn't followed his own advice. Victoria had been shot in the body and was still alive. Just.

He read my mind. "Yeah, she took me by surprise. Still, I would have normally done better. Must be rusty, or getting soft."

"Rusty and soft; like urine soaked bed-springs. How very apt."

What on earth was I saying? Insulting this murderous bastard! There really was a time and place for abuse. And here was neither. Not that he reacted. Indeed, he almost appeared not to be listening. He seemed to be mulling over what he had said as opposed to what I had. Did this give me a chance? Telepathy though appeared to a requirement in the corridors of espionage, as before I had a chance to move even a millimetre, he advised me not to correct my aim or he would be *forced* to fire. His voice was charismatic as ever. His aim was very much at my head. Even when threatening you, he sounded like a regular guy, indeed, the type of person who called people *guys*. From his tone you might have expected him to be discussing the arrangements of a social event down at the cricket club. A spot of net practice, a shower, some snacks at the bar, and then some pints to wash it down. All jolly good fun.

It was so incongruous. Dressed in his trademark denims and cheesecloth shirt and surrounded by the paraphernalia of the party, he was in his natural habitat. Here was the key man of the administrative centre of our organisation, who helped oil the mechanics of our activities. He was, I should say, *is* the administration! And yet here he was, pointing a gun at me. Here was Simon, not as an important and popular member of the party, but as a class enemy, someone who worked for MI5. Someone who had killed three times in the last fortnight, and judging from the fact that Victoria's pained moans were decreasing in volume, if she did not receive urgent medical aid, it would be four. There was, of course, a very real possibility that I would make it five.

For a second or two, we just looked at each other. Like a pair meeting at a pub for the first time, feeling a little shy and unsure of how to start. It was surprising that he would be feeling like that, considering he was far more experienced at this sort of thing. It was down to him to take the initiative. Pointing guns at people was an essential element of his chat up line, so he would, I presume, have some strategies in place to deal with situations like this. I had never as much as pointed a Biro at anyone until this minute. It wasn't the type of scenario which I had often encountered at the National Gallery archives. My concern was that in Simon's world "to hit on someone" had a very different meaning to the rest of us and that his preferred move was to press the trigger of the weapon he was holding steadily in his hands. I assumed the gun in question was an Alavares Azevedo 12D, the same one that had butchered the Wiltshires.

Finally, because I was finding the tension of us gazing lovingly at each other somewhat oppressive, I broke the silence. If I was going to die, then I might as well show how clever I was. "It makes sense," I told him, looking straight at that affable, but increasingly punchable, face of his, "that it would be someone like you. Kye Toulson joked that he could not have been the spy because his position relies on getting elected, and so MI5 could not be certain that he always would. There was always a chance that a more mainstream Labour candidate from the centre of his union or even some right-winger would get more votes."

Grinning, he interrupted. "Ahh, Kye, that loveable, down-to-earth guy, ready to stand tall for 'his members.'"

I ignored him. "That's something you don't need to worry about, is it, Simon? You are a worker for the party; you are employed by the party. No one will judge you or deselect you. You can stay as long as you want, or rather, as long as *they* want. But you are not just a lowly printer or van driver but the person who runs the national office; someone who may not be an elected official but who is *in the know*. You know everyone and everything that goes on. You have the ear and mouth of the party and would know everything that was going on. You are the ideal candidate."

"That was the idea, Peter. I must say that I thought I was safe. You two appeared to be crashing around, getting distracted by silly details and accusing everyone. You were positively obsessed by the Defence Committee. I have to say, that at times it was quite amusing watching you see spies under the beds of Reds. Anything that you didn't understand, you took to be a sign of guilt. It was funny."

I was glad he had been entertained.

"So why get Alan involved?"

You would never have known that he was still pointing a gun at my skull by the way he talked. He sounded like he was discussing the merits of the purchase of a particular sports car. But instead of its speed or energy consumption, it was deception and lies. "What can I say, comrade? I am expensive. Far too expensive to be kept in an organisation that for most of its time, had difficulty getting a handful of comrades out of their hangovers to sell *Revolutionary Worker* at the local shopping precinct. Even the intelligence services have to be cost-efficient."

That made sense. For years we had been merely a minor irritant to the ruling class. "That's why you only ever turn up at times of heightened class struggle. I've been looking at the membership records and comparing them with the coverage of *Revolutionary Worker*, and there is an exact fit: when there is an upturn in class activity, you reappear. When it drops, off you go. You have created the image of the adrenalin junkie who stays for the action and gets bored by the routine, but in reality it had to do with the priorities of your real masters—MI5."

He smirked. "Absolutely, Peter. Carry on, I am enjoying this." If he had had a pint of expensive import lager, he might have given me a toast.

Wishing he did have, rather than that gun, I filled in the gaps. "So Alan would be useful to stand in for you when you were off somewhere else, pretending to be somebody else, betraying other poor sods. I assume you managed that by getting Jenny Underhill, or Jelena Jacobs, if you prefer, into his life. What did you do—introduce them at a meeting and let young love take its course?"

He smiled, relishing the memory. "Something like that. Poor old Alan; he was a mess back then, what with his partner and kid gone. We figured he'd be vulnerable, and he was. She went all wide-eyed at his political brilliance, and he was smitten. Jelena—I always called her Jelena—was a superb actress; we hooked him very easily."

I couldn't bring myself to say anything more than a curt, "So what did you do?"

"Do?"

"What did you do to 'hook' him?"

Smugness answered. "What do *you* think, Peter? What are *your* theories?"

"I'm more interested in what you have got to say." Almost before the words had left my tightly pressed lips, he spilled it all out. He spoke with childlike pride at the whole thing.

"Jelena had been working with him for a while, but we were drawing a blank as to ideas of how to corner him. We were almost at the point of giving up, when one night they had a row. She was tiring of his pomposity and after a few drinks, hinted that she was fed up with the relationship. More drinks were drunk, and voices were raised, and the hints got stronger. Now she shouldn't have been doing that, as her role was to be ever so in love, not tell him what a boring bastard he was.

"Anyway, they stormed out of the pub, well over the limit, and he drove them home. Emotion, coupled with the booze, dulled his critical facilities, and he came off the road, ploughing straight into the side of a block of flats.

"Ironic, really; it all came about because of her acting unprofessionally. Months of playing by the book gets her nowhere, and then just as it looks as if she has blown it—she snags him!"

I had no idea what he was talking about. Snagged him—how? Blackmail him for drink-driving? What did MI5 say—"work for us or face twelve points on your licence?" In that case, they had been really keen on road safety in those days. I kept my mouth shut, though, because I wanted him to continue, not solely because I was interested in the answer to this nightmarish riddle that I had found myself in, but also the alternative to talking was shooting. Shooting me. So I let him talk. Peary obviously could see my puzzlement and explained, "He was knocked unconscious in the crash. Jelena was injured but stayed conscious. As she untangled herself from the airbag, she dialled 999 and then me. I was kind of the fourth emergency service."

He stopped. Whether for acclamation for his wit, for dramatic effect, or simply reliving the memory, I couldn't say, but I wanted him to go on. I smiled faintly to encourage him. He was all too happy to oblige.

"I arrived at roughly the same time as the paramedics did. Alan and Jelena were taken into the back of the ambulance. I wasn't quite sure what all this meant or indeed what had actually happened. He was out cold, but she was able to talk. With one of the ambulance guys in with us, we had to watch we said, but she still managed to tell me the night's events. As she did so, an idea occurred to me. It was pretty obvious that she was not going to carry on with it any longer. In her words, she was going to be 'dead to that bore.' I remember her exact words because that was the light-bulb moment." He chuckled, smiling as he reminisced about his greatness. "Because Alan had been knocked out in the impact he would have had no idea about how injured she was. So I decided to change the narrative: he had been injured, but she had been killed."

Once more he paused, ready for the standing ovation. I would have obliged, but I was still confused. He jumped to enlighten me further with the lurid details. "When Alan came to, we arranged for a couple of paid-for nurses to break the news that she was dead. Any chance of him requesting to see her body to say a tearful farewell was headed off by informing him that it had been taken away for an autopsy. The nurses were swiftly followed by two police officers who did work for us from time to time. They sat by his bedside and told him that his blood level was three times the legal limit and that he would be charged with murder.

"With a bobby stationed outside his room, we kept him effectively in isolation and let him stew in his own self-pity and guilt. Then, when he was bubbling, a member of our department arrived and spent quite a time discussing with him as to what befalls Lefties in prisons and, shall we say, the rather partisan attitude of prison wardens to the health and safety of such people as him. It was quite a picture he painted. He then helpfully offered him the way out…"

"You made him believe that he had killed the woman he had loved!"

Demons clenched their fists and hammered the inside of my skull. Their brothers kicked my rib cage. I spat venom. "You sick bastard!"

A look of commiseration softened his face, and he spoke with honey-sweet concern. "I realise that this might be painful for you, Pete, what with *your experience…*"

The words "your experience" hung in the air.

I remembered Alan's sympathy and unusually gentle attitude to me when Li and Li had died. At the time, I had been rather taken aback to receive calls from him offering support. They had shown a human side I hadn't been aware that he possessed. But obviously it was because he believed that he had gone through a similar thing. Even now, I still felt the heavy suction of the feeling of guilt for their deaths and the abyss of grief. Alan, in his fragile state and believing that through drink-driving he had murdered her, must have endured far worse. It must have been almost overpowering.

"So you convinced him that he had killed her and blackmailed him into working for you," I mumbled.

He seemed almost hurt that I had so simplified his master plan. "Peter, it wasn't *just* blackmail. Oh, heavens, no. If it had simply been that, he wouldn't have gone along with it. No, it was far more complex. He felt so guilty and angry at himself, that he almost wanted to punish himself and betray what he had helped build; damaging the party was his punishment."

Once more he stopped, so I could appreciate his brilliance. I had Sigmund Freud standing right in front of me, the professor of the mind. Not that I was aware that Oedipus ever carried a lightweight automatic.

"But why would he have believed that she was dead? His distrust, indeed hatred of the operations of the state, surely would have inclined him to disbelieve anything they said to him. He could have enquired about what had happened to Jenny, Jelena, whatever her bloody name was. He would have asked around and checked the records. All he had to do was just ask one of the nurses; Jesus, they couldn't have all been on MI5's payroll! Otherwise, they'd never have gone on strike for better pay! So why believe a spook? Surely, it was too far-fetched to be true!"

"And that was why he believed it!" he shrieked. "It was so OTT that he could not believe that it was made-up. I think he did ask a few questions, but we had easily had them covered. You know—she seemed all right and then took a turn for the worse. With health staff on shifts, it was easy to counter. The main thing in our favour was that he believed that Jelena was his new love, so it wouldn't have entered his head that she would be in on it. If she was not dead, then where was she? The answer to that conundrum: that she was an intelligence agent who had faked her death was so ludicrous that he would not have given it a second thought. And let's face it: even if he had rooted about, he would have only drawn attention to his involvement and face imprisonment."

"You did those kinds of things?" I asked, believing that this was too fantastic for words.

He gently shook his head. Presumably, he didn't want to move his head too much so as not to take his attention from me. Sweet, I should have felt flattered, apart from the gun pointing at me. "Not usually. Our routine operations were surveillance, but I was young then and fancied myself as cutting a dash, so the theatrics appealed to me. Can't say my superiors were too impressed. They considered it infantile, expensive, and liable to blow up in our faces. If Alan Wiltshire guessed the truth, then we would be for it. The press would have had a field day, and Parliament would have been forced to look into what we were up to. They were livid, but by the time they heard about it, I'd done it. Of course, they got their revenge and sent me to a whole number of bland, brain-numbing offices, logging data. It was the service's equivalent to Siberia; death by admin."

Poor didems. If he gave me a minute, I would find a hanky.

"Boy, were they pissed off. Senior supervisor, Ian Kerridge…"

My mouth opened, and before my brain could control them, words spewed out. "Yeah, yeah, Simon. Don't take this badly, but I'm really not interested in your petty office problems. What I can't understand is—why bother? Why did they go to all the trouble of dropping you on us? OK, if it was now, it would have made sense. I guess the ruling class is chucking everybody at us. But back then? We were tiny and fairly inconsequential. We'd been involved in a few campaigns, but so what? We weren't even the biggest left-wing organisation. There was…" I tried to remember the other Socialist parties and movements of the time, but whether it was the gun pointing at my forehead or the thought of Vic bleeding away, my memory must have been mislaid. All I could say was to repeat the question—"Why?"

He nodded. "They felt the same; that's why they wanted a way to keep an eye on us without much cost. A mole was exactly that—budget surveillance."

"But to go to such lengths to entrap him?"

Shrugging, he replied, "Like I said, I was young, keen, and impetuous. I wanted to get some juicy assignments and not just tread water with half-wit Lefties. Having Alan was an economical way of keeping tabs on what the party was doing. My action may have been rather adventurous, but it achieved the end they wanted. Must say, though, the powers-that-be changed their attitude, and the ridicule subsided, when the first upturn in industrial unrest occurred, and thousands started to get radicalised."

Whilst he was revelling in how clever they had been, I weighed up my options. He was still aiming at me and seemed worryingly relaxed. He knew full well that he could simply press that trigger, and I was dead. Until now, for some reason he hadn't and appeared to be content to chew the fat whilst we nostalgically discussed a past triumph.

Meanwhile, Vic was sounding worse. I wasn't sure how long she had. But what could I do? I had tried to work out the angle and thought he was right; my aim was well off his head. Could I slowly readjust? If I tried, he might change his mind and shoot. But then, what was stopping him from doing that anyway? Whatever it was, I was grateful for it and it was in my interest to use it and just keep him talking and hope something came up.

"How much did Alan give you in the way of information?" I asked, as if that really mattered; as if there was a scale of treachery.

"As it happens, not really that much at all. Indeed, there were a few periods when we had to remind him what we could do. He would neglect to keep in touch or at certain times give us duff info. He tried his best to fob us off. I have no doubt that he sincerely wanted to manage the situation. Amusingly, he was also trying to use us. A couple of times he convinced us to halt proceedings against comrades in return for his continued help…"

"That was why the assault charges were dropped against Marie?"

"Yes, we gave him that one. Well, I like old Marie too and didn't want to see her banged up. Trouble was, that he was dealing with professionals who could pull any string we wanted. We had him on the murder frame, and once he had passed on such information, we had that on him as well. Even if he had grown to believe that he could live with her death, he now had his treachery to deal with."

The ironies of ironies, that just when he would have been at his most useful, when the country was on the brink of revolution, he realised what had happened. "So then he sees her in the police magazine—very much alive and in uniform and realises he has been duped."

"Indeed, poor guy. A tragedy."

I did not know whether to laugh, throw up, or see if I could wing him with a bullet. "A tragedy? *You* call it a tragedy?"

His cheeky-boy disposition took the look of being affronted. Hearing him, I think he really was. "Of course! Alan was one of the greatest Marxists of his age. His contribution to both the theory and practice of Socialism is immeasurable."

Clocking my look of disbelief, he tried to explain his view. His self-importance bounced off the warehouse racking. "That is irrefutably true. Oh yes, I know he worked for the agency, but as I said, he did his best to minimise his contact. Frankly, he gave us bugger all. Even then, I know it pained him in the extreme. I think that was why he did kill himself when he saw Jelena. He suffered mental anguish from even the little contact he had with the service, but then when he saw that he had been doing so because of a con, it pushed him over the edge. His pride, his dignity, as well as his principles, lay in ruins. It was too much, so he had to end it, so close to possibly achieving his life's work. As I said, it was a tragedy, but then not one totally unexpected. There were a few times when he was so racked with guilt that he considered suicide. Of course he never said why, but I knew; I felt honour-bound to help him. Of cou—"

"Honour-bound?" I spluttered, dodging the bombast. I was really, I mean REALLY, wishing I had a better aim so he couldn't miss the bullet. "You?

Honour? You spend your life grubbing about secrets, living a lie, and destroying people's lives—all for a morally, economically, politically, socially, and spiritually corrupt and bankrupt system, and you talk about honour! What a jumped up little prat you are!"

He grinned. "Language, comrade, language."

"Piss off!"

I must have involuntarily twitched my hand, because suddenly his mood changed. The grin left. His jaws clenched. His eyes fixed. "Don't move a hair's width. A bullet will be lodged in the wall behind you after smashing through your skull before you even have a chance to touch the trigger."

I froze. I believed him. He wasn't charming now.

Then his mood lightened and affability returned. "Sorry about that, mate. There's no need for me to get so touchy. Judging by way you're pointing that thing, you'd only hit the floor. I guess it's getting heavy. They do if you are not used to them. After a while they feel like you are holding a stone, even with these modern lightweight models. It's the physics of it all. Why don't you put it down?"

I told him that he must be joking because as soon as I did that, he'd shoot. He replied matter-of-factly that he could have killed me already if he wished to *and still* could. To make his point and seemingly doing so without moving, I felt a warm spot on my forehead. I guessed that it was an aiming device. He even suggested that I turn mine on and told me how to do it. It was that patronising help that convinced me. I realised that I had no chance of a shoot-out in this situation, and my only option was to use my chat to get me out.

To emphasise his complete control of the situation, he proposed that we could both lay down our guns as he was enjoying "our little chat." He nodded to a waist-high pile of *Revolutionary Worker*s by me, saying that he thought it would make for a "comfy place to sit." He would elect to sit down on the large brown box on his left.

"OK, but can I see to Vic?"

That perplexed him. "Unless you are a secret surgeon which is possible, as we do sometimes have alternative professions," he laughed at his own witticism. "I don't think there is much you can do, but why not. Put the gun down—slowly—and do what you can."

I laid down my gun on top of the pile of papers and saw the headline—"United for Peace." That was grimly ironic. I did not really have time to read it right now, as I was otherwise engaged, so I had no idea what it had been about; it certainly was not about the situation I found myself in.

Before I took more than one step, he barked, "Stop there, so you do not get any ideas about making a lunge for her weapon. Stretch your left foot out, and with your toe kick the gun over to me. Do it *slowly*, please, Peter."

Clearly, he had forgotten about the deal of both of us putting down our weapons. His was still very much in his hands. Hell, if you couldn't trust double-dealing spies, who could you trust? There was no way I could reach mine with my hands, so I had no choice but to do he had commanded.

Victoria was in a bad way. There was now a substantial pool of blood around her. My shoes stuck to the floor as I knelt down. My knee grew damp as it seeped into my trousers. She looked what could only be described as deathly pale. Thankfully, though, she was still breathing. Just. Of course, Peary was right; I could do nothing, but I wanted to at least touch her face and talk to her. If we were both to die here, then we would not do so alone, and we would do so together.

I stroked her cheek. If he was surprised by this sign of affection, then he didn't mention it. But something had taken him aback. "I hadn't expected her. I thought you'd be on your own, but that was the idea, wasn't it? That was clever; I hadn't expected that from you—the trick or *any* semblance of cleverness. I suppose the idea was to ambush me." Unbelievably, he did sound genuinely impressed. "That was why you made such a song and dance about the time of meeting and that only you were the one who knew who it was—nice one. I turn up at the appointed hour, and you two jump me. Nice one, indeed. What you did not know about me is that I like to suss out any meeting place as early as possible. It's good to check out the angles, the exits, you know, get the vibe of the place. And then I was going to wait for you. I was on my way here immediately. But as I said, I expected an empty warehouse and not a snooping cop."

"Can I get her some water?" I asked.

He scoffed. "Er, like I am going to let you wander off on your own! Sorry, friend, that will have to be a no. Anyway, why the big concern? I would have thought that one less copper would have appealed to you, Pete."

I did not answer but ran my palm over Victoria's wet, sweat-soaked hair. I whispered to her, telling her that we would be OK and that I was staying. She swallowed hard and forced out a murmured command. Even now, she was trying to give orders! She told me to run.

Peary piped up again. "I guess she and I are two of the same peas in the proverbial pod. Or should it be plod?" he joked. "Both of us choosing one side of the class divide, of course, from the best of principles, but both of us realised that they had been mistaken."

That really narked me. I stood up and faced him—too quickly. He pointed the gun at me and commanded me not to try anything foolish.

"There's a world of difference between you two," I sneered, *very* foolishly. "God knows I'm no cop-lover, but at least you know where you are with them—they're the ones in uniforms and badges, and they are plainly on one side. You could almost say that they are honest in their choice. But you? You pretend to be on one side, whilst working for the other. At least Vic has changed sides and risked her personal safety by doing so. I can see her principles but you? Well, Simon, you're a scholar on language, what word would you choose for yourself? Scum? Coward? Shit-head? Or all three?"

Peary did not like being confronted with hard truths. It hadn't been a wise move. A Marxist should always recognise the balance of class forces, and the balance here was very much in his favour. I would not gain anything by antagonising him and needed to keep him sweet and preferably talking. There needed to be chillin' here, not aggravatin.' If I did, then maybe I could buy enough time for Asher and Roijin to arrive.

His jaws clenched. Anger burnt from his eyes. His fingers tightened. Like I said, not a wise move.

Trying to diffuse the heat, I put forwards an idea. I thought he'd either be impressed with my intelligence at solving the mystery, fall over laughing at my ignorance, or waste time illustrating his own brilliance.

"So when Dave rang Jackie, you immediately understood that you were in trouble. You must have been desperate to keep track of the repercussions. The surveillance software, Popovs, was placed on mine and Victoria's computers as soon as Jackie asked us to get involved. The timing of the installation was before anyone else knew. And you were right to have been worried. Alan had recorded a message specifically for Dave. I'm certain that he would not have killed himself without saying good-bye to Dave. He loved him too much for that. It must have been something more than an expression of love as otherwise Dave would have not erased it. Alan told him everything, including that he had seen Jelena in the magazine. Dave tracked her down, and she told them about you. You had to eliminate all three as they were a threat to you."

Peary did not shoot me, but I had guessed correctly; he simply could not resist the chance to show off. After curtly telling me to sit on the pile of papers, he explained. "Oh, she didn't say a word to him. She was too much of a pro for that to happen. I made pretty sure that Dave and Yasmin were talking honestly, telling me truthfully, what Jelena had said and what they had found out, and they were, er, *insistent*, that she had not told them about me."

For the first time his demeanour changed and a distant look appeared. It was almost one, which could be described as being one of regret. His bottom lip lowered just a fraction and his voice softened.

"I had no choice with Dave and Yas. They were good people, lovely people. I've known both for years. But I had no choice. I had to be certain…"

His voice trailed off into the memory of the hideous act he had committed. Was he trying to justify it to himself? If he was, then his mental defence barrister must be pretty shit hot. My mind went back to their bedroom and the brutal and barbaric nature of how he had made sure that they had told him the truth. Total torture. He hadn't just wanted to know what they had found out but if they had told anyone. To protect himself he had inflicted agony on them.

I didn't say anything because I felt gagged by the memory. A good part of me just wanted to curl up in a ball, but that was not a great survival strategy. I just remained silent, guessing that he wanted to say more.

"After one particular economic crisis, which had led to troops being introduced onto the streets, operatives under cover were told that the rules of engagement had changed. Due to the heightened emergency we were to take any measure which we felt was necessary to protect ourselves. It was drummed into us. Call it brainwashing if you like. Any measure whatsoever. Hearing that they had talked to Jelena just sent me into autopilot." He paused. "I can't believe that I did that. It went by as a blur. From start to finish it must have just been under half an hour but I've relived it ever since. It was like a nightmare which I only awoke from after it had finished."

He stopped and looked at me. What was he expecting? Forgiveness? Did I look in a priest? In *this suit?*

"I haven't slept properly since. Every time I drop off, I see Yasmin and Dave suffering. I do regret it. Really, I do. I just had to…"

His voice was now no more than a whisper. I couldn't decide which I was more impressed with: his breath taking self-justification and wallowing in self-pity or that he could look so good with so little sleep. I know my face dropped like a basset hound after just one bad night. I didn't understand why he appeared to want to elicit my sympathy. The mention of the nightmare had been an obvious ploy to get it, but emotional manipulation wasn't really required when you had a gun in your hand.

"So what 'forced' you to kill Jelena herself then?" I hissed.

"Because their visit to her and their subsequent deaths—which straightaway she knew was down to me—gave her an idea. She contacted me and tried to blackmail me. Now there was an irony! Blackmail me! She wanted enough money to secure an escape route from the country. She also made it plain that if the revolution did succeed and she was unable to flee, then I was to do everything in my power to help her, otherwise she would tell all. She was a potential risk, so yes, Pete, I had to eliminate her. It was a shame; I liked Jelena, she'd been a pretty and quite intelligent girl. She had aged a bit when I met her again, mind you.

"It was a pretty simple thing to organise. She even gave me her address. With my position at the party national centre, it was dead easy just to slip in and out without anyone noticing. That was the beauty of my role—in the know but basically anonymous. I had no problem just taking one of the party cars. I told her that I was bringing the loot. I was in and out in less than five minutes."

The level of remorse appeared to have lessened a little. Maybe because she wasn't quite the bright young thing she had once been, had made it easier. "So she had to be eliminated," I said, "because the situation in the country has reached a crucial point and with the prime minister planning a military coup, MI5 cannot risk losing any of their agents. The balance of power could be delicate with just the finest factor tipping it in favour of one class."

"Well, now, Peter, that's half right. I know that Jackie told you about it. Word is, that the PM and his circle of senior generals and financial backers have a fair amount of support from the military and the vast majority of the police forces. They can also call on the foot soldiers of the far right. They have been cowed in past battles, but in this situation they will be of use as expendable shock troops."

Trying very hard to ignore the severe dampness of my shirt and the growing feeling that my body was going into meltdown, I tried to stay calm. "And in your knowledgeable and professional opinion, who will win? Us—the movement of equality, of fraternity, of liberation, and of hope, or yours? Yours—of oppression, of cretinism, reaction, and of pessimism?" I couldn't help scoring political points, even when my life depended on not doing so. I must remember that there was a time and place for such things.

A strange look crossed his face. His reply was slow and deliberate. Earnestness was now the preferred mode of communication. "Now listen, Peter. The party has massive support but has not won the argument as widely as many would have liked in such a showdown, but then the party has not chosen the time, and I would say that the coup organisers have a number of things in their favour. But it will be very close. Be in no doubt; the ruling class is taking a huge risk. They know that. However, a significant section of them believe that they have no other place to go to. It's a gamble from start to finish."

It was hard to believe, impossible even, but the man was giving me a political lecture! He of all people was keen to enlighten and educate me on the perspectives of the next stage of the revolution. Simon Peary was a man who appreciated his own worth. Obviously, we were more alike than I would like to admit. He continued with my education.

"The question is," he said, "has the prime minister's cabal enough social forces to take control in the first place? One key factor will be those in the middle who are not die-hard NWC supporters—will they just sit back and let the coup occur? Will they see his way, the lesser of two evils or will they be polarised into supporting revolution? Then there's the role of the military who are in the position to tip the balance one way or another? If the coup does manage to get a toehold in the country, using the military, they might be able to remove the National Workers' Council's leadership and by occupying the important communication and control centres paralyse the revolution."

He paused and blew out his cheeks. He was assessing the probability of such a strategy being successful. It was a fascinating, frightening, and problematic situation that, whatever the outcome, would change the course of human history. Normally, I would have loved to discuss it and to debate the chances we had of stopping them. It was a severely terrifying scenario, or should have been, if I hadn't perched nervously here on a pile of Socialist newspapers, with a murderous MI5 psycho keeping me prisoner. Not that it was bothering him; he was evidently happy to discuss current events.

"The question needs to be asked—how long would the military coup organisers be able to keep power? And then if foreign troops are brought in, what will that provoke? Will those people who are opposed to what has been going on welcome them as liberators or oppose them as invaders? What will be the attitude of the neutrals in the British Army then?"

It was as if he was addressing a meeting, succinctly laying out the position and raising the possibilities. I noted that he had laid his gun on his lap. He was actually enjoying this revelling in political reasoning. Would he be expecting a vote? Still, it was good that he was relaxing. I stood a chance at handling him in this mode. I looked around for my borrowed gun and saw that he had put both it and Victoria's to one side of the box he was sitting on.

He continued with his analysis. "Coupled with whether the revolutionary movement is strong enough to stop them, the problem is that even if we are able to, at what cost will it be? One of the first targets is to behead the leadership, and there is no way we can wrap them in cotton wool. For the Central Committee to go into hiding means that they would have already partially succeeded in neutralising them. I've talked to Jackie several times, but she refuses to take any action; one extra bodyguard is as much as she will go for. Not that it's just about the guys at the top. The battles will be bloody; a lot of people could perish."

I tried to look down at my watch but felt that I could not do so without Peary noticing. I had totally lost track of time. It seemed like I had been here for days, but I could still hear Victoria, and I greatly doubted whether she could have held on for too long.

"And what if neither side can win an outright victory?" I asked, joining in with the Q and A with Simon P.

"A bloodbath leading to a long civil war? The failed state becoming overrun with competing militias? Then what? A strong man comes along and takes over. It won't be the prime minister but another dictator coming to aid the ruling class." He ran through the Napoleons, Stalins, and Francos of past eras. As he did so, I sat looking around for other types of answers than his dialectical, materialist history of civil wars. None jumped out at me. All I could see were cardboard boxes, iron racking, and old leaflets. Out of the corner of my eye, I could see a yellow trolley, which we had used to move bulk copies of the paper around. Quickly, I assessed my chances of it being any use and came up with the probability rating of zero. Apart from that, assuming that I would not be able to knock him out with an advertisement for a pro-choice meeting, I did not see much in the way of anything that would be of use.

Sensing that he was coming to the end of his discourse but wanting him to continue, hopefully for the odd hour or two, I turned my attention back to him. "Shouldn't that please you?" I asked. "I mean, the eventual victory of pure Capital imposing order must be MI5's wet dream. I notice that you refer to the party as 'we,' but surely the state is your 'we?'"

The look I had seen before reappeared. It soon became apparent what it indicated. "I think you misunderstand me, Peter. I no longer work for MI5, because quite simply, I no longer believe in what they stand for. I am a committed member of the United Revolutionary Socialist Party and one who believes in the perspectives of the party."

He was feeling insulted. Good grief! And they call me vain!

"I haven't had any contact with my seniors for about two years. One reason why Alan stopped any semblance of cooperating with them is that I informed the service that both he and I were opting out of doing their dirty work."

"And they let you? Just like that?" I said, surprised that secret intelligence was such an easy going affair. I never imagined that you could just ring up and resign because you had found a better job offer. They sounded like the model employers. I mean, did you have to give notice or put it in writing?

He smiled. "Let's just say, I had certain persuasive arguments."

To be honest I wasn't bothered in the slightest what these were. What got me was the suspicion that he was trying to appear more militant-than-thou.

"So you are saying that you no longer work for them and that you are a committed and hard-working member?"

I had slandered the poor love. "Oh, Peter, I have always been one of the hardest-working members in the party. What was it the old man always says? If we have moles, then keep them, as they will be the hardest-working members of all. You will be able to rely on them to keep the blog updated, attend the sales, and go to every meeting. They will do the donkey work."

I was almost choking on this. "True, but you were never what you could call a *loyal* member, were you?"

He did not answer for a minute or two. The silence was unpleasant, but I was running low on topics to discuss with him. My stock of conversation starters with homicidal loons was sadly lacking. What would interest him? An amicable meander down memory lane, discussing his many and varied jolly japes in Her Majesty's service, was what might be required, but how do you engage someone in that? But then perhaps the silence wasn't so bad. There was no rush. Whilst he pondered whatever it was he was pondering, I again tried to calculate the time. But I had no idea whatsoever. With tremors tearing up and down my nervous system, the whole notion of seconds, minutes, and big hands and small had crumbled. Was time flying or standing still? How long did I have before the comrades arrived? I looked down, but my shirt, peaking out from under my jacket, was covering the watch. Why did I not wear short sleeves?

My thoughts were disturbed when Peary started talking again. His urge to explain swept over me. "I have always been loyal to my central belief of doing the honourable thing. I was nineteen years old when I joined the service."

He must have registered my reaction on hearing how young he had been when he had signed up for them, because he sought to explain the fact, but he had misunderstood what I had been thinking.

"The service recruited me because they thought that someone my age would be a useful asset to use in any student unrest."

No, I was thinking what a sad git you must have been, not why they had recruited you. I was thinking what a geek you must have been to join. Most nineteen-year-olds are thinking of things other than queen and country; sex and beer is the norm.

"My mother was involved in military intelligence, so it was like a family tradition," he chuckled.

Yep, sad git.

Evidently, he felt the need to tell me the reasons that had convinced him to join the security services. It appeared to matter to him to explain. "I didn't join because I loved the monarchy—it was Elizabeth then, of course—or that I supported any of the prime ministers of the time. Nor, Peter, did I have any illusions about the system. I never thought for a second that capitalism was nirvana. I have always been quite aware of the disparity of the wealth that capitalism creates; you do not need to be a Marxist to know that. Any fool can see that it is responsible for oppression, war, and famine. But for all that, I believed that the western version of capitalism with democratic governments was, if not the best possible type of government, then, as someone said, it was the least worst. Looking around at the alternatives I saw *a lot* worse, so I felt it was important that I should do what I could to protect a system that was humanity's only chance."

Well, that cleared all that up, then. I asked myself why he felt the need to tell me all this. I really must be giving off an ecclesiastical vibe. Certainly, I felt like praying to some God or other for help, but that didn't make me a candidate for the confessional. But again, his time was my time. Questioning his explanation might take more of it up. Plus the fact that his excuses and self-aggrandisement were grating, so I felt a powerful urge to say something. "By spying on small, left-wing organisations? When you joined, the average party branch consisted of three students, a couple of teachers, a council worker, and some bloke who had turned up by mistake. So to protect this wonderful system, you spied on rooms of usually badly dressed types supping lagers?"

I had been sharper than I had intended. If rule number one in the hostage guides was, don't annoy the hostage taker, then number two must be to avoid sneering at their life's work. Thankfully, Peary had not read the book and seemed unperturbed. "Not all the time. I mean, I had other roles in other organisations, and when my talents were not needed, then I worked at HQ. But yes, even though it was obvious that the Socialist dream was just that, one of the needs of the system was to get rid of petty annoyances. Or rather to make sure that they remained petty. Capital needs regulation, sure, but it has to have the freedom to create the wealth that the NHS, education, the transport infrastructure, housing, and the welfare system needs. OK, it is not perfect, and some people got very rich whilst others starved, but there are still millions, billions even, of people who have homes, food, water, and, usually, jobs. Capitalism has its crises, but it also has an incredible capacity to reinvent itself, and because of that, it is ultimately a stable system."

It was touching. Pass the tissues.

Forgetting rule number two, I couldn't resist myself and gave him a little poke. "Simon, I really don't want to upset you—as you are the one holding the gun—but for someone who says that they have become a loyal party member, you sound very much like someone who still supports capitalism, and I don't know if you missed that meeting, but we are kind of a little bit *against* capitalism."

He chuckled. "Peter, you do make me laugh. I am talking about what I *used* to believe."

My jeering tone continued unchecked. "So when did this road to Damascus moment take place?"

His keenness to elucidate and describe his political journey bounded on like a puppy running down a hill. "Doubts started coming in during the first factory seizures a few years back when the party's ranks started swelling. It was funny; the guys in the service were panicking, but I was, to my surprise, getting rather thrilled by it. Inspired, you might say. Then the movement grew, and things started happening. The NWC was created and elections held. The police and troops were driven off the streets. It was then when I started to wonder if the party was not just a bunch of do-gooders and dreamers, but in actual fact, could be close to achieving its goals. Something might actually happen! The last big financial meltdown, you know the one that brought down the Higgs coalition, made me start to realise that capitalism might not be able to continue."

Woof, woof. He was wagging his tail.

The glorious epiphany became even more heavenly. "I suppose it made me go back and read and think about all the meetings I had sat in. Previously, I'd sat there, ignoring the politics being discussed, just focussing on the actions proposed and who was saying them. This time I reflected on the ideas. It was then that I came to the conclusion that there was a better system for humanity than capitalism. We could achieve world Socialism and build a society on need rather than greed. Once I had decided that, I left the service."

He was in full flow. Comrades always did like to reminisce how they had come to revolutionary politics and who had recruited them; what was unusual was that it did not usually occur after they had decided to stop working for MI5.

He ploughed on about how the fundamentals of his beliefs had remained the same: the belief that the role of society was to do the best for as many people as possible. All that had changed was his idea of which type of society could deliver it.

What did he want me to do—cheer? No doubt, rule number three was always try to flatter the hostage-taker, so it would have been sensible to say something positive or to have praised the way he had changed so dramatically his world view. Instead, I said, "So you're on our side now, are you, Simon? Well, here's another meeting you might have missed, the one that was about the issue of comrades killing other comrades. How the hell can you marry up butchering Dave and Yasmin with what you have just said? If you have switched sides why did you murder them?"

Had I a death wish?

"It was only days ago you were firing bullets into them!"

Seemed so.

But he didn't seem put out by the comment. Indeed, he gave the impression of finding the point an interesting one. "I think it was the final act of my previous life. I'd been brought to it by circumstances beyond my control and in order to leave it behind I had to take them out the equation. By sacrificing them I could devote my life to building a better future."

God help me. Did he believe this crap?

"What about your former comrade – Jelena Jacobs? I have no idea whether she deserved to be punished, but I am pretty sure she didn't deserve a bullet in the skull. And I'm certain that even if she did, it wasn't down to you to deliver the judgment. Was that a part of your new life? I guess it must have been. And now? Is shooting Victoria a way to help the revolution?"

He waived aside my comments. "In the scheme of things, Jelena didn't matter. As for your friend there," he pointed to Cole, "I don't consider her a comrade. Not a newly-joined who saw the light only when it was expedient to do so. She's not like me."

No, indeed, she is not.

He sighed and made a good impression of sorrow. "But like I said, Dave and Yasmin were regrettable. They were good people, but I had to be one hundred percent certain that they knew nothing. I was forced to do that. I had no choice. I want to make up for what I have done in the past and if they had told the party what they had found out then there was no way that I would have a chance to do that. I need the chance to use my skills to genuinely create a better world. I feel that I have much to offer. Remember, Peter, central to our thought is the belief that people can change; well, I did."

Un-bloody-believable.

"So when you saw the light and decided to hold *Das Kapital* to your heart rather than Capital, did you tell Jackie about your past? Have you tried to help us in this difficult situation by sharing your knowledge? No, I bet you didn't. Did you tell her who else in the party is working for the state? I assume there are others; they wouldn't just leave it to you—as great as you are."

His stomach-churning self-justification was so sickening that any thought on what would have been the diplomatic course of action was not even considered; I really could not let all this sanctimonious waffle go unchecked. You had to wonder if *he* really believed what he was saying.

"Oh, sure," he nodded. "I would expect that right now the entire security network is devoted to the NWC, especially the party. You can bet on that, and it is highly likely that they are people that you know and even respect. As for who they are, that is something I don't know, but it is obvious that they will hold senior positions either in the party or the workers' councils. Or, of course, both."

Not for a second did I believe that he was little brother innocent and not know at least a few names. "Come on! You have been working at this for decades—of course you know the others. Who are they? Olivia? Youssef? Who?"

"Really, Peter, I would love to help you, but I honestly don't know. The service, for obvious reasons, restricts the identity of any field operatives. Of course, I have my suspicions."

"Who?"

He laughed, and he had a point. The question of what other agents of the state were working in the party was not the most pressing one I faced. "Oh, I am not going to tell you, Peter."

My mouth was running well ahead of my brain. "Why not? I thought you were working for us now? Didn't you just give me a stirring speech on how loyal to the cause of human liberation you are? Simon, you convinced me—I *believe* that you are on our side, but that's why I am puzzled by your reticence to name names. Why the loyalty to them? I thought they were the enemy now?" I was in full Olympic sprint. "Or are they?" I sneered.

His arms widened as if to embrace me. Was he going to hug and shoot me? No, my mistake, it was more explanation. "Of course! Of course! As I said, I have broken all links with my former employers, but I'm not going to tell you that certain comrades are security officers, just because I think they are, because—"

"Have you shared your suspicions with Jackie?" I snapped.

Bizarrely, he shrunk a little at the barb. Had I hurt his feelings? Almost apologetically, he replied, "Ah, now look, it's like I said, I am not going to point the finger at anyone and everyone, just because I think they might be MI5 agents. That just wouldn't be right. Look at the uproar you caused."

"Ah, but you're far too modest; unlike me you've got skills and knowledge in this area. After all, for years you have been looking in both directions. You must know loads of stuff to pass on, stuff that might help us. Or at the very least, it would prove that you have really changed sides."

"Well, it's not that easy."

It was strange that, despite firmly believing that someone like me was a Class A Coward, the fear that I was very much feeling was getting shunted, if not out of the picture, then aside, to the edges of the frame, by the revulsion of this self-serving twaddle that he was peddling. Burning hatred was helping to propel it."'Course not! You don't want the party to know the shit you've been shovelling for so long, the comrades you have betrayed, the class you have betrayed. Dave, Yasmin, and who now? Victoria and me? Hah, that would tarnish your halo, wouldn't it, *comrade*! You are right, you are different from Vic. She's swapped sides but has done so openly and publicly and used any benefits to be gleaned from her previous employers for the good of the struggle. But you? Your priority is Simon Peary—if, of course, that's your real name—"

He went to say something.

"No, I really couldn't give a toss. It's as I said—you haven't changed your views; you've just seen the winning side and wanted to join."

Despite the fact that it wasn't in my best interests to do so, I had a desperate urge to antagonise him, to wind him up. I *really* wanted to wind that smug bastard up. I really hoped that I had hit a nerve. But to my surprise, all he did was shake his head as if I had made a mistake filling in an incorrect answer to a crossword clue. "Sadly, Peter, I don't think it is quite as clear-cut as you make out. I think it's going to be a pretty tight fight. Oh, I think and sincerely hope that we will eventually triumph, but it's hardly a forgone conclusion. It's just as likely the military coup, backed by their foreign armies, will crush the workers' movement, and we will have Pinochet's Chilean military dictatorship right here in the British Isles. And what would that mean to me, Pete? Hey? What would that mean to guys like me? I don't think I'm taking the easy option—do you?"

So now he was the great class hero. I couldn't bring myself to say anything despite the fact that with the clock ticking, it was a bloody good time to use that love of talking I was so proud of. But my lips were clamped shut.

For several moments we both just sat there looking at each other. The only sound I could hear was Cole's breathing. It was faint and laboured, but it was there. But for how long was another question. I sat there, perched on the *Revolutionary Worker*s and looked at him. All those years he had been such a fixture of the national office, organising, managing, and running it. Not the politics or the perspectives, but taking care of the nuts and bolts of the party. "Simon will see to it" had been a virtual catchphrase. He was just so good at his job—efficient and unflappable; that was why, even with his disappearing acts, he was welcomed back. We had thought he was travelling. Ha! How ironic—he was no fellow traveller. So we sat and stared at each other.

The smell of oil and dust with musty paper brought back so many memories. Of coming here, enthusiastic and keen, often feeling mashed from the night before, but on arrival the total buzz would lift me. Simon would be here, acting beyond his years and in total control.

I could feel Victoria's blood soaking into the top of my shirt and the sleeves of my jacket where I had held her. Involuntarily I stroked my arm with the former tattoo. Li Li, I might just be joining you. And now the blood of another woman was soaking into my arms. I glanced sideways and could see that she had managed to move her head and was looking at us. Her face was translucent, and her eyelids were drooping as if sleepy after a long journey.

It was he who broke the silence. He sounded disappointed, sighing, "Oh, Peter, why didn't you just stick to pottering around at home and looking at your art books? Why did you have to get involved? Why didn't you just do as Jackie told you and let it lie?"

His back straightened, and hopping off the box, he faced me. "I've always liked you—for all your faults; I wish you had just stopped."

The internal battle took another turn, as fear hit back. I had never been a card player; that had been Caroline's thing, and right now I did not have too many cards to play, but it was time to play what I had. "Do you really think that we would come alone here—knowing what you are capable of? We knew enough to let you believe it was just me here. We contacted—by landline so you would not know—Asher Joseph and Roijin Kemal, two comrades in the police, to arrest you. We also rang Zoe and January, two young comrades. I don't know their surnames, but I am sure that you know them; they, too, will be here."

He nodded. I had his attention. "I'm listening."

"We told them all about you, and they are on their way here. They'll be here in minutes. Simon, don't you think we would want more firepower than Cole? The first time I have ever touched a gun was a couple of hours ago. We wanted two more pros to take you in, with Zoe and January as witnesses."

The lie sounded so plausible that I wished that we had in fact told them in advance. In fact, why hadn't we?

I babbled on. "You don't have to do anything stupid here. Shooting me is not going to save you. It will just add another charge against you. Instead, you could return to MI5; they would have you back. Bearing in mind what you've done in the past two weeks, they would welcome you with open arms. You'd be a hero. And let's not forget all the goodies you could pass on about us. With them you have a future, because surely you must know that your time in the party is finished."

He stood in front of me. The pistol was pointing towards the floor, but quite obviously he was ready to use it. Ridiculously, I asked myself whether I should stand or sit. I could forget about running or lunging at him, as I stood no chance. My days of one-hundred-metre sprint starts were long gone, if they ever had existed. Instead, I pondered the etiquette of being murdered.

"And why should I believe you?" he asked.

"Like I said, if we were so certain it was you, why would we come alone and make us so vulnerable? All that happened was that you got here early and caught us out. OK, we're not pros, but we are not stupid!"

Well, it could plausibly be said that we were, but I was hoping that even old George Smiley here, would not appreciate just how stupid we were.

He thought about what I had said. The gun stayed pointing towards the torn lino and not at my head. Meanwhile, I was still trying to guess what the time was and weighing up the pros and cons of looking at my watch. Then there was what to say if he asked what time they were due. Did I tell him the truth? What if we had hours to go, and he reckoned on killing us and lying in wait and blowing them away as well. This could turn into a blood-fest.

On top of that, there was the unresolved question of what position I was going to be in if the end came. Funny man. It was all very well trying to be flippant, but I was terrified. But typical me, I was facing death, and no, my life did not flash before me; instead, it was just me being my normal smart-aleck self: flash not flashing past.

All my thoughts stopped when his distant look changed to one of staring right at me. His hand moved and then so did his arm. It was slowly moving upwards.

Oh no. No. Li Li!

His voice was perfectly calm, thoughtful almost. "No, I cannot go back. I meant what I have said; I *believe* in the party. I believe that we stand a chance of the working class creating a whole new future. The MI5 belongs to the past. I have rejected that. I have made my choice, and my choice is for liberation. No, Peter, I can't do that."

Silence returned. All I could hear was the sound resembling a mosh pit, with my heart crashing around my rib cage. It was a nice accompaniment to the sweaty smell of my fear. He stood and did not say a word. These quiet times were growing in oppression, and I was almost beginning to yearn for him to speak.

His facial expression went from blank thought to decision. He raised his arm.

My jabbering jabbered on. "Simon, for God's sake! How is killing me going to help the struggle? Murdering comrades is not our way. We're not Stalinists, *for God's sake!* You used to be the one who insisted on decorum between comrades—you hated us even being rude to each other, let alone killing each other!"

"You're right, Pete, and that's why I need to do this."

"Simon, we can work this out…"

"I know. Take it!"

To my astonishment, he flipped the gun round and passed it to me, handle first.

He smiled. Then came the announcement. "I am handing myself over to the jurisdiction of the National Workers' Council."

I was lost for words. Something which rarely happened. This I had not expected. Finally I made a decision, the decision concerning to sit or stand. I stood. I was using all my concentration to keep my hand still. Even with the pretence of a steady aim, it was only loosely pointing at him. It was incredible—he was surrendering—to me!

He was speaking in a tone of moral righteousness, of high-minded integrity, of principle. Who was in front of me? Did I have Martin Luther King, Mahatma Gandhi, or Jesus Christ standing there? "You are right," he asserted. "I cannot live both lives anymore. There's no way I can just carry on and hope the past will stay hidden. I need to come out and come clean."

I mumbled agreement. Feeling shocked.

"I will let the party judge me; history will pass sentence. I know that I will have a lot of explaining to do, but I hope how much I have done for the party will be weighed in my favour."

In the corner of my eye, I could see Vic's blood smudged from my trousers on the bold black print of *Revolutionary Worker*, making it look like a Bauhaus collage. A sweep, like a large teacher's tick, crossed the page. It didn't, though, look correct, let alone, inspiring—quite the opposite.

He continued with his highbrow reasons for surrender. My wonder subsided and changed to the thought that maybe it had slipped his memory that he had put Dave and Yasmin through hell in their final minutes alive. But then, he said something that told me that, no, he had not forgotten the hell he had put them through. "I know that it will not be easy for the comrades to forgive or forget Yas and Dave, so perhaps there will have to be some kind of recompense…"

Some kind of recompense? Was he equating the excruciating agony he had put them through with a cancelled holiday flight?

His insanity swirled on. "But the revolutionary tradition has always been one based on justice and forgiveness rather than revenge and retribution. Weren't the Bolsheviks in the early days after the Russian revolution forgiving of even those who had taken up arms against them? So whilst I am prepared to answer for my crimes, I hope the good heart of the struggle will understand. Of course, we will have bigger problems than ex-spies. Our attention should be outwards and not inwards!"

So he was hoping for a slap on the wrist. And perhaps it wasn't so crazy. At any other time, it would have been, but now—maybe he had a point. I was fast giving up on any pretence of knowing what was going on. After all, the party would soon be fighting for its life; the revolution was in peril. The movement was going to face its ultimate test. The choice facing us was dramatically the choice Rosa Luxembourg had put: Socialism or barbarism. Perhaps he could pass on valuable information that would help us in that fight.

There was no doubt that he had done much good for the party and had played a part in furthering the struggle. Simon was a popular man, and whilst no one would forgive him for his crimes, it was maybe just possible that his punishment would be minimal. Against the lives he had ended might be weighed the lives he had helped save. Whatever his motives, his work had furthered the cause: a cause that could mean true and total freedom. For that, forgiveness and understanding might be greater than otherwise might be expected. He had repented and turned his back on his past. Many would praise him for that.

I pulled the trigger and fired.

Punishment was required here. Not praise.

Stuff his repentance. This wasn't a confessional.

Comrades Come Rally

I had expected a big bang and smoke, but the inbuilt silencer gave out a noise similar to a spitting sound. The real noise came from Peary, shouting first in shock and then in pain. A lump of his right hip seemed to have gone. He spun with the impact and twisted like a human corkscrew, landing on his left knee. Blood splattered against the box.

So the poor man had suffered a few sleepless nights had he? Did he think that was punishment enough for ending innocent lives? Were my nightmares an adequate penance for Li and Li?

Two people said my name. Both cried, "No, Pete!" Both said them with weakness and urgency. Vic's behind me was barely audible. Peary's in front was louder, amplified by fear.

My jacket, already damp with Vic's blood, now had this scum's splatter. I moved forwards, seeing him lollop against the box. His face pressed against its side. Blood was everywhere.

No Pete, regret and guilt were not enough.

He was right. He had done a lot for the struggle for Socialism. But what should also be considered was what had he done for MI5 to give him the space to do so? What had been quid pro quo? It must have been an awful lot for them to think it was worth it. Had he been involved in the police raids on comrades a few years back? Those rounded up had been instantly extradited to other legally compatible countries through the speeded-up legal process on trumped-up charges, which in reality allowed the government to get rid of annoying Lefties. They had ended up in high-security prisons or oblivion. Strangely, many of those in hiding had been found. The cops had been able to locate them. Had this shit coughed up their names?

Fear had vanished. Pure undiluted hatred was now in control.

He was reaching up to get one of the guns. I aimed at his hand and fired. The weapon hissed. He screamed. Three fingers vaporised.

He fell back, howling. He was spluttering blood and begging. "P-P-P-Pete, I give up. You have won. T-T-Take me in as a prisoner. Try me in a revolutionary tribunal."

Yeah, try him. Like he had tried Yasmin. I remembered her shattered limbs, her blood splashed up the walls. Who had been the defence lawyer in that particular trial? Had Dave been able to plead mitigating circumstances when he witnessed her being shot? Was Victoria bleeding because of due process? And what about the torment he had put Alan through for decades? Of thinking he had killed a woman, of committing a heinous crime. And then forcing him to betray the Socialist principles in which he believed in. Had a tribunal decided that?

"Pete, have m-m-ercy…"

What mercy had he shown Dave and Yasmin? Oh yes, by first shooting them in their legs.

I aimed down and fired into both of his.

Looking at him, I had no doubt he would trade the names of the agents of the security forces employed in the NWC for clemency. That and the fact that our members who had been at the rough edge of imprisonment and state sanctions would be reluctant to use such methods on him, meant that he had a good chance of avoiding what he deserved. He didn't deserve the goodwill or decency the revolution would show him.

Here he was—Simon Peary—the man of refined manners and civility; a comrade who always spoke eloquently and passionately about how revolution would raise us to a new and higher cultural plane. I remembered those honourable words. Language itself, he said, would evolve and flower. Evolve and flower.

Fuck that. Wilt.

What had he told me when he had cornered me here? Ah, yes. "Professionals fire head shots." I pressed the trigger, aiming right between his eyes.

Five head shots.

Professional.

Extinction.

Wanker.